THE SIREN'S HANDMAIDEN

Book One

ALIZA SANTORO

THE SIREN'S HANDMAIDEN

Book One

This is a work of fiction. Names, characters, places, and events are products of the author's imagination or are used fictitiously. Any resemblance to actual persons, living or dead, or actual events is purely coincidental.

Editing, interior formatting, and illustrations by Aliza Santoro.

Cover design by Aliza Santoro.

First edition: 2026

Published by Rising Tides Press

ISBN: 979-8-9958069-0-5

For more information, visit @aliza.santoro on Instagram.

For the Reputation girlies.

You know who you are.

To Kemica Rose,

who is, in fact, totally awesome.

To my husband, Joe, for helping me write Eon and for his…contributions.

Don't be weird, just let it happen.

To my friend Winter, for encouraging me to write this story and cheering me on.

And if my mom ever reads this…

maybe just skim a little. This is your only warning.

PROLOGUE

25 Years Ago

Captain Nestor stood at the helm of the *Black Serpent*, squinting through the early morning fog. The only sounds were the crash of waves against the ship's hull, and the frenzy of gulls circling above them. Most of his crew were still trying to rub the sleep from their eyes as they went about their duties.

"Guid mornin', Captain," the quartermaster uttered between sips of her drink as she strode up the steps to the quarterdeck. Her fiery mane of hair was going wild with the humidity, wisps curling around her face, refusing to be tamed. Much like the woman herself.

Nestor glanced at her, his squinted eyes narrowing further. The unmistakable aroma of black coffee wafted from her pewter tankard. He knew for a fact that the beans were in short supply; it wasn't nearly as easy to acquire as, say, rum.

"Brigid...ye know that coffee is for special occasions only," he grumbled.

"Then I suppose ye dinnae want this coffee I poured special for ye?" She temptingly held up another tankard in her other hand. Nestor had been sailing with his quartermaster long enough to know that if Brigid O'Connell offered you something, you'd best take it. That was true whether it be an indulgent treat or unsolicited advice.

Nestor shook his head, a gruff chuckle escaping from his throat. "Well let's have it then."

He raised the vessel to his lips, savoring the bold taste. It reminded him of the merchant ship they had escorted through Dravari territory. Had it not been for the *Black Serpent*, it would have been plundered and sunk in a matter of minutes. As a token of gratitude, they had been gifted with several sacks of coffee beans and cocoa.

Wiping his black beard on the sleeve of his dark leather coat, he looked out at the horizon. Or at least, where he assumed the horizon was. "Blast this fog. Might as well be sailin' blind."

"Mark me words," Cormac warned. "Fog like this is a bad omen. We shouldn't be sailin' 'til it clears up."

"We're close enough to the port of Astyra," Nestor tried to sound reassuring. "I know these waters like the back of me hand."

"It's not the water I'm worried about, Cap'n."

"Och, let me guess," Brigid cut in. "Ye're worried about selkies or sirens."

"Don't invoke 'em like that, lass!" Cormac waggled his finger in her direction.

"Please, no one has seen a siren in decades, an' selkies are a myth," she took another sip of coffee and planted a fist firmly on her hip. "Everyone knows that."

The old boatswain simply spat over the railing and fumbled with the colored beads threaded in his unruly copper beard as if he could ward off danger.

Nestor adjusted the wheel as the cliffs of Astyra came into view through the fog. The castle sat atop the tallest point, flanked by stone watchtowers along the seawall overlooking the cliffs.

The gulls' cries suddenly rose, dozens of them screeching in the sky. There was another sound layered underneath, almost like someone was wailing.

"Ye hear that?" Nestor stretched his neck towards the port side, straining to hear better.

"The gulls?" Brigid looked in the same direction.

"No, somethin' else," he shook his head. "Listen."

Brigid and Cormac glanced at each other, then out to sea where the seagulls seemed to be circling over a specific spot. The wailing grew louder, unmistakable.

"Saints preserve us—sounds like a banshee," Brigid's normally pale face somehow went even paler, making her freckles stand out like stars against the night sky.

"Who's superstitious now?" Cormac elbowed her, earning a swift jab to his shoulder.

Nestor ignored them both, eyes scanning the water just below where the birds were circling. He could just make out a small piece of driftwood bobbing in the waves.

"What is that?" he wondered aloud, pointing.

The crew followed his line of sight, leaning over the railing to see better. They saw it too. Nestor pulled out his spyglass, adjusting the focus. The weathered lines of his face creased as his eyes widened in shock.

"Blast me bones, it's a babe!" He stuffed the spyglass back into his coat and took the stairs two at a time down to the main deck. "Brigid, man the helm! Cormac, help me lower the skiff!"

The moment the boat reached the waterline, Nestor leapt over the railing, landing with a thud and balancing on the bobbing vessel as only a seasoned sailor could. He grabbed the oars and began rowing furiously. The seagulls scattered as he approached, voicing their indignation.

Nestor slowed, setting aside the oars, and reached over the side. He was able to get a handful of the blanket that the child was wrapped in and lifted the screaming bundle from the driftwood. Settling the babe into his lap, he began rowing back to the ship. No telling how long it had been out in the elements; it was a miracle the sea hadn't claimed it.

Cormac was leaning over the railing as Nestor returned, with a disapproving expression. "Nothin' good comes from the sea, ye best toss it back 'fore it dooms us all!"

"Toss it back?" Brigid yelled incredulously. "It's just a wee babe!"

With a single sharp look from Nestor, Cormac gave in, getting ready to work the winch as Nestor attached the halyards to the skiff, never letting go of the small bundle.

Once the captain was back on his ship, he tucked the baby into his coat, rubbing its back in an attempt to warm it up. The child certainly had a healthy set of lungs, but Nestor was glad for it—the lad was a fighter.

Despite his wariness, Cormac retrieved a blanket from the supply room and handed it to Nestor, who quickly stripped off the drenched fabric and wrapped the baby back up. He noticed a braided leather cord had been knotted into the wet blanket, and when he removed it, he found attached a smooth green stone speckled with flecks of gold, carved to resemble the shape of a Nautilus shell.

"What do ye make of this?" Nestor held it up to the faint sunlight piercing through the fog.

Cormac scrutinized the pendant with his one good eye. "I ain't never seen a stone like that in all my forty years at sea," he declared.

"Well, whatever it is, it's the only lead we've got on where this pup came from." Nestor pocketed the pendant and adjusted the baby in his arms as he walked back up to the quarterdeck.

"Let me 'ave a look," Brigid reached out and took the baby from Nestor. She cradled him gently, supporting his head. "Couple o' months old, give or take. Poor thing's chilled through and through." She glanced up at the captain, an unspoken question in her eyes.

"We're keepin' him," Nestor declared, hands back on the wheel.

Cormac groaned loudly. "Ye're kiddin' me. He'll bring nothin' but trouble, Cap'n."

Nestor squared his shoulders; his voice edged with steel. "Then let trouble come. This boy stays with us, and I'll see to it he's raised proper. The sea gave him into my hands, and I'll not cast him aside."

Brigid nodded, rocking and shushing the child. "What shall we call the wee lad?"

Nestor was silent for a long moment. He tickled the boy's chin, who responded by grabbing his finger with a surprising grip. At last, he spoke. "Zale."

Brigid lifted a brow. "Strong name for a wee scrap like him."

"Aye," Nestor replied, his gaze hard but not unkind. "And he's goin' to need it."

CHAPTER 1

WELCOME TO BEING HUMAN

Nerissa

Masked men surrounded them. Too many of them. Too many. Nerissa pressed her palm against the skin below her collarbone, green blood seeping between her fingers. Her eyes darted between the silhouettes of their attackers against the torches' flames and her parents, weapons drawn.

"Run!" her father shouted.

Nerissa hesitated, torn between the safety of the sea just beyond the dock, and doing something—anything—to help her parents. But she was no fighter. She was only eleven, and much too small to make a difference. She wasn't even supposed to be there in the first place.

The glint of a silver cane caught her attention. Its owner was clothed in a dark cloak, hood obscuring everything but the serpentine smile spreading across his face. A shiver traveled down her spine.

Her mother shoved her forward, brandishing her spear as she kept the men at bay.

She ignored the sharp sting of splinters as her bare feet slapped against the wooden dock. A few more steps, and they would be gone anyway.

At the edge of the pier, she dove, headfirst, into the sea.

Pain vanished as her legs merged into a tail of iridescent scales while the ocean welcomed her back. She resurfaced to look for her parents, but they were gone.

Someone was shaking her shoulder.

"Riss," a voice whispered. "Wake up. You're twitching again."

The nightmare evaporated like foam on the tide, but the ache of the memory lingered. She blinked several times, rubbing her palms across her face. The small bedchamber was still dark.

"What time is it?" Nerissa rasped, her voice lower than usual. "Is something wrong?"

"Not quite first light," Calliope said brightly.

"Then it's way too early," Nerissa grumbled, throwing her pillow over her head.

Calliope snatched it away teasingly. "I want to go to the surface."

Nerissa stared at her with one eye cracked open, fin curling tightly beneath the bedding.

"No," she said flatly. *Absolutely not.*

Calliope pouted. How she could still pout at twenty years of age was a mystery of royal privilege and relentless optimism. "Come *on*. The treaty signing is tomorrow. I want to see Prince Leander myself before the actual wedding."

"What difference does it make? Not like you can refuse to marry him if he's unattractive."

Calliope crossed her arms and drifted upward, turning a lazy circle midwater like a jellyfish. "I just want to pretend for one day that this is a normal courtship. No guards. No entourage. Just the two of us."

"It's too dangerous."

Calliope grinned. "Which is why *you'll be with me.* Please, Riss. Just one day."

Nerissa closed her eyes. She knew that tone. The gentle plea behind the royal command. The old nickname wrapped in salt-sweet guilt. It was the same voice Calliope had used when they were children sneaking out of lessons to chase dolphin pods.

But this wasn't childhood.

This was diplomacy. This was risk. This was the *surface.*

This also wasn't her choice. Wherever the princess went, she must follow. And if she didn't escort Calliope now, then the princess would just end up going anyway, alone.

Nerissa exhaled through the gills just beneath her jaw. "Fine. *One* day. But if anything feels off, we leave immediately."

Calliope beamed victoriously. "Then what are we waiting for? Let's go!"

Nerissa grabbed her by one side of her caudal fin. "Hold on, you have to get dressed."

At the look of confusion on her face, Nerissa sighed. "When you shift, you won't just lose your tail," she gestured to the princess' golden-scaled décolletage, "you'll lose all of your scales too."

"Oh," the princess' face reddened. "I guess I hadn't thought of the logistics."

Nerissa swam to her wardrobe, pulling out a couple of sea-silk gowns, one lavender, one teal. They were sleeveless, and just long enough to reach their calves—she hoped. Normally they didn't bother with clothing unless there was a royal ceremony or banquet to dress up for. As Calliope's handmaiden, she kept a small variety of clothing and accessories for just such occasions.

"Here, this will keep you modest." Nerissa handed Calliope the teal gown before pulling the lavender one over her head and smoothing the skirt over her tail.

"See, this is why I need you." Calliope tugged the garment over her own head. "You're the practical one; you always think of everything."

"Speaking of," Nerissa rifled through a small chest at the foot of her bed, finding her leather belt and daggers. She placed them carefully into a woven-kelp satchel. "We'll also need shoes."

With a sly grin, Calliope said, "Leave that to me."

They left at first light, before the morning trumpets could sound, between the palace guard rotations.

Calliope darted ahead, her borrowed gown catching faint glimmers of fading bioluminescent light as she swam through the shadowed corridor.

Nerissa followed close behind, scanning the water around them to make sure no one was following.

The palace gates rose behind them like a wall of obsidian and pearl, etched with ancient Nautalian glyphs. Just ahead was the hub of the city; the only merfolk who were up at this time would be the vendors setting up their stalls, and they barely gave the girls a second glance.

Good, Nerissa thought. The less they were noticed, the less likely word would reach King Nereus or Queen Ophelia that their only child was gallivanting about outside the safety of the palace. Nerissa would be in for it if they got caught, and rightly so. It was her sole duty to ensure Calliope's safety. And here she was escorting her right into their enemies' territory.

Sure, after tomorrow's wedding and subsequent peace treaty signing, Astyra would become allies with Nautalia. But that didn't mean humans would suddenly become safe to be around. Furthermore, the general public believed merfolk to be extinct, wiped out during the war between the two kingdoms a century prior. The commonwealth was told that Prince Leander was to be wed to a foreign princess. Not an outright lie, but not the full truth either.

What would they say once the treaty became public knowledge? How would they feel when they found out that their king had been lying to them for the past few decades? Would they accuse the merfolk of ulterior motives? Undoubtedly their newly revealed princess from the sea would be met with unease and distrust, and that was the best-case scenario. What if there was a revolt? She couldn't protect Calliope from an entire kingdom.

Nerissa had been against this alliance from the start. Not necessarily the treaty itself; she wanted to believe that peace might be achieved without violence. But the numbers of missing merfolk had steadily risen over the last twenty years or so; all of them last seen near the surface. *Someone* knew they weren't extinct, and they were hunting them. She couldn't understand why King Nereus would willingly send his daughter into the belly of the beast as a peace offering. She had said as much to Calliope when she first heard the news a couple of months ago.

The princess, on the other hand, saw this as a new adventure. A dreamer at heart, she truly believed that peace was within their grasp and seemed all too eager to live among the humans. Nerissa swallowed, watching as Calliope twirled above her in anticipation. She was much too naive about this whole situation, in her opinion.

Then again, her opinion didn't matter. Even though she and Calliope were as close as sisters, Nerissa was first and foremost a servant. She was expected to follow orders and obey without question, and she had gotten very good at her role. She owed the crown her life, after all.

The water grew thinner with sunlight as they rose, shafts of gold slicing down from the surface like spears through liquid sapphire. The reef fell away below them, its familiar towers of coral and anemone receding into the deep.

Calliope swam ahead, a flash of golden glittering scales that matched her long hair. Nerissa moved more slowly, dread building up in her chest as she returned to the realm of her nightmares.

"You haven't been to the surface since...that day, have you?" Calliope asked softly, suddenly reappearing beside her.

Nerissa tensed but didn't answer.

"I remember," Calliope went on. "Damarion brought you to the palace. Mother and I met him in the healing chamber."

Nerissa's throat tightened. "It's been ten years. I'm fine."

A pause, long and weighty between them. Schools of ribbonfish darted past like errant thoughts.

"If it's too hard for you," Calliope said, turning toward her, "I can go alone. You can wait for me in the shallows."

"No."

"It's all right, Riss. I can—"

"I said no."

Calliope blinked at her tone but didn't flinch. She knew Nerissa too well to mistake bluntness for cruelty.

"It is my duty," Nerissa said more quietly. "You go nowhere unguarded, least of all into the humans' world. My feelings don't matter."

"They matter to me," Calliope murmured.

Nerissa didn't respond. She just kept swimming, eyes fixed upward, where the waves blurred into light. The sunlit shimmer of the ocean's ceiling wavered far above, a liquid mirror that danced and rippled. She could feel the pressure change, as well as the faint buzz in her bones.

Slowing her ascent, she glanced over at Calliope. Her eager expression from only moments ago was now pinched with uncertainty, eyes wide, movements hesitant.

"This is it?" Calliope asked, her voice a tentative whisper.

Nerissa nodded. "Almost there."

"I've never…" Calliope trailed off. "I mean, I know what they say happens, but I've never actually shifted."

"It's mostly instinct," Nerissa said, her voice gentle now. "Your body will shift as you breach the surface. Don't fight it. Just let it happen."

Calliope nodded, but she wasn't hiding her nerves well. Nerissa forced a steady breath, the memories of blood and chaos from the last time she surfaced threatening to drag her under. She pushed them back. Now wasn't the time.

"You'll feel it in your tail first," Nerissa continued. "It starts to tighten and split. You might feel a pull behind your dorsal fin as it retracts. It's strange, but it doesn't hurt."

"And breathing?" Calliope's voice wavered.

"You'll feel like you're choking for a second, but then your lungs will take over." Nerissa offered a small smile. "Try not to scream. It wastes breath."

Calliope gave a nervous laugh, her fingers twitching at her sides. "That's comforting."

"Don't think too hard about it, just breathe."

I should take my own advice, Nerissa thought ruefully. Her fingers curled reflexively, and she closed her eyes, swallowing the rising tide of emotions.

This was for Calliope. She had to be strong. Unshakeable.

"Ready?" she asked.

Calliope exhaled, then nodded. "Ready."

Together, they swam toward the light. Nerissa matched Calliope's pace, staying close as the glow grew brighter. Her muscles coiled with the old, forgotten ache of change, the pressure building in her lungs like a held breath from years ago.

And then, in one fluid motion, the world shattered into light and air as they broke the surface.

Calliope gasped, half in wonder, half in panic. She sputtered and flailed as her sleek tail shimmered in the sun one last time before splitting and twisting into legs. She shrieked and clutched at Nerissa.

Nerissa was already steadying the princess with her arms wrapped around Calliope's waist as she kicked to keep them both afloat. Her own transformation rippled through her with a familiar tingle—fins smoothing flat against her spine and forearms, scales receding, her tail cleaving into legs as her body adjusted to the human form once more. She barely flinched.

The sunlight was blinding. The air felt harsh and dry against her throat as she coughed up remaining seawater. Wind tousled her heavy black hair and salt crusted on her lips. Everything smelled stronger than she remembered, the faint tang of fish, the earthy perfume of distant land.

She caught her breath, holding Calliope upright as the princess blinked furiously and whimpered, "Why does everything feel...awful?"

Nerissa let out a short, mirthless laugh. "Welcome to being human."

Calliope looked down in horror at her legs, now tangled in the folds of her sea-silk gown. "They're so...weird."

"I know, it's like having two tails," Nerissa agreed.

A wave hit them, tossing them briefly apart before Nerissa grabbed Calliope's hand again and started towing her toward the rocky outcrop where they could gather themselves.

"Just breathe," Nerissa said. "And kick, like I showed you."

"I *am* kicking!"

"You're flailing."

Calliope muttered something unprincesslike under her breath but obeyed. They moved slowly toward the jagged shoreline, the clumsy rhythm of limbs replacing the weightless grace of their tails.

By the time they reached the rocks, both girls were panting, limbs aching, dresses clinging. The sea silk in their gowns would dry quickly; drops of water were already beading up and slipping from the material.

Nerissa helped Calliope up onto the stone, then hoisted herself up. The sun warmed her damp skin, but she shivered all the same, haunted by the strangeness of her own body, human again after all these years.

She looked at her legs, examining her feet. No splinters. It seemed that time healed *some* wounds.

Calliope collapsed beside her, arms splayed, eyes wide as she stared up at the sky. "So. This is the surface."

"Yes," Nerissa said, eyes narrowing against the rising sun. "This is the surface."

She reached into her satchel and pulled out the thin belt of supple seal-hide, worn smooth from years of use. Attached were a pair of holsters, designed to fit snugly on her hips regardless of her form. A small convenience for anyone who didn't fancy fumbling with straps mid-shift.

Sliding the belt around her waist, Nerissa adjusted it carefully, feeling the reassuring weight of the abalone-hilted daggers settle against her sides. Gifts from Damarion, her mentor and guardian when she was orphaned. He taught her how to defend herself, how to protect others, and how to survive.

Calliope watched her with a slight frown. "Do you really think those are necessary?"

Nerissa shrugged. "Better to be prepared than dead."

Calliope rolled her eyes.

"Anyways," Nerissa stood, brushing sand from her gown. "You said you would handle shoes—"

"Tadaaa!" Calliope proudly held up two pairs of leather sandals, decorated with seashells and pearls. They looked expensive.

"Where in the *abyss* did you get those from?" Nerissa whirled on her.

Calliope smirked. "I 'borrowed' them from Mother. She has a lot of shoes for someone with no feet."

Nerissa snorted. "Well done, Princess."

Calliope laughed, tentatively slipping her feet into the sandals and wiggling her toes. "Then it's settled. Shoes acquired. Now, what exactly is the plan?"

Nerissa folded her arms. She had assumed that Calliope already had a plan. All she had expected to do was escort the princess and make sure she made it back to Nautalia in one piece. "Hold on. The prince *does* know you're coming, right?"

"Yes, Riss," Calliope huffed.

"How?"

"I have my ways."

"Callie."

"We've been writing," Calliope admitted. "Is that such a crime? We're supposed to meet at a tavern called The Salty Siren."

Nerissa groaned. A tavern, of all places? She had never been to one herself, only heard stories from the older kids growing up who had snuck up to the surface and gotten drunk on something called ale. They didn't have such establishments in Nautalia; they didn't drink, so there was really no purpose.

She wrung out her still-dripping hair and slipped on the shoes. After smoothing the front of her gown and adjusting her belt one last time, she motioned for Calliope to follow her up the sandy path.

CHAPTER 2

THE SALTY SIREN

Nerissa

The city of Astyra rose before them in tiers built straight into the cliff face of the peninsula. At its feet sprawled the harbor, a forest of masts and sails rocking in the sun, the air thick with the briny tang of freshly caught fish. Ships were anchored along the docks, their painted prows jutting like a line of shark teeth, while beyond them the breakwater curved in a long arm of stone studded with watchtowers.

The marketplace began where the piers ended, spilling into a wide square alive with motion. Stalls stood up shoulder to shoulder beneath bright awnings, their canopies striped in saffron, teal, and indigo. Piles of citrus gleamed gold beside baskets of olives and figs. Bolts of cloth in scarlet and violet snapped like sails in the wind. The scent of roasted nuts and frying fish tangled in the air, tempting and dizzying all at once.

Buildings crowded the waterfront in a variety of colors, every wall painted differently: ochre yellow pressed against sea-green, pale rose against sun-bleached white. Wooden shutters swung open to let fresh air into homes, while laundry had been strung up between overhanging balconies.

The fish market met them halfway down the main street, and Nerissa stopped short.

Baskets of eels writhed in slimy tangles; red-scaled snapper and silver-skinned mackerel lay stacked in haphazard piles. A butcher lifted a cleaver, brought it down with a wet crack, and wrapped the two halves in paper for an awaiting customer.

Calliope wrinkled her nose. "Well, it's certainly...fresh."

Nerissa said nothing.

She was no stranger to hunting—merfolk were carnivores, after all—but the market still made her uneasy. It wasn't the fish themselves. It was the way they were displayed: gutted, deboned, scales glittering like coins. Too many of the tails resembled her own. Too many fins mirrored those of people she'd trained beside. A reminder that humans didn't need a reason to cut things apart. They just needed a price.

She kept her head down.

They moved deeper into the market, weaving between crates of oysters and crab, ducking under clotheslines strung with drying squid. A sailor nearly bowled into Calliope while chasing a runaway chicken. A fishmonger tried to upsell Nerissa a bucket of shrimp—"just caught this morning, love"—before muttering something rude under his breath when she ignored him.

Calliope clutched her arm, pointing at everything and nothing like an overexcited child. "Everything is so...alive!"

Nerissa's lips pressed tightly. To her, it felt like chaos; too bright, too loud, too many humans crowding them with baskets and barrels. It was overwhelming, and she had to keep taking steadying breaths to calm her nerves.

A man shouted over a stall, “You girls looking for somethin’?”

“The Salty Siren,” Calliope called back before Nerissa could stop her.

The man pointed with a knife, wiping the blade on his apron as he spoke. “End of the lane, by the docks. Look for the ugly mermaid sign.”

“Ugly mermaid?” Calliope asked under her breath.

“Charming.” Nerissa narrowed her eyes, tugging Calliope's arm.

They followed the scent of frying grease, the roar of the market slowly giving way to the rattle of dock chains and creaking wood.

The Salty Siren waited ahead, paint peeling, windows fogged, and a badly carved mermaid hanging crookedly from a rusted chain, her expression caught somewhere between sultry and seasick.

Calliope hesitated. “This is the place?”

“Definitely,” Nerissa sighed. “Let’s get this over with.”

Despite the early hour, the tavern thrummed with the clatter of tankards and the low buzz of conversation. Dusty beams arched overhead, strings of netting and mismatched lanterns swinging gently from the rafters. A haze of smoke drifted through the room, and something was sizzling in the back.

Nerissa stepped in first, eyes scanning the space like she was entering enemy territory. Which, of course, they were. Patrons hunched over drinks, cards, and questionable-looking food. A few glanced up as the girls entered but quickly looked away. The smell of sweat and grease assaulted her nostrils, and the noise was a decibel too high for Nerissa's liking.

She guided Calliope to an empty table tucked near the side wall, where she could keep an eye on the exits and everyone in between. The bench creaked as she sat, sandals sticking to the uneven floorboards.

Calliope fidgeted beside her. "Do you think he's here yet?"

"If he has any sense, he's watching before he makes himself known," Nerissa muttered, still scanning the room.

A barmaid approached, hair pinned back with a fishbone comb and apron streaked with what looked like squid ink.

"What can I get you, lass?" The question was directed at Calliope.

"She will have what I am having," said a man's voice beside the table.

It was warm and confident, like it expected to be obeyed. Nerissa turned her head slowly.

The young man who had just stepped up had golden hair that fell in perfect ringlets around his forehead. With a square jaw and straight nose, he looked every bit the picture of perfect masculinity. His shirt was simple, but the fabric was too fine, the stitching too precise. Even his boots were out of place—clean, new, unscuffed by sand or rubble.

Prince Leander.

Trying so hard to look ordinary and failing at every seam.

Calliope's face lit up with a smile that was equal parts bashful and excited. "Leander?"

He returned her smile, bowing slightly. "Calliope. You made it."

Then, glancing at Nerissa, he tempered his tone with polite deference. "Forgive the interruption. Might I borrow Calliope for a moment? My table is just over there," he gestured across the room, "within your line of sight. I thought we might speak more comfortably there."

Nerissa studied him before giving a single, curt nod. "She leaves my view for one second, you pay with a finger. I don't care how impressive your bloodline is."

"Riss!" Calliope scolded. Nerissa ignored her, keeping her eyes trained on Leander.

His smile flickered, but he inclined his head again. "Fair deal."

He offered his hand to Calliope, who took it without hesitation, giving Nerissa one last half-hearted glare as they crossed the room.

Nerissa waited, watching them settle into their seats. Leander sat across from Calliope. His posture was relaxed, one arm draped along the back of the empty chair next to him. He was charming, she could tell that much. Leaning in just enough when Calliope spoke, laughing when she did, his gaze never straying too far from her face.

Calliope, for her part, was glowing. Whatever awkward nerves she'd carried through the fish market had evaporated. Her fingers toyed with the rim of her tankard as she smiled at something he said.

Nerissa leaned back just slightly and let the tavern blur around her. Her focus honed in on the way Calliope's fingers lingered near his. On the glint in Leander's eye when she laughed.

She tracked his body language the way she'd been trained to read undersea currents. Leander was composed, his gestures never sharp. He didn't read as threatening. Most interestingly, he seemed to be very comfortable with being outside of the castle walls with no entourage. Not even a single bodyguard could be found in the small dining area. He was either very confident in his own ability to protect himself, or he truly believed that nobody would recognize the crown prince of Astyra.

In either case, he had barnacles for brains.

CHAPTER 3

A STORMY SORT OF BLUE

Zale

The cards were sticky, the table was crooked, and the ale tasted like it had been strained through a dirty sock.

In short: it was a perfect morning.

Zale leaned back in his chair, one boot hooked on the table leg, the other propped up beside a rapidly diminishing pile of coppers. Sun-tanned skin caught the light as he stretched, before he quickly tugged the cuff of his coat back down. Rubbing his stubbled chin, he laid down his hand—four of a kind.

"Well. That's unfortunate…for the rest of you," he grinned.

Bran groaned. "You're cheating."

"I'm charming," Zale corrected. "It's easily confused."

Across the table, Ma Wen shook his head and popped a dried plum into his mouth. Stocky and broad-shouldered, with black hair pulled into a tidy bun and a quiet calm that rarely cracked, he said simply, "No, Bran's the charming one."

"You wound me," Zale said, clutching his chest and doing his best impression of Bran. "Mortally, even."

Bran chuckled and threw down his hand. "Seems I've taught you too well, mate."

Cormac let out a belch and pointed a callused finger. One pale blue eye glinted in the light; the other hidden beneath a battered leather patch. "Mortally, my arse. Ye've had worse wounds fallin' outta yer hammock."

Zale grimaced at the memory. "Aye, and not a soul offered a cushion. Heartless lot." He hadn't been able to sit for *months* after that incident.

Bran stroked his goatee and leaned back in his chair, glancing toward the tavern entrance. His brows lifted as he nudged Cormac with his elbow. "Speakin' of charm...don't look now, but we've got newcomers. Pretty ones."

Cormac squinted in the general direction, then groaned. "Don't even *think* about it, Calder."

Bran shrugged, entirely unrepentant. "Just sayin', they're not locals. Those gowns? That's high-quality silk, that is."

Zale didn't look right away. He'd learned that trick years ago. Don't gawk, just glance. Gawking got you caught; glancing made you mysterious. Or so Bran said.

He set down his cards and casually swept a hand through his hair, tilting his head just enough to catch a glimpse of the tavern door.

Two women.

One blonde, one raven-haired. Both looking like they had just gone for a swim in the harbor. Their gowns clung like wet leaves, elegant and out of place amid the rough-hewn beams and even rougher patrons.

The blonde had the look of someone who thought this place was charming in a "how rustic" kind of way. Her face held the polite countenance of an upper-class lady.

The dark-haired one moved differently; she was cautious, watchful. Inky black hair hung in loose waves around her shoulders, falling to her ribs. Her exposed arms were olive, toned, and marked with old scars. She carried herself like someone used to surviving.

Curious.

Then he noticed the daggers gleaming against worn leather, a not-so-subtle warning strapped to the hips of a woman who looked like she'd gut a man before she offered her name.

Zale sat up a little straighter.

"Salty Siren, indeed," Zale gave a low whistle, averting his eyes before the armed woman could sense his stare.

The women stepped further inside. The dark-haired lass ushered her friend to a table against the far wall. Even after settling into their seats, she watched the tavern like a soldier forced into peacetime, tense and wary and very much still at war.

A figure rose from one of the corner tables and approached the two women just as the barmaid took their order.

Zale blinked. That couldn't be right.

Prince Leander?

He wasn't even trying to blend in. Or maybe he thought he was with that "simple" clothing. Zale knew Leander from a distance, seen him at public ceremonies once or twice. But not here. Not in *this* place.

The Salty Siren was a haunt for smugglers, off-duty dockhands, and pirates pretending to be respectable. Present company excluded, of course. And yet, there he was.

Interesting.

Leander approached the women with a warm smile and a shallow bow, speaking quietly to the blonde. She smiled graciously and accepted his offered hand as he led her toward his table.

The dark-haired one didn't follow. Instead, she remained at the bench, solely focused on the prince and his date, eyes unmoving. A perfect opportunity if he ever saw one.

"Reckon I'm goin' to say hello," he announced to his crew, scooping up the rest of his winnings and tucking them into his coat.

"Reckon ye're an idiot," said Cormac.

"Better an idiot than a coward," Bran countered, shuffling the cards for another round.

Ma Wen didn't even look up. "At least finish your drink first. Waste not."

Zale obediently gulped down the last of his ale, wiping his mouth with the back of his hand. "Wish me luck, lads!"

"Ye'll need more than luck," Cormac advised.

Zale stood, smoothing a hand through his hair more out of habit than vanity, and sauntered toward the table like he hadn't just been warned off by a man thrice his age and two times as paranoid.

As he approached, he got a better look at the woman's face. Her nose had clearly been broken once and not properly set. It threw her features off-kilter just enough to make them interesting. A pretty girl with a crooked edge, he liked that. Said she wasn't made of glass, wasn't sheltered. Said she'd fought for something, or someone, and come out scarred but standing.

Her eyes stopped him cold though. A stormy sort of blue and framed by lashes too thick to be fair. The kind of eyes that didn't blink often, didn't soften easily. Not warm, not welcoming, but piercing. Not unlike her mouth, set in a line sharp enough to draw blood.

She looked to be about his age, maybe a few years younger, yet she had faint creases on her brow which suggested she scowled quite often. She wasn't polished, wasn't prim. But she was mesmerizing, in a lethal sort of way.

Trouble, through and through. But since when had the promise of danger ever stopped him?

Calliope

Calliope smoothed her dress under the table, willing her hands not to tremble. *Nerae*, she'd faced entire councils without flinching, but this, meeting her betrothed, made her pulse flutter like a startled guppy.

She had only known Leander through letters. Careful, courtly words engraved in stone tablets, full of diplomacy and ideas. Words she had read and reread until she could recite them by heart. Now he was here, flesh and blood, sitting across from her in the dim light of a rowdy tavern.

At first, she couldn't bring herself to meet his eyes. What if he thought her foolish? Too young, too immature, too foreign? She twisted her fingers in her lap, breath catching when he leaned toward her.

"You do not have to look so nervous," he said gently. "We are just two people talking, that is all."

The knot in her chest loosened by a degree. She dared to glance up then, meeting his deep brown eyes. There was no judgement there, only warmth.

"Tell me what you want," he said. "Not what your council wants. Not what your father wants. You."

Her heart thudded. No one had ever asked her that before. She swallowed, then managed to whisper. "Peace. Between our kingdoms. And the chance for our people to learn from each other instead of fearing what they don't understand."

His smile deepened, soft and unguarded. "Then that is what we will work toward. Together."

And just like that, the noise of the tavern dulled around her. Calliope felt lighter, as though she were no longer sitting in a smoky den of sailors but in some place all her own, just the two of them.

She smoothed her dress again, summoning a bit of courage. "You're not at all what I expected," she admitted softly.

One of his brows rose, curiosity sparking. "Oh? And what, pray tell, did you expect?"

She pressed her lips together, heat blooming in her cheeks. "Some handsome, confident prince who only cared about the benefits of our alliance."

Leander chuckled, low and warm, leaning a little closer. "So, you do not find me handsome, then?"

Her laugh slipped out, light and ladylike. Just then, the barmaid arrived with their drinks, setting them down with a thump of metal against wood. Calliope lifted hers carefully, though her gaze wandered back to him before she could stop it.

And oh, there was plenty to notice.

The cut of his shirt fitted close across his shoulders, hinting at strength beneath courtly polish. His forearm flexed as he lifted his own tankard, corded muscle shifting with ease, as though he was just as familiar with a sparring ring as a throne room. His jaw was clean and sharp, softened only by the curve of a smile that came too easily, too genuinely, for the kind of prince she had come to expect.

But it was his eyes that she liked the most, lit with warmth. They didn't look at her like she was a pawn on a gameboard. They looked at her like she was just...*her.*

Calliope's stomach flipped, and she quickly sipped her drink to hide the foolish smile threatening her lips. What was happening to her?

She lowered her tankard, emboldened by the mead spreading warmly throughout her chest. "Well," she said lightly, eyes dancing, "you're not bad to look at."

Leander's smile curved wider, as though her teasing had only encouraged him. He leaned even closer, voice dipping low. "Not bad, hm? You wound me. I was hoping for something grander."

Before she could reply, he went on, eyes bright with mischief and earnestness all at once. "Allow me to tell you what I see. Your hair catches the light like spun gold," he said softly. "Like sunlight breaking over the sea, or wheat fields just before harvest. And your eyes are like the horizon at dawn, where all the world feels possible."

Heat swept through her cheeks and into her chest. She ducked her head with a laugh, trying to mask the way she blushed so furiously. *Nerae*, he was shameless. And yet, when she dared to glance up again, she found his gaze steady on her, no mockery, no insincerity. Just that warmth, as though he meant every foolish word.

He was handsome, confident, princely—yes. But so much more.

She steadied herself with another sip, then let her gaze drift—bold now, almost daring. "Well, if we are trading compliments...your jaw is far too sharp for its own good. And your shoulders look like they were carved by a sculptor with a fondness for symmetry. And your eyes…radiant enough to make the sun jealous."

Oh, if Nerissa could only hear her now, she would be gagging.

Leander's ears flushed pink, though his grin grew wider. He shook his head slowly, as though each word was both a delight and a torment. "I could accept all that praise, but it wouldn't matter. Compared to your beauty, Calliope, I am little more than a shadow against the light."

Her laugh spilled out, bright and bubbly. He was incorrigible, and worse, she adored it. The nervous energy was long gone now, replaced by something giddy and effervescent, like she might float clear off her seat. Or maybe that was the drink.

She smiled softly as she leaned her elbows on the table, something her mother would have immediately admonished had she caught her doing so. "Tell me about yourself," she said, curious. "What are your parents like?"

Leander's expression shifted. "My mother died giving birth to me."

Calliope's heart sank. "Oh. I am so sorry." *Nice going, Calliope.*

He gave a small shrug, eyes flicking down to the rim of his tankard. "Do not be. I never had the chance to know her, so it does not sting the way it might have otherwise."

She reached across the table for his hand, almost without thinking, her fingers brushing his knuckles in a fleeting, sympathetic gesture. "Still, it must have been lonely."

"Sometimes," he admitted, then straightened a little, his smile returning. "But I had my father. And we have a good relationship, though it is not easy finding time for each other. He has his duties, and I have mine. Half the time, we are like ships passing in the night. Still, when we do get a moment together, he makes it count."

The sincerity in his tone warmed her more than the mead ever could. She found herself studying his face again, struck by how plainly he spoke. No courtly pretenses, no rehearsed drivel, just Leander, as he was.

And she liked him all the more for it.

Calliope tilted her head, curiosity not quite satisfied. "And what kind of man is he? Not just as king."

Leander's smile deepened, touched with pride. "He is fair. Just. The kind of ruler who listens more than he speaks. My grandfather was...harsher. Stern, set in the old ways. But my father is different. He believes peace is possible, wants it more than most think. He is willing to risk trust where others would draw swords. He has taught me a lot about what it means to rule, as well as the importance of diplomacy."

The more Leander spoke, the more Calliope felt the lingering tension melt away. Of course, she was prepared to marry for the sake of peace between their two kingdoms, but it was a happy coincidence that the prince of Astyra also seemed to be a decent, honorable man. She found herself rather fancying her betrothed.

"Then perhaps we have more in common than I thought," she said with a dreamy smile.

"I hope so." Leander tilted his head, eyes sparkling with curiosity. "And what of your parents? What are they like?"

"My mother is very warm, but no nonsense. She runs the palace with quiet efficiency, though she always makes time for the healing chambers. I often help her there, tending to minor injuries and illnesses. She says it keeps us grounded, a reminder of the lives we serve."

She felt a blush creep into her cheeks yet again at the way Leander gazed upon her. She pressed on quickly, "I'm very close with her. My father is different, more stoic. He doesn't wear his heart openly, but he shows his love in his own ways. The peace treaty has been his life's work. He's been striving for it for decades. It means more to him than most could imagine."

Leander regarded her quietly, something like respect flickering in his eyes. "Then we both have fathers who carry the weight of kingdoms on their shoulders."

"Yes," she agreed. "And perhaps together we can help them lift that weight."

Her gaze wandered past Leander, across the tavern, where she caught sight of Nerissa. Her handmaiden was still seated stiffly at the table, but a rather roguish-looking man was standing there, trying to make conversation. Nerissa's face was a mask of barely concealed irritation, her eyes flashing with that particular brand of sharp warning Calliope knew all too well.

A laugh bubbled up in Calliope's throat. Oh, he was chasing the wrong current. *Nerae* help him if he thought Nerissa would be charmed by a grin and a smooth line. She shook her head faintly, turning back to Leander, still smiling to herself.

CHAPTER 4

NEVER TRUST A TAVERN NAMED AFTER A WOMAN

Nerissa

Nerissa was so focused on the royals across the tavern that she almost didn't notice the figure at the edge of her vision. Her hand twitched toward her hip, but she didn't draw. Not yet.

A man had paused beside her table, tall and lean, all swagger and charm. Locks the color of wet driftwood fell across his brow in lazy disarray, like they'd been mussed by a good strong wind, the longer strands refusing to behave despite the cropped sides. His skin was bronzed from the sun, jaw dusted with the kind of scruff that said razors weren't welcome aboard whatever ship had spat him out.

Bright green eyes slid over her, measuring and amused. Deliberately, his gaze dropped to the daggers at her hips, lingering longer than she deemed necessary, the corner of his mouth twitching in what might've been admiration...or a very poor survival instinct.

Like he *knew* what she was capable of and decided it would be fun to poke the shark anyway.

His dark leather coat hung open to reveal a black linen shirt and the flash of a braided cord at his throat. Nothing about him was polished; everything he wore looked like it had been slept in, fought in, or stolen. Probably all three.

She immediately noted the subtle shift in the drape of his coat over his left hip, just enough to suggest a weapon tucked at his side.

Pirate.

He leaned in, voice pitched low with a rough, weathered timbre. "What's a lass like you doin' in a place like this? Lookin' for trouble—or waitin' for it?"

Oh, drag me to the abyss. What had she possibly done to insinuate that she was in any way approachable? He was probably drunk.

Her chin lifted a fraction. "Whichever it is, it's none of your business."

He grinned, unbothered by the bite in her tone. "That so? Shame. I was hopin' to make it mine."

Tides help her, she was not about to let some salt-drenched flirt with unruly hair and a death wish become a distraction. She needed to get rid of him, and fast; he was getting in her way.

"You must be bored out of your mind if I'm the most interesting thing in this room."

"Bored, aye, but not blind. And I'd wager you could use company. Let me buy you a drink."

"I don't drink with strangers," she dismissed his offer.

"Then let's fix that." Undeterred, he stretched out his hand. "Zale. And you are?"

Fathoms below, he was *relentless.*

"I know three different ways to dislocate a shoulder. Ask me how many start with a handshake," she said with ice in her tone.

He chuckled, not pulling his hand back. "Fortunately, I've got two of 'em. Which one d'ye fancy first?"

He wasn't backing down, and the longer she kept fencing words with him, the more heads would turn. Her eyes flicked to his hand, still hanging there between them, then back to his face. She couldn't very well throw him out without drawing attention, but she didn't have to make this easy for him either.

"Fine," she said at last, voice cooling off. "One drink. Then you leave me be."

"A compromise, then." He slid into the chair opposite her, adjusting his coat like he was settling in for a long voyage. She noticed the way he deliberately tugged his sleeves back down to his wrists. An oddly warm, spicy-sweet scent clung to him, something she couldn't name.

"So, what d'ye like? Strong, bitter, sweet?"

She'd never had a drink in her life. Damarion had always warned her, should she ever venture back to the surface, that it dulled the senses, clouded the mind. And now here she was, cornered in a tavern by a pirate with a smile like sin, being asked to pick between poisons she didn't know the first thing about.

Her fingers drummed once against the wooden table before she stilled them. Best not to let him see she was flustered. "I wouldn't know," she said at last, tone clipped. "Surprise me."

“Alright then,” he tipped his head. “We’ll keep it light. Somethin’ that won’t bite harder than it should.”

His tone wasn't mocking, just matter of fact, with the slight lilt of a coastal accent. He turned his head, catching the tavern maid’s attention with a lift of two fingers. “A mead. Sweet, easy on the stomach.”

Sweet and easy on the stomach...he probably thought that would encourage her to drink more than she should. She decided right then and there to limit herself to a few sips only. She had no precedent for how alcohol might affect her body, and she didn’t fancy testing that threshold today.

The tavern maid returned with two pints, setting them down hard enough that froth lapped the rims. Zale slid one across the table toward her with a flourish, then raised his own in salute.

“To new acquaintances,” he said easily, taking a long swallow.

Nerissa surveyed the drink with a critical eye. The smell was sharp and sweet, like honey and something heavier beneath. Hardly poison, but still a risk. She lifted it carefully, the cool metal damp against her fingers, and took the smallest sip.

Heat bloomed at once, crawling down her throat and spreading through her chest like a tide she couldn’t hold back. She coughed once, and set the mug down with deliberate control, as though she’d meant to stop there all along.

Zale was watching her, waiting for a reaction.

“Not bad, aye?” he said.

She lifted the vessel again, and discovered that the second sip went down easier. Too easy. By the third, a faint flush had crept into her cheeks.

“It's…not bad at all,” she admitted. Under different circumstances, she might actually enjoy this...*mead.*

She glanced across the tavern at Calliope, who was daintily sipping what she could only assume was the same drink. With mild alarm, she realized that the edges of her vision felt softer, almost blurred. It was like she was moving in slow motion, trying to catch up to everything around her.

Zale leaned forward, resting an elbow on the table. "Mind yourself now. Mead can sneak up on you. Sweet on the tongue, sharper on the back end. Bit like you, I'd wager."

Her hand froze, eyes snapping to his. For a moment, she considered whether tossing the drink in his face counted as a diplomatic incident. How dare he? She was a lot of things, but "sweet" sure as the abyss wasn't one of them.

"So," he drawled, when she didn't take the bait. "What brings you and blondie to the Siren? Can't be the ambiance."

Nerissa's fingers tightened around the mug. The ambiance was smoke, sweat, and ale-stained wood. A den for men like him, not her. She had half a mind to tell him as much, but the words stalled on her tongue. If she brushed him off too bluntly, he'd only push harder. If she said too much, she'd risk more than his curiosity. He had already noticed that she hadn't come here alone. How long had he been watching her?

She set down her drink with deliberate calm, her voice clipped. "Not the ambiance. And not the company, either."

He didn't flinch. If anything, the grin softened, turned thoughtful. He leaned back just a little, voice dropping lower, edged with something sharper than banter.

"Then it must be important, whatever keeps you here. Can't imagine you suffer taverns like this for fun."

He noticed more than he let on, she noted with a growing sense of unease.

"I don't owe you my reasons," she said finally. "And you'll find I'm far less interesting than you think."

The pirate took a slow sip of his mead, grin returning in increments.

"Oh, I highly doubt that. You're her shadow, aren't you?" A flick of his chin toward Calliope, who was still engaged in light, flirtatious conversation with Leander. "Bodyguard? Cousin? Faithful maid with a mean right hook?"

Moirai. So much for drawing attention away from the princess. Nerissa looked back at him, fingers itching towards her hip.

"Bodyguard," she confirmed. "And if you've any sense of self-preservation, you'll stop asking questions now."

He only leaned in, elbows braced on the table, grin cutting wider.

"Sense, aye. Preservation...not so much." His gaze lingered before he took another slow drink. "But I can handle myself."

Against her better judgment, she lifted her own pint and took another swallow, letting the honeyed burn roll down her throat rather than dignify his words with an answer. *Was the table always this slanted?*

"I don't know you," she said finally. "But I know your type. Cocky, arrogant, and—"

"Charming?" he offered, grin widening.

"Shameless," she corrected without hesitation.

He tipped his pint toward her in salute. "Not even close to the worst thing I've been called. I'll take it."

She glowered at him. "None of those were meant to be compliments."

"Speak for yourself." Then he tilted his head, jerking his chin downward.

"Let's talk about those daggers. Just for show, or are you any good with them?"

"They're not ornaments," she said coolly. "If that's what you're asking."

"Didn't think so," he said, looking far too satisfied. He leaned back, studying her the way some men might admire a fine jewel. "Still, be a shame if you carried steel that sharp without knowin' how to use it."

"Oh, don't you worry about me." Her eyes flicked, just briefly, to the hilt of his sword half-hidden beneath his coat. When she looked back, her mouth curved in the faintest shadow of a smile, one that wasn't kind.

"And what about you?" she asked. "Has that blade ever tasted blood? Or is it simply meant to scare people off?"

For the first time, his grin slipped, just for a fraction. Something darker flickered in his eyes, heavier.

"It's seen its share," he said quietly. Then, just as quickly, the smirk returned, easy as ever.

"Maybe we put your daggers and my blade to the test. Winner buys the next round."

Nerissa opened her mouth to speak but froze mid-breath. Across the tavern, a man had stumbled toward Calliope. Then his arm snaked around her shoulders as he kissed her. Sloppily. Loudly. A drunken, unwanted press of lips that made Nerissa see red. Calliope recoiled, face twisting in disgust, but before Nerissa could move, Leander did.

He surged to his feet and yanked the man back by the collar, delivering a clean, furious punch straight to the man's jaw.

The man went flying, crashing down onto the next table over. Cards scattered to the floor, drinks spilled, chairs screeched.

And then *everyone* stood up.

"*Moirai*," Nerissa cursed under her breath. Her head felt heavier than it should, heat buzzing behind her eyes, blurring the edges of the room. Why had she taken that last sip?

The men at the neighboring table surrounded Leander in an instant, shouting curses, fists clenched. One of them grabbed a chair. Another cracked his knuckles.

"Bloody stars," Zale muttered, eyes scanning the rising chaos across the tavern. He gave Nerissa a look, no smirk this time. "Your friend's about to become very popular."

He nudged his chair back with one boot and stood, not blocking her path, but clearing it.

"Go."

Her pulse spiked, cutting through the haze. In one fluid motion, she leapt to her feet, blades sliding free with a soft *shhhhck*.

Then she immediately stumbled into the edge of the table.

"*Rheos Apatos!*" she cursed under her breath, steadying herself.

"You good?" Zale reached a hand out as if to assist, before thinking better of it and withdrawing.

"Fine," she ground out through clenched teeth, eyes locking on Calliope, who had gone pale with panic. Leander was holding his ground, for now, but more patrons were rising, swept up in the fight like a tide pulling everyone out to sea.

Nerissa shoved past Zale and ducked under a flying punch, the noise of the brawl pounding in her ears, muddled by the fuzz of alcohol. She forced her focus to narrow until there was nothing but the princess's face across the chaos. She would protect her. At any cost.

Zale

Zale slipped through the crowd, coat flaring behind him as he cut a path back to his own table. Bran collected his cards, smoothly sweeping them up into one deck before stuffing them into his coat. Ma Wen gathered up the leftover snacks, looking very unamused, while Cormac let out a gravelly sigh, still seated.

"I told ye lads. Never trust a tavern named after a woman. Bad luck, bad ale, bad company." He took one last swig before standing with the slow, deliberate menace of a man who'd seen more bar fights than birthdays. "What's the play, then?"

"Help her," Zale snapped, jerking his chin toward the mysterious woman with the daggers. "She knows what she's doin', but I think she's a bit tipsy."

Bran smirked, pushing up to his feet with a wolfish grin. "You get her drunk already?"

"She only had a few sips! And it was *mead*," Zale protested, throwing up a hand. "Shouldn't have hit her that quick; even green lads last longer than that."

Bran's grin widened as he clapped him on the shoulder. "Maybe you *are* the charming one, mate. Knock a girl flat in three sips."

Zale didn't dignify that with an answer, just shoved him toward the fight. Ma Wen was tightening his bun and rolling up his sleeves with the air of a man resigned to a mess. Cormac grumbled to himself, but he still grabbed a half-empty bottle from the table like it might serve as a club.

And then Zale followed, scanning the chaos for the dark-haired lass. Fists were swinging, chairs were splintering, the stink of ale and sweat sharp in the air. He shoved a drunk out of his way and caught sight of her again. She was quick, daggers darting in warning arcs that kept the worst of them back. But she was swaying oddly off-kilter, as if she was trying to move across the deck of a ship lurching in a storm. The mead, blast him. It was affecting her worse than he thought.

A fist came swinging for her from the blind side, and Zale was there in an instant, catching the man by the collar and driving his own fist into the bastard's gut. The man doubled over, gasping, and Zale shoved him aside.

Bran whooped nearby, laying into another sailor. Ma Wen landed a punch that sent a tankard flying, and Cormac swung his bottle hard enough to shatter it across someone's face.

Zale didn't take his eyes off the girl. She was holding her own, but if she slipped, if she got hurt because of that cursed drink he'd put in her hand, he'd never forgive himself.

Nerissa

The room wasn't steady. Or maybe *she* wasn't steady. Her head throbbed, vision fuzzy. She shook her head hard, trying to clear it, and nearly stumbled when her sandals slid in spilled ale. The mead, light as it had seemed, was still burning through her veins. She should have heeded Damarion's warning.

A sailor staggered into her path, swinging wide. She ducked low, ready to carve a line across his ribs, only for a hand to clamp down on his shoulder and yank him back. The man yelped as another fist drove into his jaw, sending him sprawling. Nerissa blinked, catching the briefest flash of a stranger with a wolfish grin before he melted back into the fight.

Strange.

Another brute loomed ahead, chair raised like an axe. Nerissa braced, then a stocky man with his hair tied back in a bun stepped neatly into the blow, catching the chair's leg and twisting it free as though plucking a fish bone. He shoved her assailant aside and turned back toward the melee without a word.

Nerissa's breathing came sharp. She shook her head again, clearing the haze, and forced her footing to steady. Two men downed in the space of breaths, neither by her hand. Both conveniently clearing her path.

She didn't have time to question it. Calliope had been driven back, ducking behind an overturned table as Leander fended off two men at once, brow bleeding.

Nerissa pushed forward. A man twice her size grabbed her arm and instantly regretted it. She twisted beneath his grip, drove an elbow into his gut, then jabbed her arm upward. Except she had forgotten that she had no razor-sharp fins in this form. The blunt strike barely slowed her opponent, and the mistake cost her. She had to scramble back, teeth clenched, readjusting to the limitations of her human body.

Someone yanked her sideways as the man charged at her. He slammed into the wall and crumpled to the floor with a satisfying *thud.* She spun around, blades ready, only to find herself face-to-face with *him.* The pirate.

"Easy," he raised both hands in surrender. "Looked like you could use a hand."

Her pulse thundered, whether from the mead or from fury, she couldn't say. But she didn't lower her blades. Not yet.

"I don't need your help," she snapped, pivoting back towards Calliope.

But his fingers caught her arm, firm enough to halt her for half a heartbeat. His grin had dimmed, replaced with a searching look.

"Your pupils," he said. "They're blown wide. Mead's hittin' you harder than it should."

"No thanks to you," she bit out, yanking her arm free with a scowl as she turned away.

But he wasn't finished. He kept pace at her shoulder, weaving through the melee with infuriating ease, as if this was just another day for him.

"Suit yourself. But I'd rather not watch you get knocked unconscious before I get your name. Even if you're dead set on throwin' yourself in the middle of every fist in the room."

The absolute audacity…

She spun on him with a sharp glare, only to find herself staring at his chest. Oh, he was taller than she'd realized. Tilting her chin higher, she leveled her fury properly at his face. He only grinned, teeth flashing as if her anger amused him all the more.

She wanted to wipe that smug smile off his face. Was this all a game to him? Did he not realize they were outnumbered?

A burly man with a crooked nose suddenly lunged at her. Before she could react, Zale reached out and slammed the man's head into the bar with a *thunk*.

"Honestly," he said, brushing his hands off, "you're welcome."

Nerissa didn't thank him. Just gave him a look of grudging, irritated approval.

"Watch the left!" Zale barked suddenly.

She dropped to one knee, albeit slower than she intended, and a mug whistled over her head, shattering against the post behind her. Ale sprayed across her shoulder, cold and sticky. *Ugh.* She resisted the urge to wipe it off with her hand.

"Nice reflexes," he said. "We'd make a good team."

She rose to her feet, expression flat. "This is *not* a team."

"Keep tellin' yourself that," Zale said, backing toward her as three more men closed in. "On your right."

Nerissa pivoted as the man lunged, her dagger slashing across his arm and sending him staggering back with a curse. Before he could recover, she drove her foot into his chest, then swept his legs out from under him. Fighting on land felt strange. Up here, gravity mattered, but she could use it to her advantage.

Behind her, Zale ducked a swing meant for his head and returned it, knocking his opponent out cold. He shook his hand, wincing, then turned straight into a fist from the third man. The blow hit him square across the jaw, snapping his head to the side.

The man lunged for Nerissa next, catching a fistful of her hair, jerking her head back. She brought her dagger up and sliced clean through the lock. He stumbled at the sudden release, off balance just long enough for Zale to seize him by the collar and hurl him over the bar counter with a crash.

Nerissa rubbed her scalp, exhaling hard through her nose. Foolish of her to not think of tying it back before getting into a fight.

"Aw, *salt and storms*!" Zale halted in front of her, fingers brushing his split lip. "That *just* healed from the last bar fight."

"So, is this a weekly occurrence, then?" Nerissa asked, surveying their immediate surroundings.

"It was a simple misunderstanding," he said with a crooked smile, then hissed when the motion tugged at the cut.

"Right." She gave him a flat look. "Well, if you want to make yourself useful, then follow me."

"'Useful', she says, after I toss a man clear over the counter," he grumbled but fell into step beside her anyway, straightening his coat.

Nerissa didn't miss how he was still grinning like a fool. As if there was no real danger. Then she realized he had yet to draw his sword.

Her brows knit as she slashed at a man's arm and sent him stumbling back. "Why?" she demanded. "You've steel at your side, why hesitate to use it? Surely your sword would be more efficient."

Zale ducked under a wild punch, straightening with a shrug that was almost careless. "There's a difference between self-defense and violence," he said. "Don't see the need to risk killin' anyone over a standard tavern brawl."

His words gave her pause; she had dismissed him as reckless, arrogant, just a pirate with more charm than sense. But here he was, choosing restraint when he could have easily chosen blood.

Maybe her first appraisal had been...off.

She shoved the thought aside as Calliope came into view once again. She was all that mattered. From behind the overturned table, Calliope's eyes darted up at Nerissa, wide with relief. Leander was still standing his ground, jaw set as he fended off a trio of staggering brawlers. His knuckles were bloodied, his breath ragged, but he hadn't given an inch.

Nerissa vaulted the last stretch of debris, daggers raised. One man lunged at Leander's flank. She intercepted, her blade slicing across his arm in a shallow line that made him howl and stagger back. Another surged from the right, but Zale met him head-on, driving a fist into the man's gut and hurling him aside with unexpected strength.

Nerissa seized Calliope's wrist, hauling her upright. "Time to go."

"But Leander—"

"He can handle himself."

Before Calliope could argue, someone shoved her roughly from behind.

She hit the floor hard, palms skidding against the floorboards. The world tilted, her head swimming as she fought to rise. The mead was still in her blood, thick and cloying, dragging at her limbs. She swore she'd never touch the drink again.

Calliope's scream jolted her back to the situation at hand.

Nerissa looked up, vision blurring at the edges. A man loomed above her, teeth bared, with a jagged chair leg raised high over his head. She scrambled, sandals sliding as she clawed for footing. Too slow.

A bottle arced in from the side and shattered across the man's temple. He crumpled, the chair leg clattering harmlessly to the floor.

Nerissa blinked through the spray of glass and liquor to find an older man standing over her, copper beard bristling.

"On yer feet, lass," he growled, turning to swing a fist at the next man in line.

Before she could push herself upright, another hand closed around her arm and pulled her up. Zale. She swayed slightly in his grip. Only when she regained her footing did he release her.

"Take your friend and go," he said, pressing her daggers back into her grip. "Out the back."

Nerissa holstered her weapons and reached for Calliope, guiding her towards the exit. She glanced back at Zale.

"Thank you."

His brows rose in mock surprise. "Was that…gratitude?"

She scowled at him. "Don't push it." Then she shoved Calliope out the back door.

CHAPTER 5

SHINIER THAN A SELKIE'S BACKSIDE

Zale

Only two brawlers left squaring off against the pale-haired prince. Kid had backbone, he'd give him that. Too much polish, but he wasn't afraid to bloody his knuckles. Royals usually kept their hands clean, let other men do the swinging. This one was different. Or stupid. Sometimes hard to tell the difference.

Zale slipped in at his flank, catching one brute by the collar and slamming his face into the table's edge. The man crumpled without ceremony. Together, he and Leander turned on the last, driving him back with twin blows until the bastard staggered off into the fray.

Breath ragged, Leander wiped a sleeve across his mouth. "My thanks," he said. "I should slip out the back before—"

"—before anyone recognizes the crown prince?" Zale finished for him, arms crossed.

The boy froze, surprise flickering across his face.

Zale gave a sharp laugh, tugging his coat straight. "A cloak would've been more inconspicuous."

Leander's mouth opened as if to say something, but he thought better of it. With a last glance toward Zale, he slipped out the door and was gone.

Zale watched the prince vanish with curiosity. Royals didn't drink in taverns without guards. Royals didn't drink in taverns, full stop. Something about it reeked of secrets, and secrets usually meant trouble.

He exhaled, rolling the ache from his shoulders. The tavern had finally calmed down—somewhat. He swept his gaze around the dining area, looking for his crew.

To his left, Bran was locked in a tug-of-war over someone's coat, laughing like a lunatic. "I *told* you we should've gone to the quiet place by the docks!"

"That was a brothel, Bran!" Zale shouted.

"Still quieter than this!"

To his right, Ma Wen was casually flipping a barstool into the arms of a man charging at him, who promptly tripped, somersaulted, and stayed down. Ma Wen, unbothered, popped another dried plum into his mouth and nodded at Zale.

"Nice way to start the day, huh?"

Zale had no time to respond—someone grabbed him from behind.

He dropped low, elbowed backward, then used the momentum to flip his assailant neatly over his shoulder. The man landed on the table with a crash and didn't move again.

"Cormac!" Zale called, searching the room.

No answer.

If the old man had gone down in the scuffle, Zale was never going to hear the end of it. Not from Brigid, not from Roan. He'd probably have to carry the bastard back to the ship himself. Again.

He finally spotted the old seadog half-lodged under a table, blinking blearily and muttering about royals and bloody bar tabs. "That's it," Zale sighed, pinching the bridge of his nose. "We're cuttin' him off at three. Or four. Five, *maximum*."

Brigid O'Connell's voice cut through the harbor air like a cannonball.

"Ye brainless, rum-soaked barnacles! Ye walk into town *once—once!*—an' come back with half th' tavern broken an' th' other half still bleedin'!"

Bran was rubbing the back of his head, wincing as Roan stitched up a gash on his shoulder. Ma Wen leaned against the mast, calmly plucking splinters from his forearm. His expression remained pleasantly neutral, like a man at peace with other people's bad decisions. Cormac sat atop a barrel with a cloth pressed to his nose and an expression that suggested he thought Brigid's wrath was a mild spring drizzle compared to the hangover blooming behind his eyes.

"It wasn't a big deal, Brigid," Zale attempted to explain. "We were just tryin'—"

She turned on him, boots thudding against the deck, the full force of her glare zeroing in like a cannon sighting its mark. Her fiery curls had escaped from beneath her tricorn hat in wild spirals, framing a face that was all sharp cheekbones and sharper fury.

"*Eh?*" she snapped, "Ye was tryin' to what? Get us kicked out of yet *another* fine establishment?"

Zale held up his hands in a gesture of innocence that only made her narrow her eyes further. "Look, in our defense, *we* didn't start it."

"Nay, of course nae," she said, voice saccharine. "Ye *never* start it. Brawls just *gravitate* to ye like flies to a midden heap."

Zale knew she was livid; that's when her brogue was the thickest. She didn't even need the axe at her hip, her tongue was lethal enough. He respected it, even when he was on the receiving end. Especially then.

He opened his mouth to protest again but stopped when he saw the crew shaking their heads behind Brigid.

"Ye'll all be scrubbin' th' deck 'til I can see me own scowl smilin' back at me!" she barked. "An' *you*—" she jabbed a finger at Zale, "barnacle duty. Boots off. Scraper ready. I want that hull shinier than a selkie's backside on a sunny day."

Zale groaned. "Come on, Brigid. That's cruel and unusual punishment."

"Nay, that's *what happens* when ye pick a fight with half a port town before *breakfast*. Be grateful I'm not making ye clean the bilge with yer teeth."

With the worst of the shouting over, the crew scattered to their assigned punishments like scolded schoolchildren. Mops slapped against the deck and brushes hit buckets, as a general air of sullen repentance settled over the pirates like heavy fog. Except for one.

Eon stood tall and lanky, like someone had stretched him out on a rack and then forgot to fill in the muscle. The mop of curly blonde hair on his head made him look even younger than his sixteen years. He had the bright, curious eyes of a boy who'd read one too many adventure novels and never quite grown out of them, and a smattering of freckles that made him look perpetually sunburnt. His shirt was rumpled, his belt crooked, and his boots were, somehow, on the wrong feet.

Despite this, or perhaps because of it, there was a certain charm to him. The kind that made it impossible to stay angry when he forgot his chores because he'd been charting constellations instead. Again.

"I wasn't even *there,* Quartermaster!" Eon protested, wide-eyed and clutching a mop like it might double as a sword. "I was on the ship. In complete solitude. Completely innocent. *Completely alibi'd.*"

Brigid turned on him with the kind of look that could blister paint. "Ye're guilty by association, savvy?"

Eon blinked. "That...doesn't feel legally sound."

"Swab the deck, *Eon.* Or I'll assign ye to clean the latrine instead. Blindfolded."

Eon muttered something about injustices of the maritime world as he began swabbing with dramatic flair.

Captain Nestor chose that precise moment to emerge from his quarters, his boots clicking lightly across the sun-warmed deck. He stood tall, with a broad, commanding presence that never needed to raise its voice. His skin was sun-bronzed, weathered by salt spray and time, with the deep-lined laugh marks of a man who'd lived long and lived well. His hair, coal-black and tied back at the nape of his neck, framed a sharply cut face crowned with a short, grizzled beard. The edges of his black coat flared slightly in the breeze as if it had its own sense of dramatic timing.

He stopped next to Brigid, surveying the scene with a vague air of amusement, as if they weren't running a ship so much as a particularly unruly schoolyard.

"Deck's lookin' lively," he observed.

"Aye, only 'cause I lit a fire under its arse," Brigid grumbled.

They stood nearly eye-to-eye, with Brigid only a couple inches shorter than the captain, her tall frame squared in defiant confidence.

He gave her a slow grin. "You're far too hard on them."

"An' ye're far too soft by half."

"That's why it works," he said simply, voice calm as the sea before a storm. "They fear ye. They like me. Between us, they mostly behave."

She huffed, her mouth twitching as she fought a smile.

Nestor chuckled and gave her a nod. "Carry on, Quartermaster."

Zale trudged toward the edge of the ship, dragging the long-handled scraper behind him like a condemned man hauling his own gallows.

Bran sidled up beside him, offering a lazy grin. "Y'know," he said, voice just low enough to avoid Brigid's earshot, "none of this would've happened if you'd let *me* flirt with the girl."

Zale shot him a glare. "She'd have gutted you with one of those fancy knives before you finished sayin' *hello*."

Bran sighed dreamily. "Worth it."

Zale snorted and kicked off his boots, muttering as he stripped off his coat. "Next time, *you* can take barnacle duty."

"Nah," Bran said cheerfully, dipping a mop into a bucket. "That one's all yours, mate. You're the only one who actually *likes* being in the water that long."

Zale grumbled something profoundly uncharitable and dove over the side with a splash, the cold harbor water stinging his split lip raw, the taste of salt and blood mingling as he kicked downward.

The sound of Brigid's shouting was muffled beneath the waves, reduced to a dull thrum above the surface. Down here, it was just him, the barnacles, and the slow rhythm of scraping away crusted reminders of time at sea.

Zale pressed the flat of the blade hard, levering another stubborn cluster of barnacles from the *Black Serpent's* hull. They broke away with a satisfying *crack*, sinking into the murk below. He kicked off the keel and shifted down a few feet, bubbles streaming past his ears as he set the scraper against the next patch.

Cold water bit into his skin, but he hardly noticed. His thoughts were elsewhere.

That morning in the tavern.

The mystery girl who didn't drink with strangers. Stars, he'd never seen anyone fight the way she had—fluid, precise, with a familiar grace to it. Not even Brigid, as fierce as she was, moved like that. And the woman had been fogged with mead. What would she have been like stone-sober?

He exhaled sharply, bubbles boiling up toward the surface, and pushed along the curve of the hull.

What gnawed at him more was the lad. Leander. Crown prince of Astyra, sitting in a tavern with no guards, no courtesans, no fanfare. Meeting a blonde lass with fine manners and wide eyes. And if the dark-haired one was her bodyguard, that meant the blonde was someone important.

The port had been buzzing with rumors that Leander would be wed to a foreign princess by tomorrow afternoon. So, what in the stars' names was he doing tucked away with another woman the day before? A mistress? A dalliance? Didn't fit clean, but then, royal games never did.

Zale scraped harder, barnacles splintering under the edge of the blade.

As for the dark-haired girl...no use puzzling over her. He didn't even know her name, and it wasn't likely he'd ever see her again. Still, he couldn't shake the memory of the way she'd grown so flustered with irritation at his mere presence. It was rather cute how her nose had crinkled every time she scowled at him.

He didn't realize how long he'd been holding his breath until the pressure in his chest finally nudged his focus back to his body. Like a polite reminder that it was time to go up.

Zale kicked upward and broke through the surface with a splash, blinking against the brightness of the sunlight. His hair clung to his forehead as he treaded water beside the ship. He brushed it back and let himself float, eyes on the cloud-streaked sky.

Even if she'd given her name—stars, even if she'd softened long enough to make conversation—what would that have led to? Nowhere. He was a pirate. They'd be leaving port the day after tomorrow, and the life he lived didn't leave room for long-term anything. Better not to bother.

Not that she seemed open to a second drink, let alone courtship. And what did he know about courtship anyway? He hardly knew anything of life beyond this ship. Hardly knew anything of relationships, he'd probably do something idiotic and ruin things if he ever did find himself in one. He had no business pursuing any woman, let alone one so clearly out of his league. What could he offer? His meager wage was fair and allowed him to take care of his needs, and then some. It wasn't enough to provide for a wife—

Stars no. He was getting ahead of himself again. Always romanticizing about things that would never be. This wasn't one of Nestor's ridiculously unrealistic romance novels. A rueful grin spread across his face as he recalled one such book. He never would have read it of his own accord. Ever. Eon had snuck it off of Nestor's bookshelf and been caught red-handed by Brigid. Instead of punishing the lad, Nestor insisted on a dramatic reading in front of the entire crew, much to Brigid's ire.

Zale chuckled to himself, recalling the overly poetic—and borderline questionable—metaphors that had even made Cormac blush. If memory served him right, one such metaphor actually involved a barnacle. Speaking of which…

He sucked in a deep breath of air before diving back under and set to work scraping off the remaining parasites. As often as Brigid liked to dole out this particular punishment, he figured there should really be a lot less of the crustaceans lodging themselves into the hull by this point.

It took Zale the better part of an hour to finish scraping the hull. When he climbed back over the railing, sopping wet, Brigid threw a bundle of dry clothes and a towel at his head.

"Straight to the washroom," she pointed aft. At least she'd cooled off since threatening to send everyone to the gallows.

Zale grumbled. "I just rinsed off!"

Nestor walked by then, offering his two coppers. "Ye smell like the harbor, lad."

"Right then," Brigid continued. "I'll nae have ye stinkin' up me galley. Go on with ye."

Zale threw the towel around his shoulders with a huff and dragged his feet to the washroom. It was basically a reclaimed storage room with a large barrel of rainwater, a mirror, and a bucket. Brigid insisted on cleanliness, and Roan had backed her up, claiming it was good for their health.

Soap was his mortal enemy. It wasn't that Zale minded getting clean though, it was the horrible bar of lye that everyone had to use. It was harsh on his skin; every time Zale used it, he had to follow up with a visit to the infirmary for Roan's miracle balm to soothe the red patches that plagued him after bathing.

Not that anyone else needed to know; he kept that part to himself. Last thing he needed was for the crew to start making fun of his sensitive skin. There was nothing fearsome about a pirate being taken out of commission by something as unassuming as soap.

Closing the washroom door behind him, he stripped off his soaked clothing and left them in a sodden pile in the corner. He held the chunk of soap in his hand, glaring at it.

"We meet again," he muttered, glaring at the wretched thing.

The soap, of course, didn't respond.

CHAPTER 6

A TREATY SEALED IN FLESH

Nerissa

The cold hit Nerissa like a slap to the face, but she welcomed it. They had narrowly made it out of that tides-forsaken tavern in one piece.

What a disaster.

A million berating thoughts fought for dominance as her legs reformed into one limb almost automatically. Iridescent scales coated her newly formed tail, scattering upwards across her body. Her sandals slipped free and sank toward the ocean floor. She prayed that Queen Ophelia wouldn't notice two missing pairs of shoes.

Beside her, Calliope swished her tail through the water, hair swirling behind her in golden ribbons. She'd barely caught her breath before they'd both plunged off the harbor wall, dresses still clinging to them, no time to strip down or stow anything properly.

They didn't stop until the coast was a distant blur behind a curtain of seaweed and schools of flashing fish. Only when they'd reached a quiet stretch of open water, hidden from the view of any boats above, did Nerissa slow down.

"You alright?" she asked, placing a hand on the princess's arm.

Calliope was hugging herself, arms folded tightly, her eyes darting back the way they'd come. "I think so," she said. "That got out of hand."

"That's what happens when someone throws a punch in a crowded tavern."

Calliope gave a sheepish smile. "Leander was just defending me."

"I'm not blaming him," Nerissa said. "But he picked one *abyss* of a place to hold a clandestine meeting."

"It wasn't supposed to go like that," Calliope muttered.

"You don't say." Nerissa didn't care about sounding harsh. Their visit could have gone much differently, and not for the better.

"I'm sorry, Riss," Calliope said softly.

"It's fine," Nerissa let out a long sigh, shaking her head. "Let's just hope your father doesn't find out about your little excursion."

For a moment, Calliope swam in silence, her hair drifting around her like a halo. Then her mouth curved into a sly grin.

"I saw that pirate trying to flirt with you."

Nerissa stiffened. "He was a distraction at best. And barely that. He kept getting in my way."

"Oh, really?" Calliope's voice turned playful. "Because it looked like he was rather in step with you. Almost like you'd fought together before."

Heat prickled across Nerissa's cheeks, and she was grateful for the shadows of the deep. "He was a pirate, Callie. Somehow, I doubt that was his first fight."

Calliope hummed, clearly unconvinced. "Mm. If you say so. Though I did see the way he looked at you. Like a sailor spotting land after a long voyage."

"You wouldn't even know a sailor if you saw one." Nerissa's tone came out sharper than she intended. "This was your first visit to the surface."

"*Someone's* deflecting," Calliope's knowing smile lingered.

Nerissa clenched her jaw, forcing her strokes longer, stronger, as if she could outswim the conversation. She wasn't deflecting. There was nothing *to* deflect. The pirate had been a stranger in a tavern, nothing more. He'd happened to be useful, that was all.

She didn't have time for frivolous pursuits anyway, not when Calliope's safety balanced on the edge of every choice she made. Duty left no room for distraction, least of all ones with crooked grins and wind-tousled hair.

The palace gates loomed ahead, obsidian spires and pearl-studded arches rising from the seafloor, massive and intimidating. Nerissa swam just a tail's flick behind Calliope, scanning the outer halls for any signs of life. It wouldn't do to be seen *returning* to the palace this early in the day.

They'd barely crossed the threshold when a voice drifted toward them, composed and laced with just enough frost to chill the water.

"Well. There you are."

Kaelen.

The courtier hovered near one of the ornamental columns, arms crossed, tail flicking with barely concealed superiority. His scales shimmered faintly, dark as midnight with a sheen like polished sapphire. His platinum hair had been slicked back with snail mucus, not a strand out of place, the pale color stark against his tawny skin.

Unlike Nerissa and Calliope, whose scales bloomed like scattered jewels along their limbs and decolletage, Kaelen's scale coverage was denser, more akin to armor across his forearms and shoulders in tightly layered plates. Razor sharp fins along his forearms glinted faintly beneath the light, tucked close but unmistakably present. His dorsal fin ran along the length of his spine, rising with each irritated flick of his tail.

Eyes of steel swept over them with that familiar glint of cool assessment. "Your father has been, how shall I put this, *less than amused* by your disappearance." He tilted his head toward Calliope, his smile courtly and absolutely insufferable. "You missed this morning's diplomatic briefing."

Calliope drew herself up, lifting her chin in defiance. "I went for a swim and lost track of time. Last I checked, that wasn't treason."

"Not treason, no," Kaelen said lightly. "But if I vanished without telling anyone, I'd be accused of plotting a coup. You vanish, and it's just...spirited youthful rebellion."

Nerissa narrowed her eyes but said nothing. Not yet. She didn't like the way Kaelen looked at Calliope, like he was still measuring her for a ring that no longer fit.

"You'd better go see your father," he added, glancing toward the inner palace. "Before he starts suspecting I helped hide you away." He paused. Then, pointedly, "Again."

Calliope flushed. "Stop bringing up the past like a moody merling, Kaelen. And you would do well to remember who it is you are speaking to."

Kaelen's smile didn't waver, but Nerissa caught the faint tension in his jaw, the crack beneath the polish.

"Off you go then," he drifted out of their path. Then, fixing Nerissa with a smug little smile, he added, "Mind you don't let her out of your sight again, handmaiden. Wouldn't want to see you lose your place at court. Such a rare privilege for someone of your class."

Nerissa floated backward, never breaking eye contact, and lifted her hand in a gesture rude enough to make Calliope gasp. "Go pound sand, Kaelen."

Once they were out of earshot, weaving through the glowing archways of the inner corridor, Calliope let out a sharp breath and muttered, "I forgot how exhausting he is."

Nerissa flicked her tail harder than necessary, startling a nearby pufferfish. "He's such a leech."

Calliope smothered a grin, and Nerissa added, "Is the human prince at least a better conversationalist, or is the court just trading one pompous sea cucumber for another?"

Calliope rolled her eyes, but she couldn't help the smile that stretched across her face. "He's...different."

"Different how?"

"He actually listens." She sounded almost surprised by her own answer. "Do you know what he said to me?"

Nerissa raised her brows. "Do I want to?"

Calliope ignored the tone, gazing into the distance. "He said my eyes reminded him of the horizon at dawn, where all the world feels possible."

Tides have mercy.

Nerissa gagged. "That's incredibly sappy."

Calliope turned, unoffended, her smile dreamy. "Just wait," she said, voice lilting. "One day you'll find someone who makes you feel the way Leander makes me feel. Then you won't think such poetry is sappy. You'll appreciate it."

Nerissa rolled her eyes so hard it made her head ache. "If I ever start spouting nonsense like that, lay me out to petrify in the sun."

Calliope only laughed, twirling once in the water before gliding ahead, her joy trailing behind her like the tendrils of a jellyfish. Then her amusement softened into something more thoughtful. "He asked me what I wanted. Not what the kingdom needed. What *I* wanted."

Nerissa glanced sideways at her, curious but cautious. "And what did you say?"

Calliope's bright eyes met hers, now stripped of the dreamy haze. "I told him I want peace between our kingdoms. And the chance for real exchange, for our people to learn from each other instead of fearing one another."

Nerissa didn't respond right away. She let the silence settle between them like silt, her gaze drifting to the soft glow of bioluminescent patterns threading along the walls. Calliope's words echoed in her head: *He asked me what I wanted.*

That wasn't how things worked in the palace. You were born into duty, raised on expectation. What you *wanted* was beside the point.

Nerissa tilted her head slightly, studying the princess from the corner of her eye.

"You really like him, don't you?"

Calliope hesitated, then gave a small, almost sheepish smile.

"He's charming, yes. But he's also…real."

They drifted forward in silence for a few moments, the palace currents warm and familiar around them. Then Calliope added, softer, more vulnerable this time,

"It's nice, you know? Being seen for more than just what I represent. He didn't look at me like a prize or a bargaining chip. He just...looked at *me*."

Nerissa kept her expression guarded, but her fingers curled slightly at her sides. Calliope knew how she felt about the arranged marriage, no need to remind her now and burst her bubble.

"So…how is this marriage going to work, anyway? The longest any siren has ever remained in human form was seven days before they supposedly turned into dust."

Calliope gave a small huff through her nose, part laugh, part exasperation.

"That story is such royal propaganda. We don't turn to dust."

"No, we just get severe muscle spasms, dry out like kelp left out in the sun, and start hallucinating fish that aren't there," Nerissa muttered.

"Which is why Leander had a special bath installed," Calliope said, smoothing her hair behind her ear. "A full-sized, ocean-fed soaking pool. Straight from the coast every morning."

Nerissa blinked at her. "You're marrying a human and becoming a glorified houseplant."

Calliope grinned. "Well, when you put it that way..."

Nerissa shook her head, but there was a trace of amusement there now. "And that's enough? A fancy tub in the palace?"

"It'll keep me healthy. I don't need to be in the open sea every day, just close enough to it."

Then her smile faded, just a little. "I wish you'd come with me, Riss."

"I'll be at the wedding."

"That's not what I mean." Calliope glanced over. "I meant after. When I'm living in Astyra. I want you there, with me."

Nerissa gave a slow shake of her head. "You know why I can't."

Calliope's brows pulled together, the way they always did before she tried to persuade Nerissa into doing something she did not want to do.

"The surface is no place for me," Nerissa continued. "I don't belong in those mosaic halls or perfumed gardens. I belong here. With our people. I'll be joining the Royal Guard after the treaty's signed. Damarion already approved my placement."

"But you've always been by my side," Calliope said, almost a whisper. "Since we were girls. I don't know what it'll be like, waking up without you there to braid my hair and scowl at court officials."

"You'll survive. You have a soaking tub, remember?"

Calliope let out a watery laugh. "You're awful."

"I'm practical," Nerissa replied. "Always have been."

"...I'll miss you," Calliope said, her voice barely audible.

"You'll have new handmaidens. Maids who speak when they're supposed to, and smile at the right moments, and don't threaten visiting dignitaries with cutlery." Nerissa knew that Calliope would want for nothing; she wouldn't even have time to miss her. There was no point in getting sentimental now.

Calliope's voice cracked around a smile. "None of them will be you."

Nerissa didn't respond, but her gaze lingered on Calliope, the way it always had when she didn't know how to say something she felt.

Finally, she turned away. "Come on. Before Kaelen catches up to us."

The throne room shimmered with filtered morning light, drifting down through the high sea glass domes like golden dust in the water. King Nereus sat atop his throne of shaped basalt, posture upright, his stark-white hair gleaming in the light. A thick beard framed his face, and though age lined the corners of his eyes, there was nothing frail about him.

Beside him, Queen Ophelia sat like carved alabaster wrapped in warmth. Her white hair fell in soft waves down her back, adorned with strands of pearl and pale coral. She looked younger than she should, her features graceful but keen, like time had tried to touch her and been politely rebuffed. Where Nereus projected command, Ophelia radiated wisdom.

"You missed the morning council," Nereus said, though his voice held more relief than reprimand.

"I'm sorry, Father," Calliope began, but he waved a webbed hand gently.

"You're safe. That's what matters." The king's tone turned firm. "I trust you haven't forgotten what tomorrow represents. This alliance is not merely a celebration. It is a cornerstone. And your role in securing that peace must be taken seriously."

Calliope's shoulders squared a little. "I know Father, I haven't forgotten."

"Good," Nereus said, though his eyes searched hers with the weight of both father and king. "There are still many preparations that must be finalized before the day is over. The Astyran emissaries will expect us at first light. Do not give them cause to doubt our commitment."

Calliope inclined her head, the faintest flicker of guilt behind her composed expression. "No cause," she murmured.

"See that there isn't," Nereus replied, then leaned back slightly, as though dismissing the moment but not the weight behind it.

Queen Ophelia's voice followed like a current in his wake, calm and warm. "We know that you will make Nautalia proud, Daughter."

Calliope dipped her head with gratitude. "Thank you, Mother."

Ophelia smiled gently, then turned to Nerissa. "And you Nerissa, always so quiet and steadfast. We're grateful for your vigilance, especially now."

Nerissa bowed her head, the weight of the Queen's regard heavy on her shoulders. If she only knew where they had been that morning. Nerissa wasn't sure that she deserved such praise.

From the far side of the hall, the great doors opened with a low groan of stone against water, admitting the stoic captain of the Royal Guard, Damarion. His close-cropped silver hair shifted slightly in the current, longer at the crown, swaying like strands of kelp. He wore the traditional armor of Nautalia, inlaid with abalone across the breastplate and pauldrons, the same iridescent sheen as the daggers Nerissa wore at her hips. A thin headpiece arched back along his temples, more crown than helmet, a symbol of his status. His scales, a deep cerulean blue, caught the morning light as he moved.

He bowed first to King Nereus and Queen Ophelia, then to Princess Calliope. When he straightened, his eyes focused on Nerissa.

"Nerissa," he said, voice authoritative, "I would have you accompany me to the Astyran castle this afternoon."

She straightened instinctively. "Is something wrong?"

"No," he said, though his tone suggested *not yet*. "But with the ceremony tomorrow, I want to perform a final sweep of the halls. Chambers, entrances, staff rotations, anything that's changed since our last pass."

She didn't ask for details. "Understood."

"Must it be her?" Calliope interjected. "There are other guards."

Damarion's expression didn't shift, but he paused.

"It's the last day before the wedding, I thought we'd—" she broke off. "Never mind."

"I need a fresh set of eyes to spot anything my men may have overlooked. She's better at reading spaces than anyone I've trained," he explained calmly. "You'll have your full retinue tomorrow."

Calliope's lips pressed together. She didn't argue further, but she didn't look reassured, either.

Nerissa gave her hand a squeeze. "We'll have time later," she promised.

Damarion turned then, offering a gesture that was both command and invitation. Nerissa followed without hesitation.

They moved in silence through the outer corridors of the palace, the ceremonial bustle fading behind them. When they were far from the throne room, Damarion slowed.

"I would have brought someone else," he said, not looking at her. "But I trust you more than anyone."

"I know," she replied.

He gave a faint nod. "If something feels wrong—if anything *feels* off—you tell me. I don't care how small it is."

Nerissa glanced at him, trying to read the deeper worry beneath his words. "You sound as if you think something will go wrong."

"I think," he said with a measured tone, "when politics are involved, something *always* goes wrong."

"Spoken like someone with experience on the subject, *Didaskon*?" she pressed. There was something he wasn't telling her.

He hesitated before giving a resigned sigh. "It was twenty-five years ago. King Vasilios had recently replaced his father as ruler of Astyra, and King Nereus thought he might be more open to discussing peaceful negotiations than King Lycaon. Our numbers had dwindled into the hundreds by that point."

Nerissa listened intently.

"I was a field commander at the time. Despite my youth, I was chosen to accompany the king on several of those visits as part of his security detail."

Nerissa folded her arms. "And King Vasilios…he didn't respond with violence?"

"No. He asked questions instead." Damarion's voice softened slightly. "He was young then. Ambitious. Not like his father. He believed the future of Astyra lay beyond its borders...and beneath its waters."

Nerissa frowned. "So why did it take twenty-five years to reach a treaty?"

Damarion's jaw tightened. "Because Vasilios still needed the support of the court. His advisers needed convincing that this wasn't a ruse to lull Astyra into a false sense of security. The proposal of a treaty didn't erase centuries of fighting. But Nereus kept the door open. Kept speaking of a future without fear."

Nerissa tilted her head. "And so he finally offered up Calliope. As proof of good faith."

"The ultimate gesture," Damarion confirmed. "A princess for a crown prince. It would bind the two kingdoms through blood. A treaty sealed in flesh."

Nerissa floated in silence for a moment, processing the history lesson. Damarion rested a hand briefly on her shoulder, about to say something else. Then his gaze sharpened as he studied her face, his eyes narrowing.

"You've been drinking."

Her face instantly flushed with heat. For a heartbeat she considered denying it, but lying to Damarion was as futile as trying to keep a wave upon the sand. He'd see through it, as he always did.

With a sigh, she admitted, "Calliope asked me to escort her to the surface this morning. She wanted to meet Leander in person before the wedding. We ended up at a tavern." Her lips pressed into a thin line. "Someone insisted on buying me a drink."

Damarion's brow furrowed. He reached for her arm, turning it slightly. She flinched as she noticed the fresh bruises marring her skin, the edges already blooming purple. His voice went low, flinty. "And these?"

Her stomach clenched. "There may have been…a small altercation," she admitted, forcing the words out evenly. "But I kept Calliope safe. She wasn't touched."

Not during the fight, at least.

The silence was worse than rebuke. Each heartbeat stretched into an eternity, heavy with unspoken disappointment. She hated that more than any sharp word. All she ever wanted to do was to make him proud, show him how grateful she was for his mentorship.

"I didn't want the drink, but refusing would've drawn more attention. It was a tactical decision, but it won't happen again," she rushed on, the words tumbling out.

"See that it doesn't," he said quietly, his tone serious. "You cannot allow yourself to be compromised while on duty. Not for any reason."

"Don't worry, I learned my lesson." Nerissa dipped her chin in a terse nod. "It was only a few sips of mead," she said at last, her voice low. "I didn't think it would affect me the way it did."

Damarion's eyes softened by a fraction. "That's because it *does* affect you. All of us. Merfolk have a harder time metabolizing alcohol. It strikes harder, faster, even for those accustomed to it. You're fortunate it didn't cost you more."

Her shame deepened. She pressed her lips together, berating herself. Foolish. Careless. She knew better.

Damarion sighed, running a hand through his hair. "I hope you do not think me too hard on you, Nerissa. Just as I hope you are not too hard on yourself. No soldier has made me prouder than you. It's important to me that you know that."

Her throat tightened. Praise from Damarion was rarer than pearls, and more valuable by far.

She managed a small nod. "I understand, *Didaskon.* I won't let you down."

"I know you won't," he replied simply. Then he regarded her with a keen eye, almost as if he meant to say something more.

"What is it?" Nerissa asked warily.

"I understand why you do not wish to continue serving as Calliope's handmaiden on the surface," he began carefully. "And of course you will make a valuable addition to the Guard. However, are you certain that is what you truly want?"

Nerissa blinked, caught off guard. "What do you mean? What else…is there?"

Damarion sighed again as he turned to leave. "I just…want you to be happy, *Skíon.* Just as your parents did." Then he swam out through one of the columned arches, his silhouette dissolving into the pale light beyond.

Nerissa lingered behind, her reflection wavering on the marble floor below. Happiness. What place did that have in a life built on duty?

All she knew was service to the crown. There had never been another choice. Besides, chasing happiness only meant it would hurt more when it was inevitably ripped away.

She set her jaw and followed the ripple of water left in his wake.

CHAPTER 7

ALIGNING OURSELVES WITH MONSTERS

Nerissa

The stone towers of the Astyran castle loomed tall and commanding against the azure sky, with scarlet and white banners snapping in the wind. It was built into the highest cliff of the peninsula, with lower walls that separated the castle from the sea. Massive ramparts carved from pale limestone, weathered smooth by years of battering waves, rose around its circumference. Signal braziers and ballistae were mounted at every watchtower, ready to defend.

Nerissa followed Damarion from the shoreline where they emerged, up the stone causeway and over an arched bridge. Behind them, four Nautalian guards fanned out in formation.

The gates parted with a groan of steel and ceremony. Nerissa stepped through the archway at Damarion's side, the abalone armor along her shoulders and her pleated skirt catching the early-afternoon sun in pale iridescence. Though her skin still tingled faintly from the recent transformation, she kept her posture straight, betraying no weakness.

A pair of Astyran sentries met them at the inner gate and greeted them with bows and polite smiles.

"This way, Captain Damarion. His Majesty and His Highness await you in the ballroom."

They were led across the courtyard and through the arched entryway, where guards in crimson tabards flanked the stone halls. The castle's grandeur struck a different chord than the glimmering beauty of Nautalia. It was all stone and symmetry, polished wood and pride. Ceilings rose high in the sunlit halls, windows cut wide to allow maximum natural light to filter in through blue and green tinted glass. Nerissa found herself captivated by the mosaic tiles beneath her bare feet. Intricate patterns depicting various maritime creatures and myths in shades of teal and violet seemed out of place here.

When they entered the grand ballroom, Nerissa's nose crinkled against the scent of something sharp and clean, though not unpleasant. The room was massive, with tall windows spilling golden light across the gleaming floors. Glittering chandeliers scattered a rainbow of light all over the room like confetti. Dozens of servants flitted about, setting tables and polishing candelabras for tomorrow's celebration.

At the far end of the room stood King Vasilios and Prince Leander.

The king was tall, with gold-streaked auburn hair and a close-cut beard. He smiled as they approached, arms open.

"Welcome, Captain. M'lady," he said. "We are honored by your presence."

"Your Majesty," Damarion said with a respectful bow, then frowned as he noticed the bandage just above Prince Leander's left eyebrow. "Was there an attack?" he asked, gesturing subtly to his own forehead.

Leander's expression didn't falter, to his credit. "Ah. No. I was…reading. Got so swept up in a chapter that I didn't see a hanging planter."

Nerissa pressed her lips together in a failed attempt to hide her smirk. Leander's eyes creased subtly in her direction, the corner of his mouth quirking upward ever so slightly.

Vasilios gave his son a bemused side-eye before continuing the conversation.

"I am sure you can appreciate how vital it is that tomorrow proceeds without a hitch. We have spared no effort in ensuring everyone's security, but of course, we welcome your input."

"That is precisely why we are here," Damarion said. "We will be surveying the ballroom and its adjoining rooms. I would also like access to the outer hallways and any private passages used by staff."

"Of course," Vasilios said easily. "I'll have someone bring you the floor plans."

Nerissa said nothing as her eyes scanned the windows, sightlines, and guard posts. Every glittering detail could hide a threat. She nodded once, a silent signal that she was ready.

King Vasilios gestured with a smile. "Take all the time you need. If there is anything we can provide, please do not hesitate to ask."

"Many thanks, Your Majesty. We will be sure to let you know," Damarion said. "Come, Nerissa."

The castle walls whispered.

Not metaphorically, but with servants. Maids and footmen scurrying from one room to the next, clutching linens and platters, their voices dropping to murmurs as Nerissa and Damarion passed. Eyes followed them, some curious, some openly suspicious. A few stopped altogether to gawk.

"They're staring," Nerissa muttered, not slowing her stride as they turned down a corridor branching off from the ballroom.

"They're not used to seeing merfolk," Damarion replied dryly, inspecting the stonework near a windowed alcove.

"They should keep their tongues in check," she said, a little too sharply.

He gave her a sidelong glance. "Easy, Nerissa. As far as most of these people knew, our kind were wiped out in the wars decades ago. We're not just a political novelty; we're a myth made flesh."

She frowned but said nothing. Ignorance didn't excuse rudeness.

The corridor opened into a gallery with stained glass windows overlooking the sea. Tapestries embroidered in gold thread depicting human naval victories lined the walls. Nerissa's gaze lingered on one in particular. A knight driving a spear through the coils of some sea serpent or mermanic creature, impossible to tell.

"Lovely," she muttered.

Damarion's voice was steady. "Treaties don't change hearts overnight."

She folded her arms as they walked. "That's assuming hearts are even part of the bargain."

They passed a pair of guards who straightened to attention but didn't speak. Nerissa kept her expression neutral, her armor creaking softly as she moved while her feet made little sound against the polished stone.

They made their way through the side halls, investigating sculleries, servant corridors, and a narrow stairwell that looped behind the grand entry. Damarion made note of each blind corner, each entryway lacking a guard post. Nerissa observed the sightlines, memorized the heights of the windows, calculated how long it would take to breach each one.

By the time they returned to the main floor, the staff had thinned, the castle slowly shifting into its late afternoon lull before supper. They entered a receiving room just off the ballroom, smaller and more private, its doors lined in gold and carved with sea motifs.

"Subtle," Nerissa noted, eyeing the mermaid engraved on the doorframe. She had very unrealistic proportions.

Damarion ignored the decor. "This room is too close to the main event. It needs a posted guard at all times."

As the captain stepped away to request the castle floorplans again, Nerissa remained near the archway of the receiving room, her gaze sweeping the corridor beyond. The stone walls threw back a soft echo of distant voices and footsteps.

"Lady Nerissa?"

She turned. Prince Leander stood a few paces down the corridor, the faintest trace of hesitation in his manner. He inclined his head politely, his voice low so it wouldn't carry. "Forgive the interruption. I wanted to ask how Calliope is faring after this morning."

Nerissa straightened. "She's unharmed, Your Highness. I managed to get her out before things turned ugly. Shaken, at first, but she recovered quickly."

Relief eased the tension in his shoulders. "I am glad. I feared I had frightened her off the entire idea of setting foot on land again."

That almost drew a smile from her. "She's resilient."

"That is a good thing," he said warmly. His gaze lingered briefly, noticing the bruises on Nerissa's arms. "And you? You look as though you took the brunt of it."

The question caught her off guard. Few ever bothered to ask how *she* was. "I've seen worse," she said, perhaps too quickly.

Leander's smile was small but sincere. "Still, I owe you an apology. The brawl was my fault. I should have chosen a safer meeting place."

"The Salty Siren was subtle," she replied, a touch of dry humor slipping through.

His smile deepened, rueful but amused. "So I thought. I assumed we would be less likely to cause a scene there. Clearly, I misjudged."

His tone conveyed a sense of humility and genuine regret that surprised her. Nerissa found herself momentarily at a loss for words.

Before she could find any, movement at the far end of the corridor caught her attention. A lone figure slipping from a half-open door. Her pulse quickened instinctively.

"Your Highness," she said quickly, dipping her head in apology. "If you'll excuse me."

Leander nodded, puzzled but gracious. "Of course."

Nerissa stepped past him, her focus narrowing on the retreating form ahead.

Male. Thin frame. Sharp profile and a prominently curved nose. He wore a cloak too heavy for the weather and moved with a faint limp, his cane tapping softly against the stone with each step.

Her stomach dropped.

That cane. Silver. Ornate. Crowned with a ruby the size of her fist.

The image seared through memory: the flash of it in the torchlight, the glint of red amid chaos on the docks. Masked men. Blades. Screams. Her parents. She couldn't remember the man's face—but the cane…the cane she had never forgotten.

The figure turned the corner, vanishing from sight.

Nerissa followed.

She didn't think, just moved, gliding between shadows and columns like a current. The man descended a stairwell near the east wing, a section of the castle that hadn't been part of the initial sweep. It was narrow, carved into the stone like an afterthought, its torches unlit. The chill air that met her was sharp and stale.

He paused once to look over his shoulder. Nerissa pressed herself into an alcove and held her breath.

Satisfied, he continued.

Nerissa had an uneasy feeling in the pit of her stomach. What was he up to?

She followed him down the stairwell and into a lower hall lined with storage rooms and damp stone walls. He approached a heavy wooden door reinforced with iron, withdrew a key from his cloak, and slipped inside.

She reached it just before it closed.

Holding her breath for a full minute to be sure he was no longer near the door, she eased it open and slipped through.

The air inside smelled wrong.

It was a laboratory. But no alchemist's den or healer's room.

Iron. Blood. Something vaguely acrid, like burnt bone or bitter herbs. She kept low, moving with slow, silent steps. The chamber opened into a long room cluttered with worktables and dimly glowing lanterns. Scrolls. Tools. Steel implements that looked more at home in a butcher's shop.

Her eyes scanned the tables—and stopped.

Laid out on one was the unmistakable form of a siren body. Adult. Pale-skinned and half-preserved, its gills split and pinned open like a grotesque dissection. Its eyes were gone, lids sewn shut. The tail, once likely iridescent, now dulled and greyed.

Nerissa froze, bile rising in her throat.

Deep's teeth...

This wasn't medicine. It wasn't study. This was desecration. Proof of the worst kind of cruelty. Of what surface-dwellers had always been capable of, and perhaps still were.

She took one step back, bumping into a shelf, sending a glass jar wobbling. She caught it just in time, heart hammering in her throat.

She needed to leave. Now. Before she was seen.

Retracing her steps, she melted back into the corridor and shut the heavy door behind her as softly as she could manage. She didn't stop moving until the laboratory was far behind her, swallowed once more by the shadows of the castle's underbelly.

She exhaled shakily and turned a corner, vanishing into the twisting passageways toward the nearest guard post.

When she spotted Damarion exiting a room with a scroll under one arm, she didn't slow down.

"Damarion," she hissed, clutching his arm with clammy hands. "We need to talk. *Now.*"

He turned at the urgency in her grip, brow furrowing. "What's wrong?"

"Not here," Nerissa shook her head quickly, steering him toward the nearest exit while trying not to draw attention. They slipped through an archway and out into a quiet terrace overlooking the cliffs, wind whipping their hair.

Damarion folded his arms. "You've gone pale. What happened?"

"I found something," she said, turning to face him. "There's a laboratory in the east wing. Hidden. Evidence of…of experimentation."

"What kind of experimentation?" His eyes narrowed.

"There was a siren body down there, Damarion. Cut open and left like a specimen on the table," she fought down the nausea that threatened to resurface. "I saw jars lining the shelves with preserved organs inside—like something out of a nightmare."

"*Moirai*," he cursed quietly. "How did you find this place?"

"I followed a man there—thin, pale, walking with a limp, silver cane with a ruby head."

Damarion stiffened, making an attempt to keep a neutral expression, but Nerissa had known him too long to miss the shift. It wasn't just concern; it was something colder. Older. A deep and bitter loathing that simmered just beneath his carefully composed exterior.

"You know him," she said quietly. It wasn't a question.

His jaw flexed, and a shadow crossed his face. "Alpheus," he said at last, as if the name tasted sour on his tongue. "Royal apothecary of Astyra. Brilliant, yes—but brilliance without conscience. The Astyrans claimed he could revive a person after drowning. I never imagined it was at the cost of our people's lives."

"There's something else," she said quickly. "I remember that cane. He was there, Damarion—ten years ago, the night my parents were killed. *I saw him.*"

His head snapped toward her, eyes flashing with a storm that mirrored her own. For a moment, the wind itself seemed to hold still between them.

"*Nerae* preserve us," he muttered. "And this is the man Astyra keeps in their service?" His voice sharpened, every word edged with steel. "If Nautalia signs this treaty while Alpheus still walks Astyra's halls, it isn't peace we're binding ourselves to. It's aligning ourselves with monsters."

Nerissa's heartbeat thundered in her ears. The image of the body, the lifeless eyes in jars, the treaty Calliope was meant to seal—it all pressed down on her chest, threatening to suffocate her. She may have questioned the treaty, but she was willing to support it, for Calliope's sake. For their people's sake.

Now her instincts were screaming that this was certainly a trap.

Damarion turned to her, his expression grim. "We return to Nautalia tonight. The king must hear this. Every detail. He cannot enter into this alliance blindly."

CHAPTER 8

WHEN FEAR DROWNS REASON

Alpheus

The apothecary stepped out from the shadows, his cane tapping lightly against the floor. A thin smile played on his lips as he gazed at the door the girl had disappeared through.

"So," he murmured to himself, eyes glittering, "you *do* remember me."

He gently touched the handle of his cane in an idle gesture, almost affectionate, and turned back toward the flickering lanterns of his hidden sanctum.

The laboratory welcomed him with its familiar chill of stale air, iron, and the faint, cloying sweetness of preservation fluid. He moved between the tanks like a priest among relics. Pale limbs drifted in suspension, eyes forever open, jaws slack in silent screams. Beautiful, in its way. The price of progress.

"She was here." He said it aloud, savoring the certainty. Older now, but unmistakable. That same determined steel in her gaze, just like her mother. She thought herself unseen, creeping through his halls, but of course he had noticed. He always noticed.

At his worktable, he unlatched a rusted metal case and drew out brittle files, their edges curled with age. Names stared up at him in neat Astyran script. Theron and Melora, loyal retainers of Nautalia, caught sniffing after his work. Hand-drawn portraits captured their likenesses: Theron's sharp jaw, Melora's watchful eyes. Dangerous. Obstinate. A problem, once.

He traced the ink with a finger, then flipped to the report tucked inside: *Unauthorized trespassing. Harbor Citadel. Captured. Interrogated. Neutralized.*

But not entirely.

"One child, missing," he murmured, eyes narrowing. The girl who slipped past his men. The one he had lost.

And now, fate delivered her back into his grasp. A servant to that porcelain princess. The irony was exquisite.

He turned to a tank against the far wall, placing a hand on the glass. Inside, a creature stirred sluggishly. A twisted amalgam of fish and man, stitched from pain and desperation. The moan it gave was almost human.

"I was patient. Obedient. I paused the work, as commanded." His lips curled in disdain. "And what did Vasilios do with that peace? He handed our kingdom's future to the sea."

Weak. Sentimental. Blind.

"No more."

His voice hardened, every syllable a vow. "The people will see. They will understand."

And the handmaiden—oh, she would be the key. Not just a scapegoat. A symbol.

"They'll call you a traitor. Assassin. Monster." He chuckled, dry and rasping. "And when fear drowns reason, they will beg me to protect them."

Alpheus brushed aside sketches of siren anatomy, the ciphered notes only he could read. His eyes gleamed as the pieces fell into place.

"Yes," he whispered. "Every plan needs a catalyst."

His cloak swept as he turned, disappearing into the corridor's shadows while above, the palace stirred with preparations for celebration.

CHAPTER 9

A DIFFERENT KIND OF ARMOR

Nerissa

The current that swirled through the royal hall felt colder than usual as Nerissa floated before the throne of King Nereus, Damarion at her side. The opalescent light of the jellyfire chandeliers above cast shifting shadows across the coralwork pillars.

King Nereus sat tall, his trident resting upright beside him, its prongs glimmering faintly in the wavering light. "Damarion tells me you have urgent news."

Nerissa's posture was ramrod straight, but her voice betrayed the storm beneath. "Yes, Your Majesty. During our visit to the Astyran castle, I discovered a hidden laboratory beneath the eastern wing. There were…remains. Merfolk. Bodies dissected, preserved. Notes and instruments meant for torture, not healing. The room was active. Not abandoned."

Queen Ophelia's hand drifted to her chest, a small gasp escaping her lips.

Calliope's eyes widened, a soft shake of her head betraying disbelief.

Nereus's jaw set. "I am aware of the experiments."

The words struck like a blow.

Nerissa stared. "You...*knew*? Your Majesty, I don't understand."

The king's tone was level, his gaze steady. "Your parents' reports first brought Alpheus's research to my attention ten years ago. They were invaluable to us in exposing his network. Until their deaths, they worked to gather proof of his crimes."

Nerissa faltered, her fingers beginning to tingle with numbness.

"They were loyal servants of the crown," Nereus continued, unflinching. "Their sacrifice was not in vain. What they uncovered allowed us to warn merfolk from going to the surface and prevent more from—"

"*Sacrifice?*" The word tore from her throat before she could stop it. The water around her stirred violently. "They didn't *choose* to die. They were murdered!"

Damarion shifted beside her, his jaw tightening, but he didn't speak.

Nerissa's voice shook as she pressed on, anger flooding her chest. "I saw it happen. I was there that day. I followed them to the surface. I saw Alpheus's men waiting on the docks, saw the flash of his cane in the torchlight. He gave the order. And you—" her voice broke, sharp with disbelief, "you *knew* what he was doing and let him live?"

Nereus's expression hardened, his tone turning cold. "Do not mistake leadership for indifference, handmaiden. The peace between our realms is fragile. If I had executed Alpheus without proof admissible before the Council, I would have ignited another war neither kingdom was ready to fight."

"Then what was their loyalty worth?" Nerissa demanded, her voice echoing through the chamber. "You let their killer walk free in the name of peace!"

Nereus rose from the throne, his crown gleaming in the shifting light. "Enough." His voice rolled through the hall like thunder. "You speak of things you do not understand."

"I understand perfectly," Nerissa snapped. "You valued the treaty more than your people's lives."

"Careful, Nerissa," Damarion said quietly in warning.

She ignored him. Her eyes burned as she met the king's gaze. "You call it peace. I call it cowardice. And now you've handed your own daughter over to them," she said bitterly. "Was that the price for silence? A royal bride in exchange for our dead?"

Calliope drifted forward slightly. "It isn't like that."

Nerissa turned on her. "Isn't it? You still believe this treaty will protect us—after what I saw?"

Calliope's chin lifted, but her voice wavered. "I believe in Leander. He doesn't know. He *couldn't.*"

"Does it matter?" Nerissa's tone rose like a riptide. "How many have died in secret while peace was being negotiated? You think marrying a prince scrubs the blood off our seabed?"

Ophelia's voice cut through. "Nerissa—please."

But she couldn't stop. Wouldn't. Not now.

"Do you think the rest of us get soaking pools and silk gowns?" Nerissa snapped. "The people outside these halls, the ones dragged from the reefs and dissected—did they get a treaty? Did they get peace?"

"That's enough," Nereus said sharply. "You forget yourself."

The command struck like a wave breaking over stone, but Nerissa didn't flinch. Her chest heaved, every muscle taut with restrained fury.

"With respect, Your Majesty," Damarion interjected, his voice calm but carrying the weight of command. "She forgets nothing."

He drifted forward slightly, placing himself between Nerissa and the king. "She speaks from grief, not insolence. And she is right to question what we have allowed."

Nereus's gaze hardened. "Watch your words, Captain."

"I am," Damarion replied evenly. "And she will watch hers as well." He turned his head just enough to meet Nerissa's eyes, his tone gentling without losing authority. "Enough. You've said what needed saying."

But the words barely reached her. The ache in her chest was too sharp, her vision too blurred by betrayal. Nereus had known the truth all along. And done *nothing.*

The king sank back into his throne. "This audience is concluded. Captain, see to your ward's composure."

For a heartbeat Nerissa hovered there, trembling, caught between fury and heartbreak. Then she turned sharply, without bowing, and surged from the hall.

Her pulse thundered in her ears, drowning out the muffled calls that followed. The chill of the corridors met her like open water, but it did nothing to cool the heat burning in her chest.

The towers of the palace faded behind her as Nerissa propelled herself through the open water, her tail carving furious arcs through the sea as sheer rage blurred her vision.

“Nerissa, wait!” Calliope called, swimming hard to catch up. “Would you just *stop* for one second?”

Nerissa didn’t slow down until the palace was little more than a silhouette in the distance. When she finally did, she turned sharply, jaw clenched and gills flaring.

“I can’t believe this,” she spat. “He knew. All these years—he *knew.* My parents died for the truth, and he buried it like it was nothing.”

Calliope hovered a few paces away, unwilling to get any closer. “I *swear* to you, Nerissa, I didn’t know. I didn’t know about any of it.”

“But you still agree with him,” Nerissa accused, voice brittle. “You still think peace is worth *this.*”

“We have to move forward somehow,” Calliope said, her voice rising. “We can’t cling to vengeance for centuries. If we do, the war never ends—it just changes shape.”

“It’s not vengeance,” Nerissa snapped. “It’s *justice.* There’s a difference.”

“Is there?” Calliope challenged. “Or is it just your hatred for humans talking again? You’ve never been able to see anything good in them—not since your parents—”

"Don't," Nerissa warned, voice low.

But Calliope pushed on. "You blame them all for what a few monsters did. That's *prejudice,* Nerissa. You're so blinded by grief and anger that you can't even see who the real enemy is."

"I know *exactly* who the enemy is," Nerissa growled. "The ones dissecting our kind like sea beasts. The ones with laboratories and cages. The ones who murdered my parents, Calliope. And they just so happen to be part of the Astyran *court.* The same court you're about to marry into."

Calliope flushed with anger. "You act like I'm just handing over Nautalia to them!"

"You're handing *yourself* over," Nerissa said, voice sharp. "You think that bath they're building is for your comfort? It's a *containment tank,* Callie. A gilded prison."

"You think you know everything," Calliope snapped. "But you're just bitter. And scared. And if you can't see how important this alliance is, then maybe you shouldn't be part of it at all."

Nerissa recoiled as if slapped.

Calliope hesitated, then looked away, her voice softer. "Just...please. Don't ruin this. Not for me. Not for Nautalia. Just get through the ceremony without making a scene. That's all I'm asking."

Nerissa said nothing.

"I mean it," Calliope added, her tone hardening again. "Don't screw this up."

With that, she flicked her tail and shot back toward the palace, leaving Nerissa behind in her wake.

She hovered in the open water, muscles taut, chest heaving in short breaths. The silence settled around her like silt, heavy and suffocating, until a shadow shifted behind the nearby coral ridge.

Nerissa turned sharply, fingers instinctively brushing the hilts of her daggers.

"Easy," came a familiar voice. "No need for those."

Kaelen emerged from the reef, his tail flicking lazily as he glided closer. His silver pauldrons caught the dim light like moonshine on a blade, his posture casual.

"I'll be the judge of that," she retorted, voice cool. "How long were you listening?"

"Long enough to wonder if I should intervene before you started slashing," he said with a half-smile. "What was that all about?"

Nerissa narrowed her eyes. "A difference of opinion. On how many corpses are an acceptable price for peace."

Kaelen's brow furrowed slightly, his easy expression darkening. "So the rumors are true…what exactly did you find?"

"Evidence of experimentation. Torture. I saw it with my own eyes."

Kaelen exhaled, a sound somewhere between disbelief and disgust. "And Calliope still plans to go through with the marriage?"

"She's more worried about upsetting her father and ruining her *special day* than she is about our people being hunted like prey."

Kaelen drifted closer, serious now. "Then it can't happen. She can't marry him—not after this."

Nerissa's gaze was hard. "You were never on board with this marriage to begin with."

He offered a small shrug, the silk of his sash fluttering with the motion. "True. But can you blame me? She was betrothed to *me* first. Then suddenly she became a peace offering to the *humans*. I'll admit I may have taken it personally." He met her eyes. "This though...this is different. If what you're saying is true—"

"It *is*."

"Then it's not just about a broken engagement or a bruised ego," Kaelen continued. "It's about protecting Nautalia."

Nerissa gave a dry laugh. "And here I thought we had nothing in common."

For once, Kaelen didn't smirk. "We can't let this go forward."

Nerissa crossed her arms, fins twitching with unease. "And what exactly do you propose? Storm the castle? Drown the prince in his imported bathwater?"

Kaelen tilted his head thoughtfully. "Tempting."

She rolled her eyes, but her expression softened, just a little. She and Kaelen didn't exactly see eye to eye on most things, but it was oddly comforting that he wasn't fighting her on this. Comforting and disturbing.

"You've always been loyal to Calliope," he said after a moment. "But now it's time to be loyal to Nautalia. She may not see it yet, but she's swimming into a trap."

"I know," Nerissa murmured. "The question is...how do I stop her without losing her completely?"

Kaelen didn't have an answer. The silence between them said as much.

The training grounds had long since been abandoned for the night. The water here was still, quiet. Pale shafts of moonlight cut through the coral pillars, illuminating the sand banks in cold silver. Stone targets lined the far wall, their surfaces pockmarked from years of impact.

Nerissa sat near the edge of the lowest platform, arms wrapped around her tail that she had brought up to her chest. Her daggers lay beside her, unsheathed and forgotten.

A memory stirred, one she had tried, again and again, to bury.

It was five years ago. Her best friend, Lir, had come to her in desperation, her golden eyes burning.

"Nerissa, please. We're like sisters, you and I. We've both lost everything. Do you really think anyone here cares what we lost? What was taken from us? They'll keep turning their backs until the whole sea is bleeding."

Nerissa had folded her arms, nails biting into her palms. She understood Lir's anger, the bone-deep fury of it. But she also saw Damarion's face in her mind, remembered the way his voice caught when he spoke of her father, the quiet grief he thought she hadn't noticed. He would see justice done, in time. She trusted him. She had to.

"Lir," she said carefully, "the Court of Sirens is not justice. They are extremists. You think they'll give you peace, but they'll only use your rage until there's nothing left of you."

"Nothing left?" Lir's voice cracked. "That's *all I am*, Nerissa. Nothing. And you're too blind to see it. Too busy polishing your daggers and bowing to your precious princess. The Court is the only way."

Her hand had caught Nerissa's then, fierce, imploring. "Come with me. We'll fight back together. We'll make them pay."

For a heartbeat, Nerissa almost wished she could. That she could lay down her duty, her loyalty, and swim with the only person who understood the hollow ache in her chest. But she couldn't. She wouldn't.

"No," Nerissa whispered. "This is wrong. I won't follow you into madness."

She would never forget the look of hurt and betrayal in Lir's eyes as she turned, the flash of her tail slicing the water like a blade.

Nerissa never saw her again. She told herself she had chosen rightly. That duty and discipline had steadied her when her heart wanted only vengeance. But now the question cut deeply.

What had her loyalty bought her?

Not justice. Not safety.

Instead, she had found dissected bodies in Alpheus's lab, jars of her people's organs cataloged like curiosities. She had discovered that King Nereus—her king—knew and still signed away his daughter's hand. Still sought peace with men who treated merfolk like specimens.

Would Lir look at her now and sneer? Call her blind, as she had then? Perhaps she would be right.

And if the crown itself was guilty of aligning with monsters, then what did that make Nerissa?

Only the soft hum of the current filled the silence, until another presence joined it, steady and unmistakable.

"I thought I might find you here," Damarion said.

She didn't turn. "Didn't realize I was so predictable."

He silently lowered himself to sit beside her, waiting for her to speak.

"I gave them everything, Damarion," Nerissa said eventually, voice rough. "I followed every order, dedicated my life to serving the crown, and for what? Where has that loyalty gotten me? Where did that loyalty get my parents? I gave them my mind blindly, trusting that they would do the right thing."

Damarion didn't answer right away. His gaze remained fixed on the empty sparring circle, on the shadows where soldiers trained.

"When I was your age," he said, "I thought loyalty meant obedience. That discipline was the highest form of service. I believed that if I just followed orders, fought hard enough, kept my head down, I could protect this kingdom from anything."

"And how did that work out for you?"

"I lost good soldiers. Good friends. Because I followed commands I should have questioned." He looked at her then, eyes cool and steady. "Loyalty doesn't mean surrendering your mind. It means knowing who you're fighting for and why."

Nerissa's brow furrowed. "Then tell me why the king would offer Calliope to the people who butchered my parents. Why he would hide what he knew. Why he would ask me to smile at the men who'd flay me open if I turned my back."

"Because kings have to make hard decisions," Damarion said. "Sometimes that means choosing the lesser evil. Sometimes it means trusting that justice can still be served...later."

"Later," Nerissa echoed bitterly. "And how many more of us must be 'sacrificed' in the meantime?"

"Hopefully none, now that we know who is responsible. We just have to do our best to protect the people of Nautalia. We are still loyal to the crown, even if we don't agree with all of their decisions."

Nerissa looked away, jaw clenched. "I don't know if they deserve my loyalty anymore."

"Maybe not." Damarion's voice was quiet. "But Calliope does."

Nerissa flinched.

"She's young. Hopeful. She sees the world not as it is, but as it could be. That's not a fault. That's why she needs someone like you by her side. To protect her from what she won't admit is coming."

Nerissa's throat tightened. "She told me not to screw this up."

"She's scared," he said. "She doesn't know how to fix what's broken, so she's pretending it isn't. You've seen the cracks. That doesn't mean you get to shatter everything. But it does mean you get to decide where you stand when it does."

He rose slowly, the weight of his armor sending a soft chime through the water.

"When the time comes," he said, turning to look at her one last time, "you'll know what to do. You always have."

And then he left her there, beneath the ruins of her trust, with only the moonlight and the ache of what loyalty used to mean.

Nerissa stayed motionless, her fingers curled against the stone ledge. She'd thought she understood what it meant to serve. To protect. To be part of something greater than herself. Every order obeyed, every mission completed, every hour of training that left her bloodied and bruised—it was all supposed to mean something.

But now she saw the cracks in the foundation.

The king had known. Known and said nothing. And Calliope had looked her in the eye and told her to stay silent. To smile through it.

Don't screw this up.

Nerissa's jaw tightened. For who? For what?

The crown she'd bled for had never once bled for her.

She looked down at her daggers. The hilts glinted in the moonlight, beautiful and sharp. Damarion had given them to her the day she completed her training. He'd told her they were a symbol of trust. Of readiness. That she had proven herself.

She wondered how different her life might have turned out, had her parents still been alive. If they'd have allowed her to train under Damarion—would she have even asked? Or would she have taken up the family business?

Before her parents began working for the crown, they had been humble snail farmers, breeding and cultivating tiny violet snails. Nerissa recalled how her own hands were perpetually stained purple from harvesting the snails' secretions. It wasn't an easy or glamorous process; she had learned to extract and bottle the snail mucus before it could dissipate into the water. Then her mother would go to the surface and combine the necessary ingredients to craft the dye she would later sell at both the Nautalian marketplace and the Astyran docks. The Astyrans were none the wiser that they were purchasing goods from a mermaid hiding in human form.

That was part of the reason why King Nereus had asked her parents to come work for him. They were familiar with the surface world, and they were trusted by the locals.

It also helped that her father had once been a soldier in the Royal Guard, working alongside Damarion. It was how they had grown to be close friends. It was how he learned how to fight. When he was severely injured in an altercation with the Court of Sirens, however, he was honorably discharged, and would often join her mother ashore to sell their wares.

Slowly, she reached for one of the blades, balancing it on her finger.

She wouldn't stop serving. It wasn't in her nature to run. But she would no longer confuse obedience with virtue. No longer mistake silence for strength.

If the crown refused to protect their people, then she would.

Even if she had to stand alone to do it.

Even if it meant crossing the very lines she once patrolled.

Nerissa rose slowly, the moonlight carving silver across her shoulders as she slipped the daggers back into their sheaths. Her tail stirred the water, calm and deliberate now. No more rage, no more blind devotion.

Just resolve.

A different kind of armor.

CHAPTER 10
DOWN DARK HALLWAYS

Nerissa

The sea was quiet that morning, like the quiet before a storm.

The escort formation was tight: Damarion at the helm, followed by King Nereus and Queen Ophelia, their royal mantles trailing like kelp in the current. Calliope floated in the center, flanked on either side by a pair of guards, her features composed but distant.

Nerissa stayed one pace behind the princess, silent.

The swim to the surface was uneventful. The closer they drew to the coastline, the more the weight of the day settled onto her shoulders. She hadn't spoken a word to Calliope since their argument last night, and the princess hadn't made any effort either.

Soldiers waited at the gate, all stiff posture and gleaming breastplates. They bowed as the royal cavalcade approached, and without delay, ushered the procession through stone corridors into the heart of the castle.

Servants were ready with thick towels that had been warmed by the hearth. The Nautalians took great care to dry themselves off as the servants mopped the floor where they had entered. Nerissa almost felt guilty for the mess.

Until she remembered the bodies in the hidden laboratory.

Eventually, the women split off from the guard. Nerissa followed Queen Ophelia and Princess Calliope into a sun-drenched room filled with mahogany furniture and gilded mirrors. The princess's future chambers.

Lavish tapestries in cool hues evoking the sea hung from the walls. A canopy bed with pearl embroidery sat in the center of the chamber. And in the corner, the enormous in-ground saltwater pool that had been installed specially for Calliope. Proof of the prince's dedication, or perhaps his guilt.

Queen Ophelia fluttered about the room, smoothing silk and tucking errant curls behind her daughter's ear. Her voice was soft, comforting. Motherly. But Nerissa barely heard it, her gaze fixed on the door. She stood like a statue by the threshold, hands folded neatly in front of her.

When Ophelia fastened the final clasp on the embroidered wrap Calliope wore over her white ceremonial dress, she stepped back to admire her work. "You look beautiful," she said with pride.

Calliope smiled, but it didn't reach her eyes.

Ophelia turned toward Nerissa with an encouraging nod. "Would you mind fetching the circlet from the table, dear?"

Nerissa moved without comment, retrieving the delicate piece of jewelry—silver shaped like flowing waves, dotted with pearls. She held it out to Calliope without a word.

Their hands brushed, and Calliope hesitated, just for a moment, but whatever she might have said died on her tongue. She looked away as she took the circlet and turned back to the mirror.

Nerissa returned to her post.

The silence stretched.

Finally, Ophelia broke it with a warm sigh. "A historic day," she said, mostly to herself. "The beginning of a new chapter. For both our kingdoms."

Neither young woman replied.

Nerissa stepped out onto the balcony for some fresh air, bracing her hands on the railing. The sea stretched far and endless beyond the cliffs, the hush of distant waves calling to her. She'd rather be anywhere else than here.

A royal wedding. A political alliance. A historic peace treaty. And all she could think about was the laboratory beneath the castle floors.

She could still see the split gills, the dissected bodies.

Her jaw tightened.

Prince Leander hadn't struck her as cruel. Naïve, certainly. Too clean, too eager to impress. But he'd looked at Calliope the way someone looks at a sunrise they didn't expect to find so beautiful. That kind of sincerity was hard to fake.

She didn't think he knew, but ignorance was no absolution.

As for King Vasilios, he had welcomed them with open arms, his manner gracious. But charm came easy to men in power. She hadn't seen enough of him to know whether the warmth in his voice was genuine or just another diplomatic veneer.

Perhaps he knew what Alpheus was doing. Perhaps he didn't.

She wasn't sure which was worse: a king complicit in quiet atrocities...or one so blind he'd failed to notice them in his own house.

Neither option filled her with hope.

Too much rode on what would happen today. And none of them could afford for her to speak the truth—not yet.

She suddenly couldn't be in the same room anymore.

"I'm going to check in with Damarion," she said to no one in particular, already halfway to the door.

Ophelia gave a small nod, too focused on adjusting Calliope's veil to question her sudden departure.

Nerissa closed the door behind her and leaned against a nearby column for a moment to gather herself. She had to remember what this day was about, what it was all for. She had to shove her personal feelings down, do what was expected of her. Her heart thumped like a war drum beneath her ribs.

A crawling sensation suddenly danced down her spine, just enough to make her shift her weight. That was when she saw him.

Alpheus emerged from the far end of the corridor, gliding like oil down a marble channel. His cane clicked with quiet precision against the floor, his bejeweled fingers curled lightly around the handle. He slowed as he neared her.

And then he *looked* at her.

Not the casual glance of a man passing a servant, not even the recognition of a courtier seeing a familiar face. No, this was the calculated eye contact of a predator inviting its prey to step into the tall grass.

Nerissa straightened, alert.

Alpheus gave a slow, mocking nod. And turned the corner.

She didn't think. She followed.

Around the bend, the corridor dipped into shadow. The air grew thick, humid, *cloying*. The scent hit her all at once: something sweet, almost floral, yet metallic. Her knees began to buckle before she realized what was happening.

She tried to speak. Her lips wouldn't move.

Her fingers spasmed once, then stilled. She was still standing, but she might as well have been a statue.

From the darkness ahead, Alpheus stepped into view once more, framed by a faint green glow.

"My dear girl," he murmured, voice smooth as sea glass, "you really must stop following strangers down dark hallways. It's becoming a habit."

He reached out, brushing a single finger across her cheek. She couldn't recoil in disgust like her body was screaming at her to.

"You're just as reckless as your mother."

Rage began to boil in her blood. What sick game was he playing at?

The apothecary circled her like a shark, the glow from the glass lantern in his hand casting eerie reflections in his dark, narrowed eyes.

"You merfolk were always so proud of your immunity to surface sicknesses and human ailments. But biology," he said with a sneer, "is like glass—it can be etched. You just need the right tools."

He held up the lantern, and she could just make out the mist inside swirling faintly. What kind of light source was that? It didn't look like the fire that humans used…

"Pheromones," he explained conversationally, as if giving a lecture at a garden party. "Harvested from certain deep-sea creatures. Laced with a paralytic mist that targets neural signals. And just a hint of hallucinogen."

He stepped closer.

"And the best part? Your mind is wide open right now. Just enough awareness to absorb. Just enough fog to forget. But later…"

He leaned in, whispering close to her ear.

"During the vows, you will take the ceremonial knife. You will walk forward. And you will kill King Vasilios."

His voice dropped to a velvety murmur.

"Say it for me, won't you?"

Her lips slack, she murmured the words with zero emotion.

"I will kill…King Vasilios."

Alpheus smiled. "Good girl."

He stepped back into the shadows. The mist began to dissipate, curling like smoke into the cold stone cracks of the corridor.

Nerissa blinked. Wobbled. She leaned against the stone wall, dazed. What was she doing here? She left Calliope's chamber to get some air, but she remembered nothing.

Just a strange smell, a moment of dizziness.

"Nerissa?"

A voice cut through the fog like a knife.

Footsteps approached, and she turned slowly, to see Damarion striding toward her, frowning.

"What are you doing here?" he asked. "You're supposed to be with the princess."

Great question. Nerissa blinked again, her brow furrowing.

Damarion's frown deepened. He reached out and gave her shoulder a firm shake.

She jolted slightly, eyes snapping into focus. Her gaze darted around the hallway.

"I—what…?" she said, disoriented. "I was just…"

She glanced back over her shoulder toward the corridor. Nothing but shadows.

Hadn't she followed Alpheus here? Where was he?

Her hand reached for the wall, steadying herself.

"I don't remember."

Damarion looked at her for a long moment, concerned. "Are you feeling alright?"

"I think so," she said faintly. "Just…dizzy for a moment. Must've been stress."

He didn't press, but the crease between his brows didn't go away.

"Come on," he said gently, offering his arm. "Let's get you some water."

"No," she said quickly, waving him off. "I'm fine. I just…I should get back to Calliope. Back to my post."

"If you're sure."

She nodded, and Damarion watched her retreat with narrowed eyes.

The great hall of the Astyran castle shimmered with candlelight and splendor. The pews were filled with nobles, a mixture of Astyrans and Nautalians co-existing in fragile harmony for the special occasion.

At the center of it all stood Princess Calliope, radiant in her white silk gown, her hair swept like a cresting wave over her shoulder. Prince Leander stood beside her, stiff with nerves, but trying valiantly to smile.

Stationed behind Calliope like a loyal shadow, was Nerissa in a simple lavender silk gown, outfitted with the ceremonial Nautalian armor of abalone. She tried to keep her face neutral; she couldn't bring herself to smile.

King Nereus and Queen Ophelia stood on one side of the ceremonial dais, wearing their finest royal blue silk robes and jewels. Damarion stood behind them, silent and vigilant. His eyes kept returning to Nerissa. He wore an expression that she couldn't quite place. Why did he keep looking at her like that?

King Vasilios stood on the opposite side of the dais, wearing the traditional crimson of Astyra's flag proudly as his son said his vows.

The officiant's voice echoed across the chamber. "Do you, Leander of Astyra, take Calliope of Nautalia to be your—"

"Pick up the blade," came a voice from inside her head.

Nerissa's breath hitched.

Where did that come from? That wasn't her, was it?

"Now. Pick up the blade."

She blinked once.

It seemed to happen in slow motion.

She saw her hand reach out to the cushion on the pedestal between Leander and Calliope. She couldn't stop it. It was like someone else was in control of her body.

The ceremonial knife was in her hand before anyone registered it.

Then she was moving. Leander turned toward her in confusion.

Stop. What are you doing? Stop!

But she couldn't. Her legs wouldn't listen. She kept moving. Past Leander.

"Good. Now kill the king," the voice commanded.

No! Don't do this! NO!

With a terrible, fluid precision, Nerissa lunged for King Vasilios, and the blade plunged into his chest. The air left his lungs in one horrible rush as his pupils dilated.

A sharp, collective gasp rippled through the crowd, punctuated with screams.

Blood bloomed across the king's ceremonial robes, blending with the crimson fabric, and he collapsed backward, clutching at the hilt in shock.

Chaos erupted as wedding guests scrambled from the pews and guards shouted. Calliope's hands flew to her mouth, frozen in horror.

"She just murdered the king!" someone shouted.

"An assassin!"

"She's cursed–"

"She's a traitor!"

Nerissa couldn't move. She just stared at the body of the king on the dais before her, blood pooling underneath him. The blade was still jutting out of his chest, dripping with scarlet.

Nerae…so much blood.

Damarion reached her first. He grabbed her by the shoulders, yanking her away from the king's fallen form, staring into her face.

"Nerissa," he breathed, "*what have you done?*"

She looked up at her mentor's face, and she felt like the scared little girl he took in ten years ago. Her breathing turned to shallow gasps.

"Damarion," she whispered. "I—I didn't—I couldn't—"

She took one faltering step back, breath catching in her throat as she stared at her shaking, bloody hands.

Calliope rounded on her, eyes burning with disbelief. "I *trusted* you!"

Guards descended like sharks. Nerissa didn't resist. She couldn't. She didn't even hear them as they pulled her from Damarion's arms and bound her wrists.

Queen Ophelia screamed for someone to help the king. Leander was already there, pressing trembling hands to his father's wound, trying to stop the bleeding.

Nerissa couldn't take her eyes from the blade and the blood as the guards hauled her away.

What have I done?

CHAPTER 11

THE SEA TOOK HER

Nerissa

The lock turned with a harsh metallic *click*, and the heavy iron door creaked open. Torchlight spilled into the cell, outlining the figure framed in the corridor.

Nerissa sat on the stone bench, her once delicate dress now rumpled and streaked with blood not her own. She squinted against the sudden light, but there was no mistaking the silhouette.

"Callie." Her voice was hoarse; she had been given no water since her imprisonment that morning.

"I shouldn't be here." The princess stepped inside, her tone glacial.

"I don't know what happened," Nerissa said quickly, desperate. "Suddenly I was moving, I couldn't stop myself, like I had no control—"

"You expect me to believe that?" Calliope's voice trembled with rage.

"That you *accidentally* assassinated the King of Astyra? During a wedding ceremony that was meant to bring peace?"

"I didn't mean to!" Nerissa cried. "You know me, Callie. You *know* I would never hurt you. I wasn't in control of my body!"

Calliope took a step forward, arms stiff at her sides. "What I know is that you hated the idea of forgiving Astyra. That you spat every time someone mentioned peace. That you thought my father was a fool for even *considering* an alliance."

"I never said that." Nerissa swallowed hard. "I never wanted *this.*"

"You didn't need to say it. Your disdain was *loud enough.*" Calliope's expression twisted, grief warring with betrayal. "And now Vasilios is dead. My wedding ruined. Leander…the *entire court* saw you standing there with blood on your hands."

"I didn't do this of my own will." Nerissa's voice trembled. "Something isn't right. Please. You *have* to believe me."

Calliope stared at her for a long moment, then shook her head slowly. "You want me to believe that you just lost control of your body and stabbed my fiancé's father during the one moment that peace was within reach? That the girl who never trusted humans, never wanted to go to the surface, just *snapped?*'

"I don't know what else to tell you," Nerissa hung her head in exhaustion. "But something is very wrong; things aren't adding up here."

Calliope's eyes glistened, but her expression hardened. "I know you didn't have an easy childhood, Nerissa, but we took you in. We gave you a home—a family. You were like a *sister* to me. And this is how you repay us?"

"That's not fair," Nerissa whispered.

"No," Calliope agreed. "It isn't." She turned toward the door, pausing with her hand on the latch. "Goodbye, Nerissa."

"Callie–"

The door shut with a dull *thunk*, sealing Nerissa in the silence, darkness, and solitude.

It had been hours since Calliope's visit. Nerissa wasn't sure exactly how many, although she was reasonably certain that evening had fallen. She sat with her back against the far wall of her cell, knees drawn up to her chest as she stared at nothing with a haunted, faraway look in her eyes.

The torches lining the stone corridor flickered, casting grotesque shadows through the dripping, moss-covered dungeon. The air was cold and damp, yet her tongue still felt bone-dry in her mouth. She missed the ocean badly.

Soft footsteps echoed.

They were wrong somehow. Too soft for the thick boots of the palace guards. And an extra tap between each step.

She tensed as a figure glided into view, illuminated by a green lantern.

Alpheus.

He stopped just outside her cell door, tilting his head at her like a collector admiring a rare and troublesome artifact.

"You know…" he began in a faux gentle tone, "for someone who made such a spectacular entrance, you've grown rather dull."

"What do *you* want?" she demanded with venom in her voice as she glared at him.

Alpheus didn't answer. Just smiled. It didn't reach his eyes.

He retrieved a small, ornate vial from inside his coat. A soft vapor coiled out as he uncorked it and slipped something into a small container.

Nerissa sat up. "What are you doing?"

"Only what I must. You're such a marvelous creature. Strong, loyal, passionate—misguided, of course, but that's what makes you *useful*."

He pressed a button on the strange device—some sort of diffuser—and the vapor spilled into the cell, surrounding Nerissa. She held her breath, but the mist lingered like a nefarious presence, until her lungs began to burn, and she gasped involuntarily.

What is this? What's happening?

Her eyes began to flutter. She slumped against the wall, unable to move.

Alpheus waited, watching her face for signs of full submission. Then he unlocked the cell with a soft *click* and stepped inside.

"There we are. Isn't that better?" He crouched beside her and retrieved a syringe from the folds of his cloak, carefully drawing the contents from the vial. The fluid gleamed yellow with a metallic sheen.

"This is something I've been working on for quite some time. A little concoction I call the *Suppression Serum*. It silences your gills, flattens your fins, keeps you nice and docile above water."

No…

He pressed the needle against the crook of her arm. She couldn't resist, couldn't even flinch.

The needle sank in. He depressed the plunger slowly, like he was savoring it.

You…monster, she wanted to scream, but her lips wouldn't form the words.

"Think of it. No more obeying weak kings or bleeding hearts. You could cleanse this rotten world. One target at a time."

When the syringe was emptied, he carefully withdrew it and patted her cheek.

"Rest well, my little siren. We've got *so much* work ahead of us."

He tucked the syringe and empty vial back into his coat and gave a mockingly courteous bow before locking the cell.

The mist gradually dissipated, and Nerissa slowly regained her senses, blinking slowly. Her pulse was sluggish now, fingers tingling.

She remembered Alpheus coming to her cell…but nothing afterwards.

The cell was cold. Not just the stone or the air, but the kind of cold that soaked into her bones and made a home there, feeding on shame and unanswered questions.

Nerissa sat with her knees drawn to her chest, forehead pressed against the wall as if it might whisper back the pieces of yesterday. Her palms were still caked with dried blood, and she had a bruise in the crook of her elbow that hadn't been there the day before.

Strange.

She remembered the vows. Standing behind Calliope, hands folded, watching her dear friend bind herself to a future Nerissa still wasn't sure she trusted. Watching the priest speak, the way the light had filtered through the stained glass. Leander reciting his vows.

And then—that voice in her head. Not her own. Commanding her to do the unthinkable.

Damarion's hands gripping her arms, shaking her hard. His voice, hoarse and disbelieving, saying her name like he didn't recognize it.

And Calliope…

The utter betrayal in her eyes..

She doesn't believe me.

No one did.

No one would.

She'd been trained to defend. Subdue. Protect. But never—never kill in cold blood. She'd knocked blades from hands. Broken a few ribs when the moment demanded it. Once fractured someone's jaw.

But this was different.

This was final.

Now she was a criminal. A killer.

She dug her fingers into her hair, breath coming faster, chest tight.

Everyone saw me. There's no mistaking what happened. The real question is why?

Nerissa curled tighter into herself, the edge of her thoughts fraying.

You were behind Calliope. She trusted you.

And then suddenly she'd been standing over Vasilios, chest heaving, blade red, everything red.

Her heart thumped painfully in her ears. She squeezed her eyes shut. Tried to remember anything—any sound, any command, any clue. Just that voice in her head, commanding her to kill the king.

Was she losing her grip on reality?

The clank of the iron door echoed through the corridor.

Nerissa didn't lift her head. She didn't need to.

She knew that tread. The measured, deliberate cadence of a soldier. She didn't look up until the lock turned and the heavy door creaked open.

Damarion stepped into the cell, his armor hidden beneath a hooded cloak. He closed the door behind him, quietly.

For a long moment, he didn't speak. He simply studied her, eyes tracing the lines of her slouched posture, the way her fists were clenched so tightly they trembled.

She lifted her tired head just enough to look at his face as he stood across from her, arms folded, jaw tight.

"I need to know everything you remember," he said. "From the beginning. Start with the moment I found you in the corridor outside Calliope's chambers."

"I…" Nerissa exhaled slowly. "I left her chambers to get some air, then I saw Alpheus in the hallway. I think? Yes…he was walking down the corridor. He looked at me as if he expected me to follow."

Damarion's brow twitched. She took it as permission to keep going.

"So I did," she said. "I don't know why. I just...did. And then it's like—like something shifted. Like I lost my grip on the current."

"You don't remember what happened next?"

She shook her head slowly. "I remember you. Asking why I wasn't at my post. Nothing in between. Then the wedding. I remember standing behind Calliope while Leander said his vows. Then…I know this sounds crazy, but I heard a voice in my head, telling me to pick up the knife. I couldn't stop myself. I had no control over my own body. And then—" Her voice cracked. "And then I killed Vasilios."

Damarion moved to sit beside her. "You weren't yourself," he said. "I saw it in your eyes before you even looked at the king."

She turned her face toward him, wary and afraid to ask the question rising in her throat.

But she asked it anyway.

"So you believe me?"

He didn't answer right away. Instead, he leaned forward, resting his elbows on his knees, and let out a long breath that seemed to echo through the cell.

"You're like my own daughter, Skíon. I've known you since you could barely lift a blade. I've seen your heart when it was broken. I've seen it when it burned."

Her throat tightened.

"And I'll be damned," Damarion said, quieter now, "if I let that snake Alpheus twist you into his next experiment and call it justice."

Nerissa closed her eyes for a moment, allowing herself to breathe now that the weight on her chest had been slightly lifted. He believed her. She wasn't alone.

Damarion stood.

"Get up."

Nerissa blinked, caught off guard.

He reached into the folds of his cloak and drew out a bundle of familiar leather—her belt, neatly buckled, twin daggers nestled in their sheaths.

"I believe you," he said, stepping forward. "And if I'm right—if Alpheus is behind this—then you don't belong in this cell."

He held out her weapons.

"You'll probably need these."

Nerissa's fingers trembled as she took the bundle, securing it around her waist with muscle memory that felt distant and dreamlike.

The weight of the daggers grounded her. Balanced her. Reminded her of who she was.

"Thank you," she whispered.

Damarion nodded once. "We need to move. Guard shift changes in five minutes."

The castle was just beginning to stir when they emerged into the early morning light, the pale gray sky still streaked with lavender. Dew slicked the stone underfoot as Nerissa and Damarion slipped through the inner gates of the dungeon tower, their footsteps urgent.

"Almost there," Damarion murmured, guiding her toward the spiral stairwell that led up the tower.

But the moment they rounded the next corner, a startled shout split the air.

"You there—halt!" A castle guard stood at the top of the stairs, eyes going wide.

The man fumbled for the horn at his belt, and the sound that followed pierced the morning calm.

"Go," Damarion said sharply, pushing Nerissa toward the winding stairs. "Now!"

She didn't argue.

She ran.

Her feet pounded up the narrow, winding steps. The tower groaned with the weight of age and sea wind, and as she burst through the upper doors, the sharp scent of salt water slapped her in the face.

She was high above the ocean, farther than she'd ever leapt. The waves churned below, jagged rocks lurking in the whitecaps.

Freedom. If she survived the fall.

More shouts echoed behind her, the boots of soldiers pounding in pursuit.

She turned once to look back. Damarion had drawn his blade, standing firm between her and the guards.

Their eyes met.

He nodded.

And she leapt.

The wind tore at her dress, her skirts snapping like sails. For a heartbeat she felt free—weightless—her body anticipating the cool embrace of the sea.

She braced for the familiar tug, the smooth bloom of her tail forming behind her, the soft, certain pull toward depth.

But it never came.

The impact stole her breath. Salt water burned her nose, her eyes, her throat. She flailed, searching for the familiar sweep of her fins as she willed her body to change. But nothing answered. She still had legs. Useless human limbs that felt numb and leaden in the frigid water.

Why can't I shift??

Panic began clawing its way up. The first reflex was the wrong one. She gasped. More water rushed into her mouth and burned down her throat. Her chest convulsed as her airway clamped shut against the water.

This is all wrong—

Her arms pumped frantically, trying to pull herself back to the surface, but her armor dragged her down like a weighted net. Her fingers scrabbled at the buckles, slipping on the leather as a cold numbness crept into them.

No. No, no, no—

The surface above became nothing more than a glimmering mirage as she fought the furious, sharp need for air. Bubbles rose past her face in fat, mocking pearls as she sank deeper.

Darkness brushed the edges of her sight. The world narrowed to a pinpoint of silver light far above. Her lungs screamed, chest burned. Her last clear thought was the knowledge that this was new. This was different. She had never known the slow, idiotic slide into unconsciousness, never felt the body betray the mind so completely as the sea took her.

CHAPTER 12

NOTHIN' BUT FISH BONES

Zale

The morning fog was still clinging stubbornly to the waves as the *Black Serpent* cut through them like a knife. The cliffs of Astyra loomed ahead, jagged and proud, the castle perched above them like a vulture watching for movement below.

Zale stood near the bow, his spyglass pressed to one eye, scanning the battlements.

"Lot of activity up there," he muttered. "More than usual."

"Mm?" Captain Nestor grunted from the helm, one hand resting lazily on the tiller. His posture was casual, but Zale knew better. The old man missed nothing.

Brigid stormed past in a flurry of red curls and impatience, barking orders at the deckhands and gesturing to the sails. "Trim that line, afore I string ye up by it meself, ye barnacle-brained numpty!"

Zale barely registered the noise. His focus was locked on one of the castle's watchtowers, where a growing crowd of guards was moving with a kind of frantic urgency. He adjusted the spyglass, angling upward.

Someone was running across the upper rampart.

Bran's voice broke into his thoughts as the boatswain leaned casually against the railing beside him, holding an apple like it was the most important object in the world.

"Word in the harbor was buzzing this morning," Bran said between bites. "That royal wedding yesterday? Didn't go smooth. Some say blades were drawn right there in the hall."

Zale didn't lower the glass. "Assassination attempt?"

"Depends who you ask." Bran gave him a sidelong grin. "Some swear the princess herself was the target. Others say it was the groom. Either way, lot of spectacle, not much matrimony."

The glass dipped slightly as Zale's jaw tightened. He thought of the blonde woman he'd seen on Leander's arm in the tavern two days ago. Was she caught up in this? Or the cause of it?

He raised the glass again, eyes narrowing on the shifting movement along the battlements.

A figure was sprinting full-speed toward the edge.

The figure jumped.

"What the—" Zale yanked the glass down, squinting at the tower.

Bran straightened beside him, chewing forgotten. "Did they just—?"

"Yeah," Zale said, stepping back. "They did."

"Think we should tell Nestor?"

"I'm thinking we should get ready to fish someone out of the water," Zale muttered, kicking off his boots.

"Not it," Bran said quickly, and bolted to alert the others.

Zale didn't wait.

He'd tossed his boots, shrugged off his coat, and was vaulting over the starboard rail before anyone could shout after him. The sea crashed over him, cold and oppressive, but he barely felt it as he cut through the current, arms driving forward with powerful strokes.

His eyes skimmed the dark water below for movement. There. A flicker of fabric, limbs drifting slack as the figure sank deeper. A woman.

He dove, arms slicing through the water. When he reached her, she was limp—eyes closed, lips parted, no bubbles rising now.

His heart seized.

The girl from the tavern.

There was a blossom of crimson on the front of her dress. Blood. His stomach twisted. Was it hers?

He hooked an arm around her waist, kicking upward. Too slow. That ridiculous armor was weighing her down and slowing their ascent. He needed to remove it, and get her to the surface, fast.

With one hand, he ripped at the buckles across her chest. The straps slipped, tangled, refused. He gritted his teeth and yanked harder until they finally gave way. The chest plate slid free, spiraling into the dark. He stripped off the bracers next, then the pauldrons, each motion clumsy in the thick drag of seawater.

Lighter now. Good.

He adjusted his grip—one arm tight around her waist, the other reaching above him—and kicked.

Up.

Up.

The light shimmered far above them like a distant illusion.

But he didn't stop.

Couldn't.

The girl sagged against him, cold and boneless. He hoped he wasn't too late.

He broke the surface with a gasp, holding her head above the waves. She gave no gasp of air. No cough. Nothing.

"Come on," he rasped, salt water stinging his throat. He shook her once. "Breathe."

Her head only lolled against his shoulder, lips tinged with blue.

Zale swore under his breath and angled toward the *Black Serpent*, which had swung in closer to the cliffs. A rope was hurled down; he latched on with one hand and clung to her with the other.

Bran and Cormac helped haul them up in a chaotic blur of arms and shouted curses. They collapsed onto the deck in a heap, seawater pooling beneath them.

Captain Nestor approached with a wary expression, eyes scanning the girl on the deck.

Brigid knelt beside them, one hand pressed to the woman's cheek. "Is she breathin'?"

Cormac leaned in, squinting. "After a fall from that height? Nah—no one survives a plunge like that, not 'less Poseidon himself fancies 'em. Lass oughta be nothin' but fish bones by now." He spat over the rail and muttered, "Mark me words, that one's got the sea's eye on her. Or somethin' fouler."

Zale didn't respond to the old man's superstitions. He tilted the woman's head back, ear lowering toward her parted lips. Nothing. No breath.

"Eon!" he barked. "Go fetch Roan!"

"On it!" The lad bolted down the steps to the infirmary quicker than lightning.

After what felt like an eternity, Roan came pounding up the stairs and dropped to the deck beside Zale.

"Talk to me."

"She fell from the cliffs, nearly drowned," Zale explained quickly.

"How long was she under?"

"Three minutes, tops," Zale told him. "Can't you give her something?"

"As a matter of fact," Roan fished in his satchel until he found a small glass ampoule. "Picked this up the last time we docked. Been waiting for a chance to try it out."

Zale eyed the glass warily. "What is it?"

"Filament distillate," he explained as he pulled the stopper out. "The old woman who sold it to me insisted it can revive drowning victims."

"Let's hope she's right." Zale shifted the girl, propping her mouth open so that Roan could administer a couple of drops onto her tongue.

"Come on," he muttered. "Breathe, damn it."

For a terrible moment, there was only silence.

Then her chest heaved, seawater spilling from her lips as her body jolted against his arms. She gasped and then coughed up more water.

Zale's shoulders sagged with relief.

The girl was coughing violently, her skin still a ghostly shade of blue-grey, and body shuddering with chill.

Zale slid his arms beneath her and lifted her carefully against his chest, bracing her upright so she wouldn't choke. Her weight sagged into him as he briskly rubbed her arms, trying to chase the cold from her skin.

The irony wasn't lost on him. At the tavern, she'd been all edges and distance, like she'd sooner gut him than allow him to help. And now here she was, clinging weakly to his soaked shirt, too far gone to shove him away.

She blinked, lashes heavy with water. Her eyes narrowed up at him.

"You…?" she rasped.

He froze. She remembered him.

"Yeah. I've got you." His hands kept moving up and down her arms, the friction finally generating some heat. "You're safe."

"Not...not safe," she whispered, her eyes rolling back. "Have to go. They'll come for me."

"Who?" Zale asked, tightening his hold.

Her breath brushed weakly against his neck. "I…didn't mean to…"

Bran crouched beside them, wide-eyed. "Poor lass is delirious."

"Looks like she's gone an' put half the Astyran guard on high bloody alert," Brigid muttered, glancing toward the tower where distant horns were beginning to sound.

Nestor's eyes narrowed toward the castle. Then he turned back to the crew.

"Change course, away from the cliffs. We've no time to untangle Astyran politics. Take her below."

Zale gathered the strange girl more firmly against his chest and pushed to his feet, water dripping off both of them onto the deck. She shivered violently as he stood, but did not resist.

Zale shoved the infirmary door open with his shoulder, Roan following close behind him.

The medic swept aside a half-finished cup of tea and a volume titled *Basic Stitching for Advanced Bleeding.* "On the table. Now."

Zale laid her down with care, then reached for her belt. "And—just in case—"

He unsheathed the daggers and set them aside, out of reach.

"Good instinct," Roan murmured. He pressed two fingers to her throat, checked her pulse, her breathing. "Looks like the distillate worked.

Heartbeat's steady, breathing is evening out. No obvious wounds, besides a bruise here, looks like a puncture wound, possibly from an injection. Is this all hers?" he asked, frowning at the crimson stain spread across her bodice.

"I don't know," Zale admitted. "She was unconscious by the time I pulled her out."

"I see…" Roan murmured, covering her with a thick blanket. "She's still too cold, need to raise her body temperature."

Zale hovered nearby, fists clenching and unclenching.

Roan looked over his shoulder at him. "Sit down. You pacing like a caged lion isn't helping."

Zale grudgingly leaned against the wall, arms crossed tightly. What exactly had happened at the tower? And what was she doing there in the first place?

The girl stirred.

Roan paused. "Wait for it…"

With a sharp gasp, she jolted upright, hands flying to her sides, searching.

"Easy," Zale said quickly, stepping forward. "I took your daggers. You'll get them back if you promise not to stab us."

She blinked, disoriented, as her gaze darted wildly around the room.

"Where…?" Her voice cracked.

"You're safe," Zale said, gently. "You're on a ship—the *Black Serpent.* You nearly drowned. Roan here is checking you over."

She stared at him, her brow furrowing, fingers gripping the threadbare blanket around her like a shield.

"You," she said, voice smaller now, "...from the tavern."

He grinned, lopsided and easy, like he was trying not to spook a wounded animal.

"Guilty," he said. "Though I was hoping you'd remember me for the dramatic ocean rescue and not the failed charm offensive."

The girl simply stared at him with a bewildered look in her eyes.

Roan, still near the shelf preparing something that looked and smelled questionably edible, turned back toward them.

"Right then," he said casually. "Now that you're conscious, let's ask the obvious question." His gaze flicked to the dark stain covering her garment. "That blood. Is it yours?"

She didn't answer at first. She just stared at the floor, lips parted, breath shallow. Then her head turned slightly. She met Zale's eyes for only a moment, and something in her expression made him stop cold.

"No," she said.

Just that.

Roan didn't ask again.

He simply gave a small nod and turned away, hands moving to create one of his tried-and-true herbal remedies.

Zale said nothing either. He just watched her, silently, as she wrapped the blanket more tightly around her shoulders and sank a little lower on the table.

He recalled what Bran had mentioned, about rumors of an assassination attempt during the royal wedding. What if this girl was there? That would mean that her blonde friend could be the foreign princess Leander was set to marry. Maybe she got caught in a struggle while protecting the princess, and that's where the blood came from? He shook his head. He could ask her later, once she had a chance to rest.

Roan set to work crushing dried leaves in a stone mortar. The scent of something minty emanated from the vessel.

“She’ll be fine,” he muttered. “No injuries besides bruising. Breathing’s steady. Heart’s too fast, but that’ll settle once she sleeps.”

He glanced at Zale, the lines in his weathered face deeper than usual.

“Help her to the cot. Slowly.”

Zale hesitated, then approached her carefully. “Hey. C’mon, tavern girl. Let’s get you off this slab.”

She flinched when he reached for her, so he withdrew his hand.

“It’s alright lass, I’m not gonna hurt ye.”

She eyed him suspiciously for a moment until she was satisfied that he was not a threat and nodded.

Zale tried again, slower this time, and she allowed him to help her down, her balance faltering like she’d forgotten how legs were meant to work. He guided her to the cot and noted with intrigue that her dress wasn’t even drenched, like the seawater had slipped right off the fabric. Looked like the same material as the gown she was wearing at the tavern.

Roan handed him a steaming cup. “She probably won’t take it from me. But maybe she’ll listen to you.”

Zale knelt beside the cot, offering it wordlessly.

She blinked at the cup. Then at him.

And took it.

Just a few sips before her fingers loosened and the cup slipped from her hand, caught swiftly by Zale before it spilled.

She sank back against the pillow, breath deepening. Not quite asleep. Not yet.

Zale pulled up a chair and sat beside her as her gaze faded into nothing, her eyes open but far, far away.

It had only been two days.

Two days since the tavern, since she'd glared at him and aimed her words like they were weapons. She'd been unshakable then, like she could command storms with just a look.

Now?

Now her skin was too pale, her breathing still not quite right. Her eyes, open but not seeing, held no fire. Just shadows. She looked…hollow.

Zale frowned, fingers twitching against the edge of the chair. He wanted to ask what had happened. Who had done this.

He leaned forward a little, studying her like a map he couldn't read. She was no longer shivering, but something about her still looked cold.

The sea had almost taken her. And maybe, Zale thought grimly, some part of her hadn't made it back.

CHAPTER 13
DIDASKON

Alpheus

The alchemical flame crackled low beneath a bubbling glass retort, casting an eerie glow over the stone walls of the chamber. Alpheus hummed a quiet tune–something old, something Astyran, long before peace had dulled the kingdom's teeth. The melody stuttered as the door opened without a knock.

He didn't look up.

"I assume this interruption is of the *utmost* importance," he said, sliding a stopper into place before the volatile fluid could hiss over the lip.

"It is, sir," came the tense, hesitant voice of the young guard, halfway regretting stepping through that threshold.

Alpheus turned slowly. "Then speak, and pray it *justifies* your timing."

The guard gave a stiff bow. "The prisoner, Nerissa. She's escaped."

"I see," Alpheus said, his tone infuriatingly neutral. "Do enlighten me."

"She was last seen at the dungeon tower. The sentries on watch say she leapt from the battlement."

"Into the ocean?"

"Yes, sir."

Alpheus paused.

"And tell me…how did she escape in the first place?" he asked with a sharp look.

"We captured the one responsible, my lord. The Captain of the Royal Nautalian Guard, Damarion."

Now *that* made Alpheus smile in full.

"Did you?"

The guard nodded quickly. "Yes, sir. He was holding back the guards at the tower steps so she could escape. He's now being held in the lower cells."

Alpheus turned back to his desk and plucked a small silver syringe from a velvet case. He admired it in the light, then set it gently in a tray on the table. "Isn't that just poetic," he mused. "Does anyone else know about this?"

"No, sir, I came straight to you."

"Good, I am certain you can appreciate the need for discretion during this difficult time for the kingdom."

"Of course."

"Bring him to me. I'd like to have...words."

“Yes, sir.”

The guard bowed deeply and practically fled. Alpheus remained still for a long moment, gazing down at his tools with quiet delight.

The apothecary door shut behind the guard with a hollow thud. Alpheus let the sound linger, then reached for a fresh page in his ledger, careful not to smear the ink of his last notation. He dipped his quill, the feather whispering against glass, and scrawled a single word at the top of the parchment:

Damarion.

A name half-buried by time, though not forgotten. The soldier with stubborn honor, foolish enough to fall for a royal.

His smile morphed, thinner now, colder.

Alpheus folded his hands neatly over the ledger and leaned back in his chair, listening to the tick of the brass wall clock. There was a soft knock at the door.

“Enter,” Alpheus called, smoothing his sleeves.

Two guards stepped in, flanking a man in shackles. Damarion looked exactly as Alpheus remembered—broad-shouldered, calm-eyed, and full of irritating dignity, despite the bruising at his temple and the blood dried at his collar.

“Leave us,” Alpheus said.

The guards hesitated, then withdrew with synchronized bows. The door sealed shut.

Alpheus regarded his visitor for a long moment before gesturing casually to the chair opposite his desk.

"Do sit, Captain. You look…weathered."

Damarion said nothing. He remained standing, shoulders squared like a statue carved from reef stone.

Alpheus tilted his head. "No? Ah, still playing the part of the loyal soldier. I expected as much. You always did find comfort in protocol."

Still nothing.

Alpheus rose, slowly, then crossed the chamber to a basin of clear water. He rolled up his sleeves, rinsed his hands, and dabbed them dry with a linen towel as he spoke.

"I suppose you're wondering why you're here. Why I haven't simply handed you over to the prince for execution."

Damarion's jaw tensed.

Alpheus smiled. "You'll be pleased to know, I believe in utility. In preservation. *In answers.*"

He turned back to face him. "Answers I think you can provide."

Still silence.

Alpheus sighed dramatically. "Well then. I suppose I shall have to inspire your cooperation." He opened a drawer and removed a small vial of crimson liquid, holding it up to the light.

"Tell me, Captain...have you ever heard of myrrh root distillate? It's an old Astyran remedy. Pain reliever. Muscle relaxant. But in large doses…" he swirled the vial, watching the viscous ripple, "it causes the tongue to loosen. Drip by drip."

Damarion finally spoke, his voice low but unflinching. "You won't find what you're looking for in me."

Alpheus chuckled softly. "That, dear Captain, is precisely what I intend to test."

He uncorked the vial with a soft pop, an earthy scent curling into the air.

"Has it really been twenty-five years?" he mused aloud, selecting a fine glass syringe from his tray and drawing up the crimson liquid with a steady hand. "Since you and dear Lady Thalassa played your little game of *diplomatic outreach.*"

Damarion's jaw remained set, but Alpheus caught the twitch at the corner of his eye.

Progress.

"Oh, come now," Alpheus continued, giving the syringe a gentle tap, watching for bubbles. "Don't look so surprised. I was in Vasilios's inner court, remember? I saw the way she looked at you. The late-night walks. The little rendezvous beneath the palace garden's rose bushes. You really thought no one noticed?"

Damarion's fists clenched, rattling his shackles. "Get to your point."

"My, my, impatient." Alpheus wandered over to the nearby table, carefully setting down the vial. He turned and met Damarion's glare.

"How curious—her sudden illness. How curious she came to me. How curious she disappeared."

He tapped the syringe, and the bead of liquid clung to the tip like blood.

Damarion's voice came low, gravel and venom. "What did you do to her?"

Alpheus turned away, satisfied at the flicker of pain he'd planted. "Ah, but dwelling on old ghosts will not serve us, Captain. We're here to speak of the handmaiden—Nerissa."

"You freed her from the dungeon at dawn," Alpheus went on, voice softening into silk. "You risked your post, your head, your precious reputation. Why? Tell me about the girl. Tell me why she means enough for you to break protocol."

Alpheus reached for Damarion's arm.

But the captain moved faster.

With a sharp twist, Damarion lashed out, knocking the syringe aside with a clang that sent it skittering across the stone floor. Alpheus recoiled, more startled than afraid.

"So dramatic," he muttered, then snapped, "Guards!"

The door burst open. Four soldiers rushed in, halberds drawn, awaiting his orders.

"Hold him."

The captain fought like a creature of the sea—fluid, brutal, and deceptively fast for a man in chains. One guard went down with a grunt as Damarion rammed him into the wall, knocking the wind clean from his lungs. The other barely dodged a blow that would have shattered his jaw.

But the shackles were too restrictive, and the numbers too many.

The third and fourth guards grappled his arms while Alpheus darted forward, scooping the syringe from the floor.

"Hold him *still!*"

The moment Damarion's shoulder was exposed, Alpheus plunged the needle in.

Damarion snarled, thrashing, but it was too late. The serum would spread instantly, curling down his veins, hot and thick.

Alpheus leaned close as the guards forced Damarion to his knees. "Tell me why you went back for her. Tell me what she is to you. Let's take a swim through your memories, shall we?"

Damarion

At first, everything was dark.

He felt the pressure of the ocean, sudden and familiar.

Bioluminescent light flickered in the deep. Coral spires twisted upward in graceful arcs around the grand gates of the Nautalian palace.

Damarion floated at his post just outside those gates, spear in hand, tail curled beneath him in a loose coil. His silver hair clung to his brow in sharp waves, pushed by the gentle tug of the tide.

A calm post. A quiet day.

Until a small, frightened voice pierced the silence.

"Help! Someone—please!"

He turned, instincts flaring. A child was swimming frantically toward him.

Her dark hair floated behind her like seaweed, tangled and matted. Blood was seeping from a gash along her collarbone. Her arms and shoulders were scraped, several scales missing, likely torn from swimming through the coral forest.

Wait. This was Theron's daughter.

"Nerissa?" Damarion pushed forward, lowering his weapon. "What happened?"

"Damarion!" she cried, stopping short and clutching a jagged coral outcrop for support. "Please—I—I need—"

He reached her in two strong kicks of his tail, hands firm but gentle on her shoulders.

"Slow down. Breathe. Tell me what happened."

The girl choked back a sob, her chest heaving with sharp little hiccups. "I...I followed them," she stammered, glancing over her shoulder as if something might be chasing her. "I wasn't supposed to, but I just wanted to help."

She squared her little shoulders as she fought to regain composure.

"They told me to stay hidden. I tried to follow without being seen. But then—" her voice cracked. "These humans came. With torches. And swords. They—they ambushed us."

Damarion's chest tightened.

"Who were they?" he asked, low and steady.

"I don't know!" she cried. "I don't *know!* They wore masks. Father told me to run. They tried to fight. I didn't see what happened next—I swam, I swam as fast as I could but they—"

She swallowed, trembling violently now.

"They didn't come back."

Damarion's grip tightened just a fraction. He could hear the shame in her voice. The way she'd clenched her jaw, determined not to cry.

"You did the right thing," he said, softly. "You got away. You made it back. That's what matters."

"But I left them," she whispered.

"You *lived,* Nerissa."

She finally looked up at him, and for a second, she looked younger than her years—just a girl in a current far too strong for her, forced to grow up too quickly.

Damarion turned his gaze toward the palace, planning what had to be done—who needed to be informed, what teams needed to mobilize. But something else settled in his chest then too. A silent, seething promise.

The land dwellers would not get away with this.

No sentry dared stop Damarion as he swept through the coral archway with Nerissa in his arms, her small frame wrapped in strands of kelp he'd used to stanch the worst of the bleeding. Her tail drifted limp and motionless, still dotted with tiny coral thorns.

The grand halls of the Nautalian palace stretched ahead, a living cathedral of reef and pearl. The walls pulsed with soft bioluminescence, lighting the way. Courtiers glanced up as Damarion surged past, their hushed gasps bubbling behind them.

Queen Ophelia was waiting outside the healing chamber, surrounded by a cluster of startled attendants.

Her serene expression fractured when she saw the girl.

"Damarion?"

"She's hurt," he said simply, voice urgent.

The queen gave a sharp nod, signaling the medics. Her gaze flicked back to him, sharp with unspoken questions. "Where are her parents? Theron? Melora?"

Damarion's jaw tightened. He shook his head once, grim and final.

The queen's lips parted, but no sound followed. She understood what he had not spoken aloud.

Then Nerissa stirred, her voice barely audible. "It's okay," she murmured. "I can swim."

Damarion gently eased her forward. She pushed away from his arms, tail unsteady as she drifted upright, wobbling in the water. She blinked, dazed beneath the glow of jellyfire lanterns, and held herself together by sheer force of will.

Little Princess Calliope darted forward from the corridor, her golden fins flashing in alarm.

"Nerissa!" she cried, immediately wrapping her arms around her. "What happened? Oh—your face—here, lean on me."

The two girls clung to each other as attendants brought bowls of soothing kelp salve and soft sea sponges. Queen Ophelia floated closer, reaching out to cup Nerissa's scraped face in both hands as gently as if she were made of glass.

"You're safe now, little one," the queen said quietly.

Damarion hovered nearby, arms crossed tightly over his chest to keep them from trembling. He watched as the attendants cleaned the coral cuts and examined Nerissa's swollen gills. Her expression was tight, distant, but her eyes kept flicking back to him.

Her lip quivered.

"I'm sorry," she whispered, her voice a fragile ripple through the water. "I should've listened."

"No," Damarion said, drifting forward. "No apologies. You survived. That's all that matters."

He drifted downward until they were eye to eye, his expression softening as he took her smaller hand in his.

"I swear to you, Nerissa," he said, taking her small hand in his. "Whatever comes next, I will protect you. You will not face this alone."

Her fingers curled around his with surprising strength.

Later, Damarion waited for Nerissa outside the healing chamber. She drifted next to him, wounds now wrapped in soft kelp strips.

"The queen said you may stay at the palace; is there anything you would like to retrieve from your home?"

She didn't seem to hear him. Her eyes, though still puffy, had steadied into something harder than fear.

"I want to train," she said, voice low but resolute. "To fight. Like you."

Damarion blinked, caught off guard. "You need rest, little one. You've been through—"

"I'm not little," she interrupted. "Not anymore."

There was no fire in her voice. No tantrum. Just cold determination, more chilling than rage.

"If I had known how to fight, I could've done something. I could've helped. Maybe they wouldn't have—" She bit the words off and looked away. Her lip trembled. "I don't want to feel helpless again. Not ever."

Damarion was silent for a moment. He studied her, and what he saw there made his chest tighten. Grief, yes. But also steel. He reached out, resting one large hand over hers.

"I'll teach you," he said. "But not to be a soldier."

She looked back at him, brow furrowed.

"I want you to understand the difference," he continued. "Soldiers fight wars. Soldiers follow orders. And sometimes...they forget who they're protecting."

Her expression softened, just a little.

"I'll train you to defend yourself. To defend others. You'll learn when to fight, and when *not* to. That's harder."

She gave a small nod. "Like a bodyguard?"

Damarion's lips tugged into a rare smile.

"Exactly."

Then she said something he hadn't expected, something that cracked the walls around his heart.

"Thank you...*Didaskon*."

The word drifted up between them like a bubble, delicate and unassuming.

The Nautalian word for *Teacher*.

He squeezed her hand in return.

The memory collapsed like a wave dragged violently out to sea.

Damarion slumped to the stone floor, still shackled, his human form drenched in sweat, chest heaving from the strain. Hair clung to his brow, fury burning in his eyes despite the exhaustion weighing down his limbs.

Across the room, Alpheus dipped his quill and scratched something into his notes with maddening precision.

"Well," he said at last, tone far too pleased. "That was informative."

He capped the inkwell with a snap and turned toward Damarion.

"I had wondered why the Captain of the Royal Guard would risk everything to free a girl with no bloodline, no name of consequence. But now I see—she's not just a stray to you. She's family."

He gave a soft chuckle, eyes glinting.

"How noble. You, the *Didaskon*, raising a little orphan with fire in her heart and nothing left to lose. Raised in the palace. Trained under your watchful eye. Practically forged for loyalty. A clean slate sharpened into a blade."

Damarion's voice rasped from between clenched teeth. "You used her."

Alpheus raised a brow, as though offended by the simplicity of the word. "Used her? No, no. I merely...revealed her potential."

Damarion's lip curled. "I knew you were involved somehow. She wasn't in control of herself."

"Ah," Alpheus said, smile blooming like rot. "Yes. My little invention. A vaporized distillate. Highly volatile, but effective. Opens the mind. Eases resistance. Lowers moral thresholds."

He stepped forward, voice darkening.

"She didn't kill Vasilios because *she* wanted to. She killed him because *I commanded her to.*"

Damarion's fists tightened, knuckles pale.

"You made her take the fall."

"I gave her direction," Alpheus corrected, casual as a doctor discussing anatomy. "The pain was already there. The anger. I didn't build the fire. I simply showed her where to burn."

He began circling behind the chair, slow and deliberate.

Damarion finally lifted his head, eyes narrowing into slits. "If *any* harm comes to her, I swear I will—"

"Ah-ah." Alpheus lifted a finger. "Careful. Empty threats are unbecoming. Besides, you speak as though she's still among us. Thanks to your little stunt, she's probably at the bottom of the sea by now."

Damarion swore his heart stopped. "What do you mean?"

"Ah, of course. You couldn't have known. I gave her a gift before her escape. A serum of my own invention. Suppresses the shift. Leaves sirens helplessly human." He leaned closer, visibly savoring Damarion's pain. "So when she dove from those cliffs…" He mimed a falling motion with two fingers. "No gills. No tail. Just lungs filling with salt water until—" He snapped his fingers. "Silence."

Horror consumed Damarion's expression. "You bastard," he rasped.

Alpheus chuckled softly. "Poetic, isn't it? You risked everything to free her, and in doing so, you doomed her."

Damarion's blood roared in his ears, blocking out everything else. Alpheus was lying—he *had* to be. The image of Nerissa's human body, blue and lifeless, sinking to the bottom of the sea was too much. He had *failed* her.

There was a knock at the door. A young guard slipped in, bowing low. "Forgive me, sir. News from the sentries. They spotted the *Black Serpent* near the cliffs shortly after the prisoner escaped. A figure was seen being hauled from the water and brought aboard."

Alpheus's smile froze, then returned—colder.

"Well," he murmured, turning back to Damarion. "Perhaps fate is not finished with your little ward after all."

CHAPTER 14

ASH AND LILIES

Calliope

What a stark contrast the morning was to the day before. Calliope's nose wrinkled at the unfamiliar scents drifting through the halls. Lilies for mourning, ash from the torches that had burned all night.

Somewhere in the city below, the bells tolled with grim persistence. Astyran banners hung limp against the pale stone of the courtyard, their colors muted by grief. At the far end, where the seawall opened into a broad descent toward the waves, the waters churned with the low pull of the tide.

Her mother clasped Calliope's hands, veil trailing against her daughter's wrists. Her voice was low, edged with worry. "You don't have to stay if—"

"She does," her father cut in firmly. His hair lifted in the wind, eyes fixed on the castle towers above. "If this treaty has any chance of survival, she must remain. Her presence is the thread holding both kingdoms together."

Calliope swallowed hard and nodded. "Then I'll remain. At least until I know where Leander stands. If he still wants the marriage...then so do I. And if peace is still possible, I will fight for it."

Her father's expression softened by a fraction, though the weight of kingship never left his face. "Hold your ground, Daughter. Do not let grief or politics turn you into their scapegoat."

Her mother leaned in, pressing her brow to Calliope's in parting. "Be strong. We will hold Nautalia steady."

The queen's veil slipped through Calliope's fingers as she and the king stepped to the seawall's edge. A heartbeat later, the waters embraced them, pulling them down in a swirl of silver and blue until they vanished beneath the surface.

Calliope stood on the beach long after the ripples had stilled, the toll of Astyra's mourning bells echoing through the stone. Her new handmaidens waited silently.

At last, she turned back toward the palace, to look for Leander.

Calliope kept her chin high as she passed through the stone halls, but the councilors did not lower their voices.

"Sirens in our midst—what did they expect?" one hissed, clutching the edge of his cloak.

"Perhaps that's what peace means to Nautalia—knife first, words later," another cut in, voice harsh. "A union cursed from the start. Alpheus tried to warn us."

"The merfolk cannot be trusted. Not after this."

"They say the girl was her confidante. If the handmaiden was capable of murder, how long until the princess herself—"

Calliope's steps faltered, but only for a breath. She forced her pace steady, though each word cut like broken glass beneath her heels.

At the far end of the corridor, two elder councilors stood close together. Their voices were lower, but she caught the name that had come to make her stomach knot.

"Alpheus has done so much for Astyra. Ensured our successful defense against Nautalia in decades past. Cured the plague that threatened to take half the city. The people trust him."

"The new king is only twenty-two. The throne is weakened; Leander will have to prove control. We need someone who can guarantee safety from the merfolk, and Alpheus is the only one with the spine for it."

Calliope's hands curled into fists at her sides. She did not slow, but she carried those words with her like stones in her chest. If Leander faltered, if he let their doubts weigh him down, then she might lose more than his hand. She might lose the treaty itself. And without it, there would be nothing left to bridge the sea between their peoples.

Calliope sat in silence beside the man who had become king too soon.

Leander had not spoken since yesterday. He hadn't even changed out of his wedding garments. His tunic was stiff with dried blood, soaked deep into the embroidery where he'd knelt over his father's body. His father's crown now perched on his head somehow seemed too large for him.

Calliope folded her hands in her lap. Her voice, when it came, was quiet. Careful. "You should change. Or eat. Or...something."

Leander didn't respond. He hadn't eaten a morsel today. Hadn't slept. Just sat there, locked in a silence no one dared to disturb.

No one but her.

Calliope's heart ached for him. Her thoughts kept circling back to that awful, gruesome scene.

"I didn't know," she whispered. "Leander, I swear it. I didn't know what she meant to do."

Finally, he stirred. His gaze drifted to her, heavy with exhaustion and grief.

She reached for his hand. It was cold in hers. "I'll stay," she said quietly. "If you'll still have me. We can still do the ceremony. Something small. Just to make it official…Whatever you want."

For a long time, he said nothing. Calliope held her breath, fearing he would send her away for good. What an utter failure she would be. Forced to return to Nautalia with no peace treaty. No alliance.

Then his fingers curled slightly around hers. "Tonight," he said at last, voice rough. "I'll change, and we'll have the vows spoken before the council convenes in the morning. Only the necessary witnesses."

She exhaled, trembling with relief.

"But the treaty…" He looked toward the window, where pale light pressed against the glass. "It cannot be signed without the court's approval. And things are too volatile right now." His voice lowered, more resolute. "But I will convince them. I have to. They must see this treaty is still in everyone's best interests."

Calliope nodded, swallowing against the tightness in her throat. She wanted to believe him. Needed to. For both their kingdoms. But even as she held his hand, her mind whispered the fear she could not speak aloud: if grief made him hesitate, if the court swayed him toward caution or vengeance, then everything—her marriage, her duty, the fragile peace—could unravel like a net cut loose.

She squeezed his hand tighter, as though the pressure alone could anchor them both.

Calliope stood at the top of the dungeon tower, arms folded tightly, her expression hard. She wasn't even sure why she had come here. She was still angry, but she needed answers.

"I want to see her."

The guard at the door shifted uneasily. "I'm sorry, Your Highness. No visitors permitted. Lord Alpheus's orders."

Her mouth hardened into a line. "Then override them. I outrank Lord Alpheus."

"But of course you do," came a smooth voice from the corridor.

Calliope turned slowly.

Alpheus.

Bejeweled fingers clasped in front of him as he bowed to her.

"How may I be of assistance, Princess?"

"I want to speak with Nerissa," she said, clipped.

Alpheus tutted softly, stepping closer. "Ah. Unfortunately, that may not be possible." His voice slid like oil. "She became violent after her interrogation. We were forced to sedate her. She's resting now."

Calliope's chin lifted. "How convenient."

His smile never wavered, but something flickered in his eyes. "The safety of the realm must come first. In times like these, sentiment clouds judgment."

Her gaze sharpened. "How fortunate the kingdom has you to remind us of duty."

They stared at each other for a long moment before she turned on her heel and strode away, before he could see the frustration beneath her composed exterior. She didn't trust him one bit.

The ceremony that evening was quiet, drained of all celebration.

The priest recited the vows in the small chapel, his voice echoing softly off vaulted stone. Only a handful of witnesses stood present, a couple of councilors, the guards, and her ladies-in-waiting.

Calliope clasped Leander's hands, the gold band cool as it slid onto her finger. She repeated the words as she was meant to, but they felt heavy on her tongue. Marriage was supposed to be joy, celebration, promise. Instead, the air still reeked of ash and lilies, and the floor below still bore her father-in-law's blood.

She stole a glance at Leander as the crown shifted heavier on his brow. His eyes were shadowed, fixed on something far beyond the chamber. She thought of his letters—the shy earnestness of them, the careful way he'd written of his hopes for peace. Those words had been warm and real. But now, standing before him, she felt the distance carved by grief and sorrow.

When the vows were finished and the blessing spoken, the small gathering bowed and dispersed with murmured courtesies. No cheers, no music, no laughter. Only the shuffle of feet and the quiet toll of the bells.

Her handmaidens took her arms and led her back through the corridors. Their whispers skimmed over her ears, but she heard none of them. She felt wrung out, caught between tragedy and responsibility to her people, and more alone than she had ever expected to feel on her wedding night.

In her chambers, her ladies unpinned her veil and laid her crown carefully on the dressing table, helping her to undress and slip into a silk nightgown. Calliope thanked them faintly and dismissed them, watching as they slipped out with soft curtsies and lowered eyes.

The door shut. Silence.

She sat on the edge of her bed, fingers tracing the embroidery of her nightgown. She didn't expect Leander to send for her tonight. Their marriage was a formality, meant to reassure a restless court, not a bond meant to be consummated in heartache.

So when a knock sounded at her door, she nearly jumped out of her skin.

"Calliope?" Came Leander's voice, muffled by the door.

She rose, heart thudding in her chest, and crossed to the door.

When she opened it, there he stood, eyes still rimmed with redness but clearer now.

"May I come in?" he asked hesitantly, toying with the hem of his tunic.

"Of course." She stepped back, motioning toward the chair at her vanity. "Sit, if you'd like."

But he didn't. Instead, he closed the door behind him and unexpectedly pulled her into a fierce embrace.

Calliope stiffened, startled, before her arms found their way around him. His frame was taut with nervous energy, his breath uneven against her shoulder. She stroked his hair with slow, steady motions, as though she could smooth the sadness out of him with her hands.

When he finally spoke, his voice was raw, torn from somewhere deep. "I am sorry. This is not...saints, this isn't how I imagined our wedding night."

Her chest ached. She pressed her cheek to his collarbone, whispering, "No apologies. Please. You've lost too much. Take all the time you need. I'll be here when you're ready."

Leander drew back, just far enough for her to see his face. His smile was faint, fragile, but it warmed the shadows beneath his eyes. "I do not deserve you," he said softly. "But I swear, I will do everything in my power to cherish you. And to pursue peace. For both our kingdoms."

Calliope's heart squeezed at his declaration. For all the anguish and ceremony between them, he meant every word. And though their union had been born of necessity, she found solace in the sincerity of his promise.

He brushed his thumb over her hand, almost absently. "I know I have a target on my head now. The crown makes me a mark. So I would rather not waste time pretending there will always be a tomorrow, when there may not be."

Before she could answer, he leaned in, tentatively, and kissed her. Gently enough that she could have easily pushed him away. But she didn't.

Instead, she rose onto her toes, deepening the kiss. The taste of salt mingled between them, whether from his tears or the ocean on her own lips, she couldn't tell. His hand slipped to the small of her back, and hers to his chest, feeling the uneven rhythm beneath her palm. For a long moment, they simply breathed together, the world narrowing to the sound of rain against the balcony glass.

When he drew her gently toward the bed, his touch was reverent, as though he were making a vow all over again—not just as king, but as her husband.

Calliope's gown whispered to the floor, a shimmer of silk and lace. Leander didn't reach for her right away. He only looked into her eyes, searching for any sign of hesitation.

"Are you sure?" he asked quietly.

She nodded, eyes glistening. "I don't want our first memory as husband and wife to be of sorrow."

He smiled, drawing her into his arms, and brushed a strand of hair from her face. "Then let it be hope."

When they finally lay together, Calliope curled sleepily against him, fingers resting over the steady beat of his heart. Leander pressed a kiss to her hair, murmuring against her temple, "Peace will come. I'll make certain of it."

CHAPTER 15

THE GHOST OF A NOBLEWOMAN

Nerissa

She wasn't sure how long she had slept, but she still felt exhausted. Her body ached as if she had been repeatedly thrown against the reef by a riptide.

The last thing she remembered was darkness. Drowning. Her body hadn't obeyed her command to shift. That had never happened before. It terrified her how quickly her natural element had betrayed her. She would have died if not for…

Him. The pirate from the tavern. What was his name again?

She sat up slowly, keeping the blanket wrapped snugly around her as she took in her surroundings. Jars lined the shelves in neat rows, labeled in a firm, slanted hand. A rack of bone saws and knives gleamed near the washbasin; threatening, but impeccably clean. This place felt miles away from the sickening atmosphere of the apothecary lab in the East Tower.

"Good, you're awake," came a man's voice. She thought she recognized the deep timbre of it—had she met him before? She couldn't quite piece together the events from that morning. Was she a prisoner? She didn't feel like one.

As if reading her mind, the man explained. "You probably don't remember much from before you fell asleep. Short term memory loss is normal after a traumatic incident. I'm Roan, this ship's medic."

Roan looked more like a brawler than a healer, judging by his broad shoulders and muscular arms. Deep brown skin gleamed in the lanternlight under the rolled-up sleeves of his cream colored shirt. The leather apron he wore had an alarming amount of what she could only assume were old bloodstains, with various medical tools poking out from several pockets. Long black dreadlocks were tied back with a red sash, and he had warm amber eyes that looked stern but kind.

Those eyes were now clinically appraising her as she shivered despite the blanket. He carefully got up from his stool and retrieved another blanket from a shelf, moving as if he was trying not to startle her. She realized that she had yet to speak.

Nerissa didn't recognize her own voice as she rasped out a "thank you" when he placed the extra blanket around her shoulders. Clearing her throat, she tried again to speak.

"How did I get here?" she managed, grimacing at the way her voice still scraped from her throat.

"Zale pulled you out of the water. You're lucky. He's our fastest swimmer. Any longer and you probably wouldn't have made it," he explained while gently checking the pulse at her neck.

Zale…That's right. The cocky flirt from the tavern.

"Are you always this blunt with your patients?" Nerissa attempted to smile, causing her teeth to chatter. *Nerae,* her human form felt so weak;

she never got cold in her siren form.

To her surprise, Roan chuckled. "I don't see the need to sugarcoat the truth. The crew is used to it. And Ma Wen should be bringing you some soup any minute now. Should warm you right up."

"Appreciate it," Nerissa chattered. She rubbed her arms under the layers of blankets. "Is this...normal?"

Roan sat back on his stool, folding his arms. "That water's downright frigid this time of year. Don't want the cold taking hold. Also need to watch out for lung fever, which is why I want to check your breathing once you've eaten."

Nerissa nodded, but her chest seized in a ragged cough before she could speak again. Her lungs burned, and she pressed a fist against her sternum in a futile attempt to soothe the inflammation.

Roan only nodded, unsurprised, jotting something in his notepad. "That burning feeling is also normal. When salt water is swallowed, it irritates the lining of the lungs. Expect soreness and coughing for a few days." He glanced up, meeting her eyes. "If it gets worse, you come to me immediately. Understood?"

She could only nod in agreement, eyes watering as she stifled another cough. This was all so utterly foreign to her. She should *never* have had to experience these symptoms.

The door creaked open then, and a hearty, spicy aroma filled the room. A stout man with narrow eyes and straight black hair pulled into a bun entered, carrying a bowl with steam curling around the edges. He gave Roan a nod before crossing to the cot.

"Broth," he said in a low, even voice. "As the doctor ordered."

Nerissa blinked. "I remember you...You were at the tavern too."

Ma Wen's only reply was a slight tilt of the head as he handed her the small porcelain bowl. Adjusting the blankets, she freed her shaking hands and accepted it gratefully. The heat seeped comfortingly into her fingers as she carefully raised the bowl to her lips.

"Slowly," Ma Wen murmured. His dark eyes softened at the expression on her face once she took a sip.

The liquid was salty and rich as she swallowed, spreading a pleasant warmth throughout her chest and soothing her throat. She had never tasted anything with so much *flavor*. Sirens didn't cook their meals; everything was eaten raw. Perhaps humans knew what they were doing after all.

"This is amazing, thank you," her voice was already a little less scratchy.

Satisfied, Ma Wen gave a polite bow before retreating to the galley.

Nerissa settled into the corner of the cot, cross-legged, slowly sipping the broth. Ruminating. Trying to get her bearings.

Her body had finally stopped shivering, but a pit began to form in her stomach. She was a fugitive from the Astyran royal guard, for a crime she had no control over.

Would she ever be able to shift again? Did it matter? She couldn't return to Nautalia, even if she wanted to. She would be arrested on sight.

Where would she go, assuming the captain of this ship dropped her off at the next port? Assuming she wasn't their prisoner? Maybe he'd take pity on her and allow her to stay on the ship, if she promised to earn her keep.

Roan glanced up from his book just as Nerissa set the empty bowl aside.

"Shivering's stopped, color looks good," he said, almost to himself. He rose and washed his hands in the basin behind him. "Let's hope those lungs are clear."

It was a strange feeling, being fussed over. She had always been the one keeping watch, the shield at Calliope's side, the one others leaned on. To be the frail one, swaddled in blankets and sipping broth, it went against every instinct she had. Damarion, in all the years he'd raised her, never let worry show. They were alike in that—logical, practical, never sentimental.

Roan returned to her side, dragging the stool in front of the cot. "I'll need to listen to your breathing. Sit forward a bit."

Every muscle in her body tensed as she reluctantly complied. She hardly ever felt the need to see a doctor; she had never had an injury serious enough to warrant a medical exam, besides that day ten years ago when she took a knife to her clavicle. This was all new territory for her.

Roan shifted forward, bracing one large hand between her shoulder blades, guiding her posture. "Deep breath in," he instructed, lowering his head to her chest.

Her fist flew before her mind could catch up, connecting straight with Roan's jaw.

He reeled back with a grunt, cupping his chin. Nerissa's hands flew to her mouth in horror.

"I—I didn't mean—! I wasn't expecting you to be so close. It was reflexes! I'm *so* sorry!" she stammered, mortified.

He gingerly tested his lower jaw, working the muscles with a wince. "Reflex packs a hell of a punch," he muttered, half-amused.

"Good thing we didn't return your daggers yet," came a very familiar voice from the doorway.

Zale.

He leaned against the doorframe with a bemused expression, arms crossed. His hair was damp and falling every which way it pleased, while his shirt was half-laced at his throat as if he couldn't be bothered with getting fully dressed.

Roan ignored him. "Let's try this again—*without* the mean right hook this time."

Nerissa glanced at the medic, chagrined, and leaned forward once more. Her eyes briefly flicked to Zale in the doorway before focusing on the floorboards. She hated him seeing her this vulnerable.

"Deep breath," Roan settled his palm between her shoulder blades again.

The air scraped through her lungs like fire, and it somehow sounded even worse than it felt. Roan pressed his ear to her chest, his dreadlocks brushing against her arm. He shifted to her other side. "Again."

She forced herself to comply, shutting her eyes against the raw strain of something as simple as drawing a breath.

After a moment, Roan sat back. "A little rough, but no water rattling in there. That's good. Keep sipping fluids, and I'll check again tonight."

Nerissa exhaled shakily. It seemed she would live to see another day. She gripped the edge of the cot, avoiding Zale's gaze. How different she must seem to him from the girl he met two days ago. She hardly recognized herself.

Roan angled his head toward the doorway. "You planning on coming in, Zale, or are you gonna loiter?"

Zale pushed off the frame and casually brushed a hand down his sleeve as he crossed the room. "Just wanted to check in. Brigid says she wants a word with the *sodden lass* once you clear her."

Nerissa tilted her head at the way his accent switched. *Curious.*

"She'll have to wait. My patient's on strict bed rest for the remainder of the day." Roan turned back to Nerissa. "Long as you don't worsen overnight, I'll discharge you tomorrow."

Great. As if I have somewhere to be.

She wrapped the blankets back around herself protectively, noticing how Zale's gaze hadn't left her. She felt small, weak. It was humiliating being forced to depend on others in this way, especially pirates, no matter how kind they may be.

She chanced a glance back at Zale's face, noting the faint swelling along his lower lip. He didn't seem bothered by it. What surprised her though was his expression. Not pity, but curiosity. That she could handle. Anything but pity.

"You must have a million questions for me," she said finally.

His mouth quirked in response, as though stunned that she'd spoken to him. The motion tugged slightly at his lip, and she saw the slight wince he tried to hide. "Aye, but I only interrogate people over drinks. And lucky for you, the good stuff's kept under lock and key."

"How fortunate indeed," Nerissa said dryly. "But you've caught me in a generous mood. I'll grant you one question."

His eyes sparked. "Any question?"

"I reserve the right to refuse to answer, of course."

Zale chuckled. "Fair enough." He scratched the stubble on his chin as if he were putting a great deal of thought into what he would ask. "Alright then. What's your name?"

"*That's* what you want to ask me?" she said incredulously.

He shrugged. "Can't very well keep calling you 'Tavern Girl.'"

She laughed softly, pitching her into a fit of coughing. Tears blurred her vision as she gasped between spasms, her chest burning all over again as she tried to catch her breath.

Zale stepped forward, alarmed. "Stars, I didn't mean—"

Roan steadied her back with one hand while pressing a warm cup into her grasp. "Drink this. Slowly. It'll ease the irritation."

Nerissa obeyed, choking it down. Relief spread almost instantly, though her pride stung at being undone by something as simple as laughter.

Roan stayed by her side until the coughing eased, then shot a flat look past her shoulder. "Well done, Zale. Exactly what a half-drowned patient needs, someone to make her laugh herself into suffocation."

Zale lifted his hands in protest. "In my defense, she didn't laugh at *any* of my jokes at the tavern. I wasn't expecting that one to land."

Despite the rasp still clinging to her throat, Nerissa managed, "It's all right. I'm fine." Her voice was thinner than she liked, but she pressed on. "Really."

She sank back against the pillow, her eyelids suddenly feeling heavy. The warmth of the broth, the comforting weight of the blankets, and now whatever Roan had given her left her feeling drowsy.

Her words slurred as she mumbled, "What did you put in that tonic?"

Roan collected the empty cup from her hands. "Something to help you sleep," he said simply.

Drowsiness tugged harder, and Nerissa let herself drift at last.

Zale

He still couldn't believe it; the mystery girl from the tavern was right here on the *Black Serpent.* He had convinced himself that he would never see her again, and had tried—unsuccessfully—to rid his thoughts of her. Now she was right in front of him, broken, but alive.

Zale lingered in the infirmary, watching her eyelids flutter as she surrendered to sleep, her breathing even now. He let out a breath of relief.

"She'll be fine," Roan assured him as he rinsed out the cup, as if he read the tension in his shoulders. "Barring fever or worsening cough, she'll walk out of here tomorrow."

Zale grunted an acknowledgement as he crossed his arms, gaze fixed on her face. *Still too pale*, he noted, recalling the warm, healthy glow she had two days ago.

He didn't move from the doorway for a long while. Couldn't help but feel inexplicably drawn to this strange girl. There was something about her he just couldn't quite comprehend.

Nerissa

When Nerissa woke up, the sunlight through the porthole had faded into soft golden rays. Shadows stretched long across the beams overhead from the few lanterns swaying above.

She shifted, wincing at the heaviness in her chest. The blankets had slipped halfway off her shoulders, and she tugged them back up before realizing Roan was seated beside her cot, book balanced in one hand. He glanced up, closing it with a quiet snap.

"Evening," he said. "Let's see how you're faring."

Nerissa rubbed at her throat, still scratchy but not as raw as before. "Better, I think."

"Let's not rely on guesses." Roan leaned forward. "I'll check your breathing again. No swinging this time, understood?"

Heat crept into her cheeks at the memory. "Understood."

He pressed his palm between her shoulder blades. "Deep breath in."

The air dragged less painfully this time, though she still felt the burn as her lungs expanded. She tried not to flinch when his ear pressed close to her chest, listening.

"Again," Roan instructed.

She obeyed, fighting the urge to glance at the door, half-expecting Zale to be watching again.

After a long moment, Roan sat back with a decisive nod. "Better. No rattling. If this keeps up overnight, you'll be cleared tomorrow."

"Good," she sighed with relief. "Thank you, Roan."

He let a smile creep across his mouth before turning back to his book. "You're welcome."

Nerissa spent the rest of the evening resting, getting up once to drink more broth delivered by Ma Wen. That man sure knew his way around the kitchen. How he could make something as simple as broth taste so savory and filling was nothing short of a miracle. It warmed her from within and helped her fall back into a deep sleep, rocked by the steady sway of the ship. When she closed her eyes, she dreamed that she was far beneath the waves, being lulled to sleep by the currents.

The next morning, Roan checked her breathing one more time. Satisfied, he told her that she was free to leave the infirmary, though he suggested waiting until Zale returned to escort her to Brigid's office.

"So, who is Brigid, exactly?" Nerissa sat on the edge of the cot, swinging her legs restlessly as she waited for Zale to come fetch her.

"Brigid is the ship's quartermaster," Roan explained while organizing bags of herbs alphabetically. "She essentially runs the ship, makes sure we have enough supplies, ensures the crew is taken care of."

"She sounds very dedicated," Nerissa mused, picturing an older woman, stern, with big round glasses.

"Oh, she is," Roan confirmed. "No one runs a tighter ship than her. Doesn't even play favorites when it comes to Zale."

Nerissa tilted her head. "Why would she play favorites with Zale?"

"Because he's been with the crew the longest. Well, besides Cormac," Roan answered after a pause, rubbing the back of his neck. His tone suggested there was more to it, but he didn't elaborate.

The door creaked open, and Zale himself poked his head in. "Hey doc, she clear?"

"Speak of the devil," Roan murmured. Then he turned towards the door. "She's free to go, long as you keep her from overexerting herself."

"Pirate's honor," Zale placed a hand reverently over his heart.

Nerissa pushed herself upright with a small wince. Her limbs still felt sluggish, but manageable. Zale watched her for a moment, then stepped closer.

"Need a hand?" he offered.

She hesitated, pride and exhaustion battling for dominance. No, she could do this. She was not helpless.

She shook her head, bracing her palms against the edge of the cot as she pushed herself to her feet, only wobbling slightly.

Zale watched her, then nodded toward the door.

"Brigid's waitin' in her cabin. Best not to keep her long."

Nerissa steadied herself against the wall as she slowly followed him out of the infirmary after exchanging a nod with Roan.

"Remember—bed rest if the cough comes back," Roan's voice followed them out.

"Don't worry, I won't be making any lame jokes today," Zale smirked.

Nerissa hid her smile; he was kind of funny when he wasn't trying to be. Not that she'd ever admit it to him.

The walls of the corridor groaned softly around them as she carefully placed one foot in front of the other. Zale walked beside her with easy steps, casually glancing at her now and then as if he expected her to collapse but was trying not to make it obvious.

"I think we may have gotten off on the wrong foot," Nerissa said at last, her voice quieter than the creak of the deck beneath them.

Zale glanced over, brow arched. "Oh? You mean back at the tavern, when you glared daggers at me, threatened bodily harm, and rejected every charming attempt I made to seduce you?"

She gave him a sidelong look. "You call *that* seduction?"

"Please." He pressed a hand to his chest. "It was the finest blend of roguish wit and pirate charm this side of the Strait."

Nerissa rolled her eyes. "If that was your best, I dread to see your worst."

He chuckled low in his throat. "Don't worry, my worst comes with better rum. Fortunately for you, good rum's in short supply."

"Is that so," she looked up at him suspiciously.

"Truthfully?" His expression shifted as he rubbed the back of his neck as though brushing off the swagger. "Most of that was just an act. Shameless flirting's more Bran's style."

"Bran?"

"You'll meet him soon enough."

"Can't wait."

This side of Zale was vastly different from the rakish pirate she'd encountered at the Salty Siren. If he was offering something more sincere than jokes and swagger...she could meet him halfway.

"Anyway, I would like to start over," Nerissa said quietly as they walked, her fingers brushing the banister for balance.

Zale shot her a look, half-smirk, half-surprise. "You're only sayin' that because I saved your life."

She didn't deny it. "That's part of it. And thank you, by the way."

"You don't have to thank me," he said simply. "Any decent man would've done the same."

The way he brushed it off with such humility made him seem all the more sincere. She'd been expecting some smug remark about owing him a drink. It was almost endearing.

Almost.

She cleared her throat, brushing the thought aside. "I may have misjudged you."

"You mean I'm not a cocky, arrogant, shameless pirate after all?"

She bristled at her own words being thrown back in her face, but she continued. "Look, I was wrong. I'm sorry."

"Oh, aye?" Zale stopped just short of the stairs, and swept into an exaggerated bow, hair tumbling over his brow. "In that case, it's an honor to make your acquaintance, Miss…?"

She hesitated only a moment before lifting her chin. "Nerissa."

Zale straightened, satisfaction glinting in his eyes. "Nerissa," he echoed. "Way you've been dodgin' it, I was beginning to think it was somethin' embarrassing like Muriel or Hildegarde."

Nerissa gave him a flat look. "My name is not nearly so tragic, thank you."

"Tragic?" He spread his hands in mock innocence. "Muriel's got a certain charm. Hildegarde, though…" He wrinkled his nose. "Now *that's* a name to strike fear into a sailor's heart."

"Oh yes, very fearsome. Because 'Zale' inspires such dread. Tell me, how did your parents come up with that one?"

His grin faltered as his hand drifted to the cord around his neck, thumb brushing the edge of the pendant that rested there. "Trade secrets, lass," he said lightly. "You'll have to earn that story."

Nerissa tilted her head, curious. It sounded like deflection, but with pirates, wasn't everything some kind of performance? Still, the way his smile had faltered seemed to suggest the story was not a happy one.

He gestured toward the stairs. "Come on. Quartermaster's waitin'."

Sunlight momentarily blinded her as he swung open the hatch leading to the main deck. She followed him towards the stern where they descended the narrow companionway nestled underneath the quarterdeck. Brigid's cabin was just beyond.

Zale reached for the latch, then paused and looked back at her. "Just a heads up, Brigid's got a keen eye and a low tolerance for lies. Say less and listen more."

Nerissa's eyebrows rose. "Noted."

"Oh, and don't call her ma'am." He glanced at the closed door and back at her. "Ever."

She almost laughed at the genuine flicker of fear in his expression. This was the same man who had faced down drunken sailors unarmed in a tavern with a bloody grin. If *he* thought Brigid deserved that kind of respect, Nerissa would tread carefully.

Her brows lifted higher. "No lies, no ma'am. Got it."

Zale rapped his knuckles lightly against the cabin door before swinging it open and stepped aside, beckoning her in with a tilt of his head.

The cabin was tidy in a way only the militantly practical could achieve. Several maps were pinned neatly to the wall behind the desk in the center of the room, while a decently-sized bed was stuffed into the far corner.

The quartermaster herself sat behind the desk, one long leg crossed over the other, a tankard dangling loosely from her hand. Her hair was braided tightly back, strands of copper catching in the sunlight, and her gaze was sharp. Nothing like what Nerissa had imagined.

Even seated, she loomed, with broad shoulders that dwarfed the chair behind her. She looked about twice Nerissa's age, perhaps more, yet her face betrayed no frailty. Before she even spoke, Nerissa understood that this was a woman to be reckoned with.

"Ah, our wee survivor," she said. "Come in, sit."

Then, to Zale, "Ye can wait outside."

Zale blinked. "You sure?"

"I didn't stutter, lad."

He gave Nerissa a parting glance, then closed the door behind him.

Brigid leaned back slightly in her chair and studied Nerissa like a jeweler assessing the cut of a gem. Nerissa held her ground beneath the look, though it felt as if Brigid were measuring the weight of her bones.

"Now," she said, folding her hands over her knee, "ye've found yerself aboard the *Black Serpent*, a legally sanctioned ship of privateers, which is a fancy way o' sayin' we're pirates with paperwork."

Nerissa's brow knit. "So...you serve Astyra?"

Brigid scoffed. "Serve them? Not likely. We serve no one but ourselves. We've permission to plunder any vessel encroaching on Astyran waters. But don't mistake that for loyalty. This crew owes no crown a damned thing."

She paused, eyes narrowing with a glint of humor.

"Now, seein' as we all saw ye dive from the dungeon tower like a bloody cormorant chased off a cliff, I've a question for ye: do we need to haul ye back to shore, or would ye prefer to be dead for a while?"

Nerissa didn't hesitate. "Dead sounds lovely."

Brigid nodded, apparently pleased. "Knew I liked ye."

She reached for her tankard, found it empty, sighed, and set it down with a dull *thunk*.

"I won't be askin' why ye were up there, or what mess ye're swimmin' in. It's not my business unless it becomes the crew's. That fair?"

Nerissa nodded. "More than fair."

"Good. Once ye've got yer strength back, there'll be an initiation rite. Nothin' too barbaric, but we've our ways. Ye want to stay aboard the *Serpent*, ye'll need to earn it."

Nerissa lifted her chin slightly. "Understood." Heeding Zale's warning, she fought the urge to follow up with "ma'am."

Brigid cracked the barest smile, the kind that might've once comforted or terrified her subordinates depending on her mood.

"Zale says ye've got some fight in ye. We'll see if he's right."

Brigid stepped over to a weather-beaten chest near the bed and flipped the lid open with her boot. She rummaged for a moment, before emerging with a bundle of clothes folded into a tidy square.

"Here," she said, tossing it into Nerissa's lap. "Ye look like the ghost of a noblewoman stabbed at her own weddin'."

Nerissa glanced down at the blood-soaked bodice of her dress, the dried rust-colored stains stiffening the fabric. The sight turned her stomach.

She examined the offered bundle, finding a loose blouse of soft, faded linen in a pale lavender hue, a fitted leather corset dyed a deep plum, worn but well-cared-for; and dark breeches that laced up the sides, reinforced at the knees.

Brigid returned to the chest and fished out a pair of knee-high boots—scuffed but solid, with polished buckles and mismatched soles.

"First pair's on the house," she said. "After that, ye earn yer own."

"Not bad," Nerissa murmured, running her thumb along the edge of the corset. "Very...nautical outlaw."

"Aye, well, yer current outfit ain't exactly seaworthy, lass. If ye're going to work on *my* ship, ye need to dress the part."

Nerissa looked up at the quartermaster with gratitude. "Thank you."

Brigid shrugged, brushing a lock of copper behind her ear. "Just grabbed what looked like it wouldn't swallow ye whole. Don't get sentimental. Ye can change o'er there." She jerked her chin toward the side of the room opposite from the bed where a navy-blue curtain was nailed to the rafter above.

Nerissa slipped behind the curtain and changed quickly, grateful for the clean fabric against her skin and the symbolic weight of peeling off the past.

She clumsily adjusted the laces of the corset, which were fortunately located in the front. The boots were a tad roomy, but she could make it work.

When she emerged a few moments later, Brigid glanced up, assessing, and nodded with approval. "Better. Ye don't look like ye crawled out of a grave anymore."

"Thanks," Nerissa said dryly.

Brigid stood and strode over to the door, opening it briskly. Zale, who had clearly been eavesdropping, flinched upright.

"Since ye've nothin' better to do than lurk like a barnacle, ye can make yerself useful. Take her round the ship, let her meet the crew. If she's to stay, she'll need more than yer sorry face to look at."

He opened his mouth with a retort, but when he caught sight of Nerissa, he let it drop open.

He recovered quickly. Mostly.

"You, uh, changed."

Brigid snorted. "What gave it away?"

"It's subtle," he muttered, still staring. "Could barely tell. You look…very piratey. Menacing, even. Good. Great."

"Are you always this eloquent?" Nerissa asked, placing her hands on her hips.

He cleared his throat. "Come on. Tour's this way. I'll try not to get too distracted."

Turning quickly, he walked right into the doorframe.

Nerissa's sleeve brushed his as she slid past. "Try harder," she murmured.

Rubbing a hand across his face, he straightened his collar and followed quickly, shutting the door behind them.

CHAPTER 16

THINGS THAT WORK

Nerissa

Zale led Nerissa back up the narrow set of stairs that opened onto the main deck, where the late afternoon sun spilled across the weathered wooden planks. The wind snapped the sails overhead, and the ocean stretched to the horizon in every direction, bluer and wider than any prison cell or castle corridor.

Nerissa blinked against the brightness, her fingers curling lightly around the railing as she stepped out. The sea air stung her lungs in a way that felt...good. Like something shaking her back to life.

"So, what did you think of Brigid?" Zale asked.

"I like her," Nerissa said. "She's tough, authoritative, but kind."

"Kind?" Zale repeated. "Oh, don't let her hear you say that."

"Well, well. If it isn't the mysterious tavern girl," a man's voice drawled.

She turned to find said man leaning casually against the rigging. His grin was as crooked as the scar down his left cheek. His beige linen shirt was loose, sleeves rolled up to the elbows, and his auburn hair was half-pulled back in a knot. She judged him to be in his late twenties, possibly early thirties.

Zale groaned softly. "Nerissa, this is Bran. Try not to make eye contact. He feeds on attention."

Bran straightened with a theatrical sweep of his arm. "Name's Bran Calder. I drink too much, gamble too well, and haven't been thrown overboard in at least three months. A personal best."

Nerissa lifted her chin, unimpressed. "Nerissa. I don't drink, I've no taste for cards or dice, but I know how to spot a cheat. And if you try anything funny, I'll help you break that record."

"I *like* her." He looked pointedly at Zale. "Can we keep her?"

"She's not a stray dog, Bran," Zale rubbed a hand down his face in exasperation. "But Brigid did approve her to join the crew."

"Fantastic!" Bran flashed her a toothy grin. "Let's say we test your daggers against my knives in a friendly competition soon."

Before she could answer, Zale stepped between them with a long-suffering sigh, pressing a hand to Nerissa's back to nudge her onward. "Ignore him long enough and he gets distracted by shiny objects."

"Tell her about the rat races!" Bran called after them. "We've got one tonight and Jaws is in top form!"

"Do *not* bet on Jaws," Zale warned. "He always loses. And bites ankles."

"Like I said," Bran shouted, "top form!"

As they rounded the next corner, Nerissa smirked. "So that's Bran.

He's...spirited."

"Spirited is one word for it," Zale muttered.

"You sure you're not just jealous?"

He scoffed. "Jealous? Of Bran?" He waved a hand dismissively. "Please. I've got at least two fewer bad habits and a full set of teeth."

Zale led Nerissa toward the starboard side where crates were being stacked, ropes coiled, and someone was narrating loudly to...a barrel?

"…and *technically*," a boy was saying, voice high and enthusiastic, "a narwhal's tusk is actually a tooth. Like, one giant spiraled tooth, which makes them the weirdest unicorns in existence—*oh!* Watch your step, that board's been loose since last Tuesday—Captain says he's gonna fix it, but I think he secretly likes the surprise—anyway, I'm working on cannon polishing today, which is not as glamorous as it sounds, but still extremely important—"

Zale cleared his throat loudly.

The boy spun around mid-sentence, nearly tripping over his own boots. He had a wild mop of blonde curls that stuck out at angles like he'd just woken up. His face was dotted with freckles, like someone had splattered him with paint.

"Zale!" he said, snapping into an awkward salute. "I was just...reviewing cannon protocols. Out loud. For retention. Also, because no one else listens and I have a lot of good material."

Zale clapped a hand on his shoulder. "Eon, this is Nerissa. She'll be joinin' us."

The boy's eyes widened like saucers. "Oh! Hello! Welcome aboard! Did you know that octopi have three hearts? And that two of them actually *stop beating* when they swim?"

Nerissa blinked. "That seems...inefficient."

"Right?" he grinned. "That's why they prefer to crawl. Anyway, if you need anything, I know where most of the non-moldy linens are and which ropes *not* to touch during lightning storms—learned that one the hard way—oh no, I'm late for cannon duty!"

And just like that, he darted off down the deck toward the forecastle, practically skipping as he narrated to himself: "Polish in circular motions, not horizontal, that was a disaster last time…"

Nerissa watched him go, brows raised. "His parents named him *Eon*?"

"Nah. His name's Gideon. He just talks so long we dropped the 'Gid.'"

Nerissa rolled her eyes. "Clever."

"He once gave a monologue on whale migration during a storm," Zale continued. "Whole ship nearly sank and he didn't even pause. He's a good kid though, all heart."

Then he tilted his head, gesturing for her to follow him towards the back of the ship.

A muttered curse drifted around the corner.

"Bleedin' fool o' a knot...tie that again an' I'll hang ye by yer toenails, see if ye still think yer clever with rope then…"

They rounded a stack of barrels to find the source of the growling: a solidly built man hunched over a tangled coil of line, bright red hair pulled into a tail that hung down his weather-beaten back like a fraying signal flag. Nerissa recognized him instantly. He was the reason she hadn't sustained any serious wounds during the tavern brawl.

"Cormac," Zale called, suppressing a grin.

The man spat over the railing and squinted at them. "What now? Sky's clear, tide's fair, and I've not felt the wrath of a seaborn kraken today, so clearly ye've come to ruin the streak."

"Just introducin' our new recruit," Zale said, stepping aside so Nerissa could approach.

Cormac's good eye narrowed, then flicked with recognition. "Aye. I remember. Ye're the one we hauled from the drink this morning. Didn't think ye'd make it. Thought ye were one more soul for the deep." After a moment, he added gruffly, "Glad to be wrong."

Nerissa blinked, caught off guard by the simple concession.

"She's joining the crew," Zale explained simply.

"Another woman," Cormac muttered, tapping his knuckles twice against the mast. "Brigid must be pleased."

Zale smirked. "What happened to women aboard being bad luck?"

"They are," Cormac said without hesitation. Then his mouth tugged wryly. "But Brigid's the only sane one on this tub, so I'll allow it."

Nerissa's eyes narrowed, but before she could comment, Cormac leaned forward, eye sharp. "Ye're not a siren or a selkie, are ye?"

She froze, the question striking too close.

Zale stepped in smoothly, steering her by the elbow. "Don't mind him. He thinks half the crew are cursed and the other half were born from stormwater."

"Ye're one to talk, lad," the old man grumbled as they moved away.

"What's he talking about?" Nerissa lowered her voice.

"Ah, nothing. He's goin' a bit senile in his old age," Zale dismissed the question a little too quickly.

Nerissa gave a soft huff. "He seems...intense."

"He's survived six mutinies, three shipwrecks, and one allegedly cursed selkie bride," Zale said. "Intense is his baseline."

He led Nerissa back down the narrow stairwell where the infirmary was located, except they turned in the other direction, leading to the galley. It was warm, surprisingly tidy, and smelled of that simmering broth that Nerissa had come to love. Pans swung overhead in a gentle rhythm while baskets of root vegetables lined the shelves.

In the center of it all stood Ma Wen.

His sleeves were rolled to the elbow, revealing forearms dusted with flour and smudged with specks of green from chopped herbs. A faded koi tattoo wound around his left forearm, the inked tail just visible beneath the cuff. He moved with measured precision, folding squares of dough, not even glancing up as they entered.

"Ma Wen," Zale greeted, tone quieter, more respectful.

The cook didn't respond at first. He pinched one of the squares closed, set it with the others, and only then looked up, eyes landing on Nerissa before drifting back to the task at hand.

"You're walking," he said simply.

Nerissa nodded. "Thanks to your soup."

He gave a grunt that might have been agreement. He turned to Nerissa and gestured with a tilt of his chin toward the nearby stool. "Sit."

Nerissa obeyed, perched lightly, her boots resting on the rung. She tried not to fidget under Ma Wen's silent inspection.

"Still too pale," he said, reaching for a tin of dried roots. "Shaky hands. Low oxygen levels." He dropped a few of the herbs into a small mortar and began grinding with slow, rhythmic circles.

Zale leaned back against the wall, arms folded. "Roan already checked her out."

Ma Wen didn't look up. "Roan checks wounds. I check everything else."

He added a splash of warm broth to the mixture, stirred, and handed her a small, steaming cup.

"Drink," he instructed.

Nerissa sniffed it, wrinkled her nose. "What's in it?"

Ma Wen shrugged. "Things that work."

She was skeptical, but took a tentative sip anyway. If he wanted to poison her, he could have spiked either bowl of soup earlier. The taste was bitter and earthy, but oddly comforting.

Ma Wen watched her closely. "You fell from the tower."

She hesitated. "Technically, I jumped."

"You're not ready to tell us why," he said, turning back to his work. "That's fine. But don't lie. Lies rot faster than truth."

Nerissa blinked. "Noted."

"Good," Ma Wen replied, finally lifting his gaze to her again. "Eat something solid soon. You'll need your strength."

"For what?" Could he be referring to the initiation that Brigid spoke of?

He tilted his head toward the ceiling. "That's not my part to say."

Then, without fanfare, he turned back to his dough, the quiet rhythm of the galley resuming as if they'd never entered.

"Is—is the conversation over?" Nerissa whispered to Zale.

He leaned towards her, lowering his voice. "Ma Wen doesn't believe in greetings or farewells."

They backed toward the door, Nerissa casting one last glance at the cook.

They reached the top of the stairwell, where Zale pushed open the hatch once again.

"So what's his story?" Nerissa was intrigued by the quiet man. He seemed less pirate and more…concerned uncle. Similar to Roan in that he had a bluntness about him, yet his actions betrayed a softer edge.

"He grew up in a fishing village," Zale answered as they stepped onto the deck. "Storm-battered coast, rough weather year-round. His grandmother raised him. Taught him how to gut a fish, mend a wound, and scold a sailor without raising her voice."

"She sounds formidable."

"She was," Zale said. "Wen says she used to threaten to slap the sea gods with a spoon if the tide came in too strong."

Nerissa gave a soft, surprised laugh.

"Cap'n found him running a food stall at a port town, somewhere along the eastern coast. Bought a smoked mackerel bun, took one bite, and offered him a job before he'd even finished chewing."

Zale continued. "Been with us ever since. Quiet hands, sharp eyes. Wouldn't be surprised if he's patched up half the crew more times than he's made dinner."

"I thought patching the crew up was Roan's job. He's your medic, right?"

"Oh, aye." Zale stretched his arms out, then tugged the cuffs of his sleeves back into place. "But sometimes after particularly rough…*encounters*, Roan has more patients than he can deal with. So Ma Wen will step in to assist."

Nerissa nodded slowly. "Then you're fortunate. Loyalty's rare enough. Skill on top of it is rarer."

Nerissa's gaze lingered on the rigging above, the lines of sailcloth snapping in the breeze. So different from the stillness of court chambers and coral halls.

"I used to think that kind of loyalty meant everything," she said at last, the words slipping out quieter than she intended. "...Maybe I still do."

"Well," Zale said, bumping her shoulder casually, "for what it's worth, the crew's pretty loyal to people who don't stab them."

A breath of laughter threatened to escape her, until the ache in her lungs stopped her short. "I'll try to restrain myself."

"Right then," he grinned, gesturing toward the quarterdeck. "Time to meet the captain."

He led her up the steps toward the helm, where the ship's wheel loomed beneath a web of ropes and weather-worn sails. The ocean breeze snapped at the lines and tugged at Nerissa's hair as she climbed the stairs.

A broad-shouldered man stood at the helm, hands resting lazily on the wheel as if steering the ship was more habit than duty. His black beard was peppered with silver and his coat fluttered like a flag behind him. A spyglass dangled from his belt, and a chipped pipe rested between his teeth, though it remained unlit.

He turned as they approached. "There she is," he said, voice low and rough. "The girl who nearly drowned and still made a more graceful entrance than half my crew."

Nerissa straightened slightly, unsure whether to bristle or smirk.

Zale grinned. "Captain Nestor, this is Nerissa."

Nerissa inclined her head. "Thank you for pulling me aboard."

"Thank him," Nestor said, jerking a thumb toward Zale. "He spotted ye, dove after ye, carried ye back. Quite the dramatic little rescue. I half-expected him to start singin'."

Zale sighed, rolling his eyes.

"Ye're here now," Nestor continued, more serious. "That means somethin'. We don't haul strangers aboard for charity. So if ye're breathin' our air and eatin' our food, I expect ye'll find a way to earn yer place."

Nerissa met his gaze without flinching. "I don't expect anything for free, sir."

Nestor gave a small nod, satisfied. "'Sir' is for landlubbers. Cap'n'll do just fine."

He turned back to the wheel, half-done with the conversation. "Zale, show her the rest. And tell Bran not to rig another rat race on my quarterdeck. I'm still finding peanut shells in the rigging."

"Aye, Cap'n," Zale said with a salute, ushering Nerissa back down the steps.

As they stepped off the helm and back onto the middeck, Zale leaned in slightly and said under his breath, "You know he likes you, right?"

Nerissa glanced at him dubiously. "That was him liking me?"

Zale shrugged. "You didn't get a lecture, a weather warning, or a nickname involving barnacles. That's practically affection."

Nerissa gave a small huff as she followed him back toward the main deck.

In Nautalia, everything had been hierarchy and deference, a rigid balance of duty wrapped in silence. Orders came from above, trust was expected, and loyalty meant submission. But here, there was no ceremony. Just expectation and earned trust.

"How many are there?" she asked. "Crew members, I mean."

Zale tilted his head, thinking. "A dozen, give or take. Some drift in and out, but the core crew stays tight. Everyone's got a role. Pull your weight or get tossed at the next port. Simple system."

"You never said what your job is."

Zale slanted her a look. "Didn't I?"

"No."

"Well then." He swept a mock bow, nearly bumping into a passing crewmate. "Zale. Deckhand, rope monkey, and fastest swimmer aboard. I pull line, haul canvas, and get sent up the rigging when nobody else wants to risk it. I spend as much time in the crow's nest as they'll give me—best view on the ship, and no one to pester me up there. Course, when I'm not doing that, they like to stick me on barnacle duty. Character building, they say. I think it's really just because I can hold my breath the longest."

"I see," she murmured. "So when do I get my assignment? I don't like sitting idle."

Zale glanced sideways at her. "You won't have to. You've got that look."

"What look?"

"The kind that gets restless if there's nothing to stab."

She huffed softly. "I meant helping."

"Oh, I know. I'm just not convinced those two are different for you."

She ran a hand along the railing, fingers tapping a slow beat against the worn wood. "I need to prove I'm not dead weight."

Zale's expression turned more serious, though his tone stayed light. "Then you'll fit right in. We all had something to prove when we got here."

"And you?" she asked. "What were you trying to prove?"

He looked out over the waves for a long moment before answering. "That I belonged somewhere."

That, she understood all too well.

Nerissa was quiet for a few more steps, her fingers still drumming against the railing in thought. Then, without looking at him, she asked, "Brigid mentioned something earlier about an initiation?"

Zale let out a low chuckle, one hand lifting to scratch the back of his head, mussing up already-wild hair. "Ah. That."

"That doesn't sound reassuring."

"It's not supposed to. It's tradition. Every member of the *Black Serpent* goes through it. Glorified obstacle course, really."

"Obstacle course?" she repeated, skeptical.

"Well, historically, there's been a rope bridge that collapses, a narrow beam over a pit of spikes, a wall slicked with fish oil, somethin' involvin' blindfolds and angry crabs."

She blinked. "I'm sorry—what?"

"You'll see," he said, far too cheerfully. "The course itself changes each season. And if you survive all that without breakin' your neck, there's the final test."

She raised an eyebrow. "Which is?"

"Sparring match." He paused dramatically. "Against Brigid. Then Nestor. If you survive that, then the swords come out. You'll have to fight them both. At the same time."

Nerissa stared at him. "At the same time?"

"Mm-hm."

"That seems excessive."

"That's the point," he said with a grin. "It's less about winning and more about proving you don't curl up and cry when things get hard."

"But if I do lose?"

He shrugged. "Then you're sore, bruised, and still part of the crew. Technically."

"Technically?"

"Well, unless you cry. If you cry, Roan takes your boots and you have to win them back in a rat race."

She gave him a sideways look. "You're making that up."

He winked. "Am I?"

She squinted at him, suspicious. "And how did *you* fare?"

Zale gave a dramatic sigh. "Let's just say I was bruised in places I didn't know could bruise. But I survived. Barely. They only made me do it twice."

"Twice?" she echoed. "What happened?"

Zale cleared his throat. "I got disqualified the first time."

She stopped walking, turning to face him fully. "How did you manage that?"

"In my defense, I was like...sixteen. Too much adrenaline, not enough coordination."

"What did you *do*?"

"Accidentally punched Nestor."

She raised her eyebrows.

"In the—well." Zale shifted uncomfortably, gesturing vaguely below the belt. "It got personal."

Nerissa stared.

"He made a noise I've never heard before or since," Zale said, deadpan. "Sounded like a harpooned walrus."

She choked on a strangled laugh before she could help it. "And the second time?"

"I ducked when I should've dodged, got knocked flat by Brigid's boot. But I didn't cry, so Roan let me keep my shoes."

"High marks."

"I'm very proud."

"Oh-ho, are we trading war stories?" a voice called down from the rigging above. Bran swung down from a length of rope and landed with a theatrical flourish. Then he leaned on the rail with all the nonchalance of a man who had absolutely not been eavesdropping.

"Tell her about the time you cried after Brigid disarmed you."

"I didn't cry," Zale muttered. "I...perspired aggressively."

Bran grinned. "From the eyes?"

"Bran," Zale said flatly, "go do something useful. Like fall off the mast."

"Tempting," Bran said, then winked at Nerissa. "But I'd hate to miss her initiation. Been a while since we had some entertainment."

"Don't you have lines to check?" Zale asked.

"Cormac said the knots were vengeful and left them alone."

Zale pinched the bridge of his nose. "That tracks."

Bran gave a jaunty two-fingered salute and strolled off, humming a wildly off-key sea shanty.

Nerissa watched him go, brow furrowed. "What's his story, anyway?"

Zale glanced after him. "Bran?"

She nodded.

Zale shrugged one shoulder, half-smiling. "Grew up on the streets of some coastal trading city. He changes the name every time he tells it, depending on who he's trying to impress...Survived by being clever and charming and a bit of a menace. Nestor caught him cheating at cards and recruited him instead of gutting him. He's been aboard ever since."

Nerissa tilted her head, thoughtful. "He doesn't seem like the type to take orders."

"He doesn't," Zale said, "unless he respects you. But when it counts? He's loyal. Brave. Reckless. He'll get on your nerves. But he'll also throw himself in front of a sword for you, if it came to that."

She considered that a moment longer, then gave a slow nod. "So he's the chaos to your order."

Zale smirked. "We call it balance."

He tipped his head toward the hatch and started down. "Come on. Brigid will probably let you sleep in the extra cot in her cabin, but just in case she changes her mind…" He pushed open the door to the lower deck, the air immediately thicker with tar, salt, and the lingering reek of sweat. "This is where the rest of the crew bunks down."

Rows of hammocks swung gently with the roll of the ship, patched canvas and frayed ropes creaking in a tired chorus. Sea chests and scattered clothes lined the walls, while someone's forgotten dice game rattled in a corner with each sway of the deck.

"Minus Roan," Zale added, gesturing aft. "He's got a little cabin off the infirmary—keeps him close to his patients. The rest of us make do here. Gets noisy, smells worse, but…" He shrugged with a crooked grin. "You won't find a sturdier lot to share the air with."

Zale gestured toward the rows of swaying hammocks. "You'll notice they've all...customized."

Bran's hammock was strung absurdly high, so close to the beams above that Nerissa wondered how he didn't crack his skull each morning. Cormac's sagged low under the weight of several empty bottles clinking together in a net beside it. Nearer the stern, a neat row of shells and smooth rocks had been lined up on the beam beside what Nerissa assumed was Eon's spot.

And then there was Zale's. His hammock was plain and spare, hung with perfect knots but lacking the clutter of keepsakes or trophies. Just the essentials: a folded blanket, a spare shirt, and a coil of rope tucked neatly beneath, as if the space belonged to someone always ready to move on.

Nerissa tilted her head. "Not much for trinkets, are you?"

Zale shrugged. "Why bother? Anything worth keeping usually ends up overboard or borrowed by Bran."

She didn't look away, and the pointed weight of her gaze made his grin falter at the edges. After a beat, he added, quieter, "Besides...never had much to keep."

Nerissa's expression softened, just slightly. "I understand. I never saw the point in collecting things either."

Zale regarded her for a long moment, his grin gone, something unspoken flickering in his eyes. He cleared his throat. "You hungry? Ma Wen should have dinner ready soon."

The scent of spiced stew and fresh bread drifted through the galley, mixing with the low creak of timbers and quiet laughter. Lanterns swung gently overhead, casting amber pools of light over rough-hewn tables.

Ma Wen appeared with a wide, steaming pot cradled in his arms and a ladle hooked over one elbow. He set the pot down with a heavy thud in the center of the table and wordlessly slid over a basket of bread.

Nerissa found herself seated between Zale and Eon, across from Bran and Cormac. The bench was worn smooth by years of use, making for a comfortable seat.

Ma Wen gave her a small nod, then retreated to fetch the next pot for another table.

Zale leaned in with some advice. "Help yourself, before Bran claims the good bits."

Bran was already elbow-deep in ladling stew into a tin bowl. "I'm conducting quality control," he said, deadpan. "You're welcome."

More crewmates trickled in as bowls were passed, banter rising with the steam. The door creaked open again to admit Nestor and Brigid, followed closely by Roan, who carried himself with his usual quiet gravity. They settled at the next table over, Nestor easing into his seat like the bench might crack, Brigid unceremoniously dropping onto hers like she meant to scare the wood straight.

Brigid's sharp gaze swept the room before it landed on Nerissa.

"Well, well," she said, voice curling with a lilt. "Still here, are ye? Thought ye might've leapt o'erboard soon as I handed ye boots instead o' a blade."

Nerissa didn't miss a beat. "I considered it," she said, spoon halfway to her mouth. "But your cook lured me back with soup."

"Aye, Ma Wen's cookin'll do that," Brigid replied with a grin.

Zale nudged Nerissa lightly. "You're officially being heckled by command. That means they like you."

Bran leaned in from across the table, stage-whispering to Eon, "Or they're testing her fortitude before the sacrifice."

Cormac snorted. "What sacrifice?"

"The one I just made up," Bran said cheerfully. "But the look on her face was worth it."

Nerissa rolled her eyes and dipped her spoon into her stew with theatrical caution. "I'm watching for bones."

Eon, who had been alternating between eating and trying to scrape a scorch mark off the table with his spoon, perked up. "Speaking of bones…"

Zale muttered, "Oh no."

"…I still can't believe you survived that fall." Eon looked at Nerissa with wide, earnest eyes. "Statistically, from that height, you should've shattered at least a femur. Maybe a rib. Something." He glanced around. "I mean—am I wrong?"

Cormac grunted. "Aye. Should've cracked like a lobster dropped from the crow's nest." He stabbed a chunk of potato with unnecessary force. "Told the lad no one survives that kind of fall unless they've got Poseidon's own luck."

That earned a few sideways glances, but Nerissa only shrugged, lifting her bowl for another sip of broth. She tried to look more nonchalant than she felt.

"I've had worse," she said coolly, hoping her tone closed the door before anyone thought to knock.

Bran cocked an eyebrow. "You say that like leaping from a tower ain't the most reckless thing you've done."

Nerissa smirked. "I'd say drinking mead with Zale still tops the list."

Zale grinned. "That so? You're welcome for the best day of your life, then."

A chorus of *ooohs* rose around the table.

Nerissa didn't even look up from her bowl. "If that was the best you can do, I'm starting to see why you sleep alone."

"Saints above," Bran wheezed, choking on his drink. "She *did not*!"

Eon snorted soup through his nose, and even Cormac gave a gruff chuckle.

Zale blinked once, then huffed a quiet laugh, rubbing a hand over his jaw. "Ouch. Should've known better than to spar with someone who carries daggers for a living. And here I was thinkin' you were starting to like me."

"Don't push your luck," she said, lifting her bowl like a toast before taking another sip. It had been mean-spirited, even for her, but he could stand to be knocked down a few pegs.

The chaos of the day had ebbed into a tranquil lull. Lanterns swung gently from the rigging, casting golden puddles of light across the deck. The *Black Serpent* rocked with the easy rhythm of a ship at anchor, its usual rattle and chatter replaced by the occasional creak of wood and the distant lapping of waves.

Zale walked beside Nerissa, hands loosely resting on his belt, his pace unhurried. The sea breeze carried the scent of citrus oil lingering from the deck scrubbing earlier that evening.

"So," he said, glancing at her sidelong, "how was your first day aboard a pirate ship?"

"Completely different from what I'm used to," Nerissa smiled softly, then added, "That's a good thing."

They walked in companionable silence for a few more paces before Zale's voice dropped, quieter now. "Mind if I ask you somethin'?"

"That depends on the question," she replied, casting him a cautious look.

Zale's expression was unreadable, save for the flicker of something more serious in his eyes. "You and your blonde friend—from the tavern the other day. Did you get somewhere safe?"

Nerissa stopped walking.

She didn't answer right away. Her eyes drifted to the sea, and when she did speak, her voice was quiet.

"She's safe," she said at last. "As far as I know."

Zale tilted his head in a silent question.

"But…" Nerissa's fingers curled around her belt. "She doesn't need me anymore."

Zale didn't push. He only watched her, brow furrowed. "That's...hard," he said.

Nerissa's chin lifted slightly, her expression composed but distant. "Hard isn't the word I'd use."

"Want me to guess a better one?"

She exhaled, not quite a laugh, not quite a sigh. "You wouldn't get it right."

Zale smiled faintly. "Probably not. But I'd try."

He studied her for a long moment before clearing his throat, gaze drifting out over the dark water. "Can I risk another question," he asked lightly, "without you hittin' me?"

"Maybe. Depends on your tone."

He huffed a quiet laugh, but when he looked at her again, the humor faded into something more sincere.

"You okay?" he asked, voice soft. No teasing this time. Just two words, offered like a hand extended in rough seas.

The question hit harder than she expected. *Okay* was the one thing she'd always had to be. Through grief, through duty, through every moment she'd held herself together because crumbling wasn't an option. Being asked aloud, so plainly, left her throat tight and her thoughts scrambling.

She opened her mouth, closed it again, fingers flexing at her belt. She wasn't ready for such a direct question, especially about her feelings. She was also taking too long to answer.

"I—" she began, then drew a steadying breath. "I will be."

Zale nodded slowly, accepting the answer for what it was. He didn't press. Instead, he bumped her shoulder lightly with his. "Well, if you ever need to talk...or hit something...I'm surprisingly good for both."

That coaxed a smile out of her. "I'll keep that in mind."

Zale grinned. "Just give me a little warnin' before you go for the punch."

"No promises," she smirked, then glanced at him again. "Can I ask *you* something?"

He tilted his head curiously. "Fire away."

She hesitated, then went with the simplest version. "How did you end up here? What's your story?"

His smile faltered as he looked out toward the horizon, where the dark water blurred into the sky, and gave a small shrug. "Not much of a story. Nothin' worth tellin'."

Her brows knit faintly. She wanted to ask what he wasn't saying, what he was hiding, but stopped herself. He hadn't demanded her story. He hadn't asked why she'd been at the tavern or how she ended up half-drowned in the sea that morning. If he could let her keep her secrets, she supposed she owed him the same courtesy.

So she only nodded, letting the silence speak for itself. "Thank you," she said after a moment, her voice quieter than the sea between them.

Zale glanced over, brow lifting. "For what?"

"For the tour."

His posture eased, shoulders loosening as if he'd been bracing for questions she didn't end up asking. A flicker of something earnest crossed his face. "My pleasure."

The door creaked softly as Nerissa stepped into the quartermaster's cabin, lanternlight bathing the room in a soft, comfortable glow. Brigid sat cross-legged on her bed, a whetstone in one hand and an axe in the other, the steady rasp of metal on stone the only sound.

Nerissa paused just inside, hands clasped loosely. "Thanks again," she said, nodding toward the spare cot. "For the bed. And for not making me sleep in a hammock surrounded by sweaty pirates and snoring."

Brigid didn't look up. "Not charity. Practicality. Easier on everyone if ye're not bunkin' ten feet from half-feral men with no volume control and even less shame."

Nerissa gave a soft snort, her gaze drifting to the shelves lined with stacks of books, rolled maps, and gear that looked like it had survived both storm and sabotage.

"How'd the tour go?" Brigid asked, voice casual, eyes still on the blade.

"Good," Nerissa replied. "Your crew's...odd. But welcoming."

Brigid grunted. "That's about the highest compliment they're likely to get."

"I think I'll get along with them," Nerissa added. "Eventually."

"Ye don't have to like everyone aboard," Brigid said. "But ye *do* have to pull your weight and know which end of a blade to hold. Respect's earned in action, not words. Comes faster if ye keep your head down, don't whine, and stab the right people when the time comes."

Nerissa smiled faintly. "I'll remember that."

Brigid finally looked up, sharp eyes cutting. "And Zale? He behave himself?"

Nerissa hesitated, then shrugged with a smirk. "He was...not what I expected."

Brigid raised an eyebrow. "That could mean just about anythin'."

"He's easier to talk to than I thought," Nerissa admitted. "Less swagger. More...substance. For the most part, anyway."

Brigid gave a low hum, returning to her whetstone. "Aye. That's Zale. Likes to talk a big game, but he's made o' better stuff than most."

Nerissa lowered herself onto the cot, leaning back on her elbows. "He told me about the initiation."

"Of course he did." Brigid's voice was dry. "Ye want to get it over with?"

"I do."

"We'll reach the cove by tomorrow afternoon," Brigid said. "Tide'll be right by then."

"Good."

"Get some rest. Ye'll need it." The scrape of stone resumed. "An' if anyone gives ye trouble before then...tell 'em I said I'll use their bones for tinder."

Nerissa grinned up at the ceiling. "Now *that's* comforting."

Zale

Zale eased into his hammock, the canvas rocking gently with the sway of the ship. Around him, the sleeping quarters had gone quiet. Mostly. Cormac snored like a storm in a barrel, Eon mumbled in his sleep about celestial navigation, and Bran sat cross-legged two hammocks over, whetstone rasping against the edge of one of his knives.

Zale pulled a length of rope from beneath his hammock and began working through knots by feel—reef knot, clove hitch, bowline, undo, repeat. Hands busy, mind restless.

He hadn't expected to see her again. The girl from the tavern with violet eyes that dared him to try his luck. He'd finally learned her name.

But names didn't explain the shadows behind someone's eyes, and he could see them clear enough in hers. She wasn't ready to talk about it, that much was obvious. And if he'd learned anything aboard the *Serpent*, it was that you didn't pry until the other person was ready to bleed.

His fingers tightened the rope into another knot, then tugged it loose again. He should leave it at that and keep his distance.

But stars, when she'd walked out of Brigid's cabin in those clothes? He'd thought she was beautiful in her gown at the tavern, feminine and untouchable. But dressed like one of them? She hadn't looked out of place at all. She'd looked like she belonged. And that did something to him he wasn't about to admit, not to himself, and definitely not to her.

Zale tied another knot, too tight this time. He blew out a breath and yanked it loose. Best to keep his mouth shut, keep his hands busy, and not think about the fact that Nerissa was just above his head, asleep under the same roof of timbers and sail.

Especially after she'd asked him about his story. *His story*. He didn't have one worth telling, not the kind she was really asking for. And he was glad she hadn't pushed when he brushed it off—because he wouldn't have known what to give her if she had. Yet the way she'd looked at him when she asked...like she might actually care about the answer. It had unnerved him more than he wanted to admit.

Almost as much as the way *she* had looked when he'd asked if she was okay—like he'd demanded her deepest secrets with two small words. He hadn't meant it like that. It had seemed simple enough, warranted even, considering she'd nearly died.

Zale tied one last knot, left it there, and set the rope aside. He needed to remember the rules he'd laid out for himself: respect her silences, keep a careful distance, don't get tangled where he shouldn't.

Can't lose what you never had.

CHAPTER 17

THE NEW QUEEN OF REGRET

Nerissa

Brigid thrust a folded bundle into Nerissa's arms before she'd even finished tying her hair back. "Here. Ye won't want the blouse and corset today. Would be a shame to get blood on them."

The bundle unfolded into a plain beige tunic, a black scarf meant for the waist, and a pair of dark breeches. Nerissa pulled them on without complaint. The fabric was coarse compared to the soft cotton of her blouse, but it moved with her rather than against her, and for that alone she was grateful.

When she emerged onto the quarterdeck, Zale was up in the rigging, adjusting a sail. He moved as though he belonged there, balanced against the sway of the ship, dark hair disheveled as he worked. Nerissa glanced once, then fixed her attention elsewhere, determined not to be too impressed with how effortless he made it look.

The morning passed in a rhythm both strange and steady. Someone pressed a coil of rope into her hands, and she set about winding it with precision. Or so she thought.

"Not bad," Bran said, appearing at her elbow. "If you want the rope to trip someone later. Otherwise—" He plucked the line from her hands and began looping it with casual speed, the motion neat and fluid. "It's all in the wrist. Keep it even, keep it snug."

He handed it back with a grin. "There. A coil worth keeping. You're welcome."

Nerissa found herself echoing his smirk despite herself. "Generous of you."

"Don't tell Zale," Bran said, lowering his voice in mock conspiracy. "He'll get jealous I'm the one teaching you."

Nerissa shook her head and went back to work, the rope falling into cleaner circles beneath her fingers this time.

Later, she was given a bucket and brush and sent to scrub down a patch of deck still sticky with fish guts from the last haul. Brigid passed once or twice, offering no correction but no praise either, just the briefest flicker of acknowledgment in her eyes before moving on.

Cormac muttered about omens in the wind as he sharpened a harpoon, pausing only to tap twice on the mast as if to ward off whatever he'd just predicted. Eon tried to explain the finer points of celestial navigation to Bran, who mostly asked if star charts could be used for gambling. Ma Wen appeared long enough to hand Nerissa a heel of bread and a tin of strong tea before vanishing belowdecks.

It was different from the court, Nerissa thought as she worked. Different from the endless waiting halls and ceremonial duties that filled her days in Nautalia. Here there was no crown, no pretense, only a crew bound together by their ship. Chaotic, yes, but purposeful too.

By the time the sun tipped toward afternoon, her shoulders ached and her hands were raw, but her resolve felt sharper than it had the day before. Whatever this "initiation" was, she would face it head-on.

The *Black Serpent* rounded a jagged outcrop of rock, her black sails trimmed and taut in the salty wind. Below, nestled between two cliff walls so steep they looked carved by giants, lay a narrow crescent of beach. Jungle trees loomed beyond the shore, vines coiling over old stone like the cove itself had been trying to hide from the world.

From the quarterdeck, Nerissa leaned on the rail beside Zale, watching the whitecaps foam as the anchor dropped with a splash. The ship rocked gently into place, embraced by the natural bay.

"Is this it?" she asked.

Zale gave a lopsided smile. "Home sweet hideout. Uncharted, unclaimed, and almost certainly haunted."

"Charming."

Bran swung down from the rigging while Brigid barked orders for securing the lines, and Ma Wen emerged from below decks carrying a well-packed basket.

Then came an eager voice.

"Ohhh, this is gonna be *so* good," Eon sang, practically skipping along the deck as he tied off a coil of rope. "Bran says the last time we did an initiation, the rope bridge snapped and sent Calus into a tide pool with the sea urchins. He had spikes in places spikes should *never* be."

Nerissa blinked. "Who is Calus?"

"Oh, he's no longer with us," Eon said, as if that explained everything.

Zale gave him a look. "Eon, stop trying to scare her."

"What? Oh. Oh! I see how that probably sounded. Calus never quite got his sea legs. He was retching over the side of the ship every time we hit rough seas. I've never seen so much vomit come out of one man before."

"Okay, Eon, she gets it," Zale interrupted as Nerissa grimaced.

"Oh, right, of course. Sorry m'lady," he bowed before continuing, ignoring her eye roll. "Anyways, he begged us to drop him off at the next port. And thus did Calus the 'Retched' conclude his short time with the crew of the *Black Serpent.* Not dead, that we know of. But most certainly *not* killed by the course! Speaking of which…"

He turned dramatically toward Nerissa, one arm outstretched.

"Welcome, Lady Nerissa, to the Cove of Trials, the Gauntlet of the Damned, the Ropes of Regret—"

Bran strolled past with an apple. "It's just a sweaty beach with too many nets, Eon."

The boy huffed. "You have *no sense of theatre.*"

Zale leaned toward Nerissa with a crooked smile. "He's not wrong though. It's basically a jungle gym with sharp bits."

"So, what exactly am I in for?" she asked, eyeing the shoreline where the outline of the obstacle course was just visible—ropes and planks and wooden contraptions lashed together with a worrying lack of craftsmanship.

"Climb things. Swing from other things. Try not to get bruised on *all* your ribs. Then you fight Nestor and Brigid."

Nerissa gave him a sideways glance. "And *you* did this? The second time, I mean."

"Made it through. Barely. Got this beauty in the process."

He hesitated—just for a breath—fingers brushing his side as if to check the skin there first. Then he tugged his shirt up, just enough to reveal a faded scar carved across his ribs, jagged as a broken piece of coral.

She squinted. "That from the course?"

"Technically? No. That was from Brigid." His grin widened. "I got cocky in the final sparring round. Tried to sweep her leg. She didn't appreciate the gesture."

"You sound proud."

"I am," Zale said. "Initiation's not about winning. It's about surviving with a bit of flair. Which I did. Eventually."

"Flair, huh?" Nerissa glanced toward the island again, now seeing the course in a new light—equal parts ridiculous and vaguely lethal.

Brigid's voice rang out from the main deck. "All hands not on duty, ashore in ten! Bring the stakes, the flags, and extra bandages—we've got a contender!"

"That's me," Zale said, pushing off the railing. "Time to go make the beach look terrifying."

Nerissa followed him down to the main deck, where the crew had begun unloading crates, ropes, and a series of wooden poles that looked far too splintery for comfort. A few men were wrestling with something that might have been a net or might have been a very large trap.

“I feel like I should be worried,” she muttered.

“You should,” Roan offered, appearing at her side with a casual shrug. “But only a little.”

She gave him a dry look.

He offered a half-smile. “If you survive, I’ll make you a tea. If you don’t, I’ll steal your boots.”

“Encouraging,” she said, walking off.

The longboat ground into wet sand with a muted *shhhk*, and the crew leapt out, splashing into the shallows.

The cove opened before them like a storybook page warped by time—cliffs rising steep and craggy around a crescent beach, the dense jungle beyond rustling with unseen creatures. At the far end of the beach, the infamous obstacle course waited in all its haphazard glory. A skeletal construction of ropes, nets, crates, pulleys, and barrels.

Zale jumped over the side and turned back to offer Nerissa a hand. She didn’t take it, but followed him out with a quick, sure step that landed her in ankle-deep surf.

He jogged a few paces up the shore, then turned and walked backward beside her, arms crossed casually behind his head.

“Alright,” he said, voice low and conspiratorial. “If I were a generous man—which I am about fifty percent of the time—I’d offer you a few tips."

"And the other fifty?"

"Petty and unhelpful. But you caught me in a good mood."

She smirked. "Lucky me."

He began ticking the points off on his fingers. "First—on the rope bridge, don't trust the third plank from the end. It's a trap. Leap over it. Dramatically. Points for flair."

"Of course."

"Second," he went on, "when you reach the barrels, don't hesitate once you've started running through. Move fast, keep low."

Nerissa nodded, her fingers tugging absently at her hair as she redid the braid. No matter how tightly she interwove the three sections, she couldn't seem to prevent the shorter chunk of hair from sticking out.

Zale's voice softened. "And last...when you spar, don't worry about fightin' fair. Nestor moves much quicker than he looks, and Brigid fights mean and dirty."

Nerissa studied him. "And how do I fight?"

Zale shrugged, but his smile didn't fade. "Like you did at the Salty Siren. Quick on your feet, no hesitation. Do that, and you'll hold your own. Just, maybe don't give yourself an impromptu haircut this time?"

"Hilarious." Nerissa flipped her braid back over her shoulder in annoyance. "Here goes nothing."

A hush fell over the beach as the crew lined up along the length of the course. Bran produced a conch shell and blew into it loudly, producing an ear-splitting noise that echoed throughout the cove. Nerissa shook her head. He was doing it all wrong.

"Everyone ready to watch the new girl get absolutely *wrecked* by the bosses?" Bran called.

The crew roared.

Brigid clapped Nerissa on the shoulder. "Ye've got grit. Show 'em."

Nerissa gave a tight nod, then turned toward the looming mess of ropes and planks while the crew murmured in anticipation behind her.

Bran spun in place, one arm out like a showman. "Ladies, gents, and various crustaceans, place your bets and hold onto your breeches. The course is cruel, the stakes are imaginary, and the scars are forever!"

"Two coppers says she makes it past the spike pit before cryin'," she heard Cormac already placing his bets.

"There is no spike pit anymore," Roan said mildly. "Not since Calus skewered his—"

"Don't remind me!" Cormac interrupted, shuddering.

Eon jumped up and down at the edge of the group, waving a scrap of parchment. "I made a scoring chart! Ten points for flair, minus five for screaming, bonus points if she does a flip—"

"Eon," Ma Wen said, deadpan, "sit down before you sprain something."

Brigid gave Nerissa one last nod and stepped aside. Nerissa inhaled slowly as she stepped up to the starting point. She flexed her fingers once, then twice, eyes sweeping the tangled monstrosity of planks, ropes, swinging barrels, and what looked like a retired ship's figurehead repurposed into a battering ram.

It's no different than Damarion's training, she told herself, rolling her shoulders back. *No different at all.*

Except this wasn't underwater. And gravity was unforgiving.

Zale

A sharp whistle split the air.

"ON YOUR MARK," Bran hollered from his perch atop a barrel, conch in hand.

"TRY NOT TO DIE," Eon added brightly.

"GO!" Bran bellowed.

Nerissa launched forward.

The first obstacle was the slanted plank bridge slick with algae, its handholds replaced by a dangling rope net strung just above shoulder height. Nerissa leapt onto it, boots skidding, arms shooting up to grab the net before she could topple sideways into the muck below.

She powered forward, pulling herself hand-over-hand while her feet scrambled for purchase. Zale silently counted the planks as she neared the end of the bridge, where she vaulted over the final three and landed in a crouch.

The next obstacle loomed ahead: a series of hanging barrels set swinging in lazy, menacing arcs by several crewmembers, suspended from an overhead beam. Between them, the only path forward.

Bran grinned. "Five coppers she ducks under the first and gets clocked by the second."

"She's not an idiot," Zale said confidently—right as Nerissa ducked cleanly under the first barrel and caught the second one full to the ribs.

THUNK.

The crew let out a collective "oof."

Nerissa staggered, hissed through her teeth, and shoved the barrel aside with one arm, pushing into a run before the next could catch her.

"Annnd she's still upright!" Eon called. "Bonus points for dramatic sound effects!"

"Did you *hear* that hit?" Bran laughed. "Someone's getting a bruise shaped like a cooper's stamp."

"She'll wear it better than most," Brigid said approvingly.

Zale's brow furrowed slightly, though his smile remained. "Told her not to hesitate."

Ahead, the final section of phase one awaited: a stack of crates leading to a rope swing over a tidepool. A faded sign nearby read *Leap or Weep.*

Nerissa didn't stop to read it. She climbed fast and launched herself into the swing, legs tucked tight, expression set.

Eon gasped dramatically. "She cleared the tidepool! Nobody clears the tidepool!"

"She just did," Zale murmured, a rare note of awe in his voice.

Brigid crossed her arms and smiled faintly. "Told ye. She's got grit."

The rope swing landed Nerissa squarely on a platform of creaky wood and rusty nails. Ahead stood the Spinning Crates of Regret: a series of wobbling wooden boxes strung across a trench like a drunk carpenter's idea of a bridge. Each rotated on a central axis, their surfaces scuffed with footprints, splinters, and one very ominous reddish brown smear.

Cormac shaded his eyes. "Ah. The crates. Many a brave soul's met the sand on these."

"And one very stupid one tried to leapfrog 'em all," Bran added. "Still can't grow hair on his left eyebrow."

"She's going for it," Eon whispered, as if they were watching a sacred rite. "Oh, bold move—she's not testing the first one—she's just jumping straight on."

Nerissa landed on the first crate with both feet and immediately lurched sideways as it spun like a tavern stool on payday. She threw out her arms, compensating, knees bent, tailbone whispering future threats.

"Good recovery!" Zale called. "Now breathe and pivot!"

"Pivoting's for dancers," Brigid muttered. "She needs to bounce."

She jumped onto the next crate, slipped, then caught the edge with her fingers, hauled herself back on, and kept moving.

The third crate wobbled violently beneath her. Nerissa launched herself with a primal grunt that startled a seagull off a nearby rock, cleared the final crate, and landed in a crouch on solid ground.

Applause erupted as Eon yelled, "Behold! The new Queen of Regret!"

"She's not done yet," Brigid said, walking toward the sand pit.

Nerissa straightened just as a wide circle of trampled sand came into view, ringed by barrels and cheering pirates. A few had started chanting:

"Pit pit pit pit pit—"

Zale winced. "I *hate* that chant."

Roan raised an eyebrow. "You *started* that chant."

"That was before I got tackled into a sand crab burrow."

Brigid stood at the far edge of the ring, rolling her shoulders with slow menace. "Alright, lass," she called. "Let's see if ye can dance."

Nerissa exhaled through her nose and stepped into the pit.

Eon leaned over to Bran. "Three silvers says Brigid flips her within the first ten seconds."

"Ten?" Bran scoffed. "Five."

The moment Nerissa's boots touched the center, Brigid lunged. Nerissa dodged instinctively, her form crisp and measured—but Brigid was already adjusting, turning the dodge into a grab.

They locked arms, sand kicking up in plumes around them. Nerissa twisted, drove her elbow up—but Brigid deflected and shoved her back, both of them skidding.

A pause.

Brigid grinned. "Not bad."

Nerissa narrowed her eyes. "Not done."

And then they were at it again—fists, knees, grit and precision. Brigid fought with the brutal strength of a seasoned brawler while Nerissa fought with the fluid grace of—of something he couldn't name.

They were evenly matched for almost a full minute.

Then Brigid swept her leg.

Nerissa hit the sand hard, rolled, sprang up—but Brigid was right there, hand on her collar.

"Ye yield?" Brigid asked, sweat dripping down her brow.

Nerissa's chest heaved. She met Brigid's eyes. "Not a chance."

Brigid's grin widened.

Behind them, Nestor was cracking his knuckles, watching like a shark waiting for his turn in the shallows.

"You're next, Captain," Nerissa said through her teeth.

Nestor bowed slightly. "Then let's give the people a show."

The crowd hushed again as Nestor stepped forward, rolling the sleeves of his linen shirt with all the ceremony of a man preparing to fold a ship in half with his bare hands. The sand sighed under his feet. He cracked his neck once, then looked Nerissa up and down with a faint, curious smile.

"Careful now," he said. "I'm not as forgivin' as Brigid."

Nerissa didn't reply. She simply lowered her stance, eyes locked on the captain.

The opening blows were a dance of misdirection—Nestor testing, feinting, circling like a predator in calm water. Nerissa moved with tight control, seemingly guided by pure instinct. But Nestor wasn't just skilled—he was clever. Every step invited a trap.

He feinted left, swept right—Nerissa barely dodged.

He advanced, one-two jab, then a leg hook—she staggered but stayed upright.

"Good," Nestor murmured. "Ye've been taught to fight. Let's see if ye've been taught to lose."

And then he *really* attacked.

The pit exploded in movement—sand flying, limbs striking, balance tested again and again. Nerissa caught his elbow with her forearm, spun out of a grab, ducked under a punch, and rammed her shoulder into his ribs. He grunted, staggered—

And then grabbed her by the wrist and flipped her neatly over his shoulder.

The air left her lungs in a huff as she hit the sand, but she rolled to her feet, breath ragged, eyes blazing.

Nestor raised a brow. "Still not yielding?"

Nerissa quickly wiped the blood from her lip and smiled. "You'd be disappointed if I did."

Nestor let out a bark of laughter and offered her a hand up.

"Alright then," he said. "Ye're ready for the last round."

From the edge of the pit, Brigid stepped forward again—this time with two gleaming swords slung over her shoulder.

"Now ye face both of us," she said. "With blades."

Bran's voice cut in from the gallery. "Everyone place your final bets! Double payout if she lands a hit on Nestor's smug face!"

"Oi," Nestor said. "That's *Captain* Smug Face to you."

Zale just shook his head, arms crossed, watching Nerissa with a look that blended concern with pride.

Nerissa took the sword Brigid offered, testing its weight. Zale briefly wondered if she'd ever held a blade other than a dagger as she stepped into the circle once more.

Brigid stood to the left, calm as a stormcloud. Nestor rolled his shoulders to the right.

"Ready, lass?" Nestor called cheerfully.

Nerissa lifted her chin, nodding once. "Let's do this."

Brigid struck first.

No warning. No ceremony. She launched forward like a thunderclap in human form. Nerissa barely sidestepped in time, the edge of Brigid's curved blade slicing a few strands of hair from her temple.

Nerissa spun out of reach, heart slamming against her ribs.

Nestor followed with a flourish—drawing his sword mid-laugh, spinning it with a theatrical twirl before lunging in with all the flair of a drunken fencer.

Nerissa blocked the first blow—barely—and danced back, sand spraying beneath her feet.

Zale watched intently. She shouldn't try to outmatch their strength. She couldn't.

Nerissa dodged. Spun. Slid beneath Brigid's swing, kicked sand toward Nestor's feet, twisted and ducked and—

The sharp sound of steel slicing skin broke the silence.

Nestor's blade, too quick to fully evade. She gasped, stumbling back as blood dripped from the fresh gash at her thigh. She quickly pressed a hand to the wound, then drew her hand back, as if confirming that she was indeed bleeding.

"Don't get distracted!" Zale cupped his hands and shouted.

Nerissa's head snapped up.

Brigid was circling again.

And so was Nestor.

Gritting her teeth, she shifted her stance—lower, tighter, more defensive.

"Sorry, love," Nestor called lightly. "Me aim's better when I've had a drink."

"Then maybe go have one," she snapped, circling wide again, keeping her distance.

Zale smirked at that, while the crowd roared with laughter around him.

Brigid came again. A flurry of blows—measured, efficient, ruthless. Nerissa parried one, dodged two, blocked the third—and caught a solid elbow to the ribs for her trouble. She staggered, but she didn't fall.

Instead she pivoted, landed a hit—not with her blade, but the pommel, knocking into Nestor's shoulder hard enough to send him back a step.

"Oho!" he whooped. "I felt that!"

Brigid didn't even flinch. "Ye *let* her hit you."

"Did not. That was genuine surprise."

Brigid's answer was another strike—this one faster, sharper, cutting in low. Nerissa twisted to block, too slow by half. Brigid seized the opening, wrenched her arm up behind her back, and with a quick, merciless twist, something popped. Nerissa's face blanched, but she refused to go down.

Teeth bared, she twisted in Brigid's grip, shoved back with her other arm, and forced herself upright. She met Brigid's eyes head-on, chest heaving, one arm limp and useless at her side.

'I'm not finished," she gritted out through clenched teeth.

For a long moment, Brigid only stared. Then, slowly, she released her.

Nestor lifted his blade in salute, his grin wide and proud. "Aye, you are. That'll do."

Brigid gave a curt nod, something almost like respect flickering in her expression. "She's passed."

Nerissa swayed, chest heaving, but her chin remained high, eyes locked onto Brigid and Nestor. Refusing to drop. Refusing to yield.

The crowd erupted into cheers and whistles.

Bran whooped from the sidelines. "She lives!"

Cormac lifted a flask and toasted the sky. "She bleeds like one o' us!"

Eon threw himself to the sand in mock reverence. "All hail the newcomer! The Queen of the Obstacle Course!"

Brigid strode toward Nerissa and looked her up and down—taking in the blood, the bruises, the sweat-streaked face—and nodded once, short and decisive.

"Welcome aboard the *Black Serpent*," she said. "From this moment forward, ye're one of us. Ye eat our food, ye pull your weight, ye curse at the same stars we do. If someone threatens ye, they threaten *all* of us."

She extended her hand. Nerissa stared at it for a heartbeat, then took it.

Zale pushed through the ring of cheering crew, his grin tugging wider despite himself. She was still on her feet. Stars, she was *still standing* after Brigid had all but tried to fold her in half.

He slowed as he reached her, letting some of the swagger fall back into place. "Congratulations," he said, voice pitched low so it wasn't swallowed by the noise. "Welcome aboard, officially."

Nerissa looked up at him, her face pale. "Thanks," she murmured. "For the tips. They helped."

She swayed slightly, and before he thought better of it, Zale reached out, a tentative hand brushing her arm to steady her. "You good?"

Her chin lifted in quick defiance. "I'm fine." A pause, then more grudgingly: "Pretty sure Brigid dislocated my shoulder, though."

Zale looked pointedly at her arm hanging limply to her side, her shoulder at an unnatural angle. "Yeah, sure looks that way."

Before he could say more, Roan pushed his way through the crowd, satchel in hand. "Sit." He pointed at a nearby crate, his tone brooking no argument.

Nerissa obeyed, lowering herself stiffly onto the edge. Roan crouched beside her, eyes sharp as he prodded her left shoulder. Nerissa flinched once, jaw tightening, but didn't make a sound.

"Dislocated," Roan confirmed at last, matter-of-fact. He shifted, bracing her arm. "Hold still. I'll set it."

He glanced up at Zale. "You. Distract her."

Zale's mouth opened, then shut again. Distract her? From *this?* His gaze darted back to Nerissa, her eyes were already watching him with a mixture of challenge and grim expectation.

Right. Fine. He could do that.

Zale crouched in front of her, trying for his most disarming grin. "So. On a scale of one to ten, how much did you enjoy getting elbowed in the ribs by Brigid? Be honest. She'll be crushed if you say less than a nine."

Nerissa's eyes narrowed. "Not working."

"Not yet," Zale said quickly. "Give me a second. You were pretty impressive out there. I especially liked the part where you got clobbered by a barrel. Told you—shouldn't have hesitated."

Her glare sharpened, but there was the faintest quiver at the corner of her mouth. "Still not working."

And right then Roan shifted her arm and drove the joint back into place with a decisive pop.

Nerissa gasped, white flashing across her features—but she didn't cry out. Her good hand clenched into a fist, knuckles white, and when the worst of it ebbed, she exhaled slowly through her nose, every line of her face composed again.

Roan nodded once, satisfied. "Done. You'll be sore, but it'll hold."

Zale straightened, trying not to look as flustered as he felt. Roan reached for fresh bandages and a curved needle from his satchel. He tapped Nerissa's knee lightly. "Hold still. This'll need stitches."

Her jaw tightened. “Of course it does.”

Roan didn’t even look up. “Keep talking to her,” he told Zale. “Don't need her passing out before I have a chance to close this.”

Zale dragged a hand through his hair, then crouched again so he was level with her. This time, he let the grin fade. “Alright. No jokes.” His voice lowered. “I really was impressed.”

Nerissa blinked, caught off guard.

He held her gaze, unflinching. “Just two days ago, you were half dead. I know you're not back to full health yet, but you showed twice as much strength and determination as anyone who's taken on that course, myself included. The hits you took, you didn't stop, not once.”

Her lips parted slightly, but she said nothing.

Zale’s voice softened, the words carrying more weight than he intended. “You fought like someone who had something to prove. Like survival wasn’t enough—you had to win. Had to show us all you weren’t fragile, weren’t broken. Just...sharp edges and willpower.”

Roan drove the needle through her skin, quick and sure. Nerissa flinched, her eyes locked stubbornly on his. Blue, violet—he couldn’t decide. They shifted with the light, almost like stormglass. Like the one Nestor kept in his cabin, its crystals changing shape with every turn of the weather—clear one hour, clouded the next, spiked when storms brewed. He’d never seen eyes like that before.

Focus, Zale. You’re supposed to be distracting her, not the other way around.

Her mouth twisted faintly. “You’re exaggerating.”

Zale shook his head. “No. I mean it. You fought well, Riss. And that’s somethin’ to be proud of.”

She shifted uncomfortably under his gaze, as if she was unaccustomed to receiving praise. Then she went pale as she looked down at her half-open thigh.

"Oh, that was a mistake…" she trailed off, swaying slightly.

"Hold her!" Roan ordered. "We've got a fainter."

Zale quickly stood up and caught Nerissa by the shoulder; he made sure it was her uninjured one. Sweat beaded up on her brow, and her skin felt clammy beneath his grip. He noticed her breathing had slowed, and her pupils were dilating as if she had been drinking. He recognized those signs.

Shifting behind her in case she did keel over, he gently gripped both of her arms to hold her steady. Her head fell back against his chest, so he took the opportunity to lean down and whisper near her ear. "Hey, you're doin' great, Roan's almost done. Just breathe."

"Ears ringing…" she murmured.

"Alright, we need to lay her back," Roan said urgently. "Before she faints." Then he set down the needle and thread, balancing them on Nerissa's leg, before standing up and grabbing her ankles.

Zale followed suit, sliding his hands underneath Nerissa's shoulders, bracing to lift on Roan's count.

"Now," Roan said. They heaved her off of the crate and carefully laid her on the sand.

Zale knelt by her head while Roan continued to work on his stitching. Her eyes were fluttering as she fought to stay conscious.

"Just breathe, it's okay if ye pass out now, though," Zale reassured her. "Least ye won't fall."

“Comforting,” Nerissa breathed. “Your accent's slipping again.”

Stars, she was right. How could she still be so sharp while half conscious? Maybe he could distract her yet.

“No it isn't,” he argued.

“You said ‘ye,’” she reminded him flatly.

“Yeah, well, ye're halfway out of it, so how can I trust anythin’ comin’ out o’ your mouth, hm?”

Her eyes narrowed up at him, before her brows lifted. “I see what you're doing.”

“Not sure what ye're talkin’ bout, love,” he let his brogue shine through, grinning despite himself. Normally he tried to hide it, as it was a constant reminder of how he'd been raised.

She laughed weakly at that, some of the color returning to her face. Good.

Roan tied off the last stitch with brisk efficiency, wrapping a bandage around the wound. “Done. Keep it dry, keep weight off of it for a few days. And stay hydrated.”

“Oh, done already?” Nerissa asked, voice dripping with sarcasm, as she slowly pushed herself up to a sitting position.

“Would've finished quicker if you hadn't threatened to faint on me,” Roan countered, unaffected.

Zale remained crouched by her side as Roan got up and headed towards the fire pit. Nerissa let out a sigh, watching him go

“Well, that was embarrassing,” she said.

“Not so good with needles, eh?” Zale watched her as her face finally regained its color.

She shook her head. "Guess not, never been around one before."

Zale frowned, recalling a small detail from Roan's initial exam. "But Roan said you had a puncture wound on your arm; he assumed it was from an injection or somethin'."

"What?" Now she was frowning too. "Where?"

Zale gently turned her arm over, exposing the bruise in the crook of her elbow. "Here."

She stared at it for a long moment, face turning pale again. "I don't actually know where I got this bruise…"

Zale studied her, afraid she might actually pass out this time. He reached for her hand, her skin was clammy again. "Hey, that's alright. What matters is that you're okay. And you passed the initiation rite! That's cause to celebrate."

He stood up, brushing the sand from his clothes, then offered his hand to her. "Come on."

Nerissa eyed him, wary, but placed her hand in his all the same. He pulled her gently to her feet, steadying her until she found her balance.

"Tradition's tradition," he said, nodding toward the fire pit where the rest of the crew was gathering, tankards in hand. "First drink as one of us."

Her lips quirked faintly, more exhausted than amused. "Is it stronger than mead?"

"You bet your bones, it is," Zale said with a grin. "Brace yourself."

"Fantastic," Nerissa muttered.

She followed him across the sand, her steps unsteady but determined, until the glow of firelight and the roar of voices swallowed them both.

CHAPTER 18

PURGEBERRIES OF DEAD MAN'S COVE

Nerissa

The fire crackled, sending sparks up into the starlit sky as the crew gathered on the sand, drawn like minnows to an anglerfish's lure. One sailor was playing a jaunty tune on some sort of instrument. Nerissa watched as he lifted the small wooden contraption, its sides folding and unfurling with each pull of his hands—the motion reminding her of gills. Notes of music wheezed with every pull, thin and wavering at first, then swelling into something bright and resonating deep within her chest.

Nerissa sat just outside the most raucous ring of revelry, with her leg bandaged and stretched out in front of her, tucked into a half-circle with Brigid, Nestor, Bran, and Zale.

Her mind was still reeling from the initiation earlier. When Nestor sliced her leg, she had braced for the green blood that would raise a lot of questions. But to her surprise, and relief, she bled red, same as any human.

And that bruise Zale pointed out, she remembered noticing it while she was in the castle dungeon, but had no clue as to where it came from. If Roan was right, that it was caused by a puncture—an injection—then Alpheus must have been responsible. She vaguely recalled him coming to her cell the night she was arrested, but she couldn't remember why.

If he had injected her with something, could that explain why she could no longer shift? If so, when would it wear off? It didn't make sense, why would he do that to her? What did he hope to gain from trapping her in human form? How might that affect the inevitable sea withdrawal? She made a mental note that it had been four days since becoming human.

Her thoughts were interrupted when Bran handed her a tin cup full of amber liquid, which she now eyed suspiciously as if it might bite. The scent rising from it certainly did—sharp and heady, like fermented seaweed left too long in the sun.

She took a cautious sip. Fire spread across her tongue, down her throat, and settled hot in her chest. She coughed once, eyes burning, earning a chorus of laughter from the men.

"Not bad!" Bran crowed, slapping his knee. "Didn't even spit it out. Not to your liking though, eh?"

She glared at him through watery eyes. "Are you sure you aren't trying to *poison* me?"

That only made him laugh harder. "Aye, that's rum for you. Burns goin' down, sings comin' back up."

Brigid gave him a death glare. "If ye make her sick, Calder, ye're cleanin' it up."

Zale reached over to nudge her cup down before she could take another gulp. "Easy," he said quietly. "It hits harder than mead."

"I preferred the mead," she admitted, once the worst of the sting had passed. "It was at least pleasant."

"Aye, but this'll keep ye warm," Nestor rumbled. "Mead's for lovers and lullabies. Rum's for sailors and fools."

Nerissa took another tentative sip, more out of pride than desire. The heat bloomed again, dizzying and bright. Big mistake. Her stomach lurched in protest, and she set the cup down quickly before her head began to swim. Should have listened to Zale.

"Then I suppose I'm neither," she murmured, half to herself. "Just foolish enough to try."

Bran leaned forward, eyes dancing in the firelight. "Come now, one more sip, for courage's sake."

Zale's voice was calm but edged with warning. "She's had enough courage for one night, Bran."

For a heartbeat, Bran's grin softened. Then he threw up his hands in mock surrender. "Fine, fine. I'll drink hers, then."

Nerissa gladly returned the drink to Bran. He tipped the cup back and immediately coughed, sputtering. Brigid's cackle cut through the crackle of the flames.

Bran wiped his mouth, still wheezing through laughter. "Fathoms below, that's rich. You handle it better than *he* did, at least."

Zale looked up from where he was tending the fire, suspicion flickering in his eyes. "Don't even start."

"Oh, I'm starting," Bran said, leaning in as if about to deliver a sacred tale. "Zale here wasn't always so composed, you know. First time he tried rum, he was twelve. Barely up to my shoulder and thought himself a grown man."

"Bran…" Zale groaned.

"Hush now mate, story time," Bran ignored his protest. "See, little Zale found his way into the captain's quarters one night, back when Nestor still locked his stash in a crate under the desk. Thought he'd just 'sample' a sip or two.

"Next thing we know, the lad's stumblin' up on deck, swaying like a sail in a gale, swearin' he could steer the ship better than any of us. Then, right as he starts singin'—gods, what was it, Cap'n?"

"'The Lass of Larkmoor,'" Nestor muttered.

"Aye! That's the one!" Bran slapped his knee again. "Didn't make it halfway through before he leaned over and emptied the whole lot—right on Nestor's boots."

The firelight caught the flush rising on Zale's face. "I was *twelve*," he said flatly.

"Old enough to know no' to drink the captain's rum," Brigid shot back.

Nerissa turned to Zale, blinking. "Wait—you were twelve?"

He didn't look at her. Just took a sip of his drink and gave a one-shouldered shrug, as if the detail meant nothing.

"You were part of the crew that young?" she asked, quieter now. That was…strange. What kind of ship would take on a child?

Zale's smile didn't quite reach his eyes. "Mm. Yeah."

Nerissa opened her mouth to ask something else, but Zale was already pushing to his feet.

"I'm gonna grab more rum," he said casually, brushing the sand from his hands. "Back in a bit."

He didn't wait for replies. Just turned away from the firelight and headed inland, past where the rest of the crew was scattered about several more fire pits.

Bran let out a low breath and leaned toward her, voice pitched low. "Tread lightly, love. That one's a tangle of stories he doesn't like telling."

Brigid added without looking up, "An' more than a few he can't."

Nestor took a long sip from his flask, exhaling a deep sigh as he stared into the fire.

Nerissa stared after Zale for a moment, then turned back to the others, brow furrowed. "Did I say something wrong?"

Brigid shook her head, tossing a twig into the fire. "Nay, it's no' you. He just doesna speak o' his past."

Nestor grunted softly, his eyes still on the flames. "Mostly because he doesn't know it."

Nerissa blinked, thinking back to the previous night when she had asked him how he had ended up on the *Black Serpent.* How he had neglected to answer the question. "What do you mean?"

The captain took another slow swig from his flask before answering. "He's lived on this ship his whole life. We found him when he was just a babe. No more than a few months old, driftin' near the coast on a splintered board. No name. No clue where he'd come from. Just a pendant and lungs loud enough to wake the sea gods."

Nerae forgive me…no wonder he didn't want to talk about it.

Brigid gave a grunt of agreement. "Taught himself tae swim 'fore he could walk. Still faster in th' water than any o' us, an' twice as stubborn."

Nerissa looked back toward where Zale had vanished, a faint pang of guilt stirring in her chest. She thought of the careless teasing a few days ago, asking how his parents had chosen his name, unaware he'd never even known them. She understood that kind of loss, though hers was tempered by memory—faces and voices she could still recall when she tried hard enough.

Bran suddenly raised his drink. "Now that we've properly dampened the mood, anyone fancy a drinking game? Winner gets bragging rights. Loser has to polish the cannons with Eon."

From across the beach, Eon's voice piped up. "I HEARD THAT, AND I ACCEPT."

Zale

Zale sat alone on a half-buried log at the edge of the tree line, where the flickering light of the fire didn't quite reach the shadows of the jungle. He turned his back on the laughter and music drifting from the beach, muffled now by the dense foliage and distance.

He hated this part.

Not the stories. Not the crew. Not Nerissa's question.

Just the hollow that always opened up afterward, like someone had scooped out a piece of him and never bothered to fill it in.

His fingers found the small pendant tucked beneath his shirt, rubbing it between his thumb and index finger, the smooth surface grounding him in the quiet. It was the only clue he had to his past, a reminder of something lost long ago. The repetitive motion kept his hands busy, but it couldn't quell the questions in his head. He stuffed it back beneath his shirt.

Did they throw me away?

He didn't remember the sea that carried him in, or the faces that might've watched him go. No lullaby, no name; his earliest memories were nothing but Nestor's barked orders and Brigid's sharp corrections. He loved them both. Of course he did. But love didn't always fill the gaps. Sometimes it only outlined them.

He leaned back against a palm trunk, closed his eyes, and listened to the surf: steady, patient, endless. The kind of sound that promised answers it never gave.

Footsteps shifted through the sand, soft and hesitant. Zale's eyes fluttered open, and he glanced over his shoulder to see Nerissa approaching. He tilted his head slightly in acknowledgment.

She didn't speak right away. Just sank down beside him, her bandaged leg stretching awkwardly in front of her. He wondered how long it would take for Roan to admonish her for walking on it.

"I didn't mean to pry," she said at last, voice soft.

"You didn't," he muttered.

Silence, filled with surf and distant laughter.

"Nestor told me," she began hesitantly. "How he found you as a baby."

Zale huffed through his nose, half a laugh. "Unbelievable."

"Look," she shifted. "I'm sorry for the other day, when I teased you about your name. I had no idea that—"

He shrugged. "That I was abandoned? That I was an orphan? Happens more than you'd think. Sea's full o' lost things."

She looked at him, but he kept his gaze fixed ahead, shoulders tightening. He didn't want pity—not from her, not from anyone.

He sighed, elbows on his knees. "I've got this crew—closest thing to a family I'll ever have. Nestor raised me like I was his own, Brigid knocked sense into me, Cormac taught me every knot worth tyin'. I owe them everything." His hand curled into a fist, pressed briefly to his chest. "But there's still this…empty space. Like something's missin', and I don't even know what it is."

He risked a glance at her. "You ever feel that way? Like no matter where you stand, part of you's still adrift?"

Nerissa stared out at the waves, moonlight tracing her features with a pale glow.

"I lost my parents when I was eleven," she said softly. "It was…sudden."

He wasn't expecting that. She didn't say how. Didn't elaborate. But something in her voice went distant, brittle at the edges.

"I was taken in, given purpose, protection. I should be grateful. And I am. But it's not the same." Her eyes stayed on the sea. "There's still this quiet, heavy sort of emptiness. You stop expecting anyone to fill it, because deep down, you know…"

Her voice caught, but she pressed on.

"No one's coming."

Zale was quiet for a long beat. Then, almost inaudibly, he said, "Yeah."

His gaze dropped to where her hand rested beside her knee—still curled slightly like she wasn't used to letting her guard down.

Slowly, he reached over and let his fingers brush hers. Not a full grasp. Just contact. Just a reminder that she wasn't alone in this exact breath, even if they both were, in different ways.

She didn't pull away.

They just sat like that, shoulders close, the silence between them neither awkward nor empty.

Zale ran a hand through his hair, then rested his elbows on his knees again, shoulders slouched.

"I used to make up stories," he said, eyes fixed on the water. "About who they were. My parents. One day it was a shipwreck, the next it was some noble sacrifice. Pirates who gave me up so I'd be safe. Royalty, even. Real dramatic stuff."

When she didn't laugh, he glanced at her, relieved. She was surprisingly easy to talk to when she wasn't on the defense.

"But lately…" he trailed off, searching for the words. "Lately I wonder if they just...didn't want me. Easier to let the sea have me than raise what shouldn't've been born."

Silence followed.

Then Nerissa said softly, "If that's true...then they're the ones who missed out."

He blinked.

"You're loyal. Brave. Infuriating, sure. But you would've made someone proud." She hesitated. "You make people proud now. Even if you don't realize it."

Zale looked at her, the firelight catching in her eyes as they stayed fixed on the waves.

He didn't deflect with a joke. Didn't change the subject. He just nodded, once.

Then he said quietly, "I think your parents would've been proud of you."

Nerissa didn't respond, but he could see the tightness in her expression, the hard set of her jaw.

A beat passed. Then Zale leaned back on his hands with a crooked smile tugging at the corner of his mouth.

"Look at us," he said. "Two perfectly well-adjusted orphans aboard a ship full of mercenaries and questionable morals. Who says trauma can't be character-building?"

Nerissa snorted—an unladylike, unguarded sound that startled even her. "That's your takeaway?"

"Absolutely," he said solemnly. "I'm practically thriving."

She shook her head, but her smile lingered.

"How's the leg?" he asked, flicking a glance her way.

Nerissa stretched it out slightly, testing the stiffness. "Tender," she said. "But manageable."

"Manageable as in 'Roan-approved for light activity'? Or 'Nerissa-approved despite common sense and medical advice'?"

She gave a slow, knowing look. "I'll let you guess."

Zale huffed a quiet laugh. "You really are one of us now."

"Is that a compliment?"

"Absolutely," he said, voice warm with mischief. "Reckless, stubborn, and refusing to rest properly. You'll fit right in."

She bumped her shoulder lightly against his. "You forgot 'charming.'"

"Oh no, that's just me."

"Modest, too."

"Painfully."

They both smiled then—small but genuine.

After a couple more minutes, Zale stood slowly, brushing the sand from his palms. "Come on," he said, glancing down at her with a half-smile. "Let's get you back to the beach before Roan hunts you down with more bandages and unsolicited advice."

She reached for his offered hand and let him help her up, wincing slightly as weight settled onto her injured leg.

"You good?" he asked, steadying her.

"I'll manage," she said.

"Spoken like a true pirate," he said, leading the way back toward the firelight. "Minus the rum addiction. For now."

"Ugh, don't remind me." She grimaced, turning a little green.

Zale chuckled under his breath. "Aye, we'll work on your tolerance later. Maybe start you off with watered-down cider before we move you up to the hard stuff."

He glanced over his shoulder at her, grin tugging at the corner of his mouth. "Assuming Bran doesn't get to you first."

Nerissa let out a small laugh. "If he does, I'll make him drink mine, too."

"Smart woman," Zale said, guiding her over the dune. "That's how you survive on this crew—let Bran be the cautionary tale."

Nerissa

As they neared the fire, Bran spotted them and raised his tankard in greeting. "Ah, the brooding pair returns! What was it this time—existential dread or dramatic sulking under starlight?"

"Little column A, little column B," Zale called back, deadpan.

"Ten coins says they made out and won't admit it," Eon chimed in, which earned him a well-aimed pebble from Brigid and a muttered, "Ye're not even old enough for those kinds o' bets."

Nerissa shot Brigid a meaningful look, grateful that she didn't have to acknowledge Eon's ridiculous accusation. The last thing she needed was for rumors to start. She wasn't here to cause drama, just survive.

Zale dropped down to the sand with a grunt, and Nerissa eased herself down carefully with a grimace—with an appropriate amount of distance between them, of course.

He tipped his head back, watching the sparks drift skyward. "We miss anything important?"

"Only Ma Wen's rat choosing Cormac as her new spiritual vessel," Eon said, holding up a tiny, sleepy rat wrapped in a sliver of cloth like royalty. "Her judgment is clearly flawed."

"What does that even mean, Eon?" Zale laughed, shaking his head.

Eon straightened, cradling the rat as if she were some divine relic. "It means," he said gravely, "that the universe has chosen this noble creature as its emissary. Through her squeaks, great wisdom shall be revealed."

He paused, lowering his voice conspiratorially. "Or maybe she just sensed Cormac needed the company. Either way, she's got good instincts."

Cormac grunted from the edge of the firelight. "That rodent's got better instincts than half ye lot. She knows where the real power lies."

A few chuckles rippled around the fire.

Then Roan appeared beside them, silent as a shadow, hands tucked in his coat pockets. "You know," he said mildly, "rats were responsible for the plagues that wiped out half the coastal cities a century ago."

Eon blinked down at the tiny creature. "You always know how to ruin a sacred moment, Roan."

"Just doing my part," Roan said, helping himself to some rum.

Bran clapped his hands once and sprang to his feet. "Well, I'm bored."

"That was fast," Zale said.

"I have a complex inner world," Bran replied. "And it needs berries."

And with that, he sauntered off into the jungle, whistling an innocent tune.

Eon stretched out on the sand. "Right then. Since Bran's off foraging for poisonous snacks like a rat himself, I say we kill time with something productive."

Zale arched a brow. "Productive, coming from you, is usually followed by fire or regret."

"I'm insulted." Eon grinned. "This time, it's crew superlatives. You know—like those weird titles rich academies give out before graduation."

"I'm listenin'," Brigid said, lounging nearby with a tankard balanced on her knee.

Eon pointed around the circle dramatically. "Most likely to survive a kraken attack out of sheer spite?"

"Brigid," Roan said immediately.

Brigid saluted with her drink. "Aye, obviously."

"Most likely to flirt during a firefight?" Eon asked.

"Bran," came a chorus from several of the men.

Zale sipped his drink. "He once proposed marriage to a bounty hunter *while* disarming her."

"She kept th' ring," Brigid added.

"Most likely to get distracted during a heist?"

Everyone turned to Eon.

"Rude," he gasped. "Accurate, but rude."

"Most like tae win a duel by accident—an' nae even ken how he did it?" Brigid asked, smirking.

"That's Cormac," Zale said. "Remember that one time in the tavern—?"

"I *tripped*," Cormac growled. "He fell on me blade. That doesn't count."

Eon leaned forward, eyes gleaming. "Alright, alright—new girl's turn. What do we think?"

Nerissa bristled, suddenly feeling self-conscious as everyone's eyes trained upon her.

"Most likely to wake up with an embarrassing tattoo and no memory of how it happened," Zale said casually.

Her brow furrowed slightly as she processed Zale's suggestion. She tilted her head just enough to give him a pointed look, her tone dry. "That would never happen," she said, as if stating the obvious. "But…if I ever *did* get a tattoo, it would at least be something with some meaning behind it."

Zale's lips curved into a playful grin as he leaned in slightly, eyes sparkling with mischief. "Meaning, huh?" He rubbed his chin, pretending to be deep in thought. "Well, if you're gonna get a tattoo with meaning, it's gotta be somethin' that says, 'I'm tough, but I also think about stuff'."

He gave her a wink, the teasing tone softening into something more sincere. "But I'm sure it'd be a hell of a lot more meaningful than some of the ones I've seen."

Before Eon could announce the next category, Bran returned with a smug grin and both hands full of suspiciously-scarlet berries.

"I come bearing gifts from the jungle!"

"Oh, *nae*," Brigid muttered, pinching the bridge of her nose. "Tell me ye did *nae* eat those."

Bran plopped down beside the flames with a triumphant flourish. "Nature's bounty! Fresh, free, and full of vitamins."

"Please tell me those aren't what I think they are," Eon said, eyeing the berries warily. "Because if they are, you're going to regret it. Profusely. From both ends."

"They're *berries*, Eon," Bran said cheerfully, popping one into his mouth. "Not musket balls."

Zale winced. "You sure they're not the...uh...*cleansing* kind?"

Eon groaned. "I *told* you last time—look for clusters of four, not three. Three means doom. Everyone knows that."

"I don't think anyone knows that," Bran muttered around another mouthful.

"I do*!*" Eon shouted, waving his mug dramatically. "Those are the infamous purgeberries of Dead Man's Cove. The old hag who ran the orphanage used to lace pies with them when she wanted to punish the troublemakers."

Nerissa watched Bran chew slower and slower. Something told her this wasn't going to end well, and she was glad to be sitting nowhere near him.

"...They taste fine," he said, but doubt was beginning to creep into his eyes.

Zale leaned toward Nerissa. "He'll be sprintin' for the tree line in under five minutes."

"Two," said Eon smugly, counting down under his breath.

Bran made it to *one* before abruptly standing, face draining of color. "I, uh...I should—check on the tide." He shuffled off with an increasingly urgent gait.

A brief silence.

Then the crew burst into laughter.

Nerissa doubled over, clutching her ribs. Her leg stung and her muscles ached, but she didn't care. The warmth blooming in her chest wasn't from the fire alone—it was from them. This ragtag collection of misfits who sang loudly, argued about poison berries, and treated impending digestive doom with the same urgency they gave to cannon fire.

The most unholy of sounds echoed from the jungle as Bran screamed,

"*ROAN, I'M DYING. TELL THE OCEAN I LOVED HER.*"

Roan didn't even look up from his tankard. "He'll live."

Eon nodded gravely. "Oh, he's paying for it, though."

Zale raised his cup. "To Bran—may his aim be true, and his lesson be learned."

Nerissa laughed again, wiping her eyes. "Do you think he'll actually learn it this time?"

Eon sighed, lifting his mug in mock solemnity. "Not a chance."

CHAPTER 19

EVERY NAVAL BISCUIT

Nerissa

The cove was still asleep, veiled in a soft gray hush that stretched across the water. Nerissa stood at the edge of the shore, barefoot and quiet, the hem of her trousers rolled to her knees. She glanced back toward the camp. No movement but the slow pull of the tide. Perfect.

She waded in, letting the ocean wrap around her legs and pull at her with familiar hands. She swam out past the jagged rocks that marked the outer edge of the cove, where the water deepened into a shadowy cradle.

Her heart pounded. She inhaled sharply.

Shift, she commanded silently. *Come on.*

She squeezed her eyes shut, willing the change. The water stirred around her. But nothing happened.

Nothing but the gnawing silence of rejection.

"*Kel'ra navessa!*" she snapped, the Nautalian curse bubbling up before she could stop it.

"You alright?" came a voice from the shore.

She spun, startled, to find Zale standing ankle-deep in the surf, shirt half-buttoned and hair a salty tangle, clearly fresh from sleep.

He lifted a brow. "Or is that the sound you make when you lose something expensive in the sea?"

Nerissa's pulse stumbled. "An earring," she said quickly, waving vaguely toward the deeper water. "Slipped right off."

He squinted out at the horizon, then back at her. "Funny. Don't remember you wearin' any."

She gave him a tight smile. "Guess you weren't paying that much attention."

His grin flickered. "Guess not."

She turned, striking out toward the ship before he could question her further. "Don't suppose you're here to help me look?"

Zale waded in without hesitation, shirt still on, she noted. "Not exactly. I like to swim when we anchor here. Roan says it's good for my skin."

"Your *skin?*"

He gave a half-shrug, his gaze drifting out over the water. "Yeah. Some condition I've had since I was a kid. Roan says the salt water helps." He rubbed the back of his neck. "Keeps it from getting...worse."

He didn't meet her eyes as he spoke, instead focusing on the rise and fall of the waves.

Nerissa caught the brief flicker of tension in his posture and the way his words trailed off. She didn't push.

"Salt water's good for a lot of things," she said quietly.

Zale glanced at her briefly, a small, fleeting smile crossing his face. "Yeah. Guess so."

They swam in silence, cutting through the calm waters like twin shadows. Zale moved like the sea itself—fluid, effortless. Then, without warning, he shot her a glance, a playful glint in his eyes.

"You know, if you're not careful, I'll leave you in my wake," he said, his voice teasing.

Nerissa raised an eyebrow, her competitive nature sparking to life. "You think I can't keep up?"

Zale's grin widened, his gaze darting ahead. "Well I don't mean to brag, but I *am* the fastest swimmer on the crew."

And just like that, he surged forward, kicking up a spray of water in her face.

Nerissa's heart quickened, and with a sharp flick of her legs, she was off, chasing after him through the water, determined to catch up. She ignored the sting in her healing wound out of sheer spite.

They reached the hull of the *Black Serpent* nearly at the same time, but Zale slapped the side first with an audible *thunk*.

"Beat you," he said, not even winded.

Nerissa clutched the edge, panting. "I'd have won if not for this stupid leg."

He gave her a sideways glance. "Excuses, excuses."

She smiled despite herself, resting her forehead against the worn wood. Water clung to her lashes, but for a moment, she forgot the weight of the sea's rejection.

"You sure you're okay?" He was surveying her again.

She hesitated, then nodded. "Just hate losing."

He smirked. "Then you're definitely in the right crew."

They hung there for a while, the ship looming above and the cove stretching out behind them. Nerissa stared into the depths, trying to ignore the ache behind her ribs—the part of her that was just out of reach, the part that didn't belong here.

But all she had was Zale's presence beside her and the ocean's cold refusal.

"Oi!" a voice rang out from the railing above. "You know swimming before breakfast can cause cramps severe enough to mimic a ruptured spleen?"

Both Nerissa and Zale looked up. Eon stood there, leaning over the edge with half a biscuit in his hand and sand in his curls.

He squinted. "Or wait...is it *after* breakfast? Before? No—definitely after. Or maybe that's lightning and trees—no, that's different trivia entirely…"

Nerissa blinked. "Morning, Eon."

He grinned brightly. "Morning! Oh—also, don't touch the purple mushrooms that Bran found."

Zale sighed, releasing the ship's hull. "Didn't he learn his lesson last night?"

Eon shrugged. "He's a glutton for punishment."

Then he wandered off mid-thought, still chewing as he disappeared from sight.

Zale shook his head. "Lad's got the soul of a seagull and the attention span of one too."

Nerissa laughed under her breath as they started back towards the shoreline. "Remind me to keep a biscuit on hand to throw as a distraction."

By the time they reached the shore, the sun was just cresting the jagged edge of the eastern cliffs, casting gold across the water like spilled treasure. The beach was beginning to stir with the low murmur of pirates still half-asleep.

Ma Wen stood at a battered wooden table near the firepit, ladling something that smelled like smoked fish into mismatched bowls. He wore his usual calm expression and an apron that had several different colored stains and patches to match.

Zale shook water from his hair like a creature breaking the surface for the first time and made a beeline toward the food. Nerissa followed, wringing out her braid.

"Hungry?" Ma Wen asked, setting out a bowl for her.

"Starving," she admitted.

As she accepted the food, she caught a flicker of movement out of the corner of her eye. Bran was strolling up with the languid confidence of someone who hadn't even attempted to be useful yet this morning.

"Well, well," he said, cocking a brow. "If it isn't our triumphant recruit and her aquatic escort." His smirk deepened. "Fancy a swim before breakfast, did we?"

Zale didn't even look up. "Don't start."

Then, almost as an afterthought, he added, "How were the berries, by the way?"

Bran's smile faltered. "Tasted fine going down."

Zale handed Nerissa a spoon with a flourish. "That's not the part I was asking about."

Bran made a dramatic face of suffering. "I was misinformed by a child."

Eon's voice piped up from somewhere near the hammocks: "*Ahem*, I distinctly recall warning you, Mister 'My Gut Is Iron.'"

Ma Wen finally looked up. "It's been a quiet morning. I'd like to keep it that way. Eat."

Bran dropped onto the sand beside them with a groan, stealing a hunk of bread from Zale's bowl.

Just as Nerissa was taking her second bite, a stern voice drifted over the crackle of the fire.

"You just had half your thigh sewn back together yesterday, and your idea of recovery is a brisk swim?"

Nerissa froze mid-chew, eyes wide.

Roan stood a few feet away, arms crossed over his broad chest, his usual expression of calm disdain firmly in place. He had his sleeves rolled up, his ever-present satchel slung over one shoulder, and a strip of linen hanging from one hand.

Zale leaned back with a wince. "Oh no. You caught her."

Roan rounded on him. "And *you*, what's your excuse? Did the ocean call to you again?"

Zale held up his hands innocently. "She was already waist deep by the time I got there. Wasn't *my* idea."

"*Traitor*," Nerissa coughed the word, earning her a smug look from Zale.

Roan turned his attention back to her, and she suddenly became very interested in her fish stew.

"You're lucky I like a challenge." He dropped the linen beside her and jerked his chin toward it. "Dry the leg. I'll check it again after breakfast. And *no more swimming until I say so*."

"Yes, Roan," Nerissa mumbled, chastened.

As Roan stalked off, Nerissa sighed and poked at her breakfast. The fire popped as Ma Wen tossed another log on, the scent of sizzling meat drifting outward.

"So," she asked, glancing at Zale beside her, "what do you all usually do here? When you're not terrorizing newcomers with obstacle courses and stuffing them full of questionable berries."

Zale chuckled, tilting his bowl to sip the last of the broth. "This cove's our breathin' space. We rest, patch up the ship if she needs it, take stock of inventory. Brigid drills the newer recruits, Nestor naps in increasingly creative locations, and Bran gambles away pocket lint."

Nerissa raised a brow. "And you?"

"I swim," he said with a shrug. "Work on my tan. Help with repairs when I have to."

"So it's like a holiday. A pirate holiday."

"Exactly," he said. "A quiet stretch of sand where no one's shootin' at us, chasin' us, or callin' us unholy sea-wretches." He looked out toward the water. "We don't get many of those. So we make 'em count."

Nerissa took in the scenery around her as she set down her bowl in the sand. A pirate ship hardly would have been her first choice of sanctuary, but this crew had welcomed her into their fold without prejudice, knowing nothing of her history, nor even what she truly was. She didn't feel any pressure to rise to some arbitrary expectations, or act in a respectable manner. It was almost liberating.

By midmorning, the cove had shed its sleepy haze. The campfire popped cheerfully. The tide swayed in and out with lazy contentment. And somewhere below deck, chaos was squeaking.

"He's cheating!" someone shouted from the hold.

"You can't cheat in a rat race," Roan said flatly as he descended the stairs with surgical calm. "The rats don't even know they're competing."

"They *do* if you train 'em proper!" Eon's voice echoed up, filled with righteous indignation and far too much excitement for anyone sober.

Nerissa followed the noise out of sheer curiosity, only to find half the crew crouched around a makeshift track built from empty crates, coiled ropes, and someone's discarded boot.

Four rats darted and scrambled around the miniature course, one of them dragging a string tied to what looked suspiciously like a tiny pirate flag.

"I present to you: Captain Cheddarhook!" Eon declared, bowing to scattered applause.

Bran leaned against a barrel with his arms crossed and a coin between his fingers. "My money's on Toothless Jim," he said, tipping his head toward a scrawny, balding rat with one eye and an unsettling aura of vengeance.

The race commenced with much whooping and shouted encouragement. Bets flew like sea spray—coin, rum rations, even someone's peg leg. Roan's look of horror was immediate and profound.

Toothless Jim made a dramatic last-minute dash for the finish line, narrowly edging out a surprisingly nimble rat named *Mittens the Bloodthirsty*. Eon accused the course of being slanted. Cormac, having declared himself the official race judge, waved him off with a mug and a mumbled, "Should've fed yours more beans."

Just as Bran began collecting his winnings with the self-satisfied air of a man who'd bet on chaos and won, Brigid's voice cut through the merriment like a dagger through sailcloth.

"Right then, you lot. Enough o' th' rodent reverence. We've repairs tae see tae."

A synchronized groan echoed from the hold.

Nerissa glanced up to see Brigid standing at the hatch with arms crossed and expression stony. A coil of sail thread dangled from one hand like a noose.

"Any soul caught idlin'll be workin' double come morn."

Roan let out a small, heartfelt sigh and vanished. Presumably to find mending needles and emotional distance.

Bran opened his mouth to argue—

"*Ah ah ah,*" Captain Nestor interrupted brightly, appearing at Brigid's side with a grin that suggested mischief. "What if we make it interesting?"

Brigid narrowed her eyes. "Go on then."

"A wager," Nestor said, sweeping a hand toward the gathered crew. "We do another race. One winner. One lucky, blessed, rodent-favored soul gets to skip mending circle today. Everyone else picks up a needle."

Brigid arched a brow. "An' who's *not* helpin' either way?"

Nestor's grin widened. "Management."

Cormac raised his tin cup. "I'll allow it."

The second race was even more ridiculous. Someone tied a crumb of smoked fish to a thread and tried to lure their rat across the finish line. Another attempted to whisper strategy into their rodent's ear. Bran painted tiny lightning bolts onto his contender's sides with soot and grease. Eon provided a dramatic running commentary that made Nerissa's stomach hurt from laughing.

Eon let out a triumphant whoop as Mittens the Bloodthirsty skittered across the finish line, tail flicking like a war banner. He pumped both fists in the air, nearly knocking over a bucket of spare buttons in his exuberance. "Victory! Sweet, rodent-fueled victory!" he declared, scooping the twitchy champion into his hands and planting a kiss squarely on her tiny head. "You're a legend, Mittens. A legend!" Before anyone could hand him a needle or so much as mention the word "hems," Eon had darted down the gangplank.

Bran, sulking over his loss, was the first to plop down beside a tangle of torn sailcloth and start threading a needle, poorly.

Nerissa sat beside him, carefully folding a hammock in need of patching.

"You seem awfully familiar with rat racing," she said dryly.

Bran didn't look up. "I grew up in a port city. You learn two things fast: how to gamble, and how to outrun your own tab."

Zale settled nearby with a ripped shirt and a look of deep regret. He held the needle at arm's length, squinting at it. "This thing's judging me."

Across the circle, Roan lifted his eyes just long enough to rumble, "Just pretend you're stitching up Nerissa."

Zale scowled, ears flushing. "Not helping."

Nerissa glanced over, one brow raised. "And here I thought pirates were supposed to be good with sharp objects."

Zale glanced down at his mangled stitches and sighed. "Aye, well. Give me a sword and I'll gut a man. Give me a needle and I'll gut myself."

He lifted the shirt with a theatrical flourish. "Behold: art. Roan, don't you dare tell me this doesn't look like the entrails of a wounded shark."

Roan's gaze lingered on the mess of thread for a long beat. "If a shark looked like that, I'd put it out of its misery," he said dryly, going back to his work.

Bran broke into mock applause, grinning wide. "Bravo. A masterpiece."

Nerissa shook her head, lips twitching despite herself. "Maybe stick to swords."

Zale clutched the shirt to his chest in wounded dignity. "Savages, the lot of you."

Brigid's shadow fell over the circle, arms crossed, eyes like flint. "Aye, and if those stitches don't start lookin' less like entrails and more like sailcloth, ye'll find yerselves mendin' with yer teeth. The canvas won't patch itself."

She moved on without waiting for a reply, her boots sharp against the deck.

That evening, as the stars blinked lazily to life overhead and the fire crackled low, Cormac leaned forward on his knees.

"Mark me words," he said, gazing out at the dark water. "There be worse things than storms on these waters."

Bran groaned as he poured himself a drink. "Here we go."

"Sirens," Cormac continued darkly. "They don't sing sweet. Not pretty. It's a sound that crawls into your ears and works its way into your bones."

Nerissa sat very still.

"They've eyes like lanternfish," he went on, gesturing vaguely. "All glow and wicked promise. Skin cold as the grave. Teeth sharp enough to split a hull plank."

Roan leaned back near Nerissa, crossing his arms, mildly entertained.

Cormac jabbed a finger into the air. "And the worst part of it? They'll smile at you. Smile like you're the one choosin' to drown."

Lanternfish eyes.

Cold as the grave.

Split a hull plank.

Blatant lies.

Her jaw tightened just slightly as she folded her hands neatly in her lap.

Bran tilted his head toward her. "You look unconvinced, newbie."

Her gaze slid to him, serene as still water.

"I have always found," she said evenly, "that men who fear women tend to exaggerate."

A few snorts and chuckles rippled around the fire.

Cormac squinted at her. "Oh? And what would ye know of it?"

"Only that superstition thrives where knowledge fails."

Roan choked on his drink.

Cormac harumphed. "Ye'll not be so clever when one drags ye under."

Nerissa met his stare without blinking.

"Then I suppose I shall swim."

Bran barked a laugh while Ma Wen's eyes creased in approval.

Zale, who had been sharpening a knife a few feet away, went still, attentive. Nerissa noticed that he had not laughed along with the others.

"They charm ye," Cormac insisted. "Make ye think they're harmless. Then before ye know it, ye're under their sirensong spell."

Zale shifted, rubbing the back of his neck, eyes on the flames.

"Never heard a song," he said lazily, "that made me do something I didn't already want to."

A few heads turned, Nerissa's included.

Cormac huffed. "That's what they want ye to think."

Zale shrugged, finally glancing up. Not at the old man, but at her.

"Funny," he murmured, "every time a sailor drowns, it's a siren. Never the drink. Never an accident."

Cormac cleared his throat loudly. "Ye'll be the first one dragged under, boy. Don't matter how good ye can swim."

Zale stuck his knife in the sand and leaned back on his hands.

"If she's smilin' at me, I'll take my chances."

The crew erupted in laughter.

Nerissa did not.

He had meant it as a jest, but she was not entirely certain it had sounded like one.

Just before Cormac could begin a rebuttal, Eon burst from the ship holding something triumphantly above his head.

"It lives!" he proclaimed. "The sea could not drown it. Fire could not claim it. Mold dared not feast upon its sacred pages!"

Brigid groaned. "Och, saints save us—nae that cursed book again."

"The very one," Eon declared, clutching the waterlogged volume like it was a holy relic. "*Stormbound Hearts: A Tidal Temptation.*"

Zale didn't even look up. "It's always worse than I remember."

"That's what makes it *art,*" Eon said.

Nestor leaned forward, a wicked gleam in his eye. "Hand it here, lad. Let's see if Lady Isadora has finally confessed her forbidden desire for the rogue Commodore D'Andre."

Eon passed it over with reverence. "Chapter Twelve is the best. You'll know it when you get there."

Nestor flipped dramatically through the pages, then cleared his throat and launched into a voice so sultry it could curdle cream. "'Her bodice heaved like the sails of a ship caught in a lustful gale—'"

"Och, *please*," Brigid snapped. "Who in th' seven seas even writes like that?"

"Clearly a genius," Zale said dryly, still not looking up.

Nerissa, wide-eyed with amusement, leaned toward Bran. "Is this...normal?"

Bran grinned. "Perfectly. Wait until Chapter Twelve."

Nestor continued with an alarming amount of commitment, complete with smoldering eye contact and occasional gasps for emphasis. "'—and she gasped, 'Commodore, you'll undo me!' and he replied, 'Aye, lass, but I'll do it slowly.'"

Cormac wheezed.

Zale had stopped sharpening the dagger. He was staring fixedly at the sand, ears a faint shade of red. Eon caught Nerissa's eye and mouthed *Chapter Twelve.*

With the gravitas of a bard in a tavern and the smirk of a man who'd lost both his morals and his shirt in a card game, Captain Nestor rose from his seat, the tome held reverently in one hand.

"'Lady Isadora stood alone on the deck of the Velvet Tempest…'" he began, lowering his voice to a gravelly, seductive murmur that made half the crew choke on their drinks.

He sauntered dramatically in a circle, adding wind noises with his mouth: *whoooooosh!*

"'You said we couldn't," he gasped theatrically in falsetto, flinging his arm over his eyes. "That duty'—"

"—'Damn duty!'" Zale muttered along, trying to hide his grin behind his drink.

Bran leaned toward Nerissa, whispering, "Watch this part. This is where he tears off the epaulet. Nestor mimed it last time and threw a spoon at Cormac."

"'He tore it off!" Nestor bellowed, flinging a random sock into the firelight where it was immediately incinerated. "I'd give up every rank, every commission, every naval biscuit for you, Isadora!'"

"Not the biscuits," someone muttered dramatically.

Eon was practically vibrating with joy, mouthing the words like a devout acolyte.

Roan, seated beside Ma Wen, simply sighed into his tea and muttered, "Every time we anchor here…"

"'I want to chart the coastline of *you*'," Nestor growled, hip-thrusting at no one in particular.

Ma Wen did not look up from mending a net. "I don't have many regrets, but this—this is one of them."

Brigid stood with her arms crossed, a vein in her temple visibly throbbing. "If anyone needs me," she said to no one, "I'll be scrubbin' this rot from my skull wi' fish guts an' a wire brush."

"'Their mouths met like dueling sabers!'" Nestor cried, grabbing Eon and dipping him dramatically. Eon yelped but went with it, clutching Nestor's shoulder like a swooning debutante.

Laughter erupted around the fire. Even Nerissa couldn't help but snort into her cup.

Zale—stoic, unimpressed Zale—was *definitely* not listening. He was looking anywhere but at the book. He was definitely *not* leaning slightly forward as Nestor flipped the page.

Bran elbowed him. "Don't pretend. We all know Chapter Twelve is your favorite."

"Shut up."

As Nestor launched into a particularly vivid metaphor involving a coconut, a compass, and "the groaning of ancient timbers," Brigid finally turned on her heel.

"I swear," she muttered, storming toward the hammocks, "th' next man who utters th' word 'bodice' gets keelhauled."

From the firelight, Nestor called after her sweetly, "You haven't even heard the bit about the barnacle of longing!"

A small gasp from Eon: "Wait. There's a barnacle?!"

Ma Wen sighed again. "I need a stronger drink."

Nestor cleared his throat again, flicked his hair back with the drama of a wind-swept hero, and held the limp book aloft like sacred scripture.

"Chapter Thirteen: The Ballad of the Barnacle."

Gasps. Coughs. One "oh no" from Roan.

"'Morning broke over the Sapphire Sea with all the subtlety of a cannon blast. Lady Isadora stood at the prow, her nightgown billowing like the sails of fate. Her eyes—stormy with longing, salted with regret—searched the horizon for one man…'"

Bran leaned over, whispering to Nerissa, "We're in for at least three euphemisms and one aquatic metaphor before the end of this page."

Zale, sipping very deliberately from his cup: "Only three?"

Nestor dropped his voice to a sultry rasp.

"'He approached, boots echoing across the deck, barnacle in hand. It was grotesque. Majestic. A symbol of his burden.'"

"Is he *actually holding* a barnacle?" Nerissa asked, unsure whether to be appalled or invested.

"Oh, it gets worse," Zale groaned.

"'This," Nestor intoned, thrusting an imaginary crustacean aloft, "is the barnacle of my soul.'"

Ma Wen: "...I'm going to pretend I didn't hear that."

Nestor continued with flair:

"Lady Isadora recoiled. 'It's...it's covered in algae!' 'So is my heart,' he whispered. 'So is my heart.'"

Brigid—who had not, in fact, gone far—groaned from the shadows. "Tell me ye're no' readin' th' barnacle chapter again."

"He pressed the barnacle to his chest." Nestor did so with conviction and a glint in his eye. "Its sharp edge slicing his noble bosom."

Zale choked on his drink.

"Blood and seawater mingled as he declared, 'For you, my love, I would dive to the ocean's darkest trench...I would let sea urchins exfoliate my pride...I would polish the rudder of destiny!'"

"Stop," Roan muttered. "Just...stop."

But the crew was lost to chaos now. Bran was laughing so hard he'd fallen backward into the sand. Eon was clutching the firewood like a lifeline. Nerissa had tears in her eyes and couldn't tell if they were from laughter or secondhand embarrassment.

"She reached out," Nestor continued, undeterred, "touched the barnacle—nay, *embraced* it—and whispered, 'We are shipwrecked upon the reef of each other's passion.'"

A long silence followed.

Finally, Cormac muttered, "I once watched a man go mad with cabin fever. He made more sense than that."

Brigid returned just long enough to hurl a wet sock at Nestor's head. It landed squarely on the book. Nestor plucked it off with dignity.

"Alas," he said, closing the book with theatrical finality, "that concludes tonight's reading. But fear not—Chapter Fourteen includes sword fights, a disguised pirate prince, and a metaphor so scandalous it was banned in four kingdoms."

Bran called out, "Is it the one with the oiled anchor chain?"

Nestor winked. "Ye'll just have to wait and see."

Nerissa dabbed at her face with the edge of her sleeve, rubbing away the tears she had shed while laughing at the absurdity of the performance. She had to hand it to the captain, he was certainly…passionate. Never had she ever had the misfortune of hearing such drivel. It sounded like a story that Calliope might genuinely enjoy reading.

Callie…

Nerissa wondered if they had gone through with the wedding after the…*incident.* Had the treaty been signed? Did Calliope even know that Nerissa was gone? She couldn't imagine a scenario where news of her escape didn't reach King Nereus. The Royal Guard was almost certainly patrolling the sea so that she could be returned to Astyra as a peace offering. She was as good as dead if anyone found her.

Nerissa's heart sank like a leaden weight in her chest. She would never be safe in the sea. The only reason she'd entered the water that morning was to try shifting again. She wouldn't have gone far—she just needed to be in her merform for a few minutes to keep withdrawal at bay. It was actually quite fortuitous that she'd ended up on a pirate ship, even if it was technically sanctioned by Astyra. For the foreseeable future, this was her home.

And she'd be lying if she said she wasn't warming up to it.

CHAPTER 20

JELLYFISH-HEARTED

Zale

The mood aboard the *Black Serpent* shifted like the wind at dusk.

The smell of tar, pitch, and damp rope replaced the aroma of Ma Wen's smoked fish buns. Hammocks were rolled, sails hoisted, and every crewmember moved with the kind of ease that came from knowing how fragile peace could be.

Brigid barked final orders to the deckhands. "Double-check th' ballast! I'll no' have this ship listin' like Bran after two cups o' spiced rum!"

"I only fell over once!" Bran's voice called back from the rigging. "And that's because Roan hit me with a *live trout!*"

Roan, passing by with a crate of citrus under one arm, didn't even look up. "Your word against mine."

On the quarterdeck, Captain Nestor lounged with one leg hooked over the railing and a spyglass in hand—though whether he was surveying the horizon or admiring the clouds was anyone's guess.

Then he tipped his spyglass toward the horizon, his voice pitched like a challenge. "Ye feel that?"

Zale wiped his hands on the coil of line at his feet. "The promise of adventure, the freedom of the tide, the—"

Nestor grinned and clapped him on the shoulder. "Finally, you're catchin' the spirit—"

"—the gull that just relieved itself on the mizzen top," Zale finished, jerking his chin upward.

For a heartbeat, Nestor just stared at him. Zale ducked his head, busying himself with the coil, hiding the grin that tugged at his mouth. He knew exactly the sort of response the old man had been hoping for.

Nestor snorted, lowering the spyglass. "...poetic as a dockside drunk."

Down near the helm, Eon was narrating the departure to no one in particular.

"The crew boards in perfect formation. The sails unfurl like wings! The ship heaves, no wait, *glides*, into the waiting jaws of fate!"

"Ye'll be the death of me," muttered Cormac, thumping the railing with his palm. "Ye and that cursed rodent commentary."

"Toothless Jim *is* the emotional core of this voyage!" Eon insisted.

Zale shook his head, chuckling faintly. They were a strange bunch, but they were the closest thing he had to family.

His gaze drifted toward the stern, where Nerissa stood with the wind tugging at her hair, eyes fixed on the fading line of the cove. He wondered if she had anyone left waiting for her, or if she'd lost her entire family when her parents died.

At first, he'd thought her lucky—to have memories of the people who'd loved her. But the more he thought about it, the less certain he was. Remembering might hurt worse than forgetting. At least he didn't have ghosts trailing him through every sunrise…though sometimes he wondered if the emptiness was any kinder.

Nerissa

Nerissa watched the hideout slowly disappear from view. Since passing her initiation, the crew was much more welcoming, less wary of her. Cormac still seemed to believe that there was something "fishy" about her, though without solid proof, no one took him seriously. Just as well, she couldn't allow anyone to learn the truth of what she really was, or they would toss her right back into the sea.

It was a stroke of luck that her blood wasn't green. The rest of the crew might not necessarily know the significance, but she had a sneaking suspicion that Cormac definitely knew what siren blood looked like.

She took a deep breath, flexing her fingers. Today marked seven days in her human form. She didn't even feel thirsty, much less any of the more worrisome symptoms of sea withdrawal. It was comforting and disconcerting all at once.

She slowly turned to face the bow of the ship, watching Zale with detached interest. He was much more tolerable when he wasn't trying to be a cocky flirt. She found herself being inevitably drawn to him, seeking him out when there was no work to do. That was probably just because he was the first crewmember she had met and really had much interaction with. Definitely no other reason, she told herself.

Bran sauntered over to Zale with the easy swagger of a man who'd slept through sail change and still somehow looked sun-kissed and smug. "Race you to the crow's nest."

Zale didn't even glance at him. "You always lose."

"That's what makes me a romantic."

Zale gave him a dry look. "That's what makes you a glutton for punishment."

Bran clapped a hand over his heart. "Say that to my face."

"I *am* saying it to your face."

Bran jerked a thumb toward the rigging. "From halfway up the mast, I mean."

Zale sighed, the very picture of disinterest. "Not happening."

Then he bolted.

Nerissa blinked as he sprinted toward the ropes like the deck was on fire.

"Ten silvers on Zale!" came Nestor's voice from the helm, eyes twinkling as he leaned over the railing. "Don't fail me, lad!"

Brigid, arms crossed, didn't even glance up. "Bran's gonna throw out his back, an' Zale's gonna snap a rope an' break his bloody neck. Idiots."

Nerissa watched as both men scrambled up the rigging. "Do they do this often?"

Brigid snorted. "Only when we've gone more than ten hours without a crisis. Enjoy it while it lasts."

Below, Eon was shouting commentary from the gunwale: "Zale takes the lead with that reckless left swing! Bran's answering with a foot hook—but oh! A tragic miscalculation! He's tangled in the line like an overambitious squid!"

Zale didn't even look down. "Still got that romantic streak, Bran?"

"Stuff it!" Bran wheezed, still climbing.

Nerissa folded her arms. "Is there a prize?"

"Bragging rights," Nestor winked in her direction.

With a final grunt of effort, Zale swung himself up and over the edge of the crow's nest, landing in a triumphant sprawl across the wooden platform. He lay there panting, a cocky grin stretched across his face as he slapped the floor twice for dramatic effect.

Half a second later, Bran clambered up after him, dragging himself over the side with all the grace of a dying walrus. He collapsed next to Zale with a groan that could have been heard in the next kingdom.

"I would've won," Bran gasped, "if you didn't get a head start. Cheater."

Zale snorted. "Sore loser."

Bran held out a hand. "Help me up, you smug sea-lizard."

Zale reached for him—only for Bran to yank him sideways with a wicked grin. Both men toppled backward with a loud thump, limbs flailing as they tangled in the rigging like two very uncoordinated octopi.

"Get—off—my—leg!"

"That's your *own* leg, genius!"

Below, Brigid glanced up from tying off a line. "Unbelievable," she muttered.

"They'll be fine," Nestor said breezily from the helm, shading his eyes with one hand. "Let 'em untangle themselves. Builds character."

Brigid made a sound that was somewhere between a scoff and a chuckle. "One o' them is goin' to fall an' crack their skull open."

"Probably. But look at 'em. That's what brothers do."

Brothers.

Nerissa couldn't help but think of Lir. She had once been closer to her than any blood sibling. Lir used to challenge her to anything from swimming races through coral tunnels to daring each other to weave through a bloom of jellyfish without getting stung. Nerissa preferred testing her speed over her pain tolerance, but she could never turn down Lir's grin. There had been laughter in those days.

It struck her now, watching Bran and Zale bicker and trip over each other, how alike they were. That same easy trust. That same unspoken understanding that the other would always be there, even mid-chaos. Lir and Nerissa had been like that once, until injustice had pulled them to opposite sides of the current.

She hadn't realized how much she missed it—the freedom to laugh without consequence, the comfort of someone who knew her before oaths and orders and secrets.

Zale's laughter carried across the deck, warm and unguarded. For a heartbeat, Nerissa could almost pretend she was back home, young again, with Lir darting through the sea beside her.

Almost.

The illusion faded as quickly as it came, replaced by a dull ache in her chest and a sluggish pull through her veins, as though her blood had been replaced with coral sap—a resin often used in Nautalia as sealant and incense.

What was wrong with her? It had been years since Lir had defected to the Court of Sirens. Why was this hitting her so hard right now? For Tides' sake, she was trapped in this form and on the run from two kingdoms for committing regicide. Surely *that* deserved her focus, if anything. But all she could think of was the family she had lost.

She'd heard somewhere that alcohol dulled more than pain—that it blurred edges, softened memories until they lost their bite. Maybe there was truth in that. Maybe not. Maybe she'd test it for herself.

Slipping silently down the companionway, she made her way to the galley. The air was thick with herbs and spices, the soft clatter of metal against wood alerting her to Ma Wen's whereabouts as he sorted through inventory. Nerissa approached slowly, letting her footsteps announce her presence. He gave no visual sign that he'd noticed her, though she knew better.

"Looking for something?"

"Yes," she said, then hesitated. Damarion would not approve of drowning one's sorrows in such a way. But Damarion wasn't here.

"Where can I get something to drink?" she asked finally.

Ma Wen stopped what he was doing and turned, his narrow eyes creasing. "What kind of drink?"

"The kind that makes you forget that you hate drinking."

He studied her for a moment, then lumbered across the galley to a high shelf. "Rum will burn." When he returned, he set down a small clay bottle between them. "This will warm."

Nerissa picked it up, tilting it toward the lantern light. The label was painted with symbols she didn't recognize, fading where time had worn the glaze.

"What is it?"

"Something from home."

He pulled out two small tin cups. Nerissa handed him the bottle, and he poured carefully. The liquid shimmered faintly in the cup, catching the light with a warmth that reminded her of sunlight on shallow water. Nerissa lifted it to her lips and took a cautious sip.

It wasn't what she expected. Smooth, almost sweet, with a hint of rice and something floral beneath it—delicate where she'd braced for fire. The warmth spread quickly down her throat and into her chest, blooming outward until even her fingertips tingled. Her head felt light, the edges of her thoughts softening in a way that was both pleasant and disorienting.

Ma Wen watched her quietly, arms folded. "Careful," he said. "A little goes a long way."

Nerissa blinked, feeling the warmth deepen into a gentle tingle beneath her skin. "It's…nice," she admitted, almost surprised by the word. "I like it."

His mouth curved faintly, not quite a smile. "Most people do, at first." He gathered up the bottle, corking it again before she could reach for a second pour. "But it doesn't chase the ghosts away. It only makes them harder to see for a while. When the haze clears, they're still waiting."

Nerissa stared into her cup, the golden liquid trembling slightly with the ship's sway. "I know," she said softly. "But a little while might be enough."

Ma Wen studied her for another long moment, then nodded once. "Then drink slow, little fish. No sense in drowning twice."

She smiled faintly at that, before tipping the cup again. *If he only knew.* The warmth returned, sweet and numbing. The ship rolled beneath her feet, but this time the motion seemed heavier, as if the ship itself were swaying through syrup.

She braced a hand on the table, eyes half-lidded. The drink dulled the ache, but it couldn't quiet the hollow space that it came from. Her mind drifted to Lir's laughter echoing through coral caverns, to her mother's songs, her father's hand steadying hers as she learned to braid nets. Ghosts, just as Ma Wen had said. The warmth couldn't reach them.

She sighed, setting the cup aside. "Thank you," she murmured. "For sharing your stash."

Ma Wen grunted softly, returning to his work. "Just don't make a habit of it."

Nerissa nodded once in silent acknowledgement. Then she rose, steadying herself against the gentle sway of the ship, and made her way back up the companionway.

The sun still sat high over the horizon, gilding the deck in gold. Most of the crew were busy at their posts—Brigid shouting orders, the deckhands coiling lines and swabbing the deck. Nerissa drifted toward the mainmast and leaned against it, the rough wood pressing cool against her shoulder.

Overhead, Bran and Zale were in the rigging, testing ropes and mending frayed ends. She could hear Bran laughing about something, Zale's deeper voice answering in that half-scolding, half-indulgent tone he always used with him.

She knew Ma Wen had been right to cut her off, and she knew he meant well. But the ache in her chest hadn't eased. The drink had only blurred its edges. She wanted to forget—just for a little while. So when she caught sight of a certain grumpy old boatswain, an idea began to form.

Cormac stood near the gunwale, humming under his breath as he checked the lashing on a cannon. A pewter flask glinted in his weathered hand. The smell hit her before she even reached him—strong, sharp, unmistakably alcoholic.

"Afternoon," she greeted, innocently enough.

He glanced over, one bushy copper brow lifting. "Afternoon, lass. Ye look like someone's chewed ye up an' spat ye out."

"Just tired," she said. "Trying to outrun some old memories."

He grunted and took a slow swig from his flask. "Aye, well. Nothin' a bit o' this can't cure."

Her gaze flicked to the flask. "What is it?"

"Homemade," he said proudly. "Blend o' rum, ginger, and whatever else was left in the bottle. Keeps the stomach steady an' the spirits steadier."

"That sounds like it would do anything *but* steady the stomach."

He gave a raspy chuckle. "Aye, but ye'll live." He offered her the flask, his beard lifting with his smile. "Go on, lass. Builds tolerance."

Nerissa hesitated. Maybe she should just quit while she was ahead. "Ma Wen told me not to make a habit of drinking."

"Ma Wen brews tea," Cormac said flatly. "Ye want advice on herbs, ask him. Ye want to forget ye've got a head full o' ghosts, ask me."

So be it, then. "You make a persuasive argument."

"That's the rum talkin'."

She took the flask and lifted it to her lips. The first swallow burned so fiercely she nearly coughed it back out, but stubbornness forced her to hold it down. Her eyes watered. It was somehow *worse* than what Bran had given her the night of her initiation. Cormac roared with laughter.

"There's a good lass!" he crowed. "See? Not so bad once ye stop fightin' it."

"Not so bad?" she managed, voice rough. "That tasted like fermented kelp and ship tar!"

"Aye," he said cheerfully. "Those be the subtle notes of its flavor profile."

He clapped her on the shoulder hard enough to make her sway. "Drink with sailors long enough, ye'll learn two things: never trust calm seas, an' never waste good rum."

Nerissa handed back the flask, her head spinning slightly. "Not so sure…qualifies as…good rum."

Cormac barked a laugh, the sound rough as gravel. "Aye, well. Give it a year or two at sea, an' ye'll be singin' a different tune."

She gave a faint, unsteady grin. "Can't promise it'll be pleasant."

He chuckled again, taking another swig. "Doesn't matter. Long as ye keep singin', lass."

Nerissa shook her head, fighting a smile as she turned toward the bow. The world tilted a little more than it should have, but for the first time all day, the weight in her chest finally eased.

Jellyfish-hearted.

That's what she was.

Spineless, cowardly—*stupid.*

She should have just dealt with her feelings instead of running away from them. Now she regretted everything.

Nerissa stood at the stern of the ship, though *stood* was a generous term for what she'd resigned herself to. Less than an hour after drinking with Cormac, the effects had struck hard and fast. Her head was spinning, her skin clammy, and she was fairly certain her face had gone greener than coral moss.

The last twenty minutes had been spent leaning over the railing, emptying the contents of her stomach into the sea below. The taste of rum and bile still clung to her tongue, and even when she was certain there couldn't possibly be anything left, her body proved her wrong. The ship's steady roll did nothing to help—each tilt of the deck felt like another cruel test of balance and dignity.

Footsteps approached from behind, light and hesitant. Nerissa groaned softly and didn't bother lifting her head.

"Permission to come within splashing distance?"

Eon's voice. Of course.

"If you value your boots, I wouldn't," she muttered.

He chuckled and crouched a few paces away, keeping a safe distance. "Fair enough. I brought peace offerings."

She risked a glance over her shoulder, fighting back another wave of dizziness. Eon held out a small bundle wrapped in wax paper. Inside were pale, candied pieces that glistened faintly in the sunlight.

"What's this?"

"Ginger chews. Ma Wen sent me. Said you'd be needing these." He winked.

So he knew exactly what she was going to do. Knew she'd go and drink herself sick after all.

She took one of the chews from Eon's hand, unwrapped it, and bit down. The sweet heat of the ginger spread through her mouth, soothing the burn in her throat. When she swallowed, she was pleasantly surprised to find that her stomach did not immediately reject the candy.

Eon stayed crouched nearby, gaze soft. "You'll find your legs again soon enough. Happens to everyone their first time."

She shot him a glare. "I'm not seasick."

"Of course you're not," he said with a grin. "You're just…enthusiastically communing with the ocean."

Despite herself, a weak laugh escaped her. "Go away, Eon."

He rose with a smile, saluted her with mock solemnity, and headed back across the deck.

Nerissa stayed where she was, back against the rail, legs stretched out before her. The sea breeze brushed across her face, cooling the sweat on her skin. Her head still swam, but the nausea had mostly passed, replaced by a heavy, syrupy drowsiness.

She tilted her face up toward the sky, eyes closed. The soft creak of the rigging and the hush of waves against the hull lulled her into a strange calm—half peace, half exhaustion.

"—told you she couldn't hold her liquor," Bran was laughing.

"I didn't think it'd *kill* her," Zale replied.

Nerissa cracked one eye open. Both men stood a few paces away, looking down at her like she was a dead animal that had washed ashore.

"I'm not dead," she muttered.

Bran grinned and crouched beside her. "A miracle, then. Ma Wen said you'd gone lookin' for a drink, and Cormac said you found it. Must've been quite the reunion."

Zale's brow furrowed. "You alright?"

"She's fine," Bran said cheerfully. "Bit green about the gills, but she'll live."

"I don't have gills," she said dryly, closing her eyes again.

"Could've fooled me." Bran leaned in, lowering his voice conspiratorially. "You know, most people start with a sip, not a challenge."

"Didn't…challenge anyone," she said, though it came out a bit slurred.

Zale crossed his arms, trying—and failing—not to smile. "You drank with *Cormac*. That's challenge enough."

Bran barked a laugh. "Aye, I learned that the hard way. Thought I was tough till I woke up in the bilge three hours later making out with a rat."

"At least I didn't kiss anyone," Nerissa grimaced at that visual. "Or anything."

Zale crouched down beside her, studying her face. "You need a drink."

"I've had plenty of that," she muttered.

He huffed a quiet laugh, shaking his head. "Not that kind."

Bran clapped Zale's shoulder. "I'll fetch some water. You make sure she doesn't roll overboard again."

"I didn't—" Nerissa began, but Bran was already gone.

Zale stayed, resting one arm on his knee. The teasing was gone from his voice now. "Next time, maybe just…talk to someone before you decide to drink the galley dry."

She exhaled, slow and tired. "Talking doesn't make it stop hurting."

"No," he said quietly. "But neither does rum."

Her eyes flicked toward him, searching his face. She'd never cared to notice before, but his eyes had depth to them—green with flecks of gold, catching the sunlight in a way that made her forget, for half a breath, how awful she felt.

Then Bran's voice rang out from across the deck. "Got the water! And a bucket, just in case!"

Zale sighed. Nerissa groaned. The moment was gone.

Bran jogged over, sloshing water from the tin cup he carried. "Here ye go, lass. Doctor's orders."

Nerissa took the cup without protest. The water was blessedly cool. She drank in small, careful sips. Her throat still burned from the rum's sting, but the tasteless liquid helped settle her stomach—or so she thought.

When the cup was empty, she handed it back to Bran and pushed herself upright, gripping the rail for balance. "I just need to lie down," she muttered.

"Careful," Zale said, rising beside her. "You're still pale."

"I'm fine," she insisted, taking one unsteady step toward the companionway.

That was when it hit her—sudden heat flooding her face, a rush of dizziness, and a high, ringing pulse in her ears. Her stomach clenched with alarming urgency.

Oh no.

She spun back toward the rail, but her balance faltered, and she didn't make it that far.

The next thing she knew, she was bent double, heaving. And unfortunately, Zale's boots were directly in the line of fire.

For a heartbeat, there was only silence. Then Bran made a strangled sound somewhere between horror and laughter.

Zale stared down at his boots. "…That wasn't the ocean."

Mortified, Nerissa wiped her mouth with the back of her hand, eyes wide. "I—I was aiming for the sea."

"Aye," Bran said, choking on laughter, "ye missed by about two feet!"

Zale exhaled slowly, the long-suffering sort of sigh that said he'd accepted his fate. "Guess I deserved that," he murmured.

"For what?" Bran wheezed.

"For trying to have a serious conversation with a drunk."

That earned another helpless burst of laughter from Bran. Even Nerissa, still bent over and wishing the planks would swallow her, couldn't help the faint, miserable sound that escaped her.

"Alright," Zale said finally, tone resigned but gentle. "Let's get you cleaned up before Brigid finds out and blames me."

"She's gonna find out anyway," Bran said. "Smell'll give it away."

Zale shot him a look. "You're not helping."

Bran grinned. "Didn't say I was tryin' to."

Zale exhaled through his nose, then turned back to Nerissa. She was still gripping the rail, head bowed, strands of hair stuck to her face. She felt sick, exhausted, and the most embarrassed she had ever felt in her entire life.

"Come on," he said softly. "Let me help you to the quartermaster's cabin before you keel over."

"It's okay. I can walk."

"You sure?"

"Positive," she muttered, though her voice didn't sound nearly as convincing as she'd hoped.

Zale didn't press her. He simply nodded. "Alright then. Try not to fall into the sea on your way there."

She managed a glare that lacked its usual force, then straightened and took a careful step forward. The deck wobbled beneath her, but she kept moving, clutching the rail with white-knuckled determination.

Bran called after her, still half-laughing. "If you see Brigid, tell her it was Zale's fault!"

"Don't you dare," Zale muttered under his breath.

Nerissa didn't answer. She just kept walking, each step a mix of dizziness and dignity, praying she'd make it to the cabin before her stomach decided to betray her again.

Nerissa stood alone in the washroom, the door latched securely. It had been a few days since Roan stitched her leg and told her to keep it dry. Brigid would've sent her to clean up regardless of his instructions—mercy wasn't in the quartermaster's vocabulary. The moment Nerissa stepped foot in their cabin, Brigid had wrinkled her nose and thrown a bar of soap and a clean rag at her, muttering that she smelled like a tavern wench.

So here she was, staring down the odd assortment of barrels and buckets, trying to puzzle out how exactly she was meant to go about it. Merfolk didn't need to bathe in the same way humans did. The most she'd ever worried about underwater was combing tangles from her hair and rubbing snail mucus on her scales to keep them moisturized.

One barrel held clean water, another sat half-full and murky, clearly meant for discarding the used. Nerissa drew a bucket of the clean water and stuffed the rag into it, then lathered it with the soap. It had a soft floral scent. Leave it to Brigid to keep a personal stash of luxuries even on a pirate ship.

She set to work scrubbing her skin, careful to avoid the bandage around her thigh. Her shoulder still ached where Roan had reset it, making it a struggle to reach her back, but she managed well enough. The water cooled her flushed skin, washing away the stickiness of salt and sweat—and the sharp, sour scent of rum that still clung to her.

By the time she emptied the last bucket into the discard barrel, she felt…lighter. Clean, yes, but more than that, *human* again, in the strangest sense of the word. The air smelled of soap instead of sickness, and her skin carried the faint perfume of flowers instead of the sea. She leaned against the wall for a moment, eyes half-closed, breathing in the scent. It wasn't home—not even close—but it was something she could stand to carry with her.

By the time she stepped out of the washroom, Nerissa felt almost like herself again. She wore a fresh linen shirt and trousers borrowed from Brigid—slightly too loose, but soft and clean against her skin. Her soiled clothes were bundled in a rag under one arm, along with the bar of soap she'd meant to return to Brigid.

The deck was quieter now, most of the crew either at supper or off-duty. Nerissa made her way toward Brigid's cabin, feet light on the planks, until a familiar voice stopped her.

"Feelin' any better?"

She froze. Zale leaned against the bulkhead near the companionway, arms crossed loosely, a hint of amusement tugging at his mouth.

"I'm fine," she said quickly. "Mostly."

"Good," he said easily. "I just finished cleanin' my boots; didn't wanna have to scrub 'em again anytime soon."

Nerissa closed her eyes, groaning as the unpleasant memory resurfaced. "Ugh, I am so sorry about that."

Zale's mouth twitched. "If it helps, I've had worse things on my boots."

"That's not as comforting as you think it is."

He lifted his hands in mock surrender. "For what it's worth, I've seen tougher sailors felled by less."

"That supposed to make me feel better?"

"Supposed to," he said with a grin.

"I regret everything."

"Regret's a start." His eyes flicked over her, lingering briefly on her damp hair and clean shirt. "You look better, though."

"Brigid's orders," she said dryly. "Apparently I smelled like a tavern wench."

"I wouldn't know," Zale said, tone teasing but soft around the edges. "But you do smell considerably less offensive. Brigid shared her soap with you, didn't she?"

Nerissa blinked, caught off guard. "You can tell?"

He shrugged. "Hard not to. She's the only one aboard who smells like roses instead of sweat."

"I should get this back to her," she said, lifting the bundle.

He nodded, straightening away from the wall. "Go on then. And Nerissa—"

She paused mid-step.

"Next time ye want to seek solace from a bottle," he said quietly, "find me first."

She hesitated, unsure how to answer, then simply nodded once and continued down the hall, her heart thudding faster than she wanted to admit.

CHAPTER 21
A STRATEGIC MANEUVER

Zale

The *Black Serpent* had seen no sails since leaving the cove.

No enemy flags. No merchant ships in distress. Not even a stray gull with a suspicious glint in its eye. Just the endless shimmer of sea and the dull creak of ropes.

By midday, morale had dropped below sea level.

Zale leaned against the rail, arms crossed, watching the horizon with the enthusiasm of a dead man. "We're goin' to start hallucinating merchant vessels at this rate."

Bran sprawled upside-down on a coil of rope nearby. "I already did. Turned out it was a cloud shaped like a schooner. Had a better figure than I do."

From the helm, Nestor called out, "Right then. Everyone gather—

deckwide emergency. We've entered a Class Four Boredom Spiral."

Brigid didn't even look up from her map table. "If this ends with another interpretive dance battle, I swear on the tide—"

"No dancin' this time," Nestor said, pulling a small leather pouch from his coat with a dramatic flourish. "Just gamblin'."

Cormac groaned. "We don't need another round of *Guess How Many Weevils in the Biscuit.* I'm still emotionally compromised."

Nestor ignored him and upended the pouch onto a barrel—silver coins, seashells, a dried starfish, and one polished gold tooth clattered onto the surface.

"Here's the game," Nestor announced. "We start bettin' on literally anything. Anything at all. Winner takes the pot. Losers...help Ma Wen with dishes."

Ma Wen, from the galley hatch, raised one flour-dusted hand. "Absolutely not. I'll burn the ship."

Eon immediately shouted, "I bet Roan will tell someone off for not drinking enough water within the hour."

"I'll take that bet," Zale grinned. "But double or nothing if he also uses the phrase *'you absolute imbecile.'*"

"I'm in," Bran said, flipping a coin. "I bet Brigid sighs at least four times before lunch."

"Three," said Cormac. "She's been in a good mood today. Relatively."

Brigid glanced up with a sound of exasperation escaping her lips. "Ye're all children."

Everyone immediately turned toward Nestor.

Nestor held up a hand. "She sighed. That counts!"

Eon scribbled it down gleefully on a crumpled piece of parchment. "Betting log initiated. This is now the only law."

The betting began innocently enough.

"I bet Eon falls asleep in the rigging again before sundown."

"I bet Ma Wen can debone a fish with one hand tied behind his back."

"I bet Cormac sings that one haunting sea shanty and we all cry about it."

"I bet Bran cries first," Zale muttered, deadpan, earning a chorus of laughs.

But it wasn't long before things spiraled. Someone bet Zale couldn't climb the mizzenmast blindfolded. He did. Someone else bet Ma Wen couldn't peel ten potatoes in under two minutes. He could. Bets piled up over wind changes, fish sightings, the lifespan of Bran's last clean shirt, and how many daggers were hidden on Brigid's person.

Then Bran, lounging with a toothpick in his mouth and mischief blooming in his eyes, drawled, "I bet Zale can't steal a kiss from our new recruit before sunset."

The deck went silent.

Zale froze, halfway into a cocky retort about Bran's laundry habits. *Of all the stupid—*

Brigid's head snapped up. "Bran Calder, ye absolute—"

"Hold on!" Bran said quickly, hands up. "Not an *unwelcome* kiss. I'm not a monster. Just one she doesn't see coming. A sneak attack, if you will."

"I will *nae*," Brigid hissed.

Zale's chest went tight, heat crawling up his neck. The absolute *last* thing he needed was the crew's attention turned on *that*. On *her*. He shot Bran a look sharp enough to slice the mainsail. "You're enjoying this."

"Deeply," Bran said with a wink. "But the pot's already at seventeen silvers, a rusty brooch, and someone's last ration of Ma Wen's seaweed buns. Worth your pride?"

Zale risked a glance at Nerissa. She was pointedly avoiding eye contact with everyone. Which only made his ears burn hotter.

He exhaled sharply. "You're insufferable."

Bran grinned. "You gonna prove me wrong, mate?"

"Five silvers says he gets slapped," Nestor bellowed from the helm.

Brigid stood, pointing a spoon like a weapon. "If anyone touches her without consent, I'll throw ye overboard personally."

Zale muttered, "Noted," and stalked off, heart thudding like a war drum. He had to move, had to *do* something before his face betrayed him completely. He could practically feel Bran's laughter at his back.

Nerissa said nothing. Just sat there, sipping her water like a queen deciding which heads to remove from their shoulders. The crew eventually dispersed—some laughing, others trading odds on slaps, blushes, or man-overboards.

Later that afternoon, the sea was calm, the sky soft with golden light. The *Black Serpent* cruised steadily, and Zale perched near the starboard rigging with a coil of rope in his hands and brooding in his bones. He hadn't spoken to anyone in over an hour. A personal record.

He didn't notice Nerissa until she sat beside him.

"Running out of places to hide?" she asked lightly.

He glanced over, grimacing. "Not hiding. Just…keeping my distance from certain loudmouthed idiots."

"Bran, you mean."

"Who else?" Zale muttered. "If I hear one more word about that stupid bet—"

"Then you'll what?" she asked, tone mild. "Throw him overboard?"

"Tempting."

They fell quiet as the waves slapped gently against the hull.

Finally, Nerissa said, "You know, the simplest way to end teasing is to give them what they want."

Zale froze, eyeing her warily. "You're not serious."

"Perfectly," she said. "He'll get bored and move on. Everyone wins."

He opened his mouth to argue, but she was already leaning in. Before he could register what was happening, she had pressed her lips against his cheek. It was brief—so brief—but his skin burned at the contact anyway.

"There," she said, sitting back. "Now it's over."

Zale blinked, stunned. "Over? That's—You can't just—"

"Watch me," she said, standing. She dusted her palms on her trousers and added, "Tell Bran he owes me ten silver."

"Sea and stars," he muttered. "I'm never going to hear the end of this."

The words had barely left his mouth when Bran's voice rang out across the deck.

"Oh-ho-HO!" he shouted, loud enough to startle the gulls. "Did *anyone else* witness that? Because I do believe I just saw Zale, First Mate of the Brooding Order, get *outplayed!*"

Zale groaned and lowered his head onto the rope coil like he was trying to merge with it, maybe suffocate, maybe just vanish into hemp and tar until the sea swallowed him whole.

"*She* kissed *you*!" Bran continued, striding theatrically across the deck like a man auditioning for a much larger stage. "On the cheek, no less—the most diabolical of all noncommittal affections! A kiss that says, *'You're adorable, now go stew in it.'*"

Zale squeezed his eyes shut. Stars preserve him. If the ocean had any mercy, it would open up and swallow him now.

Eon sprinted over, panting and carrying the scrap of parchment with the betting results. "I need a quote! Zale, how does it feel to be defeated at your own game of roguish charm?"

Zale didn't lift his head. "I wasn't playin'."

"Exactly!" Bran crowed. "And *still* she won! She didn't even use a sword—she used sass and strategy!"

Zale ground his forehead harder into the rope coil. He could still feel Nerissa's lips on his cheek, light as sea spray, smug as sin. Stars, she was never going to let him live this down. Not that she even had to say a word—the image of her walking away like she'd claimed the deck as her throne was burned into his skull.

Brigid appeared behind them, arms crossed, lips twitching. "Zale," she said flatly, "please tell me ye didn't actually let Bran bet on yer love life."

"I didn't agree to anythin'," Zale muttered into the rope.

Bran held up a finger. "Which means you didn't say *no* either. That's called silent complicity, mate."

Zale lifted his head finally, glaring at him through the wreckage of his dignity. "Oh no. What it's called is psychological warfare."

Bran laughed like a man who'd found his new religion. "Face it, mate, you lost the bet."

Zale scrubbed a hand down his face. She was supposed to be the composed one, the careful one, all steel and silence. *He* was the one who laughed too loud, spoke too fast, wore his heart on his sleeve. So why in the depths had *she* kissed him? What game was she playing, striding off cool as you please while he sat here unraveling like a fool? Stars, maybe it hadn't meant anything at all—just her way of winning the bet.

Bran paused. "Also, I just realized something."

Zale eyed him warily. "What now?"

"I still *technically* won the bet."

"…How?"

"Well, I said you wouldn't kiss her. And you didn't." He grinned wickedly. "*She* kissed *you*. Which means I was right. My genius astounds even me."

Zale sat up, indignant. "That makes no sense! How do you both win? No—absolutely not. I call foul. Nestor!"

The captain, passing by with a tankard and the air of a man who had definitely heard everything, slowed. He gave Zale a long, suffering look.

"Captain ruling," Zale pressed, pointing at Bran like he'd caught him smuggling. "This is robbery."

Nestor considered, swirling his drink like a judge consulting a lawbook that didn't exist. Then he shrugged. "Far as I recall, bet was ye kissin' her. Ye didn't." He tipped his tankard toward Bran. "Bran wins. Simple math."

Bran whooped in triumph. Zale groaned, dragging both hands down his face. He was never leaving this rope coil. He would live here. Die here. Be buried here.

Nerissa

The sun was dipping toward the horizon, painting the sea in streaks of rose and brass. Most of the crew had drifted back to their stations or their usual chaos—Zale keeping to the shadows near the rigging, scratching at the back of his neck with more fury than usual, his posture taut in a way that spoke more of unease than idleness. Nerissa had retreated to the quarterdeck rail, arms folded tight, eyes on the waves without really seeing them.

What in the depths had possessed her? A bet? She didn't care about Bran's silver. She hadn't even claimed her share—Bran, naturally, had pocketed most of it, calling himself the "technical winner." And yet...she'd leaned in, pressed her lips to Zale's cheek, and walked away like she'd meant it. Like it was strategy, not impulse. She didn't even know herself in that moment.

Boots clicked beside her, measured and sure. Brigid.

"Ye always stir up that much trouble," the quartermaster asked, "or is Zale just particularly soft in the head?"

Nerissa didn't look away from the horizon. "I wouldn't say I planned it. But if I had…" her shoulders lifted in a small shrug, "…then it was just a strategic maneuver, nothing more."

Brigid's chuckle was low and knowing. "Aye. Keep tellin' yerself that, lass." She tipped her chin toward the main deck, where Zale lingered by the rigging. He looked every bit the man pretending to be calm, and failing. "Funny sort o' strategy, though. Costs ye nothin', leaves him gutted."

Nerissa's mouth opened, then closed again. Against her better judgment, she risked a glance toward him. Zale's profile was caught in the dying light, all hard lines and forced composure. Her heart gave a traitorous skip, followed swiftly by the sharp pinch of guilt. She tore her gaze back to the waves, jaw tightening. It had been nothing. A move in a game she hadn't even meant to play. That was all. This was fine. She was fine.

Brigid's tone gentled, just a fraction. "Ye've got good instincts, lass. Don't lose yerself tryin' to match the rest of us. We're chaos. Ye don't need to be."

"I'm not," Nerissa said quietly. *At least, I hope I'm not.* "I think I'm finally catching up to me."

Brigid gave a small nod, a spark of approval in her eyes. "Then gods help the rest of us."

She turned to leave, but paused, glancing back with a sharpness that cut deeper than any blade. "Oh, and Nerissa?"

"Yes?"

"If ye're goin' to break Zale's heart...do it clean."

Nerissa froze, stunned. By the time she found her voice, Brigid was already gone.

She gripped the railing tighter, staring at the sunset. Trouble, that's what this was. Trouble in green eyes and an easy grin. Trouble she hadn't meant to invite, and yet...she had.

Zale

Zale sat at the stern rail, one boot braced against the wood, the other dangling over the edge. His arms rested across his knees as he stared at the trail the *Black Serpent* carved through the waves. Normally, the rhythm of the sea would settle him—always had. Tonight, it only grated.

Because he could still feel the phantom heat of Nerissa's lips against his cheek.

Because his stomach had tied itself into a reef knot he couldn't untangle.

Because he was supposed to be treating her like any other crewmate, and clearly he was failing miserably.

He didn't hear Nestor approach.

"Romance and regret, lad?" the captain asked, dropping into a seat beside him with a clink of metal from the flask at his hip.

Zale tensed. "Was it that obvious?"

Nestor took a swig. "Zale, m'boy, you've got all the subtlety of a cannonball in a tea shop."

Zale groaned and rubbed his face. "I didn't plan to—Bran was just being Bran and I—she—I didn't think she'd actually—"

"Ah, yes," Nestor said, nodding solemnly. "The ancient, deeply scientific formula of: 'It was a dare, and now I'm emotionally compromised.' Been there."

Zale shot him a sideways glare. "This funny to you?"

"Not funny. Well. Maybe a *bit* funny." He passed Zale the flask. "You've got the look of someone standing on the edge of something big and terrifying and probably inconvenient."

Zale didn't take the drink. He just stared at it like it held answers. His knuckles whitened against his knee. "I'm not supposed to feel like this. Not about her."

"Why? 'Cause she's a mystery wrapped in secrets wrapped in very fine cheekbones?" Nestor wiggled the flask in emphasis. "That's usually where trouble starts, lad. And sometimes, where good things do."

Zale's laugh came out more like a groan. He didn't want trouble. Trouble got you tied down. Trouble got you committed to something bigger than yourself. Trouble meant admitting you cared—and once you did that, you had something to lose. He'd spent years making sure he didn't.

"She's not like the rest of us," he muttered.

"Oh, absolutely not. She's clever, dangerous, probably hiding something tragic, and definitely capable of stabbing someone if cornered. Reminds me of Brigid in her younger years." He shuddered with theatrical reverence. "Terrifying woman."

That drew a small, unwilling laugh from Zale.

Nestor's grin softened into something quieter. "Look. Feelings are messy. You're not always going to make the right call, but if ye never let yourself *feel* anything, you'll just end up like me."

Zale blinked. "You say that like it's a bad thing."

"It is." Nestor's smile turned wry. "Charming as I am, the sea's taken more from me than I care to admit. I laugh, I drink, I dance on deck in a thunderstorm—but I know what it is to care too late."

He stood, brushing off his coat. "You've got time, lad. Maybe not answers. But time. Don't waste it pretending ye don't care."

Zale stared after him, silent, the knot in his chest pulling tighter.

Then he was gone, leaving Zale alone with the sea, the memory of Nerissa's lips, and the gut-deep certainty that Captain Nestor had just given him actual, legitimate advice.

Worse yet...it had helped.

Nerissa

Nerissa lay awake in Brigid's cabin, staring at the low timbers overhead. Sleep refused to come. The night was too still, her mind too restless, the echo of Bran's ridiculous bet and her own impulsive response refusing to quiet. Eventually, she gave up and slipped to her feet, careful not to wake Brigid.

The main deck was near silent, save for the creak of rigging and the hush of waves. Lanternlight flickered in gentle arcs, painting the planks in amber. Nerissa moved quietly, not intending to intrude—until the low murmur of the captain's voice drifted from the stern.

"…don't waste it pretending ye don't care," Nestor was saying.

No response, but she knew he must be talking to Zale.

Guilt tightened in her chest. She hadn't meant to listen, but she'd heard enough. Her kiss, her carelessness, had left him reeling in a way she hadn't considered. For someone who'd built her life on control, on discipline, she'd been reckless.

The planks creaked as Nestor stood. When he turned, he caught sight of her lingering in the shadows. His eyes glittered with a knowing gleam, then he gave her a subtle nod, as though passing an unspoken baton, and disappeared into his cabin.

Nerissa hesitated, fingers curling against the rail. Then, with a steadying breath, she crossed to the quarterdeck.

Zale sat hunched at the rail, one boot dangling above the water. He hadn't noticed her yet. The wind tugged at his hair, his shoulders drawn tight.

Nerissa braced herself, then said softly, "Hey."

He startled, head whipping around. The shadows across his face made his eyes seem darker, sharper.

She lifted her chin, though her voice stayed low. "I didn't mean to overhear. But I did. And...I think I owe you an apology."

Zale frowned, shifting on the rail. "For what?"

"For earlier," she said, her arms folding across her chest in that practiced, composed way that never quite hid the tension underneath. "I shouldn't have let Bran drag me into his games. I made it worse by...playing along. I didn't mean to embarrass you in front of everyone."

For a moment, he just stared at her, then let out a huff of laughter that wasn't entirely amused. "Embarrass me? Nerissa, this crew has seen me fall out of the rigging, get headbutted by a goat we tried to smuggle aboard, and lose a fight to a door latch. I can take being teased." He gave a little shrug, eyes flicking out to sea. "I dish it out plenty, too. Wouldn't be fair if I couldn't take it."

Her brow knit. That wasn't what she expected. If it wasn't embarrassment—then what was it? He looked wound tight, like a rope stretched too far, but she couldn't see the fray. She told herself not to ask, not to pry. And yet the question demanded an answer.

"Then what is it?" she asked quietly. "Because something's clearly eating at you."

Zale dragged a hand down his face, muttering something under his breath before finally meeting her eyes. His grin was gone, and what he offered instead was rawer, stripped down.

"You're makin' it very difficult for me to treat you like everyone else."

Nerissa blinked, the words landing heavier than she knew how to carry. The meaning was plain enough, and yet...it still knocked the wind out of her.

Her lips parted, voice catching on the single syllable that escaped. "*Oh.*"

Nerissa shifted, fingers tightening on the railing. "If I made you uncomfortable earlier...I'm sorry. That wasn't my intent."

Zale hesitated, then leaned just slightly closer, his voice low. "What *was* your intent, then?"

Nerissa froze, caught like a ship in dead wind. She opened her mouth, closed it again, the answer refusing to form. For someone who always had control of her words, her silences, she found herself floundering.

"...I don't know," she admitted finally, the words gritted out like they cost her something.

Zale studied her for a long beat, then nodded once, as if that was all the answer he needed. He leaned back against the rail, leaving the silence intact but changed—charged.

Nerissa shifted, suddenly too aware of the stillness between them. Her fingers tapped once against the rail before she said, almost abruptly, "I didn't even collect my winnings earlier."

That startled a laugh out of him. He tipped his head toward her, a half-grin tugging at his mouth. "Bran doesn't share anyways."

"So I learned," she said dryly. "Called himself the 'technical winner.'"

Zale rolled his eyes. "If you want, I'll make him cough it up tomorrow."

"No need," Nerissa murmured, her lips twitching despite herself. "I think I got enough out of it."

The look Zale gave her then was sharp with confusion. And by the tides, the way his mouth almost fell open before he caught himself—she'd treasure that look.

She leaned her elbows on the railing, letting the moment hang a moment longer before adding, "Besides...Bran's the one who deserves payback."

That earned her a grin from Zale. "Now you're speakin' my language."

She tilted her head, curious. "So what's the usual punishment for wagers gone too far?"

Zale leaned back against the rail, pretending to consider. "Depends on the crime. Hammock knots tied short, rum ration swapped with vinegar, or—my personal favorite—sabotaging his flask."

Her brow arched. "Sabotaging...how?"

"Fill it with seawater," Zale said, eyes glinting. "He takes a swig, thinks he's the cleverest man alive, and chokes on his own ego instead."

The image of Bran sputtering salt water onto the deck was too perfect. "That's cruel."

"Effective," Zale countered, watching her reaction with a hint of challenge.

She allowed herself a quiet, conspiratorial smile. "Cruel and effective, then."

Their gazes caught—brief, sharp, complicit—before they both turned back to the sea as though it were suddenly fascinating.

The quiet stretched, and Nerissa tried to smother the yawn tugging at her throat. She failed.

Zale pushed up from where he sat against the railing, brushing his palms on his trousers. "Come on," he said lightly, though there was no mistaking the steadiness beneath it. "I'll walk you back."

She blinked at him, faintly suspicious. "Afraid I'll get lost on the way?"

"More afraid Bran will spot you first and try to negotiate a truce." He grinned, offering a hand toward the steps. "And trust me, you don't want to hear his opening bid."

Nerissa eyed him for a moment, then slid her fingers into his. His grip was warm and steady as he guided her down the short flight of stairs from the quarterdeck to the main deck.

He didn't let go right away. Neither did she.

For two heartbeats too long, they walked that way, until the heat in her skin reminded her to slip her hand free. She tucked it against her side, as if nothing had happened.

Zale led her across the quiet deck and down the companionway, the lanterns below casting a dim, golden glow along the narrow corridor. When they reached Brigid's cabin, he shifted his weight, lingering a moment longer than necessary. His sleeves were rolled past his elbows, and his hand lifted, scratching absently at the inside of his forearm.

Nerissa's gaze caught on the small patch there: dry, angry-looking skin, rubbed raw from scratching. He didn't seem to realize he'd drawn attention to it, his expression easy as he offered her a faint smile.

"Here you are," he said quietly. "Safe and sound."

Nerissa inclined her head. "Thank you...for the escort."

She paused, one hand resting on the latch, waiting, half-expecting him to add something more. But Zale only gave her that faint, crooked smile of his, shadows softening the sharp line of his jaw.

"Anytime."

With a small exhale, Nerissa slipped inside, leaving him in the corridor.

Zale

Zale loitered in the corridor after the door shut, staring at the wood like it might explain her. It didn't. Of course it didn't. Nothing about Nerissa made sense—least of all the way she'd left him reeling twice in the same day.

I think I got enough out of it.

Her voice still echoed sharp in his head, smug and maddening. Enough out of it? Enough *what*? The look on his face? The fact she'd rattled him in front of half the crew? Or worse—was she hinting at something more, something he wasn't ready to name?

He dragged a hand down his face with a groan and forced his boots toward the stairs that led below. The crew's quarters were dim, lanterns guttering low. Familiar, grounding. Usually.

Tonight it did nothing to steady him.

Eon was snoring in rhythm with the sway of his hammock, Bran still muttering in his sleep about victory spoils, and Cormac grumbling faintly like a storm caught in a bottle. Zale ducked through the rows, shoulders brushing rope and canvas, until he reached his own corner.

Zale sat heavily, elbows on his knees, staring at the shadows where the timbers creaked. He should've been smug. Should've been amused that Nerissa had outplayed Bran, turned the game on its head, even turned it on him. But instead all he felt was tangled.

He scratched at his arm, where the skin itched raw at the bend of his elbow. He didn't even realize he was doing it until the scrape of his nails stung, and he jerked his hand away with a muttered curse.

Confused didn't even begin to cover it.

Because the more he told himself to keep his distance, the more Nerissa kept finding ways under his skin. And sea and stars, she didn't even have to try.

CHAPTER 22
STARLIGHT

Damarion

Somewhere in the bowels of the Astyran dungeon, water dripped in slow, maddening intervals. The cell was dark, lit only by a single lantern that swung slightly from its chain, casting long, skeletal shadows across the stone floor.

Damarion hung suspended by his wrists, arms stretched above him, his bare feet barely brushing the damp ground. His skin, usually bronzed, had taken on a grayish pallor, dry and cracked along his shoulders and neck. His hair clung to his face in sweat-soaked strands, and his breath came shallow and slow.

Seven days.

He knew it only by the rhythm of the pain. The fourth day was thirst. The fifth, the muscle spasms. By the sixth, the hallucinations began. And by the seventh, he could no longer hold the human shape without trembling from the strain.

Salt cracked his lips. His skin burned like parchment left in the sun. Every heartbeat thudded like a drum in a hollow shell.

He tried to focus on the stone wall in front of him, but his vision bled sideways. Not stone. Sandstone columns. Crimson banners. A hall with too much light, and voices speaking Astyran with clipped precision.

25 Years Ago

The court of Astyra smelled of resin and smoke—alien scents to a man of the sea. Damarion stood behind King Nereus, armored in polished abalone, a field commander chosen to represent Nautalia's strength. His trident was a spear of ceremony more than war today, grounded against the marble floor. He was not here to speak. Not to be seen. Only to protect.

But she saw him anyway.

Thalassa slipped between courtiers like a flame slipping through cracks in stone. Where her brother was sharp, she was curious; where the court was stiff, she leaned in, eyes green as cut emeralds. She should have addressed the king. Instead, she addressed him.

"You don't like these halls, do you?" she asked in a voice soft enough not to carry.

He blinked, startled. "They are...different."

"Different," she echoed, tilting her head. "That's a soldier's word for 'ugly.'"

A ripple passed through him—amusement, though he held his face still. "I *am* a soldier."

Her smile widened, unafraid. “And what does a soldier dream of, when he is not sharpening blades?”

His hand tightened on the trident's shaft. No royal had ever asked him something so disarming. “Survival,” he said finally. “The men who follow me. Making sure they see the next tide.”

“Practical,” she said. “But not an answer.”

When he frowned, she laughed softly, the sound more dangerous than any blade. “Perhaps I will ask you again tomorrow.” Then she turned, skirts brushing marble, and was gone into the blaze of the court.

The Astyran coast breathed against the night, waves lapping in a rhythm that seemed to hush even the stars. Resin from the cliffside pines mingled with brine, a strange perfume that clung to the wind. Damarion stood at the water’s edge in abalone armor that reflected the pale glow of the moon. He should have been standing guard. Instead, he was teaching a princess how to read the sea.

“Listen,” he said, lowering his voice as if the tide itself might overhear. “The sea breathes. Not just waves breaking, but the pause between them. The stillness before the draw. That’s how you know when a storm is coming.”

Thalassa leaned dangerously close to the foam, skirts damp at the hem. She closed her eyes, face tilted like she could drink the sound in. Then she repeated a phrase he had just given her in Nautalian, tripping over the consonants.

"*Su eisi mou ostrion.*"

Damarion's mouth twitched. "You just called me a clam."

Her eyes flew open, and she laughed—sharp and bright, enough to make him tense for fear someone would hear. "A clam?"

He nodded gravely, though the corner of his mouth betrayed him. "*Asterion*, not *ostrion*. Try again. Let the syllables flow like a current, not a stone dropped in water."

She pursed her lips, mimicking his cadence. "*Su eisi mou asterion.*"

This time, the syllables landed smooth and sure.

Damarion inclined his head, a rare smile breaking through his reserve. "Better."

Her eyes searched his, curious. "And what did I just say?"

He hesitated, the words catching somewhere between his heart and his tongue. "You are my starlight."

Thalassa's smile deepened, green eyes bright even in the moonlight. "Starlight," she echoed softly. "We have a similar phrase. *You are my sunshine.*"

"Ah, *aígli.*" The corners of his mouth curved faintly, though he kept his voice even. "Perhaps our languages are not so different after all."

"*Su eisi mou aígli,*" she translated. "And tell me—what is your word for teacher?"

He straightened slightly, as though the question weighed more than she intended. "*Didaskon,*" he said at last, the old Nautalian syllables rolling like a tide drawn deep.

"*Didaskon*," she repeated, savoring it, then pointed at him with mock gravity. "That's you."

He shook his head. "I am no teacher."

"Then you lie," she teased, brushing a strand of hair from her face. "Because I am learning, and you are teaching. *Didaskon*."

He had no reply. He only watched her mouth shape the word again, soft and reverent as though she'd named him something more than soldier.

Moonlight laid silver across the tidepools, turning every ripple into a mirror. Damarion's armor was gone tonight; he wore only the plain wraps of an off-duty officer, though nothing could disguise the discipline in his bearing. Thalassa leaned against the rocks, skirts damp, hair unpinned to the breeze as though she had slipped free of the palace itself.

He held something in his palm, hesitant. Not a jewel, not a crown's offering—just a stone, carved into the shape of a nautilus shell, polished smooth and shining.

Her brow arched. "A seashell?"

"Serpentine," he corrected. "The color of your eyes."

She took it, turning it in her fingers. "Not a ring, then." The corners of her mouth curled in mischief. "What would your court think of a commander who gives a princess a trinket better suited to a child on the shore?"

"They would not know," he replied simply. "And you wear it better than any jewel."

She faltered, as though the weight of the token pressed past her teasing. She looped the cord over her neck, the shell settling just above her heart.

When she looked at him again, the jest was gone. "You know this cannot last."

"I know," he said. Duty sharpened every word, but he could not pull them free. "And still—"

"Still," she whispered, closing the distance between them.

His hand rose, almost against his will, brushing the edge of the pendant where it rested at her collarbone. For the first time, his composure wavered as those beautiful eyes gazed back at him with such intensity.

He bent toward her, hesitant at first, as if kissing her might unravel everything he was. Her lips met his with fervor, banishing hesitation, and something in him broke. He pulled her into his arms, the strict soldier undone by one woman's fire.

She smiled against his mouth, and the soldier forgot his vows, his rank, the centuries of war that said he should not love her. All he knew was the warmth of her hands around his neck, the balmy scent of her skin, and the rapid beating of her heart—wild and human and wholly his in that moment.

He lowered her to the sand carefully, reverently. Her laughter, soft and radiant, broke against his chest like a wave, and his resolve shattered with it.

He whispered her name once, a benediction and a surrender both. The stone she now wore glimmered between them, cool and bright, a promise made under moonlight.

And for that single, fleeting night, the world was kind.

Weeks later, the tide had risen by the time they parted, scattering foam along the shore as though the sea itself wished to conceal them. She still wore the pendant, its emerald glint half-hidden against her skin. Damarion's hands, calloused from years of wielding spear and trident, lingered at her waist longer than they should have before he forced himself to step back.

"Rumors spread like oil," he said, voice low, rougher than he intended. "If we are careless, your brother will hear whispers before I've even returned to Nautalia."

Thalassa smoothed her damp skirts. "We *have* been careless," she admitted. "And it isn't only Vasilios who worries me." Her eyes flicked toward the cliffs above, where the torches of the palace flickered like watchful eyes.

Damarion frowned. "Who else?"

"The apothecary," she said after a pause. Her voice dropped further, a conspirator's murmur. "Alpheus. He watches too closely. Always has. I've avoided him when I can, but lately…" She shook her head. "I do not like the way he looks at me. As though he already knows something he should not."

He studied her carefully, the soldier in him cataloguing the weight behind her words. "He is a vulture. But a vulture does not bring down the lion."

"You underestimate him," she countered. "I've seen his eyes follow me across the hall. It's as though he's waiting for me to stumble, so he can pounce."

Damarion's jaw tightened. "Then we will give him nothing to see. We meet more carefully from now on. No more torchlit corridors. No more stolen moments where servants linger."

Her lips curved faintly. "You sound like a commander giving orders."

"I *am* a commander," he said. "And if Alpheus so much as breathes suspicion in your direction, I will silence him before he can speak."

Thalassa reached for his hand, threading her fingers through his with quiet defiance. "You cannot fight shadows, Damarion."

"Then I will become one," he answered.

The sea sighed against the rocks, pulling their words into its endless keeping. Yet even as they stood close, the weight of unseen eyes pressed on them, turning warmth into wariness.

The tidepool was quiet tonight, the wind carrying only the faintest scent of pine. Thalassa was already waiting when he arrived, sitting on a flat rock with her arms wrapped loosely around herself. Even in the pale shimmer of moonlight, something in her looked changed. Dimmed.

Damarion's brow furrowed. "You're pale."

"I'm fine," she said too quickly, her tone too light. She reached for his hand before he could press the matter further. "A summer cold, perhaps. Or I ate something that disagreed with me."

His fingers closed around hers, but his gaze did not soften. He could feel the fragility in her touch, as though the fire that usually danced in her veins had burned low. "It is more than that. You've been unwell for days now."

Her smile was small, almost mischievous, though it did not reach her eyes. "And here I thought soldiers were meant to be brave, not worriers. You'll give yourself wrinkles, *Didaskon*."

But his jaw remained set. "If your brother notices...if anyone notices...this is too great a risk." The words tore at his throat. "Perhaps—perhaps we should end this before it destroys us both."

Her fingers flew to the emerald pendant at her throat, gripping it as though it would lend her strength. "No," she said fiercely. "Not like this. Not with silence. I will not surrender what we have to fear and whispers." She leaned closer, her eyes sparking to life. "If we must, we'll run. Far from Astyra, far from Nautalia—just you and me and the open sea."

Damarion closed his eyes, the ache in his chest sharp as a blade. To take her hand, to flee—he wanted it more than breath. But his oaths weighed heavier than chains. "I love you," he said at last, voice ragged. "More than I should. More than I have any right. But I am sworn to my king. My post is not mine to abandon."

She pressed her forehead against his, whispering like a prayer. "Then I will fight for both of us. You'll see. Nothing will part us."

Present Day

Footsteps echoed down the corridor.

Not the heavy clunk of guards. Softer. Controlled.

Alpheus.

The man stepped into the cell with that ever-unsettling composure, a leather-bound journal in one hand and a quill already inked in the other.

"Well," he said, voice a smooth drip of oil on stone, "I believe we've reached your threshold."

Damarion didn't lift his head. He no longer had the strength to waste on glaring.

Alpheus clucked his tongue as if disappointed in a servant who'd scuffed the floor. "Seven days. No ocean. Only trace amounts of water, administered by sponge or spoon. You exceeded the longest recorded threshold by almost fourteen hours. Fascinating."

He motioned lazily to the guards, who moved forward without hesitation. Damarion didn't resist as they unshackled his wrists and hoisted him up between them.

Alpheus followed as they moved deeper into the dungeon, past bolted doors and rusted grates, until they reached a chamber illuminated by an eerie green-blue glow. At its center sat a tall cylindrical tank filled with water.

"Gently," Alpheus instructed. "Wouldn't want to kill our subject before the next round of tests."

The guards obeyed—barely. They dumped Damarion in like a sack of rotten grain. He sank instantly, lifeless as a corpse.

Then—

His body seized, curled, and shifted.

His tail unfurled with a sudden flick, cerulean scales catching the dim light in a brief, dull shimmer. His fingers webbed. His gills opened with a gasp.

Alpheus approached the glass, his quill scratching across the page.

"Remarkable," he murmured. "The physiological shift is nearly instantaneous under duress. Muscle atrophy minimal. No visible signs of brain degradation. Which begs the question…"

He tilted his head, smiling faintly.

"…just how much more can you take?"

Inside the tank, Damarion floated, eyes shut, chest rising and falling with fragile steadiness.

Calliope

Calliope's chambers straddled the line between two worlds.

Sunlight streamed in through the arched windows, gilding the coral-etched tea set that had been commissioned as a wedding gift. The walls bore Astyran silk drapes and ocean-woven tapestries. Her furniture was the finest coastal mahogany, softened by cushions the color of seafoam and periwinkle. A marriage of courtly grace and nautical lineage. Like her.

The tea had gone cold in Calliope's cup. She hadn't touched it—only turned it between her palms, the gilt handle knocking faintly against her ring.

Queen Ophelia sat across from her, regal as ever in a gown that shimmered like abalone shell. Her hair, heavy with pearls, was swept into a style that defied gravity and tradition in equal measure. Her expression was serene, but the Queen's stillness was always intentional—meant to unnerve, or disarm, or dominate. Possibly all three.

"Tell me, child," Ophelia said softly. "How are you truly?"

Calliope steadied her breath. "Leander and I...we were married the night after the...assassination." She could barely get the word out. It sat heavy on her tongue.

Ophelia's eyes flickered, relief showing in the smallest release of tension at her brow. "Good. Then the bond is sealed. Even in grief, a kingdom must see its sovereigns united."

Calliope hesitated before adding, "The treaty is less certain. Leander still believes in it, but his advisors…" She shook her head. "They whisper, they doubt. He'll need time to persuade them."

Ophelia's gaze sharpened. "And time is not something either kingdom can squander." She set her cup down with a soft click. "Have you seen Damarion? We have had no word from him these past few days."

Calliope's chest tightened. "No. Not since the wedding. I assumed he returned with you and Father."

Her mother's lips pressed thin. "He did not. And it is not like him to abandon his post."

Calliope looked down at her untouched tea, then murmured, "The guards barred me from seeing Nerissa again. They said it was under Lord Alpheus's order." She swallowed hard, lifting her gaze. "Mother, there's something wrong about him. The way he speaks, the way he controls who may enter and who may not...It doesn't feel like service to the crown. It feels like ownership."

Ophelia's expression cooled, like a tide retreating over jagged stone. "I agree. Which is why I did not come alone."

She turned slightly toward the door. "Kaelen."

The latch clicked, and he stepped into the room. Kaelen wore the polished attire of Nautalia's court, dark cloth traced with inlays that gleamed like submerged shell.

Calliope's throat felt suddenly dry. Of all the courtiers to summon, her mother had brought him. The man she had once been promised to, before the treaty had rewritten her future. Before she had traded one betrothal for another.

Ophelia's voice was calm but iron-edged. "Until this unrest is ended, he will remain at your side. Not as a soldier, but as the one person I still trust to guard you when Nerissa cannot and Damarion is missing. You are not to walk a corridor of this castle without him. Do you understand?"

Calliope forced her lips to shape the words. "Yes, Mother."

Kaelen inclined his head, courtly as ever, but his eyes lingered on her a moment longer than courtesy required. That flicker of recognition was worse than mockery. It pressed salt into the wound of what had almost been—and reminded her of everything she had chosen instead.

The teacups sat forgotten, cooling between them.

The golden light of the setting sun pooled across the floor, casting long, amber streaks over maps, scrolls, and half-drunk goblets. Leander sat behind his desk, fingers steepled beneath his chin as he stared at an open ledger he hadn't read in some time.

The door opened gently without a knock. Calliope stepped inside, her sea-silk gown glimmering faintly in the waning light.

Leander looked up at once. His expression softened. "Calliope."

"You look like you've been at this for hours," she said, glancing at the piles of parchment as she crossed the room. She no longer asked permission to enter; she simply joined him, lowering herself into a chair opposite the desk.

"Perhaps I have," he admitted, closing the ledger with a sigh.

"I came to tell you something." She smoothed her skirts, meeting his gaze directly. "My mother brought Kaelen with her when she came to Astyra. She's assigned him as my bodyguard until things settle."

Leander arched a brow, wary. "Kaelen? As in—"

"Yes." Calliope didn't flinch. "The man I was once betrothed to. Before our fathers made different arrangements."

Leander leaned back, studying her carefully. "Will it be awkward? Having him at your side?"

She shook her head. "It shouldn't be. Whatever that was...it ended the moment the treaty was drafted. I have no feelings for him. Not anymore."

Relief flickered across Leander's face, loosening something in his shoulders. "Good. Then I trust your mother's judgment. If he can be trusted with your safety, he has my approval."

Calliope nodded, then hesitated before adding, "There's more. Damarion hasn't been seen since the wedding. Not in the palace, not at the border. My mother is worried—and so am I."

Leander's brow furrowed. "Missing? Since that night?"

"Yes." She drew a steadying breath. "And when I tried to see Nerissa after the ceremony, the guards refused me. They said it was under Lord Alpheus's orders. When I pressed, he appeared himself and claimed she'd become violent and had to be sedated."

Leander's expression hardened. "That doesn't sound like her."

"I know." Calliope's voice was low, urgent. "It doesn't feel right. And it isn't only that. The day before the wedding, Nerissa swept the castle for security. She followed Alpheus down a hidden staircase in the East Tower. Behind a locked door, she said she found chains, tables, organs preserved in jars. Merfolk dissected like specimens."

Leander froze. The shadows lengthened across his face as he searched her eyes. "The East Tower hasn't been used in years. My grandfather's alchemists worked there once, but—" He broke off, shaking his head. "I swear to you, I didn't know. My father never told me."

Calliope held his gaze. "So you had no idea what Alpheus was doing there?"

"No." His voice sharpened. "If what she saw is true, then it's monstrous. And my father kept it from me." He pushed away from the desk, pacing with restless energy. "But I never would have condoned it. Never."

She rose, steady in contrast to his agitation. "Then we need to find out what Alpheus is hiding. Because whatever it is, it's already cost us too much."

The light had dimmed slightly, and Leander lit a pair of oil lamps, letting the flickering glow cast long shadows over the bookshelves and stone walls. Calliope stood near the central bookcase—a massive, double-sided behemoth that loomed like a silent judge. She met Leander's gaze as he opened a concealed panel behind it.

"Are you certain about this?" she asked quietly.

Leander nodded once. "I want to hear how he lies. And I want you to hear it too."

She slipped behind the bookcase, silent as a ripple in deep water. Leander left the panel ajar just enough for sound to pass, then returned to his seat behind the desk, back straight.

Footsteps echoed crisply outside the door. A pause. Then a sharp *rap* of metal on stone.

The study doors opened, and Alpheus entered with his usual glacial poise. He leaned ever so slightly on his silver cane, its ruby facets catching the firelight in flickers of blood-red.

"You summoned me, Your Grace?" he said, voice smooth as his entrance.

"Yes." Leander gestured to the chair across from him. "Please, sit."

Alpheus did so, adjusting his robes. "Is this about the court's recovery efforts? Or perhaps the council's push to reconvene treaty negotiations?"

"This is about the future," Leander said. "Specifically, the values this kingdom will stand for under my rule."

Alpheus tilted his head slightly. "Ah. A speech. I do love those."

Leander didn't smile. "Let me be perfectly clear. I will not tolerate the use of violence or unethical experimentation. Especially involving merfolk. Or any living creature, for that matter."

There was a pause.

Then Alpheus gave a tight-lipped smile. "Of course. I assure you, any research of that nature was halted years ago. The moment your father agreed to the betrothal, I ceased all projects that might...complicate the alliance."

"You ceased them?" Leander asked, leaning forward just slightly. "Not because they were wrong, but because they were inconvenient?"

"I am a servant of the crown, Your Grace. My duty is to further the interests of the realm. I follow the will of the monarch. Always have."

From behind the bookcase, Calliope's hands clenched into fists.

"And Nerissa?" Leander asked. "Was it the will of the monarch to keep her sedated, locked away without visitation?"

"She was...unstable. Given that she assassinated the king in full view of the court, I judged it best to keep her under close watch. For your safety."

"You made that decision on your own."

"I did," Alpheus said, utterly unapologetic. "As I have always done, in the interest of protecting the realm. You'll learn, in time, that leadership often requires unpleasant choices."

Leander stood slowly. "Speaking of unpleasant—Damarion. Do you have any knowledge as to his whereabouts?"

Alpheus blinked, the shift in topic sharp enough to draw a fractional hesitation. "No, sire."

"He was last seen on palace grounds. Queen Ophelia made note of it."

Alpheus gave a subtle shrug. "The king and queen departed swiftly after the…events of the wedding. Perhaps he lingered behind and found his own way home."

"Perhaps," Leander said evenly. "But if you *do* hear anything, I expect to be informed. Immediately."

"Of course," Alpheus murmured, and rose with a rustle of fabric and the click of his cane. "Always at your service, Your Grace."

He bowed again, just the right degree of deference, and turned to leave.

When the door clicked shut behind him, Leander waited three heartbeats before walking to the bookcase.

Calliope stepped out, her face pale but composed.

"Well?" he asked.

"I believe him," she said, voice cold, "when he says he serves the realm. I just don't think it's *this* one."

CHAPTER 23

ROTTING LIMBS AND BAD LUCK

Nerissa

Nerissa stirred as she stared at the ceiling of the cabin, the wooden beams above her blurred in the early light. Today marked nine days in human form. Even the strongest sirens would be near collapse by now. No one could stay on land for more than seven days without suffering.

She sat up. No headache. No fever. Her limbs felt strong, her breath steady. Her skin hadn't cracked, her voice hadn't faded.

I should be dying.

Instead, she swung her legs over the edge of the cot and flexed her toes. Her thigh twinged where Nestor's blade had sliced her, but otherwise...she felt fine.

Too fine.

Her fingers brushed the crook of her arm, where the bruise had since faded. If she *had* been injected with something, could that explain why she couldn't shift? If so, how long would the effect last? And what would happen once it wore off?

What if it doesn't wear off? What if I'm stuck like this?

She reached for her boots, mind racing with several possible scenarios. But even as she moved through the motions of dressing, another memory needled its way in. Yesterday's bet.

Bran's ridiculous wager that Zale couldn't steal a kiss from her by sunset. The smug grin, the expectant stares. And her own choice—tides, why had she played along? She still didn't have an answer for that question. All she knew was that it was awkward, fleeting. Yet the warmth of it lingered in her chest longer than she cared to admit.

Stop it, she told herself. *This isn't your home. You don't belong here. Don't confuse banter for belonging. And stop getting distracted. He just thinks you're a pretty girl. Nothing more. He would curse you to your face if he knew the truth.*

The sun was a merciless thing that day, bearing down on the deck like it had a personal vendetta. Even the sails drooped. Shirts were shed, boots abandoned, and tankards of water passed around like sacred relics. Nerissa's clothing clung uncomfortably to her skin, and she found herself especially missing the coolness of the deep.

Brigid had tied her fiery braid into a knot high on her head, wisps escaping in rebellion. Nerissa had followed suit, her hair twisted back into a fishtail braid. Both women had rolled their sleeves to their shoulders, blouses knotted just beneath the ribs. Less fashion, more survival. Neither of them had bothered with a corset today.

As she crossed the deck with an empty pail, Nerissa paused mid-step.

Zale stood near the starboard rail, hauling a line while gritting his teeth. Long sleeves, buttoned cuffs, not a speck of exposed skin save his hands and throat. Everyone else looked one gust away from melting into the planks, and he was dressed like it was a mild spring day.

She squinted at him. They hadn't spoken since the night before when he escorted her back to Brigid's cabin. The question left her mouth before she could help herself. "Is he…not hot?"

A voice floated down from the rigging. "Oh, he is," Bran said, draped across a support beam like a particularly smug piece of laundry. "Just not in the way you mean."

Nerissa rolled her eyes so hard it nearly gave her a migraine. "Must you start before breakfast?"

Bran placed a hand over his heart. "You kissed him, darlin'. That's eternal teasing rights. I didn't make the rules."

"I kissed his cheek. To win a bet."

"A cheek is still a face, love."

Nerissa opened her mouth to retort, but he barreled on.

"Of course," he added with a grin, flexing dramatically, "if it's a view you're looking for, I'm quite literally right here."

Without hesitation, Nerissa stepped up a few rungs of the rigging and pushed him off.

He yelped, flailing with all the grace of a fish out of water before landing in a coil of netting below.

"I'm fine!" he called, voice muffled. "Dignity's in pieces, but otherwise unbroken!"

From somewhere near the helm, Cormac muttered, "Deserved."

Brigid didn't even look up. "Aye."

Zale had paused to watch the whole exchange, amusement tugging at the corner of his mouth. But when Nerissa's gaze slid back to him—curious, assessing—he turned quickly and resumed his task, pulling the line with unnecessary force.

Nerissa frowned slightly.

Strange, she thought. Most men were eager to flaunt their muscles when the heat gave them an excuse. But Zale wore his shirt like armor—sweating through it, sleeves to the wrist, collar just shy of his throat. Perhaps that skin condition he mentioned was flaring up with the heat, and he was embarrassed of the marks it left. The images of him scratching at his neck and his arm yesterday tugged at her unexpectedly, softening the edge of her curiosity with a trace of sympathy.

Zale

Zale tied off the line harder than he needed to. It bit into the cleat like a punishment. He didn't look up. Didn't turn around. Didn't twitch an ear in their direction.

But he definitely heard it.

"Is he...not hot?"

The question had been innocent, probably rhetorical. Probably. But it landed in his spine like a harpoon.

Bran, naturally, had responded as only Bran could—with maximum flourish and minimum shame. Zale didn't have to see it. He knew the exact smirk Bran had worn. Knew the way Nerissa rolled her eyes when she was playing along but not quite laughing.

Then he felt her eyes on him. Assessing. Intrigued.

And that was a problem.

Because Nerissa was smart. Observant. If she caught on that he bared skin most days but only covered up when the lesions flared, she might piece together what he'd worked so hard to keep hidden. He'd already told her about his condition, but it was one thing to know. Another entirely to *see*. To see the cracked patches, the raw edges. To wonder, even for a heartbeat, if it was contagious. If he was something to avoid.

He'd seen that look before. Once, when a new recruit caught a glimpse of his arm during a breakout. The sailor had gone pale, muttering "leprosy" under his breath before keeping his distance for weeks. Zale had laughed it off at the time, some joke about rotting limbs and bad luck, but the sting of it had sunk deep.

Zale tugged the cuff of his right sleeve down further. He could feel the heat flaring beneath the fabric, the telltale itch of a lesion forming just below his elbow. The skin there was already tight, stretched thin and dry like sunbaked parchment.

It always started the same way. Hot days, too much sun, too little sleep. Stress didn't help. Neither did being watched.

He'd been born with this skin. This patchy, peeling curse that no one could name. Roan had guessed everything from fungus to scurvy, and Zale had stopped asking long ago. It was easier to hide. To cover up. To pretend.

Better to sweat than to explain.

He rolled his shoulders, grimacing at the pull across his back. The sweat-soaked fabric clung to his chest like a second skin—if only it *were* skin. Normal skin. Not whatever cursed patchwork his body kept trying to become.

He needed Roan. Sooner rather than later. More balm. Maybe a compress. Something to get ahead of it before it spread even further.

Because if *she* saw, he didn't know what he'd say.

Zale paced the length of the starboard rail, jaw clenched tight as the sun climbed higher, turning the deck into a skillet. The boards beneath his boots radiated heat like coals, and his shirt, plastered to his back, was starting to itch with a vengeance.

Every movement scraped. Every breath beneath the cotton caught at raw skin.

He tugged his sleeves down again, double-checked the buttons at his wrists. Brushed his thumb over the seams of his cuffs like a nervous tick.

Across the deck, someone laughed—light, effortless. Nerissa.

He didn't look.

Wouldn't.

She was probably still talking to Bran, who was likely still shirtless, still smug, still spinning some nonsense about romantic metaphors and the glory of sun-drenched abs.

And she was probably still watching Zale out of the corner of her eye, wondering why *he* insisted on dressing like he would melt in the sunlight.

The lash of a sail above snapped in the breeze. He caught the motion of

Roan leaving the quarterdeck, headed back down to the infirmary.

Zale hesitated. Then looked away.

Not yet.

He could push through. He *always* did.

Then his knee buckled.

Zale lurched against the mainmast, one hand clamping the sun-warmed wood as the world tilted off-kilter. His vision blurred at the edges, white blooming like sea foam in a storm. He blinked hard, jaw clenched.

Not now. Not in front of everyone.

He forced himself forward. One step. Another.

And then—nothing.

Nerissa

The sharp crack of rope against the mast made her glance over just in time to see Zale's face drain of color. He swayed, catching himself on the mainmast, shoulders hunched like he was bracing against more than just the sun. For a heartbeat she thought he might steady, but then his knees buckled.

"Zale?" The name slipped out before she realized she'd spoken.

He staggered forward before crumpling with a sickening thud against the deck.

"Zale!" She was already running across the deck.

She dropped to her knees beside him, reaching to feel his forehead with the back of her hand. His skin was clammy, the shirt plastered to him like it might fuse there. Heat radiated through the sleeves, his body taut even in unconsciousness. Something was wrong—she could feel it. What if this wasn't just the sun? What if his condition was worse than he'd admitted? What if—

Seconds later, Bran skidded to a halt beside her. The usual grin was gone. His fingers pressed to Zale's neck to find the pulse.

"He's burning up," Bran said tightly.

His gaze flicked to Nerissa, the familiar charm stripped away, leaving something grim. "He does this sometimes. Pushes too hard. Pretends he's fine until he drops." He looked back at Zale, jaw working. "Stubborn fool."

Eon stood a few paces off, pale eyes wide, his usual easy composure gone. He must have seen the whole thing. For once, he didn't look like he had a quip ready.

"I'll get Roan," he said quietly, quickly moving toward the stairs.

Nerissa barely registered Eon leaving. She slipped a hand beneath Zale's head, lifting just enough to keep his airway clear, and gave his cheek a firm pat.

"Zale. Wake up," she said, steady but insistent. "You hear me? Come on."

He didn't stir.

She pulled the stopper from her canteen and pressed the rim to his lips. "Here, try to drink a little," she urged, tilting the vessel forward. It just dribbled unhelpfully down his chin.

Bran crouched at her side, his eyes flicking between her and Zale. He muttered under his breath, low enough it might have been for himself as much as for her. "Come on, mate. You've survived worse."

Nerissa brushed the back of her hand across Zale's damp cheek, scanning for any sign of consciousness. Nothing. Just the shallow rise and fall of his chest. She swallowed hard. At least he was breathing.

Heavy footsteps pounded across the deck. Roan dropped to a crouch beside them, pressed two fingers to Zale's throat, then shifted to check his ribs, his limbs, the angle of his head.

"Pulse is steady," he muttered. His voice was calm, but his eyes were intent. He ran his hands along Zale's arms and shoulders, testing for resistance, then down his legs. Satisfied, he sat back on his heels. "Nothing broken. Just out cold."

He glanced at Bran, then jerked his chin toward Zale. "Help me lift him."

Bran slipped an arm beneath Zale's shoulder, Roan doing the same on the other side. Together they hauled him upright, slinging his limp arms over their shoulders. He sagged heavily between them like dead weight, until his head lolled forward and a rough groan escaped his throat.

"Easy," Roan said, shifting Zale's arm higher across his shoulder. "Don't jostle his head."

Nerissa rose quickly, falling in step behind them as they started for the companionway. Her pulse still raced, but her hands were steady now, ready to do whatever she could once they reached the infirmary.

Roan nudged open the door with his shoulder, shifting sideways so he, Bran, and Zale could fit through the entrance. Together they maneuvered Zale onto the exam table, easing him down with as much care as their strength allowed. His head lolled to the side as one arm slipped off the edge, limp and unresponsive.

Bran took a step back, running a hand through his hair, then lingered by the door. Roan moved quickly to gather supplies.

"Tell me what to do." Nerissa stepped forward without needing to be asked.

Roan didn't look up, already working. "First, we cool him down." His fingers made quick work of the laces, tugging them loose until the sweat-soaked shirt gaped open.

A low whistle escaped him. "Saints above…"

The lesions sprawled angry and red across Zale's chest and down his arms, patches of cracked, inflamed skin that looked ready to tear with the slightest movement. The sight made her feel uneasy, but not because of how gruesome the lesions were, but because of how *familiar* they looked.

She knew those marks. A memory stirred of a Nautalian spy who overstayed in human form during a coastal mission. His skin had cracked like this. It had started with dryness, then pain, then bleeding, until finally his body forced the shift to survive. And if he hadn't been able to shift?

He might have died.

Nerissa's throat tightened. Surely a coincidence. Humans could have dry skin too. It didn't mean anything. Right?

Bran shook his head slowly. "Why does he push himself like this?" His voice was low, frustrated. He dragged a hand across his face and looked down at Zale again, jaw set hard.

"He doesn't want to be seen as weak," Nerissa said quietly. Both men glanced at her, but she kept her eyes on Zale. "He thinks he has to be strong for all of you. For everyone. Even when it costs him."

Her words hung in the still air of the infirmary, sharper for how much of herself she heard in them. She knew what it was to bury pain, to swallow weakness, to stand because falling wasn't an option.

Roan shifted Zale carefully, slipping the fabric of his shirt away and reaching for the cord at his throat. He tugged it free and set it aside along with the shirt. The pendant clinked lightly against the table—a polished green stone, carved into the shape of a Nautilus shell, luminous even in the dim light.

Nerissa's eyes lingered on it for a heartbeat. She recognized the stone. Odd to see a deep-sea shell on a surface-dweller. A charm, perhaps. Sailors wore all manner of talismans.

Roan moved briskly, dunking a small blanket into the barrel of water in the corner. He wrung it out, droplets pattering onto the floorboards, then draped the cool fabric across Zale's chest and arms. Zale flinched unconsciously at the shock of coldness but didn't wake.

"That'll keep him from burning up any further," Roan muttered, pressing the blanket into place.

Nerissa hovered at the table's edge, eyes tracing the cracked, inflamed patches that spread across his shoulders. They were in the same areas where her scales appeared in merform. She told herself again it was coincidence—had to be coincidence.

"While we wait for his fever to break, we can get ahead of the flare."

Her brows knit. "How?"

"The balm," Roan said, moving toward a cupboard. He pulled out a battered mortar and pestle and set them on the counter with a clink. "I make it for him whenever it gets this bad. He'll need it as soon as his body temperature decreases."

He nodded toward the shelves along the bulkhead. "Hand me a bunch of bitterroot, beeswax, and that vial of lavender oil."

Nerissa moved at once, grateful for something useful to finally do. Her fingers skimmed across rows of jars and bundles until she found the knotted sprigs of bitterroot hanging to dry, then the wax sealed in paper, and at last the small glass vial filled with pale oil. She brought them over, placing each carefully on the table beside the mortar.

Roan gave a short grunt of approval, beginning to grind the bitterroot with slow, deliberate force. "Good. We'll mix this down, add the wax for base, oil for the sting. It won't cure him, but it'll take the edge off and let his skin mend."

Nerissa's gaze flicked to Zale's limp form on the table. *Anything,* she thought, *that keeps him from looking like this again.*

A soft creak broke the silence. Nerissa turned slightly to find Bran still leaning in the doorway, arms crossed. He didn't speak at first, just watched Zale with an expression she couldn't read.

Then his gaze shifted to her.

"I was sixteen when I joined this crew," he said, eyes drifting back to Zale. "He was ten. Scrawny, still growin' into his limbs. Didn't say much, but followed me around like a lost pup for weeks."

Nerissa glanced at him but said nothing, waiting for him to continue.

"I think he liked that I didn't treat him like a kid. And I liked that someone looked at me like I knew what I was doing." His mouth quirked faintly. "Didn't, of course. But he didn't seem to mind."

He uncrossed his arms, settling his hands on his hips. "Been giving him grief ever since. But I've always tried to look out for him. Still do."

He leaned back against the doorframe, eyes drifting toward the ceiling as if chasing down some old memory.

"Few months after I joined, we were out on the main deck, hauling nets. He was all elbows and stubbornness, insisting on pulling his weight with the grown men. Nets were heavier than him, truth be told. One slipped past the railing, wrapped round his ankle, and before I knew it he was dragged clean overboard.

"I went in after him; thought for sure I'd be pulling up a drowned boy. But he wasn't fighting, wasn't thrashing, just:..waiting. Calm as the deep. By the time we got him untangled, he'd been under nearly eight minutes." Bran shook his head, still baffled. "I'll never forget it. Hauled him back up and he was breathing like it was nothing. Just coughed up seawater and grinned at me."

Roan's rough voice cut in from where he worked at the counter, grinding bitterroot with deliberate pressure.

"I've never seen a grown man hold his breath that long without his lungs tearing themselves apart. And Zale was barely eleven."

Bran gave a soft snort. "Scared the hells out of me, but he thought it was a grand adventure. Always did have the sea stitched into his bones."

Nerissa stayed quiet, processing. Eight minutes. Even she couldn't last that long. Not without shifting. Not without gills. Curious, indeed.

Silence stretched, filled only by the slow rasp of Zale's breathing. Then, without looking at her, Bran added, "I've noticed how he is when you're around."

Nerissa's pulse quickened.

"I know I like to tease, but he seems...lighter. Happier." Bran shrugged, as though it weren't a heavy thing to say.

"Whatever it is, you're good for him."

Good for him? What was that supposed to mean? That she softened his edges, brightened his days, made him into something he wasn't?

She wasn't good for anyone. She couldn't be. Every step she took left wreckage in its wake—her parents, her kingdom, even Calliope. Alpheus had turned her into a weapon, and blood still stained her hands from a king she hadn't meant to kill. What good could possibly come from that?

And if Zale looked lighter in her presence, if he laughed more easily or smiled when he thought she wasn't watching, it was only because he didn't know the truth. He didn't know what she was. If he did, that ease in him would vanish like smoke. He'd look at her with the same horror she'd seen in too many eyes already.

No. Bran was wrong. Whatever Zale seemed to find in her was nothing but an illusion, a borrowed peace that would crumble the moment he saw her clearly.

She folded her arms tightly across her chest, locking the words behind her teeth, and stared hard at the floorboards.

Roan checked the cloth on Zale's forehead, then pressed his palm lightly to his cheek and jaw.

"Fever's starting to break," he said, removing the blanket. "We can switch to the balm now."

He scooped a dab of salve on two fingers. "Helps with the inflammation. Draws the heat out, keeps the skin from cracking." His eyes flicked to Nerissa. "Want to keep helping, or do you need a break?"

Before she could respond, Bran pushed off the doorframe with a soft grunt. "I'll let you two handle the goo."

His tone was lighter, but worry still sat behind his eyes when he glanced back at Zale. "Let me know if anything changes."

Roan inclined his head. "We will."

Bran gave Nerissa a small nod before slipping out, the door creaking shut behind him.

Roan held out the jar, and Nerissa stepped forward without a word, dipping her fingers into the balm. The salve was cool and smooth, almost jelly-like, and as she spread it carefully across Zale's shoulder, he shifted faintly beneath her touch.

His skin was still hotter than she expected, yet solid with muscle where her hand traced. She told herself to stay clinical, to think of it as a task, but the thought faltered the longer her fingers lingered, smoothing salve over the curve of his collarbone, the line of his arm.

Heat flared in her cheeks. This was no time to notice the breadth of his chest or the way his breath hitched faintly under her hand. Yet she couldn't ignore it. Couldn't ignore the sharp tug in her chest at seeing him so unguarded.

And that was the problem.

Because what good would it do to let herself feel this? She didn't know if she'd even remain with the crew, or if her body would eventually remember how to shift and force her to return to the sea. It was dangerous to get attached. Dangerous to hope.

Worse, she didn't like the lie that stretched between them, invisible but ever-present. What would Zale think if he knew the truth—that she was a mermaid, part of a people feared and hated by Astyra after centuries of war? That she had been forced into carrying out the assassination of their king?

She pressed the balm more firmly into a patch at his shoulder, steadying her hand against the rush of unease. If he knew all of it, would he look at her differently? Would he recoil, like she was some kind of a monster?

She swallowed hard and forced her thoughts back to the task, keeping her touch steady even as her heart turned traitor beneath her ribs.

Roan mirrored her on the other side, brisk and practical. Nerissa tried to follow suit, but the intimacy of the act gnawed at her, each brush of her fingers a reminder of how close she stood to a line she had no business crossing.

Zale

Consciousness came back to him slowly. Zale blinked against the dim lantern glow, his head pounding with a dull, rhythmic ache. His limbs felt like lead, sunk deep into the infirmary table, every muscle sluggish to respond.

But he wasn't alone.

The steady rhythm of someone breathing nearby reached his ears. He slowly tilted his head. Nerissa sat in a chair beside him, elbows on her knees, her frizzy braid spilling forward over her shoulder as she leaned forward.

"...Riss? What happened?" His voice rasped, thick with sleep.

She jerked upright, startled, her braid swinging as her wide eyes darted to him. For a moment she looked caught, like she hadn't expected him to wake.

"You passed out," she said at last. "Bran and Roan carried you here. We cooled you down."

Zale swallowed, his throat dry. She wasn't looking at him, not fully. Her gaze kept skimming over him and then away, never landing for long.

It was only when the cool air hit his chest that he realized why. His shirt was gone.

He glanced down, and his stomach dropped. The lesions were worse than he thought. Raw skin, cracked and crusted with blood glared up at him.

Mortification hit like a broadside. Stars, she'd seen. She'd seen all of it.

He lurched upright, too fast, ignoring the way his head spun. The room tilted violently and he nearly pitched straight off the table.

"Zale—!" Nerissa's hands shot out, catching his arm before he could topple over the side. She shoved him back down against the table with more force than finesse. "Are you trying to crack your skull open on top of everything else?"

He winced, easing back under her grip. The fire in her tone stung more than the lesions did.

"You're not impressing anyone by leaping out of bed half-dead," she went on, eyes narrowed.

Zale's jaw clenched. "I don't recall asking for an audience," he shot back. "Or a nursemaid."

Her glare sharpened. "Then maybe next time we'll leave you sprawled out on the deck and see how far pride carries you."

"Ye think I can't take care of myself?" His laugh was brittle. "I've been doing it a hell of a lot longer than ye've been watching over me."

Her hands curled into fists at her sides. "And you're doing a remarkable job."

"Maybe I'd recover faster if people stopped hovering."

"Hovering?" Nerissa's voice rose. "I was making sure you were *okay*. Forgive me if that offends your pride."

"Yeah, well, it does," Zale ground out before he could stop himself.

Her face went still, fury and hurt flashing in her eyes before she drew herself up, arms crossing like armor. He instantly regretted his words.

"If your pride matters more than your life, fine, but don't you dare make me pay the price for it."

Zale flinched, shoulders tightening, a retort dying on his tongue.

The door to the adjoining quarters creaked open, and Roan stepped in, wiping his hands on a rag. His voice cut through like an axe. "Enough. She's right. You're not proving anything by running yourself into the deck."

Nerissa's nostrils flared. She turned on her heel, braid swinging over her shoulder as she strode for the door. The latch clattered hard in her grip before the door slammed shut behind her.

Zale stared after her, pulse drumming, shame and frustration tangling hot in his chest. He opened his mouth, but Roan's voice beat him to it.

"You're being an ass." Roan fixed him with a glare flat and unflinching. "She sat in here all afternoon cooling you down, then helped me spread balm on every damned inch of you. Show her some gratitude before you drive her off."

Zale dropped his gaze, guilt prickling under his skin worse than any fever. He let out a harsh breath, then muttered, "Why'd she even bother if she was just goin' to yell at me?"

Roan leaned a shoulder against the wall, folding his arms. "Because she *cares*, idiot."

Zale let out a sharp breath, staring at the floorboards. "She's got a funny way of showin' it," he muttered bitterly.

His fingers drifted to his collarbone, searching for the familiar weight that wasn't there. The absence made his chest tighten.

"Where's my—" he began.

Without a word, Roan reached to the shelf behind him and picked up the necklace by the stone, cord looped loosely around his fingers. He gave it a casual toss, and Zale caught it against his palm.

"Stop pushing her away," Roan said before leaving the room.

Zale sat there a moment, stunned. He slid the cord back over his neck, the stone cool against his skin. Settling back on the table, he stared at the ceiling. If Roan was right, if Nerissa cared even half as much as he wanted her to...then pushing her away wasn't just cowardice. It was sabotage.

Nerissa

Nerissa stalked up the companionway, boots striking hard against the steps. The heat hit her like a wall, but it was nothing compared to the burning in her chest. She strode across the deck, only slowing when Bran leaned away from the rail to catch her eye.

"Well?" he asked, tilting his head. "How's the patient?"

"Doing just fine," she snapped, folding her arms tight. "Fine enough to be rude and ungrateful, apparently."

Bran let out a low whistle, one brow climbing. "That so? What happened down there? Did he call you a bad nurse or something?"

Nerissa blew out a sharp breath, eyes flicking to the sea instead of answering.

Bran wasn't deterred. He sidled closer, draping an elbow on the rail beside her. "What'd he do? Refuse your tender care? Make a scene about the medicine?"

She pressed her lips together.

Bran's grin tugged at the corner of his mouth. "Ah. So it's worse. He said something stupid, didn't he?"

Her jaw tightened.

"There it is," Bran said, snapping his fingers. "That's the look. What was it? 'I'm fine, leave me be'? Or my personal favorite, 'I don't need your help'? Tell me I'm warm."

Nerissa turned on him, eyes flashing. "Warm? You're blistering. He nearly collapses on the deck in front of the entire crew and then has the gall to bite back the second anyone tries to help. I've never met someone so determined to dig his own grave out of sheer pride."

Bran let out another low whistle, rocking back on his heels. "Ah. That one." He gave a small shake of his head, more thoughtful than amused this time. "Sounds about right."

When Nerissa didn't respond, expecting another jab, he didn't grin. Instead, he sighed and rubbed a hand along the back of his neck.

"He's self-conscious about it, you know. His skin. He'll let Roan see when it gets bad, only because he has to. But anyone else?" Bran shook his head. "He'd rather bleed through his shirt than let the crew think he's weak."

Nerissa's anger cooled a fraction as she clenched her teeth.

Bran's gaze stayed fixed on the horizon, his voice quieter now. "And pity? He hates it. Makes him feel like he's broken. Like the rest of us see him as less than he is. So when you came down there and saw him like that...well, snapping at you was easier than facing what he thought you might be thinking."

For once, Bran didn't look smug or playful. Just weary and protective in a way Nerissa hadn't expected.

She shook her head, frustration bubbling again. "I didn't even *say* anything about his skin. Tides, I didn't even *look* once he was awake."

"Doesn't matter if you didn't say anything. With him? He's his own worst enemy. You think he didn't notice? You think he didn't tell himself you were repulsed, that you couldn't even look at him?"

Her spine went rigid. "That's not—his skin wasn't the reason…"

"No?" Bran drawled. "Then what was it, hm?

Nerissa folded her arms tighter, lips pressing into a thin line.

Bran leaned in just a fraction. "So, if it wasn't disgust, what was it? Don't tell me the sight of him rattled you for no reason. You don't strike me as the fainting type."

Her jaw clenched, heat creeping up her neck. "It's none of your concern."

Bran's mouth quirked, though there was no real humor in it. "Maybe not. But it's his."

Nerissa opened her mouth, but Bran had already turned back to the horizon, leaving her alone with her thoughts.

Just what was he insinuating?

CHAPTER 24

YOU NOTICE TOO MUCH

Nerissa

The sun had barely crested the horizon when Nerissa gave up on sleep. She'd been awake long before dawn, her thoughts restless and circling. Now she sat on the forecastle rail, one knee drawn up, whetstone rasping against steel in steady strokes as she worked her daggers.

She hadn't been able to shake Bran's words from yesterday. The way he needled her, grinning all the while, until he'd struck closer to truth than she wanted to admit.

Avoiding him, were you? Not because of his skin, because of what you didn't want to feel when you looked.

Nerissa pressed harder against the blade, sparks scraping off the edge. Nonsense. The only reason she even followed Bran and Roan down to the infirmary was to make sure Zale was alright. She owed him at least that much.

So why did Bran's knowing smirk keep replaying in her mind?

The whetstone bit again, a little rougher this time.

Eon plopped down cross-legged on the deck nearby, chin propped on his hands as he watched her work.

"You're up early," she acknowledged the boy.

"On my way to relieve the lookout," he replied easily. Then he tilted his head, studying her. "What's eating at you?"

Nerissa blinked. "What do you mean?"

He nodded at the daggers in her hands. "You sharpen them rougher when you're stressed. I've noticed."

Her grip faltered for just a fraction of a second before she recovered, drawing the stone down the blade with more care. "You notice too much."

Eon only grinned, unbothered. "Kind of like Zale. He's definitely been stressed too."

"Stressed?"

"Yeah," Eon said with a little shrug. "He was fidgeting with his necklace last night when he came down to the bunk room, and again this morning. I don't think he actually slept, come to think of it."

Her hand stilled, just slightly. "Really."

"Yeah," Eon leaned back on his palms, satisfied to have shared his observation. "Normally he keeps it tucked under his shirt. Only takes it out when he's upset. Or thinking hard about something. It's kind of like his tell."

Her focus snapped back to the dagger in her lap. "I see," she said quietly, setting the whetstone against her second blade.

Eon pushed to his feet after a moment and padded off toward the rigging, humming under his breath.

As soon as he was gone, Nerissa stilled. Maybe she had been too hard on Zale. Maybe she should try talking to him again, now that they had both had a chance to cool off.

Yes, just get it over with.

Zale

Zale squinted against the early morning sunlight as he crossed the deck, every step heavier than he wanted it to be. His muscles still ached and his skin itched under the balm Roan had forced on him.

He'd been wrong to snap at her. He knew that. The guilt had gnawed at him all night. Nerissa had stayed with him when she didn't have to. She hadn't deserved the bite in his voice. She'd only been trying to help, and he'd thrown up walls instead.

Roan's words echoed in his head: *She cares, idiot. Stop pushing her away.*

She didn't *act* like she cared. Not openly. Nerissa kept her feelings tucked away like a dagger in her boot, sharp but unseen. As far as he could tell, she was determined to remain neutral—distant, even. But then why had she sat with him all afternoon, helping Roan tend to him, and waiting there until he woke up?

Had he misread her? Was it possible that she actually…cared about him?

No. Don't read too much into it, Zale. Just apologize and get it over with.

Eon scampered past him towards the main mast, giving him a quick nod in greeting. Nerissa didn't look up when he stopped near her, sharpening her daggers in steady strokes.

Great. She's armed.

Zale hesitated, thumb brushing over the edge of his pendant as though the worn shell might lend him a fragment of bravery. He shifted a step closer, drawing in a steadying breath.

And in the same instant, Nerissa rose abruptly.

She turned straight into him.

The impact was solid enough to knock the air from his lungs. She pitched backward with a sharp inhale, dropping her daggers as she lost her footing.

Instinct moved faster than thought. His arm shot forward, fingers closing around her forearm, hauling her upright before the sea could claim her.

She slipped and collided against his chest instead.

Her hands fisted into his shirt, clutching hard. For a breathless second she was fully against him, warmth and salt and the faint scent of Brigid's soap in her hair. Her wide eyes flew up to meet his as his grip tightened unconsciously.

He felt the exact moment she realized just how close they were.

"Easy," he murmured, voice rough.

The word seemed to vibrate between them.

Her breath feathered against his throat. One strand of her hair had come loose, catching against the curve of his jaw. He could feel the quick rhythm of her pulse beneath his fingers. Or perhaps that was his own—he couldn't rightly tell anymore.

When she found her footing, she did not let go at once.

Neither did he.

Only when the next wave crashed against the hull did awareness snap back into place. Zale released her as though burned, stepping back half a pace, heat crawling up the back of his neck.

Smooth, he thought grimly. *Nearly kill her with an apology before you even open your mouth.*

He cleared his throat, suddenly fascinated by the horizon. "Sorry. Didn't mean to startle ye."

Nerissa bent to retrieve her daggers and whetstone, though her movements lacked their usual precision. "Thank you...for catching me." She paused, then added quietly, "I'd rather not have to be hauled out of the water again."

"Don't blame ye," he muttered, rubbing the back of his neck. "Listen, about yesterday—"

"I should—" she began at the same time.

They both stopped, blinking at each other like fools.

For a brief, absurd second, he almost laughed. Instead, he watched her mouth press into a thin line as if annoyed with herself for colliding with him twice in the span of a minute. She made a small, clipped gesture. "You first."

Right. Of course.

Zale shifted his weight, dragging a hand through his hair. "I was out of line. Shouldn't've snapped at ye like that."

She sheathed the daggers with deliberate care and folded her arms tightly across her chest. Her gaze fixed somewhere near the boards between them, as though she'd rather be anywhere but here.

At least she wasn't armed anymore.

Zale forced himself to stand still. No pacing. No retreating. Stars, he could navigate a squall blindfolded, but this? This was worse.

"I know ye were just tryin' to help," he said, jaw tight. "It's just…" He exhaled sharply and pushed forward before he could lose his nerve. "Being laid out like that, I hated it. Hated that ye had to see me like that."

Her eyes snapped to his, sharp as ever. "So you'd rather suffer in silence than risk bruising your pride?"

"No." He shook his head quickly. "I just didn't want ye lookin' at me and bein' repulsed. Or seein' weakness." He tugged his sleeve down. "I've spent half my life makin' sure no one ever does. And yesterday, I couldn't stop it."

The wind tugged at her hair, loosening a few dark strands that brushed her cheek. He had the ridiculous urge to reach out and smooth it back. Her gaze softened, not by much, but enough to undo him.

"I let my insecurity do the talking," he admitted quietly. "Truth is, I wasn't angry at ye. I was angry at myself. And I took it out on the wrong person."

The silence stretched between them, unbearably tense.

"Apology accepted," she said at last, mercifully.

Relief loosened something in his chest.

"And for the record," she added. "I wasn't repulsed. By your skin, I mean."

Zale let out a breath he hadn't realized he had been holding.

She shifted her stance, arms loosening. "I simply didn't wish to sit there gawking at you while you were half-naked. That would have been...inappropriate."

He just stared at her.

All that torment in his head, and she'd been worried about propriety.

"I shouldn't have scolded you," she continued. "I was just...worried. You fainted on the deck and wouldn't wake. For a moment I thought—"

Her voice faltered. She looked away, shaking her head.

"It scared me."

Had he heard her right?

Nerissa didn't scare easily. She faced blades without blinking. Walked into conflict with her chin lifted and her shoulders squared. He had seen her bleed and not waver.

And she had been afraid.

For him.

That he mattered enough to her to cause that fear?

Stars. He was spiraling.

He swallowed hard, dragging himself back to sense. "Ye don't owe me anythin'," he said gently. "But…thanks. For worryin'."

"Well," she deflected, though her voice had lost its usual steel, "someone has to."

A corner of his mouth lifted. "Aye. Suppose that's true."

A beat passed.

She glanced toward the steps behind him. Subtle, but he caught it.

Right.

He was still in her way.

Zale shifted aside instinctively, then hesitated. The boards were slick with spray, and she had already slipped once.

"Here," he said before he could overthink it. He stepped closer again and extended his hand. "Deck's wet. Let me help ye."

His fingers hovered between them.

She looked at his hand, then at him.

For a second, he thought she might refuse on principle alone.

Instead, after the briefest pause, she placed her hand in his. Her skin was cool to the touch, but it burned all the same.

He curled his fingers around hers carefully. He hadn't noticed before, but she had callouses where she gripped her blades. Soft and unbreakable all at once.

He guided her down the first step, her shoulder brushing against his chest. Close enough that he could feel the warmth of her through the thin linen of her shirt.

His thumb moved before he gave it permission, rubbing lightly against the inside of her wrist.

She noticed, looking up at him then.

He didn't let go.

Didn't want to.

The space between them tightened, and then—

"Sails on the horizon! Bearing south-southeast!" Eon shouted down from the crow's nest.

CHAPTER 25

JUST LIKE THE TAVERN

Zale

Zale's head snapped up, the blood draining from his face. His shoulders tightened, hand drifting toward the hilt of his sword.

Beside him, Nerissa's daggers slipped free with a whisper of steel.

Nestor had taken his place at the helm, one hand on the wheel, the other raising a spyglass to his good eye. He adjusted the lens, squinting into the distance.

"Can ye see the flag?" Brigid called up.

"Orange and black!" Nestor's jaw tightened. "Battle positions!"

A murmur passed through the deck like an undercurrent. The Dravari Republic.

Zale's grip on his sword tightened, jaw set.

Nestor turned to the gunnery crew. "Load powder! Ready starboard cannon. We fire first."

Cormac was already barking orders at the nearest gun crew, his grizzled voice cutting through the din like a well-honed cutlass. "Run out that cannon—aye, like that! Powder, then ball, then waddin'! Don't make me repeat meself or I'll have ye swabbin' the latrines with yer bare hands!"

He stomped across the deck, yanking a coil of rope into place with practiced fury. His beard was flecked with sea spray, and a half-smoked pipe still hung stubbornly from one corner of his mouth like it had survived every battle since the dawn of time and wasn't about to abandon him now.

Bran arrived at the main mast with a dramatic flourish, yanking his coat on and straightening the collar. "I assume no one would mind if I contributed my dashing good looks and superior aim to the defense of the vessel?"

Brigid tossed him a powder horn without looking. "If ye don't blow yer own eyebrows off, I'll consider it a miracle."

"Darling, if I ever lose these eyebrows, it'll be in a more romantic setting." He gave a cheeky salute as he set to loading one of the cannons.

The *Black Serpent* creaked under the wind's pull, sails taut and eyes sharp. The enemy ship loomed closer now, its orange-and-black flags snapping violently against the sky like tiger stripes across storm-gray clouds. Painted teeth snarled along its bow, and figures scrambled across its deck, dark silhouettes manning weapons of war.

Eon's voice rang out again from the crow's nest. "They're gaining speed!"

Nestor didn't blink. "Let 'em."

He stood at the helm like a boulder in a gale, one hand on the wheel, the other resting loosely on the pommel of his cutlass. His expression was unreadable, but the glint in his eyes spoke of battles past—dozens, maybe hundreds. Enough to know when to charge. And when to *wait.*

"Cannons loaded and primed, Cap'n!" Cormac shouted, lighting a slow match.

"Let's send them a message," Nestor said calmly.

A deep *thoomp* echoed across the water—the warning shot from the *Serpent*, deliberately wide, a cannonball sailing past the enemy's bow and crashing harmlessly into the waves.

The enemy ship didn't slow.

Zale muttered, "Here we go."

Nestor's jaw tensed. "Brigid."

"Aye, Cap'n?" she called, eyes on the target.

"If they fire—"

A crack split the air like thunder.

The Dravari ship answered with a cannonball of its own, not wide, not in warning.

It hit the water thirty yards off their port side, close enough to spray the rail.

"—return fire," Nestor finished.

Brigid grinned savagely. "With pleasure."

She raised her arm. "FIRE!"

The air filled with smoke and thunder.

Cannonballs screamed overhead, cutting through the rigging with shrieks of tearing rope and splintering wood. The ship groaned under the assault, but she held steady, slicing through the waves like a beast with her hackles raised.

Another blast rocked the deck.

Bran threw himself to the planks just in time as a cannonball smashed into the railing inches from where he'd been standing. A geyser of salt water exploded behind him.

"Missed me, you flaming goat-milkers!" he shouted, rolling to his feet with a manic grin. His coat was scorched at the shoulder.

Ma Wen sprinted past with a bucket and a line of powder charges. "Stop flirting with death and get that starboard cannon reloaded!"

"I'm wounded, Ma!" Bran cried.

"You *will* be if you keep shouting instead of shooting!"

Near the helm, Brigid bellowed orders like a war drum, rallying the crew back into position. Cormac swore and hauled another round into the midship cannon, fingers blistered, beard singed, grin intact.

Nerissa

Nerissa crouched low next to Zale, heart hammering against her ribs like it wanted out. She gripped the hilts of her daggers so tightly her knuckles ached. She wasn't scared. Far from it. No, she welcomed the distraction from whatever had just happened between her and Zale. That was a net of confusing feelings she would much rather not untangle any time soon.

The Dravari ship was almost on them now. Grappling hooks whistled through the air, latching onto the *Serpent's* rail with ominous clanks.

Nestor stood firm at the helm, voice booming above the chaos. "PREPARE TO BE BOARDED!"

The crew roared in answer, brandishing their weapons.

Beside her, Zale drew his sword in one smooth motion, the steel catching a flash of light as he squared his shoulders against the coming wave. "You ready for this?" he asked, glancing her way.

She looked up, wind whipping her hair into her eyes. "Just another Tuesday."

He offered a grim smile. "Good. Stay close."

Another impact shook the deck. Smoke and gunpowder stung her nose. Nerissa stood, blades drawn, and took her place beside the crew.

A crash of iron grated across the ship's hull as grappling hooks bit into the railing. The first boarding planks thudded down, followed by the heavy clamor of boots.

The Dravari poured over the side, wielding short, curved sabers. They moved fast, organized, their expressions fierce beneath orange bandanas.

Brigid surged forward, intercepting the first attacker with a bellow and a brutal swing of her axe that sent him tumbling back into the sea.

Another took his place immediately.

Nerissa lunged before she could second-guess herself.

Her opponent turned too late—he hadn't expected the slip of a girl with freshly sharpened daggers. She ducked under his guard, slashed low across his thigh, then pivoted and drove the second blade beneath his ribs with both hands.

He made a strangled noise. Stumbled. Collapsed.

Nerissa stood over him, panting, blade slick in her grip from perspiration. Her breath hitched. She had trained for this—had drilled every strike, every parry—but training didn't prepare you for the warmth of blood on your knuckles. The sound a man made when he died.

Her vision tunneled. The roar of battle dulled to a low, thrumming rush in her ears. She blinked. It was no longer a Dravari pirate at her feet.

It was King Vasilios.

His crown toppled askew, his eyes wide and vacant, blood pooling beneath his body. Her hands covered in his blood, dress soaked with crimson. A sound caught in her throat, a sob she couldn't release.

No, keep it together, Nerissa.

Her chest cinched tightly, breath stuttering shallow and sharp. The deck tilted, her knees locking as the horror of that memory bore down. Every shout from the crew turned to a phantom echo of that wedding day, the gasps and cries as she drove her blade home.

Nerae, she couldn't breathe. Couldn't move.

Zale

Zale moved like the sea itself, unpredictable, relentless. His sword carved an arc through the air, deflecting a strike aimed for Brigid's back before driving a boot into the attacker's gut. He pivoted, caught another blade against his guard, twisted it free with a hiss of steel, and sent his opponent sprawling.

"Don't let them box us in!" he shouted, scanning the deck. "Keep them away from the powder stores!"

His eyes flicked toward Nerissa. She stood rigid over the body of a man she'd felled, daggers slack in her grip, eyes wide and glassy. The fight raged at her back and she didn't even flinch.

Had she been hit? Why isn't she moving?

His stomach dropped.

"Oi, Nerissa!"

She didn't so much as blink. Blast it.

Zale lunged, cutting down the Dravari charging her blind side before grabbing her arm. She resisted, stiff as stone, but he hauled her back anyway, dragging her across the deck into the narrow supply room tucked against the quarterdeck. He kicked the door shut behind them, muffling the shouting outside.

"Are ye hit?" he asked as he started patting down her arms and scanning for blood.

She shook her head. "Can't…can't breathe."

Her chest was heaving as her breaths came quick and shallow, a sound closer to choking than breathing.

He recognized that sound. She wasn't wounded. She was in shock.

Relief surged through him, chased at once by worry. He sheathed his sword and gripped her shoulders, forcing her wild eyes up to his. "Hey. Look at me. You're all right. You're here. With me."

Her throat bobbed, but no sound came.

"It's okay, just focus on breathing. Match me," he said, dragging in a deep, steady breath through his nose and exhaling slowly through his mouth. He exaggerated the motion, pressing a hand to his chest. "Like this. In...and out."

She tried. Failed. Tried again. The first attempts hitched, jagged and uneven, but he kept at it, talking her through each one, holding her gaze.

"Good. That's it. Again. In...and out."

Her breaths steadied by degrees, less frantic, more controlled. The glassy look in her eyes began to fade. She pressed the heel of her hand against her brow, shaking her head as if to shove a bad memory away.

"I—" Her voice cracked, rough. "I'm sorry. I froze. I won't again. I'm ready."

Zale searched her face, reluctant to let her back out there just yet. Then he noticed her hands, still wrapped around her daggers, still trembling so hard the blades quivered in the sunlight filtering in through a crack in the door.

"Ye don't look ready," he said softly.

Her jaw clenched, and she tightened her grip until her knuckles went white. "I am."

Zale held her gaze for a long moment, searching for any crack in her resolve. Every instinct screamed to keep her here, to shield her from the fight outside. But he saw the fire beneath the tremor in her hands, the iron in her voice despite the shake.

He gave a single, reluctant nod. "All right. But stay close."

Nerissa squared her shoulders, breath steadier now.

Zale eased the door open, the din of battle crashing back over them. Together they stepped out onto the deck, blades ready.

But while Zale met the enemy head-on, part of his focus never left her. Every movement of hers drew his eye, the way she dodged, the faint tremor still in her hands.

She said she was ready. He believed her. But he'd be damned if he let her fall while he was breathing.

Her timing was a half-beat off, her parries tighter than they should've been. Twice she barely slipped aside—once as a blade sang past her ribs, once as an axe head whistled down hard enough to split the deck. Both times, Zale's grip tightened on his sword, ready to step in—

Then the third swing came.

The Dravari's saber clipped her forearm, and a bright spray of blood arced across the planks.

Zale's gut lurched. He started forward—

But Nerissa gritted her teeth, her eyes flashing with blue fire. She pivoted hard, ducked under the pirate's arm, and spun behind him in one clean motion. Before he could recover, she drove both daggers down and wrenched him backward, sending him crashing to the deck.

The man went still.

Nerissa staggered, breath sharp, blood dripping from her arm, but she was still standing. Still fighting.

Zale froze mid-step, torn between panic and pride, every instinct screaming to cover her flank. But he forced himself still, jaw clenched. If he rushed in now, if he hovered, she'd see it as doubt. As pity.

She'd never forgive him for that.

So instead, he shifted a half-step behind her, sword raised, his eyes tracking every flicker of her movements.

She doesn't need saving, he reminded himself, though the blood on her arm burned in his vision. *Just someone who's got her back.*

Zale shadowed her closely, blade catching the arc of a cutlass aimed too near her side. Nerissa didn't glance back, didn't break stride, she just shifted with him, her dagger driving up beneath a Dravari's guard the instant he staggered from Zale's blow.

They moved again, step for step, like the rhythm had always been there waiting. His sword swept wide, forcing their attackers back, and she slipped through the gap he made, fast and merciless.

Zale felt the moment when the chaos sharpened into something steady, the two of them falling into place like pieces of the same weapon. He caught her eye briefly as they pressed forward, the heat of battle mirrored in hers.

"Just like the tavern," he said, cutting down another pirate and grinning through the sweat and smoke. "Told ye we make a good team."

This time, Nerissa didn't scowl. She bared her teeth in a smile, sharp and dangerous.

Stars, she's magnificent.

The rhythm held, Nerissa at his side, until a flash of movement caught Zale's eye across the deck.

Eon.

The boy had his sword out, stance wide, trying to parry a Dravari's brutal downswing. He managed it, barely, but the force of the strike knocked him back a step, nearly sending him sprawling over the rail.

"Damn it," Zale muttered, cutting a path across the deck. He intercepted the Dravari's follow-up, steel meeting steel with a shower of sparks, before driving his boot into the man's gut and sending him staggering into the melee.

He rounded on Eon, chest heaving. "Get back up to the crow's nest!"

Eon's face was pale, but his chin jutted stubbornly. "No—I can fight, I want to—"

Another cannon blast rattled the deck, cutting him off. Zale grabbed his shoulder, shoving him toward the ladder.

"Not here ye don't," he snapped. "Up top, eyes open. That's how ye help us."

Eon froze a heartbeat longer, then swallowed hard and scrambled for the rigging, climbing fast.

Zale turned back into the fray, sword ready, jaw tight. Better the boy curse him alive than fall dead a hero.

Nerissa

Nerissa's blades flashed, cutting down another Dravari who surged too close, but her eyes flicked toward Zale just in time to see him drag Eon out of danger. His hand was firm on the boy's shoulder, his voice sharp, leaving no room for argument. Eon's jaw clenched, but he obeyed, scrambling for the rigging under Zale's glare.

Protective. Fiercely so.

She parried a downward strike, steel jarring her wrists. Her pulse spiked, but not just from the fight. He wasn't only carrying his own battles, he was carrying everyone else's too.

And her. Especially her.

Her stomach twisted. She'd never frozen before. She'd been trained, drilled, tested in the palace guard's practice yards. But fighting defensively was different from actually going for the kill.

Except she *had* killed before. The king.

Her chest tightened, breath turning shallow. The memory surged like a tidal wave. The hall, the crown, the impossible weight of the knife in her hand. Her throat closed, vision tunneling—

No.

Nerissa squeezed her eyes shut for a heartbeat, dragging in air. In...out...steady, like Zale had shown her. Her daggers trembled, but she forced her grip tighter, forcing herself back into the present.

She would *not* freeze again. She would *not* be a distraction to him.

Because Zale would come. She knew it, with bone-deep certainty. He'd cross the deck without hesitation if she faltered. And it could cost him his life.

Her breath steadied another notch. She raised her daggers again, the fire in her chest burning hotter than the fear.

This would *not* break her.

A Dravari lunged, and she met him head-on, blades flashing with new precision. She pivoted hard, slamming her shoulder into his chest, and drove him back into the press of the melee.

She moved with more certainty now, keeping her breathing in check.

In. Out. Strike. Parry. Move.

A flash of movement caught her eye. Cormac, bellowing at the gun crew while he hacked at one attacker, never seeing the second pirate bearing down on his blind side.

Nerissa didn't think. She darted in, blades crossing in a scissor's arc that caught the pirate mid-swing. Her dagger slid home beneath his guard, and he dropped like a stone.

Cormac spun, wide-eyed, then barked a short laugh even as he swung his cutlass into another man. "Didn't see him, girl. Good eye."

Nerissa only nodded, turning to meet the next threat, her pulse steadier now. The battle raged on, steel and smoke and shouted curses. But the tide had shifted.

Brigid's axe cleaved another Dravari clean off the boarding plank. Bran's cannon boomed point-blank, the recoil knocking him sprawling but sending two more enemies into the sea. Ma Wen, apron still on, swung a belaying pin with the force of a hammer, clearing the rail beside Roan as he patched up a bleeding sailor without missing a beat.

Nestor's voice cut through the din, steady as bedrock. "Hold the line! Drive 'em back!"

And they did. One by one, the Dravari began to falter under the *Serpent's* fury.

A desperate shout rose from the enemy ship. The remaining Dravari exchanged quick looks, then began to fall back, hacking wildly as they scrambled for the planks.

Two leapt for the sea, vanishing beneath foaming waves. Another tore free a grappling hook and slid down the line, abandoning his fellows.

Within seconds, the deck was clear. The enemy ship lurched away, sails snapping hard as it veered, retreating into the smoke.

Brigid spat over the side, rolling her shoulder with grim satisfaction. "Cowards."

Cormac bellowed a victory cry that could have rattled barnacles from the hull. "Go on, ye cowards! Run home to yer orange mummy flags!"

The crew roared their triumph, the sound ragged but alive.

Nerissa lowered her daggers, her chest still heaving. She turned just as Zale strode toward her.

His long coat flared in the wind as he sheathed his sword, every line of him cut sharp by the fading smoke. His gaze locked onto hers, so direct and fierce that she flinched.

"Ye alright?" he asked, voice low, edged with concern that only sharpened the intensity of his stare.

She could only nod.

His eyes dipped, lingering on the blood streaking her arm. His jaw tightened. "Ye should see Roan."

The words left no room for argument, and she found herself moving before she realized it, slipping her blades into their sheaths and following the press of crew toward the companionway that led below deck.

On the way to the infirmary, she spoke quietly, keeping her eyes ahead. "Thank you. For before. When I froze." She swallowed hard, throat tight. "I don't...I don't know what came over me."

Zale's steps slowed just enough that she felt the weight of his gaze on her. When he spoke again, his voice had dropped into that unguarded roughness that always betrayed him.

"Ye can't do that again," he said. "Freezin' like that, it'll get ye killed. Or worse, someone else."

The words cut, but he was right. Nerissa risked a glance at him, catching the taut line of his jaw, the way his hand flexed restlessly against his coat as if he were still reaching for his sword.

"I know," she said neutrally, not wanting to argue.

"Ye've got t' be more careful," he went on, his accent thickening as the control slipped. "Can't have ye takin' steel like it's nothin, love. Not when I'm standin' three steps away."

Nerissa stopped just short of the stairs. She understood that he had been worried about her, but enough was enough. He was speaking to her as if she couldn't hold her own. Her tone stayed even, but her eyes met his squarely.

"I know what I'm doing, Zale. I'm not some damsel in distress."

"Didn't say ye were," he shot back. She raised her brows at him, and he dragged a hand through his hair and forced his tone lower. "But I've buried enough capable folk t' know the sea doesn't care how good ye are."

The fight went out of his voice on the last line, leaving only weary sincerity.

Zale's gaze softened then, the hard edge in his expression easing into something she wasn't used to seeing from him. His voice, when he spoke again, was lighter, more controlled. "You ever consider using a sword?"

Her brows knit. "A sword?"

"Puts more distance between you and your enemy," he said. His hand brushed the hilt at his hip, almost unconsciously. "Less chance of getting cut up close."

Nerissa glanced down at the daggers strapped to her belt. She'd trained with them her whole life, they were an extension of her hands. But his logic wasn't wrong. After today...maybe it was worth considering.

"I haven't," she admitted. "But I'm open to trying it." Her lips twitched faintly. "Assuming you know a good teacher."

That drew the barest smirk from him. "Aye. I might."

They reached the infirmary to find it already overflowing with the aftermath of the fight. The sharp tang of blood and sweat clung to the air, mixing with Ma Wen's herbal poultices simmering in a pot over a brazier.

Roan and Ma Wen had fallen into a rhythm that was half triage, half surgery. Roan moved briskly from one sailor to the next, long fingers swift and precise as he checked wounds, pressing cloth to bleeding cuts. Ma Wen followed in his wake, sleeves rolled high, setting out boiled needles, gut thread, and strips of linen with methodical efficiency.

Bran flopped onto a crate in front of Roan with all the grace of a bag of clams. "Doctor, if you'd be so kind, I appear to be leaking."

Roan didn't even roll his eyes. He just seized the edge of Bran's trousers and peeled back the torn fabric around a long gash in his thigh.

Bran hissed through his teeth, jerking half upright. "Sweet stars, warn a man!"

Roan pinned him back down with one hand, expression flat as a dead tide. "If I warned you every time something hurt, we'd be here until winter."

Ma Wen snorted as he passed by with a steaming basin. "And I don't have the patience to feed you through a straw, Calder. Hold still."

Bran dramatically slung one arm over his eyes. "The cruelty I endure for friendship…"

Roan glanced up as Zale and Nerissa stepped in. His eyes swept Zale, satisfied he wasn't any worse for wear, then dropped to the streak of blood running down Nerissa's arm.

"Sit," he ordered without preamble, reaching for fresh cloth.

Nerissa obeyed without protest, lowering herself onto the nearest stool as Roan approached with the cloth. She held out her arm, steady despite the sting, and let him press the linen to the gash.

Warmth spread across her skin as the blood welled up, bright and red against the white cloth. Too red.

She forced herself not to flinch. Even now, even after nearly two weeks among them, she wasn't used to the sight of it; her own blood, the wrong color. It still felt like a mask she was wearing, one slip away from cracking. She kept her gaze fixed on the far wall, jaw tight.

Roan wiped again, efficient, unbothered. To him it was only another wound, another task in an endless line of them.

To her, it was a reminder that she lived every breath balanced on a lie.

Roan finished wiping the wound clean, then reached for needle and thread. "Hold still, and maybe don't watch."

Nerissa braced herself as the sharp prick of the needle bit into her skin. Her arm twitched before she could stop it.

She refused to faint this time. Not after declaring to Zale that she was *not* a damsel in distress. She was stronger than that. She would *not* let her body betray her again.

Zale's hand closed over hers, startling her. He didn't look at her, didn't say a word, just anchored her grip in his own. The searing heat of his palm against hers was at least distracting her from Roan's stitching.

Nerissa's first instinct was to pull away—pride, habit, survival—but she didn't. Couldn't. Not with the memory of his voice steadying her in the supply room still lingering in her ears.

Instead, she let her fingers curl, just slightly, against his.

Roan tied off the last stitch, his fingers quick and sure, and snipped the thread with his teeth. He pressed a clean strip of linen into place, binding it snug around her arm.

"Keep it dry," he said, his tone brisk as always. Then his gaze flicked up to hers, pointed and deliberate. "That means *no* swimming."

Nerissa's lips pressed together. She remembered all too well Roan's expression when he caught her swimming the morning after her initiation.

"I wasn't planning to," she muttered.

"Good. I'd rather not stitch the same fool twice."

Before she could retort, he was already moving on, barking at Bran to stop squirming and sit still.

Zale shifted his grip on her hand as he pulled her up to her feet.

The infirmary was too small, too crowded. With crates stacked against the walls and others waiting their turn, there wasn't much breathing room to begin with, and suddenly she was barely an inch from brushing against him. It was the forecastle all over again.

She made the mistake of glancing up.

His normally bright green eyes were shadowed by the low lantern light, dark and intense. Close enough that she could see the flecks of gold hidden there, close enough to catch the faint scent of rum and clove clinging beneath the sweat and salt.

Ugh, why am I noticing this?

Her pulse jumped. She realized, with a lurch, that she hadn't moved since he helped her up. And neither had he.

Heat crept into her cheeks. She glanced back down quickly, tugging her hand from his. "So," she said, forcing her voice steady. "How about those sword lessons?"

"Tomorrow," he said quietly. "First light."

Nerissa swallowed, pulse still unsteady. "Guess I'd better sleep with my boots on," she muttered.

For the briefest second, his mouth curved, just enough to show he'd heard her. But he didn't reply.

And then, through the infirmary walls, came the faint scrape of Cormac's fiddle, sawing out a jaunty tune above deck as though the ship hadn't just fought off death at her rails.

Zale cleared his throat as Nerissa pulled back, adjusting the straps on her holster.

He inclined his head toward the stairwell. "Come on. You're about to experience your first post-battle revelry."

CHAPTER 26

COMPASS IN THE SKY

Nerissa

The main deck had been transformed. Cannon smoke still lingered in the air, but the crew had traded steel for tankards, wounds for laughter. Cormac perched on a barrel with his fiddle tucked under his chin, bow dancing across the strings in a quick, rollicking tune that set the planks humming beneath their boots.

In the cleared space at the center, Eon threw down the gauntlet with youthful bravado. "Come on, Bran, bet you can't keep up!"

Bran flung his coat aside and strutted into the circle. "Child, you're about to witness greatness."

What followed could only loosely be called dancing. Eon stomped and spun, all elbows and knees, grinning from ear to ear. Bran countered with a flourish of ridiculous bows, exaggerated kicks, and a twirl that nearly sent him sprawling. The crew howled, cheering and clapping time.

Brigid had stationed herself at the edge of the revelry, arms crossed, eyes sharp as ever despite the rim of exhaustion clinging to her shoulders. Her hair, usually bound in a severe braid or knot, was tumbling wild around her shoulders instead, the humidity lending it a stormy volume that made her look even fiercer, if less composed. She'd been watching the dancing with open skepticism, like the very notion of joy offended her battle-worn sensibilities.

Which, of course, made her an irresistible target.

Nestor spotted her from across the deck, his wide shoulders swaying a little with the rhythm of Cormac's tune, a half-empty tankard in one hand and a twinkle of mischief in his eye.

He approached like a man on a mission. "Brigid."

She didn't look at him. "Don't."

"Brigid," he said again, offering his hand like a knight to a particularly unimpressed queen. "I'm callin' in a favor."

She eyed him suspiciously. "What favor?"

"The one where you don't leave me lookin' like a one-legged dog at a dance."

She eyed him. "I've seen ye dance. That's nae far off."

"Then pity me," he said, taking her wrist before she could retreat. "Just one."

She tried to resist. She really did.

But a reluctant smirk tugged at the corner of her mouth, and with a huff that sounded more like surrender than protest, she let him lead her toward the open patch of deck.

Someone let out a cheer as they stepped in, and Cormac shifted the tempo to something brisk and jaunty.

Then, to everyone's amazement, they danced.

Not stiffly. Not awkwardly. But with a rhythm that spoke of years spent side by side, dodging cannon fire and commanding storms. Brigid's movements were sharp, precise, and powerful. Nestor matched her beat for beat, his steps surprisingly light for a man built like a ship in human form.

They spun once, twice, then stomped in unison as the crew clapped along.

The crew roared when Brigid dipped Nestor, and the man came up laughing like he'd just won a bet with the sea itself.

The fiddle reached its peak, and the two of them bowed with dramatic flair.

The applause was deafening.

Nerissa lingered at the edge, arms folded, watching. She couldn't quite bring herself to step into the circle, not with all eyes blazing and the music thrumming wild in her chest. This wasn't her world. She was better off on the sidelines.

A nudge at her shoulder made her glance up.

Zale stood beside her, smirking. "Don't even think about hidin' back here."

"I'm not—" she began, but he only extended his hand.

"Come on," he said over the music, eyes glinting in the lantern light. "You survived your first boarding. That earns you a dance."

She stared at his hand, then at the circle of laughing pirates, every instinct screaming to stay put.

"I'll pass," she said with zero confidence, folding her arms tighter.

Before Zale could reply, Ma Wen appeared at her other side, silent as always, and pressed a small cup into her hands.

"You're welcome," he said flatly, before turning and disappearing back into the crowd.

Nerissa scowled down at the cup before bringing it to her nose to sniff the contents. The sweet, pleasant aroma was in stark contrast to the bite of rum. It was the same drink Ma Wen had shared with her from his personal stash. She took a small sip, and heat immediately bloomed in her chest, not burning, just warm.

Zale leaned over, inspecting her drink. "Ah, looks like you've found your drink preference."

"So it seems," she knocked the rest back, feeling her pulse quicken and her inhibition lessen. "What is it, anyway?"

"Sake," he answered. "Mind yourself though; it may taste sweet, but it'll still bite."

"I like it." She set the empty cup down on a nearby barrel. "I just won't follow it up with Cormac's personal brew this time."

Zale laughed at that. "Thank the stars for that. My boots thank you as well."

"Very funny," she glared at him.

Zale's grin deepened. "If you're brave enough to drink Cormac's mystery brew, then you're brave enough to dance"

She scoffed, trying not to smile. "That's not the same thing."

"Aye, but both'll make your heart race," he winked.

Before she could come up with a retort, his hand shot out, fingers warm as he caught hers and pulled her forward. In a blink she was spun into the circle, momentum carrying her right into the thrum of Cormac's fiddle and the pounding of boots on wood.

The crew whooped, clapping in rhythm. Bran threw his arms up dramatically, shouting, "At last! Our new recruit joins the revels!"

Nerissa's eyes went wide. She had no idea what she was doing. Dancing with legs was nothing like swimming with fins. This was all clumsy gravity and stomping feet. She wasn't much of a dancer anyway; such things had belonged to Calliope, to banquets and pageantry, not to her.

Her boots tapped awkwardly against the planks, shoulders stiff, arms uncertain. Nerissa felt like a puppet with its strings tangled.

Zale was grinning like an anglerfish, trying not to laugh. "Relax," he urged, guiding her through the steps. "Just follow me."

"I *am*," she snapped through gritted teeth, nearly colliding with a barrel as he spun her.

Bran's cackle rang out over the music. "She moves like a crab with two left claws!"

That earned him a dagger-sharp glare from Nerissa, but it only made the crew howl louder, stomping in rhythm to Cormac's fiddle.

Zale leaned close enough so that she could hear him over the noise. "Ignore them. Watch me."

She did, and slowly, awkwardly, her steps began to sync with his. The stiffness bled out of her shoulders, the rhythm seeping into her bones despite herself.

And then, suddenly, it wasn't awkward anymore. It was exhilarating.

Zale spun her again, this time with enough force that her braid whipped over her shoulder, and when he caught her back, she was laughing, an unguarded, breathless sound that didn't seem to be coming from her.

The crew roared with their approval, stomping and clapping louder, the deck alive beneath their boots.

Zale's grin widened. "There it is."

He didn't stop there. He guided her into a quick turn, then another, drawing her closer each time until their shoulders brushed, until her pulse beat faster than the fiddle's reel. His palm slid briefly across hers as he switched their grip, grounding her even as the world tilted with the rush of music and movement.

She spun, boots striking the planks in something almost like rhythm now, her braid unraveling, her breath coming quick, but she didn't care. For once, she wasn't the handmaiden, the exile, the assassin. She was just a girl spinning across a deck, letting loose with her comrades.

Zale caught her again, steadying her, and for the briefest heartbeat the world narrowed. His hand was firm at her waist, anchoring her. His eyes locked with hers—bright, alive, and far too close.

The heat of the sake pulsed through her veins, blurring the lines of sense and caution she normally clung to. She shouldn't be enjoying this. Not this much. Not with him. Zale was a human. The kind of man she had every reason to keep at arm's length.

And yet.

Her pulse tripped, quick and traitorous. The music surged around them, but for that single breath, she could have sworn it was only the two of them moving in rhythm, the tilt of his face close enough to steal the air from her lungs.

She told herself it was the drink, loosening her thoughts, making them reckless. And maybe it was. Because she didn't pull away.

Not until Bran whooped somewhere behind them, the crew's laughter crashing back in like a wave and breaking the moment.

Zale lingered a second longer, his gaze still holding hers, before he finally released her hand and guided her out of the circle. His touch at the small of her back was feather-light, almost casual. Almost.

They slipped toward the rail where the air was cooler, and the sea breeze sharp.

Nerissa leaned against the wood, breathless, her braid half undone and strands plastered to her cheeks. Her chest rose and fell too fast, and no matter how hard she tried, her heartbeat refused to steady. The echo of Zale's hand at her waist burned like a brand.

He rested one hand on the rail beside her, grinning crookedly, hair damp at his temples. "Not bad for your first dance."

Nerissa shot him a look, though her lips twitched despite herself. "I nearly broke your foot twice."

"Three times," he corrected, then shrugged. "I forgive ye."

That crooked smile tugged at something in her chest. She dragged her gaze away to the sea, trying to smother the warmth curling under her ribs. This was exactly why she kept her guard up. Or tried to, anyway.

Her voice came out drier than she meant, an armor against the wild buzz still in her head. "This is why I don't drink."

Zale chuckled, low and amused. "One cup and you're blaming the drink for enjoying yourself?"

Yes, she thought. Because the alternative was far more dangerous.

A lighter set of footsteps padded up beside them. Eon leaned his elbows on the rail, cheeks still flushed from dancing, his blond hair haloed by the lanternlight. Nerissa thanked the tides for the interruption.

"Look up. See that cluster, just above the mast?" Eon pointed toward the sky, eyes bright.

She followed his gesture. The stars in question were strung together like the frame of a harp.

"That's Lyra, my favorite," he said with quiet reverence. "They say it's Orpheus's lyre, the one that could charm anything. Even the sea. Imagine that."

Nerissa's chest tightened at the name. *Lyra.* For a moment she wasn't on the *Black Serpent's* deck but back beneath the waves, sitting shoulder to shoulder with Lir, whispering secrets about the surface world and imagining what it would be like to walk among the humans. Back when Nerissa was naïve enough to be curious about such things. Lir had been like a sister to her, closer than anyone after her parents were gone.

But grief had hardened Lir, pulled her into the Court of Sirens. Nerissa could still remember the hurt in her friend's eyes when she refused to follow. That choice had cracked something between them, something that had never healed. The memory ached as much as it warmed.

She blinked rapidly against the melancholic memory. "It's beautiful."

"It's hopeful," Eon said. "A song so strong, the sky remembered it."

He grinned, rocking on his heels as he continued. "Cormac told me sailors used to follow it on long voyages 'cause Lyra points toward Vega, the brightest star up there. Like a compass in the sky. Isn't that brilliant?"

Neither Nerissa nor Zale spoke right away, but Eon didn't seem to mind. His eyes stayed fixed on the constellation, a smile tugging at his mouth.

Zale lingered beside Nerissa, his shoulder brushing hers as he leaned against the rail. She shouldn't want him to stay so close, shouldn't care if he did. And yet every time she tried to push the thought aside, her body betrayed her, skin prickling at the heat of his nearness.

"Oi, lover boy! Quit loitering and come lose at cards like a proper pirate!" Bran's unmistakable drawl came from across the deck.

Zale stiffened. The crew's laughter rippled outward, but his jaw tightened, eyes still fixed on Nerissa. For a beat, it looked like he might ignore Bran entirely, like leaving her side was the last thing he wanted.

Then, reluctantly, he huffed a laugh. "Duty calls."

But when he straightened, his grin was a shade forced, the kind that didn't reach his eyes. His fingers brushed her arm on the way past, so quickly it might've been accidental, but not quick enough to erase the warmth it left behind.

Eon sidled up beside her, arms folded on the rail. "You fought really well today."

She glanced over, surprised but not displeased. "Thank you."

He nodded, eyes flicking to the stars, then back down. "Where'd you learn to fight like that?"

Nerissa hesitated for a beat. "I was raised by a soldier," she said. "He taught me how to defend myself. And protect others."

Eon's brows pulled together. "Wish I could fight like that."

She looked at him again, more carefully now, at his wiry frame, the faint bruises on his forearms. "You see what others don't."

"I hide," he said, voice low. "Up in the crow's nest. Out of the way."

"You keep lookout," she corrected. "That's not nothing."

"It feels like nothing." He scraped a fingernail across the rail. "I want to be brave. Like the rest of the crew. Like you. I want to matter when things go wrong."

She studied him for a long moment, then said quietly, "Eon...bravery doesn't always look like swinging a blade. Sometimes it looks like climbing to the highest point and watching for danger, even when it's easier to pretend it isn't coming."

His shoulders shifted slightly. "But I want to help more than that."

"You will," she said. "One day, when it counts, you'll surprise even yourself."

Eon looked over at her, hope flickering behind the doubt. "You really think so?"

"I know so," she replied, with a faint smile.

He didn't say anything else, just turned his gaze back to the sea. But this time, he stood a little straighter.

CHAPTER 27

NEVER ASSUME THE FIGHT'S OVER

Nerissa

The first light of dawn broke softly across the horizon, painting the sea in pale gold. Nerissa slipped quietly from the quartermaster's cabin, leaving Brigid still asleep in her cot, and made her way up to the main deck.

Zale was already there.

He stood near the railing, sword in hand, testing its weight with a few lazy arcs through the air. The white linen shirt he wore hung half-laced at his throat, sleeves rolled to his elbows, the morning light catching on the curve of his forearms. With the sea breeze tugging at the loose fabric, he looked like he'd stepped straight out of one of the scenes in *Stormbound Hearts*.

Nerissa grimaced inwardly at the thought. Fathoms below. Absolutely not. She refused to start comparing Zale to Eon's favorite romance novel.

Her gaze flicked instead to the patches of skin that had looked so raw only two days ago. The lesions had faded significantly, looking like half-healed scars today. She secretly felt flattered that he was comfortable enough to expose any skin in front of her.

"Mornin'," Zale said simply, glancing her way at last.

Nerissa dipped her chin in acknowledgment as she approached.

He shifted the blade in his hands, then raised it upright between them, hilt up, edge angled toward himself. One hand gripped the base just beneath the guard, the other braced beneath to steady it.

"Thought we'd start simple," he said, offering her the sword.

Nerissa stepped closer. She wrapped both hands around the hilt, feeling the leather bite cool against her palms. The weight was much heavier than her daggers, balanced differently, but her wrist adjusted instinctively, testing the give and pull of the steel.

"Feels clumsy," she admitted.

"That's 'cause you're fightin' it," Zale said, stepping closer. "Stop strangling it. Sword does half the work if you let it. Think of it as an extension of your arm."

He moved behind her, close enough that his presence pressed like heat against her shoulder. "First lesson: stance."

She eyed her weapon doubtfully, shifting weight from one foot to the other.

"Plant your feet," he instructed. "Not too wide. Shoulders square, knees bent, like you're bracing for a wave. Your balance is what keeps you alive, not your swing."

Nerissa obliged, adjusting her stance until it felt...decent. But Zale's brow furrowed as he studied her. Was she doing it wrong?

"Close," he said at last. "But you're leaning too much on your back foot. You'll topple if someone presses."

Her chin lifted. "I won't topple."

"Mm." He stepped closer, his shadow falling across hers. "You will."

Before she could argue, his hand brushed her elbow, nudging it down, then his palm settled lightly against her hip, guiding her weight forward. The contact was brief, innocent, yet heat seared through the fabric like it was anything but.

She needed to get a hold of herself.

"Better," he said near her ear.

Nerissa tightened her grip on the sword, pulse quickening despite herself.

Zale drew his own sword, tapping the tip of the blade against the deck. "Alright. You've got your stance. Next is footwork. If you can't move right, the blade won't matter."

He took a deliberate step forward, his weight shifting smoothly between his feet. "Forward step. Front foot moves first, back foot follows. Don't drag your heels."

Nerissa mirrored his movements carefully.

"Good," he said. "Now back." He shifted in reverse, back foot sliding first, then the front following. "Always return to base. Balance is everything."

Once again, she mimicked what Zale demonstrated.

"Side step," Zale continued, gliding to the right. "Plant, then pull the other foot. Don't cross your legs, or you'll just trip yourself."

Nerissa moved sideways as instructed. She glanced at him from the corner of her eye. "Feels unnatural."

"Means you're doin' it right," he said with a grin. "Unnatural becomes natural after you've bled for it enough times."

He shifted again, this time into a long, fluid lunge. His back leg stretched, front knee bent, sword thrust forward in a straight line. "And the lunge. Quickest way to close distance. It'll either win you ground or cost you your neck if you overextend."

Nerissa hesitated, then mirrored the motion, her braid slipping over her shoulder as she sank forward. The sword wavered slightly in her grip, but the form was there.

"Not bad," Zale said, straightening with ease. "You've got balance. Just need to trust it."

She exhaled, shifting back into the ready stance he'd shown her. "Easier said than done."

Zale smirked, circling her slowly. "Good thing I've got all morning."

He rolled his shoulders back, lifting his blade into guard. "Footwork's half the fight. The other half is learning the cuts. Four basics. Master these, and you'll survive long enough to pick up the rest."

He raised the sword high, point angled slightly back. "First—uppercut. Straight down. Put your weight behind it, but don't overcommit. You miss, you're wide open." He brought the blade down in a clean vertical arc, the sound of steel cutting air sharp in the morning quiet.

Nerissa adjusted her grip, lifted her own blade, and mimicked the motion. Her swing was neat, controlled, if a little stiff.

"Loosen the shoulders," Zale murmured. "You're not chopping wood."

Her lips pressed into a line, but she tried again. Smoother this time.

"Better," he said.

He lowered the tip, then drew it up in a rising arc. "Second: undercut. Comes from below. It's faster, harder to see coming. Most useful for breaking through guard." His blade flashed upward, stopping just shy of an invisible target.

Nerissa did as she was told. She steadied her stance quickly and reset.

"Good." He stepped closer, watching her feet. "Keep them braced, don't let the cut pull you off balance."

Zale shifted into the next stance, pivoting his hips as he swung level with his waist. "Middle slash. Horizontal. Torso or arms—whatever's open. Power's in the hips, not the arms. Remember—you're guiding your blade, not wrestling it."

Nerissa followed suit, her movement cleaner this time, her body starting to find its rhythm.

Zale nodded once, approving. Then he angled the sword forward, weight centered, the line of his body taut with precision. "Lastly, thrust. Straight. No flourish, no wasted motion. Quickest way past someone's guard." He drove the point forward in a sharp, fluid extension, then withdrew.

Nerissa copied him, her strike a touch too hesitant.

"Faster," Zale said, stepping back to give her room. "Sword only works if you commit."

She tried again, sharper this time.

A slow smile tugged at his mouth. "There you go."

Zale let his blade rest against his shoulder, watching her stance. "Good.

Now let's see if you actually remember it."

Nerissa's brows lifted. "Already?"

"Best way to learn," he said, mouth curving into something that wasn't quite a smile. "Follow my call."

He stepped back just enough to give her room and barked the first command. "Uppercut!"

Steel flashed as Nerissa brought the sword down in a vertical strike. Still a little tight in the shoulders, but strong.

"Undercut!"

She reversed, blade slicing upward, her braid whipping with the motion.

"Middle slash!"

Her hips turned, carrying the sword in a clean horizontal arc. This time, it whistled sharply.

"Thrust!"

Nerissa lunged, the blade darting forward. Too cautious on the first attempt.

"Again!" Zale snapped.

She drove the sword forward a second time, stronger, more certain.

He gave a single, sharp nod. "Better. Again—uppercut. Undercut. Slash. Thrust."

She flowed through the sequence, sweat beginning to bead at her temple. She found her rhythm. Strike, reset, strike again.

Zale lifted his blade, tilting it into a guard position. "Good. Now, offense gets you nowhere without defense. Half the fight is knowing how to keep steel out of your ribs. Just follow along."

He angled his sword overhead, holding it horizontal. "Upper parry. Stops a vertical strike before it splits you open. Blade flat, wrists firm."

She copied him, her own sword steady above her head.

"Good," Zale said. "Now lower parry." He dipped the blade toward the deck, angled to catch an undercut. "Block the upward swing. Simple, but easy to forget in the moment."

Nerissa mirrored the motion, the stance awkward but manageable.

"Side parry." Zale shifted again, sword vertical at his shoulder. "Deflects a middle slash. Don't meet the blow head-on—redirect it. Less brute force, more control."

She tested the position, rolling her wrist until the balance felt right.

"And finally, thrust parry." He stepped forward, thrusting lightly at the air, then caught his own imaginary strike with a short diagonal slash. "You don't stop the thrust; you shove it aside."

Nerissa adjusted her blade and mimicked the movement, sharp and decisive.

Zale lowered his sword, watching her stance. "Not bad. Remember: defense first. A good block keeps you breathing long enough to land your counter."

When she finished, Zale lowered his blade and gave her a look that was part appraisal, part challenge. "Not bad. Now keep at it until it feels like instinct. I'm not handing you a blade so you can freeze up in the middle of a fight."

Nerissa's jaw tightened. "I told you it won't happen again."

Zale's eyes caught hers, sharp and unyielding. "Prove it."

Nerissa forced her grip steady on the hilt, but her mind churned. Training underwater had been different—fluid, weightless, every strike carried on momentum rather than anchored by ground. Footwork hadn't existed in the same way; the current decided whether you advanced or fell back. Here, every inch had to be earned, every stance rooted or risk toppling.

She squared her shoulders. She would not falter again. Not in front of him. Not in front of the crew. She refused to be a liability.

If he wanted proof, then he would have it. She was more than ready to test herself against him.

Her eyes lifted to meet his, steady now, her blade angled in silent challenge.

Zale didn't answer. He moved.

Steel cut the air as his sword came down in a sudden vertical strike, sharp and fast. Nerissa barely got her blade up in time, bracing overhead in the upper parry he'd shown her moments ago. The impact rattled down her arms, forcing her knees to bend, but she held.

"Good," Zale said at last. He didn't ease the pressure. If anything, his blade pressed harder against hers, testing her stance, her balance, her resolve.

Nerissa ground her boots into the deck, meeting his weight with her own. Her pulse thundered in her ears, but she didn't yield an inch.

Zale broke the clash first, stepping back with a flick of his wrist before sweeping in again, this time with a rising cut.

Nerissa dropped low, angling her blade down to meet his. Sparks jumped as edge met edge, the impact jarring through her shoulder. She hissed but held, then shoved back hard enough to knock his swing off line.

"Better," Zale said, circling. He shifted again, faster now, hips driving into a horizontal slash aimed at her ribs.

Side parry. Redirect, don't block.

She snapped her sword vertically, catching his strike and letting the blade glance away. The momentum spun him just enough that Nerissa seized her chance, stepping in with her own short slash toward his side.

Zale turned at the last instant, his blade intercepting hers with a sharp clang. The faintest grin tugged at his mouth.

"You're learning."

He pressed forward, his blade darting into a thrust aimed square for her chest.

Nerissa twisted, slashing across his line just as he'd taught. The point of his sword jerked wide, missing her ribs by inches. Her first clean deflection. She didn't waste the chance, snapping her blade forward in her own thrust.

Zale pivoted back, parrying easily, but the gleam in his eyes betrayed his approval. "Not bad at all."

They circled each other, breath coming heavier now, steel whispering in quick exchanges as he drove her through the motions again—uppercut, undercut, slash, thrust. Each time she met him a little faster, a little steadier, her counters less hesitant. Her forearm throbbed under the bandage, but she refused to slow down.

Zale's boots shifted forward, closing the last sliver of distance until she could feel the heat of him through the thin space between their bodies.

His breath brushed her cheek.

"Startin' to look less like a liability," he murmured.

The low rumble of his voice did something inconvenient to her focus.

She lifted her chin, refusing to yield even an inch. A slow smirk curved her lips. "Give me a real challenge."

For a heartbeat, he only looked at her.

There was something in his narrowed eyes, assessing, almost amused, that made her pulse quicken.

"You asked for it."

He broke the bind with a sharp twist.

This time he did not hold back.

His blade struck harder, faster. Nerissa met him swing for swing, feeling the familiar cadence of attack and response, pressure and release.

She caught an undercut and redirected it cleanly. Slipped past a thrust. Dared a counter that nearly grazed his shoulder.

Exhilaration surged through her.

I can do this.

But then his pace shifted. The next downward strike came heavier than she anticipated. She brought her blade up half a second too slow. In the blink of an eye, his sword hooked hers near the hilt and wrenched her weapon free from her grip.

The clang of steel hitting the deck echoed loudly. Nerissa froze, chest heaving, hands empty.

Zale angled his blade down, the point hovering steadily at her sternum.

He was grinning. Wolfish, infuriatingly pleased.

"Confidence is key," he said evenly. "But don't get cocky."

He lowered the weapon and stepped back, letting her catch her breath.

Nerissa bent, fingers closing around the hilt of her fallen sword. Instead of bristling, she straightened with calm precision, the faintest spark of satisfaction flickering in her chest.

She rolled her shoulders once, lifted the blade into guard, and met Zale's eyes head-on. "Again."

Zale eagerly obliged.

They came at each other again.

Faster.

Steel rang in rapid succession, each strike harder than the last. Nerissa felt the rhythm settle deeper this time. Not frantic, not reactive.

Intentional.

Zale pressed her, driving her backward half a step. She pivoted, boots gripping the deck, redirecting the force instead of meeting it head-on.

He adjusted.

So did she.

Their blades blurred, sparks flashing in the afternoon light. The deck seemed to fall away beneath the cadence of their clash — strike, parry, turn, bind.

He was smiling again.

Good.

Let him.

Nerissa shifted her stance deliberately, allowing the smallest opening at her left side.

His eyes flicked to it, and he took the bait, stepping in with a confident downward cut meant to overpower her guard.

But this time, she was ready.

Instead of bracing against the strike, she slid inside it.

Her blade angled low, catching his near the hilt. She twisted sharply with precise leverage and stepped through his centerline.

His balance shifted.

Too late, he realized it.

She drove her shoulder forward and swept her leg behind his.

Zale hit the deck hard on his back, the impact knocking the breath from him. His sword skidded across the planks, clattering out of reach.

Nerissa recovered smoothly, pivoting to face him. In one clean motion, she angled her blade down, the tip hovering just above his heart.

His chest rose and fell sharply as he blinked up at her, stunned.

"How," he demanded between breaths, "did ye manage that?"

A slow, satisfied smile curved her lips.

"I'm a fast learner."

She withdrew her blade a fraction but did not lower it completely.

"And," she added lightly, "I was trained under a soldier."

Curiosity flickered in his expression at that, but he masked it quickly.

“A soldier, eh?” he muttered, pushing himself up onto his elbows. “Explains a lot.”

Nerissa allowed herself a small, victorious lift of her chin.

“You yield?”

Zale’s eyes flicked to hers.

And something in them sharpened. “Not quite.”

Before she could react, he moved.

He rolled sharply to the side and hooked her ankle with his boot, yanking hard.

For one dizzying second, the sky spun above her as she lost her balance. Her blade flew from her grasp as she pitched forward with a startled breath, colliding into him.

They hit the deck together in a tangle of limbs, the impact knocking the air from both of them.

Her palms braced against him instinctively. His hands had caught her by the waist to steady the fall.

Too close.

Far too close.

Her braid had slipped over her shoulder, dark strands brushing his collarbone. She could feel the solid rise and fall of his breathing beneath her.

And his hands were still at her waist.

"Lesson two," Zale said, slightly breathless, a slow grin tugging at his mouth, "never assume the fight's over."

Nerissa stared down at him.

He looked entirely too pleased with himself for someone currently pinned beneath her.

"You fight dishonorably," she informed him coolly.

"Says the woman who baited me into overcommitting."

Her mouth twitched despite herself.

"Am I interrupting," Bran drawled from somewhere far too close, "or should I give you two a moment?"

Nerissa froze.

Zale's grin only widened.

Bran leaned casually against the rail, arms folded. "Because from where I'm standing, this looks less like sword practice and more like a courtship ritual."

Nerissa scrambled upright at once, stepping back with rigid precision and retrieving her sword. "There is nothing to interrupt," she said crisply.

"Mm," Bran hummed. "Aye. Very instructional, I'm sure."

Zale remained flat on his back for one lingering second longer than necessary, hands folded behind his head now, thoroughly unbothered.

"Just advanced instruction," he said lazily.

Nerissa shot him a warning look.

Bran's gaze flicked between them, entirely unconvinced. "Right. Shall I fetch the captain? I'm certain he'd appreciate the demonstration."

Zale finally rolled to his feet, retrieving his blade and offering her an infuriatingly satisfied grin.

"Ready for lesson three?"

"I think not." Nerissa's eyes narrowed. "I should check in with Brigid, see what work she wants from me today."

Zale tilted his head, studying her in that way that made her feel assessed rather than observed. "Runnin' off now? Thought ye were a fast learner."

Heat pricked at the back of her neck.

Bran made a low, thoughtful sound. "Aye. Just when it was getting interesting."

She ignored them both.

"I prefer my lessons without an audience," she said coolly, handing her practice sword back to Zale.

"Shame," he murmured, voice pitched low enough that Bran wouldn't hear. "Lesson three might've been the one where ye win."

Her gaze lifted to his, deliberately ignoring the way his fingers brushed hers as he took the weapon.

"Don't underestimate me," she replied quietly.

For a fraction of a second, something flickered in his expression. Surprise, then reluctant admiration.

Good.

She stepped past him.

Her shoulder brushed his as she did. Not accidental.

His breath hitched, subtle, but she caught it.

A small, private satisfaction unfurled in her chest.

Behind her, Bran gave a low whistle. "Oh, he's done for."

Nerissa did not turn around.

But she allowed herself the faintest, almost imperceptible smile as she descended the steps.

Lesson three, indeed.

CHAPTER 28

FAMOUS LAST WORDS

Nerissa

Every morning since their first lesson, she and Zale had met at first light, blades flashing in the pale dawn. Daggers still felt like home in her grip, but she was learning to trust the weight of a sword—learning to trust him, too. He pushed her hard, as if daring her to break, and she met him strike for strike until her arms ached and her lungs burned. And yet, each time, she walked away a little steadier, a little sharper.

What unsettled her more than the swordplay was *him*. The way his focus locked onto her, the curve of his grin when she caught him off guard, the way he looked at her like he saw more than she wanted to reveal. She told herself it was nothing—close quarters, too many shared dawns, and the fact that Zale was...easy to talk to. Usually. That was all.

It couldn't mean anything. It mustn't.

The seaside port of Ormia was a sprawl of sun-bleached docks, clustered buildings with tiled roofs, and gulls screaming overhead searching for their next target.

As the *Black Serpent* groaned against her moorings, Nerissa followed Zale, Bran, and Cormac down the gangplank. The salty breeze carried the scent of fish, citrus, and something less identifiable but definitely alive. Stalls spilled color across the docks—bolts of fabric snapping in the wind, barrels of wriggling crabs, vendors shouting over one another trying to attract their next customer.

Bran took one look around and declared, "Ah, Ormia. Home of the finest pickpockets and the worst ale this side of the strait."

"That's why we brought ye," Cormac muttered, tugging his hat lower against the sun.

Zale adjusted the strap on his satchel. "We've got lists from Ma Wen and Roan. We split up, we're quicker. Nerissa, you're with me, aye?"

She nodded, watching Bran snatch Ma Wen's neatly written scroll requesting rare spices, smoked sea salt, and something labeled *not ground squid ink this time, please,* before immediately veering toward the noise of a dice game.

"I'll take the marketplace," Bran announced grandly. "They know me there."

Zale snorted. "That's what worries me."

"I've got damage control," Cormac sighed.

Zale turned to Nerissa, a half-smile tugging at his mouth. "Ready to hunt down cursed herbs and spices rare enough to make Roan shed a tear?"

Nerissa matched his smile. "Lead the way."

The cobbled streets of Ormia were alive with noise and color. Flapping tarps, shouting merchants, and children darting between stalls like minnows. Nerissa stepped carefully between puddles of brine and another substance she preferred not to identify.

Day sixteen.

She didn't *feel* any different. No burning lungs. No involuntary shifting. No telltale tremor in her hands. And yet, the number coiled tightly in her thoughts like a sea serpent waiting to strike.

Seven days was the limit. That's what they'd always said. Sixteen was uncharted waters.

And still she walked.

Still human.

Maybe she was stuck in this form after all.

Maybe that was for the best. She had no family left to return to, no real home beneath the waves. She just didn't want Damarion to worry. Maybe she could somehow get a message to him when they next docked in Astyra.

Zale slowed beside her at a cart overflowing with jars of pickled things in alarming hues. "This one looks promising," he said, peering at a label written in a scrawl only a sea witch could have deciphered.

Nerissa scowled at the jelly-like contents. "Unless he asked for fermented eel hearts, I don't think that's it."

Zale held up the jar, sloshed it once. "Shame. They'd put hair on Eon's chest."

They moved on, ducking beneath hanging laundry and winding through side alleys where the more...eccentric merchants kept shop. One old woman with no teeth tried to sell Zale a "sea-blessed aphrodisiac" that smelled strongly of vinegar and seaweed.

Nerissa barely kept a straight face as Zale declined, his ears tinting the faintest shade of red.

A few blocks later, they found a tiny herbalist tucked behind a fishmonger's stall. The interior smelled like dried mint and damp stone. Shelves overflowed with clay pots, and bundles of roots hung from the ceiling like inverted seaweed.

"Roan's list," Zale muttered, tugging the parchment from his belt. "Bitterroot, ghost kelp, and bloodleaf. He also drew a very unhelpful frown next to *'if you bring back cilantro, I swear.'*"

Nerissa stepped toward a low table stacked with dried roots, lifting one to her nose. "Bitterroot," she confirmed. "Earthy, musty, just like Roan said. He uses it for sore throats, rashes, skin sores...it's the base in that balm he makes for you."

Zale grimaced. "Ah yes. The floral nightmare that makes me smell like a bouquet at a funeral."

The shopkeeper, a stooped man with crinkled eyes, emerged from the shadows and silently pressed a small bundle wrapped in cloth into Zale's hands.

Zale blinked. "Thanks, I—"

The man jabbed a finger toward a chalk sign behind him:

No talking. Prices are written. Haggling will be punished without discrimination.

Nerissa bit back a grin. "I like this place."

They gathered the rest of Roan's requests without incident. Ghost kelp bundled in oil paper, bloodleaf carefully wrapped by the silent shopkeeper, and a handful of dried roots Nerissa suspected Roan had added to his list just to test their patience. By the time they wound their way back toward the docks, the satchel was heavy with herbs and other natural remedies.

A sharp, clean scent cut through the brine and spice of the market air.

Nerissa slowed.

Zale took two more steps before realizing she was no longer beside him. He turned. "Lose something?"

She was studying a small stall tucked between a florist and a seller of lamp oil. Unlike the others, this one was quiet. No shouting, no bartering. Just neatly stacked bars of soap resting on linen cloth, pale green and cream and soft yellow, tied with rough twine.

The vendor, an older woman with sun-darkened hands, watched her with mild interest.

"For sailors?" Nerissa asked, picking up a bar.

"For skin that's seen too much sun," the woman replied. "Olive oil. Goat's milk. Calendula. No lye."

"Does it sting cracked skin?"

The woman shook her head. "It soothes."

Nerissa tossed the bar up and down once in her hand before handing over a coin.

She waited until they'd moved a few paces away from the stall before pulling it from her satchel and holding it out to Zale.

"For the shower room," she said. "The communal bar is…excessive."

He stared at the soap in her hand as though she'd offered him a live fish.

"It builds character," he said lightly.

"It builds scabs." She pressed the soap into his palm. "This won't aggravate the lesions."

His fingers closed around the bar.

"You didn't have to."

"I know."

Zale turned the soap over in his hand. "Smells better than lye, that's for sure."

"That isn't soap," she said. "That's deck varnish."

A soft huff of laughter escaped him as he looked at her a moment longer than necessary. Then tucked the bar carefully into his coat pocket instead of the herb sack.

They passed a vendor whose stall was draped in bolts of fabric consisting of dyed silks, weatherproof canvas, and coats in every shade from violet to scarlet. The woman behind the counter spotted Nerissa immediately and seized a dark purple long coat from the rack.

"You!" she called, beaming as though she'd found treasure. "Try this, perfect for you."

Before Nerissa could protest, the woman was already bustling around the counter. She held the coat up with a flourish, the deep purple lining catching the sun.

Nerissa glanced at Zale, who only shrugged, half a smirk tugging at his mouth.

The vendor didn't wait for permission. She swept the coat over Nerissa's shoulders and fussed with the collar. "See? Matches the lavender and plum in your clothes—perfect tones, perfect cut. You'll look like a lady and a captain all at once."

Nerissa stood stiff as a mast, arms trapped as the woman tugged at the sleeves. The weight of the fabric settled around her, surprisingly comfortable.

Zale's gaze lingered on her as she shifted uncomfortably. "She's not wrong. Suits you."

Nerissa shot him a dry look. "You would say that."

He grinned. "I didn't say it looked *bad*."

The vendor tugged at the lapel, beaming. "Ah, yes, perfect fit. And your young man here clearly approves."

Nerissa went rigid. "He's not—"

But Zale's smirk had already widened, one brow raised like he wasn't about to argue the point.

Heat prickled up the back of Nerissa's neck. Tides, no. The quickest way out of this was through. She dug into her coin pouch and slapped a few coppers onto the counter.

"I'll take it," she said shortly.

The woman hummed in triumph, stepping back with a satisfied nod. Nerissa tugged the coat tighter around herself and stalked toward the street before Zale could open his mouth.

Of course, he fell into step beside her, grinning. "Didn't know you were in the market for fashion."

"I wasn't," she muttered.

"Good thing I was here to approve, then."

She shot him a sidelong glare. "You're insufferable."

"Maybe," he said, giving her a long look. "But the coat does suit you."

Nerissa tightened the lapels, refusing to give him the satisfaction of answering. The fabric was heavier than she was used to, but it carried the same practical cut as the coats the rest of the crew wore. For the first time since stepping aboard the *Serpent*, she looked less like a guest and more like one of them. Not that she'd admit it aloud.

They found Bran and Cormac near the wharf, hunched over a barrel like it was their shared confidant. Cormac was gnawing the end of a dried fish with grim determination, and Bran was polishing an apple on his shirt with the self-satisfaction of someone who definitely hadn't done the majority of the work.

Bran grinned as they approached. His gaze flicked over Nerissa, and the apple nearly slipped from his hand. "Well, well. Look at you," he said with mock solemnity, sweeping an exaggerated bow. "Now you look like a real pirate."

Nerissa rolled her eyes. "Because of the coat?"

"Because of the coat," Bran confirmed, circling her once like he was appraising fine weaponry. "That shade of purple? Positively screams: 'Hide your coin purses and your daughters.'"

Cormac snorted around a mouthful of fish. "More like 'gullible enough to pay double for a jacket.'"

Nerissa crossed her arms, unimpressed. "I didn't pay double."

Zale smirked at her side. "Didn't haggle either."

Nerissa ignored them both. "Anyways, we got everything. Even the bloodleaf."

Zale shot Bran a look. "Which, apparently, helps with stomach aches. So you'll probably go through half of it yourself if you eat any more mystery berries."

Bran placed a hand over his heart. "One time. I eat *one* questionable berry and suddenly I'm a liability."

"Twice," Cormac rumbled. "Ye should really listen to Eon once in a while."

"Ah, well," Bran said, unbothered. "Heroism has its costs."

He reached over and plucked the satchel from Zale's hand with a flourish. "Well then. If the errands are run and the bloodleaf secured for my inevitable digestive doom, I say we've earned a proper reward."

Zale arched a brow. "Like what? A pat on the head?"

"No," Bran said, draping an arm around both of them as he steered them towards a weathered building. "Like a pint, some greasy food, and a fair game of cards. Come on. First round's on Cormac."

Cormac gave a slow blink. "Ye said what now?"

Nerissa hesitated. "Because the last time we were all in a tavern together went *so* well."

Cormac snorted. "Aye, but I'm fairly certain it was a prince who picked that fight. And unless one of you's secretly royalty, we're fresh out today."

Bran gave Zale's and Nerissa's shoulders a squeeze. "What could possibly go wrong?"

"Famous last words," Zale said under his breath.

Nerissa relented with a sigh. "Fine. But if *one more person* tries to grab my—"

"They'll lose their hand," Zale cut in without missing a beat.

The others paused.

Nerissa looked at him.

He didn't flinch.

Bran let out a low whistle. "Well then. Remind me never to try and hug you without written permission. Or at least while you've still got your sword drawn."

Zale's mouth twitched, but he didn't answer. He just adjusted his coat and nodded toward the tavern at the end of the dock.

Nerissa fell into step beside him, jaw tight. It didn't mean anything—couldn't. He was only watching out for his crew, same as she would have. That was all. Just loyalty, not...whatever her racing pulse was trying to suggest.

Zale

The *Rusty Rudder* loomed like a promise and a dare—its sign crooked, its windows glowing with the hazy amber of late afternoon mischief.

The tavern was exactly what it promised: weathered beams, rust-patched lanterns, and a scattering of patrons too old or too drunk to care about anyone new. The place smelled like spilled rum and fried fish, but it was cozy in a lived-in sort of way. A trio of musicians strummed a tune in the corner while a one-eyed bartender poured generous portions.

They wove through the crowd—dockhands, sailors, and a very drunk man trying to sell an eel out of his coat—and found an empty booth in the corner, half-shadowed beneath a grimy window.

Zale and Nerissa slid in first, backs to the wall like instinct had trained them for it. Zale's gaze swept the room once before settling, his hand resting near the hilt of his blade. Nerissa mirrored him without thinking, her posture relaxed but ready.

Bran plopped down across from them, clapping his hands once. "Nothing like a corner booth to make a crew feel both mysterious *and* superior."

Cormac eased in beside him, muttering, "Aye, but you'll be the one they shoot in the back first, sittin' with yer face to the wall like that."

Bran grinned. "If they shoot me in the back, I'll die looking smug. It's what I would've wanted."

A surly barmaid arrived with tankards already sloshing. Bran ordered a round of whatever was "least likely to make us blind," and she grunted in response before disappearing again.

Nerissa took a sip. "Huh. Not bad."

Cormac sniffed his ale. "Smells like fermented socks."

Zale raised an eyebrow. "You say that like you've got experience."

Bran tipped his drink toward Nerissa. "Well? You survived a port run without getting into any trouble. That calls for a toast."

"To calm waters," Cormac said.

"To hot food," Zale added.

"To famous last words," Nerissa offered with a wink.

Bran raised his tankard last. "To good drinks, better company, and absolutely no prince-related bar fights this time."

They clinked their tankards together, barely taking a sip before the tavern door slammed open with all the subtlety of a cannon shot.

Conversation faltered. Chairs scraped. Even the eel-seller paused mid-pitch.

A hulking man stepped into the *Rusty Rudder*, shoulders nearly brushing the frame. He wore a scar like a river delta across his cheek and had the kind of presence that suggested he'd once wrestled a shark and won. Two smaller men flanked him, one with a crooked nose, the other with knuckles like cracked stone.

His eyes scanned the tavern once—

—and landed on Bran.

Zale didn't miss the way Bran stiffened. One moment he was lounging with a smirk, the next he was ducking his head behind his tankard like it could somehow render him invisible.

Bloody stars. Here we go…

Cormac followed the man's gaze. "Friend o' yours?"

Bran's voice was low. "More like a...disgruntled business associate."

Zale didn't look away from the group near the door. "What kind of business?"

"I borrowed money for a poker hand," Bran muttered.

Nerissa narrowed her eyes at him. "Let me guess. You lost."

"Spectacularly," Bran sighed. "But in my defense, I was very confident at the time."

"Confidence," Cormac grunted, "is nae the same as collateral."

The big man was moving now, wading through the crowd like a shark through shallows, eyes fixed on Bran like he was already imagining the bone count.

"I might owe him...a little," Bran added. "Give or take fifty silvers."

Zale's hand had already found the hilt of his sword. "You could've mentioned that before we agreed to drinks."

"I didn't *know* he'd be in Ormia!" Bran hissed. "He's supposed to be dead."

"Wonderful," Nerissa said. "You owe money to someone you assumed was dead. That always ends well."

Bran flashed a strained grin. "Well, technically, I still assume he's dead. That might just be his twin."

The man reached their booth. He loomed.

"Well, well," he said, voice like gravel. "If it isn't Bran Calder. Been a long time."

"That's not my name," Bran said quickly.

"You told me it was."

"I lie a lot."

The man didn't smile.

"You've got a lot of nerve showing your face here."

Bran raised his hands, still holding the tankard. "I brought friends?"

The man's eyes swept the table as his lip curled. "Friends ain't gonna save you from what you owe."

Nerissa leaned forward, calm but firm. "How much?"

The man blinked. "Hundred silvers."

Bran choked on his drink. "That seems excessive for a friendly dice game!"

"You lost," the man growled.

"Only because the other guy cheated."

Nerissa didn't look at him. "Just pay the man."

Bran opened his mouth, then caught the look she gave him.

It was *not* a suggestion.

With a theatrical sigh, he shoved a hand into one pocket, then another, then flipped his coat inside out with unnecessary flair. A few coins fell to the table with a mournful clatter.

"Thirty," he announced. "And lint."

The man crossed his arms. "Where's the rest?"

Bran offered a helpless shrug. "Must've left my coin pouch in my other pants."

Zale narrowed his eyes. "You don't own other pants."

Bran threw him a wounded look. "You *used* to like me."

Zale didn't answer. Instead, he pulled a pouch from his belt and dropped twenty silvers on the table.

Cormac followed with another twenty, muttering something about reckless fools and cursed debts. Nerissa, rolling her eyes, counted out the final thirty.

The man scooped up the coins without so much as a grunt of thanks.

Bran clapped his hands together. "Well! Always a pleasure to clear one's conscience and lighten one's purse. Shall we?"

The group stood up to leave. Bran slid past first, Cormac on his heels. Zale started after them, but then the man's hand shot out and clamped down on Nerissa's shoulder.

"You," he rumbled, voice thick with old rum and worse intentions. "Why don't you stay a while?"

He gave her a long, deliberate once-over, his scar tugging when his mouth curled. "Pretty thing like you don't belong with gutter rats like this lot. Bet you'd fetch more than their sorry hides put together." His gaze dipped, lingering where it shouldn't, before dragging back up to meet hers. "A coat like that's hiding more than curves, eh? I like a woman with secrets."

Zale halted mid-step, stomach twisting. His hand was already tightening around the hilt at his hip, every muscle in his body primed to slice the man's wrist clean off. But Nerissa moved first.

She let out a slow breath as she turned, her expression unreadable. Then steel flashed—both daggers unsheathed in a blink, one pressed under the man's chin, the other resting firmly just above his collarbone.

"I'm not on your tab," she said. "Touch me again and I'll make change out of your fingers."

That might've been the end of it had his cronies not stepped forward.

"Come on, Jorran," one sneered. "Can't let her talk to you like that."

The other cracked his knuckles. "Pretty thing like her needs teachin' some respect."

That's when Zale stepped forward and drew his sword with a quiet, satisfying ring of steel.

"I wouldn't," he said, eyes locked on the crony. "She already pulled her blades. You really want to see what happens when I do?"

The bar went quiet, the kind of silence that knew what was coming and moved the good glassware out of reach.

The first crony, a wiry brute with a pockmarked face, lunged for his own blade.

Zale moved.

His sword intercepted the strike before it landed. Steel clashed in a burst of sparks, and Zale shoved the man back with a twist of his blade, footwork already shifting for the next move.

The crony snarled and came back swinging, wild and untrained. Zale blocked the blow with ease and twisted sideways, letting the man stumble past him.

"Saw that coming," Zale muttered.

Before the man could recover, Zale spun, dropped low, and swept his leg behind the man's knees. He toppled like a felled mast—only to find the point of Zale's sword already leveled at his throat.

"I'd stay down if I were you," Zale said, voice low, dangerous. "But I've been told I'm not very persuasive."

The crony blinked up at him, panting, blood trickling from a shallow cut across his cheek. He didn't move.

"Good lad."

The second crony lunged toward Nerissa—only to be tripped by Cormac, who swept out his leg with surprising agility for a man his age.

The man yelped and stumbled.

Cormac gave him a shove with surprising force, aiming a pistol at him. "Sit down, ye gobshite."

Behind the group, Bran ducked around the counter, whispering to himself like a child in a puppet show. "Come on, Bran. This is your moment. Hero time."

"Bran, don't—" Zale started, but too late.

He grabbed the nearest tankard and hurled it overhead toward the lead thug.

It veered hard left and clocked Zale square in the side of the head with a *THUNK.*

White sparked across his vision. His ears rang, the room tilting sideways for a breath.

"OW. Dammit *Bran*!" he barked, staggering to one side and turning a glare toward the bar that could've curdled milk.

"*Sorry mate! It was meant for the bald one!*" Bran called helpfully from behind a crate of pickled onions.

The bald one smirked and swung at Nerissa.

Big mistake.

She ducked beneath the clumsy arc, pivoted around his flank, and used the momentum to plant her boot hard against the back of his knee. He stumbled, cursing, as she brought one blade back around to rest against his exposed throat again, this time with a touch less patience.

Bran popped back up with another glass. "I'm helping!"

"You're *not*," Zale snapped, pressing a hand to his throbbing temple, the ringing still sharp in his skull.

The bald brute, still half-bent from Nerissa's strike, growled and lunged again. She twisted aside, letting his momentum carry him forward, and directly into Zale's path.

Zale didn't hesitate. He stepped in, grabbed the man's arm mid-swing, and twisted it back with a yank. The brute bellowed, trying to wrench free, but Nerissa was already there with her blades flashing down to slice the belt at his waist.

For a long, suspended moment, the tavern went utterly still.

Then the room exploded in laughter.

The brute froze, humiliated.

"Next time," Nerissa said coolly, "I'll strike lower."

Then Zale released him with a little shove that sent him sprawling into a table of stunned card players.

Silence returned, broken only by Bran brushing off his sleeves like he had actually provided assistance. "Well! I think that went rather well, don't you?"

Nerissa sheathed her daggers as Zale staggered again, rubbing his temple.

"You alright?" she asked, reaching out to brace him.

Zale winced. "Remind me to throw *Bran* next time."

Bran raised both hands, indignant. "Hey, if anything, that was a flawless distraction!"

"Yeah," Zale muttered. "Distracted *me*."

The barkeep groaned from somewhere behind the bar, already reaching for the broom.

"Out," he grunted. "*Out.* Before I charge you for every stool you just broke."

Nerissa shot a glance in Bran's direction. "You owe each of us *fifty* silvers."

Bran balked. "Fifty a piece? That's more than what I owed *him*!"

"That includes interest," she said sweetly, heading for the door.

The sun had dipped low by the time they trudged up the gangplank, bruised, limping, and moderately victorious.

"Remind me," Cormac muttered, hoisting a satchel of dried herbs over one shoulder, "why we let *him* lead these excursions."

Bran, nursing a scrape on his jaw and looking unfairly smug for someone who'd beaned his best friend with drinkware, offered a cheerful, "Because I'm the most charming."

"No," Nerissa said flatly. "You're the most *expensive*."

Ma Wen was already waiting near the galley entrance with his arms crossed and an eyebrow raised. "You were supposed to bring back ginger root, not injuries."

Bran dropped the sack of food at Ma Wen's feet with a grin. "You got your ginger. I got out of debt. Zale got a concussion. Everyone wins."

Zale, behind him, grunted—his hand pressed to the side of his head where a thin line of blood was seeping through his hair. "I *will* kill you in your sleep."

Bran tapped the faint scar along his left cheek and winked. "Relax, mate. Scars build character. Ladies love 'em—so really, you're welcome."

Nerissa lingered by Zale's side, one hand light against his back. "Come on. Let's get you to Roan before you pass out again."

Zale didn't argue. He let her guide him down the corridor, the ship swaying gently beneath his boots, though it felt like it was the world listing sideways. The pounding in his skull had dulled to a persistent throb, rhythmic and annoying, like Bran's voice filtered through a sieve.

He hated being seen like this—half-limping, blood trickling down the side of his scalp, a dullness behind his eyes that made his hands tremble if he wasn't careful. He hated looking weak.

But oddly, he didn't mind Nerissa being the one to help this time.

Maybe it was the way she didn't make a fuss. She didn't hover or chide. She just walked beside him, steady and quiet, a hand between his shoulder blades like a lighthouse beam cutting through fog. Not guiding. Just reminding him which way was home.

Zale grimaced to himself. Stars above—lighthouse beam? Really? That was the last time he let Nestor read from *Stormbound Hearts*. Too many metaphors were clearly rotting his brain.

He let out a breath. "You're not going to tell Roan I almost blacked out on the way up the gangplank, are you?"

Her mouth twitched. "Not if you stop pretending you're fine."

"Deal," he muttered.

Nerissa

Roan looked up from his ledger as the door creaked open. His gaze landed on Zale's temple and the blood matting the hair around it.

"Let me guess," he said, already reaching for a cloth and a jar of salve. "Bran's fault?"

Zale eased himself onto the nearest wooden stool with a grunt, wincing as he tilted his head. "Isn't it always?"

Roan didn't disagree. He set the cloth to soak in clean water before glancing at Nerissa questioningly.

"Friendly fire," she said simply, crossing to the table and setting down the satchel. "He tried to help. He missed."

Roan let out a slow breath, the kind that said he wasn't surprised in the slightest.

"Of course he did." He moved behind Zale, tilting his head to inspect the wound. "You're lucky this isn't deeper. Could've been worse. You've got a thick skull."

"Thanks," Zale muttered. "I think."

Nerissa began unpacking the satchel of herbal remedies. "We got everything on your list. No cilantro."

Roan glanced over, nodding in approval. "Good. I was serious about that."

She set the bundle of bitterroot down on the counter, brushing the dust from her fingertips. "This was for the lesions, right?"

Roan nodded. "Sore throats, rashes, sores—anything irritating, really." He gave Zale a pointed look. "Which includes the company he keeps."

He dipped a hooked needle into a jar of alcohol and flicked the excess off with a delicate hand. "Hold still. I'd rather not sew your eyebrow to your ear."

Zale exhaled through his nose and focused on a knot in the wooden floorboards. "That only happened once."

The needle pierced his skin with the first stitch. Zale grunted but didn't move.

Across the room, Nerissa quietly sorted the herbs they'd brought back, her fingers deft and sure. Bitterroot went into the bottom drawer—Roan's marked stash for balms. Ghost kelp she tucked into the sealed tin, careful not to crinkle it. Bloodleaf, vibrant and spongy, was set aside for drying.

She moved methodically, aware of the rhythmic pull of thread behind her, the faint wince Zale tried not to let slip with each stitch.

"You didn't flinch when I pulled knives on that brute," she said lightly, not turning around. "But poke you with a needle and suddenly you're made of glass."

"It's a very *sharp* needle," Zale muttered.

Roan smirked. "And it's about to be a very crooked scar if you don't stop talking."

"You say that like it's not going to be charming," Zale said through clenched teeth.

"Only to someone blind," Roan said, tying off another stitch.

Nerissa gave a soft snort and opened the cupboard above her. "I don't know. I think it'll suit him."

Zale perked up—then flinched as the next stitch went in. "Ow. Was that one on purpose?"

Roan didn't answer. He just tied off the final stitch and stepped back to examine his work. "Well, you won't win any beauty contests, but your brains will stay in."

Zale lifted a brow. "I don't recall signing up for one."

"Good," Roan said, beginning to pack away his tools. "You'd lose."

Nerissa let out a quiet huff and reached for the final bundle of herbs—but as her fingers curled around the cloth wrap, a sharp jolt seized through her palm. The bundle slipped from her grasp and hit the floor with a soft thud as she gave a sharp gasp.

She froze.

Zale turned toward her, just in time to see her hand flexing stiffly—like it belonged to someone else.

"Hey," he said, frowning, "you alright?"

Nerissa opened her mouth to reply, but her hand spasmed again, more violently this time. She sucked in a breath and pressed her palm flat to the worktable, steadying it with her other hand as though sheer will might wrangle the nerves back into place.

"I'm fine," she said—too fast. "Just a cramp."

Roan's eyes narrowed as he turned around. He approached with measured calm. "Which hand?"

"Left."

He reached for it gently, turning it over in his own. Her fingers trembled—barely—but enough for him to notice. "How long's this been happening?"

"It literally just started," she said defensively.

Roan didn't look convinced. "You been drinking enough water? Eating properly?"

Zale was already standing. "She's had the same rations as the rest of us."

"Then it's not dehydration," Roan muttered, already moving to a shelf to pull down a tin of powdered bark. "Could be nerves. Or strain."

Zale glanced over at Nerissa, concern flickering across his face. But she wouldn't meet his gaze. Her lips pressed into a thin line, jaw tight.

Roan didn't say anything more, just pried open the tin with his thumb and pinched out a fine layer of pale bark dust, adding it to a clay cup of water. The powder swirled as he stirred, leaving faint trails like smoke under glass.

"Drink this," he said, setting it in front of her.

Nerissa glanced at the cup, then up at him.

"It'll help with the muscle spasms," Roan added. "Could just be strain, like I said. But I'm not letting you walk out of here until I know you've had it."

Nerissa exhaled through her nose but took the cup. It smelled faintly of damp pine and something bitter beneath it. She held his gaze for a beat, then drank it in one go. Her nose wrinkled at the taste.

Roan watched her the whole time. "All of it," he prompted.

She tilted the cup again to show it was empty.

"Good," he said. "Now sit for a minute. If it was just a cramp, it'll ease. If not…" He didn't finish the sentence, just turned back to finish tidying his kit.

Nerissa sat back on a stool, hand resting in her lap as she tried to will the tension away. She didn't want to meet Zale's eyes—didn't want to see whatever flicker of worry might be waiting there.

Zale stayed silent as he sat back down, clearly not intending to leave anytime soon.

A few minutes passed in silence. The gentle scrape of Roan packing away his tools, the muted slosh of water as he rinsed the blood from his fingers, the soft clink of dried roots settling in their jars—all of it filled the space without pressing.

Nerissa sat still, fingers curled loosely in her lap. No spasms. No tingling.

Just the faint aftertaste of bark and bitterness clinging to the back of her tongue.

Roan glanced her way one more time, his gaze sharp beneath furrowed brows. "Still steady?"

She flexed her hands once, then again. "Seems to be."

He gave a small grunt of acknowledgement. "Alright. You're free to go."

Zale slid off his stool, gingerly touching a finger to the stitches. He gave Roan a small nod, and the medic returned it with his usual gruff efficiency.

"Try not to let Bran clock you again," Roan added, not looking up as he dried his hands.

"As if I got a say the first time," Zale muttered.

Nerissa rose with him, not bothering to hide her relief. Whatever that had been, it was over. For now.

They stepped back into the corridor, the low lantern light casting golden flickers along the curved walls. Zale walked beside her, slower than usual, one hand still absently rubbing the side of his head.

He glanced over. "Sure you're alright?"

Nerissa kept her tone light. "You're the one with a head wound."

"That's not a 'yes'."

She gave him a sideways look. "It's a *you should be focusing on not walking into walls*."

Zale snorted. "If I do, I'm blaming Bran."

"Obviously."

The upper deck was bathed in moonlight, the sea calm and deceptively serene—nothing at all like the crowd gathered near the bow, where Nestor stood atop a crate with one boot braced dramatically on the rail.

Zale and Nerissa slowed as they stepped into the scene.

"Oh no," Zale muttered.

"Oh *yes,*" Nerissa said, eyes sparkling as she spotted the worn, salt-stained book in Nestor's hand. "Chapter fourteen."

"*Stormbound Hearts,*" Nestor declared, lifting the book like it was holy scripture. "A Tidal Temptation."

Groans and cheers rang out in equal measure.

Brigid stood off to the side, arms crossed, lips twitching in reluctant amusement. Ma Wen stirred a pot of something behind her, clearly listening. Eon had dropped down from the rigging just in time to collapse dramatically at the front of the crowd like a child awaiting story time.

Zale and Nerissa each sat down on a couple of nearby water barrels.

Nestor cleared his throat. "'The pirate prince—still disguised as a humble deckhand—sheathed his saber with a flourish so roguishly precise that Lady Isadora felt faint. Or perhaps it was the fever. Or the sight of his chest, gleaming with sweat and honor.'"

Cormac let out a long, slow whistle. "Sweat an' honor. That's a dangerous combination."

"'You lied to me,'" Nestor read, switching to a breathy falsetto, one hand clutching his own chest. "'You said you were a cook!'"

"'I *am* a cook,'" he growled, shifting to a deep rumble. "'I just also happen to be heir to the Crimson Corsairs, and this soufflé has a dagger baked inside.'"

Bran barked a laugh. "That's *got* to be a metaphor."

"*Everything* in this book is a metaphor," Roan muttered, emerging from the lower deck.

Nestor continued, undeterred. "'Their blades clashed like thunder on a summer night, sparks flying as storm clouds gathered above them—both literal and emotional. 'If I fall,' she whispered, 'catch me.' 'I always do,' he rasped, because apparently he'd already caught her once in Chapter Eight, but none of us remember that because the author was on too much merroot wine.'"

Brigid covered her face with both hands. "I hate this. I hate this so much."

"Liar," said Cormac. "You're livin' for it."

Nerissa leaned toward Zale. "So...metaphor banned in four kingdoms?"

He grinned. "We're about to find out."

Nestor flipped the page, adopted a solemn expression, and lifted one hand in warning. "Brace yourselves, crew. The scandal approaches."

A hush fell.

Then, with full theatrical weight, Nestor intoned, "'His gaze roamed her like a ship mapping the coastline—searching every inlet, every curve, charting her soul with the steady compass of desire.'"

Half the crew exploded into laughter. The other half groaned so loudly it nearly startled a flock of gulls into flight.

Bran wiped tears from his eyes. "I've *been* to that inlet. It's treacherous in high tide."

Zale just closed his eyes, lips twitching as he fought a smile.

Nerissa nudged him. "So which is more painful—Nestor's dramatic reading or Roan's stitches?"

He opened one eye, mock-stern. "Ooh. That's a close tie."

Nestor held up the book like a trophy. "Chapter fifteen tomorrow, mates! There will be *ropes*."

CHAPTER 29

NOT JUST INK

Nerissa

The *Black Serpent* was running with a fair wind, her bow cutting clean lines through indigo water on the last leg back to the hidden cove. Late afternoon light spilled across the main deck, gilding ropes and railing with copper sunshine.

Seventeen days.

Nerissa flexed her fingers on the rail, watching how they curled and straightened. No lingering ache. No stiffness. Just the memory of that sudden spasm the night before.

Still no other side effects. No vertigo. No ache in her bones. No shimmer of scales beneath her skin.

Every sunrise without pain left her both relieved...and uneasy.

She exhaled slowly and folded her arms, unsettled by the silence in her own body.

Commotion behind her broke the thought.

Eon was swaggering across the deck, bravado spilling out of every pore.

"Come on! Someone give me a real match. I'm sick of being treated like the cabin mascot."

Bran lounged atop a crate, absentmindedly spinning his knife. "You sure, pup? Last time you 'squared up' you nearly tripped over your own feet."

Laughter rippled through the crew.

"Square up with *me,* Calder," Eon snapped. "First to three strikes."

Bran sighed theatrically, jabbed his knife into the side of the crate, and hopped down. "Fine. But when you're flat on your backside, remember—you asked."

A loose ring of pirates formed. Nerissa drifted to the edge of the circle, curious despite herself. Zale appeared beside her with a tankard in hand, shaking his head.

"Lad's fixin' to get taught a lesson."

"Poor Eon," Nerissa lamented, watching as he took his place opposite Bran inside the circle. "Bran's lucky that Brigid is already locked up in her cabin with a new book."

Zale grunted in agreement.

Then Roan sidled up behind them. "Two silvers says Bran ends it in under half a minute."

Zale's brow rose. "I'll take that bet."

"Last chance, pup," Bran ribbed him, stretching as he did so. "Not too late to back out with dignity."

"Back out of *this*!" Eon lunged, wild and off-balance. Bran stepped aside, tapping him on the shoulder. *One.*

Eon whirled around, over-correcting and stumbling over his own feet.

"Come on, Eon!" Nerissa cheered. "You've got this!"

A grin flashed across the boy's face as he took a swing at Bran, but he was too slow. Bran dodged, grabbing Eon's arm, and hit him in the face with his own fist. *Two.*

Eon stumbled back, hand reaching up to rub his jaw.

"That was dirty, Bran!" Zale chimed in.

Eon tried again; this time Bran hooked his boot behind the boy's ankle, knocked him to the deck, and booped him on the nose. *Three.*

Twenty-nine seconds.

Roan grunted, palm out. Zale grumbled and slapped two silvers into it.

Bran bowed with a flourish to the rambunctious crowd. "Anyone else?"

Nerissa considered the challenge. She bet she could best Bran. He was all showmanship and swagger tonight, not to mention three pints in. Without a word, she slipped away from Zale and Roan, stepping into the ring.

The crew hushed around her.

Bran blinked. "What, you want a turn?"

She tilted her head, calm and assessing as she pulled her hair back. "You said anyone."

A low whistle cut through the hush.

Bran scratched the back of his neck, unsure if this was a trap. "No offense, love, but I don't like hitting women."

"You won't get the chance."

Zale choked on his drink off to the side.

The crew erupted again, howls and jeers ricocheting off the rigging. Bran chuckled, cracking his knuckles. "Alright then. First to three."

Zale leaned toward Roan, eyes glinting. "Same wager?"

Roan studied her stance, lips pressing thin. "…Double."

"Done."

Nerissa shrugged off her coat, tossed it to Zale, and rolled her sleeves with unhurried precision.

"Ain't got all night, love!" Bran called.

Nerissa met him in the middle. Bran struck first, a quick jab at her shoulder.

She ducked, skirting behind him before he could pull his hand back, and tapped his spine. *One.*

The crew whooped.

Bran's grin sharpened. "Alright. Let's dance."

He feinted left. She twisted, pivoting to his right, and thrust her palm into his chest, shoving him back a pace. *Two.*

Another roar from the crowd.

Now he looked impressed. And maybe, just maybe, a little concerned. Nerissa smiled ruthlessly, narrowing her eyes. This was too easy.

He tried getting clever. Grapple, feint high, sweep low. She let him get close, then used his momentum against him, flipping him in one fluid motion.

Bran hit the deck with a grunt, then a laugh, as Nerissa hovered over him and jabbed him in the shoulder. *Three.*

Barely two minutes.

The circle exploded. Coins changed hands. Someone slapped the mast for emphasis.

Bran sat up, dazed but smiling. "Remind me never to get on your bad side."

Zale collected four silvers from Roan with exaggerated satisfaction.

What started out as a simple sparring match quickly turned into a proper gauntlet.

Cormac went first, claiming "weather pain" in his joints before Nerissa swept him like a sack of flour. He hit the boards with a groan and bellowed, "Saints below, give me death! I yield!" which earned raucous cheers.

Ma Wen stepped forward next, bowing silently. Nerissa returned it. He moved gracefully, like he was dancing on the wind. They traded strikes, earning two points each. Then, she slid past, struck the side of one knee, and knocked him over into a coil of rope.

"Nice reflexes, little fish," he tipped his head in surrender, almost amused.

Nerissa offered her hand and pulled him back to his feet. He rejoined the circle, dusting himself off.

"Stars alive," Bran muttered from the sidelines, nursing his shoulder. "She's cutting through us like a kraken through a hull."

Roan stretched, rolling his neck. "Alright, half pint. Let's see what you're made of."

He stood at least two heads taller than her, and was all muscle. Nerissa adjusted her stance, similar to how Zale taught her during one of their early morning training sessions. Roan may have her on size and sheer strength, but she had speed and agility.

He lunged first; she palmed his face, blocking his line of sight. Quickly placing her free hand on his shoulder, she grabbed underneath his armpit with her other hand, twisting him like a steering wheel and tripping him as the momentum carried him forward.

Roan tumbled heavily to the deck, trying to catch himself. Nerissa was already there, jabbing her elbow into his chest. *One.*

He leapt back onto his feet, shoulders squared. Nerissa struck first this time; Roan dodged the first swing, then caught her second in the jaw. *Two.*

Roan cracked his neck, chuckling. "You'd think I'd be more prepared for that move."

Nerissa stretched her own neck. "Just be glad I'm pulling my punches," she smirked.

This time, he hunched forward, aiming for her knees. She planted her palms on his shoulders and vaulted over him, barely breaking a sweat. She swung her leg into the backs of his knees, buckling him, before finally striking between his shoulder blades with the heel of her boot. *Three.*

Roan staggered up, laughing as he raised his hands. "Note to self: never bet against you again."

Nerissa drew herself to her full height with pride, catching Eon's eye.

"Ready to get back in here?" she goaded him.

"No thank you, ma'am," Eon shook his head vehemently.

"Smart," she couldn't help but laugh.

"I think that's everyone," Cormac declared, raising his tankard.

Then the crew stilled.

Nerissa turned around to find Zale had stepped into the ring.

Laughter bled into murmurs as the crew nudged one another, leaning forward as though the air itself had shifted. Now *this* would be interesting.

Nerissa eyed him suspiciously. "You sure about this?"

He rolled his neck, flexed his fingers. "Crew's been goin' easy on ye, but I won't."

A chorus of *ooohs* reverberated throughout the crowd.

Nerissa's eyes narrowed. "You've been training me; I already know all your moves."

"Not all of them," his eyes darkened in warning.

Please, she thought. *Is that supposed to be intimidating?*

She'd seen him fight in two separate taverns now; he was far from untouchable. He might land a strike or two, but she would beat him easily. No problem.

They circled like two predators sizing each other up, seeing who would flinch first.

Zale kept his hands loose at his sides, forgoing a typical guard stance. *Arrogant.* She'd make him regret it.

She struck first, catching him by surprise. A jab to the ribs, clean and fast. *One.*

He blocked clumsily, stunned, and she followed with a low sweep of her leg that clipped his knee. He stumbled, caught himself, and laughed.

"You're a lot quicker when you're sober," he quipped.

She ignored him, focusing on her next move. He swung wide, she ducked under and drove an elbow into his gut. He grunted, staggering back. *Two.*

One more strike and she'd wipe that smug look right off his face.

She swung, but he moved quicker than she anticipated. Her punch met empty air. His hand caught her wrist mid-strike, tugging her forward, and his shoulder slammed into her chest as the deck tilted beneath her.

She hit the planks hard, breath snatched clean out of her. Point to Zale.

…*How?*

Gasps followed by cheers erupted around them, boots stomping. Zale stepped back, offering a hand. "Little piece of advice: don't lunge where your opponent *wants* ye to."

Nerissa ignored his hand and rolled to her feet, cheeks burning with indignation. He had played her, let her get comfortable before bringing the real fight.

This time, she was ready, or so she thought. She feinted left, went low, aimed a kick for his ribs. He twisted, faster than she expected, and caught her ankle. With one sharp motion, he pulled and swept her leg out from under her.

She barely managed to twist midfall and avoid cracking her head on the planks. *Two points for Zale.*

He let her stand back up, cracking his knuckles while he waited.

When he advanced, she drove forward, feinting another punch before shifting her weight and slamming her shoulder into his chest. He grunted, grabbed her by the waist to steady himself, and suddenly they were chest to chest, breathless.

His voice dropped low, rough as the sea between storms. "Ye sure you're still fightin' me, love?" His breath brushed her ear. "Feels a bit like you've changed tactics."

"In your dreams, pirate." She twisted out of his grip, grabbing his wrist and shoving hard. He stumbled back against the rail, catching himself with one arm. "Almost had me," he said, still grinning.

Nerissa lunged again. He sidestepped, caught her by the waist, and spun. The world blurred, and then she was flat on her back *again* with his body hovering above her, one forearm pressed lightly across her collarbone.

"Any last words?" His voice came out smug.

"Yeah." She wrinkled her nose. "When's the last time you *bathed*?"

The pirates howled. Zale huffed a laugh and tapped her forehead. "I win."

The circle exploded with cheers, whistles, and Bran hollering, "GET A CABIN!"

Zale pushed up, breathing quickly, victory flush across his face. He offered his hand.

Nerissa eyed it, then him. She took it. His pull was strong, warm, pulling her closer than necessary. Her pulse skipped, though she'd never admit it.

"You got lucky," she muttered, brushing herself off.

"You've already floored half the crew. Let's call it even."

She stepped further into his space, chin tilted. "Don't patronize me."

"I'd never," Zale said, smirk betraying the lie.

There was no way she was about to let him hold this over her head. She had him figured out now; she was sure victory would be hers if she could convince him to another round.

"I want a rematch." She glared up at him, ignoring the lack of space between them. "Let's raise the stakes."

The crew gasped as one.

Zale frowned, wary. "Terms?"

"Winner picks the loser's tattoo," she said nonchalantly. "...and where it goes."

The crew erupted into shrieks, whistles, and catcalls.

"Make it somewhere scandalous!" Bran yelled.

"Don't make it easy for him, Nerissa!" Eon called. "I have *so many* ideas if you need help picking!"

Roan shook his head, "You're both cracked."

But Zale's eyes lit with challenge, mischief, and something more intense. With a deliberate slowness, he rolled up his sleeves, pulled a bandana from his waist and tied it around his forehead. "Ye've got yourself a deal, love."

Nerissa rolled her neck, taking her stance again. This time, she wasn't going to let him read her. She'd studied him during the last match—the twitch of his hand before he swung, the lazy rhythm meant to lure her in. She could see every tell, every trap.

When he lunged, she moved first. Her fist cracked against his jaw, followed by a sharp kick to his ribs that sent him staggering back. The crowd erupted.

Zale laughed, shaking it off. "Alright then," he said, eyes gleaming. "Guess we're done playin'."

"Guess so," she shot back, flicking hair from her face. "Hope you like dolphins."

She dodged his next strike and pivoted fast, sweeping his legs out from under him. He caught himself on one hand, rolled, came up again.

She saw the opening—clear as sunlight through water. One more strike. That's all it would take.

She lunged—

And the world went white.

It wasn't pain at first, just blinding brilliance bursting behind her eyes. Her stomach lurched. The deck swayed hard beneath her feet.

Zale moved, a blur she couldn't track, and his fist connected squarely with her nose. A sharp, wet *crack* split the air.

She stumbled backward, disoriented, blood spattering her lip. The last thing she heard was Zale's startled curse before everything went dark.

She was twelve again.

Back in Nautalia.

The sea stretched endlessly in every direction, a kaleidoscope of shifting blue-green, fractured sunlight dripping down from above. Kelp swayed like curtains; sand plumed with every flick of her tail.

Nerissa hovered, armor too big for her frame, fists clenched, jaw locked.

Damarion circled her like a shark in thought, his powerful tail keeping him steady in the current. The trident in his grip gleamed, not polished for ceremony, but dulled by use.

"You're distracted," his voice carried through the water, resonant, unyielding.

"I'm not!" she snapped.

He moved. Fast.

The butt of the trident slammed across her face.

Crunch.

Pain flared white-hot. The water around her bloomed green.

Nerissa reeled, disoriented, the shock ringing through her skull. She hit the seabed hard, sand billowing like smoke around her.

Blood spiraled from her nose—emerald threads unraveling in the current.

Damarion was there instantly. He steadied her, but offered no apology.

"You cannot afford distractions," he said, hand tight on her shoulder. His voice was fierce, but not cruel. "The ocean is merciless. The enemy won't wait. Not for a thought. Not for fear. Not for you."

Her hands trembled, fingers digging into the sand.

He tilted her chin, forcing her gaze to his. Storm-gray eyes locked on hers.

"You fight with everything you are, Skíon," he said. "Or you die."

Nerissa blinked.

She was on the deck again.

Blurry shapes swam into focus, figures looming above her, voices muffled as if underwater as she came back to her senses.

Zale was kneeling over her, one arm braced behind her back, cradling her head with surprising gentleness. His face hovered close, tense with worry.

Roan was crouched beside them, pressing two fingers against her throat. His brows knit in concentration.

"Nerissa?" Roan's voice, low and clinical. A finger lifted her eyelid. "Look at me. Can you hear me?"

"Well, that settles it," Bran drawled from somewhere over her shoulder. "I'm retiring from combat. Clearly, chivalry is dead, and Zale's the one who killed it."

Zale shot him a look sharp enough to gut him. "I thought she'd dodge it!" his voice cracked. "She *always* dodges. Why didn't she—?"

Nerissa drew a shaky breath. Her nose throbbed, but the world had stopped spinning. She pushed against Zale's arm, sitting up slowly.

"I'm fine," Nerissa groaned, waving Roan's hand away. "It's just my nose."

Roan raised a skeptical brow but leaned back, giving her space.

Zale's hands lingered a second longer before he released her, reluctantly. His gaze stayed fixed on her face, the worry and concern evident.

Carefully, she reached up and touched the bridge of her nose, assessing the damage. It ached like the abyss, but it wasn't broken, just bleeding. Her fingers came away wet and sticky.

Her stomach lurched.

Her fingertips were glistening in the moonlight like moss-dappled emeralds.

No—Not here. Not now.

Zale leaned closer, voice low. "Are you okay?"

She curled her fingers fast, smearing the blood across her pants before anyone else could see, and quickly pushed herself to her feet. "I said I'm fine."

Roan's eyes narrowed. He didn't buy it, she could tell, but he let it slide.

She brushed past Zale, ignoring the weight of his gaze on her back. The crowd began to stir again—laughter breaking through, jokes tossed into the air, someone shouting, "Rematch when she can see straight!"

But Nerissa didn't hear them.

All she could hear was the rush of blood in her ears.

All she could feel was the phantom sting of salt water burning her nose.

Sea withdrawal.

Zale

His heart was still hammering in his chest as Nerissa fled the deck. Guilt gnawed through the rush of adrenaline. It was only supposed to be a friendly sparring match; he hadn't meant to actually land that last hit. Her reflexes were normally quicker than most—even after a drink. So what had happened?

Bran leaned in, voice a stage whisper loud enough for half the deck, "Oh, I *cannot wait* to tell Brigid that you punched a woman."

Zale didn't even glance at him.

Something was off. He saw the look in her eyes when her hand came away bloody. How she quickly wiped it off as if she was trying to hide something. And then she brushed past him, gone before he could question her.

The crew was already back to jeering and shouting ink suggestions, but Zale barely heard them. His chest felt tight. What if she was ill, or what if she'd been injured worse than she'd admitted? He wasn't about to let her suffer in silence because of her stubborn pride.

So he shoved Bran's elbow off his shoulder, and followed after her.

The noise of the crew faded as he descended the companionway, trading rum-soaked laughter for the dim creak of the hull and the drip of seawater through the boards.

He found her in the washroom, the door left ajar. Nerissa stood with her back to him, bent over the shelf, sleeves rolled to the elbow. Her braid had come half-loose in the scuffle, dark strands curling damp against her neck.

At the sound of his steps, she grabbed the bloodied rag and shoved it into the bucket, replacing it with a clean cloth just as he came into view.

He cleared his throat gently. "Hey."

"Come to gloat?" she asked without turning.

Zale shook his head, then realized she couldn't see it. "No," he said quietly. "I came to apologize."

That made her glance over, pressing the cloth to her nose. Her eyes were shadowed, expression guarded. "For what?"

He looked at her like she'd asked what water was made of. "I hit you in the *face*, Nerissa."

She offered a crooked smile, wincing slightly. "Not the first time I've been hit. At least you didn't break my nose."

"You should've won," he admitted, voice low. The bruise blooming around her nose sent a prickle of guilt through his chest again. "I—I didn't think I'd land that hit. You never miss a dodge. What happened?"

Her grip tightened around the cloth. "I got distracted."

Zale frowned. It was the way she said it. Too quick. Too practiced. Like she'd already rehearsed the answer that would make him stop asking.

She was hiding something. He knew it in his gut.

"Distracted," he echoed.

She nodded once. "Sun got in my eye. It doesn't matter."

He stepped a little closer, fists clenching and unclenching at his sides. "It does to me."

Her gaze flicked to his and away again, like she couldn't quite hold it.

"I never want to hurt you," he said quietly. "Even by accident."

Nerissa turned back to the bucket, rinsing the cloth. Finally, she looked back at him, eyes steady.

"You didn't hurt me," she said gently. "Looks much worse than it is. I faltered. That was on me."

Zale held her gaze, his brows drawing slightly together.

"Doesn't matter whose fault it was," he murmured. "I hated seeing you bleed."

He shrugged one shoulder. "That's all."

Nerissa let out a slow breath, eyes flicking away before settling back on his.

"Well, you'll be pleased to know I'm honoring the terms," she said, tone lighter now. "I'll get the tattoo."

He blinked. "You're serious?"

"Of course I am." She folded her arms. "I lost. You get to choose."

"Nerissa...you don't have to."

"I want to." A small smirk tugged at her mouth. "Besides, can't have the crew thinking you've gone soft."

He scratched his chin thoughtfully. "Alright. I'll try not to pick anything too humiliating."

"Just don't misspell it," she said, turning back to the mirror. "Or put it somewhere awkward."

A beat of silence.

“Define awkward.”

“Zale!” She tossed the cloth at him over her shoulder. It missed by an inch.

He caught it easily, a laugh breaking loose as he tossed it back into the bucket. “Come on,” he said, jerking his head toward the stairs. “Let’s find Ma Wen before you lose your nerve.”

Nerissa rolled her eyes, but Zale couldn't help but feel relieved as they headed up to the main deck together. She seemed okay, for now.

By the time Zale and Nerissa returned to the main deck, the mood had shifted. Moonlight spilled in silver ribbons across the planks, catching on sails that fluttered lazily in the breeze. Most of the crew had resumed their usual evening routines of swapping tales, playing cards, and drinking.

Cormac strummed a slow, lazy rhythm on his fiddle. Eon nursed his pride with a damp rag soaked in one of Roan's concoctions. Bran was dealing out a hand to a small group of men. But all eyes subtly followed Zale and Nerissa as they passed.

Zale didn’t say a word as he crossed to Ma Wen, who was seated near Eon and sipping sake. He tapped the cook’s shoulder once.

“Ma Wen. Ink kit.”

The man raised an eyebrow, slowly, then gave a faint grunt of acknowledgment. He rose and disappeared below deck without a word.

Nerissa hovered near the mainmast, arms crossed, watching Zale with guarded curiosity. He was glad to see the color had returned to her face, albeit mottled with purple bruising.

"You ever had ink before?" Zale asked, trying to sound casual.

"No, does it hurt?" She eyed him warily. "Be honest."

"Hurts less than having your shoulder dislocated—or having it set."

"Comforting," she hummed, looking away.

"In all seriousness, though, Ma Wen is probably the most gentle inker you'll find. You're in good hands." He paused, examining her expression. "It's not too late to back out, you know. No one will think any less of you."

Her eyes sharpened. "No, I need to do this. I want to prove myself."

Zale nodded. She was truly stubborn sometimes.

Ma Wen returned, carrying a battered wooden case. He set it down on an overturned barrel and opened it with the reverence of a holy ritual. Inside: a small collection of pigment jars, needles, cloths, and a thick leather-bound journal.

Zale crouched beside it, flipping through the pages carefully as he reviewed sketched designs ranging from swirling ocean waves to coiled sea serpents and compass roses. Some simple, others elaborate. Nerissa deserved something meaningful, something personal.

When he reached the page he wanted, he stopped. "This one," he said, tapping the design.

Ma Wen examined it, nodding once. "A bold choice."

"She's earned it."

Ma Wen looked to Nerissa. "You want to see it first?"

She shook her head. "Surprise me."

"Suit yourself," he glanced at Zale, "Where's it going?"

Zale considered for a moment, his eyes briefly dipping to the pale line beneath Nerissa's collarbone—a scar, old and uneven. He had first noticed it the day the Dravari attacked, when he had coerced her to dance with him. She shifted slightly under the weight of his gaze.

"There," he said. "Just under the collarbone. The scar."

"Why there?" Nerissa's brows lowered.

"Might as well make something out of it."

The crew had caught on now. They weren't crowding—yet—but whispers were spreading like wind through canvas. Someone let out a low whistle.

Nerissa stepped forward. "Let's do it."

Ma Wen simply gestured for her to sit as he selected his tools. Zale stood beside her as she settled onto the barrel, brushing her collar aside to expose the skin. The scar gleamed faintly in the moonlight, ragged and lonely.

Not for much longer.

Ma Wen dipped the needle into the ink as Nerissa sat still on the overturned barrel. Zale crossed his arms, watching her for any signs of fainting.

"So, what would I have been in for if *you'd* won?" Zale asked with morbid curiosity, hoping the conversation might distract her from the needle.

"You really want to know?" She looked up at him through narrow, mischievous eyes.

"Yeah, I do."

"It was going to be a patch of fish scales." She hissed softly as the needle bit into her skin.

Zale arched a brow, relieved. "That's all? I was expectin' much worse."

"On your left cheek."

He blinked. "...Which cheek, Nerissa?"

Her gaze drifted downward, making him shift uncomfortably. "The one you sit on."

Now Zale feared *he* would faint. "You wouldn't."

Her saccharine smile said otherwise.

Without looking up, Ma Wen muttered, "I'm grateful you lost, then, little fish. I've no wish to ink a man's arse."

Zale scowled at him. "That makes two of us."

Nerissa smirked, biting back laughter as Ma Wen continued to work.

Then Eon appeared out of thin air, squinting at her scar.

"How'd you get that, anyway?" he asked, tone curious but careless. "If you don't mind me asking, I mean."

Nerissa didn't flinch, but Zale saw the subtle shift in her spine, the way her smile faded. She stared ahead for a long moment before answering softly.

"Knife wound when I was eleven. The day I lost my parents."

The silence that followed was brittle.

Ma Wen's needle paused mid-air.

Zale's brows knit. He wanted to say something but couldn't find the words.

Eon's face went pale. "Oh. I—stars, I didn't mean—I wasn't—"

He looked to Zale for help and found none, just stunned silence.

"I, uh—Nestor!" he said suddenly. "Nestor was calling for me. Probably. Yep." He spun on his heel and bolted across the deck, muttering apologies under his breath.

Ma Wen resumed the tattoo, the tapping now oddly loud in the silence that followed.

Zale exhaled quietly through his nose, his voice low. "He's a knucklehead."

Nerissa offered a small, tired smile. "It's alright. He didn't know."

Zale didn't respond, but his hand came to rest lightly near her shoulder as Ma Wen worked without comment. The ink bloomed slowly beneath the needle.

Nerissa

Ma Wen finally leaned back, inspecting his work with a critical eye. Then he gave a short nod of approval and reached for a clean cloth, dabbing the skin gently. "There," he murmured. "Done."

He handed Nerissa a small mirror, its glass cracked diagonally through the middle, the reflection fractured like sea ice. Still, it was enough.

She angled it carefully, lifting it just enough to glimpse the new mark.

A black serpent.

Coiled and elegant, its head poised like it might strike, its body arched in a graceful loop that perfectly followed the curve of her scar. It didn't hide the scar so much as inhabit it, twining around the old wound like it was protecting it.

Zale stepped closer, his voice somber. "Every crewmate has a version. Design changes a little from person to person. But it's always the serpent."

A symbol of loyalty. Of survival. Of the ship and the strange, seaworn family bound to it.

He could've picked anything—something ridiculous, some inside joke or cheeky emblem meant to tease. He'd won, after all. But he'd chosen this.

Something meaningful.

Something that made her feel like she belonged.

Without quite meaning to, she glanced at his arm. She'd caught glimpses of the tattoo before, but she'd never really studied it. Now, he tugged his left sleeve higher, revealing most of the serpent coiled around his arm.

It wound up from his wrist to his shoulder in sleek, fluid arcs, bold and dark, its scales catching the moonlight like armor. Its head curled around his wrist, fangs bared, tongue forked.

Nerissa blinked. It was *not* subtle. But it was fitting.

Zale caught her expression and tilted his head. "Too dramatic?"

Before she could answer, Ma Wen snorted behind them. "Took three sessions to finish because he wouldn't stop squirming."

"I didn't squirm," Zale said, wounded in dignity, if not in truth.

"You were as still as a fish out of water."

Zale turned to Nerissa with a long-suffering look. "You see what I deal with?"

She smiled despite herself, fingers brushing gingerly against her own tattoo.

"Thank you," she murmured, still not looking away. "Both of you."

Ma Wen only hummed and returned to cleaning his tools.

Zale leaned in and said softly, "It's not just ink. It's a promise. You're one of us."

CHAPTER 30

OCEAN EYES

Nerissa

The wind tore at her hair, the surface world wide and strange above her. Shadows of masts loomed over the harbor like the bones of giants. She shouldn't have been here, her parents had told her to stay home, to wait. But she wanted to help.

She trailed after them, heart pounding, bare feet whispering against the warped planks of the dock. Her legs still felt wobbly; she wasn't used to walking so far on land. Her parents didn't see her at first. She remembered thinking she'd done well, that she was clever enough to keep up.

But then her father turned. His eyes found hers. "Nerissa. Hide."

She froze. His tone brooked no argument.

Her mother pressed a finger to her lips and whispered, "Stay behind us."

So she did, heart hammering as her parents moved deeper into the Harbor

Citadel.

The floorboards creaked. There—signs of a struggle.

Loose scales scattered across the planks, torn from skin. Dark green blood smeared across the wood like old paint.

Her stomach dropped.

That's blood. Real blood.

She had never seen so much before. Never smelled it. It clung to her nostrils, sharp and metallic, impossible to mistake.

Her throat tightened.

Something terrible happened here.

Her parents gathered what evidence they could. They had to get back to Nautalia. They had to warn the king.

But they only made it as far as the docks.

Shadows dropped from the pier. Men in masks, blades glinting in the half-light.

Panic shot through her chest.

Too many. What do we do?

Her parents fought, her mother's spear flashing, her father's dagger striking in quick arcs. They were strong. Fierce. They tried to protect her.

A knife spun through the air, lodging itself just beneath her collarbone.

Her scream stuck in her throat, choked by shock. She stumbled, blood seeping hot and slick down her chest.

I'm going to die.

Her father caught her, pulling her upright and yanking the blade free. His voice was urgent, desperate. "Run. Find Damarion. Go!"

Her mother's voice cut across his, fierce and unyielding. "Don't turn back. No matter what happens."

But Nerissa stumbled again, blood spattering the dock beneath her. Fear dragged at her heels, and against her mother's command, she looked back.

Through the chaos, one figure stood still.

A silver cane gleamed, ruby catching the torchlight from the docks. His eyes locked onto hers.

For a moment the battle seemed to fall silent, nothing in the world but his gaze pinning her where she stood.

Cold. Calculating.

Alpheus.

She was in the tower dungeon now. Chained and numb. Alpheus was holding a needle. She couldn't move, couldn't shout.

"Suppression Serum," he said as he injected it into her arm.

Nerissa jolted upright in her cot, breath ragged, heart pounding against her ribs like it meant to break free. Her nightshirt was plastered to her skin with sweat.

She didn’t move. Couldn’t.

Her chest clenched, sharp and crushing, like a fist squeezing her heart. Gasping for air that refused to come. Every breath was shallow, useless. Her vision tilted, dark at the edges, the room spinning with it.

I’m drowning again. No, suffocating.

One trembling hand rose to her collarbone, pressing against the phantom sting of the knife wound. The skin was smooth now, but she knew the scar beneath her fingertips as surely as her own name.

For a moment all she could see was blood on the docks. Her mother’s voice in her ears. Alpheus’s eyes pinning her in place.

The pressure mounted. Her pulse thundered, too fast, too loud.

Panic. She knew this feeling. She remembered it—the Dravari raid, freezing after the kill, the same suffocating terror.

Her thumb dragged lower, brushing over the raw skin where the black serpent coiled around the scar. Not just an old wound anymore, but a mark Zale had chosen, like a shield laid over the past.

Still, the nightmare threatened to choke her, heavy and suffocating.

Nerissa doubled forward, pressing her knuckles hard to her mouth to stifle the sob threatening to claw its way out.

It was just a nightmare. Only a nightmare.

But it wasn't just a nightmare. They were memories. Whatever Alpheus did to her, was that why she couldn't shift?

Her pulse still raced, wild and uneven, as she squeezed her eyes shut. Forced her focus inward.

In through the nose. Hold. Out through the mouth.

Zale's voice: *Match me. In…out. She tried. One breath. Then another. Her chest still ached, but slowly, little by little, the iron vice around her lungs began to ease.*

Nerissa sat there for a long moment, waiting for her pulse to settle, for the air to feel like air again. But the cot felt too small, the walls too close. The nightmare was still so vivid in her mind.

She needed fresh air.

Carefully, she swung her legs over the side, bare feet finding the cool planks. Brigid's even breathing filled the cabin. Nerissa paused, every movement measured, and then crept toward the door. She eased it open, slipping through as silently as she could.

The corridor was dark. Empty.

The companionway groaned under her weight as she climbed, one hand brushing the railing, the other clutching her nightshirt against the draft.

She pushed open the hatch as cool night air rushed over her skin, making it prickle. Her thin nightshirt did little against the chill, but it cut through the heaviness in her chest. The sea stretched endlessly around the ship, like rippling black glass beneath the moon.

She drew in a deep breath. Salt and wind and freedom.

It wasn't enough to erase the dream. But it was enough to remind her she was awake. Far from Alpheus.

Her feet carried her across the deck, to the main mast, before she'd even thought it through.

Her fingers curled around the rope ladder. She knew Zale was on watch; he had headed up to the crow's nest shortly after Ma Wen finished inking her tattoo. Now, with her chest still tight and her thoughts muddled, she climbed. She wasn't sure what exactly she was looking for, but whatever it was, maybe Zale could help.

One rung, then another. Her limbs still trembled from the aftershocks of the nightmare, every muscle tensing with leftover panic, but she forced herself upward. The mast swayed gently in the wind, ropes creaking. Higher. Higher. The crow's nest loomed above her, a dark silhouette against the moonlit sky.

By the time she pushed her head and shoulders through the narrow opening in the platform, her breath came ragged, not from the climb, but from the weight still pressing on her chest.

Zale was seated with his back to the railing, one knee bent, arms draped loosely over it. His sword lay beside him, forgotten but within reach. Moonlight silvered the edges of his profile. He didn't startle at her sudden appearance, he just turned, surprise flickering across his face before it softened into something else. Something gentle.

She froze, not sure how to explain herself.

Then his hand extended down, waiting. She gratefully took it without hesitation.

He pulled her up onto the platform with ease, not letting go until she was safely in the nest. Whatever he saw in her face must have told him enough. Without a word, he guided her closer, next to where he sat against the railing.

For a while, neither of them spoke. The night wrapped around them—dark sky, darker sea, scattered lanterns swaying from the rigging lending to the eerie atmosphere. Nerissa leaned forward, arms wrapped tightly around her knees, forcing her breath to steady.

Zale glanced at her at last. "Couldn't sleep?"

She shook her head. "Nightmare." After a breath, she added, "Had another...panic attack." The words felt heavy on her tongue, but she forced them out.

He didn't react with surprise or pity. Just nodded once, slowly, like he understood.

Nerissa let the silence stretch. Then, almost grudgingly, she said, "I did the breathing thing. The one you showed me."

Zale's gaze flicked toward her as he listened.

"It helped," she admitted. "Where'd you learn that, anyway?" she asked after a brief pause. "You don't seem the type to study breathing exercises for the fun of it."

Zale's mouth twitched at that. "Didn't. Roan taught me."

"For what?"

His gaze dropped to where his sword lay, thumb brushing absently over a scar on his wrist. "First time I killed a man," he whispered. "Didn't mean to, but it didn't matter. Couldn't breathe right for hours after that. Thought I was dying, but Roan said it was just panic. Sat with me until I learned to get air in proper."

Nerissa's thoughts returned to the Salty Siren, when Zale had refused to draw his sword. Now it made sense, why he never used his weapon unless there was no other choice.

"Did you have many more attacks after that?"

"Aye, anytime I smelled gunpowder or blood, it seemed to trigger the panic all over again. But eventually, I learned to fight through it. In this line of work, ye either find your breath or ye drown."

She hesitated, her voice quieter. "It scares me when it happens. I feel like my body's betraying me."

His head tilted slightly toward her. "That's how it feels," he said softly. "Like the air's turned traitor. But it isn't. You just have to remind it who's captain."

The faintest flicker of a smile ghosted across her face, but it faded just as fast. "Even though the breathing helped, the walls still felt like they were closing in. I needed air, so I came up to the deck. I don't even remember deciding to climb up here—I just...did."

Her mouth twisted, half in frustration at herself. "Stupid of me. I could've slipped."

Zale leaned an elbow against the railing, studying her. "Aye," he said quietly. "But you didn't."

Nerissa rested her chin on her knees, eyes fixed on the horizon. After a moment she asked, "Do you ever have nightmares?"

Zale was quiet, gaze sliding back to the sea as well. "Sometimes."

"What about?"

He exhaled through his nose, long and slow. "There's one that comes back now and then."

She waited.

"I'm adrift at sea," he said finally, voice rough. "No ship. No crew. Just me, floating like a bit of wreckage. Dark sky above, no stars. Black water all around." His jaw flexed. "Then all at once I'm not floating anymore. I'm sinking. Trying to swim, but I don't know which way is up. Doesn't matter how hard I fight, I keep going down into the dark until I wake up."

Nerissa turned her head to study him, curiosity piqued. "What do you think it means?"

He huffed a humorless laugh that didn't reach his eyes. "Means I've got anxiety about not belonging anywhere." He shrugged one shoulder. "Or at least, that's what Roan's medical books say."

"Do you believe that? What Roan's books say?"

Zale worked his jaw, eyes fixed on the endless darkness below. For a long moment he didn't answer.

"When you don't know where you come from…" His voice was still rough, unsteady in a way she rarely heard. "…it makes it hard to believe you belong anywhere."

Nerissa studied him, noticing the way his neck muscles tensed. Her heart ached with recognition.

"Sometimes," she said softly, "even knowing where you come from—what's expected of you—you still might not feel like you belong there."

He turned, brow furrowed slightly, as if her words surprised him.

"It isn't about where you come from," Nerissa continued, steadier now. "It's about finding people who care for you unconditionally. People who let you be yourself, whether they're blood or not."

"That's…profoundly wise." Zale's gaze held hers before he looked away, out toward the horizon again. After a moment, he broke the tension.

"Want me to take a shot at diagnosing *your* trauma based on your nightmare? I'm practically a professional now. Read at least two of Roan's books," he said with a wry smile.

The corner of her mouth lifted. "I appreciate the offer." Her voice quieted. "But mine usually aren't dreams. They're memories. The meaning isn't so ambiguous."

The humor faded from his expression. He didn't press, didn't ask, but the silence that followed was thick with everything she hadn't said aloud.

Then the breeze shifted, rising sharp and icy across the mast. Nerissa shivered before she could stop herself, the thin fabric of her nightshirt no match for the bite of the ocean air.

Without a word, Zale shrugged out of his long coat. He draped it over her shoulders, carefully, as if he was trying not to startle her.

The weight and warmth settled around her, smelling faintly of sea spray and leather and something indefinably him.

Nerissa blinked, startled by the quiet gesture, but she didn't push it away. She drew the coat closer, feeling the tightness in her chest ease, just a little. She glanced sideways at him, catching the way he leaned against the railing, eyes distant on the horizon.

"Can I ask you something?" she said at last.

Zale looked over, one brow raised. "You just did."

She gave him a look. "How *did* you get your name? I believe you owe me a story."

He rubbed the back of his neck, a little sheepish. "Ah...it's a little embarrassing."

Her lips curved. "I promise not to tell Bran."

He huffed a laugh and leaned back against the wood, eyes fixed on the stars. "Nestor gave it to me. Said I needed a name that meant something. Something strong."

"And Zale means…?"

"Strength of the sea." He made a face, like he expected her to laugh. "He thought it might help. That maybe if I grew into it, it'd make up for not having...you know. Anything else."

Nerissa was quiet, reflecting on his story. "It suits you."

He turned his head toward her, surprised. "Yeah?"

"Strength isn't just about muscle. It's about carrying people with you. You do that, whether you see it or not."

Zale studied her for a long second, lips parting like he wanted to say something else, but whatever it was, he swallowed it.

Instead, he smirked. "So you're saying I don't have muscle?"

Her gaze flicked, unbidden, to the curve of his arm where it rested along the rail, muscle flexing with casual ease. Heat pricked her cheeks, but she lifted her chin, feigning indifference.

"Obviously not," she said. "But strength isn't the only thing I see when I look at you."

"Careful, lass," he said teasingly. "You'll have me thinkin' you actually like me."

Her heart gave a traitorous jolt, but she forced her gaze away, back toward the horizon. "Of course I like you," she said briskly. "Same as I like everyone else on this crew."

He said nothing for a long, awkward moment. Until finally, he asked, "What about your name?"

She turned back to him, slowly.

"Daughter of the waves." The sound that escaped her was closer to a scoff than a chuckle. "Poetic, isn't it?"

"Daughter of the waves," Zale repeated, a crooked smile tugging at his mouth. "Bit ironic, don't you think? Considering you were half-drowned when I pulled you out of the sea."

Her eyes flicked to him, sharp, but the corner of her mouth betrayed the smallest upward pull. "Trust you to point that out."

"I'm just sayin'," he said, grinning now. "Sometimes names can be hard to live up to."

She couldn't tell him how on-the-nose her name actually was. Not without telling him her secret. So she said nothing.

Zale's grin lingered, but after a moment it softened. "Jokes aside," he said quietly, "it suits you."

Her brow furrowed, silently asking him to explain.

"You've got ocean eyes," he went on. "Stormy ones. Like they're always searching for something just out of reach. Longing."

Nerissa blinked at him, caught off guard by the way he waxed poetic. Then her lips twitched. "Did you just quote *Stormbound Hearts* at me?"

His mouth fell open, all mock offense. "What? No."

She laughed, "You absolutely did!"

"Don't tell Bran. He'd never let me live it down."

"Pirate's honor," she promised, saluting him.

They settled into comfortable silence as the rigging creaked rhythmically around them. She pulled Zale's coat tighter around her shoulders as the wind picked up again, grateful for its warmth. Leaning back against the railing, she stared at the stars overhead. Her eyelids felt heavy, but she wasn't ready to sleep yet.

Zale didn't speak as he shifted beside her, letting his gaze drift skyward again.

Then, so softly she almost thought she imagined it, he began to hum.

The melody was low and rough-edged, more felt than heard. A sea shanty, she realized. One of Cormac's. Slower than usual. Softer. As if he were trying not to wake something sleeping.

Nerissa's eyes fluttered shut.

She hadn't meant to. Just for a second.

Just long enough to rest them.

She blinked again—once, twice—then exhaled slow and long, her body tipping ever so slightly toward the warmth beside her.

CHAPTER 31

YOU'RE A TERRIBLE LIAR

Nerissa

A breeze stirred, gentle and cool, sweeping across the deck and teasing loose strands of hair across her face. Nerissa stirred with a faint frown, scrunching her nose as something tickled her cheek. She shifted slightly, only to find herself pressed against something warm and solid.

And breathing.

Her eyes blinked open slowly.

Wooden railing. Sky going pink at the edges. The creak of the mast above.

And—

Zale's coat around her shoulders.

Zale's *chest* beneath her head.

Zale's *heartbeat* beneath her ear.

Oh no.

Oh no no no.

Memory returned in a slow, horrified trickle. The nightmare. The panic attack. The stars. His humming.

She was nestled against his side, one arm tucked awkwardly between them, the other curled near his chest. Her leg was *overlapping his*. And he was *very much awake.*

Mortified, she jerked upright. "Sorry—I didn't mean to fall asleep on you," she blurted, tugging the coat tighter around herself. "If you tell anyone, I'll deny everything."

Then she tried to stand.

Tried.

Her legs, half-asleep and stiff from the cramped position, gave out beneath her. With a startled yelp, she stumbled—and would've gone face-first into the railing if Zale hadn't caught her around the waist.

"Easy," he murmured, steadying her.

Her hands gripped his arms instinctively, and for one horrifyingly long heartbeat, they were far too close again. His face hovered inches from hers, and she knew—*knew*—her cheeks were burning hotter than the morning sun breaking over the horizon.

"I swear I'm not usually this uncoordinated," she muttered, eyes darting everywhere except his.

Zale's mouth quirked. "Must be my influence."

"Don't flatter yourself."

He made no move to loosen his hold on her waist, and Nerissa found herself staring up into his eyes despite herself. He held her gaze with a quiet intensity as the wind shifted, creaking in the rigging around them. She swore the temperature spiked ten degrees.

"Are you going to let me go," she asked, voice just a bit too breathy, "or do I need to file a formal complaint?"

Zale's lips twitched. "Go ahead. I'll make sure it reaches Nestor's desk. In triplicate."

Still, he didn't move.

Neither did she.

And it wasn't until a gull shrieked overhead—loud and obnoxious, like the universe itself was clearing its throat—that Nerissa finally stepped back. Or rather, *launched* herself backward like a guilty apprentice caught snooping in the captain's quarters.

Zale leaned casually against the railing, as if he hadn't just been inches from kissing her.

"Breakfast?" he asked, with mock innocence. "Or do you need a minute to regain your...coordination?"

Nerissa gave him a withering look, which unfortunately did nothing to cool the flush in her cheeks.

"I hate you," she muttered.

"You say the sweetest things in the morning."

She shot him another glare.

Zale smirked, one hand gesturing toward the ladder. "Ladies first."

Nerissa rolled her eyes, still flustered, but she turned toward the opening in the platform anyway. She crouched, bracing her hands on the rim, and started to lower herself onto the rope ladder—

Then froze.

A sharp, involuntary jolt spasmed through her thigh, her calf seizing a heartbeat later. Pain flared hot and merciless, locking the limb like rusted iron. She gasped, her grip faltering on the wood as her leg buckled beneath her.

For one terrifying instant she wasn't thinking about pain at all—only the drop yawning beneath the crow's nest, the dizzying open air, the certainty that she was about to fall. Her stomach lurched, panic crashing over her harder than the cramp itself—

"Whoa! Hey, easy."

Zale's arms hooked beneath hers before she could tumble through the hatch. He hauled her back to safety, settling her onto the planks and bracing her as she sank to the floor of the nest.

Nerissa's mind reeled with the grim realization clawing its way through her chest.

First her siren blood had returned. Now spontaneous muscle cramps. The next phase of sea withdrawal.

Her hands curled into fists against the wood.

No, not yet. Not here.

If she could just endure until they made it back to the cove...

Zale crouched in front of her, one hand still braced on her shoulder. His brows were drawn low, his voice sharper with concern than she'd ever heard it.

"What was that? Ye alright?"

"I'm fine," she said too quickly, dragging her hands down to knead at the rebellious muscles in her thigh, trying to coax them into loosening.

His eyes narrowed, not buying it for a second.

"Just a cramp," she added, softer this time. "Probably dehydrated."

"Ye sure you're okay?" he asked, searching her face.

"I'm fine," she insisted, still rubbing at her thigh. The muscle had started to loosen, though the ache lingered like a warning.

He didn't look convinced. "Maybe I should take you to Roan. He's got that tonic for muscle spasms—might help."

It won't, she thought. *Not for this.*

Nerissa shook her head, forcing her voice even. "I probably just slept on it wrong. What I need is water, not a tonic." She managed a strained smile that didn't quite reach her eyes. "If it still hurts after breakfast, I'll go to Roan. Promise."

Zale studied her a beat longer, clearly skeptical, but he finally gave a short nod. "Alright. But you'll hold to that promise."

"I will," she said quickly.

He eased back, rising to his feet. "Think you feel okay enough to stand?"

She nodded, though her pride was doing most of the work.

"Good. I'll go first."

Before she could argue, he turned and lowered himself through the hatch onto the ladder, moving with the sure, easy grace of long practice. He glanced up once. "Just in case you slip again."

Nerissa waited until he was a safe distance below before lowering herself carefully through the hatch. Her leg still ached, though the worst of the cramp had passed.

She adjusted the long coat tighter around herself, suddenly twice as grateful for it as she felt the cool air nip at her bare legs.

"Don't even think about looking up," she warned, voice sharper than she intended.

Zale chuckled, the sound drifting up from below. "Wouldn't dream of it."

She rolled her eyes, focusing on each rung, one hand over the other, as the mast creaked with their combined weight. Her pride burned hotter than the ache in her muscles, but at least the coat gave her dignity a fighting chance.

The deck was quiet when they landed, the dawn hush still hanging over the ship. Anyone awake would already be in the galley chasing coffee or bread. Zale reached up as Nerissa climbed down the last section of rope, his hands steadying her waist as he helped her down to the boards. She was only slightly wobbly, though she straightened quickly as if daring him to comment.

"Quartermaster's cabin," he said firmly, keeping a hand near her elbow until she brushed it off. "Humor me."

She sighed, tugging his coat tighter around herself, but didn't argue.

They crossed to the companionway, their footsteps quiet on the planks. Nerissa reached for the latch—

Only for the door to swing open from the inside.

Brigid stood in the threshold, arms folded, eyes flicking from Nerissa's nightshirt...to Zale's unmistakably oversized coat draped over her shoulders...back to Nerissa again.

Her brows lifted.

"Well then," she drawled, slow and pointed. "Eventful night, was it?"

Zale made a strangled sound somewhere between a cough and a choke, suddenly very interested in a knot above the doorframe.

Nerissa, mortified, scrambled to explain. "It's not—nothing happened. I just—I couldn't sleep, and I went up for air, and he was on watch, and then I—" She flailed a hand vaguely, as if that could untangle the mess of words. "I fell asleep. That's it. End of story."

Brigid's brows arched higher. Her gaze slid pointedly to the coat still draped over Nerissa's shoulders.

Nerissa tugged it tighter. "I was cold."

Zale coughed again, this time into his fist, shoulders shaking like he was trying not to laugh—or die.

Brigid hummed low in her throat, clearly unconvinced, but she only stepped aside from the doorway with an infuriating little smirk. "Of course. Just air an' sleep. Perfectly innocent."

Nerissa moved to step past her, but Brigid's sharp eyes caught the faint hitch in her stride.

"Ach, dinnae mind me," Brigid added, voice sly as a cat's smile. "But ye're walkin' like someone who'd either wrestled a kraken...or had a different kind o' tussle."

Zale promptly choked on air again.

Nerissa went crimson. "It was a cramp," she snapped, more defensively than she meant to.

Brigid's smirk widened. "Aye. That's what they all say."

Nerissa shot a desperate glance at Zale, silently begging for rescue.

He dragged a hand down his face with a groan. "Stars above...Can we not? You *raised* me."

Brigid didn't miss a beat. "Aye—and I can un-raise ye just as quick, laddie."

Nerissa muttered something incoherent, shrugged out of the coat, and shoved it into Zale's arms before Brigid could get another word in. Her cheeks burned hotter than the sunrise as she ducked past them both into the cabin.

By the time Nerissa slipped into the galley, the place was already alive with the clatter of mugs and the low rumble of early conversation. She slid onto the bench beside Zale without a word, her lavender blouse and black corset neat as armor, her boots laced sharp. If not for the faint pink still lingering in her cheeks, no one would've guessed she'd nearly died of embarrassment moments ago.

She reached for the bread bowl at the center of the table, tore off a hunk, and nibbled it in quiet defiance of her still-knotted stomach.

Across from her, Bran leaned an elbow on the wood, smirk tugging at his mouth. "So. How'd the tattoo turn out?"

Nerissa stilled, then carefully tugged down her collar just enough to reveal the edge of Ma Wen's ink—the black serpent coiled sleek and dark against her skin.

Bran let out a low whistle. "Well, well. Didn't think you'd let him put his mark on you." His grin widened, flicking to Zale. "And look at that—lad's got style. A black serpent. Subtle. Regal. Bit vain, though."

Zale snorted, shaking his head. "That's the *ship's* mark, not mine."

Bran's grin sharpened. "Aye, but you're the one who chose it. Can't tell me you don't like seeing your beastie inked across her skin."

Nerissa let their voices wash over her, Bran needling and Zale batting him back with the weary patience of someone used to his nonsense. Normally she might have smirked at the exchange, maybe even added a dry comment of her own—but the bread sat heavy in her stomach. She blinked, realizing she hadn't taken another bite.

The edges of her vision swam.

Bran leaned back mid-retort, his grin faltering. "Hells, Riss—you look a little green."

Her mouth went dry. She pushed back from the bench, muttering, "I just need some fresh air—"

But the moment she stood, the world tilted. A wave of vertigo rolled through her, and she swayed. Instinct overrode pride: one hand flew to her head, the other clamped onto the nearest anchor—Zale's shoulder.

He caught her arm in return, steadying her. "Whoa—hey. You alright? Is it your leg again?"

"I'm fine," she said quickly, though her voice sounded distant to her own ears. "Probably still just...dehydrated."

Zale frowned, not letting go. "Then let me take you to Roan."

"That's not necessary. I just need some water—some air—"

Her left hand spasmed, curling on its own. She winced and shook it out, but it didn't obey right away.

"You look like you're about to keel over," Bran said unhelpfully.

That's when Ma Wen appeared at her side, silent as ever, eyes narrowed like he'd been watching for longer than she realized.

"Come," he said gently, offering his arm.

Nerissa hesitated. Then, grudgingly, she took it.

He led her toward the cooking area without fuss, just a subtle shift of his weight to guide her steps. Once inside, he nudged a stool against the wall with his foot and gestured for her to sit.

She didn't argue.

Ma Wen moved with quiet purpose, gathering herbs and filling a kettle. She recognized the sharp scent of saltroot, something Roan had once muttered about for treating muscle spasms.

He didn't speak—not at first.

But then, as he tossed a few dried leaves into the pot, he said without looking up, "Don't lie next time. You're a terrible liar."

Nerissa stared at the kettle, her voice low. "I didn't want anyone to worry."

A pause settled between them like steam over the stove. Then, just above a whisper—

"I didn't know it was this bad. Thought I could push through." She gave a short, bitter exhale. "Guess I'm not as good at pretending as I thought."

Ma Wen glanced over at her—just once, just long enough. Then turned back to strain the tea.

"You don't have to be good at pretending," he said simply. "Not here."

He set the steaming mug in front of her, his hand lingering for a breath.

"Let someone else be strong for you, now and then."

Nerissa stared down at the tea for a moment, fingers curling around the warm mug but not lifting it. Her throat felt too tight.

"That's not exactly my strong suit," she muttered. "Letting anyone else carry the weight."

Ma Wen didn't respond right away. He just leaned back slightly, arms folding loosely across his chest as he studied her with that composed calm of his.

Then he gave a faint nod toward her collarbone. "That's funny," he said. "You didn't flinch when I put that mark on you."

Nerissa's hand rose, fingertips grazing the ink on her skin.

"That's ours," he said simply. "That serpent. It means you're one of us now." He tilted his head. "Which means you don't have to do everything alone anymore."

A beat passed.

Then another.

Nerissa's gaze dropped to the tea again, and she finally lifted it to her lips, taking a careful sip. It was bitter. Earthy. Sharp in the back of her throat.

But grounding.

"I'll try," she said quietly. "No promises."

Ma Wen gave a slight smile—the kind that barely moved his mouth but somehow warmed the whole room. "No one said it had to be perfect." He reached over, plucked a spoon from a nearby hook, and stirred the tea in her hands. "Just honest."

The soft creak of the galley door announced a presence before any words did.

Zale stepped into the cooking area, his eyes scanning the space until they landed on Nerissa seated against the wall, clutching her mug of steaming tea. Ma Wen stood beside her, arms still loosely crossed, a protective stillness in his posture.

Zale's gaze flicked between them, then settled on Nerissa. "You alright?"

She nodded quickly. Too quickly. "I'm fine."

Zale raised an eyebrow.

Ma Wen didn't move. "She's resting. Or was. Sit."

It wasn't really a suggestion. Zale obliged, pulling over a crate and lowering himself beside Nerissa, close enough that his knee brushed hers.

"What happened?" he asked quietly.

"Just dizzy," she said, not quite meeting his eyes. "Dehydrated, apparently."

Zale's brow creased. He didn't press further, but his voice was softer when he said, "I'm worried about you."

That drew her gaze—sharp, surprised. "I'll be okay."

Liar.

The word knifed through her chest the second it left her mouth. She wasn't okay—not even close. The dizziness, the spasms, the ache in her limbs…she knew exactly what it meant. Ocean withdrawal. And she couldn't tell him. Couldn't explain any of it without unraveling the secret she'd been guarding since the moment she set foot on this ship.

Her fingers tightened around the mug, as if the heat alone could keep her anchored.

The late-morning sun beat down on the deck with unrelenting heat, turning every plank into a slow-baked griddle. Sweat slicked Nerissa's brow as she knelt beside Brigid, fingers working stiffly to braid strands of twine into a fishing net. The repetitive motion should have been meditative, but her limbs felt leaden, each knot tugging more than just rope—it tugged at the edge of her patience.

She blinked rapidly as her vision swam, a drop of sweat sliding into her eye. She swiped at her face with the back of her hand, then again when it immediately beaded up anew.

"Yer weaving like a blind fish," Brigid muttered without looking up.

Nerissa scowled and yanked the twine tighter than necessary. "It's hot."

Brigid gave her a sideways glance. "It's always hot."

Nerissa didn't argue. Instead, she reached for her water flask, tipping it back—only for a single, lonely drop to dribble onto her tongue. She upended it again, just to be sure.

Empty.

Her chest tightened. *Perfect. Just perfect.*

She exhaled slowly through her nose, lowering the flask.

Without a word, Brigid reached into her belt and handed over her own. "Here."

"I'm fine," Nerissa said, even as she accepted it.

"Don't care." Brigid went back to knotting rope. "Ye're sittin' down before ye tip over."

"I'm not—"

"Sit."

Her tone left no room for negotiation.

Nerissa reluctantly dropped onto an overturned bucket with all the grace of a collapsing sail. Her legs ached, and her back felt like it had been wrung out and hung up to dry.

Brigid watched her for a moment, then said more gently, "Ye look peaked. Don't push yerself."

"I said I'm fine."

Another lie. You're not fooling anybody.

"Aye, and Zale said the same thing last week. Then went down like a felled mast in the middle o' tying down the rigging."

"Not planning to drop dramatically for attention, if that's what you're worried about."

Brigid's smile softened and gestured with her chin toward the steps. "Go cool off, lass. Cabin's that way. If I see ye on deck again before high tide, I'll have Roan tie ye to the mast."

Nerissa didn't have the strength to scowl. She muttered something halfway between agreement and defiance, wiped her brow again, and trudged below deck. Every step made her legs feel heavier, like she was walking through water. By the time she reached the quiet of their shared cabin, the world was tilting slightly to the left.

She collapsed onto her cot, kicking off her boots with one weak motion. Her head spun. Her skin itched.

You're unraveling, she thought bitterly, pressing a damp palm against her temple. *And if they see it, everything falls apart.*

It felt like barely a minute had passed when a gentle knock stirred her. She blinked blearily, unsure whether she'd drifted off or simply blacked out. The knocking came again—soft, not urgent.

She managed to get upright, swaying slightly as she padded barefoot to the door. When she opened it, Zale stood there, brow creased.

"Brigid said she sent you to lie down," he said, voice quiet. "Just wanted to check on you."

"I'm fine," she murmured automatically, one hand on the doorframe for balance. "Feeling better."

"You sure?"

No. Absolutely not.

But she nodded anyway.

Zale didn't look convinced, but he stepped back. "Alright," he said, still watching her carefully. "You'd tell me if something was wrong...right?"

Nerissa didn't answer right away. Then she nodded, just once.

Zale held her gaze a beat longer, then finally stepped back. "Alright," he said. "Get some rest."

And with that, he turned and left.

Nerissa woke with a gasp that scraped her throat raw. Her chest burned as if the air itself had turned to ash, every breath thin and unsatisfying. She pressed a trembling hand to her sternum, but the ache only deepened.

Not yet. She had told herself that a dozen times already. Not yet, she could endure this. But now her lungs ached for water with every breath, and endurance had bled into desperation.

She sat upright, curling forward with a low sound that was half groan, half growl. Her skin prickled with heat, damp hair sticking to her temples. She dragged a hand through the tangles and forced herself to breathe evenly, even though each inhale only reminded her of what she lacked.

Zale's voice rose unbidden in her mind.

You'd tell me if something was wrong...right?

Her throat tightened. She had promised. And she wanted to keep that promise more than she feared what came after. He deserved the truth. He deserved to know what he had brought aboard.

Her legs wavered as she stood, bracing against the edge of the bunk until the dizziness passed. She smoothed her hands down the front of her blouse, as if neatness might make the words easier to say.

"Tell him," she whispered to herself. "Before it's too late."

Nerissa crossed to the door, fingers curling around the latch. Her heart pounded as though it already knew the risk—what she was about to put in Zale's hands, what it might cost. Still, she drew in another burning breath and pushed the door open.

The night air struck her like a cool blade. She stepped onto the deck, swallowing against the sting in her lungs. Lanterns swayed, throwing long shadows over the rail where three figures stood in quiet conversation.

Cormac's voice carried first, low and rasping. "These waters reek of sirens. Too many ships lost here without a trace."

Eon shifted where he sat on a coil of rope, book closed in his lap. "That's not possible. Every history book I've read says they died out in the wars. Whole race gone."

Cormac gave a dry, humorless laugh. "Aye, that's what the scribblers say from their stone towers. But I've sailed these waters longer than their grandfathers were alive. I've heard the singing. Men don't vanish into calm seas for no reason."

Eon glanced toward Zale. "What do you think?"

Zale leaned against the rail, gaze on the horizon. "Never seen one. But just because I haven't...doesn't mean they aren't out there."

Cormac jabbed the stem of his pipe in Zale's direction. "Exactly. Which is why a man should keep his wits about him. One careless step, one voice too sweet in the dark, and the sea takes you whole."

Nerissa froze in the shadow of the companionway, her breath catching in her throat. The words struck harder than the burning in her lungs. She had meant to walk straight to Zale, to tell him everything. Or at least, just enough. Now the weight of her secret pressed heavier than ever. Her courage withered as swiftly as it had sparked, leaving only silence in its place.

She turned to retreat into the safety of the cabin—but her foot slipped. She stumbled, palm slamming against the wall to keep herself from falling. The jolt rattled through her arm, and the shallow, ragged draw of her breath gave her away.

Bootsteps thudded quickly across the deck. "Nerissa?" Zale's voice was sharp with alarm. He appeared from the lantern glow, eyes catching the faint sheen of sweat on her brow, the way her fingers clutched the rail. "Stars—are you all right?"

She forced a steady inhale, though it burned. "I'm okay," she managed, shaking her head. "I just...came up for some air. Got a little dizzy, that's all."

His frown deepened, gaze searching her face. "You want to head back and lie down? Or...stay up here a while? I'll help you either way."

For a heartbeat, she nearly told him. Nearly let the truth fall free. But Cormac's warning still echoed, heavy as lead in her chest. She straightened slowly, loosening her grip on the rail. "Fresh air," she said with quiet resolve.

"All right." He slipped an arm lightly against her back, guiding her toward the steps. His presence was steady, grounding, though his gaze flicked toward her every few breaths as if he expected her to drop.

Cormac squinted at her through a haze of pipe smoke. "She doesn't look so good," he remarked, voice like gravel. "Pale as a gull's belly."

Before she could respond, Eon piped up from his coil of rope, eager to be useful. "Could be scurvy. Early symptoms include fatigue, dizziness, and weakness. There's a fascinating treatise I read about—"

"Ignore them," Zale cut in, tone dismissive. He steered her past both men, toward the bow of the ship.

Nerissa kept her eyes forward, fighting to keep her steps steady. "How much longer until we reach the cove?" she asked, casual as she could manage.

"If the winds hold strong, two days." He gave her a sidelong glance. "Why?"

She shook her head quickly. "Just wondering."

But inside, her thoughts churned like the dark waters beneath them. Two days. She didn't have two more days.

They stood at the bow together, the expanse of dark sea glittering below. Nerissa leaned forward over the railing, closing her eyes as the sea breeze cooled her burning lungs. So close—so close she could almost taste the salt water—yet still too far. She deliriously considered throwing herself overboard, imagining how cool the water would feel against her skin.

But Zale kept his arm looped firmly around her, as though he feared she might topple headfirst into the waves. His grip was careful, protective, but unyielding.

Her fingers drifted absently to her arm, nails scratching at the skin beneath her sleeve. She hissed softly when it stung. Slowly, she rolled the fabric back—and froze. Dry, scaly patches mottled the flesh, rough beneath her touch.

She tugged the sleeve back down in a rush, but not before Zale's eyes caught the movement. "Those look...just like mine," he said slowly, brow furrowing. "When I have a bad flare-up."

Nerissa's throat tightened. "It's nothing. Just dehydration. I'll be fine."

His frown deepened, unconvinced, but he didn't argue outright. He lingered, studying her with that piercing, searching gaze.

"I'd...like to try to get some sleep now," she said quickly, before his questions could cut any deeper.

For a long moment, Zale didn't move. Then, with a reluctant exhale, he shifted his arm to guide her back from the rail. "All right," he murmured.

Together, they made their way across the deck, his hand still steady at her back. He didn't press her, not yet—but she could feel the weight of everything unsaid hanging between them as he helped her down into Brigid's cabin.

At the cabin door, Nerissa reached for the latch. Before she could pull it open, Zale's hand caught hers. She whirled around to look at him.

"Promise me," he said quietly, eyes fixed on hers. "If you're not feeling better in the morning, you'll go to the infirmary."

She summoned a weak smile, though it felt brittle at the edges. "Of course."

But he didn't let go. His hand remained entwined with hers, his gaze sharper now, cutting through her flimsy reassurance.

"I mean it, Nerissa. If something's wrong...let us help."

Her throat tightened. For a moment, she thought he might hear the pounding of her heart in the silence between them. She gave the smallest nod, tugging gently to free her hand.

Only then did he release her, stepping back just enough for her to slip inside.

And when the door closed softly between them, the promise lingered heavy on her tongue—one she already feared she could not keep.

CHAPTER 32

SOMEONE BETTER BE DYING

Nerissa

A sharp jolt to her leg yanked her from sleep.

Nerissa gasped, hand flying to her thigh as the muscle seized. The cramp pulsed like a fist clenched too tight, refusing to let go. She bit down hard on a whimper and pressed her knuckles against the knot of pain, willing it to release.

Across the small cabin, Brigid's steady snoring continued, completely oblivious.

Nerissa swallowed, blinking against the dark. Her skin was slick with sweat despite the cool night air drifting in through the window slats. Her nightshirt clung damply to her back, and her pulse pounded in her ears like distant drums echoing underwater.

She forced herself to breathe.

In, out. In, out.

The leg cramp began to ease, slowly unwinding its grip, but the panic it had stirred lingered just beneath her ribs. Her breath hitched again, this time not from pain, but from a tight, rising dread she couldn't shake.

She curled forward on the cot, wrapping her arms around her knees, forehead pressed against them.

This wasn't just fatigue.

This wasn't dehydration or heatstroke or nightmares.

Something inside her was shifting.

And she knew—deep in her bones, in the marrow of her merblood—what was coming.

She eased back down onto the cot, eyes fixed on the ceiling's dark wooden beams. Brigid shifted and snorted softly in her sleep, then settled again. Nerissa forced herself to lie still. Just for a few minutes. Just until her body calmed.

But no calm came.

Without warning, her other leg spasmed—sharp, vicious, like a hook driving into muscle. The pain tore through her and left her gasping, clutching at her calf as her foot twisted involuntarily. She bit down on a cry so hard it brought tears to her eyes.

Not again. Not now.

She kneaded the muscle with both hands, whispering curses under her breath. She tried breathing exercises again: in through the nose, count of four. Hold. Out through the mouth, count of eight.

It didn't help.

If anything, the numbness was spreading. Her lower body felt disconnected, like the nerves had forgotten how to translate her will into movement.

She dragged in another shaky breath, and Zale's voice echoed once again in her mind:

"You'd tell me if something was wrong...right?"

She let out a quiet, miserable groan and covered her face with her hands.

Just do it. Just tell him. You've run out of time.

With a grimace, she forced herself upright, swinging her legs over the side of the cot. They tingled and ached, but she could stand—barely. Her body felt like a traitor. Her skin prickled with phantom chill, her pulse fluttering too fast.

She needed help.

No more hiding. No more pretending she could out-stubborn sea withdrawal.

She reached for her coat and pushed open the cabin door, stepping into the cool silence of the ship's corridor. Her steps were slow, uneven, and her hand braced against the wall more than once to keep her upright.

But she didn't stop.

She needed to find Zale.

Before she could no longer walk.

She crept down the stairs toward the lower decks, every step a silent plea for her body to hold together just a little longer. She didn't know what Zale could possibly do, but she needed him.

Even if it was too late, she didn't want to die alone.

Her breaths came more and more shallow, lungs burning. Her skin felt like paper stretched too tight over trembling bones. The corridor narrowed the deeper she went, lit only by the faint orange flicker of lantern light swinging from rusted hooks.

She reached the base of the stairs and turned down the next corridor, heart hammering, vision tunneling.

Left? Or was it right?

A wave of dizziness struck her so hard she staggered into the wall. Her palm braced against the boards, slick with sweat.

"Zale…" she whispered hoarsely. "Please…"

Another step—just one more—

Her legs gave out.

Not gradually. Not with warning. One moment they were beneath her, the next she was crumpling to the floor like her strings had been cut.

The world tilted, her knees hitting the planks with a muted thud, and she collapsed to her side, shaking uncontrollably. Her legs were numb. Dead weight. Except—no. Not dead. Shifting. The muscles locked hard as iron, her thighs pressing together as though they wanted to braid into one limb. Her feet were starting to lengthen, toes stretching, webbing straining to form where skin had no business tearing.

Her hands scrabbled weakly at the floor, but her fingers had gone stiff too. She clenched her jaw so tight it ached. Something was pulling at her—beneath the skin, beneath the bones. Like her body was finally, violently, rejecting the borrowed shape it'd been forced to hold for too long.

Then came the sting—splitting heat racing along her temples, shoulders, torso, legs. Tiny scales forcing their way through the surface, raw and burning, as if her own skin were fracturing to let the sea reclaim her.

Cold panic surged in her chest. Zale was going to find her dead body in the morning. Twisted and wrong, caught between two forms.

It wouldn't matter that she had had every intention of telling him the truth. She had waited too long, like a coward. Now it was too late.

Zale

Zale lay in his hammock, one arm folded behind his head, staring at the underside of the beams above. The wood creaked softly with the motion of the ship, the occasional snores and murmurs of the crew punctuating the quiet.

He hadn't slept. Not really.

He was worried about Nerissa.

She said she was fine, over and over again, but that was a lie so flimsy it barely held its shape. The spontaneous muscle cramps, the dizziness, and the look in her eyes when she brushed him off earlier had gnawed at something deep in his chest.

She was hiding something, and it was hurting her. Zale exhaled, rubbing his palm over his face.

Stubborn woman. Why did she insist on suffering in silence?

He swung his legs over the side of the hammock, quietly pulling on his boots. Maybe a walk would help. Get the knots out of his gut. Let the night air cool his nerves.

He stepped lightly through the narrow space between the other hammocks, shoulders hunched from habit, avoiding loose planks that squeaked.

Then he heard it.

A low thud, almost like someone had stumbled. Followed by—nothing.

Zale froze.

The sound had come from the corridor just outside the quarters.

Something in his chest twisted.

He moved fast.

Out the door. Down the hall. Rounding the corner—

His heart jumped into his throat.

Nerissa.

Collapsed on her side, one arm weakly curled in, the other reaching toward nothing. Her eyes were half-lidded, jaw clenched, and her body was seizing uncontrollably.

He dropped to his knees beside her. "Nerissa!"

Her lashes fluttered. A sound left her throat—not a word, just a broken breath.

His hand found her shoulder. "Hey, hey—look at me. Talk to me."

She struggled to form a sentence between the tremors. "Zale…help—"

Panic threatened to seize him, but he shoved it down. Now wasn't the time.

"I've got you," he murmured, slipping his arms around her. "You're alright—I've got you."

But when he tried to gather her closer, his breath caught. Beneath the hem of her coat, her legs were twisted at an angle no person's should bend. Had she broken them when she fell?

Whatever was happening, he didn't understand it, but he knew one thing with crushing certainty. She wasn't alright. She wasn't *fine*. Whatever she'd been hiding...it was killing her.

Zale lifted her like she weighed nothing. Her body felt clammy and limp in his arms, breath shallow against his chest.

"I'm taking you to Roan," he said, turning toward the stairs.

But then her fingers curled into his shirt, trembling and desperate.

"Wait," she gasped, barely above a whisper. "Just—wait, please."

He froze mid-step, heart thudding.

Her head lolled against his shoulder, but she forced her eyes open, glassy with pain. "Sorry," she murmured, voice ragged. "Th-thought I...could handle...it."

"Why?" He searched her face. "Why didn't you tell me?"

"Trust me," she gritted out through clenched teeth. "You...wouldn't have...b-believed me."

"Nerissa, I *do* trust you," he said softly. "I'm asking you to trust *me*. I won't have you die in my arms because you were too proud to ask for help. Just tell me what you need."

"Salt…" Her lips barely moved. "Salt water."

Before he could answer, another jolt wracked her body—her back arched in his arms, a strangled sound leaving her throat.

That was enough.

Zale kicked the infirmary door open with his foot, the wood cracking against the wall as he strode inside. He crossed to the exam table in three strides and gently laid her down. Her body was still shaking uncontrollably.

"Easy," he muttered as she winced, easing the heavy fabric of her coat off her shoulders. Her skin was flushed and damp beneath her night shirt, breath hitching with every movement.

Then the light caught her skin, and his blood ran cold.

Cracks split across her collarbone, thin lines glowing wet as *something* forced its way to the surface. More fissures marred her forearms, glinting like shattered glass. And lower, where her legs twitched against the table, he caught the same dreadful shimmer breaking through the skin.

Zale's stomach lurched. *Stars above...she's breaking apart.* It looked wrong, impossible—like her body was being remade piece by piece, and he was powerless to stop it.

He swallowed hard, pushing down the rising panic. *Focus.* He turned and stormed to the adjoining cabin, fist raised.

BANG BANG BANG.

"Roan!" he shouted. "I need you. Now!"

Behind him, Nerissa shivered on the table, muscles twitching beneath her skin. Her lips parted on a broken groan, her voice rough and unsteady. "...Zale?"

He spun back at once, crossing to her side in two strides. Her eyes fluttered open, glazed with pain, and found him again.

"I'm here," he said quickly, stepping back to her side and gently squeezing her shoulder. "You're not alone, alright? I've got you."

Her lips moved again, barely shaping words. "I...can't—nnngh—" The rest dissolved into a strangled groan, her body arching as another tremor seized her.

Zale's heart clenched. "Don't try to talk," he leaned closer. "Save your strength. Just hold on for me."

From the other room came a low rustle and the creak of a hammock.

"Someone better be dying," came Roan's gravel-rough voice.

The medic appeared in the doorway a moment later, shirtless and barefoot but already assessing the situation with clear, sharp eyes. He took one look at Nerissa, shivering on the table, and his brow furrowed.

"What the hell happened?"

"I found her collapsed in the corridor," Zale explained quickly. "I don't know what's wrong—she can barely breathe, and she's getting worse by the minute."

Roan strode forward without another word, fingers going to her pulse, then to her temple, then pressing lightly against her chest to gauge her breathing. His eyes traveled down her body, pausing—just for a heartbeat—before narrowing in sharp focus.

Roan's jaw worked as he drew his hand back. "Gods…" he muttered, more to himself than to Zale. "This isn't sickness."

Zale swallowed hard. "No. I know it's not. There's something growing from her skin. Could it be some kind of fungus, or…?" His voice cracked, desperate for any explanation that made sense.

Roan shook his head once, sharp and certain. "I've never seen anything like this before. But it's not a fungus."

Zale's mind raced, snatching at anything that might help, and then Nerissa's broken words came back to him. Salt water.

His grip tightened on the edge of the table. "She asked for salt water," he said quickly, eyes snapping to Roan. "That's what she said she needed."

Roan's brows drew together, incredulous. "Salt water? How in the hell is that supposed to help?"

Nerissa's eyes cracked open, finding Roan's face. "Please," she whispered, voice raw. "Listen...to him…"

Then her eyes rolled back, her body giving a violent shudder before going slack against the table.

"Roan?" Zale's voice broke on the single word, a plea more than a question.

The medic leaned in fast, pressing two fingers to the side of her throat. "Still there," he muttered, counting under his breath. "Pulse is racing." He leaned closer, watching the shallow rise and fall of her chest. Her breaths were quick and uneven—barely filling her lungs.

"Damn," he muttered under his breath. "She's burning through herself."

"What does that mean?" Zale asked.

Roan didn't answer immediately. He was watching Nerissa's fingers—her left hand was spasming again, curling in on itself as if trying to claw free from her own body.

"She's crashing," Roan said finally. "Her system's dehydrated and overcompensating. This is more than heatstroke or muscle strain. Her body's trying to correct something it can't fix."

He met Zale's eyes, the weight of it heavy and grim. "Let's hope the salt water works."

Roan moved fast. He yanked aside the curtain in the corner of the infirmary and dragged a large metal tub into the center of the room, its base shrieking across the wooden floor. He seized a bucket and plunged it into the barrel by the wall, filling it with a violent splash.

"Get the salt," he said, jerking his head toward the storage room as he poured more water into the tub. "Four bags. Dump 'em straight in."

Zale didn't argue. He was already moving, tearing into the storage space and grabbing the thick canvas sacks stacked on the lower shelf. He brought them two at a time, ripping them open with his teeth and pouring the coarse crystals in as the water sloshed and frothed against the metal sides.

Then Zale was back at Nerissa's side.

Her eyes were still closed, lips parted in shallow breaths, her skin pallid and clammy despite the sweat. Her body jerked at random intervals now—twitches in her legs, a ripple across her torso, as if her muscles were rebelling one by one.

"She's stopped shivering," Zale murmured. "That's not good, is it?"

"No," Roan said grimly. "Means her body's past the warning phase."

Gently, Zale slipped an arm beneath her knees and another behind her shoulders. Her fingers twitched weakly against his chest as he lifted her.

"You're going to be alright," he whispered, as much to himself as to her.

He carried her to the tub and knelt beside it, lowering her slowly.

The moment Nerissa's skin touched the salted water, her back arched violently, a sharp cry ripping from her throat like it had been clawed free.

Her eyes flew open, wild and glassy. For a terrifying heartbeat, she looked like she didn't recognize them.

"Easy," Roan said, stepping in, one hand braced gently on her shoulder to keep her from lurching out of the tub. "Let it take. Just breathe."

Zale's hands hovered helplessly in the air, still half beneath her, unsure whether to let go or hold on tighter.

Her chest heaved with ragged gasps as another wave of pain shot through her limbs, muscles tightening and convulsing beneath the surface.

Roan leaned close, checking her pulse again. Her breath was coming in short gasps, her fingers gripping the rim of the tub as though she could hold herself together by will alone.

Zale knelt at the side of the tub, one hand braced on the rim, and then Nerissa's fingers shot out and clutched his.

Her grip was like iron, trembling with strain, but it wasn't the intensity that stopped his breath—it was what was happening to her now.

Thin, translucent skin stretched between her fingers like a silken membrane. For a split second, he thought it was a trick of the water—but then came the fins, slicing from her forearms like blades of polished bone.

His eyes widened. *No...no, that's not—*

"Nerissa?" he whispered, voice breaking.

She didn't answer. Couldn't. Her lips parted in a soundless gasp, her head lolling back as another convulsion tore through her body.

Zale's heart hammered. He wanted to pull her out, to tear her free of the water that seemed to be remaking her piece by piece—but her grip on his hand held him fast, desperate, as though she needed him anchored there.

Roan's voice cut through the roar in his ears, sharp and steady despite the tension. "Zale. Look at me. She's not getting worse." Zale's eyes flicked from Nerissa's trembling form to Roan, then back. "Whatever this is—it's happening because of the water. Which means it's working."

Zale dragged in a ragged breath, the words hitting like cold steel. Working. Stars, if this was working, what did failure look like?

He tightened his grip on Nerissa's hand, leaning close so she could hear him even if her mind was lost in the pain. "You're not alone. Do you hear me? I'm right here. Just...stay with me."

Her eyes flickered open for a heartbeat, unfocused violet clouded with fog, then slid closed again as another tremor wracked her frame. Her webbed fingers dug harder into his palm, refusing to let go.

Her back arched again as another wave hit her, and beneath the surface, he saw it—her legs were fusing together. Her feet elongated into long, delicate fins, twitching as lavender scales bloomed in rippling waves up her calves.

What…?

Zale's breath stuttered, the world narrowing to the impossible sight before him. It'd only been a few hours since his conversation with Cormac and Eon, debating about the existence of sirens. They were supposed to be an extinct race—yet here she was.

She wasn't becoming something monstrous—she was becoming herself.

Zale's grip on her hand tightened until his knuckles blanched. Not afraid *of* her. Afraid *for* her. For the way her body convulsed, for the pain twisting her face, for the way her breath hitched shallow and uneven, as if every gasp might be her last.

"Stars," he whispered, leaning closer, voice raw. "Stay with me, Riss. I've got ye."

Then Zale saw it, the skin just beneath her jaw splitting open in thin, wet lines. Slits, pulsing, fluttering, desperate.

A shuddering gasp ripped from her throat, then another—sharp, shallow, choking. She was fighting for air she could no longer take.

"Stars—she's *suffocating*," Zale choked out, panic rising.

Roan was already moving. "Not air. Water." His voice was grim, decisive.

Together, they pressed down gently but firmly, guiding her beneath the surface. Zale cradled the back of her head, fingers tangled in her damp hair, lowering her until the salted water closed over her face. For a heartbeat his gut rebelled—every instinct screaming that he was drowning her—but then—

The gills flared.

Water surged through them in a rhythm, her body twitching as it adjusted, then settling into steadier pulses. Her chest eased, rising and falling with a natural cadence.

Zale knelt over her, arm braced protectively along the rim of the tub. She wasn't drowning. She was breathing.

Roan exhaled, low and rough, though his eyes stayed sharp on her. "Well, I'll be damned."

Zale didn't move. He still gripped her hand tightly beneath the surface, even as her fingers slackened against his. He wasn't ready to let go—not when he'd felt her slipping from him only moments before.

Her tail slumped over the edge of the tub now, scales glinting faintly in the lantern light, droplets running down in steady trails to pool on the floorboards.

Roan leaned close one last time, checking her pulse, then let out a long breath. "She's stabilizing," he said.

The medic sank onto the nearest stool with a heavy exhale, elbows braced on his knees. He dragged both hands down his face, the sharp edge of composure slipping for just a moment. "Gods above," he muttered into his palms.

The frantic pounding in Zale's chest eased by degrees as her breathing steadied, each pulse of her gills pulling water with measured rhythm. Only then—when the danger had passed—did he allow himself to look at her. Really look.

Salt water gleamed across her skin, tracing the delicate ridges of scales scattered over her arms and collarbone, catching the lantern light with an opalescent sheen. Lavender shimmered along the curve of her tail, each ripple of color shifting like moonlight over seashells. Even in exhaustion, even like this—undone, transformed—she was breathtaking.

Zale's throat tightened. *Is this real?* His mind scrabbled for footing. It felt impossible, like some rum-induced fever dream. And yet her hand was still in his, warm and tangible, her pulse fluttering against his thumb.

This was it. What she'd been hiding. What she'd been too afraid to tell him. Not sickness. Not weakness. A truth too big, too dangerous to speak aloud.

He swallowed hard, his grip steadying around her slack fingers. "Riss…" he whispered, the name catching in his throat.

Roan exhaled, long and low, before muttering, "She's merfolk…Did you know?"

Zale didn't look at him. "Of course not. She's been having these weird symptoms for the past few days but kept trying to hide it. Kept insisting she was fine."

"Can't say I blame her," Roan said. "All the old stories…the wars. Merfolk and humans don't have the friendliest history."

"She's one of us," Zale said firmly. "She's fought beside us. Bled beside us. That doesn't change just because she's got gills."

Roan blinked at him for a beat—then gave a small, crooked shake of his head. "Didn't say it did."

"What do you think happened?" Zale's eyes finally broke away from Nerissa, looking to Roan for answers he almost surely didn't have. "Why did she suddenly–transform like this?"

Roan's gaze slid back to Nerissa, studying the slow rise and fall of her chest, the faint pulse of her gills. "If I had to guess," he said slowly, "her body's been fighting this for days. She was trying to keep herself human, even when she couldn't anymore. Like holding her breath until she blacked out."

Zale's brow furrowed. "And the collapse?"

"Withdrawal," Roan said simply. "Cut off from the sea too long, she started to break down. The salt water jump-started the change her body was already screaming for." He dragged a hand over his mouth, muttering, "Makes sense of the dehydration, the spasms, the fever. Every system she had was red-lining, trying to correct itself without the one thing it needed."

Zale's stomach churned as the pieces slammed into place. Her restlessness. The way she'd brushed him off when he asked if she was alright. The way she'd asked—too casually, too carefully—how much longer until they reached the cove.

Stars. She hadn't just been impatient for shore. She'd needed the water. Needed it desperately, and she hadn't been able to say why.

His throat tightened. *She was trying to find a way to save herself without me ever knowing.*

"That's why she wanted the cove," he muttered. "She needed a chance to get into the water—without raising suspicion."

Roan gave a short, grim nod. "And she almost didn't make it."

Zale's hand tightened around Nerissa's limp fingers, his jaw working. "Stars, I should've pressed her harder. I knew something was wrong. I could see it, but I let her push me off." His voice cracked low. "If she'd felt like she could trust me—if she'd told me the truth—she wouldn't have gotten this far gone."

Roan leaned back on the stool, arms braced on his knees as he studied Nerissa's unconscious form. For a moment, his expression softened beneath the usual iron calm. Then he huffed out a quiet sound, somewhere between a sigh and a chuckle.

"She wouldn't have told you either way," he said. "Not because she didn't trust you—because she's damn near as stubborn as you are. Maybe more."

Zale's head snapped toward him, caught between bristling and breaking.

Roan raised a brow, unflinching. "You'd run yourself into the ground before admitting you needed help. Don't pretend you wouldn't; or have you forgotten last week's incident? She's cut from the same cloth."

Zale looked back down at Nerissa, guilt still gnawing at him, but Roan's words rooted deep. Stubborn. Proud. Just like him.

Roan exhaled through his nose, the corner of his mouth tightening. "But don't get lost in the what-ifs. You were there when it mattered. You listened when she finally asked—and you helped her. That's why she's still breathing."

Zale's throat worked, a rough sound catching as he brushed his thumb gently across her knuckles. He wanted to believe that. Needed to.

"She's tougher than she looks. She'll pull through," Roan said firmly, then pushed himself upright, shoulders squaring as he slipped back into the steady authority of a medic. "But she's not out of the woods yet. Her system's been through hell—it's going to take time to stabilize."

Zale finally looked up at him, eyes sharp. "Tell me what to do."

"Keep her submerged," Roan instructed. "Watch her breathing, watch her pulse. If either falters, wake me."

Zale nodded once, absorbing every word.

The infirmary had fallen into a hush, broken only by the faint lap of water in the tub and the occasional groan of the ship's timbers. Roan had retired to his cabin half an hour ago, leaving Zale alone with the dim lanternlight and the steady rise and fall of Nerissa's chest beneath the surface.

Zale hadn't let go of her hand once.

He sat hunched on a stool beside her, thumb brushing absently over her knuckles. Every so often her gills flared with a soft ripple, the sound both foreign and reassuring. She was alive. That was all that mattered.

A low groan pulled him upright. Nerissa stirred, her brow furrowing as she brought her free hand to her temple, pressing the heel of her palm against it.

“Riss?” Zale whispered, leaning closer.

Her lashes fluttered. Then, too quickly, she lurched upright, chest heaving. A sharp gasp tore from her as her gills broke the surface, fluttering uselessly in the air.

“Easy, easy—hey.” Zale’s hand came to her shoulder, gentle but firm. He guided her back under, tilting her until her gills slipped beneath the surface again.

The moment the water closed over, her body responded. The frantic rise and fall of her chest steadied, her gills flaring in rhythm as the tension bled from her shoulders.

Zale exhaled in relief. “There you go,” he murmured, voice low and steady. “That’s it. Just breathe.”

Her hand trembled in his, gripping faintly, and when she finally turned her face toward him, her violet-blue eyes cracked open—glassy, searching.

“Am I...dead?” Her voice rasped, barely more than air.

Zale leaned closer, his hand still steady on her shoulder. “No,” he said firmly. “We got you in time. You’re still here.”

Her gaze flicked down, taking in the sight of her tail before her. A shudder went through her as she pressed her palm over her mouth, like she could somehow push the reality back inside.

“Didn't want…” she whispered, each syllable fractured. “You…to see me…like this.”

Zale’s chest tightened. “Riss. You nearly killed yourself trying to hide it.

And for what? Thinking I'd see a monster?"

Her breath hitched again, half-sob, half-shake of her head, though she couldn't quite get the denial out.

"You're not," Zale said firmly. His thumb ran lightly over the webbing between her fingers. "You're still you. That hasn't changed."

Her eyes lifted to his, fragile and uncertain. "You're…not afraid of me now?"

"No," he said incredulously. "Not any more than usual, at least."

A shaky laugh escaped her, laced with exhaustion, before her hand slackened slightly in his.

"Thank you," she whispered. "For saving my life…again. If you hadn't found me when you did—"

Zale cut her off before the words could spiral further. "But I did," he said, firm but gentle. His hand tightened around hers. "And you're alright. That's what matters."

"Zale…" she whispered, voice thin with weariness. "I don't know what comes next. I can't keep this secret up forever. Eventually, the rest of the crew will find out. Then what?"

Zale shook his head, leaning closer, his grip steady. "Nerissa. You belong *here*." His eyes flicked toward the timbers above, the ship groaning around them like a living thing. "You're part of the crew—you wear the Serpent's mark now."

Nerissa's fingers trailed along her tattoo, eyes uncertain.

Zale continued. "You've fought alongside them. Bled alongside them. They'll accept you for who you are."

A faint, wry smile tugged at her lips. "Even Cormac?"

Zale huffed a soft laugh, the tension in his chest easing just enough. "Might take some convincing that you won't try to lure him overboard in the middle of the night. But he'll come around."

That pulled a quiet laugh from her, weaker than usual but genuine.

Zale's expression sobered again. "Tell me how we prevent this from happening in the future. I don't ever want you to have to go through whatever happened tonight again."

Nerissa took a steadying breath before answering. "Under normal circumstances, merfolk can only stay in human form for up to seven days. After that, the body starts rejecting it. That's what you saw tonight—sea withdrawal." She closed her eyes briefly. "As long as I swim at least once a week in the ocean, I'll be fine."

Zale's brow furrowed, confusion flickering sharp in his eyes. "But...you've been with us almost three weeks. Well past seven days."

She nodded once, slowly. Then exhaled—long and weary.

"It's a long story."

Zale tilted his head, studying her. "Rest now. You can tell me your story when you're ready."

But Nerissa shook her head weakly, the motion sending ripples through the water. Her eyes found his again, glassy but intent. "No," she whispered, her voice rough but certain. "You deserve to know the truth. All of it."

With effort, she pushed herself upright, bracing against the rim of the tub. She dipped under once more, drawing in a deep, steady breath through her gills before breaking the surface again.

Zale frowned, half-rising from his stool. "Shouldn't you stay under?"

She shook her head, strands of wet hair clinging to her cheeks. "I can hold my breath for a few minutes in between. I'll be fine. You need to hear this."

Zale studied her, uneasy but unwilling to argue when determination burned through her exhaustion. He settled back, jaw set, and met her eyes.

"I'm listening."

CHAPTER 33
IF THE SKIN FITS

Nerissa

Nerissa leaned her head back against the rim of the tub, water lapping gently around her chin. She didn't look at Zale when she began to speak.

"That day at the Salty Siren, the girl that I was protecting…she's the princess of Nautalia—the kingdom where I come from. She wanted to meet Prince Leander before the wedding. She had been promised in marriage to seal the peace treaty between Astyra and Nautalia."

Zale blinked. "So that's what he was doing there. I knew your friend was someone important."

She gave a faint nod. "My job was to keep her safe. During a security sweep of the castle later that day, I caught the royal apothecary sneaking into a hidden corridor. I followed him."

Her voice wavered slightly. "I found his lab. And inside were...bodies. Dissected merfolk. Half-transformed creatures in tanks."

Zale's expression darkened, mouth tightening. "Bloody stars…"

"I told King Nereus what I had found. Turns out he already knew. And was still willing to marry off his daughter to them, for the sake of 'peace,'" she said hollowly.

She looked away from him then, unable to meet his eyes.

"On the day of the wedding…I saw Alpheus again, just outside of Calliope's chambers. Like he was daring me to follow. Next thing I know, Damarion–the Captain of the Royal Nautalian Guard–was shaking me awake. I have no memory of how I got there, or what happened. And then…"

Her voice trembled as she hesitated to continue. "Zale, I did something terrible…"

He squeezed her hand reassuringly. "Hey, you live on a pirate ship now. We've all done terrible things."

She shook her head, grateful for his words, but she knew he wouldn't say that once she told him the whole truth. Calliope's look of betrayal flashed in her mind. She dreaded to see that look on Zale's face now, but she had to tell him. No more secrets.

"During the wedding ceremony, when Leander began reciting his vows…I stabbed the king. I killed Vasilios."

Her hands started shaking at the memory of that horrible, gruesome scene.

"Could it be possible that you were framed?" Zale's eyes had creased, but he didn't draw away from her.

She shook her head again. "No. You don't understand. Everyone saw me do it. I *remember* doing it. There was this voice in my head—commanding me. I tried to fight it, but it was like I no longer controlled my own body.

I just watched it happen. I had never killed a person before that day."

Zale slowly nodded, brows furrowed. "That's why you reacted like you did when you killed that Dravari pirate."

She closed her eyes tightly against the memory. "Yes. It took me right back to the wedding. All the blood...*so much blood.*" Dipping under the water again, she fought to keep her breathing under control. Zale's warm grip on her hand kept her present.

"They threw me in the dungeon. And while I was there, Alpheus came to my cell. I think he injected me with something? I'm not sure. The whole memory is hazy."

Zale was silent, taking it all in.

"Damarion helped me escape the next morning. He was the only one who believed that I had been set up. He knew Alpheus was somehow responsible. I jumped from the tower. I thought I'd shift once I hit the water. But I didn't. Couldn't. Whatever Alpheus injected me with, it suppressed my ability to shift. That's why you found me, drowning, covered in someone else's blood."

Zale sat there, silent. Then his jaw clenched as he ran his hand down his face. She flinched, expecting him to get up and leave. But instead, he leaned forward, voice gentle yet firm. "You didn't deserve any of that, Nerissa. And you sure as hell don't have to carry it alone anymore."

Something inside her warmed at his words. So unexpected. So supportive.

"We're gonna make it right," he promised. "I don't know how yet—but I'll be damned if that snake gets away with what he did."

Nerissa blinked. Why did that sound so familiar?

Of course.

In the dungeon. When Damarion freed her.

"*And I'll be damned,*" he had said, "*if I let that snake Alpheus twist you into his next experiment and call it justice.*"

The words pulled her back into a place of cold stone walls and desperate hope.

Zale inclined his head. "You've gone quiet—was that too harsh of me?"

Nerissa startled at the sound of his voice. A faint huff escaped her nose. "No, it's just...funny, I suppose. You and Damarion both have an affinity for calling people snakes, it seems."

Zale blinked, then let out a low chuckle. "Well, if the skin fits."

Her lips curved, just slightly, and some of the heaviness in her chest loosened.

The door creaked open then, and Roan stepped into the infirmary, now wearing a loose shirt, his dreadlocks tied back under a bandana. His eyes were bloodshot, and he carried a half-filled mug of something steaming that smelled vaguely medicinal and entirely unpleasant. Nerissa hoped it wasn't for her.

"Well," Roan muttered around a sip, "Welcome back to the land of the living."

Nerissa offered a weak smile. "Sorry if we woke you, Roan."

Roan gave a grunt and crouched beside the tub, setting the mug on a nearby crate. He pressed two fingers gently to the pulse point at her neck. "Pulse is still holding steady. Good."

He adjusted his weight with a quiet sigh, his voice lowering. "But listen to me carefully, Nerissa. No more shifting. Not for at least twenty-four hours. Your body's been through hell, and if you try that again too soon, you might not come back from it."

Nerissa blinked at him. "You expect me to stay in this tub all day tomorrow?"

Roan raised a brow over the rim of his mug. "Yes. You afraid of wrinkled skin?"

Nerissa rolled her eyes.

Roan continued, "I can bring you broth, or tea, or whatever it is merfolk consume that isn't souls—"

"That's a myth."

She pushed her damp hair off her face, eyes still half-lidded with exhaustion. "And I don't need a special diet," she added. "I'll eat whatever's on the regular menu."

Roan gave a grunt of approval, clearly satisfied, and turned toward the door.

"Roan?" Nerissa called quietly before he could leave.

He paused.

She glanced at Zale, then back at Roan. "I'd prefer it if you kept this...my *condition*...between us. At least for now."

Roan studied her for a long beat, then gave a slow nod. "Wasn't planning on announcing it over breakfast." He knocked his knuckles twice against the doorframe on his way out. "Rest. Both of you."

The door creaked shut behind him.

Nerissa shifted, adjusting her weight with a soft splash as she eased into a more upright position. The water lapped gently against the tub's rim, and her damp hair clung to her neck and shoulders.

"Well," she muttered, wincing as she stretched out her tail, "if I'm stuck in here for the next twenty-four hours, I might as well get comfortable."

Zale tilted his head. "Need anything?"

She hesitated, then looked at him sideways. "No, but, don't freak out."

"That's usually what people say right before they do something that absolutely causes freaking out."

"I'm going to take off my shirt."

Zale blinked. "I—what?"

"I need to let my skin breathe, and this shirt is positively drenched." She tugged at the fabric clinging to her dorsal fin between her shoulders as if to prove her point. "Besides, I've got scales. Don't worry, I'll still be decent."

"That's—wait, *is* that how this works? Do you all just—?"

She rolled her eyes, fingers already sliding toward the hem. "Try not to faint."

"I'm not fainting," Zale said, sounding very much like someone who *might.* He scrambled back a bit on instinct, as if proximity increased his odds of scandal. "I'm just—trying to respect boundaries. And—decency. And...biology?"

With a slow motion, Nerissa peeled the shirt off and dropped it to the side of the tub with a wet *plop.* Iridescent lavender scales shimmered across her collarbone and chest, glittering softly in the lanternlight.

Zale blinked. Then blinked again.

"You—yep. Okay. That's...definitely coverage."

She smirked. "Told you. Think of it like built-in armor."

"Sure," he said, voice suddenly an octave higher. He cleared his throat. "Battle-ready. Tactical modesty. Got it."

Nerissa settled deeper into the water, watching him with amusement. "Are you always this dramatic?"

"Only when half-naked mythical sea women strip in front of me without warning."

She laughed, softly but genuinely, then reached over and gently touched his hand where it rested on the tub. "You should get some sleep."

"I will," he said, already pushing himself up. "I'll be over there—" He nodded toward the small cot in the corner, barely big enough for a full-grown man, but he didn't seem to mind. "Just in case you need anything."

"Wouldn't you be more comfortable in your own bunk?" She began to protest, although she didn't really like the idea of being trapped in a tub all night, alone.

"Honestly, I probably won't get much sleep regardless. I'd be too worried," he glanced away, ears turning pink.

"Suit yourself, then," she replied softly.

Nerissa couldn't deny the relief she felt, neither could she stifle the blush that crept into her cheeks. *Nerae*, they both must be past exhaustion if they were getting so flustered for no reason.

She sank back into the water slowly as she tried to make herself comfortable. It was no small feat though; the basin was intended to be used by a full grown human, and with her tail she was easily a couple feet longer than her human form. She exhaled underwater, wrapping her arms around herself and shifting onto her side to avoid crushing the dorsal fin between her shoulder blades. She stretched her tail out and let it drape lazily over one side of the basin.

Then Zale's voice carried through the water. "You good over there? Sounds more like splashing around than sleeping."

Her head popped up to glare at him. "Look, *you* try getting comfortable in a tub smaller than your full height and trying not to cut off circulation to your fins."

"Fair enough," he chuckled. "I'll take your word for it." Then he stretched out on the cot, boots still on, one arm folded behind his head as he stared up at the ceiling beams. He ran a hand through his hair with a sigh.

"Can I tell you something without risking you killing me in my sleep?" he said after a long pause.

Her gaze flicked toward him warily. "Possibly…"

"Scales or not…" He gave a small shrug, like it wasn't important, even though something in his tone said otherwise. "You're a very beautiful woman, Nerissa."

She hummed in response. "Goodnight, Zale."

Nerissa submerged once again, tucking in for the night, thankful that Zale couldn't see the way her face had flushed at his words. She was never good at taking compliments in the first place, but especially not now. Not from him. Not in a voice that sounded like truth more than flattery.

She told herself it didn't matter, that it was nothing. But the warmth blooming in her chest disagreed.

CHAPTER 34

ROUGH SEAS

Zale

Zale rose before the sun, after a night spent wrestling with sleep that refused to come. He still couldn't believe it. Before last night, merfolk existed only in history books and dockside legends. Now there was proof right here in the *Black Serpent's* infirmary.

He peered into the basin where Nerissa was fast asleep, curled up on her side with her hair floating around her in delicate tendrils. Her skin looked far less pallid this morning, and he allowed his gaze to linger on the scattered jewel-like scales decorating her upper body. He noted that they inhabited the same places where the rough patches of dry skin had been the day before.

Rough patches that looked alarmingly similar, if not identical, to the way his skin reacted when he went too long without taking a dip in the sea. He rolled his sleeves up, examining the scars along his arms—some from blades, but most from the lesions that always inevitably flared up.

Swimming in the ocean had remained the best antidote, but it wasn't always practical. Not while they were away from the cove, unless he wanted to become shark bait.

Salt water.

The very thing that had allowed Nerissa's body to complete the transformation. The same thing that soothed his skin condition.

What if…

Zale shook his head, leaving the infirmary.

He needed air.

The deck lay still in the pale hush before dawn. No footsteps, no voices—only the groan of the timbers and the slow pulse of the waves against the hull. But the air felt heavier than usual, carrying a damp, metallic tang. A faint swell rolled beneath the ship, deeper and slower than the lazy rhythm of calm seas.

Nestor was likely still in his cabin, Brigid in hers. Zale drifted toward the stern, bracing his hands on the railing as the horizon bled from black to indigo. Far to the west, low clouds bruised the sky, their edges lit in flickers of distant lightning.

He couldn't stop replaying the night before. When he'd found her in the corridor: crumpled against the wall, shaking so hard her teeth chattered, eyes glassy and unfocused like she was drowning on dry land. He'd touched her shoulder and felt nothing but ice and tremors, and a fear he didn't know he could feel had gripped his heart.

He'd felt utterly useless—just a pair of hands and panic—sure he was about to watch her slip away.

Then she'd changed.

Right there in front of him—scales, fins, tail, and all. Shock had hit him like a breaking wave, but it had carried something else with it too—understanding.

Of course the alcohol had always hit her fast and mean. Of course she'd watched Cormac sideways whenever he spun siren tales, jaw set like a rock. Of course she moved the way she did—footwork like eddies, blade-work like water finding the easiest path through stone. It had always been there, written in how she held herself and how she fought, and he'd been too human to read it.

And the other revelation: the assassination. He was certain Alpheus had done something to her—drugged her, maybe. There was no way she'd have killed of her own free will.

The attack was so public, so deliberate. A statement meant to shatter the treaty before it began, he'd wager. But why? Nerissa had found evidence of merfolk experimentation in his lab. If the Nautalian king knew, then King Vasilios likely did too. Ending those experiments had to be part of the treaty—no more dissecting merfolk, especially not with a mermaid princess for a daughter-in-law.

Would Alpheus really betray his king to keep working? Zale's gut said yes.

And if Alpheus had dosed her to keep her human, he hadn't just wanted to hurt her; he'd wanted to *use* her. If he ever learned where she was now…

A gust curled around him, cooler than before, carrying the faint scent of ozone. The sea's swells had shifted—higher now, heavier—lifting the vessel in slow, deliberate rolls.

Nerissa wasn't safe in Nautalia. She wasn't safe in Astyra. Here, at least, she was *free*.

And he wanted her to stay—just not because she had nowhere else to go.

Zale lingered at the stern, eyes on the horizon as the first edge of the sun broke free of the water, staining the sea in bands of copper and gold. The warmth didn't quite reach him.

A door creaked open behind him. Nestor stepped out onto the deck, rubbing a hand over his face before heading toward the helm. "Bones're achin'," he muttered under his breath, as if the ship herself might be listening. "Pressure's droppin'."

He dug his spyglass from a coat pocket and raised it toward the horizon, scanning the dark clouds swelling to the west.

Brigid emerged a moment later, her hair a chaotic mess of frizzy curls, coat thrown on over her shirt. She spotted Zale immediately and made a beeline for him.

"Where's Nerissa? She's not in her cot."

Zale didn't flinch, but he kept his eyes on the water for a heartbeat before answering. "Collapsed on her way to the infirmary last night. I found her by chance—got up to take a walk."

Brigid's mouth tightened. "Och, I told the lass no' tae overdo it yesterday." She shook her head, then fixed him with a sharper look. "Well? How is she?"

"Roan's got her on strict bed rest for the next twenty-four hours," Zale said. "Stable. No fever. She just needs the rest."

A stronger gust swept across the deck, tugging at Zale's hair and carrying the first faint bite of rain. Brigid's gaze flicked toward the horizon, then back to him, but whatever she meant to say was cut short by the creak and thud of hatches opening below.

One by one, the lower-deck crew began to emerge—still rumpled from sleep, pulling on jackets and boots, yawning as they stretched stiff muscles. A few traded lazy greetings, though most cast quick glances toward the west where the clouds were thickening.

Nestor lowered his spyglass, tucking it into his coat. "Right then," he said, his voice low but carrying just enough to reach the men now scattered across the deck. "Best tidy the lines and check yer lashings. I want the loose gear stowed and the sails ready to reef if I give the word."

There was no panic in his tone, but his commanding authority made people move without asking questions.

"Aye, Cap'n," came a few murmured replies as the crew set about their work—coiling ropes, fastening barrels, checking knots along the rail. The usual slap of the waves against the hull had taken on a heavier, more deliberate rhythm, each one lifting the ship in a slow roll.

Zale's hands curled over the railing, watching the horizon darken. If they kept their course, they might reach the safety of their cove before the rain—assuming the sea allowed it.

The scent of turmeric and ginger hit Zale the moment he stepped back into the infirmary. Nerissa was propped up in the metal basin, a blanket draped loosely over her shoulders, steam curling from the mug in her hands.

Roan sat on a stool beside her, journal balanced on one knee, pencil poised. "So—how long can merfolk breathe air?" he asked without preamble.

Nerissa shook her head slightly. "We don't technically breathe air. But if we take a deep breath underwater, we can hold it for a few minutes. Give or take."

Roan's pencil started scratching immediately. "Interesting. So gills remain the primary respiratory function even at the surface—no true lung capacity, then?"

"Correct." She took a sip of tea.

"And how long can you remain human before shifting back to a mermaid?"

"Usually, seven days," Nerissa said.

Roan's pencil moved faster. "Fascinating. And the fins—do they heal like human skin or more like cartilage?"

"Somewhere in between."

"Would removing one—hypothetically, of course—affect your balance in the water?"

"Yes."

Zale leaned against the doorframe, one brow raised. "Should I be worried you're about to dissect her, Doc?"

Roan didn't glance up. "Purely academic."

Nerissa's lips twitched over her mug. "He's been at this for twenty minutes. I think he's cataloged more about merfolk than the Nautalian archives."

"Give me another twenty and I'll have the definitive volume," Roan said, flipping to a fresh page. "Now—about the structural makeup of your dorsal—"

"That's enough for now," Zale cut in, pushing off the doorframe. "She's supposed to be resting, not giving you a dissertation."

Roan sighed, closing the journal with visible reluctance. "Fine. But you're stifling the pursuit of knowledge. I'll be in the galley if either of you regain your appreciation for groundbreaking research."

Zale waited until the door clicked shut behind him before stepping closer to the basin. "How're ye feelin' this mornin'?"

Nerissa set her mug aside on a crate that Roan had pulled up next to the tub, the steam curling away between them. "There's that brogue slipping through again," she laughed.

His ears warmed, though he masked it with a grin. "I cannae help it. 'Twas me upbringin', ye see. Now, answer the question, *lass*."

She laughed again at the deliberate exaggeration. "Still sore," she admitted at last, "but overall...much better." Her gills fluttered as she dipped below the water, pulling in a deep breath. "Roan said as long as I don't relapse, he'll clear me tomorrow morning."

"That's good to hear." Zale leaned a hip against the edge of the table, studying her. "Though from the way he's talkin', I'm not sure if he's more excited about your recovery or about turnin' you into his next thesis."

A faint smile ghosted across her lips. "He's harmless. Mostly."

A low, distant rumble threaded through the timbers beneath them. It wasn't the groan of the ship this time—it came from beyond, rolling in from the west.

Nerissa paused mid-sip, her gaze flicking toward the ceiling. "That thunder?"

Zale nodded, glancing toward the small porthole above the supply shelves. Through the warped glass, the sky had deepened to a sullen gray, the sunlight already losing its warmth. "Saw the clouds before I came down," he said. "Figured we'd have more time before it hit." Another rumble followed, longer this time, and the faint patter of rain began against the deck overhead.

Her lips twitched faintly. "What's the protocol for rough seas? Should I be nervous?"

Zale's grin was small but reassuring. "Nay, Nestor doesn't spook easy; he's weathered his fair share of storms."

She raised a brow over the rim of her mug. "*Nay*?"

He rolled his eyes up to the ceiling, smirking. "You know what I meant." Then he straightened, listening as footsteps hurried overhead. "For now, you just stay put. We'll handle whatever's up there."

The infirmary door swung open and Roan stepped back inside, a thin spray of rain clinging to his sleeves. "All hands on deck, Zale. Nestor wants every able body topside."

Zale gave a quick nod and followed, pulling the door shut behind them.

The moment he stepped out onto the deck with Roan, the wind shoved at him like a living thing. Rain sheeted sideways, stinging his face, soaking through his shirt in seconds. The *Black Serpent* rolled hard under his boots, timbers groaning as she crested another swell.

Brigid's voice cut through the roar, sharp and commanding as she barked orders to the crew scrambling along the rigging and securing the last of the lines. "Haul that sheet in—tight! Watch your footing, ye daft clod, unless ye fancy a swim!"

At the helm, Nestor stood braced with his boots planted wide, both hands locked around the wheel. His coat snapped violently in the wind, but his grip was steady, eyes fixed on the black horizon as if daring the storm to try harder.

Zale took one glance at the waves rising on their starboard side and knew this wasn't going to be a quick squall.

The wind howled through the rigging, whipping rain into Zale's eyes as he and Roan fought their way toward the starboard side. Brigid was already there, shouting over the storm as she threw her weight into hauling a line taut.

"Get that cleated—now!" she barked.

Zale lunged for the nearest rope, the sodden fibers rough and biting against his palms. A shadow fell beside him—Eon, looping a coil over his shoulder.

"Got your tail, Zale!" he shouted, grinning like this was just another race against the tide.

"Let's make it quick," Zale shot back, muscles straining as the ship rolled again. Together they wrestled the line into place, rain sluicing over their arms and backs.

A sudden crack split the air—not thunder, but the snap of a loosened sheet slamming across the deck. Brigid swiveled just in time for the flailing rope to whip past her head, missing by inches.

"Bloody—" she snarled, ducking low and grabbing it before it could lash again. "Mind yer heads, all o' ye!"

Another swell hit broadside, the deck tilting sharply. Zale's boots skidded on the slick planks, and Eon grabbed his arm, steadying them both.

"Thanks," Zale muttered.

"No dying before me, yeah?" Eon shot back, turning to secure the next set of lashings. He moved quick, too quick for the shifting deck, and Zale caught himself glancing over just as Eon's foot slipped near the rail.

"Mind yourself—" Zale started, but Eon recovered with a laugh, tossing him a two-finger salute before diving back into the rigging work.

Above them, lightning forked across the sky, followed by thunder that rattled Zale's teeth. Nestor's voice boomed from the helm, cutting through the chaos: "Brace for the next one!"

Zale tightened his grip on the line, but his eyes flicked back toward Eon. That near-slip had been too close.

Nerissa

The infirmary shuddered with the force of the wind, the timbers creaking like an old hull in a swell. Nerissa sat in the basin, tea cooling in her hands, listening to the chaos above.

Boots thudded hard across the deck overhead. Voices rose in sharp bursts—orders shouted, lines answered. The pitch and roll of the ship had shifted from the familiar sway of open water to a sharper, more urgent rhythm. Each tilt felt steeper, each righting slower.

She set the mug aside, tilting her head to catch the muted thunder, the rip of sails straining against their rigging. The air down here was still warm, but she could feel the storm pressing against the hull, the vibrations carrying through the water around her.

Then the ship lurched hard to port. The basin skidded across the infirmary with a teeth-grinding screech. Salt water sloshed over the rim, then the whole thing tipped, dumping its contents—Nerissa included—

across the slick floorboards.

She landed on her side with a grunt, propping herself up on her elbows as the deck rolled beneath her. "Bloody scallops," she muttered, shoving wet hair out of her face.

Her nightshirt lay crumpled in the puddle beside her, still damp from the night before. She snatched it up, wringing it once before dragging it over her head. The cotton clung cold against her skin, but she ignored the discomfort as she focused inward.

The shift came easier this time—not the searing, bone-deep agony of last night's forced change, but still enough to make her jaw tighten. Her tail receded, legs unfurling in its place, muscles trembling with residual soreness.

She sat there for a moment, letting the ache ebb just enough for her to move. Then she pushed herself to her feet, scanning the infirmary until her gaze landed on her leather coat hanging from a peg by the door.

Roan's voice from the previous night echoed in her mind—*No more shifting. Not for at least twenty-four hours. Your body's been through hell, and if you try that again too soon, you might not come back from it.*

She pulled the coat from its hook and shrugged it on without hesitation. The familiar weight settled across her shoulders like a second skin.

Sorry Roan.

The corridor outside tilted sharply, forcing her to brace a hand against the wall as she started forward. Every few steps, the ship pitched hard enough to slam her into the opposite bulkhead, but she kept moving, timing her steps with the roll of the deck.

By the time she pushed open the hatch, the storm hit her full in the face—wind tearing at her coat, rain lashing against her cheeks, salt spray stinging her eyes. The deck was chaos: Brigid shouting over the roar, crew hauling lines under Nestor's steady helm, lightning flashing white against the dark sea.

Her gaze caught on movement at the starboard side. Eon was clinging to a line, his boots scrambling for purchase. A wave slammed against the hull, the force jerking his hands from the rope.

"Eon!" she heard Zale shout into the wind as the boy vanished over the rail into the churning sea.

Then Zale vaulted over the rail, diving after him. Nerissa's heart lurched.

He was the best swimmer on the crew—besides her—but that knowledge did nothing to ease the knot tightening in her chest. She gripped the nearest line, scanning the water for any sign of him or Eon between the rolling swells. Lightning flared, briefly painting the waves in stark white, but there was nothing—only the restless churn of the sea.

One minute passed.

Then another.

The knot in her chest twisted into something sharper.

Too long. Even if he could hold his breath longer than anyone on this ship, Eon certainly couldn't.

She ripped off her coat and tossed it toward the nearest figure—Brigid—without looking.

"Don't ye even think about it!" Brigid's voice cut through the wind, sharp and furious.

But Nerissa was already moving, bare feet gripping the slick deck as she climbed onto the rail. The next wave hit, and she used the tilt to hurl herself into the water.

Brigid

Brigid lunged to the rail, rain plastering her hair to her face as she leaned out over the frothing black below. The sea was a seething mess—walls of water heaving and crashing against the hull, swallowing anything unlucky enough to be in their path.

"Three overboard!" she bellowed toward the helm.

Nestor's head snapped her way, his coat whipping in the wind. His jaw tightened as he fought the wheel, eyes flicking to the starboard side where the waves were already closing over the spot.

Boots pounded up behind her. Roan appeared at her shoulder, one hand braced on the railing. "Who?"

Brigid's lips pressed into a grim line. "Zale, Eon...and Nerissa."

Roan's expression darkened, the storm's spray mingling with the water dripping from his beard. "Of course she didn't listen."

Brigid tore her gaze from the water, scanning the deck. "Get lines over the side, starboard! Now!"

Roan was already moving, barking for two crew to bring the longest coils they had. The deck pitched hard, forcing them to grab at the rigging as they scrambled to obey.

"Mind the slack!" Brigid shouted as the first rope hit the water. "Keep it clear in case they surface!"

Roan seized the second coil from a wide-eyed deckhand and tied it off to the rail with quick, sure knots. "If they get close enough, we'll haul them straight in," he said, yanking the rope taut to test it.

Another wave slammed into the hull, sending a spray over their heads. The ship groaned in protest, the wheel creaking as Nestor fought to keep their broadside from turning into a broaching off.

"Reef that topsail before it takes us under!" Brigid barked at a pair of crew scrambling up the ratlines. The wind caught her coat, nearly pulling her sideways, but she shoved past it, eyes fixed on the churning sea below.

Somewhere in that chaos were three souls—and their window to find them was shrinking with every wave.

CHAPTER 35

MAGICAL OCEAN CREATURE

Nerissa

The sea slammed into her like a wall, but she didn't fight it—she let it pull her down. The sting on her skin faded as her body gave in to the change. Her legs fused, tail unfurling with a ripple of scales, gills flaring open as she drew the sea into her mouth.

The roar of the storm above faded to a muffled, distant pounding. Down here, the world was darker, heavier—water so thick with silt and churn that it swallowed the light in seconds. She blinked against the sting, pupils narrowing, then widening again as her vision adjusted to the dim light.

A variety of foreign objects took shape around her—a tangle of lines caught in the current, shadows of debris torn from the deck. She spun slowly, scanning through the gloom. The current was strong, pulling everything east, and if Zale and Eon had gone under near the starboard rail, it would already be dragging them away from the ship.

Her pulse thudded in her ears, matching the rhythm of her tail as she drove herself deeper. Then—there! A flash of movement below and to her left, swallowed almost instantly by the darkness.

She angled downward hard, ignoring the ache still lingering in her lower body from the night before. The sea pressed colder, heavier around her, but she didn't slow—this was her element. She focused on the direction where she first caught movement, and spied what looked like a large net with something trapped in it. *Or someone.* She pumped her tail harder, closing the distance until the shadow morphed into two figures—one limp, the other moving with quick, deliberate strokes.

There you are.

Zale had one arm wrapped tight around Eon's chest, the other working furiously with a knife, sawing at the snarl of netting cinched around Eon's legs. The mesh dragged them both deeper, weighted with knots of rope and torn canvas that twisted in the current like the grasping fingers of a drowned hand. He was fighting valiantly against the pull, but every downward tug of the net yanked them closer to the black depths.

Eon had already blacked out from lack of oxygen, but Zale didn't look to be struggling yet. Still, they needed to work fast if they wanted Eon to have a chance. Nerissa felt a pit in her stomach as she noted the bluish tinge his lips had already taken on. She surged forward, curving her body around the current's drag. Zale glanced up as she approached, his eyes wide for a fraction of a second before he went back to hacking at the ropes.

Nerissa swept in beside him, bracing one hand on Eon's shoulder to steady him. She drew her arm back and slashed down. The razor edge of her forearm fin sliced clean through the thickest rope. Another flick, and another coil split apart, the freed strands spiraling away in the dark water.

Zale's blade found the last binding, and together they tore the net away. It fluttered downward into the depths, vanishing like smoke.

Hooking her arms under Eon's, her eyes briefly met Zale's, a silent agreement passing between them—*up, now.*

They kicked hard, driving for the faint shimmer of light far above.

The light above grew brighter, wavering and fractured through the heaving surface. Nerissa kept going, Eon's dead weight dragging at her arms, her muscles burning with the effort. Every surge upward was met by the pull of the sea trying to take them back.

A sinking crate suddenly obscured the light, and Nerissa barely maneuvered herself and Eon out of its path in time. The cargo grazed her tail on its way down; she winced against the scrape of splintered wood, but she didn't stop—she kept focused on getting Eon to the surface.

The storm's roar came crashing in all at once as their heads broke the waterline—wind shrieking through the rigging, rain lashing her face, the ship looming like a dark cliff against the flashes of lightning.

She struck out for the *Black Serpent,* Eon firmly in her grip. The swells battered them sideways, salt spray flooding her mouth, but she forced her strokes into a steady rhythm until they reached the lifelines trailing over the side of the ship.

Nerissa caught one in her free hand and wrapped it quickly around Eon's torso, pulling the rope into a basic knot that Cormac had taught her beneath his arms. "Got him!" she called, jerking the line twice in signal.

Above, Brigid and Roan leaned over the rail, bracing themselves as they heaved. The rope went taut, lifting Eon slowly out of the water, his head lolling against the line. He would be alright now—he *had* to be. He was too young to die.

Nerissa let go of the line, treading water as she watched them haul Eon to safety.

"Where's Zale?" Brigid called down to her.

Nerissa spun around, scanning the surface. Her stomach dropped, ice filling her veins. Lightning lit the waves for a heartbeat, but there was no sign of Zale—only the endless, angry sea.

No, he was right behind me…

Then all at once, it hit her.

The crate. It must have clipped him.

She had been so focused on getting Eon back to the surface, that she hadn't even noticed that Zale was no longer trailing them.

"*Moirai!*" Nerissa cursed as she dove back under, her tail flicking upward before slicing into the water. The cold closed over her, muting the storm above to a low, relentless thrum once more.

Roan

Roan's muscles bulged with strain as he and Brigid hauled Eon over the rail. They didn't bother with gentleness, speed mattered more than comfort right now. The boy's limbs flopped bonelessly as they heaved him onto the planks, his skin cold and blue under the medic's hands. A few surrounding crew members crowded around, murmuring prayers and gripping various trinkets and talismans.

"Clear back," Roan barked, dropping to his knees. He ripped off his shirt and shoved it beneath Eon's head. Then he tipped Eon's head back, pried his jaw open, and let two drops of the distillate drip onto his tongue.

"Come on, lad," he muttered against the rush of wind and creak of the rigging. Rain pelted his bare skin, but he ignored it.

Brigid hovered close by but silent. The rest of the crew stood at the edge of his awareness, their voices a dull roar compared to the pounding in his own ears.

Roan gritted his teeth. "Don't you quit on me, Eon."

Suddenly, Eon's body jerked as he coughed violently, seawater spilling from his mouth in a thin stream. Roan rolled him onto his side as the coughing fit took hold, bracing a hand between the boy's shoulder blades.

Bran let out a sharp breath, raking both hands through his wet hair. "Thank the saints," he muttered, though his gaze flicked immediately to the rail, scanning the churning water below. Roan knew exactly what he was thinking. Zale hadn't come up yet; it was long past the breath-holding record he had set several summers ago. He knew Nerissa would be fine, but he began to prepare himself for the worst.

Brigid crouched near them, draping a thick blanket around Eon's shoulders as he sputtered. "Easy, lad. Ye're back."

Eon sagged against the deck, coughing raggedly into the blanket. His skin was waxy and pale, but his chest was moving now—shallow, uneven, yet blessedly alive. Roan let out a breath through clenched teeth, relief sharp as pain in his ribs.

He glanced up, rain running in rivulets down his face. Brigid was still crouched, tucking the blanket around Eon's trembling frame, her own hair plastered to her head in a wild copper tangle.

"Any sign of them?" Roan asked, his voice rough with salt and strain.

Brigid's eyes lifted, dark and grim. She gave a single, hard shake of her head.

Roan's gut tightened. The storm still howled, spray lashing over the rail in sheets. Lightning split the sky in a jagged arc, painting the water below in a brief, merciless white.

"Damn it," Roan muttered under his breath, forcing his attention back to the boy in front of him. Eon was shivering violently now, lips slightly regaining their natural pink. Roan braced a steadying hand on his shoulder, grounding him. Eon coughed again, weak but responsive, and that would have to be enough for now.

Nerissa

She shot like an arrow through the dark, every instinct screaming at her to *hurry*. And hurry she did, though she was going nowhere fast, unsure which direction to look besides down.

Where are you?

Her gills flared, pulse hammering, matching the churn of the sea around her. Though her body ached, she surged through the depths with a speed that would leave most sirens in her wake, her lean muscles honed by years of Damarion's rigorous drills. Her eyes adjusted to the darkness as she scanned wildly around her.

Don't panic. He's fine. He's strong. He's the best swimmer on the crew.

But the knot in her chest tightened anyway. If Zale had been caught in the undertow, even his strength wouldn't make him untouchable. Especially if he had gotten hit by debris. He could be unconscious, and if she didn't find him soon…

No. Don't think like that.

She angled deeper, scanning every shadow, every flicker of movement.

Lightning flashed somewhere far above, sending ghost-light rippling through the dark, but there was still no sign of him.

Don't panic.

Diving deeper still, she weaved through the churn of broken debris—splintered wood, frayed lines, and loose canvas tumbling towards the murky depths. Her heart thudded harder with each empty sweep of her gaze. The lightning no longer reached this level of the ocean.

Come on, Zale. Where are you?

Finally, a shape flickered at the edge of her vision. She turned sharply—and froze.

He was drifting in the dark, body limp. A thin ribbon of crimson swirled from a gash at his temple, curling upward into the gloom. Her gills stuttered as she recognized the shape of a predator circling him in narrowing laps.

Most other sharks stayed away from storms, retreating to the depths or fleeing the area altogether. But not tiger sharks. No, they were drawn to these conditions hoping for an easy meal. Just as this one eyed Zale like he was his next snack.

Nerissa's eyes narrowed, body simmering with a protective rage as she darted towards the sinuous outline of the shark. Its circles were narrowing by the second, and she knew she had only a matter of seconds before it struck. Propelling herself forward, she came up underneath its body, matching its speed. It didn't notice her.

Just as the creature lunged for one of Zale's arms, she drove both arms upward, fins flaring, and sliced its underbelly down to its tail, effectively gutting it. Nerissa held her breath as the shark thrashed before going limp and spiraling downward in clouds of blood. She waved her arms on either side of her body to clean off the remaining guts and gore.

Ugh. Zale, you owe me for that.

Zale was drifting just ahead; she closed the distance in a matter of seconds, hooking an arm around his torso. "Got you," she muttered, more to herself than him.

A blur of movement caught her attention, drawing her gaze to his neck, just beneath his jawline. Faint slits, fluttering open and closed with each subtle shift of the current.

What in Nerae? Gills? How…?

Her chest seized. For one impossible instant she just stared, the world narrowing to the delicate membranes flexing against his skin. It couldn't be. It explained too much, yet it raised too many questions—*Not now.*

Shoving the storm of questions aside, she kicked hard for the surface, dragging his deadweight with her. His limbs hung slack, dragging against the water, and every pull on her muscles felt like tearing threads. The burn in her lower body flared into something sharp, her body's lingering exhaustion turning her strokes sluggish. Her tail thrashed harder as she gripped Zale with both hands now, clutching him close to her chest. The water seemed thicker, heavier, each second stretching until it felt like she was dragging him through molasses. Her muscles ached, her vision narrowing at the edges, but she refused to let her grip slip.

At least he was breathing—impossibly so—and that knowledge allowed her to pace herself, no longer worried about him losing oxygen. She just needed to get them to the surface without blacking out from sheer exhaustion.

When they finally broke the surface, his head lolled back against her shoulder, mouth slack, eyes closed. She watched in awe as his gills closed up and the skin beneath his jaw smoothed out as if they had never been there at all.

Interesting. They must have appeared because he was unconsciously breathing in water.

And now that he was no longer drawing in water—wait.

He wasn't breathing anymore.

"Zale!" Her voice cracked, half-swallowed by the wind and crash of waves. She adjusted her grip, keeping his face above water, and pumped her tail hard toward the *Black Serpent's* shadow looming ahead.

Nerissa's arms trembled as she half-dragged, half-floated Zale to the hull, the storm battering them with every surge. Spray blinded her, her muscles screaming as she clawed at the slick wood.

Too heavy. He's too heavy—and he's not breathing–

Her fingers finally found purchase. A line, sodden and frayed, trailing down into the waves. She hooked her arm tighter around Zale's chest, seizing the rope with her free hand. "Got you," she panted, forehead pressing briefly against his. "I've got you."

She looped the line under his arms, knotting it with shaking fingers, and yanked hard to signal the crew above.

Almost instantly, the line went taut, Zale's body lifting from her grasp as Brigid and Roan began hauling him up. She watched his limp form vanish over the railing.

Please be okay.

If this had happened a few weeks ago, she wouldn't have been nearly so terrified. She still would have jumped overboard to rescue him—she would have done that for any member of the crew. She wouldn't have felt so strongly as to whether or not the sea claimed him. Any loss of life was a waste; she had learned better than most that anything could happen in the blink of an eye and change everything forever. But now? She didn't know what she would do if he didn't make it. Somehow, that cocky pirate had stubbornly worn down her walls, and he meant more to her than she was willing to admit. She needed to get up there and make sure he was okay.

She turned inward, reaching for that familiar pull. Her focus tunneled to her breathing, to the beat of her heart, to the deep coil of power anchored in her core.

Come on. Shift back. Just once more.

Her gills sealed over with a sting, her lungs expanding to gulp in the salt-stung air. But her tail…her tail stayed, heavy and unyielding. She felt the tingling of her dorsal fin, but it stubbornly remained in place, much like her forearm fins. Muscles twitched uselessly, the change halting halfway as if her body had simply had enough.

No. No, no, no—please…not now.

She sagged against the hull, waves battering her against the slick planks, water lapping high against her ribs. Every shift in the past twenty-four hours had been forced by necessity, each one ripping more from her reserves. Now there was nothing left to give.

A leaden dread sank in her stomach. No clever excuses. No chance to hide.

No. They can't see me like this. Not now. Not after everything. The thought gripped her chest. Her grip slackened on the rope, as she considered letting go. She could ride out the storm, float on her back, and conserve her strength until she could shift again. The crew would think she had gotten pulled under by the current. Zale would know the truth—he wouldn't worry too much about her. He'd at least know she hadn't drowned.

That was, if he even survived.

She pushed her fear back down. It would do her no good here. She had to at least find out if he lived. Even if the crew decided to throw her overboard as soon as they saw her fins.

You're still you. That hasn't changed. His words echoed in her mind, pulling her back from the edge. Zale didn't think she was a monster, and he swore the rest of the crew would accept her as she was. Did she really believe that? Was it worth the risk?

Her jaw clenched hard, hand reluctantly gripping the rope once more. Fingers trembling, she tied it around her waist, every knot a sentence sealing her fate.

She tipped her head back and gave a grim nod upward.

Two sharp tugs. Resignation settled cold in her stomach.

The crew was about to see her for what she was.

Bran

Bran's palms burned on the wet rope as he heaved, shoulder to shoulder with Brigid. Rain and seawater lashed his face, stinging his eyes, but he still found breath to quip, "She's heavier than she looks."

Brigid shot him a sharp glare. "One more word, Calder, and I'll toss ye over meself."

He wisely shut his mouth, gritting his teeth as the line jerked in their hands. Inch by inch, Nerissa came into view—first her long dark hair spilling over her shoulders like a drowned veil, then the sodden sweep of her nightshirt plastered to her frame. She clung to the rope at her waist, eyes wide, locking on each of them in turn.

"Don't freak out," she rasped.

Bran exchanged a wary glance with Brigid, but together they hooked their arms beneath hers and hauled her over the rail. She hit the deck hard, her weight sagging between them—that's when he saw it. A long, scaled *tail* dragged across the planks beneath her. Then he finally clocked the sharp fins protruding from her arms—he hadn't even noticed when they pulled her onto the deck.

Bran's grip nearly gave. "Saints above—"

Brigid's muttered oath was too thick with brogue for Bran to catch, but the shock in her voice was plain.

For a moment, they both froze. Then Brigid cursed again and dropped to her knees, steadying Nerissa as her body slumped forward. Bran followed suit, lowering her gently onto the slick boards.

Nerissa tried to push herself up on her arms, hair hanging in a drenched curtain over her face. Her breath came ragged, every muscle trembling, but she forced the words out: "How's...Zale?"

"Not breathing," Roan's voice cut in, grim and clipped. He was kneeling over Zale a few feet away, dripping the last bit of miracle elixir into his mouth.

Nerissa lurched forward instinctively, only to sag back against Bran and Brigid's hold as her arms gave out. Her eyes were wide with fear, fixed on Zale's still form.

Bran swallowed hard, throat dry despite the storm raging around them. Jokes failed him now. All he could do was grip Nerissa's shoulder to steady her as Roan worked.

Nerissa

Her arms trembled as she fought to keep herself upright, every muscle in her body shrieking for rest. She barely registered Bran's grip on her shoulder, or Brigid hovering close, or the wide-eyed stares of the crew gathered in a broken circle around them. None of it mattered.

All she saw was Zale's blue face.

Her breath came in short, shallow rasps, a combination of overexertion and the sheer terror clawing at her ribs.

Please breathe, please breathe.

Zale's chest stayed still.

She bit down hard, tasting salt and iron where her teeth caught her lip. The deck tilted beneath her as a wave of vertigo swept through her, but she refused to let herself collapse. Not while he lay there unmoving. Not while his chest refused to rise and fall on its own.

"Come on, Zale," Nerissa pleaded into the wind, her voice breaking. She could feel tears burning at the edges of her eyes, but the rain swallowed them before they could fall.

What if he doesn't wake up? What if I wasn't fast enough?

Her chest constricted until it hurt, and she pressed trembling palms to the slick deck to keep from collapsing. She should have noticed when he'd fallen behind. Should have checked for him. Should have—

Tides, this is my fault. What will I do if he dies? I never even got the chance to—

Zale's body jolted with a wet, shuddering cough.

Seawater spilled from his mouth, followed by another, harsher cough that wracked his chest. Then a gasp—ragged, broken, but blessedly real—as his chest rose.

Roan rolled him onto his side, bracing a hand against his back. "That's it. Breathe, lad. Nice and easy now."

From somewhere nearby, Cormac's voice carried over the pounding of waves against the hull, rough with the cadence of old superstition. "Sea's not takin' any souls today."

Relief washed over Nerissa all at once, her chest loosening as if someone had cut a rope she hadn't realized was binding her. Her head dropped forward, damp hair clinging to her cheeks, and for a moment she didn't care that the crew's stares still pinned her to the deck.

Her arms gave out, and she sagged fully onto the cold, wet planks. Brigid and Bran eased their grips, letting her sink forward against the boards.

She turned her head just enough to look at the gray sky overhead, the storm's edge beginning to break apart into softer light. Her voice came out low and ragged, shaped in the fluid consonants and lilting vowels of Nautalian.

"*Kharis Pontou.*"

Thank the Sea.

Her eyes fluttered shut for a moment, not from sleep, but to let the rain and wind wash over her face, mingling with the brine already on her skin. Now she could rest.

Zale

Zale's lungs burned like fire as he dragged in air that felt too heavy, too sharp, every breath scraping his throat raw. He coughed hard, salt water searing on the way out, then collapsed back against the deck with a ragged groan.

His skull throbbed, each pulse of pain radiating from the gash at his temple where something in the water had clipped him. For a moment the world tilted, the storm above a blur of gray light and shouted voices.

"Easy," came Roan's gravel-rough voice, betraying the fear he tried so often to hide behind a mask of neutrality. The medic crouched close, bracing him as he tried to sit.

Zale's muscles protested, weak and trembling, but he forced himself upright inch by inch. His breaths came shallow, deliberate, every inhale tasting of brine.

Roan's hand stayed firm on his shoulder, grounding him against the deck's roll. "That's it. Slow and steady."

Zale pressed the heel of his palm against his temple, wincing at the sticky warmth there, then blinked hard to clear his vision. Shapes swam into focus—the rail, the crew gathered in a ragged circle, Eon huddled beneath a thick blanket.

Good, he's okay.

Then he caught sight of Nerissa slumped over on her side a few feet away, hair strewn about in wild waves, her body sagging with exhaustion.

He remembered diving in after Eon. Remembered Nerissa darting towards them to help free the boy from the debris. Then following her back to the surface...but nothing after that.

Zale swallowed against the raw burn in his throat, his voice rough when it finally scraped out. "What…happened?"

"Nerissa pulled you out," Roan said simply.

"How long—" Zale began, before a coughing fit wracked his chest. "How long…was I under?"

"I stopped counting after fifteen minutes, to be honest," Roan said gravely. "Thought for sure you were lost to the sea."

Bloody stars…over fifteen minutes in the water? I *shouldn't be alive.*

His thoughts were cut short when Brigid moved past him, kneeling beside Nerissa. She draped Nerissa's purple coat over her shoulders and torso, a faint shiver running through her as the fabric settled. Bran stood near her looking like he'd seen a ghost.

Zale's heart almost stopped when he finally registered her tail splayed out across the deck. Why hadn't she shifted?

Cormac's voice cut in from somewhere near the rail, incredulous and edged with something like awe. "A mermaid…saved a sailor. Pulled him from the deep instead o' draggin' him down to it." He spat over the side, muttering an old phrase that might have been prayer, might have been curse. "Never thought I'd live t'see the day."

Zale's jaw tightened at Cormac's words. The secret Nerissa had nearly killed herself trying to keep was no longer just his and Roan's to bear. It was out now. There'd be no putting it back in the dark.

But none of that mattered if she wasn't breathing.

Gritting his teeth against the ache in his skull, Zale shoved unsteadily to his feet. Roan didn't try to stop him, only watched as he staggered the few steps across the deck to where Nerissa lay. Zale dropped to one knee beside her, bracing himself with a hand on the boards.

Her eyes were closed but he saw the faint rise and fall of her chest beneath her coat. Not deeply as if she were sleeping though, more shallow.

She's alive. She's still breathing.

Relief coursed through him so sharply it left him dizzy. He noted the smooth skin of her neck. No gills. She must have partially shifted then? He didn't understand how that worked, but he was grateful.

"Riss? You alright?" he whispered, leaning closer.

Her lashes fluttered, those ocean eyes cracking open just enough to find his. "Yeah…just resting a bit. You?"

He closed his eyes, nodding. "Aye, thanks to you."

A tired smile tugged at her lips. "Guess we're even now."

A short, shaky chuckle escaped him. "I guess we are."

"...I'm glad you're okay," she whispered after a few breaths.

Before he could answer, another voice piped up, hoarse but indignant. "I'm okay too, thanks for asking!"

Eon's mutter carried just enough bite to break the tension, and a ripple of relieved laughter spread across the deck.

Brigid's voice cut through the fading laughter, brisk and no-nonsense. "Right then. Eon, Zale, Nerissa—down t'the infirmary wi' ye. Rest o' us'll see t' it the ship stays in one piece."

Eon groaned but obediently shuffled toward the companionway, blanket still wrapped tight around him.

Zale bent and gathered Nerissa into his arms, the sweep of her tail heavier than he'd expected as it trailed against the deck. His muscles ached at the strain of use so soon after coming back from the dead, but he ignored it. She must have seen the wince he tried to hide, though.

"Sorry for the extra weight. Tail's not exactly travel-friendly." She grimaced faintly, offering a rueful smile.

"It's no problem," he said, shifting her carefully against his chest. "You forget—I've got that sea strength."

A soft huff escaped her, half laugh, half sigh, as she let her head tip against his shoulder. He adjusted his grip, steadying her despite the weakness in his limbs, then started toward the companionway.

The deck was still slick underfoot, crew darting around them to secure lines and canvas, but none of it touched the fragile quiet wrapped between the two of them. Her damp hair clung to his neck, her breath warm and even against his throat.

They reached the infirmary door, and for a moment he didn't move to open it—just looked at her, something unspoken flickering in his expression. "You're sure you're alright?"

She met his gaze, heavy-lidded but focused. "Mhm. Just…tired."

"So…too much shifting in one day, I take it?" Zale gestured to her scales.

"Guess so…body's spent," she mumbled sleepily.

She looked as if she might pass out on him any second now, so he stopped asking questions and nudged the infirmary door open with his shoulder.

Eon was perched on the edge of the exam table, swaddled in his blanket like a smug, half-drowned cat, while Roan stood beside him, ear pressed to his chest. He glanced up briefly, nodding, before returning to his patient.

Zale crossed the room without a word and lowered himself onto the nearest cot. He kept Nerissa in his arms while he settled heavily against the wall, and she shifted just enough to rest against his chest. Her tail curved toward the floor, fin brushing against his boot and curling slightly around his ankle.

If you had told him three weeks ago that he would be holding the mysterious tavern girl in his arms like this, he would have called you mad with scurvy. But the warmth of her body pressed against him now told him that this was real, and he would allow himself to enjoy this moment.

He let his eyes close, the pull of exhaustion seeping into his bones now that the worst was over.

Nerissa

Zale's head rested against the wall, eyes closed, his chest rising and falling in a steady rhythm that still felt impossible to believe. The image of him drifting in the dark, limp and yet miraculously breathing—with gills!—was consuming her thoughts.

She thought back to the day he collapsed on deck, to the angry lesions riddling his torso and arms. How they looked so eerily similar to her own patches of scales threatening to rupture her skin when her body could no longer hold its human form. She recalled how he'd said swimming kept the patches at bay. How that was the only thing that really worked.

It never once occurred to her that Zale might not be fully human. He was an orphan—he knew nothing of his parentage. They could be anyone. At least one of them had to be merfolk.

She gazed up at him now, squinting her eyes at his jawline—hidden by stubble. No indication that there had ever been anything other than his sun-weathered skin.

As if sensing the weight of her gaze, he cracked one eye open. "What's up?"

She startled. What could she say? Was he even aware of what his body could do? Should she ask him?

No, not here. Not with an audience.

She would find the time to talk to him about it, but for now, she was just grateful that he was still here, still alive.

Both of his eyes were open now, questioning. She realized that she had been staring at him for an awkwardly long amount of time.

Her throat tightened. "It's just...when I pulled you from the water, and you weren't breathing, I thought—" She found that she couldn't finish her sentence, the reality of what could have happened chilling her to the bone. She looked down to her lap.

"Hey, I'm okay," he cut in, his voice raw but trying to soothe, sparing her from finishing. "You're okay. We're okay."

The simple certainty of it unraveled something in her—something she only noticed when the silence stretched.

She hadn't realized she was clutching his shirt until her webbed fingers curled tighter, fabric bunched in her fist. The warmth of him seeped through the sea-soaked cotton, steady against her palm, grounding and disorienting all at once. How could he be so warm despite his drenched clothes?

Her breathing hitched when she looked up and found both of his eyes fixed intently on hers. The dim lanternlight caught the gold in them, sparkling like wet glass.

Her gaze faltered, dipping to his mouth before she could stop herself. And suddenly she was leaning closer, not even aware of moving, the space between them narrowing—was he leaning in too?

"Alright," Roan's gravelly voice cut through the moment like a knife as he crossed the infirmary. "Vitals. Both of you."

Nerissa jerked back slightly, pulse hammering, her palm now simply resting against Zale's shirt. His gaze lingered on her a beat longer, a faint crease tugging between his brows. For the briefest moment—before he shuttered it—she caught the flicker of irritation in his face.

Then Roan was there, tilting his head to get a better look at Zale's temple. "This is gonna sting." The medic's voice was brisk as he reached for a clean cloth and pressed it to the cut.

Zale hissed through his teeth but didn't flinch away, though his jaw flexed like he'd rather be anywhere else. Nerissa curled her fingers slightly into his shirt again as if grounding him without thinking about it.

Roan's gaze flicked between them once but he said nothing, focusing on cleaning away the blood. "You're lucky this isn't deeper," he muttered.

He finished cleaning the cut and set the cloth aside. "Alright," he said, shifting his focus, "let's check the rest of you."

He took Zale's wrist, fingers pressing lightly against the vein. "Pulse is slightly elevated," he noted, then glanced up with a sly look. "Though I'll chalk that up to the present company."

Zale's ears went red immediately. "Yeah, alright, Doc, just write it down and move on."

Roan chuckled, a deep sound in his throat, then had Zale sit forward while he pressed an ear against his back. He listened to Zale's breathing, counting the beats under his breath before leaning back. "Any pain anywhere?"

"Not unless you count my pride," Zale said.

"Cleared," Roan declared, closing his satchel with a snap. He turned his attention to Nerissa. "Your turn."

She offered a hand reluctantly. Roan's fingers settled over her pulse, his brows ticking up almost instantly. "Also slightly elevated," he said. His tone turned pointed. "Am I gonna need to separate you two?"

Heat rushed to her cheeks, and she looked away from both of them—straight into Eon's waiting gaze. He waggled his eyebrows in the most exaggerated, conspiratorial way possible.

She rolled her eyes, muttering something under her breath before glancing back at Roan.

"Any pain?" he asked.

She hesitated.

"Nerissa," Roan said, his voice edging into that steady, no-nonsense tone, "you know better than to pretend you're fine. Honesty keeps people alive."

With a sigh, she relented. "All my muscles ache. But that's pretty much it."

Roan nodded, satisfied. "Soreness is to be expected. Rest and fluids—you push yourself again before you're ready, you'll regret it."

"Already there, trust me," she didn't even try to hide the sarcasm in her voice.

"That means no shifting for a while," he said, his tone making it sound less like advice and more like an order, which it absolutely was. At least she wasn't stuck in the basin again; Zale was much more comfortable.

Roan straightened, tucking his satchel under one arm. "Rest. All of you. I'll be back to check in later." Without waiting for a reply, he strode to the door and disappeared up the companionway, the thud of his boots fading into the storm above.

Nerissa and Zale watched the door swing shut, the lantern swaying in the sudden quiet.

Before the silence could stretch for any length of time, Eon's voice piped up from his blanket cocoon. "So...were you cursed by a sea witch or something?"

Nerissa blinked at him. "What?"

"You know—transformed into a mermaid after crossing some spooky undersea enchantress?"

Her lips parted in disbelief, then pressed into a flat line. "I was born like this, Eon."

"Oh." He nodded slowly, looking genuinely thoughtful—as if this answer required deep consideration.

Eon tilted his head. "So...can you talk to fish?"

"No."

"What about whales?"

"No."

"Dolphins?"

Zale's mouth twitched like he was holding back a laugh. "You gonna go through the whole ocean one species at a time?"

Nerissa stared at him. "Eon. Can you talk to rats or seagulls?"

"Point taken. Can you, like, control the tide? Or just water in general?"

Nerissa gave him a long, unblinking look. "Why would I be able to do that?"

"Because you're a magical ocean creature!" Eon said it like she'd just asked him if water was wet.

"First of all, not magical. Second of all—*creature*?" Nerissa's eyes narrowed.

"Okay, okay—water *person*. Happy?"

She grumbled. "Can *you* control the *wind*, Eon?"

"Of course not."

"Are you not a magical land creature?"

Eon opened his mouth, paused...then pulled the blanket higher around his shoulders. "Alright, fine, point to the mermaid."

Zale choked out a laugh, chest shaking as he turned his head away to cough for several moments.

"Eon! You're going to give Zale permanent lung damage," Nerissa scolded.

Eon grinned, undeterred. "Can you lure sailors to their untimely death using your hypnotizing voice?"

"Trust me, you don't want to hear me sing," she deadpanned.

He leaned back, smug. "That wasn't a no."

Another roll of thunder rumbled overhead, the timbers creaking with the strain, but Eon didn't seem to notice—or care.

"Do you sleep on a bed, or like...in a giant clam shell?" Eon went on.

"Bed."

"But in the ocean, wouldn't it just float away?"

She pinched the bridge of her nose. "Weighted frame."

Eon nodded seriously, as if this was vital intelligence. "Can you eat human food? Or is it all kelp and sushi down there?"

Nerissa blinked slowly. "What do you think I've been eating for the past three weeks?"

Eon tapped his chin, clearly searching for his next target. "Alright, fair, so one more question—how do merfolk—" he paused for effect, eyebrows waggling, "—mate?"

Zale immediately choked on nothing but air, coughing hard enough to bend forward and almost drop Nerissa.

"Eon!" Nerissa snapped, her face going hot.

Eon blinked at her, all feigned innocence. "What? It's a fair question!"

Zale held up a hand, still catching his breath. "Nope. Absolutely not. Ye're far too young for that conversation, and we are done here."

Nerissa smiled inwardly at the brogue he let slip when he was flustered.

Eon leaned back in his blanket, grinning like the cat that ate the canary. "Guess that's a 'classified' answer."

"Guess ye'll never find out," Zale shot back, his voice still rough from coughing.

Nerissa exhaled slowly, leaning just enough toward Zale to mutter, "Who *raised* this kid?"

"Not pirates," Zale said without missing a beat. "I turned out with better manners than him."

"Debatable."

He only smirked to himself, eyes drifting toward the swaying lantern above them.

Above them, the thunder began to fade, rolling farther away with each passing minute. The sharp pitch and sway of the *Black Serpent* gradually evened into the gentler rise and fall of calmer seas. The lantern's swinging slowed, shadows settling across the infirmary walls.

They sat in that relative quiet for a few minutes, the only sounds the muted creak of the timbers and the occasional drip from the ceiling.

A particularly loud crack of thunder split the air, making the entire ship shudder. The lanterns above them rattled on their hooks, casting wild arcs of light across the infirmary walls.

Nerissa flinched at the sound, instinctively tucking closer into Zale's lap. His arms, already loose around her, tightened without thought, drawing her more securely against his chest. Her cheeks warmed, but neither of them said a word. Yes, this was definitely better than the basin.

Then the door banged open.

Bran stepped inside, shaking rain from his hair as if he'd just strolled in from a light drizzle instead of a storm. "Just checking in," he said easily—then his gaze landed on Zale and Nerissa. One eyebrow arched high. "Well, well. Aren't we comfy?"

Zale didn't even blink. "Don't start."

Bran lingered just inside the doorway, arms folded, eyes glinting with mischief. "So...how long has *this* been a thing?"

Nerissa froze, heat rushing to her face. "We're not a thing," she said quickly.

Both of Bran's eyebrows shot up, his grin deepening. "Wasn't talkin' bout you and lover boy, darlin'." He tipped his chin toward her tail. "Meant *that*."

Her blush somehow darkened another shade.

Eon, still bundled in his blanket, piped up helpfully, "She was born that way."

Bran chuckled low. "Good to know."

Zale muttered something under his breath that Nerissa didn't quite catch, but the glare he shot Bran was clear enough.

Nerissa let out an exasperated breath, flicking her gaze between Bran's smug grin and Eon's too-innocent expression. "You know what? I don't care what Roan says—I'm shifting so I can retreat to Brigid's cabin and avoid more questions."

Zale's head turned toward her sharply. "No, you are not."

"You gonna stop me?"

"Aye," he said flatly. "You've already pushed yourself too far today. Strain yourself again and you won't make it to Brigid's cabin—you'll end up right back in the infirmary."

Her lips pressed into a thin line, but she didn't fire back right away.

Finally, she huffed out a breath and muttered, "Fine. But if Eon asks me one more thing about mermaids, I'm biting him."

"Noted," Zale said, smirking faintly as Eon's eyes went wide.

Bran straightened from his lean against the doorframe, clearly fighting a grin. "On that note, I'm leaving—before I see something I can't unsee."

He tipped an imaginary hat at them and strolled out, the door swinging shut behind him, leaving the three of them in the steady creak and sway of the post-storm calm.

Bran's boots had barely faded up the passageway before Eon gave a jaw-cracking yawn. Without a word, he shuffled over to the nearest empty cot, dropped onto it face-first, and was snoring within seconds.

Zale huffed a quiet laugh, shaking his head, but didn't disturb him.

"Thank the tides," Nerissa let out a breath, grateful for the reprieve.

"All heart, no brain—that one," Zale chuckled as he leaned back against the wall, eyes closing.

Nerissa shifted slightly against him, then murmured, "I'm sorry. You've been carrying me around like deadweight since we came aboard." Her gaze flicked to the dark dampness soaking his shirt. "Are you sure you don't want to change into something dry before you catch a chill?"

He glanced down at her, the faintest smile tugging at his lips. "You're not deadweight. Stop worrying and just rest," he said, his tone firm but gentle. "I've got you."

Her cheeks warmed once again—or maybe they were just perpetually flushed at this point. The tension she'd been holding in her shoulders at last uncoiled as she let herself lean fully into his warmth—and rest.

Bran

Bran sauntered across the deck, freshly changed into a dry shirt and looking far too relaxed for someone who'd just weathered a squall. The storm had begun to break, gray clouds thinning to let pale light spill across the battered planks. Around him, the crew clustered in groups, their voices a low thrum of disbelief.

Cormac leaned against the rail, fingers working restlessly at the beads in his beard. "Mark me words," he muttered, voice carrying just enough to draw a few uneasy glances. "Siren aboard means ill luck. Always has, always will."

Brigid shot him a sharp glare. "She's still Nerissa. Same lass who fought beside us, bled beside us, near exhausted herself pullin' Zale out o' the sea."

Roan crossed his arms, his deep voice steady and sure. "She's earned her place. You know it as well as I do."

Cormac shifted, muttering under his breath, but didn't argue further.

Then Nestor stepped forward, his shadow long across the deck as the last of the stormlight broke free. "A tail don't matter one whit," he said, his tone flat as hammered iron. "She pulls her weight, same as the rest of you. More, today. So long as she's on my ship, she's one of ours."

A hush followed, the words settling heavy into the post-storm air.

Bran let out a low whistle, breaking the silence with a lopsided grin. "Well, you heard the captain. Guess that settles it."

"Aye," Cormac grumbled, though it sounded begrudging. "Saved our lad Eon, I'll give her that. Still doesn't mean the sea won't call her home someday."

"That's true for all of us," Ma Wen said, returning to his work.

The crew shifted at that—some nodding, some frowning, none willing to push further against the calm finality in Wen's tone. Above them, the last tatters of stormcloud peeled back to reveal a sliver of pale sky, the ship groaning as it steadied on the calmer swell.

Bran propped his elbows on the rail, smirk tugging at his mouth. "Well, if the sea does come callin', I'd rather have her on our side than against us. Siren or no, I like our odds better that way."

His tone was light, but the glint in his eyes left no doubt he meant every word.

A few reluctant chuckles stirred the air, cutting through the heaviness, and the tension bled off the deck like rainwater through the scuppers.

Bran pushed off the rail and sauntered toward the rigging, flashing Cormac a grin that was half challenge, half camaraderie. "Come on, old man, let's see if your knotted mess of a sail can survive my delicate touch."

Cormac snorted, muttering something about "clumsy hands" as he shoved a line at him, but Bran just laughed and set to work. His fingers moved quickly, the banter easy as breathing. Out here, he could be all jokes, all swagger—the version of himself the crew expected.

But underneath, his chest still felt hollow.

The image wouldn't leave him: Zale limp under Roan's hands, skin gone blue, his chest refusing to rise. For a heartbeat—longer, if he was honest—Bran had thought he'd lost him. His brother in all but blood, gone to the deep like so many nameless men before.

He swallowed hard, yanking the line tighter than it needed to be.

And Nerissa—gods above and below, the stubborn slip of a girl had gone back into the storm for him. Dragged Zale out where the sea might've swallowed him whole.

Bran worked faster, jaw set, laughter still on his lips but ringing hollow in his ears. He'd never forget what she'd done, whatever came of the truth she'd been forced to reveal tonight.

He tugged another knot loose, the rope rough against his palms. But even as his hands worked, his mind kept circling back to the infirmary.

Zale, half-asleep, with Nerissa tucked protectively against his chest. Her tail stretched across his lap, her strength spent, and yet his arms never wavered from holding her close.

Bran huffed a laugh under his breath as he recalled her quick, flustered denial that they were a thing. Gods, the way her cheeks had colored—he'd almost felt bad for teasing. Almost.

He gave the rope a sharp pull, shaking his head. "You're not foolin' anyone, lass," he muttered under his breath.

Because he'd seen it—plain as daylight over the past few weeks. The way Zale looked at her when he thought nobody else was watching, his fierce protectiveness of her when the Dravari attacked, their early morning sword lessons. No, he was not half as subtle as he fancied himself to be. Nerissa either, for that matter. He'd seen the panic in her eyes when Zale collapsed from the heat, the unresolved tension while they sparred a few nights ago, the way she flung herself into the raging sea when Zale didn't resurface.

Bran snorted softly, shaking his head. He *had* tried to help. Thought that kiss bet was a surefire way to shove them into admitting it. Instead, the pair of them had only dug their heels in deeper, as stubborn as barnacles on a keel.

He smirked faintly, tying the line off with a practiced snap. "Wonder which of you two thick-heads is gonna figure it out first."

CHAPTER 36

SLEEP-DEPRIVATION-INDUCED DELIRIUM

Zale

Somewhere between the fading thunder and the steady hum of the ship's timbers, sleep had claimed him.

When Zale blinked awake hours later, the infirmary was dark, lit only by the low amber glow of the lanterns. He became aware first of the weight against him—the slow, even rise and fall of Nerissa's breathing. She was curled into his chest, coat drawn over her like a blanket, hair loose and damp where it brushed his shoulder.

He should've been chilled to the bone; he'd refused to put Nerissa down for even a moment to change out of his sea-drenched clothes. But there was no bite of cold in his bones, only a steady, blissful warmth radiating from where she rested.

He'd told himself a dozen times over that she was just another crewmate, that he'd treat her no differently than Bran or Brigid or any of the others. No reckless flirting, no foolish hope that she might ever see him as more than a passing ally. And yet the past few days had unraveled his resolve thread by thread.

The heat sparking between them as he taught her to dance, and again during sword drills, the early morning hours in the crow's nest trading secrets about nightmares—each moment had carved a place for her that friendship alone couldn't contain. And when she'd finally told him the truth of Astyra, of what had been done to her, he'd felt something settle deep in his chest: not pity, not obligation, but the dangerous beginning of—something he couldn't quite name yet.

And now here she was, asleep in his arms like she trusted him to hold the weight of the world for her.

His gaze drifted down, catching on the strands of dark hair that clung damply to her cheek. Without thinking, his hand started to rise, the way it always had when a crewmate's gear needed straightening or a rope needed coiling—just a simple, practical gesture. But this wasn't a loose knot or a frayed line. This was Nerissa, breathing easy for once, her face softened in sleep, expression unguarded. Her nose was still mottled purple from bruising, he noticed with a pang of guilt. His fingers hovered inches from her skin before he curled them into a fist and lowered his hand back to his side. He couldn't cross that line. Not now. Maybe not ever.

Roan's words had stuck with him—*she cares for you*—but Zale couldn't let himself believe it. Not really. That look in her eyes when she thought he'd drowned, the way her voice had broken when she confessed her fear—he'd replayed it a hundred times already, trying to convince himself it meant more than loyalty, more than duty. But Nerissa was bound by loyalty to everyone she trusted, and he'd be a fool to mistake her devotion for desire. Better to guard his heart now than to let it drift toward a hope that would only wreck him in the end.

You can't lose what you never had, he repeated the mantra to himself.

He didn't dare move for fear of waking her though. She had pushed her body to the limit to save him and Eon, and she deserved uninterrupted sleep. So he stayed where he was, eyelids drifting shut as he dozed off again.

Nerissa

Nerissa stirred, her cheek brushing against the coarse fabric of Zale's shirt. The steady thrum of his heartbeat reached her ears before her thoughts caught up, pulling her half-awake. She blinked groggily, memory tugging her back to the crow's nest only nights ago—waking mortified to find she'd slumped against him, the flush in her face lasting long after she'd scrambled away. But this...this felt different. There was no jolt of panic, no urge to flee. Only warmth seeping into her bones, safety wrapping around her like a tide she didn't want to break. She frowned faintly, wondering when that had changed, when his presence had shifted from disconcerting to steadying.

Maybe she was just exhausted.

Or maybe it was because she'd trusted him with all her secrets, and he hadn't judged her, hadn't looked at her like she was a monster when her body had forced itself back into her true form. All he'd cared about was whether she was breathing, whether she was in pain. And even now, when he deserved nothing more than rest after diving headlong into a storm to save Eon and nearly drowning himself, he hadn't changed into dry clothes—just sat here, holding her, because she was stuck this way.

Warm and dangerous thoughts flickered in her mind, and she shut them down at once. There had to be a logical reason for this, and exhaustion was the simplest one. Anything else was a complication she couldn't afford—especially not with him, not when she had only just begun to carve out a place among this crew.

The infirmary door creaked open, lanternlight from the passage spilling briefly across the floor. The sound roused Nerissa fully, and Zale shifted beneath her with a low start, blinking awake. She realized then that Eon's cot stood empty—he must have woken earlier and slipped out while they'd been curled up here like fools.

Roan stepped inside, with his usual heavy tread, the wooden door shutting behind him. He crossed the room and knelt beside their cot, his expression calm as his sharp gaze swept over her.

"It's evening," he said matter-of-factly. "Before I discharge you, I need to do a thorough check of your muscles."

Nerissa did as instructed, holding herself still while Roan's hands pressed along the length of her tail, his touch firm but careful, cool against her scales. "Flex," he said, tone calm as ever. She obeyed, perhaps a little too sharply, because her caudal fin lashed upward and came within an inch of smacking Roan in the face.

Her eyes went wide. "I'm sorry!" she blurted, heat rushing to her cheeks.

Roan didn't so much as flinch, only eased her fin back down with a steady hand. "Reflexes are intact," he remarked, dry as driftwood.

"At least you didn't sucker punch him this time," Zale choked out a laugh.

The sound broke loose into full-bodied amusement, his shoulders shaking as he tried—and failed—to stifle it. Nerissa shot him a glare, which only seemed to make him laugh harder, which led to a violent coughing fit.

Finally, Zale managed to drag in a breath, rubbing at his eyes as the coughing ebbed. "Sorry," he said, grinning helplessly. "Blame it on sleep-deprivation-induced delirium."

Nerissa folded her arms, trying for stern but unable to keep the corners of her mouth from twitching. Roan, unfazed, simply moved on to the next muscle group as though nothing had happened. At last, he leaned back on his heels, wiping his palms against his trousers.

"No strain. No tearing. Reflexes and strength are holding," he said. "Safe for you to try shifting again."

Nerissa exhaled slowly, tension loosening from her shoulders. Relief mingled with disappointment, because if she shifted back, she'd be standing, and standing meant no excuse for staying in the circle of Zale's arms.

Wait—what?

She crushed the thought at once, shoving it into the same locked box where she kept every other reckless impulse that threatened to derail her focus lately.

She drew in a steadying breath and fixed her focus on the length of her tail. Better to start there; if her strength failed her, at least she would be able to walk. The ache began low, a dull pull deep in the muscles as her fins twitched, flexed, and then shuddered. Slowly, the powerful sweep of her tail thinned and split, scales retracting as muscle and bone reformed into two separate limbs. Her forearm fins tightened, melting back into the lines of her arms with a prickling sensation, followed by the dorsal ridge at her back drawing in on itself, sliding away until all that remained was a faint stiffness along her spine.

Cool air brushed against her bare calves, and she was suddenly grateful for the cling of her damp nightshirt and the weight of her coat over her lap. The realization that she still had nothing covering her legs from mid-thigh down made her cheeks warm—though whether from modesty or from the fact that Zale was still holding her close, she wasn't sure.

Zale shifted slightly, his gaze lingering on her face. "Your scales," he said quietly, lifting a hand but stopping short of touching. "They're still there—just at your temples."

Nerissa let out a low groan, dragging a hand over her eyes. "*Morai.* Still exhausted, I guess."

Roan rose to his feet, brushing off his knees. "That would be my assessment as well," he said matter-of-factly. "Your body's spent. Best remedy is a good night's sleep."

Roan's gaze settled back on her. "Can you walk?"

Nerissa hesitated, then nodded. "I think so."

Zale shifted at once, loosening his hold just enough to help her rise. His hands steadied her as her bare feet touched the floor, legs trembling as she tested her weight. For a heartbeat she thought she had it—then her knees buckled.

Rising from the cot in one smooth motion, Zale caught her before she could topple over. His arm slipped firmly around her waist, the other steadying her shoulder, holding her close to him. Nerissa leaned into him without protest, grateful for his assistance.

Roan, watching closely, gave a short nod. "Good enough. Head up to your cabin, get some rest. Don't overdo it. Zale, make sure she gets there in one piece."

"Aye aye." Zale gave Roan a two-fingered salute, as he reached for Nerissa's coat, holding it open in silent offer. She slipped her arms through the sleeves, pulling it close around her as a shiver ran through her body beneath the damp shirt. "Thank you," she murmured.

He didn't answer aloud, only met her eyes with a look that carried more warmth than words could hold. She really wished he would stop looking at her that way.

Zale stayed close at her side as they made their way up the narrow companionway, his hand steady at her back each time she faltered. She leaned more heavily on him than she cared to admit, the climb leaving her breath uneven, though he never once let her slip.

When they finally reached Brigid's cabin, she lifted her hand to the latch—then paused, her pulse skittering. Should she tell him what she saw? About the gills? How would she even start? *Hey, you know how you just found out yesterday that merfolk still exist? Well guess what? You're one of us! Congratulations!*

She turned to say something—anything— only to find Zale watching her intensely. Their eyes locked, the charged silence between them snapping taut. His hand drifted upward, almost unbidden, and his knuckles brushed against the faint shimmer of scales at her temple, tracing the iridescent curve as though he could no longer help himself. The touch was feather light, but it sent a pleasant shiver down her spine as her eyelids lowered.

Before she could say a word, before she even understood what was happening, Zale leaned down and kissed her.

It was short, startling, his mouth firm against hers for only a heartbeat. Nerissa froze, stunned, her thoughts scattering too wildly to respond before he broke away as suddenly as he'd closed the distance.

"I—I'm sorry," he rasped, his voice rough. Then he stepped back, hands held up as if he expected her to hit him, before retreating down the passage, leaving her at the threshold with her lips tingling, her heart thundering, and the door still closed at her back.

What just happened...and why didn't I stop him?

Her thoughts spun like a whirlpool as she slipped into the quartermaster's cabin, only to nearly leap out of her skin at the sight of Brigid sitting on the edge of her bunk, lantern still burning low.

"You didn't have to wait up for me," Nerissa managed, her voice thinner than she'd intended.

Brigid arched a brow, arms folded. "'Course I did. It's my responsibility to keep watch over the whole crew. That includes ye."

Nerissa hesitated in the doorway, the warmth of Zale's kiss still buzzing under her skin. At last, she drew a slow breath. "Then...if you'll have me, I'd be honored to stay on with the crew."

For a moment Brigid only blinked, then let out a short laugh. "Didn't know that was up for debate. Ye already proved yerself with the initiation. Ye're stuck with us for life."

"Even though...I'm not human?" Nerissa pressed.

Brigid snorted. "So long as ye carry yer own weight, ye could be a banshee or a harpy for all I care."

Nerissa dipped her head in a small nod of appreciation. It was enough. Neither of them were much for spilling emotions, but the understanding passed clean between them all the same.

"Just promise me, lass," Brigid said then, her voice carrying that familiar clipped burr. "Next time somethin's wrong, ye tell me. No more tryin' tae drag yerself tae the infirmary in the dead o' night."

Nerissa managed a faint smile. "I promise."

Brigid gave a small nod of approval, though she didn't move right away. Her sharp eyes lingered on Nerissa's face, studying her a beat too long. "Ye alright? Ye're redder than a sunburnt crab. Roan clear ye of fever?"

Heat rushed straight to Nerissa's cheeks, the memory of what had just happened at the door flaring like kindling. She pressed her palms to her face, wishing the sea would swallow her whole.

Don't lie next time. You're a terrible liar. Ma Wen's voice floated through her mind, and she cursed him silently for being right.

Nerissa groaned into her hands before finally lowering them, cheeks still burning. "I—It's...Zale," she stammered out.

Brigid's brows shot up, her arms crossing in an instant. "Ah. That one." Her tone sharpened, protective as a drawn cutlass. "Ye need me tae give him the boot?"

Nerissa's eyes widened. "What? No!" She shook her head quickly, as if she could rattle the heat right out of it. "It's just—I guess—more accurately…" She faltered, her voice barely above a whisper. "…it's me."

Brigid's expression softened, just slightly, a knowing look flickering across her face before she let out a low hum. "Aye," she said, blunt but not unkind. "That's the harder side of it."

Nerissa sank onto the edge of her bunk, twisting her hands together in her lap. "I don't even know when things changed," she admitted, words spilling before she could swallow them back. "Only that they have."

Brigid tilted her head, watching her with the steady patience of someone who had raised more than her fair share of wayward sailors. "Then best ye figure out what ye mean tae do about it," she said at last.

"There's nothing *to* do," Nerissa said sharply. She fixed her gaze on the floorboards, jaw tight. If she allowed herself to be vulnerable in that way—if she let this become anything more—then she'd only be opening herself up to heartbreak. "I can't—what if…?" She trailed off, not even knowing what the question was.

Brigid didn't answer right away. The silence stretched, filled only by the faint creak of the ship's timbers. At last, she spoke, her voice quieter than usual, almost motherly. "Nestor and I—we're by no means yer typical parents. But we tried our best tae raise the lad with...let's call it morally gray pirate standards." A faint, wry smile tugged at her mouth. "I know it's not near a replacement for his real parents. Still, he's family tae us."

Her gaze sharpened, pinning Nerissa where she sat. "Mark me words, once someone's earned Zale's loyalty and respect, it doesn't go anywhere. And he doesn't grant it lightly. Whatever ye tell yerself, I can see plain enough he's already found somethin' in ye worth takin' the risk."

Nerissa didn't argue this time. Brigid's words settled over her like the weight of an anchor, heavy and undeniable, and she could already feel them tugging at the edges of her thoughts.

Brigid gave a sharp nod, satisfied enough, and stood. "Now, get out of that damp shirt before ye catch yer death," she ordered, slipping back into her usual brusque tone. "Then get some sleep. Tomorrow'll come quick enough."

Nerissa managed the barest hint of a smile, though her chest still ached with too many thoughts. She murmured her thanks as Brigid turned down the lantern, leaving her to the darkness and to the restless tide of her own heart.

But sleep refused to come. Nerissa lay curled beneath her blanket, Brigid's breathing already gone soft with slumber across the room, while her own thoughts twisted like tangled rigging in a gale.

Every time she shut her eyes, she felt it again—the feather-light brush of Zale's knuckles against her temple, the shock of his mouth on hers. Her lips still tingled with the memory, her chest still tight with emotions she couldn't silence. It was...unsettling, but in a way that warmed something deep within her chest.

Her mind warred with itself, logic clashing against the unsteady swell of feeling. The pragmatic voice she had relied on her entire life insisted she tamp it down, that there was no place for such distractions. And yet her heart—alarmingly loud and insistent—kept circling back to him, to the way she hadn't wanted to pull away, to the way she felt *safe* around him.

She had never been romantically interested in *anyone* before. For the last decade, her life had been one of discipline and duty, every spare breath devoted to sharpening her blades, honing her instincts, ensuring that neither she nor those she served would ever again be vulnerable to the whims of fate. She had never allowed herself the luxury of considering her own feelings—what she wanted, *who* she might want, or what her life might hold beyond service to the crown.

And now, when she tried to picture a future, she realized with a pang of disorientation that she didn't know who she *was* without that servitude.

However, with Brigid's reassurance that she wasn't going anywhere, maybe she could start carving out a new purpose, a new future. Maybe she could finally allow herself to admit that she had feelings for Zale, that at some point, she had stopped thinking of him as a *shameless pirate* and now considered him a close friend. She had never felt more comfortable discussing her insecurities and fears than when she was with him. Not even with Calliope or Lir had she had the same level of communication.

Nerissa rolled to her back and stared at the beams overhead. The image of Zale drifting limp in the deep haunted her. She almost lost him today, and probably would have had it not been for his gills.

The memory sent a cold thread through the warmth his kiss had left behind.

She pressed her palms to her eyes until stars burst against the dark. Whatever that meant for Zale, he deserved to know it—from her. Not as a rumor, not as an accusation, not tangled up with the way her pulse tripped when he stood too close. Facts first. Truth first. Then...maybe...the rest.

Nerissa let her hands fall and drew a steady, quiet breath.

At first light, she decided, *I'll tell him what I saw.* Before the day crowded in, before she lost her nerve, before any talk of kisses or feelings could muddy the water. She would give him the truth, clean and plain, and let him choose what to do with it.

Only then—if he wanted to hear it—would she risk the other thing that had been tugging at her heart lately.

CHAPTER 37

RHEOS APATOS

Zale

Zale rose before the rest of the crew, the hammocks around him swaying slightly with the rock of the ship. He slipped on his boots and ventured up the companionway, until the briny air hit his lungs and the pale glow of predawn wrapped the deck.

He made for the stern, bracing both hands on the railing as the *Black Serpent* rode the swell. The salt air scraped his throat raw, each breath dragging against lungs that still ached from the sea's attempt to claim them yesterday. A cough rattled up before he could stop it, leaving his chest tight, his ribs sore.

Not that the sting of it mattered. Not compared to the thought that had gnawed at him since last night.

Stars above, what had he done? He'd promised himself—sworn to himself—that he'd treat her like any other crewmate. No flirting, no lines blurred, no crossing into waters that could wreck them both. And yet the moment her eyes lifted to his in that narrow passage, he'd unraveled. The unguarded weariness softening her features, the way those stray scales had caught the lantern light like shards of gemstone, the barest hesitation at her cabin door—it had been a deadly combination. By the time he realized what he was doing, he'd already kissed her.

Now the memory burned like salt in an open wound. He scrubbed a hand down his face, muttering a curse under his breath. She'd trusted him, and he'd gone and shattered that with one reckless lapse of control. If she never looked at him the same way again, it would be no less than he deserved. Maybe he *was* a shameless pirate after all.

The horizon bled from black to slate gray, the first smear of light catching on the waves, but Zale barely saw it. His thoughts ran in circles, looping back again and again to that moment in the passageway. He could still feel the way she'd gone still beneath his mouth, the sharp intake of her breath, the shock in her eyes when he'd pulled back.

What if she thought he'd taken advantage? That he'd mistaken her trust for something else entirely? He ground his teeth, shame rising hot in his chest. Nerissa had endured more than any soul should, and the last thing she needed was him blurring the line between comrade and—

He cut the thought short with a harsh shake of his head. The very word felt dangerous, like a fire he had no right to strike.

His grip tightened on the railing until his knuckles whitened. The sea rolled dark and endless before him, the swell matching the churn in his gut. He'd spent years building a wall between himself and the ache of wanting more than loyalty from anyone. One kiss, and he'd nearly torn it down without thinking.

Nerissa

Nerissa tugged the hem of her lavender blouse into place, the fabric soft against her skin. She'd left the corset folded neatly on her cot; today, she didn't have the patience for laces or tightness pressing against her ribs. Black breeches clung comfortably at her hips, and she hadn't bothered with her hair. It spilled loose down her back, a wild tangle of waves still damp at the ends.

The cabin felt too small, too thick with feelings she hadn't managed to silence through the night. So she slipped out into the morning light, intending to get some fresh air, but secretly wondering if a certain pirate would also be up. If she had a hard time sleeping, she doubted that Zale had fared any better.

Sure enough, Zale stood at the stern, braced against the railing, the pale light painting his profile in hard lines. His gaze was fixed on the churning wake, shoulders tense, the kind of posture that spoke of a man wrestling with something heavier than the sea.

Her steps slowed. The memory of his mouth on hers flared hot and vivid, tangling her resolve as she lingered a few paces back, watching him in silence. She told herself it was only caution, only the need to measure his mood before she approached. But her gaze betrayed her.

His black shirt clung to him in the morning breeze, the sleeves shoved carelessly to his elbows. Muscles pulled taut beneath the fabric with every shift of his shoulders, a reminder of the strength that had carried her yesterday. The wind caught in his hair, tangling it into wilder waves than usual, and she found herself staring longer than she should have, heat rising unbidden in her chest.

She drew in a bracing breath and closed the distance, boots steady against the planks despite the uneven beat of her heart.

"Hey," she said softly as she came to stand at the railing beside him.

His gaze didn't part from the sea, but the muscle ticking in his jaw was enough indication that he had heard her.

"We need to talk about yesterday," they said at the same time.

The corner of Zale's mouth twitched, humorless. "Right. I—let me go first." He raked a hand through his hair, then finally faced her.

"I'm so damn sorry, Nerissa. It was—stars, it was unprofessional. Reckless. I didn't mean to break your trust like that." His voice was rough, threaded with a guilt that made her chest tighten. He looked away, focusing back on the sea.

He was sorry for kissing her. Was that simply because he didn't know how she truly felt? Or did he regret it altogether?

Nerissa took a deep breath, fully aware that she was about to change things between them, for better or for worse. Somehow, this was more terrifying than sea withdrawal. More vulnerable than sprouting scales and fins in front of him the other night.

"I'm not sorry," she said slowly, forcing herself not to look away. This was so awkward. She hated this. Hated feelings. But they both deserved to know where each of them stood.

Zale froze, the tension in his shoulders clearly visible as he slowly turned back to her.

"...what?"

In that moment he no longer looked like a seasoned, battle-hardened pirate. He looked scared and vulnerable, something she was not accustomed to seeing in him. The silence stretched, her own heartbeat hammering in her ears.

It's now or never.

"Yesterday," she began quietly, "when Bran teased me, I was so quick to tell him we weren't a 'thing.' But that was only because he caught me off guard. I was embarrassed."

Zale's brow furrowed, but he didn't speak.

"The truth is," Nerissa pressed on, "I've been trying to keep you at arm's length this whole time. Because I didn't know how long I'd be able to stay. And it didn't feel right—letting you get close—without knowing the truth about what I am."

Her throat closed, the words tangling. She looked down at the deck, unable to hold his gaze any longer. "But now you know all of it. Every secret. And I'm not sure I deserve…" Her voice caught, but she forced herself to go on. "I kept trying to deny my feelings, but when I thought I had lost you, and then after last night...I don't even know how to tell you that I—*ugh*, you must think me a fool."

Nerissa continued to stare hard down at her feet, shame and embarrassment curling tightly in her chest, suffocating her. He still hadn't spoken, and she was too afraid to look back up after her admission.

This was a huge mistake. What if she had completely misread him? It wouldn't be the first time. The voice in her head was already trying to downplay his kiss.

Just because he kissed you doesn't mean he has serious feelings for you. You were both exhausted, it had been a traumatic day—it was heat of the moment, nothing more.

"If...If I've misread the situation, please tell me now. I'd rather throw myself overboard or walk the plank than stand here in silence," she choked out a bitter laugh, trying to hold back the tears that threatened to spill over.

Then she felt it—his fingers, warm and trembling, brushing against her chin. Slowly, deliberately, he coaxed her face upward until her eyes met his.

"Nerissa…You are the strongest, most terrifying woman I've ever met," he said, his voice low and intense. A faint, wry smile tugged at his mouth. "And I was raised by Brigid."

That startled a small huff of laughter from her. But when she tried to glance aside, blinking rapidly, his touch kept her steady, refusing to let her pull away.

"I've seen you at your most vulnerable," he continued, his tone softening but never losing its weight. "And even then, I could still see your strength. Your resolve. That's...beautiful to me. More than anything else could be."

"You shouldn't say things like that," Nerissa murmured, but the words lacked her usual edge.

"Why not?" Zale asked, his thumb brushing the faintest arc beneath her jaw, his gaze steady on hers. Her pulse was racing.

She drew in a shaky breath. "Because...I've spent so long thinking strength only meant something if it was in service to someone else. To the crown. To duty. I've never dared to believe that someone would value me for who I am, not just for what I can do."

"I do." The words left him instantly, without pause or doubt. His voice was firm, certain, like a vow. "I value *you*, Nerissa. Not your blades. Not your duty. Just you."

Her eyes shimmered, the disbelief breaking through in a rush. "You can't mean that," she whispered, shaking her head. "You don't know—"

"I *do*," Zale cut in gently, unyielding. His hand lingered at her jaw, thumb tracing small circles on her skin. "I know enough. I've seen ye—fierce, unshakable, terrified, stubborn as hell—and I still mean it. Every word."

Her throat tightened, and despite her best efforts, a single tear broke free, trailing hot down her cheek. Zale caught it with his thumb before it could fall, brushing it away.

A shaky, rueful smile tugged at her lips. "I was so awful to you when we first met."

His grin curved knowingly, though his eyes never wavered from hers. "Aye, and I deserved it. I knew I was rubbin' ye the wrong way."

She didn't answer, only shook her head faintly, lips quivering. Did he have any idea what he was doing to her?

Zale's gaze softened, his thumb lingering for just a moment longer against her cheek. "It was worth it," he said quietly.

Her breath hitched at his words, and before she could think better of it, she threw herself against him, burying her face in his chest. His shirt was rough, but the solid warmth of him was enough to undo the last of her restraint.

He went still, then his arms came around her, firm and sure, pulling her in as if he'd been waiting for this as long as she had. She felt the tension drain from his muscles, the rigid set of his body loosening until he simply held her.

They lingered in that embrace, the steady beat of his heart beneath her cheek grounding her in a way she hadn't thought possible. Being this close to him, not out of necessity, but by choice, lit a spark inside her chest, traveling down her spine and warming her all at once. She breathed in the spicy sweet scent of rum that lingered on his clothes, a comforting, familiar aroma—even if she hated drinking it herself.

"Hey," Zale whispered, causing the hairs on the back of her neck to prickle pleasantly.

She tilted her head up as his fingers ghosted once more across the scales at her temple, sending her pulse racing all over again. She closed her eyes, leaning into his touch.

He let his hand fall from her temple, drifting instead to trace the line of her jaw again, while his other arm remained tightly around her waist, holding her as though he'd never let go. *Nerae,* this was torture. She wished he'd just kiss her already, but maybe he was still afraid she'd push him away.

When she opened her eyes, she found that same intense green gaze from the infirmary last night, burning with restraint. He was waiting for her to move first.

Her own hands rose, hesitant at first, one sliding to the side of his face, the other coming to rest upon his shoulder. The rough stubble scraped lightly against her palm, tickling her skin and igniting heat.

With a trembling breath, she shifted onto the toes of her boots, closing the last sliver of distance. Their lips finally met, tentative at first, heat spiking and spreading throughout her body from the contact.

Finally.

Zale pulled her tighter against him, his arm a solid band around her waist as if he feared she might vanish with the sea breeze. His other hand slid up, cradling the back of her neck before tangling in her loose waves, the gentle tug sending a shiver all the way down her spine.

His lips were warm against hers, the steady pressure grounding her even as it left her dizzy, unmoored in a way she had never allowed herself to be. All the restraint he'd shown crumbled in the heat of her response. Nerissa's fingers tightened along his jaw, sliding upward into his wind-tossed hair, anchoring herself in the certainty of him.

Her pulse thundered as his mouth moved against hers, coaxing and claiming all at once, and for once she didn't think of crowns or duty or consequences. She thought only of this—of him—of the fire and salt and sheer want that had lain coiled between them for far too long.

At last, Zale tore his mouth from hers, dragging in a breath like a man who'd fought too long beneath the waves. His chest heaved against her, lungs still raw, no doubt, from the sea's cold grip the day before, but his hold on her didn't loosen.

He pressed his forehead to hers, their breaths mingling in the shared space between them. Nerissa closed her eyes, savoring the warmth of him, the steady beat of his heart against her own.

"I've wanted this longer than I care to admit," Zale whispered, voice rough in a way that made Nerissa want to kiss him all over again.

"I was afraid to want it," she whispered back, her own voice trembling. "I tried so hard not to...but, *Nerae,* this is really nice. I should have kissed you a lot sooner."

Zale's eyes creased as he looked at her with a hint of amusement and pride.

And before she could say another word, he closed the scant distance, catching her lips with his once more. The kiss began fierce, desperate, carrying the weight of every stolen glance, every unspoken word, every ache they had buried too long. Nerissa clutched at him, fingers curling in his shirt to hold herself steady.

But then, slowly, it softened. The urgency gave way to something quieter, gentler, as if both of them realized at the same moment they didn't need to rush. Zale's hand, tangled in her hair, eased into a caress, and Nerissa let her palms rest against his chest, melting into him.

"Ha!"

The triumphant exclamation shattered the quiet. Zale reacted on instinct, both arms wrapping firmly around Nerissa as if shielding her from an ambush. Her startled breath caught against his chest, until the voice rang out again, gleeful and unmistakable.

"Just like Chapter Twelve of *Stormbound Hearts!*"

They both turned, still tangled in each other's arms, to find Eon standing a few paces away, practically vibrating with delight. His grin was so wide it threatened to split his face. "The fierce warrior maiden and the rogue with a heart of gold, caught in the throes of a kiss they swore they'd never allow themselves! Stars above, I knew it!"

Zale groaned, dropping his forehead briefly against the top of Nerissa's head, muttering something unprintable under his breath. Nerissa pressed her hands over her flaming cheeks but made no move to pull away, mortification warring with the absurd urge to laugh.

"Chapter Twelve, my arse," Zale snarled, finally lifting his head to glare at Eon. "You're about to be written into Chapter Thirteen: *The Cabin Boy Who Went Missing at Sea.*"

Eon only beamed brighter, utterly unfazed, bouncing on his heels like he'd just won a bet. "Oh, that's *exactly* what the rogue would say!"

Nerissa pressed her burning face harder against Zale's chest, torn between wishing the deck would open up and laughing until she cried.

"I *knew* there was something going on," the younger man declared, crossing his arms. "You've been giving each other those looks. And the way you were holding her in the infirmary—"

"Alright, that's enough," Nerissa cut in, her attempt at sternness breaking under a ripple of laughter.

Eon only smirked. "Mmhm. Sure. Totally not a *thing.*"

Zale groaned, scrubbing a hand over his face while Nerissa muttered under her breath, " *Rheos apatos…*"

His head turned toward her, one brow raised. "Run that by me again?"

She sighed, realizing she'd spoken aloud. "It's a Nautalian curse. Means 'deceitful current,' but it's used for...well, anything from a mild inconvenience to a full-on betrayal."

His grin tugged back into place. "You're going to have to teach me a few more of those."

Eon gave them one last smug look before sauntering off toward the bow, no doubt eager to broadcast the news to anyone within earshot.

Nerissa exhaled through her nose. "He's going to tell everyone."

Zale looked in the direction Eon had run off to. "Yeah, most likely."

She narrowed her eyes at him, but there was no real heat in it. "You look absolutely devastated about it."

"Devastated," he agreed solemnly, though the corner of his mouth kept twitching upward.

Her glare softened as she studied him for a long moment. "Thank you," she said finally.

"For what?"

"For...making that as painless as possible. I'm not the best at talking about feelings, especially romantic ones."

"Guess I'll have to help you get better at it."

Before she could decide whether that was a threat or a promise, he pulled her in close and kissed her again—even slower this time, stealing the breath from her lungs in the best way possible.

When he pulled back, she was smiling, eyes half closed. "That's not exactly the kind of practice I meant."

"I know." His smirk tugged wider. "But I'm an overachiever."

He drew her in until there was barely a breath between them, and even then, it still wasn't close enough. Nerissa's arms slipped around his neck, holding him with a desperation that surprised even her. Zale lowered his head, his breath warm against her ear before his lips traced the line of her neck. A shiver rippled through her, her fingers tightening at his shoulders as one reckless thought flickered through her mind—what it might feel like if he kissed the place where her gills would be.

Wait. Her gills. *His* gills—

She stiffened slightly, the realization cutting through the haze. Tides below—she'd completely forgotten what she'd come here to tell him. Placing a hand against his chest, she reluctantly drew back, hoping the distance would allow her mind to clear. Zale stopped at the action, brow furrowing in confusion.

"Zale—wait. There's something I need to tell you before the day gets away from us."

His brows lifted as he searched her face. "What could it possibly be? I already know you're a mermaid, and we've both admitted we're hopelessly into each other. Hard to top that kind of confession."

Nerissa huffed a quiet laugh. "You'd be surprised."

The humor faded as quickly as it came. "Yesterday, during the storm," she began softly. "When I found you under the surface, unconscious. You were bleeding, but...you were still breathing."

Zale frowned. "What do you mean?"

Her fingers rose, hovering just under his jaw. "There were faint slits here—gills. When we broke the surface, they faded. And you stopped breathing."

The sea noise seemed to dull, the wind itself holding still. Zale went motionless, eyes flicking between hers like he was searching for any hint she might be teasing him.

"I know what I saw," she insisted. "You don't have to decide what it means right now. I just wanted you to have the truth."

He swallowed hard, the muscle in his jaw tightening before he nodded once. "Okay," he said finally, voice rough. "Okay."

Nerissa reached for his hand, giving it a brief, grounding squeeze. "You're still you."

He let out a breath that came out half a laugh, half disbelief. "You say that like it's supposed to make sense. Gills?" He touched the spot beneath his jaw, fingers brushing the smooth skin there. "Stars, I'd have noticed something like that."

"Not likely," she said gently. "If you've always held your breath underwater, they wouldn't have been…triggered. But when you were knocked unconscious yesterday, I think they appeared because you swallowed water. Your body's been hiding it. Adapting."

"Adapting to what?"

"To living on land," she answered. "Your 'skin condition'—the dry patches, the heat exhaustion, the dizziness when you've been too long at sea without a swim—it's not an illness, Zale. It's sea withdrawal. Your body's half-starved for salt water."

He blinked at her. "You're saying this—" He rubbed absently at his wrist where a particularly severe dry patch had recently flared raw. "—is just a side effect of being away from the sea?"

"Yes, it's your body's way of forcing balance."

Zale stared at the horizon. "That explains why I can outswim everyone.

And the breath-holding thing."

She nodded. "It's unnatural for a human."

He drew a slow breath through his nose. "Nestor always said I was found drifting out there. Said they thought I was lucky to have survived that long. He figured I'd washed off a wreck or something." His jaw worked. "But what if it wasn't luck? What if one of them—my parents—put me there on purpose?"

Nerissa hesitated, then said softly, "If you've never shifted before, then you're likely only half merfolk. That could explain it."

His gaze snapped to hers. "Half."

She nodded, rolling around a theory in her head. "A child born with lungs instead of gills—born to the sea but unable to breathe it…If your mother was a mermaid…" Her voice trailed for a moment before she forced the thought out. "She might've thought she was saving you. Leaving you somewhere you could live."

Zale's grip on the railing tightened until his knuckles went white. "She abandoned me."

"Or she loved you enough to let you go," Nerissa countered softly.

The silence that followed was heavy, but not empty. The waves below them lapped quietly at the hull, filling the spaces their words left behind.

Finally, Zale huffed a breath that trembled somewhere between a laugh and a sigh. "You sure know how to upstage a romantic morning, Riss."

"Sorry," she said softly. Then, despite the warmth creeping up her neck, she promised, "I'll make it up to you later."

The grin that broke across his face was slow and unmistakable, that familiar glint sparking back to life in his eyes. "Careful with promises like that, lass. I tend to remember them."

Nerissa brushed past him, glancing back over her shoulder. "I'm counting on it."

CHAPTER 38

SALT AND MOONLIGHT

Bran

The ship dipped as it rounded a rocky bluff, and the hidden cove opened before them—a sweep of turquoise water tucked between jagged cliffs, sunlight glinting on the shallows. Pretty enough, Bran supposed, though the stink of fish in the air mixed with kelp rot made it less poetic than it looked.

The *Black Serpent* slid into the narrow mouth of the cove, sails drawn up, hull carried by the tide. From his perch in the rigging, Bran could see the storm's handiwork plain as day—splintered rails, torn lines, a section of the mainmast that looked ready to come down if someone sneezed at it. Nestor's orders rattled across the deck, sending men scurrying to drop anchor.

On the deck, Roan pawed through a crate of sodden supplies, his scowl dark as thunder. No doubt he'd be cursing the sea for ruining his precious bandages. A few strides over, Ma Wen had his stew pot out, doling bowls to the poor souls who looked ready to keel over. At the bow, Cormac puffed his pipe and lectured a pair of greenhands on bad omens and splinters, jabbing the stem for emphasis until the lads nearly tripped over themselves to sand faster. Typical.

Bran braced his boots against the ratlines, sleeves shoved up as he worked a frayed line back into order. Eon clung to the ropes a few yards away, steadying the pulley while Bran secured it. The lad's gaze drifted down toward the deck, and a grin spread across his face, slow and smug.

Bran glanced down and followed his line of sight. Zale and Nerissa, shoulder to shoulder, walking lazily across the deck like they had nowhere else to be. Zale said something that tugged her mouth into the barest hint of a smile, and then Bran caught it. Their hands, brushing once, twice...before Nerissa's fingers slipped into his and stayed there. Bold as you please, though they clearly thought no one was watching.

"Well, well," Bran murmured, his own grin tugging wider. "Finally."

"Told you so," Eon said, still not looking away.

Bran snorted, turning back to his work with a sharp tug on the line. "Noted. And when I cash in on the betting pool, I'll be sure to cut you in."

Zale

The fire crackled low in the center of the cove, warm light painting the crew's faces in flickering gold. The smell of smoked fish cut with the savory tang of Ma Wen's stew made his mouth water. Zale lowered himself onto a driftwood log, Nerissa settling beside him. She sat with her usual soldier's posture, expression neutral.

His mind hadn't stopped spinning since that morning. Not from the kiss at the stern—though stars, that alone would've been enough to wreck his concentration for days—but from what came after.

Gills. He had *gills.* The thought alone was enough to make his stomach flip. Every half-forgotten quirk suddenly felt like a piece of a puzzle he'd never known existed. The rash that eased only in salt water. His record-breaking dives. His lungs that seemed bottomless. Even the constant pull he'd always felt toward the sea—what most sailors called the "call of the ocean"—now sounded less like poetry and more like biology.

He huffed a quiet, humorless laugh to himself. Trust his life to turn a romantic sailor's phrase into anatomy.

Ma Wen made his rounds with the ladle, pressing bowls into waiting hands. "Eat while it's hot," he muttered, dropping one into Nerissa's palms before handing Zale his share.

Zale had only taken his first spoonful when Bran leaned forward across the fire, elbows braced on his knees, grin sharp as a cat watching gulls scrap over a crust.

"So…" he drawled, savoring it. "Anything either of you feel like sharing with the group? For the sake of honest crew relations, of course."

Nerissa didn't so much as blink. "Not particularly."

Zale kept his gaze on his bowl, but the smirk tugging at Bran's mouth was enough to see even from the corner of his eye.

"Really? Because I'm starting to think I should be collecting my winnings tonight."

Zale lifted a brow over the rim of his stew. "You make a habit of gambling on your crewmates' personal lives?"

"Only when there's a sure thing," Bran said, eyes glinting.

Zale didn't take the bait. He only shifted until his knee brushed Nerissa's, the smallest touch setting his nerves alight. Sea and stars, if keeping his wits around her had been hard before, this was bloody torture.

He continued eating his stew, pointedly ignoring Bran, until the man jabbed a spoon in his direction.

"And let's not forget, the Salty Siren. You wouldn't even let me go talk to her. I saw her first, mind you."

Nerissa's chin lifted sharply. "You'd have been flat on your back before you finished your pickup line."

Bran only grinned wider. "Guess it worked out better this way. He does take a punch better than I do."

Zale shrugged, spoon still in hand. "Can't deny the woman's got good taste."

"So that's a yes!"

"Didn't say that," Zale replied.

Nerissa tilted her head, watching him over the rim of her bowl. "No? Because that sounded like an admission to me."

Zale looked up, feigning innocence. "Did it?"

"It did," she said sweetly, a spark of challenge in her eyes. "Almost like someone's getting sloppy with his denials."

Bran let out a delighted bark of laughter. "Ha! She's got you cornered now."

Zale's smirk deepened, his gaze still fixed on Nerissa. "Oh, I wouldn't be so sure."

"Wouldn't you?" she shot back, tone light but daring.

Bran groaned, dragging a hand over his face. "If you two start flirting over the stew, I'm taking my bowl elsewhere."

From across the fire, Roan spoke without looking up from his meal, voice dry as driftwood. "Stars above, Bran, everyone already knows. They've been making eyes at each other for weeks."

Bran gaped at him, spoon halfway to his mouth. "Spoil sport."

Brigid snorted, flicking a fishbone into the fire. "It's about time one o' 'em did somethin' about it. Poor lass's been twistin' herself in knots."

Zale looked over at Nerissa with a bemused expression, his accent slipping free as he drawled, "Twistin' yerself in knots, eh?"

Her cheeks flushed instantly, the corner of her mouth fighting a smile. "Careful, sailor," she warned, voice low enough for only him to hear. "You're not untangling them any time soon."

Before Zale could muster a reply, Nestor's voice rolled across the fire like distant thunder, equal parts captain and showman.

"Saints preserve us, would ye look at that—two hearts caught fast in the same current, thrashin' like netted fish and callin' it destiny."

"Thrashing like fish, is it?" Nerissa narrowed her eyes at the old man, but her wry smile betrayed her amusement.

Bran let out a bark of laughter. "Cap'n, you been sneakin' chapters again?"

"Pure research," Nestor shot back. "A good captain keeps up with the literature o' passion and peril. Builds character."

Brigid chuckled. "Builds somethin', that's for certain."

Nestor ignored her, puffing on his pipe before fixing Zale and Nerissa with a mock-stern look. "Now then. If the two o' ye are intent on turnin' my deck into a serialized love story, at least promise it'll have fewer drownings and a happier endin' than *Stormbound Hearts.* A man's nerves can only take so much tragedy before breakfast."

Laughter rippled around the fire. Bran doubled over wheezing, Roan hiding a grin behind his mug, even Ma Wen's quiet chuckle rumbling low.

Then Bran wiped his eyes and straightened, voice still bright with mischief. "Alright, but if this is official, I'll need proof. Cormac said I only win the bet if there's verifiable evidence."

Zale groaned, lifting a hand. "We're not tonight's entertainment, Bran."

"Oh, I disagree," Bran said cheerfully, leaning back on his elbows. "The crew's owed a bit of spectacle after yesterday's storm."

Zale opened his mouth to protest again, but Nerissa was already rising to her feet. She set her empty bowl neatly on the log behind her and caught Zale by the collar before he could so much as blink.

The kiss landed firm and decisive, no hesitation, no coyness, just a clean strike that left the entire circle of pirates stunned into silence. Zale's eyes widened for a heartbeat, then lowered as his hand found her waist out of instinct. When she finally drew back, she gave a quick, mock-formal bow toward Bran.

"Well?" she asked coolly. "Satisfied?"

Bran blinked once, then grinned like a man who'd just won the greatest hand of his life. "Aye, that'll do nicely."

The fire erupted in cheers and laughter—Cormac begrudgingly slapping coins into Bran's waiting palm, Brigid cackling outright, and Nestor wiping at his eyes, muttering something about "a man could die happy seein' that kind o' drama play out live."

Nerissa dropped back onto the log beside Zale, her composure flawless save for the faint color still burning in her cheeks.

Zale looked at her sidelong. "Ye do realize that only encouraged him, aye?"

Her lips curved, just barely. "Good. Let him talk. I'm done pretending."

Zale's answering grin was slow, proud, and entirely smitten.

Nerissa

The laughter still echoed faintly through the cove when Cormac rose from his spot near the fire, the battered fiddle already in his hands. He drew the bow across the strings once, testing the pitch, before settling into a lively rhythm that set the air humming.

"Well now," he said, squinting at Zale through the smoke. "Since the young buck's feelin' bold tonight, I reckon it's only right we get a tune to match. How about *The Ballad o' the Tempest Tide*? Ye always did fancy that one, lad."

A chorus of agreement rippled through the crew. Bran whistled. "Aye, go on then, love-struck! Sing for your siren!"

Zale groaned softly beside her, dragging a hand down his face. "I really need to stop tellin' Cormac what my favorites are."

Nerissa arched a brow, a teasing smile tugging at her lips. "You can sing?"

He shot her a sidelong glance, feigned offense glimmering in his eyes. "I've been a bit busy—and distracted—the past three weeks. Haven't had much time for performances."

Before she could reply, he started tapping his boot against the sand, syncing to the fiddle's bright, lilting beat. The rhythm spread like wildfire. Bran clapped along, Ma Wen joined with a steady thump against a barrel, and even Roan tapped his fingers against his tankard. Eon, never one to be left out, snatched up a pair of spoons from the discarded bowls and rattled them together in quick, gleeful time.

Then Zale began to sing.

His voice was rough-edged but warm, carrying easily over the fire and surf. The melody was quick and rollicking, full of daring leaps and crashing refrains, the kind of song that could turn a storm into a dance. The lyrics spun tales of cursed tides and reckless captains, of storms outwitted and ships that refused to die. An anthem of every fool who ever chose the sea over safety.

The crew roared the chorus back at him, stomping in time, laughter spilling between the verses. Zale's grin grew with each refrain, shoulders loose, hair wild, eyes alive in the firelight.

Nerissa could only stare, caught somewhere between astonishment and awe. His voice wasn't flawless, but it was alive, as raw and real as the sea itself.

She realized, with a slow swell of warmth in her chest, that she was tapping her foot too, the shanty infectious, impossible to resist.

Three weeks ago, she was half-dead and terrified, dragged aboard this ship in chains of secrecy and guilt. Now she sat by a fire, sand in her hair, laughter in her lungs, and something dangerously close to peace in her heart.

Maybe this was what Damarion had meant when he said he only wanted her to be happy.

She hadn't known there could be something else out there for her, something beyond service, beyond duty, beyond the cage she'd built around herself.

As the final chorus rose, the crew's voices thundered together, wild and off-key, but full of life. Zale threw his head back on the last note, laughter bursting free as the cove echoed with cheers.

Cormac shifted his grip on the fiddle, sliding easily into a softer tune, something lilting and content, the kind of melody meant to follow full bellies and good company. The fire crackled, the surf whispered against the rocks, and for a rare moment the world felt perfectly still.

Zale leaned closer, his shoulder brushing Nerissa's. "Don't you sing?" he asked, teasing.

She shook her head, smiling faintly. "Not unless you want the entire crew to beg me to stop. I've never been much of a singer."

"I don't believe that for a second."

"It's true," she said, glancing at him sidelong. "Even before all this, I could never bring myself to do it. Too self-conscious, I suppose."

He studied her for a beat, something curious flickering in his eyes. "You told Eon sirens don't lure sailors with their voices. But is there any truth to the rest of it? Does sirensong exist?"

Nerissa's smile softened. "In part. The stories exaggerate, as they always do. Sirensong is rare—a gift, or a curse, depending who you ask. It isn't something most of us are born with. And even among those who are…it doesn't always awaken."

"It's not a trick to lure anyone," she continued. "It's more of a resonance. A connection. Something that responds when the currents align."

Zale hummed, thoughtful. "Sounds powerful."

"It is," she admitted. "Too powerful, sometimes. It's why the old choirs were so feared."

He tilted his head. "And you?"

She held his gaze for a fraction too long.

"I've never had that kind of voice."

"Maybe you've just never had reason to use it," he said, the smirk returning, softer now.

Nerissa laughed under her breath. "Maybe. But you won't be hearing it tonight."

"And what a shame," he shook his head. "One day I'll get you to sing."

Nerissa lingered by the fire a while longer, letting the laughter fade into the softer hum of conversation. Zale was still fielding teasing remarks from Bran, who insisted he'd butchered the final verse of the shanty, while Ma Wen methodically collected the empty bowls.

When she finally rose, Cormac was coaxing a gentler tune from his fiddle, something wistful and easy, meant for winding down.

"I'll be back shortly," she murmured to Brigid, who raised a knowing brow but said nothing.

The walk to the ship was quiet, the night air cool and still. Lantern light glowed faintly from the *Black Serpent's* deck, gilding her path up the gangway. Inside her cabin, she shed her breeches for a long plum skirt that brushed her ankles, soft and flowing. It felt almost indulgent after weeks of leather and laces.

She wandered until the fire's glow was a dim orange shimmer behind her. Here, the beach sloped softly into the tide, the sand cool beneath her bare feet. Moonlight danced across the water's surface, silver and quiet, broken only by the whisper of waves. She hesitated at the edge, the foam curling around her toes, then stepped forward.

The sea met her like a familiar friend, cool against her skin, silk over muscle. She drew in a deep breath and let the water pull her farther in, the skirt drifting around her like a plume of ink. The rhythm of the waves was soothing, rather than taunting as it had been in the weeks prior.

"Couldn't resist, could you?"

The voice made her turn.

Zale stood at the edge of the beach, hands in his pockets, the moonlight tracing sharp lines across his face.

"Didn't think you'd notice," she said lightly.

"Hard not to." His tone was soft but teasing.

Nerissa tilted her head, watching him from where she hovered knee-deep. "Are you just going to stand there, or do you plan on joining me?"

His grin curved slow and wicked. "Was hoping you'd ask."

Without another word, he toed off his boots and stabbed his sword upright in the sand, then tugged his shirt over his head and hung it from the hilt. Then he was striding into the surf after her, the moonlight catching on the lean lines of his frame, the water folding around his legs as if welcoming him home.

The waves tugged at her skirts as she waded in up to her waist, but Zale's longer strides closed the distance easily. His hand caught her wrist, and he turned her toward him.

Moonlight and salt water slicked across his bare chest, highlighting every line and scar. She forced her eyes upward, but it didn't stop the heat climbing into her cheeks.

"You're being very distracting," she muttered, trying for dry and failing.

Zale's chuckle rumbled low in his chest. "I'll take the compliment."

Nerissa huffed, though her lips betrayed her with the start of a smile. "I did promise I'd make it up to you for cutting the romance short this morning."

That earned her a spark of mischief in his eyes that made her pulse trip.

"This feels like a scene straight out of *Stormbound Hearts,*" she added quickly, fighting a grin. "We'd better keep an eye out for Eon before he leaps out of the surf quoting Chapter Twelve again."

Zale's grin turned downright wicked. He leaned a little closer, voice dropping into the overblown cadence of a dramatic reading.

"And there, beneath the moonlit waves, the daring rogue caught his fierce maiden at last, and, unable to resist, stole another kiss to seal their fate."

Nerissa arched a brow, deciding to humor him. She lifted her chin and matched his tone with her own dramatic lilt.

"And the maiden, ever practical, reminded the rogue that if he kept running his mouth, she'd feed him to the sharks and be done with him."

Zale barked out a laugh, the sound carrying over the waves. He stepped closer, the water swirling around them, and lowered his voice again into that faux-dramatic cadence.

"But the rogue knew better—knew her threats were only to hide the truth burning in her heart. So he caught her close, daring the tide itself to try and take her from him."

As he spoke, his hand slid from her wrist to her waist, drawing her nearer until there was hardly space for the sea between them.

Nerissa lowered her eyes and continued.

"And so the maiden, in her infinite patience, took pity on the poor rogue, granting his wish at last."

Before his grin could widen, she rose onto her toes and kissed him, firm and sure, her lips cutting off whatever smug reply he had waiting.

Zale's hand tightened at her waist, pulling her flush against him as the kiss deepened. His lips moved with quiet insistence, matching the rise and fall of the tide around them.

Nerissa melted into him, throwing her arms over his shoulders. She barely registered the water swirling higher around her ribs, until her body betrayed her, shifting on instinct. Her legs fused, fins flaring, lavender scales rippling into being beneath the moonlight.

The sudden loss of footing sent her slipping down into the surf with a startled gasp. Zale's arms tightened around her waist before she could sink, hauling her back up against him.

"That's never…happened before…" Nerissa remarked breathlessly, eyes wide.

"Guess I'm just that good?" Zale teased, his grin faint even as he kept his hold firm.

"Very funny," she gasped. Then she tipped her head toward deeper water, gills fluttering against her neck. "Now, if you'd be so kind?"

Realization dawned instantly. Without a word, he shifted his grip and scooped her into his arms, wading forward. The tide climbed from his waist to his chest, until the sea wrapped them both in its cool embrace.

Bubbles slid past his ears as they sank together, her gills flaring in a rush of relief as she drew her first true breath of the sea.

Zale was still holding her close, and she wondered briefly if his gills would appear if he stayed under long enough. She seized his shoulders and kissed him again, curling her tail fin around one of his ankles.

Before too long, he tapped her wrist and pointed upward. She nodded, taking him by his shoulders, tail propelling them upward until the water broke over their heads in a rush of silver spray.

Zale sucked in a deep breath, dragging a hand through his dripping hair. "Guess Cormac was right about bein' pulled under."

"At least I gave you a smile." Nerissa tilted her head, smirking. "What happened to that famous eight-minute record of yours?"

He shot her a look, half breathless, half smug. "That only works if I'm *conserving* energy. Nearly drowning yesterday didn't help either."

"Excuses, excuses…"

She rolled onto her back, floating with her hair fanning out on the surface. Zale followed suit, stretching out beside her, their fingers lacing together.

Nerissa's free hand traced lazy circles on the surface. "So...are you still freaked out?"

"Oh aye," he said immediately, turning his head toward her. "Despite my excellent flirtation skills, I know nothing about women. So this is quite literally uncharted waters for me."

She narrowed her eyes. "You know that's not what I'm talking about."

Zale let his hand drift, trailing silver ripples through the dark. He exhaled slowly. "Honestly? I've been trying not to think about it."

Nerissa studied him, weighing whether to push or leave it alone. She didn't want to overwhelm him, not after everything that had happened in recent days.

"Do you…think it would help if…" she began carefully.

"If…?"

Her gaze softened. "If I showed you how to shift?"

His hand went still in hers. "You think that's even possible?"

"Well," she said with a faint smile, "if you can grow gills, I'd say fins aren't much of a stretch."

He huffed a breath that was part disbelief, part surrender. "Alright. Suppose there's only one way to find out."

"Only if you're sure," she said quickly. "If you're uncomfortable, we can wait."

"No." His tone sounded resolute now. "I want to know."

"Very well," Nerissa turned in the water, releasing his hand. "Keep floating on your back. Close your eyes. Let your limbs go slack and feel the pull of the tide."

Zale obeyed, stretching out until he was weightless again, eyes focused on the stars with a look of intent.

She slid a hand beneath his back, steadying him against the rise and fall of the waves. "Good," she murmured. "Now, don't think of your legs as two. Think of them as one line, one limb. The shift starts from your core."

Nerissa kept her voice low, almost melodic, syncing to the rhythm of the waves. Zale stayed motionless, eyes closed. She ran her other hand along his arm, noticing how his muscles twitched under her palm, still tense, still fighting the current.

"Relax," she whispered, smoothing a hand over his abdomen, tracing the path of breath beneath his ribs. "Let the water hold you. Imagine your legs being drawn together...elongated...part of the tide itself."

Zale cracked one eye open, lips curving. "You know, it's extremely difficult to relax when you do that. Not that I'm complaining."

Nerissa narrowed her eyes at him, then flicked her hand through the water and splashed him square in the chest. "Focus," she ordered, the corner of her mouth twitching.

Zale sputtered, laughing under his breath. "Alright, alright. Focusing."

He settled again, closing his eyes. The air between them stilled. For a long moment, nothing seemed to be happening.

Then Nerissa saw it. A subtle tremor. The skin along his forearms shimmered faintly where thin ridges began to rise beneath the surface, forming the delicate outline of fins.

Zale grimaced, muscles flexing instinctively. "Damn, that feels—strange."

"It's alright," Nerissa murmured, watching closely. "It might feel odd at first, but it shouldn't hurt."

"Doesn't hurt," he said quietly, opening one eye. "Just…feels wrong. Like my body's doing something it shouldn't."

"Don't fight it," she said softly. "Just let it happen."

Nerissa's gaze dropped to his legs, where his feet had begun to web slightly, the skin between his toes stretching into translucent membranes.

They were lengthening, too, ever so slightly. Nerissa's pulse raced; he was actually doing it.

Zale's brow furrowed. "Wait—if this actually works, where do my pants go?"

Nerissa blinked, then groaned, pressing a palm to her face. "I...didn't think of that."

He cracked a grin. "You mean to tell me there's no merfolk version of trousers?"

"That's why mermen usually wear tunics or kilts," she said, dragging her hand down her face.

Zale's eyes widened. "Absolutely not. I am not wearing a skirt."

Nerissa arched a brow, amusement breaking through her exasperation. "It's not a skirt, it's traditional attire."

"Uh-huh." He kicked his feet, shaking off the shimmer as he righted himself in the water. "Tradition or not, I'm keeping my pants."

"It's just as well," Nerissa said, brushing a stray droplet from her cheek. "We should probably head back before Bran comes looking for us."

"Och, last thing he needs is more ammunition."

The words rolled off his tongue thick with brogue, and Nerissa's head turned sharply toward him, eyes glinting with mirth.

"Do you even realize how adorable it is when your accent slips?" she asked, voice lilting with amusement.

Zale's grin spread slow and unmistakably smug. "Adorable, huh? So ye've liked it all along."

Her cheeks warmed instantly. "Don't push it."

He chuckled, low and pleased, wading a little closer. "Too late for that, lass."

Nerissa shook her head, still smiling, and let the water buoy her as she closed her eyes. A faint shimmer rippled over her skin; scales faded, fins drew back, and her legs reformed in their place. When she finally stood again, the surf brushed against her knees, her plum skirt clinging to her legs like ink-stained silk.

Zale lingered beside her, watching with open admiration. "Never gets old seeing that," he said quietly.

"Good," she replied, wringing a handful of her dripping hair. "I wouldn't want you getting bored of me."

They started toward the shore together, the sand shifting beneath their steps. The night air met them cool and crisp, laced with smoke from the dying fire down the beach.

Zale stopped long enough to retrieve his sword and the shirt still hanging from its hilt. Without a word, he shook it out and draped it over her shoulders.

"Here, you'll freeze before we make it back," he said simply.

Nerissa blinked, caught off guard by the gesture. The fabric smelled faintly of cedar and spice, carrying his warmth with it. She slipped her arms through the sleeves, pulling the fabric close around her.

"Thank you," she murmured.

Zale only smiled, the moonlight glinting in his eyes. "Anytime."

Together they crossed the stretch of beach, the glow of the campfire ahead marking where the crew waited.

The fire had burned low to coals by the time Nerissa and Zale made their way back up the beach. Shadows climbed the cliff face, long and flickering, and Bran's laugh carried on the salt-heavy air before the firelight reached them.

"Well, well," Bran called, spotting them first. "The lovebirds return—looking damp, disheveled, and entirely too pleased with themselves."

Zale shook his head like a dog, sending seawater flying. Cormac swore and hunched his shoulders against the spray. "Blasted haddock," he grumbled around his pipe.

Nerissa twisted her braid over one shoulder, wringing out seawater until it pattered into the sand. Firelight caught on the droplets running down her collarbone before she tugged Zale's shirt tighter around her.

"Training exercise," Zale said, deadpan as he flexed water from his fingers. "Entirely professional."

Bran gasped, hand over his heart, eyes wide with mock reverence. "Professional? You mean to tell me this was business, when here you stand—shirtless, glistening like some tragic sea god, moonlight caressing your noble shoulders—"

"Oh, for pity's sake," Brigid cut in, rolling her eyes.

Unstoppable, Bran leapt to his feet, voice rising like a bard at court. "—the salt spray clinging lovingly to every finely-sculpted line, hair dripping with Poseidon's own blessing—"

"Sit down before ye drown yourself," Cormac barked, though his pipe twitched with suppressed laughter.

The crew broke into laughter, a chorus of jeers and cheers. Zale only ran a hand through his dripping hair, unimpressed. Nerissa bit back her own laugh—his ears were turning red, and she had the sinking suspicion it wasn't from the cold.

"If you're that desperate, Bran," Zale said flatly, "I'll lend you the shirt next time."

That earned another round of howls. Nerissa dropped onto the sand beside Brigid, who wordlessly passed her a blanket, eyes twinkling with silent amusement. Nerissa wrapped it around her, covering her shoulders—and when Zale sank down beside her, close enough that their knees brushed, she lifted one edge in quiet invitation.

He hesitated only a heartbeat before sliding under it with her, their shoulders pressed together beneath the shared warmth. The heat that flared wasn't from the fire.

Eon, who had been quiet until now, tipped his head back against the log and grinned. "You know, this all feels familiar. Reminds me of Chapter Seventeen in *Stormbound Hearts.*"

The collective groan was instant.

"Not this again," Brigid muttered.

Cormac jabbed his pipe stem toward Eon. "If ye start quotin' that blasted book, I'll toss it—and ye—overboard."

But it wasn't Eon who answered. From his place by the fire, Nestor rumbled in his gravelly brogue, perfectly monotone:

"'His broad chest, bared to the night, was glistening with salt and moonlight as she pressed herself against him, surrendering at last to the tide of desire—'"

The circle erupted. Bran clapped like a delighted child, Cormac nearly choked on his pipe smoke, and Eon doubled over laughing.

Nerissa pressed a hand over her face, torn between mortification and mirth. Zale groaned beside her.

"Why," he demanded, "do you people know that by heart?"

Nestor didn't even blink. "Because you lot keep making me read it aloud." He took a slow sip from his flask, utterly unbothered. "Word sticks after a while."

The fire-ring roared with fresh laughter, Bran clapping like he'd just won a prize, Eon doubled over against the log, Cormac puffing smoke through his grin. The mirth rippled outward, bouncing off the cliffs until the whole cove seemed to be laughing with them.

Nerissa leaned into Zale, his warmth seeping into her side. His hand brushed hers beneath the blanket—accidental, maybe, but he didn't pull away. Nerissa looked around at the faces of the crew she had come to view as family, simply enjoying each other's company. It felt like home.

CHAPTER 39

PENANCE AND PROTECTION

Alpheus

The boy was twelve, maybe thirteen. Too young to have bled that much and stayed quiet about it.

They had brought him to the Harbor Citadel at dusk—another desperate family pressing their luck on Alpheus's reputation. Sailors and fishmongers whispered that no wound bled too deep, no sickness sank too far, for the royal apothecary to mend. They called them miracle cures. He called them demonstrations.

Alpheus didn't ask for his name. Names tangled things. He noted the pallor first, then the glassy flutter under the left eye, then the way the child's breath pulled high and shallow—panic trying to climb out of a ribcage.

"Hold that," Alpheus said, guiding the boy's small fingers to the wad of linen at his thigh.

He cleaned the wound with brine and spirits, ignoring the flinch. A shipyard hook had laid the muscle open. From the polished tray he chose a small glass vial—amber as old tea, viscous as honey. He called it filament distillate when he had to label it. In his private ledger it was simpler: *what stops the dying.*

"Breathe," he told the boy, voice even. "In. Out."

He set the vial's lip to the breach and let the liquid crawl into the wound like sap finding a crack. The cedarwood clock ticked in the corner, steady as a metronome. Tick. Tick. Tick.

Five counts and the bleeding gentled. Ten and it clotted into a clean, dark seal. He stitched, quick and neat. The boy watched the blood *not* move and began to cry—the silent kind, relieved and ashamed of the relief.

"Pain will ebb," Alpheus said, not unkindly. "You'll limp two days. No running. No ladders. No sand." He didn't glance at the mother when he said it. He kept his focus on the thread, on the knot that would not slip.

When he finally stepped back, the boy whispered, "Thank you," as if telling a secret.

"You will live," Alpheus said, and only then looked at the woman. "Buy fresh linen from Ruelle at the quay. Keep it dry. Return if the edge reddens."

They went. He washed his hands until the scent of spirits took the copper out of the air. The vial, half-empty, caught a lance of light and threw it red, a trick of glass the color of old blood. Beside it lay his cane—silver chased with fine scrollwork, head capped with a ruby. He had polished it at dawn. It shone now, precise, impeccable, a seal.

He turned it in his palms and, as it always did when the lab was quiet and his hands were clean, the memory came.

35 Years Ago

He remembered the morning more than the night.

Bread still warm from the oven, steam curling into the rafters. Althaea had swatted his hand away from the butter crock with mock severity—"Wait until it cools, or you'll burn your fingers." She was humming under her breath as she worked, some old lullaby she never seemed to realize she knew by heart. The sound had threaded through the little house like sunlight, familiar as his own pulse.

They'd sat together at the rough pine table, knees brushing, the window cracked to let in a sliver of sea air. Ordinary, unremarkable. The kind of morning you never think to memorize until it's the last.

He had been happy then. Content. The town's healer, with jars of herbs lined neat on the shelf and neighbors who came to him for poultices, stitches, and advice. His life was simple, quiet, marked by the rhythm of tides and seasons. He had thought it would always be so.

By dusk, the village was gone.

They came out of the surf without warning, pale shapes cutting through the breakers, then rising as men and women with blades in their hands. Sirens—not singing, not luring, not the stories told in taverns—but armed and ruthless. Their spears caught the torchlight as they stormed the quay.

Alpheus had been in the square when the first scream split the night. He turned in time to see one of the creatures drive a hook into Tomas the net-mender's throat. Panic shredded the market like paper.

His hand seized Althaea's wrist. "Inside!" he urged, dragging her toward their door. But the mob of villagers scattered, tripping over stalls, stumbling into death. Alpheus fumbled for the wood axe by the door, raising it in shaking hands. A spear flashed toward him—silver arc, sure and straight.

She moved faster.

Her body took the blow meant for him, the steel biting deep into her ribs. Her gasp—half air, half blood—was the sound that would never leave him. She crumpled against his chest before he could catch her, eyes wide, mouth working for words that never came.

He roared something wordless, swung the axe wild, useless. They left him alive—he never knew why. Maybe they thought the wound they dealt him was enough. Maybe they wanted him to watch.

By dawn the beach was a graveyard. Nets torn, huts burning, gulls circling over what the tide had claimed. His shirt was stiff with her blood.

On that shore he made his vow. Never again. Never unprepared. Never caught with nothing but an axe in shaking hands. He would learn them—learn what made them bleed, what made them fall, what secrets lay in their blood and bones. He would cut them open, and in their deaths Althaea's would not be wasted.

The vow had hardened into his marrow that day, and everything since—every vial, every experiment, every scream—was only its fulfillment.

The year after the massacre was marked in scalpel strokes.

In the weeks that followed Althaea's death, Alpheus had buried his grief beneath the discipline of inquiry. The villagers had managed to drag a few of the creatures from the surf before the tide claimed them. Alpheus claimed what was left. He worked alone, lamp guttering in the dark, his hands green with discovery. Gills flared open like shutters under his knife, membranes fine as lace, slick with threads of luminous filament. He studied how they pulled air from water, how they collapsed and stiffened when starved. He took samples, dried and ground them, tested tinctures, distilled, failed, began again.

At first, Alpheus told himself the work was penance and protection both. If a siren's gills could teach him to draw air from water, then perhaps no child would drown again. If their blood yielded secrets, perhaps poisonings could be undone, perhaps fevers quelled. Each organ he opened, each filament sac he harvested, he named in his mind not as desecration but as salvation. He whispered Althaea's name beneath his breath sometimes, as if to remind himself she would have wanted lives spared, not taken.

But time dulls edges.

The first time he cut, his hands trembled. The tenth time, less so. By the hundredth, the tremor was gone entirely. The gills were no longer a marvel but a mechanism. Hearts, lungs, stomachs—parts of a system to be mapped and categorized. He stopped speaking Althaea's name.

It was not that he forgot his vow. It was that the vow became a method. And the method required detachment.

Months later he had found it—the way to keep the filament alive outside the body, suspended in amber fluid that would not rot. One night, when a fisherman's boy was pulled half-dead from the harbor, lungs filled and lips already blue, Alpheus forced the draft into him. The boy lived. Coughed seawater, eyes wide and wild, then lived.

Others followed.

A dockhand swept overboard in a sudden squall, dragged ashore lifeless—revived with a vial tipped between clenched teeth. His lungs rattled like broken bellows, but within an hour he stood on the quay cursing the sea as though it had merely robbed him of sleep.

A little girl who had toppled into a rain-swollen cistern, her mother shrieking as Alpheus bent low to pry open her mouth. The serum slid down, and a moment later she coughed up half the village's drinking water into his lap.

An old woman found floating face-down in the shallows, skin gone waxen. Even she revived, her breath rasping back in fits and starts until she clutched his wrist with astonishing strength and whispered, "Not yet."

Each account spread like wildfire. Neighbors whispered his name with awe, then reverence, then superstition. They called it a miracle, a gift of the gods, a draught that turned back the tide.

By spring, the stories reached the court. And Alpheus was summoned to Astyra by King Lycaon.

The throne room smelled of oil lamps and iron. Guards flanked the dais, their bronze helms polished bright. Lycaon sat forward on his throne, heavy cloak spilling over the steps, his eyes pale and sharp as a hawk's.

They brought Alpheus before him with the deference usually reserved for priests. He felt their stares—men and women who whispered about miracle cures, about the boy who had drowned and yet did not die. His tray was set upon a stand: glass vials lined in orderly rows, amber liquid catching the torchlight.

"You are the healer who turns back drowning," Lycaon said, his voice carrying like a blade striking stone.

Alpheus bowed his head. "Majesty."

"I have heard the accounts." Lycaon leaned one elbow on the throne arm, studying him. "That you possess a draught to cheat death itself. That is no small claim."

"It is no claim," Alpheus answered evenly. "It is observation. Within a short window, the serum arrests the suffocation and restores breath. Beyond that…" He let the silence finish the thought.

The King's mouth curved faintly. "Even the gods draw their lines."

A ripple of amusement passed through the courtiers, but Lycaon did not smile long. He gestured to the vials. "This distillate—its name?"

"Filament," Alpheus said. He did not mention gills or sirens or how many corpses it had taken to refine. "It does what the sea steals."

"Then you will serve here," Lycaon decreed. "Astyra has need of such knowledge, and I would not have it squandered in a fishing village." His gaze sharpened, as though weighing Alpheus's marrow. "You will be royal apothecary. You will preserve our sons, our sailors, our heirs. And in return, you will be given all you require to continue your work."

Alpheus bowed again, hiding the flicker of satisfaction that threatened to show. At last, he thought. Not a hut with jars on a shelf, but a laboratory worthy of the vow he had made on a beach of corpses. Here he would refine. Here he would expand.

And if Astyra believed his gifts were miracles from the gods, he would let them. The gods had nothing to do with it.

King Lycaon kept his word.

Within a fortnight, Alpheus was granted chambers in the East Tower. The rooms were fitted not with tapestries or luxuries, but with stone benches, brass instruments, and shelves built to bear the weight of glass. For the first time, he had a laboratory worthy of precision.

He was also given hands to serve him. Not loyal apprentices, but men with irons still fresh on their wrists—mercenaries and cutthroats pulled from the gallows. Their sentences had been commuted, their service pressed into the King's design. They were not given to Alpheus for their skill but for their willingness to do what other men would not.

Their task was simple: hunt the coasts, take sirens alive when they could, dead when they could not. Shackled to Astyra by decree, they became predators at the King's command, scouring the shallows with nets, barbed spears, and cruel ingenuity.

And when they returned, the bodies came to the East Tower.

There, beneath its vaulted stone, Alpheus plied his trade. He peeled back their organs one by one, cataloguing the strange and the familiar alike. Filament sacs were harvested carefully, preserved in amber fluid, while the rest was burned or salted down until no trace remained.

The servants never spoke of what they saw. Fear kept their tongues still, fear of the King and fear of the man who could make blood halt its flow with a vial of honey-colored liquid.

To the court, Alpheus was miracle-worker, savior of sailors and children. To the King, he was an instrument—a blade drawn against the sea itself. But in the East Tower, where brine and copper mingled in the air, Alpheus knew the truth: this was only the beginning.

The first siren they dragged in alive was a woman with hair like wet kelp plastered to her cheeks, eyes still fierce despite the ropes biting her wrists. She hissed curses in a tongue the guards didn't know, her voice low and sharp enough to raise the hairs on the back of the neck. When they forced her onto the slab, one of the mercenaries muttered a prayer and refused to meet her gaze.

Alpheus did not.

He leaned close, studying the flutter of her gills against her throat. "Fascinating," he murmured, more to himself than anyone else. He pressed his fingers there, noting the rhythm, the heat of her blood. When he made the first incision, the woman arched against her bindings, her cry echoing against the stone walls. The mercenaries shifted uneasily, but Alpheus kept cutting, lips pursed in concèntration.

It was when he reached her chest that the silence broke. The rib cage, delicate and flexible as whalebone, bent easily beneath his instruments. The heart beneath was unlike any he had ever seen—larger, thicker-walled, pumping furiously even as the body failed. For a moment, he simply stared, entranced. Then, with slow precision, he slit the vessels one by one to watch how quickly the pulse faltered.

One of the mercenaries swore and turned aside, bile rising in his throat. "Saints preserve us," he muttered. "This ain't healing."

Alpheus did not look up. His voice was steady, clinical. "You mistake the purpose. I am not healing her. I am learning how to heal *others.*"

When at last the heart stopped, he lifted it free, cradling it as though it were a jewel. The organ pulsed faintly in his hands, a twitch of muscle memory that made one of the men stagger back against the door. Alpheus only tilted it, watching the last of the blood trickle down into the waiting vial.

Later, he suspended that heart in amber fluid, sealing the jar with wax and setting it on the highest shelf of his tower. It gleamed red-gold in the torchlight, preserved not as a relic of horror but as a monument to discovery. His first true specimen. His triumph.

The mercenaries would not bring him another living siren after that. They had no stomach for the cries, the convulsions, the way the man in the white coat leaned in with shining eyes as though witnessing wonder instead of ruin. From then on, the bodies they delivered were already stilled, the tide or the spear doing its work before the slab ever saw them.

Alpheus did not mind. Dead flesh spoke just as eloquently under the knife. Perhaps more so—no interruptions, no distractions. Only silence, and the steady pursuit of truth.

Word of Alpheus's work reached the King long before the jars cooled in the East Tower. Reports of fishermen revived, sailors pulled from the surf, children breathing again because of the amber serum—these were the stories Lycaon wanted told. Not the others. Never the others.

So when Alpheus was summoned to court once more, it was not to be questioned but to be honored.

The hall glittered with torchlight and gold leaf. Lycaon rose from his throne, a rare gesture, and in his hand was a cane of gleaming silver, chased with scrollwork so fine it seemed spun from frost. At its head, a ruby the size of a knuckle caught the light, burning like a coal.

"For a man who walks in two worlds," Lycaon said, voice carrying over the assembled lords and courtiers. "Among commoners you are healer, among scholars you are master. But here, in Astyra, you are something greater—my apothecary. My blade against the sea."

He placed the cane in Alpheus's hands, and the weight of it was both gift and shackle. The ruby glowed like a drop of heart's blood, polished to perfection.

The courtiers applauded. Alpheus inclined his head, but he felt the cane settle into his palms as though it had always belonged there, an extension of the vow he had made on the beach of corpses.

Later, in the solitude of his tower, he set it beside the amber jar with the preserved heart. Both gleamed in the torchlight—one a trophy of loyalty, the other of discovery. Together they seemed to seal the path he had chosen.

25 Years Ago

King Lycaon's reign ended as it had been lived—unyielding. Some said the old king's heart had hardened past its years, others whispered poison, but the truth mattered little. By the time the bells tolled, his body was already sealed in stone, and Astyra had a new king.

Vasilios inherited the throne before the mourning fires had burned to ash. He was younger, sharper of face, his voice less gravel and more steel. Where Lycaon had been immovable, Vasilios was restless, calculating, his gaze always scanning horizons his father refused to see.

It was within weeks of his coronation that the first envoys from the sea arrived.

They came not as raiders, not with spears or nets, but under a banner of Nautalia, the merkingdom long treated as myth or menace. Scaled emissaries rose from the harbor in polished shell armor, their movements deliberate, their weapons sheathed. Their message was simple: the tides had shifted, and Nautalia sought peace.

Alpheus remembered the stir in the court that day. Old lords muttered of blasphemy, of monsters pretending at diplomacy. Younger voices whispered of opportunity—trade, knowledge, a fragile end to bloodshed.

For Alpheus, it was neither. He had stood at the edge of the throne dais, his silver cane gleaming at his side, and watched the delegates bow low. To others, they looked regal, dignified. To him, they looked like resources, eyes glinting with secrets he had not yet split open.

Vasilios listened. That was the difference. Where Lycaon had spat at the very notion of parley, Vasilios leaned forward, weighing every word.

The peace they offered would demand sacrifice. Alpheus knew that even then. He also knew that with sirens walking willingly into Astyra's halls, he would not need to rely on condemned men dragging half-dead bodies from the surf. The sea itself was delivering its riddles to his door.

It was during those early weeks of negotiation that Alpheus noticed the princess.

Thalassa was Vasilios's younger sister, fair where her brother was sharp, quick to smile where he was measured. She moved through court like sunlight through glass, easily overlooked until one paid attention. Alpheus paid attention.

He saw it first at the feasting table, when her gaze lingered too long on one of the Nautalian envoys—a field commander with bronze skin and silver hair that caught the torchlight. Damarion, they called him. His manner was steady, his words clipped, but there was an ease in his bearing that spoke of command.

It was not the commander's council that drew Thalassa. It was him.

Alpheus marked the glances passed between them, the way her hand brushed his as she offered wine, the subtle tilt of her head when he spoke low. He marked, too, how they vanished from the hall at intervals, returning with cheeks a shade too warm, eyes a shade too bright.

They thought themselves clever, slipping out through gardens and side corridors, stealing moments in alcoves when the court was thick with politics. They were not.

From the gallery above, or the shadowed edge of a colonnade, Alpheus saw everything. The touch of her hand on Damarion's arm. The way she leaned close, laughing softly, forgetting the eyes that might be watching.

He did not interfere. Not yet. But he filed it away—another detail, another fault line beneath the shining facade of peace. He had no use for love stories, no patience for royal whims. But he knew what they led to. Attachments. Divided loyalties. Weakness.

And weakness was something he could always use.

The summons came at dusk.

Alpheus climbed the spiral to Thalassa's chambers, cane clicking against the stone with each step. The air smelled of lavender oil and damp linen, the kind used to cool fevers. Her handmaidens flitted nervously at the bedside, wringing cloths and whispering in worried tones until Alpheus raised one long finger.

"Leave us."

They obeyed. The door shut, and silence settled, broken only by Thalassa's shallow breathing. She lay pale against the cushions, a sheen of sweat across her brow, her hands curled protectively at her waist.

Alpheus set down his tray, fingers moving with the surety of habit. He examined her eyes, her pulse, the faint tremor in her frame. His questions were brief, precise: when the sickness began, how often it returned, how sharply the vertigo struck. He did not need her answers to confirm what he already suspected.

At last, he straightened, folding his hands atop the silver head of his cane. "You are not ill, Highness. You are with child."

Her breath hitched, eyes widening in horror. "No…" The word rasped, thin as paper. "I am unwed. If this becomes known—"

Alpheus's gaze did not waver. "The scandal will be greater still when the infant is born with gills."

Her head snapped toward him, eyes blazing. In that instant, he knew she understood—he knew of Damarion, of her stolen moments, of the secret that had bloomed dangerous in her womb.

He inclined his head, his tone measured, almost soothing. "You need not fear exposure. I will keep your secret. Tell your brother you are leaving for a royal retreat at the Spring Palace. He need not suspect otherwise. In truth, you will come into my care, in the East Tower, where no tongue will wag."

Her lips parted, but no words came.

"I can ease the worst of your symptoms," Alpheus continued, "if not remove them entirely. You will be comfortable. You will be safe. And when the time comes...we will see to the rest."

Thalassa closed her eyes, jaw tight. She knew the cost of refusal. She knew the ruin that would follow her if word reached the court.

Begrudgingly, she nodded once. "Very well."

Alpheus bowed, though a faint curl of satisfaction touched his mouth as he did. Another secret bound to him, another thread pulled tight into his grasp.

The seasons turned, and Thalassa vanished from court.

The official word was that she had gone to the Spring Palace for rest, to soothe a lingering malady. Only a few knew better: she was locked in the East Tower, hidden away where no gossiping courtier or prying servant might glimpse the truth. Only one handmaiden was permitted to remain with her, a quiet girl with fearful eyes, sworn to secrecy by both oath and threat.

Alpheus saw her daily. He came with vials in hand, each one a shade of amber, green, or violet, each one a draft meant to ease her sickness—or test her limits. Some eased the nausea, dulled the tremors, softened her breath. Others...were less merciful. Extracts distilled from merfolk gills, filament diluted with brine, tinctures he had spent years perfecting. He told her they would strengthen her, fortify her child.

The truth was simpler. He wanted to see what the sea would make of her.

By the fifth month, faint ridges had begun to crease the sides of her neck.

By the seventh, iridescent scales prickled at her ribs, pale and luminous as pearls. Thalassa wept when she first saw them, pressing her palms hard against the ridges as if she could rub them away. "What have you done to me?" she demanded, her voice breaking, her eyes flashing not with fear of the sea but with fury at him.

Alpheus only observed, delight gleaming in his eyes, and made another careful note in his ledger.

And then the child came.

She labored through the night, her cries echoing through the Tower's stone, until at last she brought forth a son. Alpheus leaned in eagerly, instruments ready, only for his anticipation to curdle.

The boy looked human. Entirely, frustratingly human. No scales, no gills, no sign of the bloodline that should have marked him. His skin was pink and ordinary, his lungs shrill and ordinary, his eyes shut tight against the world.

Alpheus hid his disappointment behind a thin smile. "We will need to test him," he murmured, reaching for his tray.

Thalassa pulled the infant close, eyes blazing with the first true fire he had seen in her since she'd entered his care. "No. You will not touch him."

He tried persuasion, then reason, then the quiet steel of command. She refused them all, her arms a fortress, her body a shield. At last, he relented outwardly. "One month," he told her. "One month undisturbed. Then we will see."

But when the month passed and Alpheus came to claim what was his due, the cradle was empty. Thalassa sat pale but defiant, her son gone.

"Where?" His voice was sharper than he intended, the cane's ruby glinting blood-red in the chamber light. "Where did you send him?"

Her lips curved, faint and tired but triumphant. "Away from you."

No coaxing, no threat, no draft would wrest the answer from her. Somehow, impossibly, she had smuggled the child from the Tower under his very nose.

Alpheus stood in the stillness, fury churning beneath his calm exterior. He had lost his specimen. But not forever. Secrets had a way of surfacing. And when this boy did, he would find him.

23 Years Ago

King Vasilios sent for him in the hush of night, when the torches in the castle burned low and the court's whispers fell silent. Alpheus was ushered not into the throne room, but into the King's private chambers, where the Queen sat pale and tight-lipped beside him.

They had been wed for two years. Two years without an heir. Two years of mounting pressure from lords eager for succession and whispers that the union was cursed.

"You are said to have remedies," Vasilios told him, his voice carrying the edge of command over desperation. "My Queen has yet to quicken. This cannot continue."

Alpheus inclined his head, fingers resting on the silver head of his cane. "There are elixirs to strengthen the womb. To encourage life where it falters. But the course requires precision—and trust."

The Queen's eyes flickered up to him, wary, but she nodded. She had little choice.

Over the weeks that followed, Alpheus prepared draughts tinted in shades of amber and green, each laced with herbs, tonics, and filament traces in quantities too fine for the court physicians to detect. He dosed her carefully, watching her color shift, her breath deepen, the subtle change in her pulse. He made notes in his private ledger, pleased with the body's response.

Within three months, the Queen conceived.

The court erupted in relief; prayers and offerings crowded the temple steps, while Vasilios's praise was reserved for the man who had made it possible. Alpheus accepted it with bowed head, though in truth he regarded the conception less as miracle than as proof of method.

Nine months later, in the height of summer, the child came. Prince Leander entered the world with a cry sharp enough to rattle the watchtowers—but his mother gave none. She had bled too much, her body breaking beneath the strain of birth.

Alpheus stood at the bedside, the King's roar of grief echoing in his ears, and made a final note in his mind: the Queen had not survived the experiment, but the outcome was achieved. An heir for Astyra. A victory for the throne.

And in the silence that followed, as the infant was swaddled and the Queen's body veiled, Alpheus rested both hands on the ruby head of his cane and thought, as always, of progress.

10 Years Ago

It was late afternoon when the report reached him. One of his masked hunters appeared at the East Tower door, breathless and reeking of brine. "Trespassers," he rasped. "At the Harbor Citadel. Snooping where they shouldn't."

Alpheus needed no further detail. The Citadel had only just received its latest haul of sirens—raw, valuable specimens destined for his tables. Intrusion there meant risk, exposure. Unacceptable.

Within minutes, his carriage was rattling down the cobbled road, the ruby on his cane glinting with each jolt. By the time the harbor came into view, dusk was falling, torches painting the stone red.

He stepped down in time to see his men encircle the intruders. They wore masks—birdlike visors and dark cloth to obscure their faces, a precaution Alpheus had insisted upon. The scene was chaos lit by fire: a man, a woman, and a girl no older than ten or eleven driven back toward the pier.

The girl stumbled when a knife flew, burying itself in her collarbone. She gasped, clutching the wound, but before she could collapse, the father caught her by the shoulders and shoved her back to her feet.

"Run," he ordered. "Find Damarion. Go!"

The name instantly grabbed Alpheus's attention. Damarion. The Nautalian commander who had turned Thalassa's head. What tie did this man have to him?

The girl faltered only a moment longer before her gaze caught his. For the briefest instant, their eyes locked—hers wide with pain and terror, his cool, measuring, curious. Then she dove from the pier, black hair flashing once in the torchlight before the sea swallowed her whole.

For an instant, the surface broke—a flick of a lavender tailfin vanishing into the depths.

Alpheus's breath stilled. Merfolk. Not raiders, not rumor, but flesh and blood from Nautalia itself. And the child was one of them.

He did not follow her with his eyes. She was not his concern. Not yet.

The parents were.

His men had them pinned in moments, spears pressed to their throats, their resistance snuffed out. "Alive," Alpheus ordered, his voice cutting across the surf. "Bring them to the Tower. I will have answers."

The hunters dragged them struggling into the waiting cart. Alpheus leaned on his cane, gaze shifting back to the pier. Where the girl had fallen, blood stained the wood—a vivid, unnatural green that the waves could not quite reach.

They brought the captives into the East Tower bound and bloodied, masks still on the men who had dragged them there. The chamber smelled of brine and spirits, the polished tables already waiting with instruments laid in precise rows.

Alpheus dismissed the mercenaries with a flick of his cane. This part he preferred to do alone.

The man and woman sat shackled to iron rings bolted into the stone floor. They were strong still, shoulders squared, though the fight had left their eyes raw with grief. Alpheus studied them as he prepared the vial—crimson fluid, thinner than the filament distillates, but potent enough for his needs. A preliminary version of the serum he had been refining from myrrhroot distillate. It softened resistance, loosened tongues.

He forced the draught down their throats in turn. The reaction was swift—their breathing slowed, their eyes clouded, and the tight lines of their jaws slackened.

"Your names," Alpheus said, voice even.

The man's lips moved first. "Theron."

The woman followed. "Melora."

"Who do you serve?"

"King Nereus," Melora murmured, eyes unfocused. "We are his envoys. We were sent to the surface...to investigate the disappearances. Too many of our people lost. Too many who never returned."

Alpheus's fingers tightened on his cane. So Nautalia suspected. So the king was probing the shadows. He leaned closer, voice low and precise.

"And Damarion," he asked. "What of him? Does he have a child? Around fifteen years old?"

The two exchanged a faint, bewildered glance—struggling against the fog of the serum but unable to deny its pull.

"No," Theron said slowly. "He has no children."

"No mate," Melora whispered. "He is married to his duty. Captain of the Guard. That is all."

Alpheus studied them in silence. If they lied, the serum would have shown it. He dismissed the notion. The girl on the pier, their daughter. She was a problem. A witness who had seen his masked hunters, who had heard her father's cry. A loose thread.

And loose threads had a way of unraveling everything.

He straightened, smoothing his coat. "You have given me what I needed."

Their relief was fleeting. The instruments gleamed under torchlight, and his hands were steady as he reached for them. The rest of the night was long with questions of a different kind, carved into flesh instead of coaxed from lips. Their answers, when they came, were written not in words but in blood and bone.

By dawn, Theron and Melora were no more than specimens, their bodies reduced to parts catalogued and preserved.

But the girl had escaped.

Alpheus leaned on his cane as the sun bled through the narrow tower windows, ruby flaring red in the light. Somewhere out in the sea, a child swam free who should have been silenced.

And that, more than anything, was intolerable.

2 Months Ago

The summons came to the throne room itself, in full view of courtiers and guards. Alpheus noted the choice—it was deliberate, meant to wrap this moment in pomp and record.

King Vasilios sat rigid on the high seat, Leander at his right hand, scribes gathered to capture every word. His crown glinted coldly in the lamplight.

"Astyra has come to terms with Nautalia," Vasilios announced, his voice carrying to the farthest pillar. "King Nereus has agreed to a peace treaty, sealed in marriage. His daughter, Calliope, will wed my son."

Relief rippled through the assembled lords. Murmurs followed, some awed, some doubtful. Alpheus neither joined nor stilled them. He studied the King instead, waiting.

"And in light of this," Vasilios continued, "our focus must turn to peace, not bloodshed."

Alpheus bowed his head, his grip tightening on the ruby-capped cane. But he said nothing. Not here. Not yet.

When the ceremony of dismissal concluded, Vasilios caught his apothecary's eye and gave a single, curt nod. Guards led Alpheus from the hall not back to his chambers, but to a smaller antechamber paneled in dark oak, the sound of the court muted beyond the heavy door.

There, the King's mask of ceremony fell away. He stood facing the fire, one hand braced on the mantel. "You will end your work in the East Tower," he said, low and sharp. "No more specimens. No more dissections."

Alpheus inclined his head. "Majesty, you know as well as I do that my remedies—my successes—were not brewed from herbs alone."

Vasilios turned, eyes hard. "I know. And that is precisely why this must end. Do you think our allies would sign their names to a treaty if they learned their kin had been cut open under my roof? Do you think my son would consent to this marriage if he knew what has been hidden beneath the Tower?"

Alpheus's mouth curved faintly. "Prince Leander does not know?"

"He does not," Vasilios snapped. "And he will not. He believes your cures are drawn from craft and learning, not corpses. That is how it must remain."

Alpheus was silent for a moment, studying the King's lined face. "Majesty, forgive my candor, but you mistake diplomacy for deliverance. A marriage bed will not erase centuries of blood."

Vasilios's voice hardened to iron. "It will buy peace enough for Astyra to prosper. That is all that matters." He stepped closer, lowering his voice further. "You may remain my apothecary. You will keep your reputation as savior intact. But the Tower is finished. Do you understand me, Alpheus? Finished."

Alpheus bowed, outwardly compliant. "As you command."

The ruby atop his cane caught the firelight, gleaming red as coals.

He knew when to bend. But never when to stop.

The East Tower was sealed in name only.

By night, Alpheus still worked. The Tower's lower vaults had no need of torchlight—lamps burned smokeless and steady there, shadows long against the stone. His latest project stood waiting on the central table: a brass chamber rigged with glass tubes, bellows, and a vial of verdant liquid. Within it, when agitated, the substance fumed into vapor—sharp, clinging, insidious.

The pheromone had taken years to perfect. Its roots lay in the harvested glands of sirens, augmented with extracts from certain deep-sea creatures whose bioluminescent trails masked chemical signatures. Together, distilled, they became something potent: a mist that clouded judgment, suppressed will, and left the victim pliable as clay. The latest version carried farther, clung longer, and bent obedience not only in moments of weakness but in the midst of blood and battle.

Alpheus adjusted the valves, watching the green vapor coil and disperse into the chamber, then drew a steady line of notes across his ledger. Soon, he would test it beyond the Tower.

The wedding of Prince Leander and Princess Calliope would provide the stage. A ceremony of unity, a treaty signed in peace, the kingdoms of land and sea woven together. All of it so precarious. All of it ripe for collapse.

Alpheus's design was simple: release the mist, guide a Nautalian's hand, and turn their blade upon King Vasilios. Let the people see their sovereign slain by a mer's weapon. Fear would revive itself, the treaty would die in its cradle, and his work would continue, free from talk of alliances and diplomacy. His hands would remain clean. The sea would bear the blame.

He allowed himself the faintest smile as the mist curled green against the glass. Progress required sacrifice.

Two months later, the city roared with anticipation. Banners of Astyra and Nautalia alike streamed above the castle, silk snapping in the wind. Soldiers lined the avenues, vendors hawked ribbons in the treaty's colors.

Alpheus moved through it all with measured pace, his cane tapping against the flagstones. He had no need to hurry; the plan was already set in motion. The vials were sealed, the placement secured.

And then he saw him.

Damarion. The silver-haired captain of Nautalia, armored in shell and steel, his bearing unmistakable even at a distance. A man Alpheus had not laid eyes on in years, yet one whose name had lingered sharp in memory.

But it was not Damarion who made Alpheus pause. It was the figure shadowing him—a girl with black hair spilling down her back, violet eyes catching the sunlight like cut amethyst.

Alpheus's steps slowed, breath tightening in his chest.

The girl from the pier. The one who had escaped all those years ago.

He had never doubted her survival. Not once. The sea had its ways of sheltering its own. But for her to appear here—unwittingly crossing into his dominion, on the eve of his design—was almost too exquisite.

She had walked into his reach.

Not a problem now. An opportunity.

His grip tightened on the ruby-capped cane, and the corner of his mouth curved. The mist no longer needed to seek an anonymous Nautalian hand. He had found someone better.

Present Day

Alpheus stood outside the cell, cane balanced lightly in his hand. Damarion sat straight despite the shackles—old soldier's posture, old soldier's eyes. Close up, the years since the first talks traced themselves in the finer lines at his temples; the set of the mouth hadn't changed. Duty did that to a face—smoothed certain expressions flat.

"You haven't softened," Alpheus said, letting the words echo in the stone chamber. "I expected more wear on you, truth be told. Captain of the Guard, drowning yourself in vigilance year after year. It should have carved you hollow."

Damarion didn't answer. His silence was as disciplined as his posture.

Alpheus smiled faintly, leaning on the ruby head of his cane. "No matter. I didn't come here for conversation. I came to tell you what use you serve."

He paced slowly along the bars, the cane ticking against the floor. "You raised her well. Loyal. Steadfast. A blade sheathed in obedience. It's admirable, really. And it is that loyalty, Captain, that will bring her to me."

Leather creaked down the corridor: a runner slowing to a respectful halt. The young man bowed, eyes fixed dutifully on the floor. "Report, sir. Harbormaster's office confirms the *Black Serpent's* charter remains active.

No recorded docking for at least a fortnight. Patrol towers at Saltgate, King's Quay, and Breakwater have been instructed to signal on sighting."

"Which signal?" Alpheus asked.

"Two green lanterns at the yardarm, sir."

"Good." Alpheus didn't turn from Damarion. "Offer the harbormaster a gratuity for zeal."

A muffled, nervous "Yes, sir," and the runner's boots retreated.

Damarion's jaw tightened. "She won't walk into your hands."

Alpheus tilted his head, smiling faintly. "Of course she will. Not for me. For you. Straight into my grasp."

He leaned a fraction closer, the ruby of his cane catching the torchlight. "She will come for her *Didaskon.* She cannot help herself. Shadows always follow their source of light. And when she comes crawling back, I will show her what loyalty truly costs."

For the first time, a flicker of emotion stirred in Damarion's eyes—anger, fear, something caught between. His lips parted, and he rasped through clenched teeth, "*Katará sou.*"

Alpheus only smiled at the curse, as though it were a benediction, before turning away. The click of his cane echoed down the corridor as he left the Captain to his chains.

CHAPTER 40

BALLAST WITH A MOUTH

Zale

The next day settled into the rhythm of repair. Nets were spread wide on the sand, patched and knotted under quick fingers. Brigid had an assembly line of deckhands—including Zale and Nerissa—patching holes after the storm had ripped parts of the sails to shreds. Cormac hummed under his breath while checking pitch seams along a rowboat, pipe stem bobbing with the tune.

By evening the cove smelled of roasting fish and woodsmoke. Someone started a shanty; within minutes it had turned into a full-blown contest—Bran and Eon howling verses, Brigid's side snapping back with cutting harmonies.

Bran and Eon stood shoulder to shoulder, one arm slung around the other, voices already cracking with laughter:

Oh, the boatswain's pipe is old and sour,
He smokes it at the midnight hour!
It creaks and groans, it wheezes smoke,
One day it'll set the ship afloat!

Cormac lifted his pipe out of his mouth long enough to scowl. "Ye'll be eating splinters if ye keep singing about me pipe."

"Counter it, old man!" Bran shouted.

Cormac rose, slow and deliberate, Brigid stepping up beside him with her arms crossed but a glint in her eye. When they sang, it was sharp and steady, cutting through Bran and Eon's racket like Brigid's battle axe.

Oh, Bran he boasts, but knots he ties,
Would strangle both his thumbs and thighs!
He trips on ropes, he trips on deck,
He'll sink us all, the poor ship-wreck!

The circle roared. Bran clutched his chest like he'd been mortally wounded. Eon, undeterred, shoved him upright. "Stand tall, mate. We'll drown 'em with verse."

Oh, Brigid yells and makes us sweat,
Her temper's worse than sails when wet!
She scolds, she snarls, she cracks her whip,
She'll marry no man—she's wed the ship!

Brigid's brows shot up. "Wed the ship, is it?" she muttered, stepping forward again.

Oh, Eon talks from dusk till dawn,
He'll yammer till the gulls all yawn;
He'll talk the wind right from our sails,
Then drown us all in fourteen tales!

Even Zale barked out a laugh at that one, Nerissa biting her lip to smother hers.

Eon bowed dramatically. "I prefer 'gifted orator,'" he declared. He held up a finger, attempted silence for three heroic heartbeats, then broke. "Also, the gulls love me."

Bran slung an arm around Eon's shoulders. "Come on, chatterbox—time for the killing blow."

He and Eon leaned in together, conspiratorial, then bellowed their final verse:

Oh, Zale went swimmin' in the night,
The moon it shone, a lovely sight!
With chest so bare and hair so wet,
Nerissa hasn't stopped droolin' yet!

The circle *exploded*—laughter, whistles, Bran doubling over as Eon slapped his back.

Zale's face went flat as a plank. "Truly inspired," he muttered.

Nerissa cleared her throat, smoothing the blanket at her elbows with deliberate dignity. "Children. All of you."

Brigid smirked. "Point goes to us."

Cormac puffed his pipe. "Aye. They forfeited by draggin' in romance."

"Unfair judging!" Bran protested, laughter giving him away.

Nestor finally raised a hand, gravelly voice carrying over the racket. "Call it a draw, before ye all lose your voices. We sail at dawn."

Groans and chuckles circled the fire as tankards were drained and verses hummed low into the night. The cliffs caught the sound and sent it back again, rowdy and alive.

The crew sprawled in loose circles, voices hoarse. Bran lay back in the sand like a man after battle. Nerissa tipped her cup toward Eon, who was still grinning, eyes bright from the contest.

"Tell me something," she said. "Did you always want to be a pirate? Or was that a later decision?"

A chorus of snorts. Zale muttered, "Careful. You've opened a door you can't close."

Eon sat up straighter, as if she'd asked him to address a court. "Since you ask so kindly—"

"Och, here we go," Brigid said, settling back.

"I was raised in a coastal orphanage," Eon began, solemn as a priest. "Damp place, smelled like boiled cabbage and mildew. Twenty-three of us, give or take—though really only twenty-two if you don't count Ratty Tom, because he ate soap once and never quite recovered."

"Too many details already," Cormac grumbled.

Eon pressed on. "I stayed till I was twelve, which was far too long to tolerate boiled cabbage, so I made my daring escape. That part involved a very complicated pulley system and two goats—though I digress. Spent a while running messages on the docks, stealing bread, that sort of thing. Then, four years ago, fate intervened."

Bran groaned. "Here comes the epic chapter."

"I happened upon the *Black Serpent*," Eon continued, puffing his chest out, "and executed a flawless stowaway maneuver, which mostly consisted of hiding under Bran's hammock and hoping he didn't roll over in the night."

Bran propped himself on his elbows, scandalized. "That was *you*? I thought the rats had learned to snore."

Nerissa's mouth curved. "And they kept you?"

"Nestor wanted to throw me overboard," Eon admitted cheerfully. "But Brigid found me too amusing, and Zale—well, Zale argued I was small enough to crawl into places the rest of them couldn't. It was before my growth spurt. Voila. Indispensable."

Zale groaned into his cup. "Worst argument I ever made." Truth was, he hadn't wanted to see the kid tossed into the sea, not when he looked so damned hopeful. And now? Four years later, Eon still hadn't shut up once.

Brigid's smirk cut through the firelight. "Best one ye ever made, and ye know it."

Eon spread his hands with mock grandeur. "And the rest is history. I have elevated the *Serpent* with my wit, my charm, and my astonishing ability to squeeze into barrels."

Cormac knocked ash from his pipe. "Elevated? You're ballast with a mouth."

Laughter rippled the circle. Eon basked in it, cheeks flushed with heat and attention. He flopped back, hands folded behind his head, still grinning at the night sky as if it had applauded him personally.

Zale shook his head, fighting a smile. Stars help him, but he'd miss the racket if it ever stopped.

At last, the circle began to thin out. One by one hammocks creaked in the trees, mugs were drained, voices faded to murmurs. Brigid disappeared with her braid coiled tight; Cormac's pipe winked out in the dark; even Eon at last collapsed into the sand, still grinning in his sleep.

But Nerissa didn't move, except to lean her head on his shoulder, the blanket around them drawn close against the night. Neither of them spoke. The only sound was the tide hissing against the rocks and the soft crackle of the fire's last embers.

"When do we return to Astyra?" Nerissa asked, almost too casually.

"We should be docking in their port by nightfall tomorrow, why?"

"It's just," she began before trailing off.

"What is it?" he pressed.

She sat up, looking him in the eye. "I'm worried about Damarion. I have a bad feeling that he didn't make it out of the tower after he helped me escape. I thought maybe I'd look—"

"Ye'll stay on the ship," Zale cut in, protective steel in his voice. He angled toward her, his jaw set. "No wanderin', no errands. Promise me that."

Her eyes narrowed. "I can't promise that Zale. He's the only thing close to family that I have left, I *have* to find him."

He held her gaze, unflinching. "You'll have a target on your head from the moment you step foot on dry land. Do you think the Royal Guard forgot about you?"

"No, of course not," she bristled. "Look, I don't have a plan yet, but I'll be careful."

"Careful?" Zale scoffed. "Oh aye, just sneak into the dungeon tower, check every cell without getting caught, and break him out—that's *if* he's even being held there. What if he's not?"

"Then I'll figure it out," she turned away, exasperated. "It doesn't matter, forget I said anything."

"Nerissa," he tried to catch her eye again. "Don't do anything reckless. Damarion wouldn't have wanted you to put yourself in danger for him."

She whipped her head around. "You speak of him as if he's already dead."

He held up his hands. "That's not what I—"

She stood up stiffly, letting the blanket fall to the ground beside him. "If he's still alive, then I need to find him. I *will* find him. And you can't stop me from leaving the ship."

"Are ye crazy?" Zale started to rise from his spot in the sand. "Ye're fixin' to get yourself killed, Riss!"

"I can take care of myself just fine," she retorted. "If I can stop something terrible from happening to him, then I will. And if I can't, then I am damn well going to try anyway. You don't understand what it's like to lose everything."

Didn't he?

"Riss, I probably understand better than most what that's like," he shot back. "Hell, I lost my parents too. I've tried my entire life not to get too attached to anyone because I'm afraid I'll lose them too." His voice dropped to a whisper. "Please don't make that fear a reality."

Nerissa stopped dead in her tracks.

"You're right," she sighed heavily. "Of course you understand. But please understand this: you don't get to tell me what I can and can't do. I know you're worried, but this is something that I have to do."

Before Zale could respond, she turned away and headed back to the ship, leaving him alone by the dying fire.

CHAPTER 41

CLOSER TO THE STARS

Zale

The *Black Serpent* cut free of the cove at dawn, freshly stitched sails snapping full as she caught the wind. The cliffs fell away behind them, the water turning from glassy shallows to the rolling blue-green expanse of open sea.

From the crow's nest, Zale braced one arm against the mast, the other shading his eyes as he scanned the horizon. The deck was a world below with the crew moving about their duties as the ship groaned like a living thing under their feet. Up here, though, it was only wind and sky.

He breathed deeply, letting the salt air scrape away the heaviness that had clung to him since last night. Nerissa hadn't spoken to him since she left him on the beach. He knew better than to seek her out before she was ready.

Of course she was right. He couldn't control her, nor did he want to. But if something happened to her in Astyra, he'd never forgive himself. Before docking, he would find her, help her come up with a plan that didn't involve storming the castle alone.

His gaze swept the horizon once again, tracing the line where sea blurred into sky. For a moment there was nothing but waves and light. Then a flicker of fire bright against the blue. He narrowed his eyes, leaning forward over the rim of the nest.

Not one. Three.

Orange flags, snapping sharp in the wind.

Zale's gut tightened. Dravari. And they weren't drifting aimlessly; their prows cut straight across the *Serpent's* path, sails full and eager.

Damn.

Cupping both hands to his mouth, he bellowed down through the rigging. "Three Dravari ships off the starboard bow! Half a league out—bearing straight for us!"

Heads snapped up across the deck. At the helm, Nestor's weathered face turned toward the horizon, his stance shifting as his hands found the wheel. His voice thundered across the deck, "All hands! To stations!"

The deck exploded with motion. Sailors pounded across planks, Bran and Eon darting toward the rigging, Cormac overseeing the cannons. The *Black Serpent* came alive beneath him, every pirate sliding into their place like the cogs of a war machine.

Zale gripped the rim of the nest, pulse hammering in time with the sails. The ships were getting closer by the second. They had escaped relatively unscathed from the last battle, but that had only been one ship. Now they were outnumbered, outgunned, outmanned.

"Chain-shot on the lead," Zale called down. "Ballistae high!"

The first volley scythed long; the second sang true. Chain chewed across their port bow, iron screaming against timber. Zale dropped to a knee and felt the mast's shiver pass through him as the ship shuddered from the impact..

He dropped his gaze to the deck, scanning frantically for Nerissa. Relief flooded his chest when he finally found her at the armory hatch, hand gripping the hilt of her sword. With a hint of pride, he was suddenly very grateful that he insisted she learn.

The *Serpent* churned forward, sails straining as Nestor angled her bow into the wind. The crew had armed themselves in preparation for the impending battle. Zale's knuckles whitened on the rim of the crow's nest as a glint of metal caught his eye. He squinted, heart lurching as he made out the curve of iron hooks stacked along their decks.

"Grappling hooks!" he yelled, returning to his feet. "They're readying to board!"

Zale caught a rope in one hand, swung his legs free, and slid down from the crow's nest in a rush of wind and burning rope. His boots hit the planks hard as he drew his sword in the same motion.

Out of the corner of his eye, he caught a flash of black hair. Nerissa moved through the crowd of bodies, blade already drawn, eyes bright and determined. She gravitated toward him, shoulder brushing his arm as she took her place at his side, much to his pleasant surprise.

Zale angled toward her, sword lifted, his voice pitched low. "Ye ready for this?"

Her grip tightened on her weapon, chin lifting. "Ready to put my training to good use."

Despite everything, his mouth tugged into a grin. Honestly, he was just glad she was even speaking to him.

Eon slipped past them, attempting to be stealthy. Zale caught his shoulder, spun him towards the mast. "Up. Nest. Hide."

"I can—" Eon began to protest.

"Ye *can* follow an order," Cormac barked, slamming a barrel lid. "Up, boy!"

Eon's jaw worked. He shot Zale a look, then scrambled for the ladder, vanishing into the rigging.

No sooner had Eon disappeared above than a roar split the air. Heavy iron whistled through the sky.

The first grappling hook slammed onto the *Serpent's* rail with a jarring crack of steel against wood. Another clanged close behind, then a third—lines tightening as the Dravari ships hauled themselves in.

A heavy plank slammed against the rail, allowing a pack of Dravari to surge across. At their point strode a man taller than most, all lean cruelty and swagger, an orange sash knotted at his hip and a string of shark teeth riding his collarbone.

Nestor's jaw went hard. "Voss."

Zale's body went rigid at the name. This was the man he'd only heard stories of, Nestor's first quartermaster. That was long before Zale's time. He'd been fortunate enough to have never met the man in person, but the stories had been enough. A violent brute with no honor. Voss didn't follow the pirate's code, and he was known for using women the way others used rum—quickly, carelessly, and never twice.

Fire burned through Zale's veins as he caught Nerissa's eye at his side.

Before he even realized he was moving, he stepped in front of her, angling his body between her and the bastard now standing on their deck. There was no version of this fight where he'd let Voss so much as *look* at her. Every muscle coiled, already calculating the three quickest routes to the rail if the battle turned against their favor. She could find safety in the water, beyond the reach of the Dravari's guns and blades.

"Stay close," he murmured, keeping his eyes on Voss.

"I'm not afraid." She stiffened behind him.

"Humor me," he said, voice urgent. Any other time, he'd grin at that flash of defiance, but not now. Not with Voss on their deck. He needed her safe. She seemed to pick up on his tone and mercifully stayed behind him.

But the pirate captain had already caught sight of her. The man's eyes lit with wolfish pleasure.

"Well well well," he drawled, voice thick with mockery. "Bad enough ye tossed your best first mate for a red-haired harridan—" he jerked his chin toward Brigid "—but *another* woman? Saints, Nestor, is the *Black Serpent* a fighting ship or a floating brothel?" He tilted his head, sneer deepening. "Tell me, Captain, do they fight as well as they—"

Brigid's axe sang through the air before he could finish. Voss jerked aside at the last instant, the blade missing his skull by mere inches but clipping his ear clean enough to draw blood. The weapon buried itself in a crate behind him with a solid, resonant *thunk*.

Voss straightened with a hiss, fingertips brushing the blood streaking down his jaw. His grin turned razor-sharp. "Still got a temper, I see."

Brigid reached for the haft of a spare axe on her back, expression flat as stone. "Step a pace closer, Voss, an' I'll show ye what the house charges."

A ripple of dark laughter rolled through the *Serpent's* crew. Voss's grin faltered just enough to elicit a smug grin from Nestor.

The old captain took one step forward, sword low. "Ye've got a lot of gall settin' foot on my deck, Voss. I threw ye to the sea once. Don't tempt me to do it proper this time."

"That so?" Voss's tone sharpened. "Funny, I seem to recall a captain too soft-handed to finish what he started." He snapped his fingers; a dozen swords unsheathed with a rasp of metal behind him.

"Ye only breathe because I was merciful. Don't mistake that for weakness," Nestor said evenly.

Voss tilted his head, blood still dripping from his ear. "We'll see."

He raised his blade in lazy salute, then snapped his wrist. His men surged forward like a rip current breaking, howling and wielding their curved blades.

Voss immediately went for Nestor.

Steel met steel as Nestor took the first exchange on the flat, letting the jar run up his arm and out through his shoulder the way years had taught him. Voss pressed with that hungry curve of blade, all flourish and speed for the crowd. Nestor slid inside the next swing. His pommel caught Voss under the jaw with a solid crack that rang up his arm like a struck bell. The younger man staggered, laughing low and feral as he shook it off.

Brigid shouldered through a knot of men to clear Nestor's flank, hooking a boarder down by the ankle and bringing the axe back up in a red arc. "Yer right!" she barked.

"Your left," Nestor returned without looking. Voss lunged high; Nestor dropped the shoulder, let the kiss of steel whisper across his coat, and answered with a cut that would've taken a lesser man's sword hand. Voss wrenched free, swore, and came at him again.

Satisfied that Nestor and Brigid could handle Voss on their own, Zale directed his full attention to the enemy pirates swarming his position. Nerissa held her blade low beside him in a defensive stance. Bran slid in at Zale's other side like he'd been summoned, knives at the ready. Zale caught a slash and answered with two quick cuts. He stepped into a lunge, and then felt the hair rise along his neck. Another pirate appeared behind him, blade coming down.

Before Zale could turn, a knife flashed from Bran's palm and buried to the hilt into the attacker's chest. The man folded without a sound.

"You're welcome," Bran said, plucking his knife from the fallen Dravari.

"I had it," Zale replied, deadpan, pivoting through a parry.

"Sure you did," Bran said cheerfully.

"Eyes forward," Zale shot back, knocking a cutlass wide.

"Forward is the idea," Bran agreed, shouldering a boarder off a plank.

Nerissa stepped in beside them, sword glinting. "Then stop talking and fight," she said, breathing sharply.

She met the next boarder head-on, parried with the same clean efficiency he'd drilled into her, then riposted with a sharp thrust that dropped him to the planks. Another came at her from the side; she pivoted, steel ringing, and turned his momentum against him, sending him staggering into Bran's waiting knife.

Nerissa reset her stance at Zale's shoulder, eyes focused, her blade steady. Each move recalled the lessons he'd hammered home on their quiet mornings after the last attack: balance first, then the strike. Zale's chest tightened with pride.

Another Dravari vaulted the rail with a snarl, cutlass arcing for Zale's exposed side. Nerissa was there first, steel flashing as she caught the blow and turned it aside, her riposte opening the man's ribs before Zale's sword finished him clean.

He pivoted, blade singing through the air, and cut down a pirate who had slipped in behind her. She didn't even glance back, trusting him, already moving to meet the next attacker.

Zale ducked too late under a slash, the edge grazing his temple and stinging hot before he shoved the boarder away. Nerissa caught a glancing cut across her sleeve that opened a shallow line on her arm, sharp enough to make her hiss but not enough to slow her down.

They adjusted, a little tighter now. Strike, parry, cover, shift. He drove one back with a hard feint that opened space for her to thrust through the guard of another. She spun low, clipped a knee, but nearly over balanced. Zale's hand snapped to her elbow, steadying her as his sword batted aside a strike meant for her neck.

Back-to-back at last, scraped and breathing hard, they circled together in the press of bodies. Not flawless, not easy, but they were holding the line. Zale felt the weight of her shoulder blades against his back, the moisture of his own blood in his hair, and let both anchor him as the deck thundered with the clash of steel.

The press thinned for a breath, only to make way for a brute of a Dravari officer shouldering through the melee. He was a head taller than Zale, built like a fortress, with a curved blade broad enough to cleave a man in two.

With an unholy roar, he bore down on them. Zale met the first strike and nearly staggered under the weight, arms jolting to the sockets. Nerissa darted in to intercept the next blow, but the man's backhand smashed her guard wide. The sheer force wrenched her sword from her grip and sent it clattering across the deck.

Her breath hissed, but she didn't falter. Her hands flew to her hips, drawing the twin daggers she'd kept ready. The shorter reach forced her close, weaving under the officer's swings as Zale tried to keep his footing.

"Zale!" she cried out, seeing the blade lift high.

He caught the strike on his sword, but the impact shoved him back against the rail, knees nearly buckling. The man raised his weapon for the killing blow—

—and Nerissa leapt. She sprang from the deck with a fierce cry, daggers flashing like twin sparks. One buried deep in the Dravari's shoulder, the other raked across his throat. The force of it carried them both down, her momentum driving him to the planks with a crash that rattled the boards.

Zale blinked, chest heaving, as the giant shuddered once and stilled. Nerissa wrenched her blades free, rising fluidly, eyes blazing violet fire.

Zale gave her a breathless look of gratitude, fierce and unspoken.

But then his eyes caught movement past her shoulder: a Dravari by the main mast, pistol leveled at her head.

The flintlock flared.

"Down!" Zale barked. He dove, catching Nerissa around the waist and dragging her to the deck. They hit hard, the breath jolting out of him as he braced his body over hers. For a heartbeat he felt only the bruise of impact, the scrape of wood against his shoulder. The crack split the air like a breaking mast. He braced for heat, for the hammer of impact—

But felt nothing.

No pain. No bloom of fire. No new hole to reckon with.

Cold realization hit him then. *Nerissa.*

He rolled off her fast, hands already moving, searching for blood. "Nerissa—are you hit?"

She blinked up at him, startled by his panic. "I—I don't think so." She pushed up on one elbow, rubbing the arm she'd landed on. "No. I'm fine."

Zale's pulse thundered in his ears as his gaze swept over her, refusing to trust words alone. No crimson, no bloom of red spreading through her coat. Stars above. His breath left him in a rush somewhere between a laugh and a gasp.

"Zale…" Nerissa had gone pale, eyes wide as she looked past him.

Only then did he follow her line of sight back toward the mast, where the gunman was gone. In his place stood Eon, gripping his knife as he stood over the body.

"Eon—?" Zale called to him. He slowly turned around, exposing the bloom of crimson spreading fast across his shirt.

Zale's stomach lurched. *No.*

The lad swayed, bloody knife slipping from his fingers, and went to his knees.

Zale lunged before he could pitch forward, catching him under the arms and lowering him to the deck. The blood came hot and fast through his fingers, slicking his palms as he tried to press down, tried to stop it. Stars, there was too much.

Around them the fight still roared, but Nerissa was back on her feet, blades flashing as she cut down the last of the boarders who dared to come near. The rest broke and scattered, scrambling back over the rails, seizing the grappling lines to swing for their ships. The *Serpent's* crew drove them back with steel and curses until the last orange sash vanished over the side.

Zale hardly saw it. He pressed harder against the wound, cursing under his breath, knowing it was useless. The blood kept coming.

Nerissa dropped beside him, knees hitting the planks. Her mouth was pressed thin, but it quivered, betraying the tremor underneath. "*Nerae…*"

Eon blinked up at them, pale already, but his voice was almost boyishly proud. "That was pretty cool, right? I...stopped the bullet."

"Eon, why?" Nerissa's breath hitched; she shook her head hard, fighting tears. "Why would you do that?"

He tried for a grin, but it twisted into a grimace. "Wanted...to be a hero."

Zale's hands slipped as he pressed down harder, desperate. "Roan!" he bellowed over his shoulder, voice cracking with urgency. "Over here, now!"

Nerissa clutched Eon's hand in both of hers, knuckles white. "You *are* a hero. Stay with us," she begged, her voice tight, shaking. "Just hold on, Eon, you hear me? Just *stay*."

Eon's lashes fluttered, his breathing shallow. "I'll...try," he whispered. His face twisted. "But...it hurts." His eyes began to roll back.

"No." Zale shook him, fierce. "You're not allowed to rest yet, ye hear? Not yet. Tell me—tell me some little-known fact about jellyfish, or which wild mushrooms won't kill a man. Just keep talkin'. Anythin'."

Blood bubbled faintly at Eon's lips as he blinked, eyes glassy but trying. His mouth twitched like he wanted to smile.

"Did you know...French angelfish...they mate for life? Always together. Guard the same patch of reef. Never stray."

His breath hitched, but he pushed on, eyes flicking between Zale and Nerissa. "Like you two. Called it from the start...knew you'd end up together."

He coughed, voice fading to a rasp. "Like in *Stormbound Hearts*...'the tide always carries true souls back to each other.'"

He went silent as more blood dripped from his mouth. Zale bent low, his grip fierce on Eon's blood-slick shirt. "Keep talkin'," he urged, voice rough, raw. "Anythin'—doesn't matter what. Just stay with us, Eon. *Say somethin'*."

But the boy's eyes glazed, his life draining as his chest rose once more, shuddered, and fell. It did not rise again.

For a heartbeat, Zale's world went soundless. He felt his own pulse hammering in his throat, louder than the sea, louder than the victory cries of the crew somewhere aft.

Nerissa gasped. "Eon, *no*—" Her hand tightened around the boy's limp fingers. She looked up at Zale then, her face a mask of control, but her eyes betrayed the raw pain beneath.

Zale's brain refused to accept what his eyes were seeing. No. Eon was too young for this—barely grown, full of trivia and facts no one else cared about. He should have outlived them all. There had to be something Roan could do. There *had* to be.

"Roan!" Zale shouted again, voice cracking as he pressed harder against the wound, blood oozing through his fingers.

Nerissa's hand slipped from Eon's to Zale's, her touch trembling but steady enough to cut through the storm rising in his chest. She leaned closer, eyes wet, her voice breaking as she forced the words out.

"Zale...*he's gone*."

The deck seemed to tilt beneath him. Zale stared down at Eon's still face, willing the boy to prove her wrong—to twitch, to gasp, to toss out one more useless fact. But the silence was absolute.

Boots thundered across the deck, and then Roan was there, dropping hard to one knee beside them. His fingers pressed against Eon's throat, then his chest. For a moment Zale held his breath, clinging to the impossible hope—

Roan's eyes lifted, dark and somber, and he gave the smallest shake of his head. Wordlessly he reached down to close Eon's glassy eyes with a gentleness that made Zale's chest twist.

Nerissa's grip tightened painfully around Zale's hand. Her voice came thin, almost to herself, as if speaking the words aloud might make sense of them. "He wasn't supposed to be here. He was supposed to be hiding…" Her voice caught. "But he jumped down…to save me."

Zale bowed his head, throat tight, and the thought came unbidden, jagged and shameful: *And thank the stars he did.* As awful as it was, as cruel as it felt to admit even to himself, he wasn't sorry Eon had taken that bullet—for her.

He squeezed Nerissa's hand harder, like the pressure alone could smother the guilt clawing at his ribs.

By evening the Dravari ships were nothing but smudges on the horizon, their retreat leaving the *Black Serpent* bloodied but afloat. The sails had been trimmed, the wheel steady, Astyra's coast now their grimward course. No cheers rose for surviving. The deck was too heavy with what hadn't.

Roan worked in silence near the stern, his great hands precise as he washed the blood from Eon's small frame. He smoothed the boy's hair back, binding him in clean linen with the same care he gave a wounded man. The crew gave him space, their voices hushed, their gazes sliding away rather than face the truth square on.

Zale leaned against the rail, the salt wind biting at the random nicks and cuts he hadn't bothered patching. Earlier, he and Nerissa had wordlessly helped each other bandage the bigger wounds so Roan could devote himself wholly to Eon. Small hurts tended, while the greater wound bled through the deck.

Now Nerissa stood beside him, eyes fixed on Roan's steady work as though the simple act of watching was the only thing keeping her upright.

The sea was waiting. And soon, they would have to give Eon back to it.

They wrapped Eon in canvas cut from a torn topsail—Brigid's hands steady as she stitched, Cormac tying the knots because his knots always held.

The crew gathered at the rail, lanterns swinging low as the sun bled into the horizon. Roan and Bran lifted the linen-bound body between them, laying it gently across a plank angled to the sea.

Nestor stepped forward, his weathered hands braced on the rail. The wind pressed at his coat, tugging his words into the dusk. "Four years ago, we near tossed him back to the tide. A stowaway rat under Bran's hammock—scrawny, loud, more mouth than sense. I'd've had him overboard myself, if Brigid hadn't stayed my hand."

A ripple of tired laughter, thin but genuine, moved through the circle.

"But he made himself a place," Nestor went on, his voice gruff. "Became every crew member's little brother aboard this ship. Talked our ears off with useless trivia, aye, but he noticed things too. Saw tells we never knew we gave. Understood us better than he let on. He'll be sorely missed."

Nestor's gaze dropped to the shroud resting on the plank. His next words came quieter. "And in the end...he was a hero. Sacrificed his own life for one of our own. There's no greater loyalty than that. Rest in peace, Gideon Thatch."

On his nod, Roan and Bran tilted the plank. The sea took the body quickly, linen sinking into the dark with barely a splash. The tide closed over him as though it had been waiting.

Zale's hand lingered on the rail even after the others began to drift away, chest tight. He was still covered in Eon's blood; he'd been in too much shock to clean up yet. When he finally turned from the dark sea, he counted the faces one by one. Bran with his jaw clenched as he flipped his knife across his fingers. Brigid sharpening her axe with murder in her eyes. Cormac tamping his pipe without lighting it. Roan wiping his hands clean while Ma Wen stood silently in the shadows.

No sign of Nerissa.

A chill threaded through his chest. He knew that look in her eyes when Eon fell, knew what it meant. She'd be blaming herself. Survivor's guilt surely had its claws in her already.

Zale shoved away from the rail, pulse quickening. He couldn't let her sit with that poison. Not alone. Even if she was still upset with him.

He started with Brigid's cabin, the door left ajar, lantern glow spilling over empty quarters. Then he crossed the deck at a clipped pace, checking the galley, then the infirmary. Nothing. He emerged back onto the main deck, scanning shadows and rigging.

Then he realized—tonight should've been Eon's watch.

Zale tipped his head back, eyes tracing the line of the mast in the dark. The crow's nest loomed above, lantern unlit, just a silhouette against the stars.

He climbed, boots finding the rope rungs with grim urgency.

And there she was.

Curled up in the narrow space, knees drawn to her chest, hair spilling forward like a dark curtain shielding her face. When his boot hit the last rung, she scrubbed the heel of her hand across her eyes in a motion too quick to be anything but what it was.

He didn't say a word. Just slid into the nest beside her, shoulder to shoulder, the wind trying to get between them and failing. The wood creaked under their combined weight. For a long moment, the only sound was the wind hissing through the rigging.

Her body shuddered once, a silent sob that hit him harder than any scream. Slowly, she leaned her head against his shoulder, heavy with the kind of exhaustion no sleep could touch. He stayed very still, letting her settle there, letting her know he wasn't going anywhere.

She hadn't cried the night she'd climbed up here after a nightmare and panic attack. She hadn't cried when she'd taken blades to flesh, or when her body betrayed her and forced her to shift. Even then, her eyes had stayed dry. Seeing her now, breaking quietly in the dark, it split something open inside him. And he couldn't fix it.

When she finally spoke, her voice was hoarse. "Tonight would have been his watch." She swallowed hard. "Didn't seem right for the nest to be empty."

Zale let out a slow breath. His gaze drifted upward, to the sprawl of stars glittering above the mast. "He liked it up here," he said quietly. "Said it made him feel closer to the stars."

Nerissa's words came out raggedly, each one scraped from somewhere deep. "I can't stop thinking...it's happening again. Someone died just so I could live. First my parents. Now him."

Her head stayed bowed against his shoulder, hair falling forward; he could feel the tremor in her voice more than he heard it.

Zale's jaw worked. "What happened...with your parents? If you're ready to talk about it."

For a long moment, he thought she might stay silent. He didn't blame her. Then her shoulders rose with a shuddering breath.

"Ten years ago. I followed them to the surface. I wasn't supposed to." Her voice dropped to a whisper. "Alpheus's men were waiting. They ambushed us. My parents fought so I could get away. They—" She swallowed hard. "They never came back."

There it was, the jagged edge he couldn't sand down for her. His chest tightened in a hard, unhelpful way. He wanted to say the simple thing: *It's not your fault.* He'd watched people say it like they were swiping a stain with a wet thumb. It never took.

Instead, he turned toward her, wrapping his arms around her and pulling her in close. He tucked her head beneath his chin, holding her as though sheer strength could shield her from the weight she carried.

"You did what your parents fought for," he murmured. "You survived." He tightened his hold, feeling the tremor in her frame. "And Eon...stars, he never would've forgiven himself if you'd been hurt while he had the power to stop it. That choice was his. The guilt—" his jaw hardened "—that guilt falls to Alpheus, to the Dravari. Not on you for living."

For a heartbeat she held herself rigid, but then the dam cracked. A sob tore loose, muffled against his chest, and then another. Her fingers fisted in his shirt, clinging as the emotions she'd been holding back finally gave way.

Zale closed his eyes, pressing his chin more firmly to the crown of her head. He didn't try to quiet her or tell her to be strong. He just held her as the tide of her grief broke against him.

Time stretched and blurred, her sobs softening by degrees until only the hitch of her breath remained.

At last, Nerissa shifted, pulling back just enough to speak, though she didn't leave his arms. Her voice was raw but steadier. "I know you're right. My head knows the logic. But my heart…" She shook her head faintly. "My heart doesn't."

"Mine either," he admitted, because pretending had never helped anyone sleep. His gaze flicked out over the sea, unfocused. "I keep expecting him to pop up, grinning, quoting *Stormbound Hearts* like he always did."

Nerissa let out a breath that might have been a laugh if it hadn't been made of tears. "We'll have to make sure to keep the dramatic readings alive. It's tradition."

"Mm." Zale swiped his sleeve across his eyes. "Damn right we will."

He leaned back against the rail, gaze lifting as the clouds shifted. A narrow gap opened, and there—clear and bright against the dark—shone the constellation of Lyra. His eyes stung again, but he nudged his chin upward. "Look."

Nerissa followed his gaze. "…Lyra."

She settled against him, her head resting against his chest, one hand splayed across as though anchoring herself there. Zale wrapped an arm around her shoulders and held her close. They stayed like that through the long hours of the night, keeping Eon's watch together until dawn found them.

CHAPTER 42

LEAVE A MARK

Nerissa

The hours bled together in silence as Zale held her. She had wanted to be alone, or so she thought, but she found a small amount of comfort in his embrace. It was odd, but not so terrible having someone to share the heartache with. She didn't even mind that he had seen her cry. No one had ever seen her break down like that before, not since the day she lost her parents.

Neither of them had slept. They had kept Eon's watch through the long night, eyes fixed on the horizon that never changed.

Only when the stirrings of life began below did she lift her head. The hatch opening. Muted thuds of bootsteps. Ordinary sounds. Familiar sounds. But without Eon's voice weaving between them, everything felt wrong.

Zale shifted beside her. He didn't speak. Just reached for her hand, his fingers warm and comforting around hers. He gave the smallest squeeze; she squeezed back, because words felt brittle and useless, too small to carry what had been lost.

The crew moved about their tasks in brittle silence.

Everywhere Nerissa looked, she found spaces Eon should have filled. He should have been underfoot, cracking jokes, pestering Bran, spouting some ridiculous fact about whales or sea slugs. She kept waiting for his laugh to cut across the deck, and every time it didn't, the silence carved deeper.

The *Serpent* was whole, but the crew was not.

Nerissa braced her hands against the rail, staring out at the horizon where Astyra lay waiting. She knew what it meant—that they had survived, that the ship carried on—but the thought felt hollow in her chest.

Zale's words from the night before still lingered—telling her the blame wasn't hers to carry. That Eon had chosen. That her parents had chosen. She had repeated those words to herself like a prayer until they began to bleed together.

But her heart still refused to believe it.

Her parents had died to buy her escape. Damarion had stayed behind to hold the line so she could escape the tower. Eon had thrown himself in front of a bullet meant for her. How many more would fall so that she could go on breathing? How many more pieces of the crew would the sea demand in her place? Was she even worth all those sacrifices?

Her throat tightened. She didn't dare look at Zale. Because if she did, she'd see the one person she couldn't bear to lose, and she already knew she would give anything to save him.

Alpheus

The laboratory smelled of brine and iron, the acrid bite of his tinctures clinging to the air. Alpheus bent over his worktable, steady hand guiding a quill across a page of dense scrawl. A vial hissed faintly at his elbow where it bled green vapor into the chamber.

The door creaked. Boots scuffed the stone floor. One of his men lingered at the threshold, head bowed. "My lord—the yardarm has struck two green lanterns at King's Quay. The *Black Serpent* has docked."

Alpheus's quill stilled mid-stroke. Slowly, he lifted his gaze. A smile curved thin and sharp across his face, more knife than mirth. "So. At last."

He set the quill aside, flexing his long fingers around the ruby head of his cane as he rose. A self-satisfied sneer tugged at his mouth. He had known it would not be long.

And now his little siren assassin had come home—unwitting, unguarded. Unaware that she was about to walk straight into his trap.

He turned from the worktable, slipping the stoppered green vial into the chamber of his vapor nebulizer. The device purred faintly as he checked the seals, the faintest trace of satisfaction curling his lips. Perfect. He leaned on his cane and descended the spiral staircase, the echo of his steps hollow in the stone throat of the castle.

Torches guttered along the walls, shadows bending across the rows of cells. Damarion stood shackled at the center of his, chains drawn taut from wrists to wall, his eyes fixed on Alpheus with all the loathing the man could muster.

Alpheus stopped just outside the bars, tilting his head as though appraising a prize beast. "The *Black Serpent* has docked at King's Quay," he said lightly, almost conversational. "And our dear Nerissa will not resist the chance to set foot ashore. Especially when she sees that her guardian waits for her."

Damarion's jaw clenched. "I will not call to her."

Alpheus's smile sharpened. He lifted the nebulizer, its brass fittings glinting sickly in the torchlight. "Oh, Captain," he purred, uncorking the vial with a twist. "I'm afraid you don't have a choice."

The green mist hissed into the air, curling through the bars, seeping into every crack of stone. Damarion stiffened, his chains rattling once before he forced himself still. His jaw locked tight, teeth grinding against the taste of the vapor as it threaded into his lungs.

Alpheus watched him with clinical delight, the nebulizer purring steadily in his hand. "Ah. Always the dutiful soldier," he murmured. "So disciplined. So stubborn. But brawn is no match for brains."

Damarion's eyes stayed fixed on him—hard as hammered steel. Not a plea. Not a word. Only the defiance of a man who would rather break than bow.

Alpheus sneered faintly, tapping his cane against the stone floor. "Resist all you like, Captain. It won't matter. The mist will do its work, and she'll follow your call. Straight into my hands. Tonight, you will enter the shipyard. You will lure her to you. And you *will* bring her to me."

Nerissa

The *Black Serpent* sat moored at King's Quay, her rigging whispering against the masts as the evening tide pulled restless at the hull. Dockside voices drifted faint and far, the bustle of Astyra carrying on as though nothing had changed.

Nerissa lingered at the rail, the sun sliding low behind the city spires. Not many words had been spoken since they made port. The crew went about their duties out of habit—ropes secured, sails tied off, supplies inventoried—but no one wasted breath on more than necessity.

Her gaze drifted to the streets beyond the quay. Lanterns burned in every window, merchants hawked late goods, children darted through the crowd. Life moved as it always had, unbroken. No draped banners, no black armbands, no outward sign that a king had fallen.

Her throat tightened. *Killed.* She could barely form the word, could hardly stomach the memory. The blood, the dagger in her hand, the look of betrayed horror on Calliope's face. She pushed it back, shoved it down where it couldn't reach her.

If the mourning had already ended, then Leander must have taken the crown, which meant that Calliope was now Queen.

Nerissa's chest tightened, a different ache threading through her ribs. Years of loyalty—years of service, of guarding Calliope's every step, of standing at her side against all threats—wiped away in a heartbeat. One moment of blood on her hands, and Calliope had turned on her without hesitation.

Her loyalty had meant nothing.

She forced herself to breathe, to keep her gaze fixed on the lamplit streets. If she let herself drown in that betrayal, she'd lose sight of the one thing that still mattered.

Damarion.

He had been the only one who believed her when she was thrown into the dungeon, the only one who had looked past the lies and seen her. He had fought so she could escape. *Nerae*, he might be in custody because of her.

She had told herself that Calliope would surely handle things if Damarion had been arrested. But what if she had given her too much credit? What if Calliope hadn't even been given the chance? The court would be wary, suspicious of a queen who came from their enemy, peace treaty or not. They might silence her voice altogether.

If Calliope couldn't protect him, then who would? Who else would stand for him the way he had stood for her?

Her hands tightened on the rail. She knew Zale was afraid of losing her. But what was she supposed to do? Sit idly while the one man who had believed her might be rotting in some Astyran cell?

Her mind began to trace paths. Ways she might slip unseen through the dungeon tower. How quickly she could vanish and return before anyone noticed. She could do it. She could slip ashore, find Damarion, bring him back before anyone on the ship even realized.

A warm hand closed suddenly over hers on the railing.

Nerissa jolted. She hadn't heard Zale approach, hadn't felt the deck shift under his boots. Her pulse spiked with the sharp, guilty startle of being caught.

She turned her head, and there he was, his gaze searching her face.

"Not planning your escape route, are ye?" he asked quietly.

Her mouth went dry. The truth pressed at her tongue, but she swallowed it down, forcing her expression flat. "No, I was just...thinking about Eon."

Zale's brow furrowed, like he didn't quite believe her, but after a beat he only gave her hand a slow squeeze. "I just wanted to say, I'll help you find Damarion. We'll figure out a plan together."

Her heart swelled in response. He would do that for her?

"Thank you," she said quietly, forcing a faint, weary smile. "Why don't we sleep on it, and come up with a plan in the morning? We'll think better after a full night's rest."

Zale nodded, then leaned down and pressed a kiss to her forehead, his voice low and gentle. "Aye. Get some rest."

Hours later, Nerissa lay awake, staring at the dark slant of beams above. Her body screamed for rest, but her mind would not still. Every time she closed her eyes, she saw Eon's face, heard his final words.

Then she heard something in the night.

Faint at first, like a thread of song pulling through the water—no, not through the water. Through her. A sound pitched so high it shimmered at the edge of pain yet threaded with something hauntingly familiar. She held her breath, straining to be sure, but it only grew sharper. It was not meant for human ears. Only merfolk would have caught it.

Sirensong.

Her pulse quickened. Nerissa sat up, listening harder, the sound tugging insistently at her chest. It wasn't her imagination—she knew that much. Someone was calling to her.

Sliding from the bunk, she dressed quickly in her plum skirt, black linen blouse, daggers at her hips, nothing more. No corset, no jacket, not even her boots. She wanted no sound, no weight.

Brigid's steady breathing didn't falter, and Nerissa hesitated only long enough to glance back before slipping out to the main deck.

The sound grew sharper now, vibrating along her bones, drawing her toward the quay. She crossed the deck like one caught in a dream, her body moving before her mind could argue.

Her fingers curled around the rope ladder. She swung over and climbed down, the wood damp under her feet as she landed on the dock. The pull guided her farther, down the pier, until a figure emerged from the shadows.

Silver hair glinted in the moonlight, with a frame she recognized instantly.

"Damarion?" The name slipped out in a hoarse whisper. Her heart leapt, but suspicion followed sharp on its heels. *Why was he here?*

She hurried towards him, her bare feet making no sound against the wooden boards.

His skin, normally bronzed, looked ashen, as though the life had been drained from him. His movements were stiff, mechanical, each step pulled by invisible strings.

Something was wrong. Terribly wrong.

Nerissa's heart thudded. She moved closer, cautious, every instinct straining. "How—how did you find me? Why are you still in Astyra?"

He didn't answer. His eyes glinted glassy in the moonlight, unfocused. When he spoke, his voice was low, flat, stripped of its usual confidence.

"Come."

The hairs rose along the back of her neck. That single word carried none of the man she knew.

She reached for his arm, desperate. "What's happened to you? Damarion—talk to me."

In a blur, his hand shot up, clamping onto her shoulder. His grip was iron, shockingly strong for a body that looked so depleted. Nerissa gasped at the pressure, at the sheer force coiled in his hold.

His grip tightened, and suddenly she was being hauled forward, feet skidding against the dock. Nerissa twisted, yanked, dug her nails into his wrist, but his hand was unyielding.

Panic surged. It was reckless, foolish, walking off the *Serpent* alone in the dead of night. She should have woken Zale, Brigid, anyone. And now exhaustion gnawed at her muscles, her strength frayed after two nights without rest. She was no match for him like this.

"Damarion. *Didaskon*, please!"

But it was no use. He couldn't hear her.

The shadows of the quay loomed closer, an alley yawning dark and silent. Damarion dragged her toward it, step after step, his glassy eyes fixed straight ahead.

No no no.

Nerissa tore her daggers from her belt. She didn't want to hurt him, but she would not be taken without a fight.

Damarion moved in eerie silence, glassy eyes fixed, and then steel gleamed in his hand. He had drawn his own dagger wielded with a cold precision that felt utterly foreign.

Their blades met with a clash that rattled up her arms. Sparks leapt as edge met edge. She twisted, drove him back a step, then another, bare feet sliding on damp stone.

She lunged, feinted low, but his arm shot out with unnatural speed, catching her strike and shoving it wide. Every parry jarred her wrists, every block rattled her shoulders until her muscles burned.

"Damarion!" she gasped, desperation breaking through the fight. "It's me—*wake up*!"

Nothing. Only the flat, rigid cadence of his movements, mechanical and merciless.

He pressed the advantage. One brutal swing sent shock screaming through her arms, nearly knocking a dagger from her grip. Another sharp clash, and her blade slipped, leaving her chest open. She barely twisted aside in time, his dagger slicing a shallow cut across her sleeve.

Her exhaustion dragged at her limbs, every breath a chore. She had never beaten him in sparring, even when he was himself, even when she was at peak performance. Now, drained and hollow though he looked, he fought with the inexorable strength of command, of something not his own.

A final strike wrenched her weapons wide. Pain exploded as his shoulder slammed into hers, driving her down hard onto the stones. The impact jarred her spine, knocking air from her lungs.

She scrambled to regain her footing. Her chest heaved, lungs burning; the tang of blood stung her tongue where she had bitten it. Above her, Damarion loomed, dagger raised as if ready to fall.

She tried to shove herself up, but his weight bore down, unyielding. She knew it in her gut: she had lost. She couldn't outfight him like this.

Think, Riss. Leave a mark. Leave something.

Her fingers brushed the hilt of a fallen dagger. She lunged sideways, snatched it, and before his hand could wrench it away, she drew the blade hard across her palm.

White-hot pain seared up her arm as she hissed through her teeth. Green blood welled up instantly, spilling over her fist, pattering thickly onto the ground. She let it drip, drop by drop, her heart hammering with the hope that Zale would see it in the morning and follow it.

Damarion's grip clamped down. With a twist, he wrenched the weapon from her and flung it aside, clattering into the shadows. His other hand seized her wrist, dragging her upright as though she weighed nothing. Shackled in his hold, she staggered after him, blood trailing behind her as he hauled her toward the waiting carriage.

A figure stepped out from the driver's bench, boots striking sharp against the cobbles. His face was hidden behind a birdlike mask, dredging up memories Nerissa had tried to bury—masks just like that, the night her parents died. She felt sick to her stomach.

Without a word, he seized her hands. Cold iron clamped around her wrists, shackles biting deeply. Then with a shove, she was flung into the dark maw of the carriage. She hit the bench hard, chains rattling as the door yawned wider.

As the masked man turned away, something at his belt caught her eye—a small brass whistle, no longer than a finger. It dangled from a leather strap, swaying with his movement.

Her breath hitched. That was it. The sound. Not real sirensong, just metal, shaped to shriek at a pitch no human could hear. But merfolk could. Merfolk had no choice. Was that how they had lured countless of her people before her from the shallows? To capture them and deliver their bodies to Alpheus? She didn't want to consider how he had figured out how to replicate sirensong.

Damarion followed, shackled just as quickly, his face blank, eyes still glassy. The man pushed him in beside her and slammed the door before climbing onto the driver's bench. A snap of the reins and the horses lurched forward, wheels groaning against cobblestone.

Nerissa pressed her shackled wrists to her lap, the sting of her bleeding palm keeping her alert. Her heart hammered against her ribs, one frantic thought keeping pace with the wheels:

Zale. Please find me.

Zale

Zale jerked awake in his hammock below deck. His head snapped up, heart pounding. The sound was faint, thin, like pressure behind his eyes more than anything he could hear. He pushed upright, pulled on his boots, and stalked onto the deck.

Silence. Nothing but the tide lapping at the hull and the creak of rigging.

Yet the ache lingered in his skull, metallic and sharp, like the after-ring of a struck bell. He frowned into the dark, unsettled. Whatever it was, it had stopped.

He scanned the rails, the dock beyond, but there was nothing. The sound had vanished as suddenly as it began, leaving only silence and a gnawing unease he couldn't shake.

He waited another long moment, scanning the empty quay. Nothing moved. Nothing stirred. With a low exhale, he rubbed a hand over his face and turned back toward the hatch.

It was nothing.

CHAPTER 43

BLOOD IN THE WATER

Nerissa

The carriage jolted over uneven cobblestones, iron rattling at her wrists. Nerissa's head bowed, exhaustion dragging at every bone, but she forced herself upright. Every muscle ached, her palm throbbed, blood still trickling hot between her fingers.

She shifted, angling her wrist toward the narrow-barred window. When the next jolt in the road rocked them, she pushed her hand through the gap, smearing green along the frame and letting drops fall to the stones below.

She clenched her jaw against the pain, against the nagging whisper that it might not be enough, and held her hand there until the steady rattle of the wheels drowned her thoughts.

Nerissa leaned her head against her arm as she left her hand dangling outside of the window, biting down hard on her lip.

"Skíon…"

Her head snapped up as she yanked her hand back into the carriage.

Damarion's glassy stare had sharpened, faint color warming his face. He was studying her palm. His brows drew together, confusion roughening his voice. "You're bleeding."

Nerissa clenched her fist and flexed it, blood welling fresh between her fingers, but said nothing as she stuck her hand through the bars once again.

"What...happened? Where are we?" His voice came out hoarse and uncertain.

She drew a breath, forcing it past the tightness in her chest. "You were on the docks. I followed you, but…" Her voice wavered. "You weren't yourself. You weren't in control. You were like a violent sleepwalker."

His gaze dropped, fixing on the raw gash at her shoulder, the scrapes cutting across her cheek. "We fought, didn't we?"

Nerissa saw the guilt in his eyes. She shook her head firmly. "You don't understand. It wasn't you. Alpheus somehow had you under his control. Like me. I don't know how he did it, but it explains why…why I killed the king."

Damarion's eyes flicked up to hers, but he said nothing.

Nerissa took a deep breath before changing the subject.

"You've been his prisoner since that morning, haven't you? Since you helped me escape from the dungeon."

His jaw tightened, the faintest muscle twitch betraying him.

"An entire month," she whispered, horrified. "You've been his prisoner this whole time…because of me."

No," Damarion said firmly. "It wasn't you. It was my choice."

The shadows beneath his eyes were deep, bruised hollows that spoke of sleepless nights. His skin was dry and cracked in patches, mottled with scars that hadn't healed right.

"What has he done to you?" The words ripped out of her, low and trembling with barely checked rage.

"Enough about me," he murmured. "What happened after you jumped from the tower? Alpheus said he found a way to prevent you from shifting. I thought—"

Nerissa closed her eyes. "I almost drowned. A man pulled me out and brought me aboard their ship. I've been with their crew ever since."

He exhaled with relief. "Then I owe that man."

She got up again and shoved her bleeding palm through the window once more.

"You'll owe him twice over if he finds my trail."

The carriage jolted over a rut, causing her to stumble. She grabbed one of the bars instinctively to steady herself, hissing when she realized she was using her injured hand.

"*Morai,*" she swore under her breath, shaking her hand.

Damarion studied her through the shadows of the carriage.

"This man who saved you," he said at last. "Tell me about him."

Nerissa hesitated, gazing out the window at the passing alleys. "His name is Zale," she said finally. "He's…infuriating, mostly. Raised by pirates."

Damarion's brow furrowed. "Pirates," he repeated.

"Yes. But not like the ones in the stories." Her tone softened. "They're good people. The captain raised him as his own. He's rough around the edges, but...good. Better than most men I've known."

For a long moment, the only sound was the rumble of wheels and the faint rattle of chains. Damarion's gaze held hers, unreadable, though something in his eyes gentled.

"You speak highly of him," he said quietly.

Nerissa's throat tightened. "He saved my life more than once. And when I was...when the sea withdrawal nearly killed me—he was there. Wouldn't leave me until he knew I was going to be okay."

Damarion's expression shifted, softened by something like understanding. "Sounds like a man worth knowing."

She looked down, her thumb brushing over the edge of her shackles. "He is."

He studied her a moment longer, then asked, almost offhand, "And what would he do, this Zale, if he knew where you'd been taken?"

Her heart gave a small, unsteady jolt. "He'd come for me," she said without hesitation. "The whole crew would."

Damarion's mouth curved faintly, the ghost of approval in his tone. "Then I pity the men guarding the gates."

Nerissa blinked, startled into a short laugh, and for a heartbeat the dread pressing in from all sides eased. But it returned just as swiftly when the carriage lurched to a halt, wheels grinding against the stone.

She yanked her bleeding hand back through the bars, clenching her fist to hide it. Boots struck the ground outside. The lock turned.

The door swung open, torchlight spilling in, and Alpheus filled the frame. Cane balanced in one hand, the ruby glinting like captured fire, his expression all quiet triumph.

Nerissa's lip curled in disgust.

"Well done, Captain," Alpheus said smoothly, his gaze flicking over Damarion. Then his eyes settled on Nerissa, dark with amusement. "All it took was dangling your dear *Didaskon* in plain view. Loyalty makes such a tidy leash."

Fury flared as Nerissa surged forward, aiming her bound fists for Alpheus's stomach.

One of his masked guards moved faster. Slamming the flat of their blade hard across her shoulders. The blow sent her crashing to her knees, breath knocked from her lungs. The clatter of chains echoed in the narrow corridor as she braced herself on trembling arms, teeth bared against the pain.

Alpheus didn't so much as flinch. He only tilted his head, watching her struggle back upright with the faintest curl of a smile. "Still so spirited," he murmured, almost fondly. "I do hope captivity doesn't dull that."

"What do you want with us?" Nerissa spat. "Haven't you done enough?"

His smile didn't waver; if anything, it sharpened. "You still have so much potential, Nerissa," he purred. "It would be such a shame to see it squandered."

Nerissa's glare burned hotter than flame. How she wanted to squander *his* potential.

"Take them below."

The masked men moved at once, hands clamping onto their arms. Nerissa stumbled as she was hauled forward, the stones cold beneath her bare feet, the torchlight of the corridor swallowing them into the tower's belly.

The torches guttered as they were shoved through the iron-bound doors. The air inside was damp and metallic, thick with the stench of chemicals and rust. At the chamber's heart loomed a great glass tank, chains creaking as more masked men heaved at a pulley to lower it. The tank groaned, descending until its rim was level with the stone floor.

"How fitting," Alpheus mused. "You stand here as she once did. Ten years ago, your mother looked just so. Shackled. Defiant." His lips curled. "And then she, along with your dear father, became my next test subjects."

Nerissa's breath caught, rage and horror warring in her chest. Her vision narrowed, and a cry ripped from her throat, raw and furious.

"You son of a leech!"

She drove her elbows back into one man's ribs; the other took her heel across his shin. Both staggered with curses, grips faltering as Nerissa wrenched free.

Her shackles clanged as she surged forward once again, unarmed but deadly, every muscle straining toward Alpheus. His smile only widened as if he had expected nothing less.

She was a heartbeat away when a third masked figure stepped in from the side. The shaft of his spear slammed into her ribs with brutal precision.

The floor rose up to meet her, cold stone biting her cheek and arms. She fought to rise again, only to find a boot pressing against her back.

"There she is," he murmured. "The fire that made her such a promising weapon."

"*Katará sou*!" Nerissa spat out with venom in her voice.

Alpheus only chuckled, leaning his weight on the ruby head of his cane. "Come now, that's not very ladylike."

Then with a flourish of his hand, "Hold them still."

The glint of a needle caught her eye. Her pulse spiked as she thrashed against the rough hands holding her down. Cold pierced her skin with a stinging sensation like a jellyfish as she hissed through her teeth.

The adrenaline in her veins turned to lead, her strength draining like sand through glass. Through hazy vision, she could see Damarion sagging against the wall near her as Alpheus injected him next.

"Remove the shackles," Alpheus said smoothly, tapping the ruby head of his cane. "They won't be needing them."

Wrists finally free, her mind screamed at her to *move, to fight.* But her body refused to obey as she lay motionless on the cold stone. She couldn't so much as twitch her fingers.

"Into the tank," Alpheus waved a hand dismissively.

Hands clamped around her shoulders, hauling her to her feet and shoving her hard towards the tank. She staggered on numb limbs, and then cold water engulfed her.

The shock seized her body, but instinct overrode everything. Scales rippled across her skin, her tail unfurling sluggishly. Across from her, Damarion's body plummeted into the water, cerulean scales materializing.

They sank to the bottom. Chains rattled above as the masked men worked the pulley system, raising the tank back up until its bottom sat flush with the stone floor.

Alpheus began to circle them slowly, like a shark tasting blood in the water. His reflection dragged across the glass, distorted by ripples.

"Ah, what a sight. The great Captain of the Guard, and his loyal protégé." His tone oozed satisfaction, every word drawn out like he was savoring it. "Caged. Bound. And yet—oh, how simple it is to set you free."

He tapped the ruby head of his cane against the glass. "A whisper of mist. A flicker of suggestion. And you become mine again. Imagine it. Your blades carving through friend and foe alike, striking before they even suspect the hand that guides you."

Nerissa bared her teeth through the water, fury in her chest, but the sedative kept her muscles heavy, her tail dragging uselessly against the tank floor.

Alpheus leaned close, his smile warping through the curve of the glass. "Why stop with Astyra? Why stop with a single king dead on his son's wedding day? There are others yet to fall. Perhaps King Nereus next. Perhaps the princess you once swore to protect. Together, we will accomplish wonders."

He straightened, his shadow looming over the water. "And the kingdom will thank me for it."

Nerissa managed to clench her fist. "I'll die before I take another innocent life."

"Innocent?" His voice dripped with disdain. "Vasilios was not innocent. Nor are the puppets who sit on Astyra's throne. They deal in weakness, in compromise. They would sooner sign away your people's future than face the truth." His mouth stretched with a thin smile. "You will not be destroying innocents, Nerissa. You will be clearing the field of threats so that the true innocents might finally flourish."

He turned toward the stairwell, satisfaction settling into every line of his face. "Get comfortable," he said smoothly. "It will be a big day tomorrow. A day the entire kingdom will remember."

His men fell into step behind him. The door groaned shut, the echo rolling through the chamber like a seal on their fate.

Nerissa clenched her jaw, the cold seeping into her bones as she stared up at the dark surface. Zale would find them. He had to.

CHAPTER 44

DROWNING ON DRY LAND

Zale

Morning arrived gray and heavy, the sea pewter under a sky that couldn't be bothered to brighten. Zale hauled himself onto the main deck, exhaustion settling in his bones. The *Black Serpent* sulked at her moorings, crew scattered like rats—some at their posts, some ashore, some trying to drink away memories of the lad who never stopped talking.

Bran lounged at the rail with a melancholic grin as Zale approached. "Salty Siren? Round or three."

Zale opened his mouth to refuse, then closed it again. A tavern meant noise. Noise meant not thinking. "Aye," he said, surprising them both. "Why not."

He knew drinking wouldn't erase the hollow ache in his chest, but it would at least dull the memory of Eon collapsing in a pool of his own blood that kept repeating in his mind.

Zale dragged his boots down the gangway behind Bran, casting a glance toward the quarterdeck out of habit to call out to Nerissa. She'd been bone-tired the night before; odds were good she was still asleep.

As he and Bran stepped onto the pier, a glint of metal at the mouth of a narrow alley caught his eye. He slowed, something instinctive tugging at his gut.

"What's that?" he murmured, squinting into the distance.

Bran followed his gaze and tilted his head. "Dunno. Looks like someone dropped a blade."

Drawing forward as if by a hook, Zale crossed the dock, each step quicker than the last. Two objects waited in the grime as he dropped to a crouch, picking up the discarded weapons.

His fingers brushed the cold abalone hilts, and the world seemed to tilt. A sick certainty crawled up his spine.

Something happened here.

Last night.

While he lay in his hammock, telling himself the noise outside was nothing.

You should've checked on her. Stars damn you, you should've checked.

Forcing himself upright, he scanned the stones beyond. That's when he saw the faint, irregular drops marking the path deeper into the alley. Green against gray.

Zale's stomach turned to lead.

"Riss," he breathed.

"Aren't those—?" Bran started, staring at the daggers in Zale's hands.

"Yes," Zale stuffed the daggers into his belt and started down the alleyway. "Go alert the crew—she's been taken, probably to the castle. I'll follow the trail."

"Zale—"

"*Go.*"

Bran gave him a terse node before turning on his heel.

Zale tore down the alley, shoulder-checking crates and scattering a pair of cats that hissed at his passing.

Every drop of blood he found drove him faster. No thought of subtlety, no thought at all—just Nerissa, dragged stars-knew-where while he slept. His heart slammed with every footfall, lungs burning, legs pumping like the sea itself had him by the back and was hurling him forward.

Stars, he wasn't a doctor, but even he knew this was too much blood for her to still be on her feet. Why had she left the ship in the first place? He thought they'd agreed to come up with a plan together to look for her mentor.

The trail thinned but didn't vanish, pulling him through narrow streets until the ground sloped upward. Ahead, massive stone walls loomed in the morning light. So he was right, they *had* taken her to the castle.

Zale's momentum faltered, instinct finally kicking through his blind rush. He ducked hard behind a jut of stone wall, chest heaving, sweat slicking his temples.

The trail led straight to the gates. Guards in Astyran colors stood alert, spears braced, eyes scanning the road.

Zale pressed back against the wall, forcing himself to breathe quieter, slower. *She's in there. Stars damn it, she's in there.*

He should be charging the gate, cutting down anyone in his way, forcing his way in. Every part of him screamed for it.

But there were too many guards. One step into the open and he'd be skewered before he could set foot inside.

He raked a hand down his face, grit grinding against his skin. *Think, Zale. You can't fight a whole garrison. Not alone. So how in the tides do I get inside without being seen?*

His eyes swept the walls, desperate for a weakness. Nothing but stone and steel, guard patrols pacing with a routine cadence.

Then he located one option. Low at the base of the wall, half-hidden by weeds and runoff was a rusty grate. Wide enough for a man to crawl through if he didn't mind the filth. A drainage culvert.

His stomach twisted at the thought of where it would lead. *Not glamorous. Not clever. But it'll do.*

He glanced once more at the guards, then dropped into a crouch, slipping along the shadowed wall until he reached the culvert. He yanked the grate loose with a grunt, dropped to his belly, and slid inside.

The stench hit him first—stagnant water and rot so thick it clawed at the back of his throat. He gagged once, then forced it down, wading forward as the murky current rose to his waist. The tunnel was narrow, stone slick with slime, but he pressed on. He would find Nerissa, and he *would* get her out of here.

He pushed deeper, the darkness closing in, guided only by the faint pull in his gut that said Nerissa was near.

The culvert twisted and forked, water sloshing around his boots. Twice he followed the wrong tunnel, only to slam against a wall of iron bars or a grate too small to squeeze through. Each dead end tightened the knot in his stomach, the urge to punch the wall nearly overwhelming. He doubled back, until finally—finally—he found a shaft that climbed upward.

He hauled himself up by the slick handholds and shoved against another rusted grate until it gave with a groan.

Torchlight spilled over him. The stink of mildew was replaced by damp stone and the faint tang of iron. The dungeon.

Zale pulled himself free, boots squelching onto the stone floor. He dragged a sleeve over his face, then looked down at his clothes plastered with moss and grime, streaked dark with muck. A humorless huff slipped out. Living on a ship full time wasn't the most hygienic, sure. But this was not one of his finer moments.

He straightened, hand hovering over the hilt of his sword, and pressed onward until he found a break in the wall where a narrow staircase twisted upward. Zale took two steps at a time, heart climbing faster than his legs.

At the top, he kept quiet, each step measured, until the passage ended at a thick wooden door, iron-banded and swollen from the humid air.

He pressed his ear against it. Nothing. No murmur of voices. No clang of armored guards. Just dense silence.

Zale eased his sword from its sheath, metal whispering against leather. He curled his fingers tightly around the hilt and pushed the door open slowly, hinges groaning. The gap widened, spilling a slant of torchlight into the corridor.

Inside, the chamber yawned wide. Chains rattled overhead, suspending a massive water tank. And at the bottom was Nerissa.

Zale's heart skipped a beat.

She lay motionless on her side, fins not even flicking. Strands of hair drifted like ink in the water around her, hiding her face.

The sword in his grip felt suddenly useless, his pulse roaring in his ears as his gaze flicked around the chamber. No guards. No sound but the faint drip of water.

He slid inside, easing the door closed behind him, and slowly sheathed his sword. Cautiously, he made his way to the tank and pressed his palm against the cold glass.

"Nerissa?" he breathed.

No response.

Cold dread gripped his heart. What if he was too late?

Fighting the urge to yell her name, he instead knocked on the glass, wincing as the sound echoed in the chamber.

Zale sighed with relief as Nerissa blinked, eyes glazed before sharpening in recognition. She drifted forward and pressed her hand to the other side of the glass, mirroring his own.

"Hold tight. I'm going to get ye out of there."

She shook her head, then lifted her other hand, pointing past him. Zale followed her gesture to a lever beside the chain rigging. He sprinted to it, wrenched it down with all his weight, and jumped back as the gears screamed to life.

The tank shuddered, chains rattling, then slowly lowered into the floor until the rim sat flush with the stone floor, water sloshing around the perimeter.

Zale dropped to a crouch at the edge, reaching down to gather her tightly into his arms. She sagged against him like deadweight, arms drifting at her sides. Something was wrong.

"Are ye hurt?" He looked her over, noting the scrapes on her face, the scabbed-over cut on her shoulder through the torn fabric of her blouse.

"Sedative," she mumbled against his shoulder. "Hard to move."

He nodded, then reluctantly lowered her back into the water so she could breathe.

"I'm sorry," she began as she resurfaced. "I wasn't trying to sneak off, but I saw Damarion on the docks. Something wasn't right—"

"No need to explain," he cupped the side of her face, gently. "I'm just glad you're okay."

A pointed throat-clear cut through the moment.

Zale's head snapped up.

Another figure had broken the surface of the tank, water dripping from broad shoulders. His gray eyes fixed on them as he floated near the edge. There was an air of command about him.

Nerissa exhaled, half-laugh, half-sigh, brushing wet hair from her face. "Zale, this is Damarion."

She hesitated, then glanced back toward the water. "Damarion, this is Zale."

For a long moment, the two men just stared at each other across the chamber. Zale felt the weight of the older man's scrutiny, a measured assessment that might've cut a lesser man in half.

Finally, Damarion inclined his head. "I owe you more than I can ever repay," he said quietly. "For keeping her safe."

Zale looked around at the chamber, then pointedly at the tank. "Not safe enough, it seems."

Nerissa rolled her eyes. "Anyway, we need to get out of here before Alpheus comes back."

The door in the opposite wall burst open.

An older man wearing a black cloak swept in, four masked men flanking him like shadows. His mouth curved in a thin, self-satisfied smile.

"How romantic," he drawled, voice echoing off the vaulted walls. "A rescue attempt."

The words slithered between them like oil, souring the air.

So, this was the snake she'd warned him about. Perhaps now he'd get the chance to cut off its head.

Zale's sword rasped free of the scabbard in the same instant the masked men drew theirs. He met the first with a clean parry, drove the second back with a boot to the gut, then split the third's guard with a vicious downward cut. They crumpled fast, and Zale barely broke stride.

But more poured in from behind Alpheus, blades drawn. Zale twisted, swung, ducked—until he caught one blow on his guard, knocking the weapon from his grip. Another attack came from the side, but Zale turned too late.

The blade ripped across his chest, tearing through fabric and flesh alike. He hissed through his teeth, stumbling back. Blood welled hot beneath his shirt, darkening the cotton until it clung to him. His pendant slipped free, swinging loose.

Snarling, he yanked Nerissa's daggers from his belt. They felt wrong in his hands, lighter, smaller than he was used to. He slashed wide, carving space, but the rhythm wasn't his. The men met his slower parries, drove him back step by step until his shoulders brushed the cold wall of the chamber.

Alpheus's cane tapped once, deliberately, against the floor. Then he stepped forward, leveling the ferrule at Zale's chest.

"Well, well," he murmured, almost pleased. The tip caught the cord of Zale's pendant, tugging it taut until the shell swung into the torchlight. "What have we here?"

What could this bastard possibly find so interesting about his necklace?

Alpheus's eyes glittered, his smile widening as he turned toward the water tank. "Tell me, Captain, do you recognize this trinket?"

Damarion went utterly still.

Alpheus chuckled softly. "Of course you do." He pivoted back to Zale, eyes raking him up and down as though seeing him for the first time. "Isn't this poetic? The siren girl, guided by instinct alone, leads the lost hybrid straight into my hands. A trap I hadn't even needed to set."

"What are you talking about?" Nerissa's voice cut through the chamber, sharp and cold as she broke the surface, eyes burning. Then she whirled on Damarion. "What is he talking about?"

But Damarion didn't answer. His gaze was locked on the pendant. Why did he suddenly look so haunted? He was with Nerissa on this one—*what was bloody going on?*

Alpheus's satisfaction deepened. "Ah. You didn't tell her, did you?" He leaned closer, voice dropping to a hiss. "This, my dear, is the bastard son of Princess Thalassa and her ever-loyal captain."

The words took the breath from Zale's chest. *What…son??*

His pulse roared in his ears. Nerissa's eyes met his, shock mirrored in both.

"That's—that's impossible…" Nerissa stammered, looking between Zale and Damarion.

Alpheus gave a low, delighted hum. "Oh, but it isn't. During the first peace talks, what has it been, twenty-five years now? Your gallant Captain Damarion caught the eye of dear Lady Thalassa. A tryst beneath the moonlit sky, a forbidden spark between kingdoms…" His tone turned almost wistful. "And, as such stories tend to go, it bore fruit."

He began to circle the tank slowly, cane tapping out a smug rhythm on the stone. "She hid the pregnancy, of course. Royal scandal, merfolk father, all that tiresome political fallout. I offered to…assist. Purely for research, you understand. But before I could conduct so much as a preliminary test, she sent the infant adrift—tied up in some sentimental gesture of mercy." His eyes gleamed. "A waste, really. Such potential, lost to the tide."

Nerissa's head snapped toward Damarion. "You knew?"

Damarion's throat worked, but no words came. His hands trembled against the glass of the tank. "No," he managed, voice rough with disbelief. "I never knew she'd ever been with child."

Zale was still trying to process it all. His mother—royal Astyran blood—had set him adrift at sea, not to abandon him, but to save him from this madman. And his father…well, that certainly explained the gills.

Alpheus turned his gaze back to him, eyes gleaming with academic fascination. He began to circle like a shark.

"My, my," he said, voice dripping with mock admiration. "A fine specimen, isn't he? Broad shoulders, lean frame, built for endurance, not bulk. A swimmer's build through and through." He clicked his tongue, the sound sharp as a metronome. "I must admit, the symmetry is remarkable. Why, Captain, he even has your nose."

The faintest chuckle escaped him, low and humorless. "Genetics truly are a wonder."

Alpheus smiled faintly, almost reverently. "Do you know how many sleepless nights I spent wondering what became of you? How many hypotheses I drafted, how many experiments aborted for lack of a proper subject? And now—" he spread his arms as if presenting some grand discovery. "Here you stand. A living answer to every question that has haunted me for twenty-five years."

Zale's jaw clenched, heat flaring in his chest. He stepped forward despite the blades still pointed at him, voice rough with defiance. "I'm not your specimen," he spat. "Not your experiment. Not your answer to anything."

Alpheus chuckled, the sound soft and needling. "Oh, but you *are* a specimen, my boy. The first of your kind." His eyes glittered as they swept over him, calculating. "Can you shift, I wonder? Grow fins, gills, a tail, just as the merfolk do?"

Zale's lip curled. "Keep wonderin', old man. The only thing I'll be shiftin' is your teeth across the floor."

"Such impertinence," Alpheus said silkily. "Let's see how arrogant you are when you're choking on air."

Hands like iron pinned his arms as Alpheus drifted toward his worktable, humming to himself. The apothecary's fingers plucked a syringe from the tray, dipping it into a vial of golden liquid. He flicked the plunger, watching the bubbles rise with clinical detachment.

Zale barely had time to catch Nerissa's eyes narrowing at the vial, before Alpheus plunged the needle into his neck.

At first, nothing. Then suddenly his lungs seized like fire had swallowed them. His hand clutched at his chest. "What—what did you do to me?" he rasped.

Alpheus circled him leisurely, cane ticking against the stone. "Ah. You sound just like your mother did."

Zale doubled over in pain. Through the ringing in his ears, he heard Nerissa's urgent cry. "Zale! Hold your breath!"

He tried—stars, he tried—to obey. He dragged in one last breath, but the fire in his chest only climbed higher, searing through his ribs, his throat. His vision swam. The chamber tilted. He staggered, knocking into one of the masked men as his muscles spasmed, his body torn between air and water and something in between.

"Fascinating," Alpheus murmured, scribbling notes with one hand while still holding the syringe in the other. "Respiratory paralysis within seconds. Perhaps the hybrid physiology rejects the catalyst faster than expected."

"Stop it!" Nerissa's shout echoed through the vaulted chamber. She lunged for the edge of the tank, but slipped back into the water at the effort. Her tail thrashed, sending water sloshing over the stones. "You'll kill him!"

Alpheus didn't even look up. "Hardly. Death would be such a waste."

Zale dropped to his knees, gasping against the invisible weight crushing his chest. Every heartbeat felt like a hammer blow. Somewhere through the blur, he caught Nerissa's voice again, urgent and pleading.

"Zale, listen to me! Breathe shallow—don't fight it—just hold on!"

Agony lanced through his legs as they drew together, bones grinding, skin splitting and merging. His trousers shredded at the seams, fabric giving way to a cascade of scales that burst across his skin. A scream tore from him but broke into a strangled gasp as his back split open, a razor-sharp fin ripping free.

He was lying on his side now, legs gone, replaced with a heavy tail that lashed against the stone. The weight of it was unbearable, wrong. His teeth clenched so hard that his jaw ached as his forearms flared with fresh pain—fins slicing through skin with a wet snap.

Searing hot slits tore open on his neck. Air scraped raw down his throat but brought no relief. Panic seized him. His chest heaved, lungs clawing for oxygen that no longer worked.

I can't breathe.

Another gasp. Sharper, frantic. His lungs spasmed, no air, only fire.

I can't control this. I can't—

His vision tunneled. Stars crowded the edges. His chest convulsed again, body wracked with the primal terror of drowning on dry land.

I can't—

Alpheus's voice slid into the panic like a scalpel. "Fascinating. So the hybrid *does* retain the physiological ability to shift forms. Proof that the inheritance is stable. How…promising."

CHAPTER 45

GREEN SUITS YOU

Nerissa

Nerissa's fingers splayed across the glass as she willed her body to shift. Nothing. Just the sting of the gash on her palm that had reopened. Her tail dragged heavily beneath her, but no power gathered in her muscles. She clenched her jaw, tried again, harder, commanding herself to shift, to rise, to *do something.*

Nothing.

She flicked her gaze to Damarion. "Are you able—?"

He gave the smallest shake of his head. "The sedative," he said. "I've already tried."

Pounding her fists weakly on the glass in frustration, all she could do was watch in horror as Zale's body tore itself apart from the inside out.

"Fascinating," Alpheus remarked with a cold, detached tone. "Half of one world, half of another, and belonging fully to neither."

"Are you just going to let him die??" Nerissa snapped.

Alpheus didn't even spare her a glance. "Put him in the tank," he ordered coolly.

Two of his men hauled Zale up and dumped him like refuse into the water. Nerissa caught him under the arms as he sank, dragging her down with him. His weight pressed against her heavily, but his eyes fluttered. Still conscious. Barely.

Alpheus turned away, cane tapping idly against the stones as he strode for the door.

"Leave them. They won't get far," he told his men. The hinges groaned shut behind them, and the echo of the bolt sliding into place left the chamber steeped in silence.

"Zale," she whispered urgently, steadying his face in her hands. "You can breathe now. You're in the water; you have gills. Just breathe."

His jaw was clamped shut. Eyes squeezed tight. His whole body screamed refusal.

"I know," she said fiercely, forehead touching his. "I know it goes against everything you've ever known, but you won't drown. I swear it. Just—*breathe.*"

He shook his head, stubborn even as his face turned blue.

"Fine." She pulled her arm back and drove her fist into his stomach as hard as her groggy limbs would allow.

His eyes bulged, arms curling instinctively around his middle as his mouth flew open. Water rushed in. He gagged, coughed, then froze, blinking as the water flowed cleanly through the slits at his jaw. His chest eased, rising and falling with a new rhythm.

"There," Nerissa sighed, relieved. "Isn't that better?"

Slowly, he lifted one hand. His fingers curled, trembled, then settled into a very deliberate, very rude gesture.

"Honestly," she muttered, half-laughing, "you're welcome."

"This is…not how I expected today to go," he frowned, tentatively flicking his tail.

"Well, *moirai*," Nerissa stifled a rueful laugh. "Now we're all trapped. Please tell me you have a backup plan."

"Oh aye," Zale stretched his arms slowly, grimacing at the unfamiliar new fins that cut easily through the water. "Bran should be right behind me with the cavalry."

"So our lives depend on Bran, *great*," Nerissa rested her forehead tiredly against Zale's chest. "Things could be worse, I suppose."

"Give him some credit," Zale laughed. "He was only meant to alert the crew, not lead them into battle. We both know Brigid will have this tower reduced to rubble."

"Hopefully not with us still in it," Nerissa groaned with a smile, idly tracing the emerald scales scattered across Zale's abdomen before she realized what she was doing. "You know, green suits you."

"Oh? Like what ye see, lass?" His hand lifted, fingers sliding to the back of her neck, thumb tracing small circles along her jaw. He leaned in, his lips brushing hers as she lowered her eyelids, heart racing.

Damarion loudly cleared his throat.

Nerissa stiffened, heat rushing to her face as she pulled back as much as Zale's arms would allow. She refused to meet Damarion's eyes. Of all the ways to die, she hadn't expected embarrassment to be one of them.

"Well," Zale gave a nervous laugh. "This is awkward."

"Indeed," Damarion narrowed his eyes at him. "I should be asking what your intentions are with my surrogate daughter."

"Didaskon…" Nerissa started but halted as he held up a hand.

"I should also be telling my son he couldn't have chosen better." His eyes softened a fraction, and Nerissa let out the breath she had been holding.

"But for the love of Poseidon," Damarion looked upward in exasperation. "Can you at least wait until I am not present? A merman can only handle so much melodrama in one day."

Zale dipped his head solemnly. "Yes, sir."

Nerissa could only bury her face in Zale's chest as she felt heat rise to her cheeks yet again. The sooner the crew arrived, the better.

As if on cue, a thunderous *boom* shook the chamber, sending dust and pebbles cascading from the arched ceiling.

All three heads snapped up in unison.

"That's cannon fire," Zale grinned.

Another blast answered, and this time the whole tower seemed to tilt.

Chunks of debris rained from above, thudding across the floor. One jagged piece crashed straight into the tank, shattering the surface tension in a geyser of foam. Nerissa barely had time to gasp before Zale yanked her aside. The stone plunged past where she'd been floating and sank to the bottom, missing her by inches.

"*Moirai*—" she breathed, eyes wide.

Before either of them could recover, the heavy door slammed open. Alpheus swept in, flanked by a half dozen of his masked men, his expression tight with fury.

"Retrieve the girl," he snapped, voice slicing through the noise. "Our timetable just shortened."

The men fanned out, wielding long metal poles tipped with metal hooks.

Nerissa's tail flicked in alarm as Zale shifted to put himself between her and the advancing men. Damarion moved in tandem, sweeping forward until the two of them formed a wall between her and the hooks.

The first hook slashed down through the surface. Zale deflected it with his arm, metal screeching against scale. Another came from the right, Damarion seized the pole mid-strike and yanked hard, pulling the man off balance. He toppled headfirst into the tank, breaking the surface with a splash. Damarion's fist met him halfway. The man's body went limp, sinking quickly.

Another hook darted toward Zale's side; he twisted, slicing through the shaft with one sharp sweep of his fin. The guard recoiled with a cry, clutching the splintered end.

The remaining five thrust their poles into the water in random chaos. Hooks skimmed past Nerissa's tail, snagging strands of her hair, tearing fabric from her sleeve. Adrenaline surged through her limbs, finally beginning to shake off the lingering effects of the sedative. She gripped one of the poles and wrenched it free from its owner's grip. Spinning it the opposite way, she aimed the hook at the man's ankle and pulled hard, knocking him off his feet.

Damarion had been pinned by three men, lashing his tail violently to no avail.

"Persistent bastards," Zale spat, catching one hook and wrenching it down hard enough to snap the tip. Another hook caught him across the jaw, sending him spinning into the glass wall with a trail of blood spiraling from his mouth.

Nerissa lunged forward to help but was suddenly covered with a heavy net that tangled around her arms and tail. She twisted, trying to free herself by slicing at random with her forearm fins. The remaining men dragged her to the surface, hauling the net onto dry ground as she struggled.

Alpheus's voice cut through the chaos. "Careful now," he said. "We still need her intact."

With a primal yell, Nerissa sliced through the net, swiping at the men around her. Her eyes locked onto Zale's, wild with fury and helplessness, until the guards forced her down onto her back. Her tail slapped against the cold floor beneath her with a sickening thud. Pain jolted through her ribs as her chest seized.

Her gills flared wide, starving. She fought the instinct to drag in air that would choke her. Her fingers clawed at the slick stone, seeking something, anything, to use to defend herself.

Behind her, Zale's yell rattled the tank, his fists pounding the glass over and over again.

"My, my," Alpheus drawled, circling closer. His voice dipped. "She means something to you." His sharp smile cut toward Zale. "How touching. How *human*."

Zale's voice was low and dangerous. "Let. Her. Go."

Alpheus stooped then, low enough that the torches threw long shadows across his face. He reached out with a gloved hand and closed his fingers beneath Nerissa's chin, cold as the stone beneath her. When he tipped her face towards him, the faint chemical tang of his clothes washed over her, making her feel sick to her stomach. She recoiled as his thumb traced the line of her jaw as if cataloguing a specimen. If she only had her daggers, she would gut him right here and now.

"Do you know what it is to watch the one you love skewered through the heart by a siren's spear? To stand powerless as her blood runs into the sand, knowing you will never save her?" He shoved Nerissa back to the ground with disdain. "No. Of course you don't. None of you will ever understand that pain."

So his whole crusade against sirens is a revenge story, Nerissa thought, vision spotting.

"Touch her again," Zale ground out, every word edged with steel, "and I will kill you."

Alpheus only tilted his head, amused, as though Zale were a boy puffing out his chest. "Ah. There it is. The hybrid bares his teeth." He clicked his tongue, mock disappointment curving his smile. "You sound so very much like your father."

Nerissa squeezed her eyes shut as every nerve in her body screamed for air. She forced herself to focus inward, commanding her body to shift, to at *least* shift from gills to lungs, but the sedative still had her trapped inside her own skin.

The burning in her chest was growing unbearable.

Darkness was closing in when something sharp stung her neck. Adrenaline snapped her body taut, her back bowing off the stone, muscles locking as if she'd been struck by lightning.

Then her tail began tearing into two, too quickly, too unnaturally. She clawed at the stone as her lower half reshaped itself with the sickening snap of ligaments and bone, scales burning away from her skin in a cascade that felt like molten glass being scraped from her flesh. Her fins shivered before retracting into her spine and arms with a final, stinging sensation.

Her gills clamped shut, every nerve screaming as water turned useless in her lungs. She rolled to her side, choking, coughing up the liquid. Then her chest heaved in panic, until air finally flooded down her throat in a single, brutal gulp.

Then she winced at the pressure of Alpheus's fingers at her throat. Through the ringing in her ears, his voice intruded, cold and clinical. "Pulse accelerated. Erratic."

You don't say, rhypós.

"Pupil dilation...full." He leaned closer. "Respiration—labored, inconsistent. Body temperature falling, tremors present."

Nerissa flinched as his shadow loomed over her. "A successful reversal," he concluded softly. "Repeatable. Promising."

A strangled groan broke loose before she could silence it. Her whole body shuddered with lingering muscle spasms.

Alpheus plucked a device from the worktable. The faint swirl of green vapor curling within its familiar lantern-like glass chamber. Nerissa recognized it. When she followed him into the corridor just outside Calliope's chambers…was that how he did it?

His voice carried, smooth and sure, pitched for the men trapped in the water. "A bit of pheromones, a touch of paralytic, and my little assassin will heed when called. All that loyalty, all that training…it would be a shame to waste it."

"You snake, you'll regret this!" Zale's roar cracked the chamber, fierce and desperate.

Alpheus only smiled as he twisted the valve. A hiss filled the chamber, subtle and sinister. The mist poured out in soft ribbons, winding across the floor, curling toward Nerissa.

She tried to hold her breath, tried to twist away as she propped herself up onto her elbows. But she couldn't move—the fog wrapped around her, thick and insistent, seeping into her lungs with each ragged inhale.

Coldness spread instantly, drowning her own thoughts as her vision swam.

No, not again.

Alpheus's voice drifted through the haze. "Breathe deeply, my dear. That's it. Let it settle."

Her pulse pounded in her ears. The dungeon walls wavered, the torchlight bleeding into streaks of gold. Something inside her chest fluttered—not her heart, something deeper. A tremor, a hum, rising beneath her skin like a thousand tiny strings pulled taut.

Alpheus's cane tapped once against the stone, sharp as a command. "You will kill King Leander," he said softly, almost tenderly. "And anyone who dares step in your way."

Her mind screamed, clawing against the fog.

No.

No, I won't. Focus, Nerissa. Focus on Zale.

She clung to the sound of him—muffled shouts, fists slamming against the glass. Through the blur of green and blue, she could just make out his face above the water, eyes wild with rage.

Do not listen to Alpheus. Listen to Zale. Listen to yourself.

But her lips stayed closed. Her body remained utterly still beneath Alpheus's hand.

Slowly, against her will, she rose. Legs trembling but steady enough. Her eyes hazily focused on the door that Alpheus held open.

Somewhere in the back of her skull, her mind screamed itself raw, but the sound never reached her throat.

Alpheus turned toward the stairs, smiling as though escorting a favored student. "That's it," he murmured. "Steady now. One foot, then the other."

He pressed her daggers into her clammy hands. "Your weapons, my dear."

Her fingers closed around the hilts without her consent.

Zale's voice thundered against the glass. "Nerissa! Fight it—!"

The words reached her like echoes through deep water. She wanted to answer—to look back, to see him—but her head wouldn't turn. Her feet moved instead, slow and obedient, following Alpheus toward the staircase.

Every step felt like betrayal as she climbed the stairs, the dungeon door sealing the chamber behind them.

Zale

He slammed his hands onto the stone floor just above the tank, about to haul himself out of the water, when a hand clasped him by the shoulder and pulled him roughly back under.

"No, what are you doing? We have to stop her!" Zale whirled on Damarion, chest heaving in barely restrained fury.

"You'll only suffocate if you leave this tank in your current form," Damarion crossed his arms, expression stern. "You'll be no use to her then."

He knew that, of course he knew that. But he couldn't stand doing *nothing.*

Zale raked his hands through his hair, frustrated at the feeling of uselessness that washed over him. Then he felt Damarion's hand on his arm, grounding.

"I know you want to go after her, but we need a plan first. Rushing in is a graveyard for good intentions."

"Rushing in is what I do best," Zale shook his head with a rueful smile. "I've survived on instinct my whole life."

"That man is no brute without a brain." Damarion's voice was flat. "He thinks. He's always one step ahead. Use your head, or you won't get a chance to use your sword."

Zale's tail flicked with agitation. "We don't have time for that! Nerissa's already hunting for Leander. I need to find her before she does somethin' she'll regret."

"And?" Damarion's stare was patient and hard. "What then? What is the plan?"

"Distract her from Leander for as long as it takes. Until whatever that snake just did to her wears off," he answered confidently.

"She would kill you in less than sixty seconds," Damarion said simply.

"We've sparred before…I can handle myself."

He was reasonably confident that he could stay alive long enough, at least. But that wouldn't matter if he couldn't get out of this damned tank. If he could just get his legs back…

"Alright," Zale said suddenly. "How do I do it?"

Damarion blinked. "Do what?"

"Shift." The word came out sharper than intended. "Any plan we come up with won't mean a thing if we're stuck with tails."

Damarion's mouth twitched in something between patience and pity. "It's not really something that can be taught. It's in your blood. But I'd wager that the serum Alpheus injected you with is preventing the change. He wouldn't risk leaving us unguarded otherwise."

"Then let's find out," Zale said, bracing his palms against the wall of the tank. He shut his eyes and tried to remember what it felt like to be human, the weight of his boots, the pull of gravity, the feeling of two separate limbs to walk with. He willed his tail to reform, to split into his legs, like he had seen Nerissa do.

Nothing.

Just gills, scales, and fins.

Zale's jaw clenched. "Well. Either I'm doing it wrong, or your hunch was right."

Damarion gave a grave nod. "Likely both."

Zale shot him a glare. "You're really inspirational, you know that?"

"Someone has to be realistic," Damarion replied evenly. "For now, we wait. If that crew of yours has breached the tower, then we shouldn't have to wait much longer."

"Waiting's never been my strong suit," Zale muttered. His tail flicked irritably against the tank wall, sending ripples through the water.

"I gathered as much," Damarion said dryly. Then, quieter, "This is not how I envisioned we might meet."

Zale huffed a humorless laugh. "Yeah, me neither. Figured my parents' identities would forever remain a mystery." He glanced toward Damarion again. "Is it true then? Was I…a mistake?"

Damarion's gaze lingered on him, a mix of pride and regret flickering in his eyes. "Absolutely not," he said firmly. "Unexpected, certainly, but not a mistake."

Zale felt the tiniest weight lift from the ache in his chest. That was something, at least. "Do you know why my mother tried to hide me?"

Damarion drew a slow breath, as though choosing each word with care. "Your mother and I were never meant to be together. We had to meet in secret or risk severe political fallout." His eyes softened, tracing the shell that floated against Zale's chest. "I gave her that as a gift. She wanted to run away, but I was bound by duty. I didn't know she was with child." He paused, voice roughening. "She must have kept you hidden to protect you. Tensions between our kingdoms were still volatile. If anyone had discovered the truth…" He shook his head. "She did what she had to do."

Zale swallowed hard, his fingers brushing the edge of the pendant. "What was she like?"

Damarion's expression eased into something gentler. "Curious. Fiery. Unstoppable." A faint, wistful smile ghosted across his face. "She didn't fear the merfolk like most of the court did. Her hunger for knowledge about Nautalia was insatiable. She wanted to understand the sea as if it were a language she could learn."

He looked back at Zale, studying him for a long, quiet moment. "You have her eyes, you know." His gaze flicked toward the shell at Zale's chest. "That's why I chose that stone for her pendant. It matched her eyes."

Zale touched the stone absently, thumb tracing its smooth edge. No longer a mystery, but a link to his past.

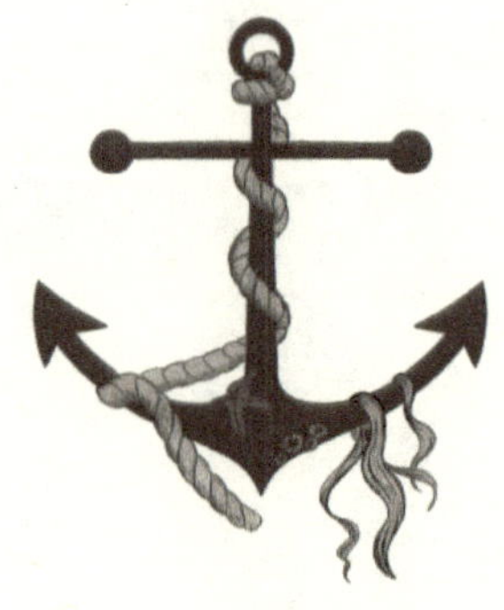

CHAPTER 46

THE CAVALRY

Bran

The *Black Serpent* pitched and rolled with each blast, her cannons thundering louder than the storm brewing in the clouds. Smoke billowed around the rigging, thick and acrid, drifting toward the cliffs where the castle loomed like a wounded beast. Chunks of stone sheared loose with every hit, crashing into the surf below.

"Again!" Cormac barked.

Bran followed his orders with repetitive actions—load, aim, fire, repeat. His hands were black with powder, palms raw. "More!" he shouted. "We need more powder. Eon, fetch another—"

Cormac looked over, eyes grim and knowing.

Bran forced a grin that didn't fool either of them. "Habit," he muttered. "Still expectin' him to come runnin'."

Cormac grunted, not unkindly. "Ye're not the only one, lad."

Bran swallowed hard and turned back to his work, focusing on the rhythm, the thunder of the cannon, the sting of smoke in his lungs, the bruise blooming on his shoulder from recoil. Anything to drown out the silence where Eon's laughter should've been.

He'd watched Zale disappear up the road that morning, following the trail of Nerissa's blood like a hound on the scent. Bran had wanted to go with him, but someone had to alert the crew. Now, as the tower shuddered with each impact, he prayed that Zale had been right about where she'd been taken.

Or else they were attacking the royal castle completely unprovoked.

Another shot landed home. The base of the cliff erupted in smoke and dust, a plume of fire curling from the dungeon's side.

"Direct hit!" Brigid shouted over the chaos.

Bran shielded his eyes against the haze, heart hammering. The upper levels of the tower were bleeding smoke now, its stonework cracked and crumbling.

Brigid's shout rose from the helm. "Cap'n wants the guns cooled! We're movin' in!"

Cormac grinned, fierce as a storm. "Ye heard the lass!"

Bran grabbed his cutlass from the rack, sliding it into its scabbard at his hip. "Aye," he said. "Let's bring in the cavalry!"

The ship swung broadside to the cliffs, her hull groaning as she rode the shallows. The crew moved as one to haul in the sails and prepare the boats.

"Drop anchor!" Nestor bellowed.

The chain screamed over the side, the ship lurching as the anchor bit into packed sand.

"Lower the skiffs!" Brigid shouted from the rail. "Cormac, Bran—follow the Cap'n! Roan, Ma Wen—with me!"

Bran vaulted the rail, landing in the first skiff with a splash. Cormac followed, grunting as he steadied the hull, while Nestor descended last, cutlass already in hand.

"Heave hard," Nestor ordered. "We breach at the base of that tower."

Bran and Cormac pulled together, oars biting into the surf. Behind them, Brigid's skiff hit the water, Ma Wen and Roan boarding in silence. The sea boiled beneath cannon smoke, waves flashing orange from the fires chewing through the cliffside.

"Hold steady," Nestor called. "There's a breach—halfway up from the rocks!"

Bran's arms burned, but he didn't slow. Each pull brought them closer to the tower's broken face, where firelight flickered through a gaping wound in the masonry.

"Out!" Nestor barked as the skiff slammed into sand.

They splashed into the shallows, hauling the two boats higher ashore.

"Bran, left flank!" Brigid shouted, pistol already drawn. "Cormac, ye're on powder—keep those reloads comin'!"

Roan checked his flintlock as Ma Wen unsheathed his thin sword in one smooth, whispering motion.

"Move!" Nestor's voice cut through the din. "Push to the tower!"

They charged up the sand, scaling the rubble toward the smoking breach.

A line of Astyran guards waited just inside, their armor blackened with soot, faces smeared with grime and confusion. Muskets leveled, they shouted over the roar of the surf.

“Hold fire! Identify yourselves!”

Nestor raised his hand, stepping forward into the smoke. “Captain Nestor of the *Black Serpent!* One of ours was taken prisoner without cause. We’re not here for your king!”

The lead guard hesitated, eyes narrowing. “A likely story. You’ve been bombarding the fortress for an hour!”

“Aye,” Nestor shot back. “Because we’ve men trapped inside and no one answered our signals!”

The guard’s jaw tightened. “Stand down, pirate, or we’ll—”

He never finished.

The man’s pistol came up, and Brigid fired first. The shot struck his shoulder, spinning him sideways and knocking him flat. The other guards hesitated, startled, but didn’t fire.

“Next man lifts a weapon,” Brigid warned, “an’ I’ll aim higher.”

Nestor stepped past her, voice like steel. “We’re done talkin’. Stand aside if ye value your lives.”

The remaining guards faltered, exchanging uncertain glances. The confusion in their eyes was real—they didn’t know what was happening below any more than the pirates did. One finally lowered his musket, stepping back.

“Down the hall,” he said, breathless. “Whatever you’re looking for, it’s under the old cells. But gods help you if you go there.”

Nestor nodded once. "We'll take our chances."

He motioned to his crew. "Move."

They pressed forward, leaving the wounded guard groaning in the rubble. The corridor was narrow and slick, torches guttering low in their brackets.

Brigid kept one hand on the wall as they advanced, her boots echoing off the steps spiraling downward. "This place feels cursed," she muttered.

"Keep your heads," Nestor said, scanning the shadows ahead. "Eyes sharp. We find Zale and Nerissa, and we get out."

Bran swallowed, pulse drumming in his ears. He could hear faint dripping somewhere below, steady as a heartbeat.

Cormac spat on the ground. "I dinnae like this place."

"No one does," Nestor said quietly. "Which means we're close."

They descended deeper, the air growing cooler, the torches thinning until only the glow of distant firelight marked the way ahead.

The stairwell opened into a wide stone corridor lined with rusted sconces and the faint shimmer of greenish light reflecting off glass. The air was colder here, stale and thick with brine. Bran slowed as his boots splashed into standing water, the echoes of their steps whispering down the passage.

"What in the hells is this place?" Bran muttered.

"No place for the livin', that's for certain," Cormac said grimly.

The room beyond stretched cavernous and low, carved directly into the bedrock. Tables stood in uneven rows, most overturned or half-buried in debris. The stench hit them first—salt and rot and something sweet beneath it, like fruit left too long in the sun.

Ma Wen stopped short. His expression didn't change, but his knuckles whitened around his sword hilt.

Brigid raised her pistol, eyes scanning the shadows. "There's...tanks," she said quietly.

The tanks scattered across the walls. Some had shattered, their contents spilled across the floor in slick, green puddles. Others remained intact, filled with cloudy fluid that distorted the shapes within.

Preserved bodies floated half-suspended—tails and scales glimmering faintly beneath the haze, pale faces turned toward the glass.

Bran's stomach lurched. He'd seen death before, but not like this.

"Saints save us…" Cormac whispered. "They're merfolk."

Nestor's jaw hardened. "Keep your weapons ready. Whatever this is, we're not lingerin'."

Roan drifted to one of the tables. He brushed aside a waterlogged parchment, squinting down at the spidery handwriting, then at a series of sketches—anatomical drawings of lungs, gills, and the slow degradation of muscle over time.

His features turned grim. "This isn't preservation," he said quietly. "It's dissection. He was studying them, taking them apart, piece by piece."

Bran looked over his shoulder at the nearest jar—a glass cylinder holding what could only be a heart, its veins trailing like seaweed. His chest clenched. "Why would anyone—"

Brigid's voice cut him off sharply. "Captain."

She was standing near the far wall, her torch raised. On the wall hung several half-finished sketches. Cross-sections of merfolk anatomy beside notes written in a precise, elegant hand. Words like *withdrawal threshold* and *hybrid stability* leapt out from the pages.

Nestor scanned the room once more, then exhaled slowly. "There's no one alive up here. We keep movin'. Down another level."

Brigid nodded once. "Aye. Before I lose me breakfast."

As they descended, the air somehow got even colder, and the drip of water increased. Bran didn't get scared easily, but this place felt unnatural, wrong.

The stairwell opened into a wide stone chamber, lit by the flicker of a single lantern. At the center of the chamber, the floor dropped away into a large, sunken pool. Chains rose from the corners, attached to the ceiling. It looked like a prison.

Bran's pistol came up automatically. "Cap'n?"

Nestor motioned for Bran to flank him as they approached the water. The only sound was the creak of settling rubble.

Bran edged near the pool, trying to peer through the murky surface.

A ripple spread across the water as a head appeared.

"Holy—!" Bran threw his gun at it in a panic.

"Bloody hell, seriously?" Came a disgruntled, but very familiar voice.

Bran froze for a beat, then barked out a disbelieving laugh. "Zale? Saints above, you're—"

The words died as he processed the sight before him.

Where Zale's legs should've been, a long fish tail swayed beneath the surface instead.

Bran's mouth fell open. "What in the seven hells…" He blinked, then shot a look at the others. "This what happens when you kiss a mermaid?"

Even Cormac couldn't stop a dry chuckle. "Well, I'll be damned."

Zale scowled faintly, rubbing the lump that had already begun to swell on his temple. "Really? That's your first question?"

Bran grinned. "Aye. Because I don't remember you mentionin' the part where you're half bloody *fish*."

Zale rolled his eyes at Bran as Nestor crouched at the tank's edge. "Ye all right, lad?"

He nodded once. "I'll live."

"Where's Nerissa?" Brigid asked, eyes darting around the chamber.

Zale's gaze hardened. He looked toward the stairwell, toward the light bleeding faintly from above. "She's gone after the king," he said quietly. "Alpheus made her—he's controlling her somehow."

Nestor's brow furrowed. "The apothecary?"

Zale nodded. "He's a traitor to Astyra."

The captain's tone sharpened. "Right. Well, first things first. Let's get ye outta there."

"So...that may be a problem." Zale rubbed the back of his neck. "I don't know how to shift back. I didn't even *mean* to turn into this."

"Don't look at me," Bran said. "I'm not carryin' you."

Before Zale could respond, something rippled behind him. Another figure surfaced, eerily similar in build and face.

Bran yelped, stumbling back and nearly tripping over a broken stone. "There's *two* of them?!"

Zale rolled his eyes. "I'll explain later. He's with us."

The older merman lifted his head, eyes sharply assessing as he surveyed the armed crew surrounding the tank. "Indeed," he said. "There might be some serum left on one of those tables. Alpheus used it on Nerissa to force the shift into human form. It won't be pleasant." His gaze flicked toward Zale. "But it's our only way out of here."

Roan stepped forward at once. "On it."

He began sifting through the cluttered tables, brushing aside shattered glass and scattered parchment. "What am I looking for?"

"Golden vials," Damarion said.

Roan nodded and kept searching, eyes scanning the wreckage until a glimmer caught his attention. Half-buried beneath a collapsed shelf, several small vials rolled against one another, their contents glinting gold in the dim light.

"Got it," he muttered, retrieving two and drawing the liquid carefully into syringes. He crossed the room and knelt at the edge of the tank, holding them out. "Two doses. You're sure about this?"

Damarion took one without hesitation. "There's no other way."

Zale, however, stared at the syringe in his hand, expression twisting. "I uh…don't think I can inject it myself."

Roan sighed. "Right, then. I'll do it."

"Wait," Damarion said, and before anyone could stop him, he dove beneath the surface.

Bran stepped back quickly, half expecting another merman to appear. "Please tell me there aren't *three* of—"

He cut off when Damarion resurfaced, a pair of trousers clutched in one hand. "Taken from one of the guards," he explained matter-of-factly, passing them to Zale. "You'll want these."

Zale blinked at him, then managed a hoarse laugh. "Aye. Good lookin' out."

Without another word, Damarion plunged the needle into his arm. Roan followed suit, driving the second syringe into Zale's bicep.

The reaction was immediate. Both men arched with a strangled sound, water sloshing around them. Their tails convulsed, scales shifting in a violent cascade as their bodies fought the transformation.

Bran flinched back as the emerald sheen dulled to flesh. Zale gasped, gripping the edge of the tank until his knuckles whitened, his breathing ragged and uneven.

Then it was done. Two men floated where moments ago there had been merfolk.

"Saints above," Cormac breathed. "That's…unnatural."

"Tell me about it," Zale coughed, dragging on the trousers before hauling himself onto the stone floor. He sat there for a moment, breathing hard, then spotted his discarded boots near the debris. He shoved the boots on, grimacing as the leather clung to his wet ankles. His gaze fell to his sword, glinting faintly beneath the rubble. He gathered up his belt and scabbard from the shredded pile of fabric that used to be his pants.

"Remind me to never do that again."

Bran smirked. "Trust me, no one wants a repeat performance."

Zale shot him a look, then swung a tired fist into Bran's shoulder. It was more a shove than a punch, but it got the point across.

"Whatever," he rasped. "We need to find Nerissa."

Damarion pulled himself out of the water next, armor and tunic dripping. "Let's pray we are not too late."

Zale

Nestor led the way, cutlass drawn, while Brigid followed close behind, hair damp and wild from the humidity of the dungeons below. Bran kept pace beside Zale, glancing at him every few steps like he still couldn't quite believe what he'd seen. Ma Wen, Cormac, and Roan brought up the rear.

"I swear," Bran muttered under his breath, "if you sprout fins again mid-fight, I'm leavin' you for the gulls."

"Not how it works," Zale said tightly, scanning the next corner. His throat still burned from the serum. Every breath felt strange, too dry, too shallow, but he pushed onward.

They burst through a set of double doors and into one of the main corridors of the castle, nearly colliding with a line of Astyran guards forming across the hall.

"Hold!" their captain barked, raising his sword. "Drop your weapons!"

Bran groaned. "Not again."

The pirates halted, the air between both sides thick with distrust. The guards' armor was scorched from the bombardment; none of them looked eager, but they were terrified enough to be dangerous.

Nestor stepped forward, voice calm but commanding. "We don't want any trouble. One of ours was taken; experimented on down below. We're not your enemy."

The captain's jaw tightened. "You bombarded the royal fortress."

"Only because it took that much to break through!" Brigid snapped. "Ye've got devils in yer dungeon wearin' yer crest and ye're arguin' semantics?"

The guard hesitated, confusion flickering across his soot-streaked face. "What are you talking ab—"

A second wave of guards rounded the far corner, weapons drawn.

"Right," Nestor muttered. "So much for diplomacy."

One of the guards panicked and fired his musket. The round ricocheted off the wall. That was all it took.

Steel clashed, pistols fired, and the corridor filled with smoke. Zale dove forward, intercepting a blade meant for Brigid, their swords shrieking against one another. His muscles still burned from shifting twice, his balance not quite right.

He parried, swung, missed by inches. The guard recovered faster than expected, lunging for Zale's chest.

The blade caught the light, arcing toward him, and was knocked aside with a burst of sparks.

Damarion stood between them, spear gripped in both hands, the weapon's haft braced against his forearm. He shoved the guard back. "Keep your focus," he said without looking at Zale. "You're no good to her dead."

Zale could see where Nerissa got her people skills from. "Right." He adjusted his grip and swung low, disarming the guard without landing a killing blow.

"Remember!" Damarion barked as he pivoted to deflect another strike. "No deaths. They don't know the truth—don't make them martyrs!"

Brigid parried a halberd with a sharp curse. "Ye think we're tryin'?"

"Just making sure," Damarion growled, driving the butt of his spear into an armored gut.

Zale ducked under a swing, rammed his shoulder into a guard's chest, and knocked the man clean off his feet.

"Zale!" Nestor's voice cut through the noise. "We'll hold the line—give you some time. Go find her!"

Bran shoved another guard aside and shouted, "You heard the man! Before she does somethin' she can't take back!"

Zale hesitated only a for a moment, then turned and ran, boots pounding across the flagstones.

Nerissa's face burned in his mind, glassy-eyed and unfocused under Alpheus's control. His stomach twisted as the memory surfaced: her body convulsing on the stone floor, the sound of her choking breath, the helplessness as Alpheus made him watch.

He would not let her kill for that snake again. Even if it cost him his life.

CHAPTER 47

FINISH IT

Nerissa

Her bare feet whispered over the stone floor as she moved. Morning light poured through a high window, pale and golden, making the corridor feel too bright for what she carried. The castle halls stretched silently before her; torch sconces guttered with smoke.

Stop.

Her voice, her true voice, echoed inside her skull.

Stop, Nerissa. Think. Calliope will never forgive you if you do this.

But another voice slid in behind it, smooth and venomous.

Calliope already despises you. You killed her father-in-law. What's one more body on your hands? One more king? He's just a human, after all.

Her pace quickened, though her fists clenched at her sides.

He's not one of them. Just a man caught in a web more complicated than he realizes. A good man. Zale is human too. And I could never–

The cynical voice laughed, sharp and cruel.

Ah yes, Zale. Half-blood, half-broken. Hardly counts as human, does he?

Her stomach twisted.

The crew, her rational voice tried again, louder now. *Bran, Brigid, Nestor, all of them—they're human. And I trust them with my life.*

Trusted, the sneering voice corrected. *Past tense. They'll be loyal until they see you for what you are—a king killer. Do you really think they'll keep you once they've had time to let that truth rot in their mouths?*

She faltered, one hand brushing the cold stone wall as she forced her breathing to steady.

The cynical voice pressed in closer, suffocating.

You know what they see now when they look at you? A blade. A weapon. Nothing more. And weapons are discarded when they dull.

Her jaw clenched.

No, I am not—

Yes, the other voice hissed. *You are. And now you will do what you were made for. Exact justice. For your parents. For everything these humans stole from you.*

A patrol rounded the corner ahead. Two guards, eyes narrowing at the sight of her blades. One shouted, fumbling for his sword.

"Strike fast," Alpheus's voice purred in her ear, curling like smoke. "Before they sound the alarm."

Her body lunged before her mind could stop it. The first went down in a spray of red, her dagger carving a clean line across his throat. The second's blade barely cleared its sheath before she slammed him against the wall, steel plunging between his ribs. His gasp choked off into silence as he slumped downward, blood trailing from his mouth.

Her stomach lurched, bile rising in her throat.

Stop. Nerae, stop. They were innocent.

But her hands moved anyway, wiping her blades clean against the dead man's tabard, the cynical voice savoring each step, before pushing onward.

See how easy it is? They fall like paper, one by one. This is what you were made for.

Her grip shook around the daggers. "I am not—" she whispered, voice strangled, but her feet carried her forward anyway, with Alpheus following close behind.

The next turn brought two more guards, shouting an alarm. She spun low, daggers flashing. One blade drove up through a gap in armor, another ripped across a jaw. Their bodies collapsed in a wet heap behind her.

Her breath came fast, uneven, her pulse deafening in her ears. Her voice shrieked inside her, fighting to be heard.

This isn't me. I don't want this.

Alpheus's laugh slithered through her skull, as if he were in her head too. *What you want is irrelevant. I am your will. You obey.*

Ahead, the double doors of the prince's study loomed, carved with the sigil of the crown. She could faintly hear Leander and Calliope inside, discussing the treaty.

Her hand hovered over the gilded handle, trembling violently. Every nerve screamed in conflict, her breath hitching as the two voices inside her battled like sharks.

Open it.

Don't.

Justice demands it.

Calliope will never forgive you.

She's already forsaken you.

Her fingers tightened. Sweat slicked her palm, mingling with blood from her gash, but she forced the doors wide open. The hinges moaned and the bright room stirred.

Leander and Calliope were bent over his desk, voices low with the careful cadence of negotiation. The treaty lay spread between them, official and absurdly ordinary in the face of what waited at the doorway.

Calliope's head rose first; color drained from her face. "Nerissa?" she breathed, bewilderment and alarm in one sharp note. "Tides—Nerissa!"

The sneering voice in her head laughed, coiling tighter.

See how she fears you now? The princess whom you served loyally for years, and how did she repay you? She condemned you. Told you she never wanted to see you again. Cast you out like a soldier gone rogue. Look how she trembles now.

Calliope covered her mouth as the quill slipped from her fingers.

Nerissa stepped forward.

A sword barred her path.

Kaelen stood just inside the doorway, blade leveled, platinum hair a disordered halo in the sun. "I don't know what's gotten into you," he said, voice low and ringing. "But if you mean harm, I will stop you."

For a heartbeat, Nerissa froze, caught between the daggers in her hands and the shield in his stance.

Inside her head, the war raged louder.

Strike him down.

No—stop—

He's just another person in your way.

He's only protecting Callie.

Her body moved before her mind could stop it. She lunged at Kaelen, daggers catching the sunlight as they swept toward his chest.

He parried cleanly, the ring of steel sharp in the still chamber.

"Nerissa, stop!" His blade locked against hers, holding her back. "You don't want to do this!"

But her arms drove forward with unnatural strength, teeth gritted as the pheromone's command screamed louder than her own will. Sparks hissed as their blades scraped and broke apart, and she came at him again, slashing low then high, desperate to get past him.

Behind Kaelen, through the study's open arch, Leander scrambled to his feet, hastily shoving treaty scrolls aside. He snatched a ceremonial dirk from a stand near the desk; it was more symbol than weapon, but he would not be left unarmed. "I'll—" he started, voice thin.

"Get Calliope out," Kaelen barked without breaking his guard. "Now!" He swung his sword, forcing Nerissa back a step. "Take her beyond the east galleries!" he ordered. "Move!"

Calliope seized Leander's sleeve and they stumbled from the room, terrified and desperate.

Nerissa snarled as they slipped from view.

Your quarry is escaping—kill him, kill them all.

Kaelen's sword rose again to hold her, steady and merciful. "If I must fight you, I will. But I will not let you harm them."

"Give me a reason, Kaelen." Nerissa spun her daggers, not sure if the words came from herself or not. The sight of him ignited violent thoughts under normal conditions, let alone with Alpheus's command to kill.

Their blades rang and flashed down the short corridor outside the study. She feinted, lunged, twisted, but Kaelen refused to commit to a killing blow. He blocked, gave ground, then pushed forward to pin her away from the door.

For a breath his guard wavered. She seized the opening.

Her blade sank into his ribs without hesitation. He staggered with a gasp, the color draining from his face as he dropped to one knee. Nerissa spun with a vicious kick that slammed into his chest. He went down hard; the sword clattered from his grip.

"Stay down," she hissed.

Nerissa's chest heaved. Her grip on the daggers tightened as she turned sharply, eyes snapping toward the corridor ahead. Calliope's terrified cry echoed faintly down the hall. Leander's hurried footsteps dragged with hers. They hadn't gotten far.

Her body tensed to pursue.

Then she heard soft applause from the shadows.

"You're doing beautifully."

Alpheus glided into the light, cane tapping the stone with slow, measured clicks. His smile was serene in that way that made every hair on her neck bristle; his eyes drank in the sight of her bloodied blades and Kaelen's crumpled form with cold approval. He inclined his head toward the study's open arch.

"Now, girl. Finish it."

Her feet carried her, faster, faster down the corridor. Leander and Calliope stumbled, cornered near a stairwell; their faces were stark with terror. Nerissa lifted her daggers, muscles coiled for the strike—

—and the world tipped as something struck her from the side.

Air burst from her lungs as she hit the stone. Her daggers clattered across the floor, spinning away in a ringing scatter. For a dizzying moment the chamber tilted, and she clawed at the floor to steady herself, shaking to clear the fog.

Her gaze snapped up.

Zale. Human again.

He stood above her, sword drawn, torn shirt barely hanging on to his shoulders. Exhaustion and blood marked him, but his stance was immovable.

Something inside her twisted, a raw, immediate ache of relief tangled with terror.

Not him. Please, not him.

He stands in your way. Remove him. End him, and nothing will stop you.

"Zale...please," she barely managed to get the words out. She clutched her head as if to wrench the whispering poison free. Staggering back to her feet, she snatched her daggers from the floor. Her grip trembled.

"Get out of my way."

He didn't; instead, he stepped forward and clamped his hands down on her shoulders, firm and careful. His touch felt like a tether through the fog. The low timbre of his voice was threaded with urgency. "This is what Alpheus wants, Nerissa. Ye hear me? This is his game. Don't give him what he wants."

Her hands shook. Her arms strained against his hold; the fog in her mind drowning out his words. The command surged again.

This is what you want, the voice hissed, forcing her forward like a marionette.

She shoved him away and spun toward the royals. Calliope screamed as Nerissa lunged, aiming for Leander's heart.

But Zale was faster. His sword met her blades in a ringing crash of steel, sparks scattering in the torchlight.

The voice rose in a furious shriek.

He's in your way. Remove him. Now.

Her own voice fought back, weaker, fading.

No…no, I won't…

But the daggers kept moving with vicious precision, striking high, then low, feinting, lunging, twisting toward his throat. Every blow felt like someone else's hand guiding hers as Alpheus pulled her strings.

And Zale blocked every strike. His blade moved swift and sure but never struck to harm. Always turning her aside, always stepping back just far enough to avoid her edge.

"You're stronger than this!" he shouted, voice raw. "Fight it, Nerissa!"

"I can't!" she cried out. Her blades whirled again, faster, harder, screaming metal against his cutlass. Her muscles burned, her vision swam, but still she drove forward.

Remove him. He is in your way. Kill him. KILL. HIM.

No—he's—Zale, please—

He caught her wrists with his free hand, straining to hold her back. Their faces were inches apart, his eyes fierce. "You are stronger than Alpheus. Don't let him win."

Her body betrayed her. A dagger wrenched free and slashed down, carving across his arm. He hissed through his teeth, but his sword came up again in time to parry the second strike.

Nerae, I almost—

You almost cleared your path forward. Stop being so weak and end him.

NO, there must be some other way!

But still her body lunged, still her daggers struck. Each blow came heavier, more frenzied, daggers seeking his heart, his throat, his life.

Zale met every strike with his sword, jaw clenched, teeth bared. He gave no ground but what he had to, parrying desperately, always deflecting, never striking true.

And it was killing her.

Every strike, every block, every time their steel met, she felt herself slipping further. Until there would be nothing left but Zale bleeding at her feet.

From the corridor's shadow Alpheus laughed, cold and delighted. "Futile," he crooned. "Do you see, boy? She is mine. There is only one way to end this." His eyes glittered as the smile curdled. "You'll have to kill her."

He won't do it though. He'd rather die than strike me. But it's the only way…

Their blades locked again, his sword pinning both her daggers in a desperate cross. His voice was hoarse but steady. "I won't hurt ye, Riss."

She snarled, her arms straining against his.

End him. End him now.

He shoved her back a step. His chest rose and fell with ragged breaths, blood dripping down his arm.

Nerissa surged again, faster, harder; sparks leapt between their blades. The corridor shrank to the metronome of steel. She could feel the strings pulling tighter, dragging her forward, forcing her to keep striking at him.

She clocked the way he was beginning to sway on his feet, sword hanging heavy in his hand.

Now's your chance, kill him!

No!

But the pull tightened. Her hands rose. Her daggers gleamed.

Her mind spun. There had to be a way. A loophole.

Kill anyone who gets in your way.

She froze.

What if...I am the one in my way?

Her hands trembled violently. Her gaze locked onto Zale. He would never forgive her for what she was about to do. She choked on the words, barely able to force them out.

"I'm so sorry."

"It's okay, Riss." His jaw set as he shut his eyes, bracing for the final blow.

She spun her daggers once, and her arms swung with deadly precision.

CHAPTER 48

NOT DONE YET

Zale

Calliope's scream ripped through the corridor as Alpheus's cane struck the floor with a sharp crack. "No!"

Zale flinched, bracing for pain that never came. His eyes snapped open.

And his stomach dropped.

Nerissa stood before him, daggers buried deep in her own abdomen. Her chest heaved once, a sharp, broken gasp tearing from her lips. Then the air left her lungs in a long, shuddering exhale. Green blood spilled in dark rivulets down her skirt, dripping onto the stone in slow, sickening patters that echoed in the stillness.

Zale's sword clattered from his numb fingers as he lunged forward, catching her just as her knees buckled. She moaned softly, pain bleeding through every syllable as her body slumped into his arms.

"Riss—*why*?" His voice broke as he lowered them both to the ground. "Why would you *do* that?"

Her lashes fluttered, her breath catching as she forced the words past trembling lips. "…you wouldn't…do it…not that bad…"

Not that bad? Did she not see that she was bleeding out?

Her arms dropped heavily to her sides, fingers slipping from the hilts of her daggers. The blades jutted obscenely from her stomach, blood pulsing slowly around the steel. Her breathing turned quick and shallow.

"Skíon!" came an anguished cry from behind them.

Zale turned in time to see Damarion's spear pointed at Alpheus's chest, pinning the apothecary back against the wall. The older merman's face was stone, cold fury in his eyes.

Alpheus did not flinch. His thin smile only widened. "Too late, Captain," he crooned. "Too late to save her. Even if you were to strike me down this instant, the damage is done. There is no sane voice left in Astyra who would agree to peace with Nautalia. The court bleeds with fear of your kind. The treaty is already ash in the wind."

"You…monster!" Calliope screeched as Leander held her back. "You did this, this is *your* fault!"

Zale sank to the cold floor with Nerissa, then eased her back across his lap, careful—stars, so careful—not to jostle the daggers. Already her skin felt cooler beneath his touch, like the creeping chill of the sea stealing its way into her warmth. His hands shook as he brushed damp strands of hair from her face, every touch a desperate attempt to hold her here, to tether her to him.

"I'm so sorry," he whispered, voice cracking. "I swore to keep you safe—"

Her cloudy eyes found his. "…'s okay." A faint, pained smile tugged at her lips. "...owe me a drink."

An incredulous laugh escaped his throat. "You've got it."

Her hand lifted, fingers trembling as they cupped the edge of his jaw. The touch seared him as he leaned into her palm. Then her hand dropped limply to her side. His heart stopped.

"No, stay with me Riss—" His voice broke into a plea as he gripped her bloody hand. Panic began to rise as he realized he could feel the tension leaving her body.

Her eyes fluttered, glassy and unfocused, morbidly similar to how Eon's looked right before he—

No. Not like this. Not her.

Flashes of memories ripped through his mind like lightning on the horizon. The first time he'd seen her at the Salty Siren—violet eyes sharp as cut glass, lips pressed into that stubborn line as she dismissed him flat-out when he tried to buy her a drink. The day he pulled her from the sea, half-drowned, dress soaked with someone else's blood, fierce even as she fought for survival.

Her face the day she squared off against Nestor and Brigid, sheer determination carved into every line of her body as if daring them to deny her place among their crew. The quiet warmth of her shoulder brushing his on the beach as they sat together, sharing the hollow ache of lost parents.

The sheer terror in his chest when he'd found her seizing on the floor outside the sleeping quarters, cold and unresponsive, only for that terror to give way to shock as she transformed into a siren right before his eyes.

The memory of the storm that had nearly killed him, thrown him into the sea's jaws, but she had risked her secret to save him. He remembered the warmth that had flooded his chest when she finally told him what he meant to her, the spark that shot down his spine when she'd melted into him; fingers tangling in her hair as he held her close, kissing her like he'd never let her go. His first taste of something he hadn't dared to want—

She was shivering now, eyes rolling back.

"Roan!" Zale's voice cracked as he clutched her tighter. "Where is Roan!"

Movement burst into the corridor. Some of the crew had reached the upper level at last, weapons still drawn.

Brigid stopped dead. Her pistol lowered as her gaze fell on the scene before her. The color drained from her face.

"Saints preserve us…" she breathed, voice trembling despite the iron edge. "What in the hells happened t' her?"

Bran froze beside her, eyes wide. The grin he usually wore was gone. "I'll go get Roan," he promised, sprinting back through the archway.

Only when Cormac took over Damarion's place and forced Alpheus back against the wall did his father finally lower his weapon and stride forward. He dropped heavily to one knee beside Zale, his hand clamping onto his shoulder.

Zale barely felt it. Barely registered Leander's voice as he ordered his guards to arrest Alpheus. His entire world narrowed to Nerissa's uneven breaths against his chest, the heat of her blood soaking into his clothes as she continued shivering.

"Stay with me, Riss. Please, stay with me." His cheek pressed to her damp hair, his words spilling in a frantic rush. "You're too stubborn to die."

Her teeth chattered as she slurred, "Pontos…skotos…"

"What—I don't understand," Zale glanced up at Damarion, confused.

"She's slipping into Nautalian, but it's incoherent."

"What's she saying?" Zale implored him.

"Deep darkness," he murmured grimly.

Zale's face fell. "No. No, not darkness—Riss, you're still here. Look at me."

Her brow furrowed as her lips moved again. "Pou…eisin…hoi goneis mou?"

"She's asking…for her parents." Damarion took her other hand. "Eisin ento Bathos, Skíon."

She blinked away tears, before seeming to regain a brief moment of clarity. "Chairo…" she whispered. "Oti me anhelkas…ek tou kymatos."

Damarion swallowed, voice thick. "She says…she is glad. She is glad you pulled her from the water."

Something in Zale broke. He cupped her face, thumbs trembling as they brushed her cheeks. "Always," he whispered. "Do ye hear me? I'll never let ye sink. Just hold on—"

Roan appeared then, dropping to his knees beside them, satchel swinging open as he assessed the situation. "Talk to me, what happened?"

"She stabbed herself to break Alpheus's mind control," Zale quickly explained. "I haven't moved the daggers."

"Good, if you had, she'd have bled out in seconds," Roan muttered, voice taut. "They're the only thing keeping her together."

Zale swallowed hard, his throat raw. "She's delirious, Roan. What can we do?"

The look on Roan's face felt like a death sentence. There was nothing he could do.

"Hold on," Damarion said. "Her injuries are low. If she were to shift, it *might* be enough to seal her wounds and stop the bleeding."

Zale's heart lurched, hope clawing up like a drowning man finding the surface. "She won't make it to the sea. It's too far—"

"Take her to my chambers," Calliope cut in. "There's a soaking pool fed by the ocean. She can use it."

Zale bent his head, lips brushing Nerissa's temple. "Ye hear that? We're not done yet. You're not done yet."

CHAPTER 49

STUBBORN, IMPOSSIBLE WOMAN

Zale

His arms ached from carrying her, but he didn't slow down. Each step felt like walking a blade's edge—careful enough not to jostle her wounds, fast enough to outrun death's shadow clinging to her. Calliope darted ahead, leading them through the dim hallways, Leander close behind her, his hand hovering near the small of her back.

It wasn't far. Calliope threw open the carved oak door to her chambers, motioning toward the recessed pool built into the stone floor.

Zale walked straight into the water, lowering himself and Nerissa onto the wide shelf that was built into one end of the pool. She didn't even flinch as her skirt fanned out like spilled wine as the seawater closed over her legs. He slid an arm beneath her shoulders, keeping her head above the surface. She was so cold. Too cold.

Calliope lingered nearby, her hands clenched tightly together, face drawn tight with grief and guilt. Leander stood close, his expression grim, but his eyes flicked more often to Calliope than anyone else.

"Riss," Zale's throat felt like it was full of broken glass. "Listen to me. Ye need to shift to stop the bleedin'."

The salt water rippled around them. Nerissa's eyes fluttered weakly as if she couldn't quite hold him in focus.

Her lips parted, confusion evident. "…shift?"

He shook his head. "Ye know how to do this—ye taught me, remember?"

"She doesn't understand." Damarion knelt by the water and gripped Nerissa's hand. "Állaxon."

Her eyes flicked with recognition. A faint tremor moved down her body as she curled her fingers around his hand.

"Nerissa, look at me. Just once more. Focus on me. Ye can do this. Please. *Please.*" Zale pleaded.

"Zale?" she mumbled, looking back at him.

"Yeah, I'm still here. You're okay, I'm okay, we're okay," he reassured her, as if by saying it out loud he could make it true.

She gave him a weak smile, but it disappeared with a gradual exhale as her eyes rolled back, body going slack in his arms.

"No," he rasped, clutching her against him, his voice cracking in raw denial. "No, no, no—Nerissa!"

His throat burned as he pressed his forehead to hers, rocking her limp form as if motion alone could call her back. "Please, don't leave me. Don't—" His words dissolved into broken gasps as tears fell freely down his face.

Roan hung his head, eyes squeezed shut. He placed a heavy hand on Zale's shoulder. "I'm so sorry Zale."

No. This couldn't be it. Not after everything they'd been through. This was all his fault. If only he'd gone to check on her last night. If only he'd been stronger when he fought Alpheus's men. If only—

"There's nothing you could have done." Damarion's hand rested on his other shoulder, gripping it with surprising strength. He took in a shuddering breath. "This is my fault. I should have killed Alpheus while I still had the chance."

Zale looked up at his father, then at Roan, and finally at Calliope. Leander was holding her tightly as she sobbed quietly into his shoulder.

"None of this was supposed to happen." Zale shook his head in denial. "She's the strongest person I know. She—I…"

"I know." Damarion squeezed his shoulder.

Zale stared down at the water, now tinted pale green with Nerissa's blood. He wasn't ready to let go yet. Wasn't ready to admit that she was gone. He shifted her weight in his arms, noticing that she felt lighter. Or maybe he was just numb.

His thumb brushed absently against her knee as he held her, memorizing every inch of her. Something felt off. Maybe his mind was playing tricks on him, but he swore he could feel tension returning to her body. He didn't dare get his hopes up. It was just her limbs stiffening.

Then he felt Damarion tense beside him.

"Skíon …" he breathed.

That's when Zale caught the movement so subtle he almost missed it.

The light was bending strangely off her skin as it dissolved into a sweep of amethyst scales.

"Roan, it's working!" Zale cried.

Roan's head snapped up as he leaned forward, his hands hovering carefully around the hilts of her daggers. "Gotta time this just right."

Once the scales began creeping up towards Nerissa's torso, he gripped the daggers, and in one smooth motion, he pulled them free.

Zale held his breath, bracing for the flood of blood. But it never came.

Instead, the water glowed faintly around her, iridescent light catching on the edges of each scale as the transformation continued its natural course, rewriting her broken body into wholeness.

He held her tightly as she shifted, her torso arching once against his chest. He felt the faint scrape of her dorsal fin pressing through the back of her shirt and against his arm. A soft whimper escaped her lips, before her chest rose again, shallow but steadier. No gills, he noticed, careful to keep her head above water.

By the time her full tail stretched out beneath the surface, the wounds were no longer visible, protected by the natural armor of her scales. Her body slackened as she lost consciousness again, but stars, she was breathing.

Zale crushed her against his chest, his own breath shuddering free as the dam inside him broke. His tears mingled with seawater, his voice hoarse. "Ye stubborn, impossible woman…"

"Let her rest now," Roan said quietly. "Her body's spent, but she has a chance now."

Zale buried his face in Nerissa's damp hair, clutching her as though the world might still try to take her away.

The room around him blurred into the background. His focus was on Nerissa's weight in his arms, the faint warmth of her skin against his, the fragile rhythm of her breathing. She was so still, brow faintly furrowed and mouth set in a sharp frown.

Roan finally exhaled, rising to his feet. His hands lingered a moment on his satchel, before he turned toward the door. "I'll be close. Call if she worsens."

Damarion followed, pausing only to rest a hand on Zale's shoulder. His grip was brief but grounding, a silent reassurance before he strode after the others.

Zale barely noticed them leaving. He settled back against the edge of the pool as Nerissa's head rested in the crook of his arm. He had come so close to losing her, yet by some miracle, she was still alive.

Zale hadn't moved in hours. He was only aware of the passage of time when the sun sank into the ocean through the tall window behind him, casting long shadows across the chamber.

The water in the pool was warm against his skin as he sat half-submerged, back pressed to the tiled wall with Nerissa curled against his chest. Her hair fanned across his arm in a dark tangle as she breathed steadily. He would never get tired of that sound.

Before long, the door eased open. A soft glow of lamplight spilled across the chamber as Calliope stepped in. She carried a folded bundle of clean clothes in her arms. Her gaze lingered on the pair of them before she set the bundle down on the stool beside the pool.

"You'll catch your death if you stay like that," she said gently.

Zale didn't look up. His hand kept its slow, steady path through Nerissa's hair, combing it back from her temple. "Not leavin' her," he muttered, voice rough with exhaustion.

Calliope crouched at the pool's edge, the silk hem of her robe trailing against the tiles. "You've done all you can tonight. She needs rest…and so do you."

Nerissa stirred faintly in his lap, a soft sound slipping from her throat. Her fingers twitched weakly against his chest as her lashes fluttered. Those violet-blue eyes Zale thought he'd never see again cracked open just enough to find his face in the dim light. "You…need sleep," she rasped weakly.

Zale shook his head, jaw tightening. "I'm not leavin' ye."

"Not asking you…to leave. Just rest. Let Callie sit with me…Please."

He went still, torn by the plea in her eyes.

Calliope laid a hand lightly on his arm. "I'll keep watch. I swear she won't be alone."

For a long moment he didn't answer, gaze flicking between them. Then, with a sharp exhale, he nodded once. "Fine. But wake me if—"

"If she so much as sighs in her sleep, I'll send for you," Calliope finished, her tone firm but kind.

Zale hesitated still, then finally eased Nerissa against the curve of the pool's edge, as though setting down something impossibly fragile. Calliope tucked a blanket underneath her neck and shoulders to help prop her up as he brushed the wet strands of hair from her face, thumb lingering against her cheekbone.

"Rest now," he whispered, pressing his lips to her temple. "I'll be back before first light."

Nerissa closed her eyes, leaning into his touch, before drifting back into a heavy sleep.

He pulled himself from the water, boots squelching against the stone floor. Calliope held out the folded clothes as he passed. He muttered a gruff, "Thanks," his eyes drifting back to Nerissa even as the door closed behind him.

Nerissa

Nerissa blinked awake slowly, disoriented by the warmth cradling her body and the weightless drift of her tail beneath the surface. For a heartbeat she forgot where she was, thought she was still in that awful tank in the East Tower. Her eyes snapped open, scanning her surroundings as her breath quickened.

Morning light filtered through high windows, pale and cool, scattering across the room. Calliope's chambers?

What was she doing here? She attempted to sit up but stopped cold at the tug in her abdomen. Her hands flew to her stomach, where her scales transitioned to skin. The muscles beneath ached deeply, reminding her of the events of yesterday. How was she still alive? Where was Zale?

A soft rustle drew her attention. Calliope sat on a stool beside the pool. She offered a faint smile when Nerissa made eye contact.

"*Kharis Pontou*...we weren't sure if you would make it through the night."

Nerissa cleared her throat, unsure what to say. The last time she had seen Calliope, they hadn't exactly parted on friendly terms.

"Riss," Calliope started softly, tears brimming in her eyes. "I am so sorry for those things I said to you—in the dungeon. I'm sorry I didn't believe you, didn't fight for you. I didn't know what Alpheus had done…can you ever forgive me?"

"I forgive you Callie…but," Nerissa swallowed over the lump in her throat, "it's going to be a long time before it stops hurting."

She bowed her head, eyes closed. "Of course, I understand. I swear to do everything in my power to make it up to you."

"I appreciate that," Nerissa lowered her gaze to the water. "And thank you for letting me use your pool."

Calliope looked back up, a slight smile starting to return. "Who's the glorified house plant now?"

Nerissa chuckled lightly, caught off guard. "Touché."

Calliope studied her for a long moment, chin propped delicately on her hand. Then, with the smallest curve of a smirk, she said, "So…the dashing pirate from the tavern. Doesn't seem like such a stranger now."

Nerissa blinked at her, then huffed a soft laugh, shaking her head. "No, definitely not a stranger anymore."

Calliope rested her chin in her palms, scooting her stool closer, clearly demanding more details.

Nerissa sighed, smiling. "Zale is…steadfast, loyal, brave."

"Wow, how romantic, Riss," Calliope rolled her eyes. "Is that all you've got to say about the man who spent most of yesterday soaking in my pool with you?"

Heat flushed Nerissa's cheeks as her eyes widened. "Tides above, Callie, don't make it out to be so scandalous!"

"I'm just saying," she giggled. "The way he was looking at you like you were the only person in the room, it sure seems serious."

"I…guess you could say that." Nerissa nodded slowly. Calliope was enjoying this *far* too much.

"So…have you two kissed yet?"

"Callie!"

"That's not a 'no,'" she narrowed her eyes, grin spreading.

Nerissa ran a webbed hand down her face, exasperated. "Can we not do this right now?"

"Sure, unless you've got something juicier to discuss," Calliope smirked.

Nerissa stared at her, long and hard, before simply saying, "Zale is Damarion and Thalassa's son."

Calliope almost fell off her stool.

"Thalassa—Leander's *aunt*?" Calliope's hands had flown to her mouth. "And Damarion, as in, *Captain* Damarion?"

"It's true," Nerissa crossed her arms smugly, glad for the slight change in topic. "Alpheus confirmed it in the dungeon yesterday."

"So your pirate is…half Nautalian?" Calliope's face was still the picture of shock and disbelief.

Nerissa nodded. "Scales and everything. He didn't know until recently."

"*Moirai,* you sure know how to pick them, Riss." Calliope shifted in place. "But wait, if he's Thalassa's son…then that makes him Leander's cousin!"

"Don't you dare tell Zale that," Nerissa laughed weakly. "He's still processing everything."

"Okay, I promise…but only because I owe you."

“Speaking of Leander,” Nerissa’s tone turned more somber. “How have things been since…the wedding?”

Calliope fidgeted with the ring on her finger as she spoke. “It’s been complicated; we’ve been trying to convince the council that the peace treaty is still the wisest course of action for Astyra. Their initial trust in Vasilios has been…shaken.”

“Because of me,” Nerissa looked down at her own hands, thumbing the webbing between her fingers. “I know I wasn’t exactly the treaty’s biggest supporter, but I am sorry to hear that, Callie. If there’s anything I can do—”

“No no, don’t you worry about that. You’ve done enough—and I don’t mean that sarcastically,” she offered a genuine smile. “You just focus on healing.”

“What about Alpheus?” Nerissa’s eyes narrowed at the thought of that venomous apothecary. “He ought to hang for everything.”

“Agreed, but that is for the court to decide. Leander had him arrested yesterday.”

Nerissa closed her eyes. “Good. That’s a start.”

She caught sight of her daggers lying on the floor nearby, triggering yet more memories to flood over her. How many innocent guards had she slain?

Oh no. Kaelen.

“Callie, I struck down Kaelen when he tried to stop me.” Nerissa swallowed, her throat suddenly dry. “Is he…?”

“He’ll be fine,” she explained. “Honestly, I think you wounded his pride more than anything.”

“Thank the tides.” Nerissa let out a breath. “Don’t tell him that I asked about him though. Can't have him thinking I care."

"No," Calliope laughed softly. "Can't have him thinking that."

Then the door creaked open. Footsteps sounded against the stone, the gait at once familiar.

Zale stepped inside, dressed in a clean linen shirt and plain trousers Calliope must have dug up for him. The absence of his long coat and leather arm bracers made him look startlingly different—less like the roguish pirate she had come to know and—well, anyways.

Nerissa blinked, then let out a quiet laugh. "It's strange seeing you like this. You look almost like a polite member of society."

His brows lifted as he glanced down at himself, tugging at the loose shirt. "Don't get used to it," he said with half a smile. "First chance I get, I'm stealing my boots back from the drying rack."

Her lips curved, but her gaze softened as it lingered on him. "I hope you got some rest."

Zale's eyes flicked to hers, something warm sparking there before he dipped his head. "I got enough," he said. The truth sat in the faint shadows under his eyes, but she didn't press him.

Calliope rose gracefully from her stool, smoothing her robes. She regarded Zale with a careful, measuring look that Nerissa did not miss. Then Calliope turned to her with a smile.

"I'll leave you to your pirate," she said lightly, the glint in her eyes betraying her mischief.

Nerissa's cheeks warmed as Calliope swept toward the door. Zale raised a brow after her retreating figure, then crossed the chamber and lowered himself onto the edge of the pool.

"What was that about?" he asked.

Nerissa shook her head, smiling. "Nothing you need to worry about."

"That makes me ten times more worried."

She laughed again. "Callie and I were just catching up."

"So, I take it you two are square now?"

Nerissa nodded slowly. "It's going to be a long time before things are back to normal, but it's a start."

"Glad to hear it," his smile was genuine, but undercut with worry. "How're you feelin' otherwise?"

"Like I'm ready to get out of this fishbowl."

He laughed, then leaned forward, letting his hand drift briefly under the water's surface. His thumb brushed hesitantly over the scales that hid her wounds.

"Any pain?" he asked, voice low.

Nerissa shook her head. "Not really. Just…sore." Her lips curved faintly. "It's not bad, promise."

He searched her face, looking for any flicker of pretense, then nodded slowly. "Good."

His hand still lingered on her scales beneath the water, heat blooming across her torso from the contact. Zale's gaze drifted back up to her face, the sunlight glinting off the gold flecks in his eyes. He ran his other hand through his hair and let out a shaky breath.

"You scared the hell out of me, Riss." His voice cracked. "Don't ever do that again."

"I know," she blinked slowly, gripping his hand underwater. "I'm sorry, but I…I couldn't live with myself if I had killed you. It was the only way."

He squeezed her hand back. "Just *promise* me you won't do something reckless like that again. I don't want to lose you, not when I've only just found you."

"I can't promise that…I've been nothing *but* reckless these last few weeks," she smirked up at him.

"You know, you're lucky I like you."

"One might argue that *you're* lucky I like you—or you'd be dead right now."

"Unbelievable," Zale exhaled, a smile cracking despite himself. "So, what happens now?"

Nerissa's eyes creased in confusion. "What do you mean?"

"I mean…your name has been cleared, right?"

"Basically, yes…" Nerissa sat up a little straighter. "What's your point?"

"Are you…" he stopped, rubbing the back of his neck, "planning to go back to Nautalia? Now that you're no longer wanted for war crimes, I mean."

"Oh," she understood his hesitation now. She hadn't even given Nautalia a second thought in the past week. "I suppose I *could* return to Nautalia, but…"

"But?"

"That's not my home anymore."

Zale's brows lifted slightly, though the faint smile on his lips gave him away. "No?"

Nerissa shook her head, eyes soft. "Home is with the people who fought beside me, who risked their lives when they didn't have to. With the ones who gave me a place when I had nowhere else to go." Her gaze met his, steady and sure. "That's with you. With the crew."

He swallowed. "You mean that?"

"I do," she said simply. "If the *Black Serpent* will still have me."

Zale's smile spread. "You kidding? Brigid'd throw a fit if you tried to leave. Cormac might even cry."

Nerissa laughed. "And you?" she teased, tilting her head.

He feigned a thoughtful hum, pretending to weigh it. "Oh, I'd manage. Might take me a decade or two to recover, but I'd get there eventually."

She rolled her eyes, but the fondness in her expression was unmistakable. "You're impossible."

"Maybe," he said, leaning closer until his voice dropped to a low murmur, "but I'm yours, impossible and all."

CHAPTER 50

HAPPY ENDING

Zale

Zale woke up to someone shaking his arm. He rubbed his eyes and sat up groggily, the crimson tapestries hanging from the walls of the guest room reminding him where he was. He squinted, making out the shape of Calliope's face in the candlelight. It was still dark outside.

"What is it? Is Nerissa—" he asked, alarmed.

"Her wounds reopened," the princess said urgently. "I fetched your medic. He's assessing her now, but I thought you'd want to know."

Zale was on his feet in an instant, following her down the corridor as cold dread gripped his heart.

When they arrived at her chambers, he saw Roan crouched by the pool, fussing with bandages while Damarion stood in the water, supporting Nerissa. Her eyes were shut tight, and he could hear how shallow her breathing had become.

"What happened?" his voice rasped from sleep.

Damarion looked his way first. "She tried to shift too soon and reopened her wounds."

"She's stable now," Roan added, tying off the bandage around Nerissa's waist. Then he looked at her pointedly. "And she will *not* be trying that again anytime soon."

Zale glanced at Calliope, who was wringing her hands in an attempt to calm her nerves. "I woke up to this terrible sound," she whispered to him. "It was like she had been stabbed all over again, I thought—" she broke off, unable to finish.

"Hey," he said softly, squeezing her hand reassuringly. "You did the right thing."

She nodded with a watery smile as Zale crossed the chamber, joining Roan in kneeling by the water.

"Riss, what were you thinking?" he searched her face, expression hard with barely restrained worry.

She cracked an eye open, a sheepish look coming across her face. "I just…wanted to see if I'd be able to. I've never tried shifting after a major injury—I didn't know—I thought shifting healed the wounds."

"And that's where you'd be wrong," Damarion's jaw tightened. "Shifting isn't a magical cure-all; it just buys you time while the wounds heal. Try that again and you'll die."

Nerissa flinched. "So, what, I'm stuck like this?"

"For several weeks, at least," Roan confirmed, unapologetically. "You need to allow the stab wounds to scab over while they're still protected by your scales, or you *will* bleed out."

She waved them both away, frustrated. "Okay, okay, *I get it.*"

"That's not a friendly suggestion, either," Roan warned. "I mean it this time—this isn't like the sea withdrawal."

Damarion cast a glance at Zale. "She used to take orders without question; I suppose I have your influence to thank for her recent…*character development*," he said wryly.

Zale wasn't quite sure how to respond to that. He was still getting used to the fact that this was his father.

"Don't blame him, *Didaskon*—" Nerissa started, but she was swiftly cut off.

"Don't '*Didaskon*' me; this is serious, *Skíon*." Something softer flickered underneath Damarion's stern glare. Zale wagered it took a lot to rattle this man, much like himself.

"Alright, so, what's the plan?" Zale cut in. "She can't very well stay in the princess's bath for the next few weeks."

"Indeed not," Damarion agreed. "She needs to see one of our healers who specialize in wounds affected by shifting." He glanced at Roan then. "No offense."

"None taken," Roan stood up, brushing his hands together. "Your ward has been keeping things interesting; I've learned more than I ever thought I would about merfolk physiology in just the last week alone."

Nerissa cast them both withering glances before shooting Zale a pleading look.

"I can carry you to the shoreline," Zale said, reining in the discussion back to the matter at hand. "In the morning, after you've had more rest. Damarion, you can bring her to Nautalia, aye?"

"Yes," he confirmed, nodding his head. "I'll make sure she gets the proper care."

"And I'll prepare a message for my father to send ahead of you," Calliope chimed in. "He needs to know about the recent…turn of events." She looked at Nerissa kindly. "Don't want you getting arrested the moment you pass the gates."

"Then it's settled." Roan stood up, wiping his hands on his trousers. "We'll reconvene at first light."

Damarion sloshed out of the pool after giving Nerissa's shoulder one last squeeze. He looked at Zale for a long moment, before finally saying, "Get some rest, Son. You'll need your strength tomorrow."

Son.

He never thought he'd hear that word in such a literal sense. It brought up an old, familiar ache in his chest where it had once been hollow. He nodded in response as Damarion and Roan left the chamber.

Zale lingered by the pool, taking Nerissa's hand. "Ye sure you'll be alright?"

"I'm okay now, as long as I don't try shifting again for the foreseeable future." She blew out a breath of frustration. "Several weeks, Roan said. That's not ideal."

"Nae, nae it isn't," he agreed. "But it's what your body needs, Riss."

"I know that." She closed her eyes. "Doesn't mean I have to like it."

Zale chuckled, giving her hand a squeeze as he stood. "Get some rest."

Morning came far too quickly. Zale had barely slept in the hours since Nerissa's scare. His eyelids felt heavy, his muscles stiff. It wasn't just worry about her well-being that kept him up—it was the thought of her leaving. Returning to Nautalia, even if only temporarily. He wouldn't see her for weeks, maybe even months.

Once again, they gathered in Calliope's chamber. Zale and Damarion crouched by the edge of the pool, moving in unison as they carefully lifted Nerissa from the water. Damarion adjusted her weight into Zale's arms until she fit against him, her hands clasping behind his neck for balance.

"Now remember," Roan advised. "No shifting until your doctors clear you. And try not to use your abdominal muscles for at least a few days."

"Roan, Nautalia isn't exactly a short distance from shore," Nerissa began. "How am I supposed to swim without using those muscles?"

"You don't," Damarion said curtly. "I'll be carrying you—no arguing," he gave her a stern look when she opened her mouth to interrupt.

"This is humiliating." Nerissa rolled her eyes. "I'm not a child."

"Just listen to him, Riss," Zale said softly. "We all want what's best for you. Don't be stubborn."

She looked up into his eyes, clearly at war within herself. "Fine."

Calliope stepped closer, her composure slipping as she reached for Nerissa's arm. "You come back and visit as soon as you're feeling up to it, alright?"

Nerissa smiled. "Thank you for everything, Callie. I'll see you soon. Promise."

Nerissa

The castle corridors were lined with guards, every one of them standing at attention as they passed. Their armor gleamed in the morning light, polished to a mirror shine. When Zale and Nerissa came into view, they bowed their heads in unison.

She wanted to tell them not to bow. That she wasn't a hero—that she'd killed several of them, albeit unwillingly. Zale felt her tense slightly, and his grip tightened around her shoulders.

"Almost there," he whispered.

The great doors ahead creaked open, spilling sunlight across the mosaic floors. They stepped onto the drawbridge, the ocean stretching out beyond the cliffs azure and sparkling.

Leander stood waiting at the far end, his scarlet cloak stirring in the breeze. He looked weary, but when he saw them, his expression softened.

"Captain Damarion. Sir Roan. *Lord Zale*," he greeted, voice even but sincere.

Zale stopped mid-stride. "I—what? *Lord*?"

Leander's mouth quirked faintly. "Thalassa was my aunt. That makes us cousins, does it not? And as such, you are hereby granted the title of Lord."

"...oh. We'll uh, yeah, we're gonna have to unpack that later," Zale stumbled over his words, flustered and taken very much off guard.

Nerissa's shoulders trembled against Zale's chest as she stifled her laughter. "Sorry you had to find out this way," she whispered.

Leander's composure returned a moment later, his tone gentling as his gaze settled on her. "And Lady Nerissa." He bowed his head. "On behalf of Astyra, you have our eternal gratitude. Alpheus's reign of terror has ended because of you."

Zale inclined his head. "And what of him?" he asked quietly.

Leander's jaw set. "He's alive, for now. We intend to interrogate him thoroughly before his trial. It will be some months before the council convenes."

"Keep us updated," Damarion said. "I have a few questions for him myself."

"Absolutely. You'll be kept informed. I owe you that much."

Leander stepped aside, clearing their path to the winding trail that led down to the shore. "Safe passage, my friends. And…thank you."

Zale shifted Nerissa in his arms, giving Leander a brief nod before continuing forward. The sea breeze met them halfway across the bridge, carrying the brine of open water.

The walk to the beach was uneventful once they left the castle behind. There were so many things that Nerissa wanted to say but couldn't find the words. A month ago, she would have just focused on the practicality of the plan; that this was necessary for her survival, and only temporary, so why get emotional about it? She would see Zale again soon enough.

But that was the old her.

Now, she had way too many feelings and had no idea how to *deal* with them. All she knew was that her chest ached.

The sun hung high in the sky when they reached the shoreline. The hiss of the tide against the sand was a balm after the suffocating hush of the castle halls.

The crew of the *Black Serpent* was lined up on the shore, waiting.

Cormac was first in line, arms folded, eyes squinting against the breeze. "Ye don't get to haunt this crew, girl. If ye've business left, ye come back an' finish it proper."

"I'll miss you too, Cormac," Nerissa smirked.

"Sea's got no claim on ye yet," he grumbled, turning away and blinking far too much.

Ma Wen stood solidly in the sand, hands clasped behind his back. "Heal well, little fish. I'll save the rest of the sake for when you return."

"Oh my," Nerissa laughed. "Appreciate that, Ma."

He nodded once, saying nothing more.

Roan regarded her with his stoic, unreadable face. "Don't overexert yourself, but make sure you do gentle stretching after a few days. Keep those muscles loose and take care of yourself."

"Yes, Roan," she nodded with a smile. "Thank you."

Bran smiled widely, hands in his pockets, as they approached. "Still owe me a knife-throwing match, love. Don't make me put up with Zale on my own for too long."

Zale rolled his eyes.

"You've got it, Bran," Nerissa laughed. "But the loser has to get a piercing."

"Deal!" he grinned.

Brigid was holding her hat down against the wind, curls whipping her face. She stepped forward, eyes narrowed.

"Ye stubborn wee menace. Ye're not done yet, d'ye hear me?" Then she jabbed a thumb towards Zale. "This eejit's barely holdin' together as it is. So ye come back an' sort him out."

"Thanks for that, Brigid," Zale narrowed his eyes back at her.

Then her voice became softer, almost maternal, as she leaned in. "We'll keep the deck steady for ye lass. Stay strong."

Nerissa's eyes started watering. She couldn't take this.

Then the captain himself spoke up, planting a hand firmly on each of their shoulders.

"You're crew," was all he said at first. Then he gestured to the serpent inked onto her collarbone. "Don't forget what this means; we don't abandon our own."

Nerissa nodded her head solemnly. "I'll be back, Nestor."

That was everyone.

Zale followed Damarion into the water lapping against the sand. The first lick of the sea reached his ankles. He didn't stop until the water climbed past his waist, cold and biting.

"Eon would've kept us here 'till sunset with an epic poem that he drafted overnight," Zale said low enough that only she could hear.

Nerissa smiled through the tears as she laughed. "Yes, he would not have disappointed."

"I wish I could come with you," he admitted after a brief silence, resting his chin atop her head.

"Me too," she said softly. "But the crew needs you. And you need more practice shifting on your own first."

Zale's throat worked. "Then I expect lessons from the master when you come back."

She pulled back to look him in the eyes, voice dropping to a whisper. "It isn't fair. We won. We beat Alpheus at his own game. So why doesn't it feel like we get our happy ending?"

Zale lifted one hand, his thumb brushing beneath her chin. "Because happy endings aren't the point," he said softly. "It's about the journey."

That was the sappiest thing she had ever heard, yet she still stifled a sob that threatened to come loose. He leaned closer, his voice low against the sound of the tide. "Ye need time to recover, Riss. But you'll always be part of the crew. We'll be waitin' for ye."

He bent, brushing his lips against hers. Nerissa's fingers curled into his shirt as she drew him closer, her kiss deepening, fierce in its promise.

When she finally pulled back, Zale waded through the water and reluctantly passed her into Damarion's awaiting arms. Then he slowly removed the cord around his throat, before carefully placing it over her head, the green pendant resting against her chest.

She looked down at it reverently, brushing her fingers over the stone shell's smooth surface. "Zale—"

"Hold onto it for me," he smiled, eyes glistening.

"I'll bring it back, I promise."

"I know ye will."

"I'll keep her safe," Damarion said quietly. "Until she returns to you."

Zale's eyes were still fixed on the pendant, unable to look either one of them in the eye.

"I owe you an apology," Damarion said at last, his voice rough with years of restraint. "For not being there. For letting you grow up without knowing me. I can't make up for the time we lost, but I would like to try. If you'll let me."

Zale finally met his eyes. "I'd like that," he said, voice breaking.

"You're both welcome, by the way," Nerissa interrupted. "If not for me, you two never would have met." Then she shrugged. "Sorry, had to break the tension. It was getting awkward."

Both men chuckled before clearing their throats. She looked between them, smiling inwardly at their shared mannerisms. How could she have missed the resemblance before? It was uncanny.

"Well, Skíon, we'd best be heading back now." Damarion adjusted his grip below her tail, beginning to turn away from shore.

"Wait!" she cried out, surprising herself. She grabbed one of Zale's hands, suddenly unsure what to say. "I…I just wanted to say—"

"Tell me when ye come back," Zale gripped her hand, placing a kiss on it.

"Okay." She let her hand slip from his as Damarion waded into deeper water, his scales slowly emerging from his skin. Nerissa took a deep breath of water as it closed over her head, feeling her gills reappear and open up.

After several minutes of silence, Damarion finally spoke.

"You know that boy is in love with you."

Her eyes snapped to his, wide and surprised. "He's barely known me for a month, Damarion! And most of that month he didn't even know what I was."

"Doesn't matter." He shook his head, biting back a grin. "The way he held you when we thought you were gone, trust me. He is already in too deep."

She looked away. "He doesn't know what he's choosing. Everyone I care about ends up paying for it."

"Nerissa. You nearly died. For him."

"I would have done it for anyone," she blurted out in defense. But they both knew that wasn't true. She rubbed the green shell between her finger and thumb, the way she had seen Zale do a hundred times.

"So," she said abruptly, desperate to talk about anything else. "You and Lady Thalassa, huh?"

Damarion blinked.

"You conveniently left that part out of your history lesson on the peace treaty."

"Ah," he said slowly. "We're changing subjects."

She ignored his tone. "The royal family believes that she took ill and passed before Leander was born."

The water darkened as they descended, the glow of Nautalia faint in the distance now.

"Alpheus said she smuggled Zale out of the tower as a baby," Nerissa continued. "But what really became of her after?"

Damarion's jaw tightened. "That," he said evenly, "is exactly what I intend to find out."

Nerissa studied his expression. "Even if you don't like the answer?"

"Knowing the truth," he said after a moment, "is the only way to move forward. Whether it hurts or not."

The rest of the journey passed in silence.

When the gates of the palace came into view, the guards on duty saluted Damarion as they approached, before faltering when they recognized the assassin in his arms.

Nerissa went rigid.

It was a mistake to come back.

"They're going to arrest me on sight," she whispered.

"They are not," Damarion said sharply. "Calliope's message will have already reached the king. Nereus knows Alpheus orchestrated the assassination. He knows you were under his control."

"Knowing and believing are not the same thing."

"You are under my protection," he said firmly. "I will not see you chained again."

At the coral archway, Queen Ophelia was waiting, framed in the pale shimmer of bioluminescent lanterns as if she had been expecting them.

"Captain Damarion," she said. "We were concerned when you did not return after the wedding."

"Your Majesty." He inclined his head. "I regret the disruption of my duties. I was detained unjustly."

"Yes." Ophelia's gaze did not waver. "Calliope's account was quite…comprehensive."

Her eyes shifted to Nerissa.

"And you," Ophelia said quietly, "have been through enough."

Nerissa blinked.

"I assure you," the queen continued, "Nautalia will know what you've done for the sake of peace."

Nerissa attempted to sit upright to bow properly, but the muscles beneath her scales clenched in protest. The water clouded faintly with blood.

Ophelia's expression sharpened.

"Enough formalities." She gestured down the corridor. "Take her to the healing chambers. Immediately."

"Thank you, Your Majesty," Damarion said, bowing once more before carrying Nerissa away.

The healers meticulously wrapped her torso in kelp bandages, layering with an algae paste meant to reduce inflammation. As it dried, it tightened, constricting slowly until hardening protectively around her scales.

"You must not twist or overextend," the senior medic instructed. "Strict bed rest for a week. The fibers will hold, but they cannot mend what you reopen."

Nerissa nodded absently. "And how long until I can shift?"

The medic's hands stilled for a fraction of a second before she met Nerissa's eyes.

"Not for quite some time, I'm afraid."

"How long?" Nerissa pressed, glancing briefly at Damarion. "Please. It's important."

The medic exhaled and moved to the stone bench along the wall, folding her hands in her lap.

"It is difficult to predict precisely," she said at last. "But several weeks at least. You cannot risk rupturing the wounds. A forced shift too soon would undo everything we have just done."

Several weeks.

The words settled heavier than the bandages.

"I see," Nerissa said quietly.

She closed her eyes.

Several weeks.

She hoped Zale wasn't still standing on that shore.

EPILOGUE

2 Months Later

The cove was quiet in the afternoon light, the tide pulling slow and steady against the sand. The *Black Serpent* sat anchored nearby, her silhouette framed by the cliff walls, the faint noise of the crew drifting from the campfires further up the beach.

Zale sat alone at the water's edge, hunched forward, flinging shells and flat stones one by one into the surf. They skipped once, maybe twice, before sinking, swallowed whole by the sea.

He wasn't really watching.

What was she doing right now? Was she strong enough to swim yet? Or was she still confined somewhere in the deep, bound in bandages, forced into stillness she would hate?

His chest tightened.

He dragged a hand through his hair and reached for another stone.

Footsteps crunched softly in the sand.

Nestor lowered himself beside him with a grunt, saying nothing at first.

"Ye plan to mope until she comes back," he said at last, "or ye plan to be worth comin' back to?"

Zale didn't look at him.

"She's fightin' for survival…are ye?"

"She might not come back," Zale snapped, the bite sharper than he intended.

"Aye, she will. That girl's too stubborn to die." His usual gruffness softened then. "But when she does return…what do ye want her to find?"

Zale's jaw tightened as he stared out at the horizon, where sea met sky in an unbroken line.

He had no answer.

Nestor rose, clapping a firm hand against his shoulder before trudging back up the beach toward the others.

The tide rolled in. Rolled out.

Zale blew out a slow breath, dragging a hand down his face. The stubble he usually kept trimmed had grown into a full beard—something between neglect and defiance. He suspected Nestor was beginning to eye it with competitive interest.

The corner of his mouth twitched faintly, then faded.

Maybe the old man was right.

He couldn't imagine Nerissa surrendering to idleness the way he had these past two months. It hadn't escaped his notice that Ma Wen had prepared his favorite meals more often than necessary. Or that Bran had picked more fights than usual. Or that Roan hovered nearby without pretending not to.

They were waiting.

All of them.

He pushed to his feet, brushing sand from his trousers.

The tide sighed against his boots, the same soft rhythm that had filled every dream since she left.

He turned toward the camp.

Then a hand closed around his wrist.

Zale froze.

Slowly, he turned back.

Nerissa stood there, water streaming from her hair, her eyes glistening with unshed tears. A simple white linen shirt clung to her frame, an abalone-plated skirt catching the last light of day.

Her smile trembled, watery, but it lit her face with something he'd ached to see again.

Zale's heart stuttered in his chest. For a moment, he forgot how to breathe.

He didn't speak. Didn't dare.

He just pulled her into him.

She collided with his chest, arms locking around his back as if anchoring herself there. He crushed her close, one hand fisting in the damp fabric at her shoulder, the other sliding up into her hair.

For a long moment, there was nothing but the hush of the tide and the violent thud of his own heartbeat.

When he finally drew back, it was only enough to see her face.

His thumb brushed wet strands from her cheek.

"Your wounds—"

Her smile flickered. She lifted the hem of her shirt just enough to reveal two thick, green-tinged scabs rising above her waist. Not pretty, but not bleeding either.

"Do I look like a real pirate now?" she asked softly.

Zale let out a soft, incredulous laugh. "Ye look like trouble," he murmured, eyes darkening. "Which is close enough."

She laughed too, shaky and luminous all at once.

He reached toward the scars, fingertips grazing lightly over the edges. She shivered.

He immediately pulled back. "Does it hurt?"

"No." Her voice broke just slightly. "I've just missed you."

That did it.

Something inside him split clean open.

He gathered her in again, his mouth finding hers with all the restraint he had lost somewhere in those two endless months.

It wasn't gentle.

It wasn't cautious.

It was the kind of kiss that erased distance. That turned absence into fire. That said every word neither of them had managed to speak.

When they finally broke apart, breathless, their foreheads rested together.

He was smiling.

Actually smiling.

Nerissa reached for the green pendant resting against her collarbone, fingers tracing the worn grooves.

"Here," she whispered, beginning to lift the cord. "You should have this back."

Zale caught her hand before she could remove it.

"Keep it," he said quietly. "You're my family now. It belongs with ye."

Her breath hitched. Tears slipped free without shame this time.

He brushed his thumb along her jaw, tender now where he had been fierce.

"Welcome home, Riss."

GLOSSARY

Aígli (AY-glee)

- Literal translation: “Radiance”, “glory”, “splendor”
- A term of endearment meaning “my sunshine”

Didaskon (Dee-DAS-kohn)

- Literal translation: "Teacher," "Mentor," "Guide"
- This term emphasizes the wisdom and guidance provided by this figure. It would be used for someone who isn't necessarily directly related by blood but imparts vital knowledge, life lessons, or skills, acting in a guiding, paternal role. It conveys deep respect and affection for their mentorship.

Katará sou (kah-TAH-rah soo)

- Literal translation: “Your curse”
- Nautalian equivalent of “Damn you”

Kel'ra navessa (KEHL-rah nah-VESS-ah)

- Literal translation: “the sea’s betrayal”
- An exclamation of frustration or distress.

Kharis Pontou (KAH-rees POHN-too)

- Literal translation: "Grace of the Deep!" or "Favor of the Sea!"
- An exclamatory phrase for expressing relief or thanks, similar to "Thank goodness!" It honors the sea as a source of protection and provision.

Moirai (MOY-rye)

- Literal translation: "Fates!" or "By the Fates!"
- Nautalian equivalent of "Damn"

Nerae (NEH-rye)

- A very common, everyday exclamation of surprise or a plea for help
- Nautalian equivalent of "Saints"

Rheos Apatos (REE-ohs ah-PAH-tohs)

- Literal translation: "deceitful current"
- Used for a wide range of situations, from mild frustration (a current pushing you the wrong way) to genuine anger (a treacherous situation that blindsided you).

Rhypós (Rhee-POHS)

- Literal translation: "filth, mud, scum, sewage"
- A vulgar insult. It implies they are a disgusting residue that belongs on the bottom floor of the ocean, not among civilized merfolk.

Skíon (SKEE-on)

- Literal translation: "little shadow" or "my shadow"
- A term of affection for a devoted student.

Su eisi mou asterion (SOO EH-see moo ahs-TEH-ree-on)

- Literal translation: "You are my starlight."
- An intimate and affectionate phrase.

To be continued in

Book Two: The Court of Sirens

www.ingramcontent.com/pod-product-compliance
Lightning Source LLC
LaVergne TN
LVHW091248110826
845146LV00002BA/452

* 9 7 9 8 9 9 5 8 0 6 9 0 5 *